Only the Wind is Free

To my family

Margaret Graham

Only the
Wind is Free

Annie's
Promise

ARROW

This edition published by Arrow in 2002
an imprint of The Random House Group
20 Vauxhall Bridge Road, London SW1V 2SA

Copyright © Margaret Graham 2002

The right of Margaret Graham to be identified
as the author of this work has been asserted by
her in accordance with the Copyright Designs
and Patents Act, 1988

Only the Wind is Free copyright ©
Margaret Graham 1988
Annie's Promise copyright ©
Margaret Graham 1993

Papers used by Random House UK Ltd are
natural recyclable products made from wood grown
in sustainable forests. The manufacturing process
conform to the environment regulations of the
country of origin

A catalogue record for this book is available from
the British Library

Printed and bound in Germany by Elsnerdruck,
Berlin

ISBN 0 09 188981 2

CHAPTER 1

Little Annie Manon was come home. Standing on the wind-whipped dune, lifting her face towards the lightening sky, she welcomed the North-East bite. She thought of the Wassingham she had known, the black streets of her childhood that seemed a million years away now.

The sand stretched clear and clean, all blemishes swept away by the tide before they had a chance to settle. God, she thought, who'd believe the pitch-black was creeping down to this beach last time I was here. She shook her head. Where did they dump the coal dust now she wondered – or had the miners been tidied away also, rationalised as though they'd never been?

But they had been there all right and somewhere the workings would be standing; stark and silent perhaps, but you could not wipe away completely years such as those or the memories that lingered.

She shivered, remembering the sound of the disaster whistle cutting through the loudest noise, bringing fear into every kitchen in the pit villages. Bet would slowly and quietly lift the latch and stand, helplessly watching the hurrying women, shawls hastily wrapped round greying faces and bowed shoulders, their breath white and thin as they struggled to go faster still. Please God, please God, not one of mine this time but none of this showing on their rigid faces and Bet hugging to her the certainty that it was not her pain this time because she had faced that long ago.

Annie could still feel the rough-textured dress of her step-mother as she clutched it, pulling it to one side so that she could also see, but not hear, for never a word was spoken on the long private walk to the pit-head. She was to nurse those miners in later years and she could never be professionally detached in

1

the face of their grimy courage and determined humour.

Annie had been called a bonny lass then with her dark hair and eyes; though the eyes were not so dark really but hazel, deeply set under arched brows that cast a shadow. Like her ma, she was hinny, she had been told. Annie frowned with the effort of remembrance. The gnarled hands of Bet had always repulsed her. How coarse and vulgar she had seemed against the slight refined frame of her father. Annie sighed. How cruel children are, she thought, condemning so easily with no mercy given, even though they knew it was being asked.

Poor Bet, no wonder her hands were distorted; whose wouldn't be, hulking great kegs up to the shop from the cellar, corking and uncorking barrels for a trade that increasingly failed to give them a living. She remembered the smell of beer, the darkness of the small one-roomed store which sold cigarettes as well as Newcastle Brown. It was set in a street which was indistinguishable from the other back-to-back terraces which made up most of Wassingham. A village which had grown into a town after a station had been built and yet more pits had been opened. The pit wheels were always there against the skyline and the slag heaps too, though hardly noticeable because they were so familiar. And there was the smell of the coal which overlaid everything.

Their father's shop was a sorry remnant of the chain of wine merchants, the ownership of which should have been handed down from her grandfather to her da and his brother, Albert. Instead her father and uncle had been forced to sell it all piecemeal to settle the debts of a business which had been destroyed by the war. Her father had then leased one back from Joe Carter for the privilege of having something to call a job.

Those First World War years had ended more than one life she knew, broken more than one heart, but perhaps you only really cared deeply about your own particular grief. The rest were merged into a greyness against which the matt blackness of the pain stood out sharply and unavoidably.

She settled herself down, spreading her Harrods mackintosh on the sand. She did not want to return yet to Tom. She wanted to remember how it had been before she left; never to return until today. Her own hands were work-worn now, the wedding ring slipped easily up and down between the swollen joints on her right hand. Ruby Red of the left would never dance for

2

anyone again. She smiled and stroked its crookedness, shaking aside the pain.

Leaning her head back, she let the wind sweep the fine hair where it chose. Her profile was strong and saved from prettiness by a chiselled nose. The lines of ill-health ran deep to the corners of her mouth and the sallowness of her skin owed as much to that as to the heat of her war years. Laughter had carved its path also. Maybe, she mulled, it was the laughter that carried her through, but only so far for it had then cracked and dried, it's husk blown beyond her reach.

She nestled deep into the mohair sweater which was too large for her slight frame but that was how she liked it; her cuffs were undone as well. The restraint of tightly buttoned clothes was unbearable to her. Strange that, she thought, remembering the long summers when they strolled in the spent warmth of the evenings, smoking and eating vinegar-soaked chips. Strange to hate such restraint when I so longed for it as a growing girl. Eeh, Annie, no one'll mind if you's late, we'll get others back first or they'll be for it else.

Tears threatened even now, so many years later, glinting like the coins they had bashed and filed from scraps of lead pipe before the fair. She laughed deeply in her throat. That was class she thought, remembering Don and Georgie choosing the stalls round which to loiter; the ones with the overworked taddy on whom they would then all surge, Tom, Grace and Annie at the front because they were smaller.

She picked up a handful of sand and let it fall through slightly parted fingers. The wind blew it back against her body. It was a good gang, she reflected, but one which yet another war has done its best to scatter. Annie sighed as she traced her salt-dried lips with her forefinger. In the beginning though, there were just the two of us, Don. And you are the one who stayed, deep down in your guts, stayed where you were and what would our da have thought of that, she pondered wryly. She could never forget her father's chronic need for his children to climb back up as he had failed to do.

Annie allowed herself then to remember the first time she had consciously seen her father but by then he was already wounded beyond endurance, with his youth long away and joy a distant memory. It was 1920 and she was 7. Don was 9.

The air had been sharp on her chapped face, much as it was now, and it had stung the roughened lips still wet from licking. The salivary warmth had eased the misery for a moment but as the wind whipped it dry again it hurt even more. She hunched herself deeper into her coat and wished Don would hurry. There was no way of ducking out of the cold here by the school gate. The railings were as dull as the iciness all around and their chill sank into her back as she changed from foot to foot, dragging her socks up with the toes of her boot. She grimaced at the thought of Aunt Sophie having to make yet another pair of garters. I don't know where you find holes to hide them in Annie, she'd say, I really don't. And you standing there the image of your bonny mother so's I don't have the heart to scold you.

Annie was glad it was Friday because Don would be here again, home from Albert's for hot scones and buttered toast. She wished he hadn't gone to live with their uncle. It was strange how things and people always seemed to disappear eventually and she rubbed her nose on her sleeve.

First it had been the light and pretty house on the hill that had gone. One day when she was 3, the light had simply fled and shadows had filled the rooms as the drapes were drawn across the windows; they were pink like plums. Everyone had spoken in whispers. Jane, the nanny, had red eyes and there had been a quiet emptiness until she and Don had moved in with Aunt Sophie but before that her father had come and gone from the big house, dressed in khaki with a black band on his arm. She knew now that he had come to bury her mother and that after her mother died, the house had too. Did the house always die she wondered, and shivered as the wind suddenly blustered down the street.

The cables were grinding up the slag-heap which had been created behind the school. She could hear the clang as the buckets emptied their waste when they reached the tipping gear.

She and Don had clambered into a black taxi when they travelled from the big house for the last time and Sophie's arms had hugged them to her. Her coat had been black and smelt of damp and they had passed the station and a church with no steeple, down street after street until they were at Sophie and Eric's, backing on to the railway line.

4

It was when she was 6 and Don was 8 that Albert had come for Don. She had thought her brother would stamp and scream and not leave as she would have done, had she been taken from Sophie and Eric's and put in that smelly old shop a good mile across town. But Albert had said he would give Don sixpence each week for running errands and he had laughed and gone.

The wind blew again bringing the noise of the cables nearer it seemed and then died away and the mist crawled in up the street. Again she searched the road for Don and she wanted someone but did not know who.

In the failing light she first heard, then saw her brother. Eeh, it was grand to see the lad but he was walking with someone, holding his hand and at this she frowned. Aunt Sophie had told her that, even though she was old enough to start school, she was never to talk to strangers and here was Don, for goodness sake, holding this big, strange hand. She faltered as they came close, unsure of what to do.

'Hey, Annie,' Don called. 'Guess who this is?'

He puffed out his chest and tried to look big. She bit back a retort and flicked the hair out of her eyes with a quick nod of her head. Eeh, you'll catch it when we get home, Don Manon, you see if you don't she thought to herself. She held the railing behind her. It was so cold it hurt her hand as she looked from Don to the man. He was not very big, she saw, and he was thin, so thin that he looked even smaller in the heavy brown coat. He squatted before her, his tired hazel eyes the same height as hers now. He held out his hands and said.

'It's me, little Annie. It's your da come home for good.'

His hands drew her towards him and held her close. Dear God, he thought, neither of my children know me and I would have passed them in the street. Annie's body was stiff against him and the brown serge hurt her chapped lips and she hoped she would not have to leave Aunt Sophie now that this man who was her father was home.

There was no colour, not even the grey of evening to help the long walk home. The hand which held Annie's was not warm but it did protect to some extent the painfully reddened wrist, which was grand. All the time though, she was aware of the soft slapping of the worn brown leather glove into which her da had pressed her other hand. Don had looked away as the warmth, someone else's warmth had stuck, clammy, to her hand. She

5

had seen the snigger though. Just you wait, she thought, you daft beggar. Just because it doesn't bother you. You'd go and roll in the muck heap given half the chance. Her skin crawled with distaste; it was as bad as sitting on someone else's warm seat. She half closed her eyes, holding her hand taut within the glove.

Maybe if she held it quite still the sodden heat would pass her hand and seep out through the top without touching her. Then, so long as the sides of the glove did not touch her skin, it would be all right. In fact it wouldn't be so bad if it was someone she knew. She sighed.

'Are you liking school, Annie?' her father asked quietly, at a loss to reach these children, aware that already there was a distance between him and this quick-eyed wary child whom he had last seen when she was barely 3. She had changed little; there was still the chin which tilted in something short of defiance when she was uncertain but the voice was Mary's. He felt the pain tense and leap at the sound of her reply.

'Yes, Da.'

Somehow in the last four years he had imagined the child but not the voice. The sound destroyed the nervous unreality of his mood, hurling the cold dark evening and the remnants of his family before him. Despair hung poised to swoop but was held at bay by the memory of his daughter's stiff embarrassed body awkwardly allowing his earlier embrace. A glimmer of feeling emerged as they silently trod the cobbles and his corrosive grief was given reason to pause.

Annie stared steadfastly at the ground as that old cat Sadie passed by. That did it; now the whole neighbourhood would know that Annie Manon was walking with some strange man. She dreaded a new round of whispers and furtive stares like those that had made her cringe with unhappiness when she had joined the school. Somehow these people were not like her or perhaps she was not like them since she was the one who had spoken differently and had struggled to understand the words which corkscrewed out so fast it had left her gaping. She smirked with satisfaction as she recalled how geordie she had quickly become and now was even as tough as Nellie, that gormless great gertie from Lower Edmoor Street.

Bye, that was a great day, the day she tripped Nellie into the steaming pile left by Old Mooney's rag-and-bone mare. She giggled softly as she pictured that face smeared with it. She had laughed so hard she'd wet her knickers but it was half fright as well because she hadn't meant to; she'd just turned at the end of the hoop run and her foot had caught Nellie's ankle. She had half thought she'd be killed by the great lump but Nellie had run off crying and Annie had been slapped on the back and given a jelly baby by Bert, the toughie of the street, and no one, but no one was given anything by Bert. She had nipped off the head first, then the legs and saved the body till last. After that she had sounded and looked the same as them and she was glad.

Even Sophie and Eric had seemed different in their own home to the people they had appeared to be on their visits to Annie's old house up on the hill. Without her hat and coat and in the compact terrace Sophie had been fuller and she smelt of lavender and Eric of the colliery smithy where he heaved and banged at glowing metal every day, singing in his deep voice the music of Gilbert and Sullivan. The difference was a good one, Annie thought, for the house always bubbled with talk and fun and Sophie would grasp her by the waist and lift her, tight and close and laugh into her neck so that she could hardly breathe for shrieking and Eric read her stories each evening before she slept. They made her body feel loose again like it used to before . . . but she wouldn't think of that now.

Sophie was watching for them, unalarmed at their lateness since Archie had written to say that he was coming home and would be in Wassingham, today. She had not warned Annie at his request and by now the headache which had been nagging all day stretched from her shoulder to her eye.

She moved to the fire and stood with her back to the heat which eased it a little but the tension that had knotted her muscles drove her to the window once more. The tears were close again and she clenched her mind against them. There had been so many shed over the last four years and now was not the time for more. But, Mary, my dear girl, she could not prevent herself calling silently, if only it hadn't happened, if only you were here now. What in God's name is to become of them?

She chewed her nail. I couldn't even manage to keep them together for you, your pigeon pair, and Don has grown away from us as I feared he would, once Albert had his way. She wondered yet again if she could have fought harder at the funeral to prevent Albert from persuading Archie to allow him to take Don when he was 8, but he seemed so determined, almost obsessed by a need to have one of Archie's children. Was it just that he wanted a messenger boy or did he really care for his nephew? Somehow Sophie doubted this.

She rubbed her face with her hands, trying to shake the past from her head and moved first to the fire to add more coal, and then to the window searching with strained eyes through the mist and, dimly, they came, three figures emerging so sparingly from the dark of the street that it nearly broke her heart.

The years since 1914 had made a mockery of so much shining promise, she thought savagely, and there is absolutely nothing I can do about it. Her impotence drew back her tension, her headache increased, but she drew herself straight and moved to the front door, spilling the light into the thick darkness and drawing the now recognisable figures into its beam.

Annie blinked, warmed by the promise of familiarity and the scones which she could smell even as she crossed the stone step that clicked against her father's shoes as he followed her into the glinting hallway.

'Go through, Annie love,' Sophie coaxed as she kissed the hair which was cold and hung with minute droplets of evening chill. She pushed the thawing child gently from behind, only patting Don on the shoulder and smiling. He had told her last time that he was too old for kisses.

Annie, relieved that tea was as usual in the kitchen and not in the starched and strange front parlour, hurried past. She grinned and, shrugging herself free of her coat, flung it and the now lifeless leather glove onto the airer by the range and lolled kneeling against the guard. Her cheek pressed against the linen towels and the smell of boiling was still deep within them. With her face protected from the heat her knees and feet roasted themselves free of numbness until the itch of chilblains drove her further back to the chair in which she usually sat.

She glanced quickly at Don who had taken her place. His thin face was blotched with cold and his brown eyes were half closed. His light brown hair was dry now and flopped down towards his eye. She reached for the winter-green from beside the clock on the mantelpiece. Its tick was loud close to, but once back in her seat at the table it became lost in the hiss and spit of the fire. The mirror above the fire reflected the gas lamps which spluttered on the walls and the pictures of Whitley Bay that Eric had found wrapped up in old newspaper on a train.

'D'you think,' she pondered, her voice muffled as she drew her leg up and pulled off her sock, 'I should let a claggy skunk like you have any of this?' She held up the winter-green and dared him to reach for it. She hoped it would gain a response and it did.

'It's that or a damn good clout,' he murmured, scratching his throbbing toes and making a lunge.

'Now, now, Don lad,' she taunted him, her voice full with laughter, her mouth rounded into posh. 'Is that any way to treat a young lady especially when her father is outside ready to save her.'

She rolled her eyes and clutched her hands to her breast and was helpless to beat off Don's attack which came and soon they were both tingling with suppressed laughter.

Don tossed it back for her to put away, as Annie knew he would. Bye, she'd get the beggar one day she vowed, happy that he was here and that, for this moment, he was as he had been before he went to Albert's. She leant her mouth against the knee she liked to hug. The smell of her skin was pleasing to her and she resisted the temptation to make a bum of it between her fingers. He might walk in.

In the pause they heard the lowered voices in the hallway and it drew their eyes to one another.

'D'you remember him, Don?' she whispered. 'And why is he here?'

Don shook his head, his finger to his lips. 'He says he's come home,' he mouthed. 'I hope so, then I can live back home.'

Annie nodded. So perhaps he didn't like it at Albert's after all. She was pleased. The winter-green was interfering with her sniffing and making her eyes water. Reluctantly she pulled her sock back on and allowed the leg to drop. She settled back into the chair, sitting on her hands and feeling warm all over, with no gaps at all. He seemed old, she mulled. It wasn't that he was different to the man she had imagined for she had never thought about him. She watched Don put more coal on the fire and didn't want this moment to pass. There was something so certain about the heat, the smell of winter-green. Something so certain about scones and Don rubbing his hands free of coal marks. It wasn't exciting but it was the same as last Friday and the Friday before. The dresser was up against the wall, the rag mat was by their feet. The walls were still cream, the scullery was through the brown door.

She looked at Don. 'But where is his home?'

Don shrugged, pulled his socks back on and searched in his pocket.

'Give over Annie, they'll tell us when they want us to know.' He held out the smooth Jack stones. 'Come on, I'll give you a game. Best of three and if I lose, I'll get a pennyworth of chips tomorrow and you can have a few.'

'You're a tight one,' she accused and smoothed the table cloth which she had rucked as she had turned her chair. Her back was now to the fire and it felt good. 'Don't you like it at Albert's then?'

'It'll do,' he said as he tossed the ball, 'but he's the one who's as tight as a mouse's whatnot. Won't let me have any sweets unless I pay for them.'

He was feeling the table cloth now.

'The stones will lie steady but it gives the ball a low bounce,' he remarked.

'Well, I think it's lovely.' She looked at him. 'Is that why you want to leave, because he's a skinflint?' Hoping that he would say that he missed her.

'It's like this see, if we've got a da, why not live with him. It's right isn't it, then I won't have to work for me pocket money.' His voice was impatient.

Annie sat back in her chair watching as he threw up and grabbed three pebbles. She couldn't see at all why it was right to live with a man she didn't know.

'But . . . ' she began.

'This is the one they used for the vicar,' Don interrupted. 'The tablecloth, you daft nellie.'

He threw again and Annie said nothing, knowing that he did not want to talk about it. It was finished as far as he was concerned and Annie wondered whether he really had feelings or just bounced like his jack ball was doing.

She heard the click of the front-room door and thought how wonderful it would be to be able to melt into invisibility, slide under the door and sit close to Auntie Sophie, rubbing her face against the softness of her jumper. She wondered if someone would feel an invisible stroke or would it be as light as gossamer. She frowned.

'What's gossamer, Don?'

'Don't talk daft, Annie.' His small blunt fingers were steady as he readied to catch the last stone. His nails were dirty from the coal and she hoped that he would wash his hands before they had tea. She traced the pattern of the satin stitch which edged the table cloth and it was smooth and raised and cool. She eyed the bare corners of the table; the cloth had never been put round that way before. So, an extra place must have been laid and there it was, at the end. It would be Uncle Eric at one end, and him, her father, at the other. She fidgeted and folded her arms across her stomach holding her breath knowing it was coming but unable to prevent it. The rumble escaped.

'For Pete's sake, Don, hurry up,' she snapped, a blind anger sweeping over her but he just laughed and dug her with his elbow.

'Still as noisy as an empty barrel,' he sniggered, handing her the stones. 'Your turn and let's have some hush while you're at it. Eeh, I'm right hungry, what are they doing in that room anyway?'

Sophie had closed the front-room door behind them. The fire was still well built up and Archie stood before it, rubbing his hands in its warmth. He turned and stood quietly looking round the room as though familiarising himself with a place he had once known but had now forgotten.

It was lit by a small table lamp which left the corners in darkness. The antimacassars showed up clearly against the dark maroon of the settee and chairs. There were just two occasional tables, one which held the lamp and a photograph of Annie and Don; the other, set to the left of the settee, held several; one of Eric in uniform before his injury, one of Sophie and Eric on their wedding day. The other was of his own wedding with his cousin, Sarah Beeston in attendance. He looked away quickly, away from his Mary, back to Sophie.

'This room's hardly changed at all, my dear,' he said after a moment.

Sophie smiled. 'But we have.'

They looked at one another and were comforted. She sat and beckoned Archie to the other fireside chair. He sat down carefully as though he were a person who had been ill.

'It was all such a rush last time,' she murmured. 'It was difficult to . . . ' she paused, searching for words, 'to approach the future.' She gestured helplessly. 'I didn't know how to help you.'

'Sophie, it's all right. I've sorted things out a bit now, made some plans.' He paused. 'They've grown so much. Don's a real lad now, though it'll be good to get him away from that shop.'

Sophie nodded, her eyes darkening. Archie continued.

'It was a mistake. Albert is not the one to look after children. I was wrong to agree but he seemed to want it so much, but that's in the past now. And Annie, well Annie's so like Mary isn't she?'

He leant forward resting his elbows on his knees, his hands clasped tightly. Sophie watched the taut face with concern. The fire's half-light accentuated the shadowed eyes.

'Damn it Sophie, I still find it so hard.'

He pressed his fist to his mouth, his eyes dark and years away. She leant across and held his other hand, saying nothing, letting the minutes drift by along with her thoughts. She knew now that he had come for the children and logically, emotionally even, it was right that he should. Dear God, he had little else and he was a good man, but how broken was he, she wondered anxiously. She pushed the thought away to the back of her mind. Eric was still talking of Australia; it had been their alternative should the worst happen and there could be nothing worse than losing Annie. They had the money saved and they would go, go as soon as Annie was gone.

Her headache was throbbing and there was an ache which filled her throat, one which she knew would spread this evening and which would always be with her no matter whether they were here or in the heat of a new land. I must not think about this now, she told herself. I will think about it in small pieces, that way I can bear it. She forced her shoulders down, taking deep breaths, composing her body into a calmness which was essential for them all.

She wished Eric would come home soon, his shift must be nearly over. It would be so much easier if he were sitting on the settee, his hands held loosely, his eyes gentle and calm.

'Tell me about your ideas, Archie,' she prompted. 'Will you stay in the army for a while. I never expected you to stay in after

12

the armistice. You could have been back two years ago. It seems strange?'

Ignoring what was really a question, Archie explained that he had finally left the service. 'There was,' he added awkwardly, 'the chance to rent back one of my father's shops.'

He brought out his pipe, knocking it against the hearth before he unfolded his tobacco pouch carefully, just as he used to, Sophie noticed. The pungent moist smell was one she had not thought of for six years. It had always been their Christmas present to him, a two ounce tin of Player's Navy Cut.

He pushed the dark shiny fibre neatly into the bowl before lighting it, relishing the absorption of the task but knowing that he must speak to her of the things he had arranged. How to tell her that in what he planned there was no disloyalty to her dead sister since he dealt only in practicalities these days. Since the war had seen fit to pass him along to the end he had to exist but his survival made him bitter.

There was that time when he should have died, the day there was no wind to blow the gas across. The day he had been called a murderer by someone whose hand he could still feel clutching at his leg. He ran his hand over his face, snapping the shutter down. Would he never shake off that voice or this tiredness which now dragged at his heels. Though it must drag even more for those who stood on street corners, filling in empty days in this land fit for heroes. He, at least, had a job to go to now and it was all comparative anyway, he told himself briskly. For God's sake though, it was hard not to think of the good years but the love of my life is not here any more so let's get on with the next bloody lifetime.

Sophie was startled when he spoke, he had been silent for so long.

'You see Sophie, this shop is owned by Joe Carter who bought it off us when we had to sell out. He's had enough and wants to lease it.'

'But what about the children?' she interrupted.

'I'm coming to that.' He smiled nervously. She was so very much like her sister. 'Elisabeth Ryan housekeeps for him.'

'So you'll employ her?' she interrupted again.

'Not exactly. You see it'd look bad, her being young and with the lad.' He finished in a rush. 'I've asked her to marry me.'

Sophie was stunned, then perturbed, at a loss for words.

13

She eventually asked slowly, 'But do you love her Archie?'

He drew on his pipe, tilting his chin as he exhaled. Her blue eyes were confused as he explained.

'No, I don't love her and I doubt that she loves me but without Joe she's homeless. Not many want unmarried lasses with bairns these days; there aren't that many men around any more. I want my children with me, then maybe I can make sense of things, and I can't have them without help. Let's just say we need one another.' He looked at her seriously. 'Barney, her fiancé, was killed at Ypres in '15. I was there but later.' His voice tailed away.

Sophie shuddered thinking of Eric's leg which had been saved even though he had been in a Somme shell-hole for thirty-six hours after being shot. They said it was the maggots which had kept it clean, free of gangrene, but she preferred to consider it a miracle. A shaft of compassion for the girl went through her. At least she'd been lucky enough to have her man return and if Elisabeth had a child of her own she would know how to care for the children. She found it helped to concentrate her mind on the facts.

'When will you take them?' she asked, meaning when is my Annie to leave me.

He stood up. 'I thought a week on Saturday might suit us all, I'll have a word with Albert about Don. I can get moved in by then and Elisabeth has agreed to marry me that morning. Don't want to close the shop longer than necessary; can't risk losing custom. I must get on my feet you see.'

She saw his hands clench and unclench at his sides and nodded though suddenly she was unable to sympathise with his reduced circumstances because a violent spasm of outrage had gripped and held her. She fought to keep it from her face but she wanted to scream at this man for taking Annie from her, just because he was her father. And it was this word which cut through the anger and made her shoulders sag and her lips tremble. She forced herself to rise calmly, banking the fire carefully and repeating that word – father – because of course Annie was not her child. Annie was Archie's. Replacing the shovel, she turned towards the door, still unable to meet his eyes but she repeated the question she felt she had a right to ask and which he had not yet answered.

'But why have you stayed away so long?'

14

Her hand was on the doorknob; she would not pass through until she had an answer.

Archie paused a moment. 'I couldn't come earlier,' he pleaded in a whisper, fearful that the children might hear the conversation, now that they were so close to the door. 'I had to sort something out first, have something to offer the children.' His long slender fingers sought her understanding. But inside he knew it was nothing so honourable, just a long blank series of weeks, months, years, where responsibilities were ignored, buried beneath the noise of ghosts. He was ashamed that it was still without any real interest that he had finally come to take up the pieces. It was simply that there was nothing else to do; he was finished as a soldier; the shaking and the nightmares were too bad. Now he needed to cling to something which belonged to him, to try to find a measure of peace. Therefore he had come to claim his family and rent his shop.

Sophie waited but he said nothing more.

'Will you tell them your news or shall I?' Her voice reflected her troubled doubts. Every breath was difficult now.

'Perhaps we both could,' he replied, laying his hand on her arm, delaying their entrance. 'And Sophie, I will never be able to thank you enough for taking Annie in for these four years. There is a spark in those eyes of hers which makes me feel,' he searched for the right word, 'interested. Heaven alone knows what would have happened to them both without you to sort it out.'

'Your cousin, Sarah, helped a great deal you know. She's always been there, should I need her and she has, without fail, sent the children Christmas and birthday presents. I thought you should know.'

Archie smiled. He was not suprised. Sarah, the daughter of his father's cousin, had always been a good friend to Mary since their marriage and to him as well.

Sophie continued. 'One thing I haven't yet done, although Annie asked so often in the early days, is to tell her how Mary died. She never mentions it now but one day she may hear from someone else.' She paused. 'Perhaps you should be the one, not some spiteful gossip.'

Glad that she had found the courage to say what she had long felt, but not hopeful about the result, Sophie opened the door into the hall and then walked through into the kitchen and the

15

throb of young life met them instantly, softening the tightness of their faces.

'Anyone for scones,' she called, smiling love as Annie won the last game of Jacks and Eric's voice called from the yard.

CHAPTER 2

Betsy leaned against the iron mangle, arching her back in an effort to relieve the ache which dragged at her body. The washroom was the last to be swept, scoured and polished and now the copper shone and she longed to run her hands over its round shine-splashed shape; it looked so warm to the touch.

The ceiling was free of webs which had cocooned spiders all through the long winters but the drab green walls would never look as sparkling as they really were. The sun shafted in from the skylight but it was still dark in this basement section of the house. She could hear, but not see, passers-by as they hurried to where they were going. She straightened, rolling each shoulder in turn, proud of the stiffness of hard work and reached for the shawl which had been flung aside as the sweat had pricked then run down her back when the scrubbing-brush and hearthstone had whitened even the back step. She clicked at herself and said out loud:

'For Pete's sake, bonny lass, they're only a couple of bairns arriving, not the princes of the land.'

'Aye,' she answered laughing at herself, 'but they're to be my bairns so they're better than the King himself.'

She winced as she dried her hands on her coarse apron, the sacking rasping and scratching her work-reddened and swollen hands. Her eyes were pale blue and her lips full and red. Her hair was brown and curled at the temples, the rest was drawn back into a bun and she tucked in the pins more securely. Her hands shamed her and she pulled her cuffs down, the same cuffs that she had nervously pulled this morning at the service. Thank the Lord there was no photographer she thought, and was relieved to see that they contrasted less against the blue cotton than they had against the stark white of her arms.

She traced the raised veins with a puffy forefinger and shook her head. Barney had kissed them and called her the Queen of Sheba and promised her rings for her pretty soft fingers. Well, that's a long time ago now she thought and it should have stayed at fine words but it had not so that was that. The clock in the upstairs hallway chimed but the number was too distant to register so she hurried up the steps, through the kitchen, then on up into the hall.

'My God,' she gasped. 'Four and the buns still not in and they'll be here soon.' Her hands flew to her hair. She could feel the thick damp strands hanging heavy with sweat on her forehead, released from the bun by her rush up the stairs. Her nose and cheeks felt greasy with the shine of labour and there was no tea ready.

She felt her body begin to shake and the hot waves of panic and fatigue swept her first to the stairs leading to the bedrooms, then to the front door until finally she rushed back down to the kitchen.

'Calm yourself, girl,' she urged. 'Just get them buns on. Tom will do at Ma Gillow's for a while longer, then when they come give them bread to toast on a fork, bairns like that.'

She looked in the pantry. 'There's the ham and pickle, they can go on the plates now. And talking to yourself is the first sign of madness.' She carried plates and breadcrumb-coated ham back to the table. Grey ash lay thick where there should have been glowing coals in the grate. The oven set into the left of the fire held barely any heat now and the hotplate on the right was only warm. Betsy shovelled coal on gently, trying not to spurt the ash up into the air only for it to settle on her polished and wiped surfaces.

'Just a few for now,' she breathed, then held up an old newspaper to try and provoke a draught. It was no good. 'Oh God damn it,' she swore and rushed to open the outside door, the paper flapping in her hand. At last there was sufficient air to try and suck the flames up the chimney and what did it matter that the cold raised goose-bumps on her flesh if only the coals roared enough to heat the oven. At last they did and before the newspaper could yellow with the heat she pushed it back into the kindling box, grimacing at the blackness of her hands, the smudges on her apron. She rushed to shut the door, confident that the fire would burn quickly now. She added more coal, still gently, then stood momentarily at a loss.

18

'Come on, get 'em washed, then do the bliddy buns. And don't you swear like that,' she aped her mother, scrubbing her hands then rushing and spilling flour and water, almost in tears. The bowl was already on the table but the buns were soon too wet and stuck to her hands as she tried to mould them.

'More flour, that's all you need, hinny,' she soothed herself but her voice was shaky and high in the chaos. 'That's right, take a deep breath and then bang them in the oven.'

The smart of the oven heat on her tender raw hands made her gasp and two of the buns lurched on to the flag-stoned floor whilst she saved the others only by steadying her arm against the open oven door. The searing white pain brought everything to a stop. The spreading whiteness of the dough at her feet barely registered and tiredly, mechanically, her panic cut through as though sliced from her by a cleaver. She slid the tray, hard and real between her thumb and forefinger, into the dark of the oven. The door clanged shut and carefully she slotted the latch home.

The earlier satisfaction had vanished and her arms ached with a weariness that seeped throughout her body and emptied her mind of even her nervousness. She pulled her coat from the back of the chair and slumped into its clammy heaviness and sat looking round a kitchen which was, from now on, her own. She felt no elation.

It would all have been so different but for the war. Then she would have married Barney and had Tom. Done things the right way round, her mother had hurled when Barney had died, and soon after his son was born. Look at the mess she had just made of a room she had spent hours cleaning and polishing; what a talent she had for little messes; and yes, her mother had said that too. Her hands lay throbbing one upon the other and the harsh pain of the tightening burn across the softness of her upper arm was almost a comfort. It was something which belonged to her and on which she could focus. She had been burned before and knew the course of the pain and that was all she wanted to know at this moment. Her head hung to one side and she lifted her shoulder to rub her cheek and that caress was better than none.

Barney Grant had been a strong young pitman but how gently he had led her to the slopes of the slag after he had arrived home on leave. She pressed her cheek closer now, deep into the cotton of her blouse and she could feel the heat of her skin and she remembered the smell and the feel of the body of her man.

Again and again they had promised that they were different, that lovers who opened their mouths to one another and knew such pleasure in one another could not be touched by war, by death. But his eyes were deep with thoughts that were his own, that he would not share and later he had cried and worried for her in case there should be a bairn, my bonny wee lass he had whispered.

She had laughed then because next week they were to marry and no God would defy her love. And he had nodded and kissed her hand fit for bloody diamonds he had said again.

They had all been recalled the next day in a rush for the next big push. His mates had told her he had felt nothing but she knew it had been raining, raining, raining because that's what the papers had said of Ypres and he hated the rain on his face.

He wasn't found for days. Wipers was such a stupid name for a grave she thought and wished she could have cleaned the mud from his eyes and carried him home, warmed him and, in time, shown him his son.

She stared dully at the fire. Here she was then, living in the same house where she had worked since she was 14 but now it was to be with a man who had today given her a name and a family, not just a job. She should be grateful but her scream for Barney sounded so real that she snapped upright and could not tell whether it had pierced the air or just her mind. The fire was solid red now, God knew how much time had passed, she must be mad to sit as though life was a holiday. She pressed her fingers to her forehead, nervous at the thought of Archie coming home before all this was straight, but she had to fetch Tom, she was already late.

Betsy straightened her coat, drew the latch and the cold of the early evening caught her again. It cooled her even as it caught in her throat and she reached for the bairn's blanket. He'd need it over his face in this chill, then she'd just have to be back in time for them to arrive. Yes, that was it, be quick and there was nothing to worry about she urged herself, thinking as she went that he was such a cold one there was no knowing how he would take a mistake. God, she thought as she undid the gate, what I wouldn't give for a cup of tea.

Archie led the way up the four steps and fumbled for the keyhole.

'The shop is over there,' he told them over his shoulder and Annie nodded though all she could see were dark forbidding shapes in the dim light. She grasped the peak of one of the railings which lined the steps to the front door and through the thickness of her glove she could feel the flakes of old paint first stick into it and then give way beneath her restless thumb. The tip of the railing was not as sharp as had first seemed and it had flat edges which swept to a modest point.

'D'you think if you fell on these they'd go right through you?' she asked her father. 'I mean so they come out the other side.'

He was on the step above her and seemed not to hear. His back was towards her, his face pressed close to the keyhole.

'Don't be daft Annie,' mocked Don. 'You'd have to be right tender and skinny to have them go through. Most people would have 'em stick halfway through and they'd wobble about with their eyes popping out.'

'Until you knocked them off in three throws,' Annie retorted. 'Hey, that would make a good fairground game. Roll up, roll up, knock off the gentleman with the funny hat and win yourself a – a what, Don?'

'Clip round the ear if you go on like this,' he whispered, nodding his head and pointing it towards their father. They sniggered together and tried to count the railings from the bottom to the top even though the gloom made it difficult. Archie looked at them in confusion. They had forgotten him and he was glad for he hadn't known how to react to their extraordinary conversation. He could not remember discussing impaled bodies with Albert as a child, far less attempts to dislodge them once they were 'set up' as these children of his had suggested. Mind you, he and Albert had never been close enough to discuss anything. The key was by now in the frozen lock though it was stiff to turn. Peering closer, working it backwards and forwards, he muttered:

'I'll have to get Elisabeth to oil this thing. It really is too slack of her.'

Annie wondered why he didn't just breathe on it instead of bellyaching about what other people should have done. He's got a pair of hands hasn't he, she thought, and in her irritation could no longer be bothered to count the railings.

She moved her toes inside her boots, her feet ached with the cold but her toes were empty of feeling and seemed heavy in their numbness. She rose and fell, pressing all her weight on to them and longed to squeeze their cold dampness between warm hands. She felt Don close to her, his breath showing white as he blew on his hands. The door loomed large as they grew accustomed to the dimness and Annie's eyes hurt as she struggled to follow the shadowed bulging shape hanging on the door which minute by minute seemed to sharpen and move even as she looked.

Well, she thought, fancy having a great big claw knocker on your door and then spending all night fiddling with the keyhole. She stood staring hard, until the knocker disappeared in a blur of cross-eyes and she felt triumphant at reducing the bunched brass to nothingness. As the door finally swung open she began to move with it. Don felt her sway and shook her arm.

'Don't be stupid,' he whispered in her ear and Annie felt the sniggers rise and shake her shoulders. Oh no, she prayed, don't let me start again else I'll never stop and she wondered where the giggles were coming from.

'Come along then,' their father directed, standing in the dark of the hall and the laughter drained from her and she held back. Why should she go first to be swallowed up by this strange dark house? Don could, the canny beggar. She twisted from his grasp and stood sideways, her eyes refusing to move until he had passed. Her feet curled in her boots for a better grip and her legs braced for battle.

'Come along Annie,' her father ordered shortly. 'Ladies before gentlemen. Donald is quite right.'

Annie raised her chin in a fury of frustration which contracted her scalp but she could do nothing but obey. It was two against one. Turning she squelched hard down on Don's foot, twisting as she did so and sailed in on his indrawn breath of pain and surprise. That'll teach you, she thought, you canny little squid.

Inside there was no wind and it seemed much warmer and very quiet but for a loud tick and there was a strange sharp smell mingling with polish but no scent of cooking or arms outstretched. She stood quite still, her heartbeat loud in her ears, not wanting to move unless it was to touch something definite, to lean against something solid. She felt no friendliness

22

about her, just thick space which could hold endless horrors. She longed for the noise of trains clattering beyond their eyes but not their ears at Wassingham Terrace and the pigeons scattering in their loft as the cats screamed.

Here, in the dark, the ache was swelling. Closing her eyes, Annie tried to remember whether she had missed any black dogs on her way here. There was only the brown one she was sure but still she had held her collar until she had counted a hundred. She had not trodden on any cracks either so surely her wish would be granted. She'd also prayed to God each night, twice, but he had seemed to be deaf for quite some time. Nonetheless her father might just change his mind or even drop dead so that Sophie could walk over and take her back.

It would have been just bearable if Sophie and Eric had stayed in the town just half a mile from this shop but to pack up and go to the other side of the world seemed like the end. There would be no more stories from Eric, no more hugs and tickles from Aunt Sophie, no more drawing on the kitchen floor while Sophie and Eric held hands and talked at the kitchen table.

Sophie had said that she and Eric were young enough to start a new life in a new country and must go straight away. She'd said how she was 29 and Eric was 30 and if they didn't go now, this minute, perhaps Australia would be too much for them. Annie had never thought of them in terms of years before and 29 seemed very old. It's the same age as Sarah Beeston, Sophie had said, but Annie was not interested in other people, only in Sophie.

'Come on in Annie,' her father's voice called and as she turned she remembered the feel of Don's foot beneath her heel and her hands went still and her fingers filled with splintered ice. Oh no, she'd broken her good luck, just when she'd done nothing wrong but everything painfully right since that day in Sophie's kitchen.

Her lip stung between biting teeth and she wanted to drop to the ground and beat it with her hands because now there was no way back to the old life. She wanted to screech to Don, to pummel him with her fists and hurt him as she was hurting. Why did you get at me and make me do it? Why didn't you leave me be, she wanted to shout, and the hate spilled out from her eyes and Don was shocked and she was glad that someone else was feeling pain. Then in turn she was shocked and frightened because she did not want the hate to remain. He was all she had if Sophie could not come for her and she didn't want to be alone with just this dark angry hole left where people had once been.

'Elisabeth, Elisabeth,' her father called into the darkness but there was no reply. 'That's strange,' he murmured almost to himself and the children stayed still. 'I think we should go down to the kitchen and see how dinner is coming along. Get your bearings first though.'

He had already lit the gas lamp and now blew out the match; then shook his arms out of his coat, helping Annie with hers when he had finished. The elastic, which ran from one glove through her sleeves to the other, caught on her cuff and she had to scramble to free herself. She looked up at him. What big nostrils he had and why did he call tea dinner and dinner lunch she wondered. She sighed. And he had not called them bairns since that first day; it made him seem very far away. But now that the smell of the gas lamp was nudging at her it seemed, together with the light, to bring the house to life and that was a surprise for it had almost been as though nothing existed beyond the darkness.

The light showed steep stairs rising with a dark glossy conker-coloured bannister which curled and stopped like the doormouse and she could almost believe she was Alice. Ahead of her was a passageway with a strip of carpet laid on black and white tiles. It ran into the hall and was the same carpet which was laid up the middle of the stairs. It drew her feet far less than the stone of the pavements. She was feeling better now that the front door was shut and the Gladstone bags were lined up at the hall-stand. Now there was no decision to be made. She was here and must stay.

She looked round the dim hall and across to the clock which stretched from the floor to way above her head; much higher than the hall-stand which was now lumpy with coats. She followed the brass pendulum as it swung from side to side disappearing and reappearing with a regularity which calmed her. She had never seen anything like it before but the deep sure sound of the tick, unchanging and predictable, made her feel that here was something that would never surprise, never shock and she was comforted. She tried to reach fifty strokes in one breath. It was five o'clock.

The eruption of sound hit her full in the face and the bone buttons of her cardigan were pulled harshly on straining thread and she jerked back her shoulders in terror. Then, hickory dickory dock her mind raced and she laughed. You'll not catch me again she challenged and it was to life she shouted.

Turning to Don, she drawled. 'Don't fret bitty bairn, it's only a grandfather clock.'

Don caught her tone and cursed himself for leaving his mouth hanging. 'Course I know that,' he snapped but they both knew he hadn't. He had been peering up the stairs, his back to the clock and the noise had been like a clap of violent thunder without a source.

They followed Archie down the passageway, Annie carefully treading on her toes to avoid the pattern. Don's hiss of irritation as she veered into his path was a small price to pay for catching up on some luck. It was dark at the end of the passage and the door to the basement was shut. Annie pulled Don back against the wall. His head was well into the wallpaper above the wooden rail which divided the bottom paint from the flock wall-covering. Hers was part in both and they grinned at one another. She needed him and she had made him feel big again and their anger was gone.

When their father closed the basement door behind them there was silence again and it was cold and dim. The light from the gas mantle outside the kitchen door was the merest glimmer but there was now a smell of baking which was gentle on them. Archie was relieved, this was an important moment for them all and he had feared problems.

'Come down these steps carefully now,' he instructed, guiding them to the rounded wooden hand rail. 'The ground drops at the back of the houses so the basement is at garden-level whilst the front door is at street-level.'

Annie loved immediately the long-grained smoothness of the rail and tried to stretch her hand round it, finger to thumb but failed. She laid her hand lightly on its surface instead and had double value by running it backwards and forwards as she followed the darkness of her father's back. He smelt of hair oil and she thought of his voice which she decided she liked, though it was different to everyone else's that she knew. It had a pattern which kept nudging at a shadow in her mind. She wished he would call them pet or hinny though, since it sounded like love.

As he opened the door, the light burst out at them, warm and tasty, and she and Don followed him quickly through. There was no one there. The fire was low but still red hot, almost clinkered and the table was covered in flour with a bowl in the centre. A boiled ham lay on an oval dish. The floor was smeared with white trails and plopped against the hearth were two dough lumps and the kettle was bubbling its head off on the hotplate.

She looked at their father who just stood there, saying nothing but feeling something because his face was pale and his top lip had thinned. She moved closer to Don who looked nervous in the mounting tension. Annie looked at the white blobs and then at Da; they were the same colour and hysteria rocked inside her.

'Well, I dare say there's a perfectly reasonable explanation,' he managed and picked up a tea towel from the peg to lift the kettle on to the table. The steam made his hand red and wet but the rattling ceased and suddenly it was quiet.

They all stood there staring in silence at the black kettle as though it was the most interesting thing, Annie thought, since Ma Henry's teeth fell out when she sang 'God Save the King', last Empire Day in front of the flag-pole. Why doesn't he just get on and make us a cup of tea like Eric would have done? She changed her weight to her other foot. At the sound of running footsteps in the yard, she stepped back; the door burst open and Betsy spun to a halt. Her laboured breath was loud in the room and she held Tom close, glad of his warm weight against her body, glad that she had a shield against the group.

The frost had turned her nose red and her face white and her hands were still swollen with cracks of deeper soreness opening. More hair had fallen from her bun and hung loosely over and around her face and there was a drip teetering on the end of her nose. Annie shrank as it dropped on to the bundle in her arms and widened and sank into the worn blanket. She saw that it was not a baby but a child with holes in its boots.

'I'm sorry, Archie,' Betsy gasped, her breath still shallow and fast. 'I fell behind and then had to fetch Tom from Mrs Gillow.' She drew away the blanket as the child began to squirm and pull to one side.

26

'There now, Tom,' she soothed. 'Say hallo to your new brother and sister.'

Betsy smiled and drew two chairs close to the fire and then Tom's which was cut down.

Annie smiled at Tom as he sat on the small chair. His eyes were a deep blue and his hair as brown as the bannister upstairs and she'd never seen that colour eyes with dark hair before. Tom ducked his head and looked at her under his brows. He was smiling.

'Come on then, pet,' Betsy coaxed Annie. 'Come on and sit by the fire. And you lad.' This was to Don. 'Are your toes frozen? Then warm them gently or you'll start chilblains.'

Annie moved to the chair nearest the fire taking advantage of the fact that Don was further away and unable to get there first without pushing and shoving and he was hardly likely to do that with her father standing there looking as though he had sucked a lemon. Her Da still hadn't said anything and she stretched her legs to the warmth, trying to ignore the tension he was creating. It made her feel as though she had a clenched fist in her stomach. Betsy leaned past her and shovelled more coal on the fire and the noise was welcome and familiar.

Don stepped to one side as Betsy crossed the room to the guard which she had moved against the wall as she cleaned. It was heavy and the strain showed on her face as she attempted to drag it back to the hearth.

'Don't want you falling on to the coals,' she said in a voice taut with effort.

Annie looked at Da; he was gazing into the fire. She looked at Don, he was looking at his feet, so Annie rose and moved to take the other end and together the two of them brought it back to the fire. By then Don was sitting in her chair, as she knew he would be. He did not move as Annie took her end past him, brushing close to the oven. Breathing hard with the effort she let it drop down, now that it was in position. She heard the thud as it hit Don's boot and she smiled, knowing that she had judged it to a nicety and that it was heavy enough to bruise a toe, even through thick leather. She heard his gasp and trod on his other one as she stepped over him to what should have been his chair.

'Oh dear,' she said, as he hugged his foot. 'Chilblains?'

'Chilblains, did you say?' asked Betsy as she hung her coat

up on the peg at the back of the door. She had noticed nothing but Tom had. He buried his face in his hand and tried to stifle his laughter. Annie grinned at him and winked, he was a bonny lad with his eyes so full of warmth.

'We'll have a winter-green party, shall we later?' Betsy laughed. 'Or at least when I've sorted out something to fill your bellies.'

She glanced at Archie who had stood silent since she entered and ran her hands over her apron, remembering too late its black smudges. She smiled nervously at him, moving over to collect the kettle from the table and realised that she must have left it on the range while she fetched Tom and flushed. Oh God, it must have been bubbling its bloody head off, she thought.

He was looking at her flushed greasy face and eyes which were smudged beneath with shadows and he turned from them and left the room.

Betsy stood and looked at the closed door and listened to his tired footsteps as he climbed back upstairs and knew he would be going to his study. She also knew that she had not fancied the flash of distaste before he had left and it hurt. What had she done that was so terrible, why had he made her feel like a gormless slaggy?

'Mam,' called Tom, 'Your buns is burning!'

Annie and Don helped her as she rushed to open the door and snatch them away from total disaster. As she tipped them onto the table, bits broke and Annie looked sideways at Betsy, her mouth rushing with saliva at the hot sweet smell and Betsy nodded and they both laughed. They were spicy.

'They're not half good,' Don said and Annie agreed as she pressed some into Tom's mouth, watching Betsy wash her hands, and felt a slackening of tension. She had a thing about snot her Auntie had said.

'How old is Tom?' Annie asked, sitting back in the chair which, this time, she had managed to reach first.

'I'm 5,' Tom replied. 'I've got ears and a mouth, you know.'

Annie laughed then, loud and long. Her feet were against the guard and not yet burning. The smell of mashed tea was thick and her hands, round the mug Betsy handed her, felt in place. Betsy's eyes were kind, she thought, but had the same blackness beneath as Aunt Sophie's. She felt sorry for her; it must be hard to be old and have sore hands with no one to pour

28

cream on to cupped palms and no one to put the stopper in or stroke coolness into heat.

She had tried to do it herself once but the cream had run all over the table as she upturned her hand putting the top in the bottle. She ran her tongue along her teeth wondering if her da would do it for Betsy and the thought of him stroking anybody seemed daft. She remembered the look she had seen on his face and shook her head. She was glad he had left because the stiffness had gone with him. He looked as though he had moved from sucking a lemon to finding a nasty smell under his nose, especially when he looked at Betsy, but she didn't really smell, she just looked sweaty.

Anyway, Annie thought, holding the toasting-fork, Betsy was full like Sophie and spoke kind words with laughter in them. It made her feel floppy and her jaw sagged. Maybe it was going to be all right after all.

CHAPTER 3

Archie sat in the cold of his study. It was not heated in any way, though there was a fireplace set into one corner. He did not notice the temperature but sat in the mahogany carver chair which had remained, together with the desk, when he had leased the premises from Joe. Bellies, he thought. It was too much. This room was naturally cold set as it was on the north side of the house and, now that it was evening, he had automatically drawn the curtains across the window when he had crossed to the desk, not completely though, because he never liked to shut out the light altogether. It was a relief to eliminate some of the down-draught from the ill-fitting sash-windows. He had hung the curtains himself as they were ones which Sophie had given him from the attic where she had been keeping them. Bellies. He tore his hands through his hair and made himself think of other things. The curtains.

They were ones which Sophie had rescued from the sale of the house on the hill and they were his and Mary's first purchase for that house. They had chosen a heavy damask drape. Oh yes, he remembered now how he had explained to Mary when they had been delivered to the house that damask was the name originally given to a rose from Damascus, hence the colour, whilst she was a rose from Wassingham. It sounded trite now in retrospect, but she had lifted her hand to his cheek and stroked him. She was so soft he could hardly feel her touch though the heat of her reached him.

The maids had hung the curtains that day in spite of the fact that they were really too heavy for that achingly hot June, the one that blazed just before the world went mad. At least, he recollected, the farmers were able to reap their harvest in time to feed the troops who were quickly blasted away, so more came to eat the supplies the others were no longer hungry for and I was one of them. Balance and counter-balance, he thought, picking up the paper-knife on his desk, that's what most things amount to. He ran his fingers either side of the blade.

The ivory handle, carved in the image of some long forgotten Indian god was as cold as it always was. It was too dark by now to see clearly but he knew its contours intimately. It had been his father's, made from the tusk of an elephant that he had shot himself when on one of his frequent forays to the Raj. Archie had always refused to go; he couldn't bear the heat and he wondered whether Albert had ever been asked.

His father had not liked Albert; not from the same mould, he had grumbled, can't think what went wrong there. Just like your mother's father, like a pot of cook's gravy. Thick and slow. I wonder if Albert noticed, Archie pondered, but dismissed the memory as unimportant to him. Blood sports had disgusted him but the knife had always appealed. It was so impervious to human warmth, to friction. So totally detached.

He turned in his chair, running the blade gently down the curtains. His ivory against her damask, his pale cold skin against her soft warmth. It was too much. He flung the knife on to the desk, burying his face against the faded worn curtains as she had done but that had been on the day when they were vibrant and new.

It's so beautiful, all of it, she had said, her voice muffled by its folds, and he had reached out, taken her shoulders, feeling her flesh beneath the light cotton day-gown and had drawn her to him. I love you so much he had murmured, his mouth in her hair, then on her neck, his hands seeking and finding her breasts, full now with her pregnancy. He could remember still how she had leant into him, pressing her laden womb against him and he had felt her down the length of him. The sounds of the summer which had filled the room through the open windows had disappeared and all that was left was her; hot, soft, urgent, leaning into him, her unborn child thrusting against him as though in protest.

I love you, I love you, she had whispered. My cool ivory blade. I want you in me and she had coloured then, hiding her face in his shoulder, embarrassed at speaking words like these in the daylight, in the drawing-room with Annie curling and turning deep inside her.

He had gripped her black hair which hung loose down her

back, pulling her head so that her face lifted from him, kissing the damp strands which had caught on her forehead and finely boned cheeks. Some swept across her half-open lips and he had kissed her mouth and then her body.

He stirred in his chair, rose and paced the floor.

She had tapped a heat in him that he had not known existed. From the moment he had seen her in his father's office, she had stirred in him a response that no one else ever had. He could at last relate to another human being. Her cool ivory blade she had called him because they both knew that this ivory could only be warm near her source of heat.

He drew the curtain back so that he could see out over the dark yard and then the passageway which ran down the rear of the terrace and looked for the stars but there were none. She had risen to the big house, moved up from Wassingham as though it was natural to her. There had been no bellies from Mary. He felt the pain and then his breath grew shallow and he fought to control the rising panic that increasingly sprang from nowhere. He knew he must push all thought of her away. He must breathe deeply, steadily. Pull into his mind the image he had built of his life from today. He repeated his words in time with the slow breaths he forced himself to make. Cling . . . to . . . the . . . image . . . he . . . had . . . built . . . of . . . his . . . life . . . from . . . today . . . Again and again he said it until his hands which had been gripping the arms of the chair became gradually less tense, his breathing more normal. His mind uncoiled. How much time had passed this time, he wondered, feeling drained.

It usually worked. It had worked when they went over the top, following the white guide-tapes. It had worked when the whizz-bangs fell too close. It worked during the long nights without her, sometimes. He would have liked to thank the captain who had shown him how it was done but his head had disappeared when he'd been on his third breath. They'd heard the shell a fraction later. And of course there was the gas, but even the breathing couldn't help with that.

I was the only one who could have helped with that but I did not. I went ahead and gave the order. He flinched then and bunched a fist, bringing it down sharply on the desk, against the edge because he wanted it to hurt, wanted it to stop. He put his head on the desk, rolling it backwards and forwards waiting for the trembling, which would have built up in his body by now, to explode into his hands and when it came he thrust them between his thighs to contain them. It was quite a little routine now he thought. I'm really becoming quite good at dealing with myself and my rather peculiar habits.

His breathing was becoming normal and his hands were still enough now to light the lamp on his desk. The wick burned blue then yellow and the smell of oil pervaded the room. Gas did not reach above the ground floor so at least he was spared that reminder.

Calmer now, he was able to think of the children and determined again that those four years which took everything else were not going to rob him of the people his children should have been. They were not going to be guttersnipes, they were going to climb out of this shop, back to the top with him and that would include Betsy's bibelot, but my God, there were going to be some changes. God blast it – bellies!

Archie Manon was not going to have a wife behaving like a damn skivvy with buns all over the floor and hair all over her face and street-talk falling from her sloppy mouth. Next it would be the children if it wasn't already. The work was going to be hard, why else did he marry her, but there was no way she was going to look as though it was. He lowered the wick now that it was burning steadily. Barney would no doubt have been happy with bairns, bellies and buns, but there was no way he would ever accept it. He flung himself back in the chair. Damn the hospital, damn their incompetence. How dare they take my Mary from me and he bit on his hand to save himself from calling aloud.

He finally heard the repeated knocking and, forming a tight smile, he rose and walked towards the door. His movements were deliberate and he paused momentarily before he opened it, preparing himself to face the present. It was Betsy.

'I'm sorry, my dear,' he murmured, his voice level, controlled. 'I remembered I had to sign some papers.'

She nodded, not believing him.

'Tom is tired now, Archie,' she apologised. 'Shall we eat without you?' She no longer wore her apron and her hair was newly brushed and coiled.

'Not at all, I'm on my way now but just one moment.' He turned and doused the lamp, replacing the paper-knife at right angles to the letter-rack before returning. He held out his hand to guide her down. 'But perhaps we could be a little better organised in future.' It was not a question but a command and one he gave without even looking at her.

Betsy had expected something of the sort but still the gall rose in her throat and she burned with anger. He had said nothing of her hours of effort and she turned to say as much but his face was closed to the subject and she lost her thoughts in a mesh of clumsiness. Perhaps, she thought as they entered the kitchen, perhaps she could draw nearer when they spent their first night as lovers.

Lying as far under the hot bath-water as possible Betsy felt tea had been better than she had feared. The children had eaten well though they'd been sent to bed early by Archie, and Betsy smiled, grateful for his eagerness.

The air was cold and she soaked a flannel in the water and laid it across her breasts. They were still firm despite feeding Tom and she stroked them and thought of the pleasure a man's hand would bring. It was hard to imagine Archie beneath his well-behaved clothes she thought. Barney's body had been broad and scarred blue from the pit but his skin had been smooth and smelt of sweat. She remembered the weight of his body and the gentleness until they had both wanted something stronger.

The water was cooling and she felt nervous. The nightdress clung to her imperfectly dried body as she slipped it hastily over her head, holding the feeling of abandonment and joy tightly to present it to her husband. What did it matter that it arose from her dead lover?

The fire hissed and flickered in the bedroom with urgent tongues and the room felt strange to her; she had only cleaned it in the daylight as Joe's maid but now she belonged here and could sink into the mattress and open her mouth beneath his. She longed for it, for the grasp of a man's arms after so long. The clinging together, the end of loneliness and shame. She was to be a wife at long last, half of a pair and she was grateful to be made complete.

Archie lay quite still on his side as she edged into the bed. Betsy trailed her hand towards him beneath the sheet and it grew cold as it passed over the emptiness between them. He felt

34

the rustle and then the hand. It lay in the slight hollow of his buttock and his body became rigid at its touch. His eyes moved rapidly in the dark and gently he took it and placed it alongside Betsy's thigh, then rolled over on to his back, closer to her and she held her breath in anticipation.

'My dear,' Archie said quietly. 'You and I have both had our difficulties during the past few years and I think we both have cause to be grateful to have found a partnership that fills both our needs. I feel however that there is one area in which I need not trouble you. After all, neither of us wants more children do we?'

He patted her hand.

'I think it is more important for us to concentrate on providing the right atmosphere within the family. I should prefer that you do not use the vernacular with the children since it won't sit well when we move back to the good side.'

Betsy lay in the dark, loose with shock, her tongue heavy and enormous with grief in her dry mouth. Yes, she wanted more children. Yes, she wanted to writhe and cling to a male body. And what the hell does the vernacular mean. She understood neither him nor his words but she said nothing and moved not a muscle and finally Archie turned towards her again.

'I mean I would rather a standard of manners and language was maintained. Belly is really a word I would prefer not to hear in my own home.'

The fullness in Betsy's throat hurt and she had to breathe cold air through tightening nostrils until they were too full with the mucus of tears. Then, through barely opened lips, she spoke and did not recognise the sound of her own voice.

'Yes, Archie, I understand.'

'Goodnight Elisabeth.'

She turned on her side away from him and, carefully, she cried silent tears for her 22 years and the countless more that were yet to come and there was a coldness in her now, a despair which soured her youth.

CHAPTER 4

Annie hung on the bar which divided the allotments from the wasteland at the back of the lanes, near to her father's shop. The rust was gritty beneath her hands and smelt of old money. At last her balance was perfect. She released her hands and opened her eyes, lifting her head slowly, savouring her success, smiling though the bar pinched her breath up into her throat and her stomach was pushed into her back. The sky was dusty blue and everything shimmered in the heat.

'All right Annie, we know you can do it, get yourself down here now. Eleven's too old for that sort of thing,' Don ordered.

She flipped over the bar, the air rushing through her body so that her face screwed up with ecstasy. It was pleasure mixed with pain and she did it again.

'Hey Annie,' called Tom. 'If you do that too often the blood will rush to your head and burst all over the ground, and I'm not clearing it up.' She laughed and stayed where she was. 'And you're showing everyone your knickers. There'll be a long queue soon.'

'Don't be daft Tom. Who wants to see these bloomers? But just think, if they did, we could charge a penny a look and save all this work.' She pointed to the lead coins which she had finished in record time so that she could be free for the bar

They laughed at her, Georgie, Tom and Don as she stood brushing red dust from her clothes, then bent again over the piping. Don and Georgie chiselling then banging, while Tom just hammered. He'd have to wait until he was 13 too, Don had told him, before he could use the proper tools. Nine was too young.

Grace had not been able to come today but would be at the fair this evening and in spite of Don's protests they were doing enough coins for her too. Tom had flared at Don that it shouldn't matter if Grace was there or not. They were a gang weren't they and Annie had kissed his thin cheek. They loved Grace, her and Tom did, but she loved Tom more. He was a like a puzzle piece. He fitted her exactly.

Bye, it was grand here in the sun she thought, but hot, very hot. When they had arrived, Don, of course, had grabbed the shaded area created by the corner of hawthorne hedge that ran round the whole of the allotment. The only other area of shade was along by her father's shed where they had found the hammer and chisel but nettles grew three feet high in this spot and Georgie had not let them beat them down to make a cool work area. Might see a Camberwell Beauty he had said and besides, the butterflies need nettles more than we need shade.

Georgie was now sitting by the rows of lettuce which were yellowing and limp from too much sun whilst Tom still sat where she had been, next to the young leeks which had wafted a strong smell as they worked.

Her da would need to water them tonight, when the sun had gone down, but most likely it would be Tom or her again as usual. She looked along the rows. There wasn't much in this year; the patch was mostly overgrown with weeds, though the runners had gone in as always. Her da liked runner beans but without the stringy bits. Shame really that it was so neglected. It was like everything else round here now and she reached down and pulled at some weeds; the ground was too hard and would not release the roots. Georgie looked up and smiled, his mouth turned up at one side as it always did. His brown hair was too long and it fell over his eyes. He flicked it back. His teeth were white against his tanned skin.

'You're always brown,' she called. 'Where do you get your tan from? Been taking the sun by the sea, like the royals?' She thumbed her nose and strutted about doing a regal wave.

Tom giggled and Georgie threw a handful of grass he had torn from the verge. It fluttered to the ground before it reached Annie, lying in a loose circle.

'A cloak for me to walk on – how kind,' minced Annie and the laughter continued. She felt a sense of delight.

'Get on with the work,' Don growled. Tom glanced across at him.

'She's only having a bit of fun,' he protested. 'And she doesn't act like a lady that often.' Annie shook her fist at him.

'Well, she's not doing it on my time,' ground out Don, his head still down. He ran his fingers round the rim of the coin, making sure it would pass without comment tonight.

Annie gazed at Tom. He raised his eyebrows, then they both mouthed, 'Bloody Albert!'

'Hope it's not catching Tom,' Annie called.

'This Albertitis, you mean,' he replied. They both turned to Don and stared. 'No, we'd have to work in Albert's shop every Saturday and the old man's not going to have us over the doorstop. We have to help Betsy in ours for nothing. Good thing we like it, ain't it, Annie.'

Don looked up and glowered at them both.

'Get on with your work.'

'I've done my share,' challenged Annie, 'and Tom's doing fine. Just keep your hair on, will you, or you'll be polishing your head in the morning. Anyway, it's just because you're the eldest you throw your weight around.'

'Only by two days,' chipped in Georgie and Don returned to his coins without a word, forgetting everything but the need to finish the job.

Georgie sat back on his hunkers, wiping his forehead with the back of his hand. His coins were perfect and Annie was intrigued that those broad hands could produce such precise work. He had worked quickly without seeming to, always calm, always accurate. She watched as he half closed his eyes against the sun and cocked his head to one side.

'I'll show you how to hang by your arms from that bar, turn inside out and dangle if you like.' His voice was soft.

She moved closer, blocking the sun and casting her shadow over him, her eyes alight with interest.

'When?' she asked.

He half smiled. 'Whenever you like,' he replied, looking directly up into her face, able to do so now that she stood as a shield between him and the sun. She could see that his eyes were almost black with small yellow flecks, like a cat's. Tom moved near to her, his small shadow cast over Georgie's neatly stacked coins. Georgie pulled a long stem of grass from a nearby clump, eased it out of its shaft and chewed the moist white shoot. His smile grew into a grin and she responded but did not know why she felt so pleased.

'Will you show me too?' asked Tom, his small face eager. He

38

moved up against Annie and she put her arm round his shoulder and pulled him close.

Georgie continued to chew for a moment while he studied Tom and through his eyes Annie saw Tom as he now was; very thin and pale, though without rickets yet, thank God. She hadn't noticed how gaunt he had become, how gaunt they must all have become but it looked worse on Tom because he was younger. She took out the last of her bread and dripping from her pocket and made him eat it. Hunger seemed always to be with them these days.

Georgie smiled. 'I reckon you're just too young Tom, but I tell you what; I'll take you to the hives, shall I? Down by the beck. Show you the bees, you'd like that.'

'You would and all Tom,' agreed Annie shaking him slightly, aware of his disappointment, wanting to make it all right for him. 'Bring your pencil and draw it. There's the beck and that willow and the shape of the hive. Georgie'll tell you all about bees, he's good on insects. I know, we'll make a day of it. I'll do a picnic for you and Don. What do you think? We'll ask Grace, she'll like a picnic.'

'Oh aye, Annie, that'd be . . . '

'Oh God,' Don broke in, 'not old fatty.'

Annie turned to him. Why could he never be easy? She felt anger growing. He knew she couldn't stand to hear him start on Grace. She felt hotter as the anger took her over, made words spill out.

'Why d'you have to be so mean?' she hissed. 'You know she can't help being plump; she's made that way and she's nice with it an' all.'

She strode over the uneven ground in a hurry to reach him, in a hurry to fight him, to make him stop it once and for all. She stood above him, hands clenched, waiting. Georgie reached out and held Tom back as he moved to follow. He was squinting against the sun now that Annie had moved. 'Stay here with me lad, it's between them two, I reckon.' Tom tugged against him but Georgie held firm so he stood and they both watched.

'Look at me Don Manon and stop poring over your bloody money for a minute.' Annie waited but he ignored her, banging with his hammer at the lead. 'Don, look at me.' She moved closer but still he ignored her and a great swamping rage cut out the banging, cut out the sun and she grabbed his hair.

'I'm not bloody Betsy and you're not me da so don't start treating me as though you are.' Her voice was low, her hand clenched his hair tighter.

Don slapped her hand away, still without looking up. She grabbed his hair again and pulled. 'Lift your head and look at me,' she shouted.

This time his slap caught her leg and she almost went down but did not. She still had his hair and at last his head was forced up as she pulled again. His eyes were watering with the pain, his face was red and sweating and full of anger.

He lashed out at her leg again, the crack echoed across the allotment. Tom struggled in Georgie's grasp.

'She's doing fine bonny lad, she's all right for now.' But though his voice was still soft, his eyes were narrowed and alert, and there was a set to his face. His legs were tensed to spring, though he still squatted like the miner he would become.

'I'll kill him if he hurts her,' Tom cried, still tugging away.

'You won't need to Tom, because he won't hurt her. I won't let him. I won't let anyone ever hurt her.' His voice was still quiet but there was something in it that allowed Tom to relax, to stand and wait.

Again Annie withstood the slap and tightened her grip. 'Grace is not fat, she is clever. She is just big for her age – got it. And don't ever let me hear you say that again, and don't let her hear you either. You made her cry last time.' She was speaking slowly, clearly, her face close to his. She could feel his breath on her cheek, see his eyes staring into hers.

'You're a cruel boy sometimes Don Manon and when you are I don't like you.'

She released him and still he said nothing, just glared. As she turned he tripped her. She sprawled on the ground and smiled, she had known he would and she had let him. It made him think he was even but she knew he would not call Grace fat again. She scrambled to her knees and looked at Tom. He would understand that she was all right. He always understood her but would Georgie? Would he think she had been defeated? She looked past Tom to him and he winked.

'For God's sake sit down and stop causing a draught,' he said and suddenly laughter played around the group again. The atmosphere was broken and Tom and Don began to bang again.

Annie sat down shaking inside, upset by the sudden fight. She raised her face, eyes closed towards the beating sun and felt the heaviness of her hair as it dropped on her back. She shook it until it brushed against her shoulder. Forget it she told herself and made the last few moments squeeze into a black box she kept at the back of her mind. She was sheltered from the slight breeze by the blackberry bushes and the allotment shed and the heat drew the creosote out to hang heavy about her face, stinging her nose with its sharpness. Her breathing was slower now, the trembling in her hands was less. She made herself look out over her da's patch to help push back the last few moments. The beans were setting bright red flowers and she could hear the murmur of bees. Yes, it would be nice to go to the hives. She lifted heavy lids and could see, or almost see, minute insects which flickered full of lightness and then were gone. The soil was baking drier with each day and she rubbed warm dust into the cracks which ran everywhere at her feet and would probably stretch down to Australia soon. Was it as hot with Aunt Sophie she wondered, but her last letter had said their winter took place during our summer. She sighed but was not unhappy with her life. It had settled into a pattern, though there was no money any more and men out of work all around.

She stretched her arms and felt loose again. The winter seemed long ago and she was right glad to be free of the liberty bodices and rough wool stockings. She squirmed at the thought; it was like living in a cinema seat for half of your life. She rose and sauntered beyond the bushes, flicking at the straying brambles with a split birch twig. They'd soon be picking the berries which were now only green and hard to the touch.

The pain from Don's slaps was receding. Her heartbeat had slowed again. The clicking of a cricket and rustle of unknown life was close and loud. Beyond that were the distant sounds which reminded her of the world beyond the allotment but nothing was real today except them and their work because he, the Lord and Master, their father, had allowed them to stay out late at the fair tonight and had actually given them each tuppence, even Tom, which was a bit like the second coming. He was tight with Tom though she made sure the lad had half of everything of hers.

She reached down and eased a ladybird off a blackberry stem

41

on to her hand, watching it until it opened its wings and flew to its burning home. She would go straight for the boats tonight, she decided. They thrust you higher the harder you pulled at the rope thronged with ribbon rags. It hauled your arms as though they would come straight from their sockets and lifted you half out of your seat, or at least they did last year but she was bigger now.

Annie hugged herself and grinned. They must have been minding their manners or something to go again this year with things as they were, but Don was right, tuppence wasn't near enough, not if you wanted to win a coconut and skewer out the sweet milk or stay on the painted horses for another go. Mind you, they could make you sick if they went on too long dipping and rising, round and round.

Yes, Don's idea of the lead coins was a good one but she felt again the sense of unease at the gap which had begun with his year spent at Albert's and had become even greater as the years passed and she did not know why. He was her brother but she could not get close any more. It was as though he was slapping her away all the time.

She watched as they worked and gradually the thrill of passing the coins pushed everything else to one side. She was half excited, half terrified and wondered if they would get caught and that was what was so much fun. Bye, just think of the row if that happened. Da would go even paler.

The shadows were lengthening across the allotment now and she called. 'Come on, you lot. That's enough. If we're late for tea we've had it.'

'Dinner you great daft dollop,' Don hissed, looking tired now and she wanted to put her arm round him and hold him to her but she daren't. 'Right, we're coming. Make sure it's all clear. Go and look and wait by the corner, Annie. Now listen, Tom, not a word to your mam about this or you don't come tonight and for God's sake be quiet. Make sure you're the same Georgie.'

Georgie threw a lazy salute and ambled along watching the ants as they scurried in and out of the cracked soil.

At the corner with the street in sight, Annie heard them coming and would have done a mile away, she thought. She stood, arms akimbo, a breeze lifting her hair and dropping it as quickly; it was refreshing. She watched as they came in single file round the edge of the last three vegetable plots, dry earth puffing up with each step, covering their boots so that they had no shine left as they reached her.

'It's no good, you'll have to wrap them in something. You sound like a load of brass monkeys, jingling about like that.' She could barely talk for laughing.

Don glared. 'Will you shut up with your daft remarks. Go on then, find us something.' But there was nothing here or further down by the entrance to the street so they retraced their steps hoping that no one was watching from the houses which faced the plot. They searched for old sacking in the shed but there was only dried disintegrating newspaper that crumbled as they touched it. There wasn't even a dock leaf with its moist expansiveness.

'You'll just have to keep your hands in your pockets and stifle the noise until you can belt up to your rooms. Will your ma be in, Georgie?' Annie asked.

'O aye, but she'll not notice over the noise of the bairns.' The grass stem was still in his mouth. 'Go on Don, you'll be late,' he chivvied. 'We'll meet in the usual place.'

Annie ran on, turning to look at them following her. She held out her hand to Tom and clasped his free one. It was hot and sticky. She was laughing so hard her stomach banged against her ribs.

Betsy turned as they stumbled in the door, the laughter making her long to be out with them and ten years younger.

'Just look at you,' she scolded, turning Annie round. 'Your skirt is filthy and screwed up in your knickers. You've dripping round your mouth. You're worse than Tom and he's no bleeding angel.' She turned to Tom. 'And you can wipe that smile off your face, that's nothing to be proud of.' Tom straightened his face and Annie saw Betsy smile as she turned away.

'Come on now, all of you, clean up and then sit down, your da will be here in a minute. Come on, Don, don't hang about outside, and leave that door open, it's too hot as it is with the fire on. Get your hand under the tap and sort yourself out.'

Don caught at the door as it swung shut and pulled it open again. The water spluttered as Annie twisted the tap. She waited for Tom to wash first then held her hands under the spurting water.

'Go on with your pocketful,' she mouthed under cover of her splashing. She was thirsty and her tongue ached with the thought of a cold clear drink but she knew she would have to wait until she was clean before Betsy would allow it.

Tom was on his way and Don moved with him.

'I'll just nip upstairs for a moment, Betsy.' He was nearly at the door, having side-stepped round the laid table when he stopped dead-still as their father entered.

Tom sat down in his seat, he had been just behind it, gripping both pockets.

'Come along, Don,' their father said. 'Sit down or I shall assume you don't want to finish your meal in time for the fair.'

Annie's eyes widened and she half turned, splashing water down the front of her dress. Don was stranded halfway to the door and had to return to the sink without rattling and giving everything away. She coughed, again and again and Don bolted over to the sink, gave himself a quick splash and moved, stiff-legged, to the table.

'For goodness sake girl, have a drink. Don't stand there looking helpless.'

'Sorry, Da.' She reached for the enamel mug and filled it. Avoiding the black chip she looked over the top to see if Don was safely seated. He was. 'I should have had a drink earlier,' she tossed at Betsy and scuttled to her seat as she caught the look in her step-mother's eye. It would be a clip round the backside if she wasn't careful. She pressed her leg against Tom's as she sat down.

Betsy looked at Annie and then at Tom. His wide-eyed look betrayed him. Just like his da when he's up to mischief, she thought. Ah well, let them have some fun, thinking all the time of the unpaid invoices she would have to deal with this evening and the partnership papers that Albert was coming to sign, though what good it would do to pool their meagre profits she could not understand. If there was no work, there was no money for traders. Even those in the pits knew they could be working today and not tomorrow so were being canny with the pennies, especially with wages going down, not up.

She shivered, looking at the rashers she had put before the family and worried about the future. For the moment they were just about fed and clothed. But for how long? She sighed. It must be time for another of Ma Gillow's readings. Maybe the tea leaves would be clearer this time. She lowered herself heavily on to the chair and played with her meal; the fat had congealed and a thick whiteness coated the bottom of her plate and she had little appetite.

'Your knife is not a pen, my dear,' remarked Archie.

Automatically Betsy shifted her grip, no longer stung to a retort. At least the bugger had been right about one thing she thought; she wouldn't know what to do if she had a string of bairns hanging off her skirts as her mother would have said. At least she did not have to suffer a husband's beer-breathed Saturday night demands and Archie's pale hands on her body. Betsy wiped her forehead with her arm. The thought of her belly full with Archie's child made her feel sick.

She stretched back in the chair. Her hands were swollen and aching again from the beer kegs and they would be worse tomorrow and the next day and for as long as she had to drag and hammer and cork hop-reeking barrels.

Again Archie broke into all their thoughts.

'I'll just get along to the study and make out Bert's invoice. He's coming along later to settle.' He rose. 'Now, be in by ten all of you and no mischief.' He looked particularly at Annie before leaving and laughed at Don who said:

'As if we would.'

They all watched as he reached the door. He seemed to hesitate, then passed through. Betsy pursed her mouth in frustration; wouldn't we all like a study to hide in, she thought, but at least this time he'd given her lad the same as the others. Annie and Don nodded to Tom to follow as they slipped from the table and made for the door.

'Before you go, please make sure you wrap those lead bits in cloth,' Betsy had spoken softly, smiling as she caught the clink when they stopped abruptly.

Annie swung round, her mouth open.

'And don't think you were the first to work out that fiddle.' Betsy laughed. 'Just make sure you're not the first to be caught.'

Don and Tom dodged out of the door. Annie remained, looking closely at Betsy who stood with her back to the light but there was enough from the fire for her to really see her and she was shocked. Her step-mother was not really old, she realised. In fact she was young where the lines hadn't dug in and spewed out wrinkles. She must once have been a child and laughed in the sun, and pity twisted inside her and drew her across the room, back to the bowed shoulders and cruelly worked hands.

Betsy was now looking at her with gentleness in her eyes. Annie touched her hands which were like the sausages in Fred Sharpe's window, blotchy and glistening. How could Betsy bear to leave behind the things that she and Tom knew. The smell of blackberries as they burst, ripe segments between thumb and forefinger, the pink mice from the corner shop. Leave them behind for this. She thought of the cooking, the washing with arms deep in water again and again as she dollied and scrubbed the same clothes week after week. The house was a prison to be escaped at all cost and so was the shop with its smell of beer and a man who never looked at you as you cleared up behind him.

'How can you bear not to be free?' she asked looking up into her face.

She allowed Betsy to place her hands on her shoulders and pull her into an apron which smelt of bacon.

'Nobody is free,' she replied. 'We all have our place and you have to make the best of it.'

Betsy was comfortable to lean into, Annie realised with surprise.

'Come on, Annie,' called Don through the door, his tone strident with impatience. 'We'll be late.'

Annie stayed. She felt that if she went now she wouldn't quite keep this moment, wouldn't be able to find her way back to it.

'I said, come on.' Don called again.

Annie pushed back from Betsy's arms then, thrusting away the feeling that this was important, then was gone, but not before she said. 'I'll be different, I'll be as free as the wind.'

Betsy stood empty, now that she had gone, but still aware of the warmth where she had been. I love her, she nodded to herself, but there never seems enough time to show her.

Archie sat in his study, arms loose and hands dangling. It was cool in spite of the heat of the day and little of the soft evening light penetrated, though the street sounds were a constant murmur and he welcomed them. There was noise but nothing

46

discernible, nothing he had to note or which demanded his attention. That was why he liked the prints on the far wall. Framed in mahogany they were so discoloured that the views were merged into the paper; totally indecipherable. His pipes were set in their stand, each in order. The paper-knife at right angles to the letter-rack. His chair was placed in the middle of his desk and the whisky was in the decanter; all could be reached without conscious thought.

The decanter stood out now like a jewel and he treasured it as such with a sensuality which was usually reserved for a smooth-skinned woman, but that was because Mary had given it to him. It was all that he had left of her now.

He set his lips as he turned to the invoices and went yet again over the last four years' trading. It seemed impossible to make any headway, there simply wasn't the money any more with the depression biting harder.

If only the war hadn't happened. It had destroyed overseas markets for the old industries because other nations had been forced to produce their own coal and steel, and now, where could the North sell their wares?

He went over all the alternatives for his own survival again, knowing that this was what he was fighting for, not any longer his dream of middle-class status. Perhaps with a family partnership one store could keep the other afloat.

To merge with Albert went against the grain somehow, though. He took a pipe from the rack and filled it, tamping down the tobacco. He did not feel easy with the man though, for God's sake, he was his brother. Was it unnatural he thought to dislike Albert, to feel nothing but irritation at his surliness; at the way he pressed close in order to use his larger size to intimidate?

Above all, was it normal to resent entering into a partnership of equals when he had always felt superior? His father had encouraged that of course, grooming him to run the business whilst sending Albert into one of his shops.

He should have objected then, told his father it was unfair on Albert, but he had not. He enjoyed too much the position of power and Albert had never objected, never complained. Even when they were at grammer school together and Archie had always beaten him in the exams, he had never appeared to register the fact. They had just grown up ignoring one another.

Albert was like Betsy, Archie thought, not aware of anything very much.

The irony was, of course, Archie sighed to himself, his father had groomed Albert to succeed in the world they now found themselves in whilst he was sinking rapidly. The golden boy was going under and, what's more, he doubted if he really cared.

He struck a match and sucked until the vapour entered his mouth and the tobacco was alight. He kept his hand half covering the bowl and turned to the window. He knew he needed more customers but where were they to come from. There were so many men on street corners making their woodbines last all day and not having a beer at all as they wondered when the air would be filled again with the noise of the pits, but there was no more work here than in the docks. At least the bloody war had kept the men off the streets, he had heard a vicar say to his companions as they waited to cross the road in Newcastle the other day. Makes it untidy for you does it, he had wanted to say. Should have finished a few more off, should I, while I was out there. As his hands began to tremble he clenched them between his thighs. His pipe was still gripped between his teeth but he had forgotten, he was falling back into the darkness again.

The trouble was that he had known nothing about gas, he pleaded silently, he had just been sent along to fill a gap. But had he known about wind? He nodded to himself. There was no excuse, he had known about the wind. God damn it, everyone knew about wind. The bloody generals knew about wind. How there had to be wind.

The shuddering in his hands was violent now and this was transmitted down the length of his legs. His pipe was cold. He had told them though, he had told H.Q. There was no wind. He had shouted it over the sound of the bombardment which preceded the attack. He was sure he remembered shouting but it had made no difference and he had obeyed the order. His eyes were open now, his head jerked back, he drew in deep breaths, he could hear again the murmur of the streets in place of the scream of shells, of men. He knew a lot about gas now.

His hands were finally still, he was too tired now to even relight his pipe, which he placed on the desk in an exact line with the paper-knife. He heard faintly the sound of the fair organ as the breeze blew up from the wasteland and he envied his children who lived every moment joyously. What did they know of 1924 and the way things were coming apart at the seams?

The shadows deepened in the room and he leant over and lit the lamp, hearing heavy footsteps on the stairs and knowing that it was Albert and he was not alone, for there were lighter, quicker ones in his wake. That would be Bob Wheeler who was coming as witness. He was a good man and worked at the colliery in the office but spent most of his time on union affairs. Archie had only met him once, briefly, but had liked the man. There was an intelligent look about him.

Albert didn't knock, just came straight in as Archie rose. He covered his irritation by reaching for his pipe and striking a match. He waved to a chair while he relit his pipe.

'Not late, am I,' said Albert. It wasn't a question. He was late and relished the fact, it was clear from his voice which had more than a hint of belligerence, Archie thought.

He turned to the man who waited in the doorway while Albert slumped into a chair. He was small and wiry in a well fitting but old dark blue suit. He held his hat in one hand and smiled as he waited to be invited in.

'Come in,' said Archie, bringing another chair up to the desk. Albert grinned.

'You know Mr Wheeler, don't you, Archie? I brought him along like I said. Equal partners at last, eh, Archie!'

Archie felt his face tighten. He nodded and turned to Mr Wheeler.

'Good of you to come. Sit down, won't you.'

Wheeler's handshake was firm but there was a slight tremble as he took the whisky that Archie offered. War, Archie wondered?

He poured one for Albert.

'Bit more in that, Archie, this is a celebration.' Albert leaned forward and grinned again. His long face looked heightened with pleasure. His large body still seemed as though it had been tipped into dirty clothes but there was an air of expectancy about him, almost a lascivious pleasure.

Archie forced himself not to visibly recoil as he poured more Scotch into his glass and listened to Albert.

'Wonder what the old man would think of this then. You and

49

me equals. He'd turn in his grave and I don't see you laughing all over your face either Archie, me lad.'

Archie was surprised. So, he thought, I've underestimated you, all these years have I, and now the question is, how deep is the grudge, for he felt sure that there would be one. He felt curiously detached; not worried, not frightened since there was little anyone could do to hurt him any more. He just felt surprised. He watched as Albert settled himself back in his chair, his shirt open at the neck, his chest hairs crawling up his neck. He really did despise the man. He turned to hide his eyes.

'Let me take your hat,' he suggested to Mr Wheeler but he refused.

'Call me Bob,' he said to Archie.

'Right we will then, Bob,' Albert said, annoyed by this instant familiarity, knowing that Wheeler had for two years preferred to stay on formal terms with him. 'Let's have another drink then, Archie.'

There was sweat on his upper lip; this was not his first drink of the day, thought Archie, but then it isn't mine either. He poured another for Albert but Bob had drunk hardly any yet. Archie noticed the tremble of his hand as he took another sip. It must be the war, he thought again.

But it was not the war, though Wheeler had been through that too. It was merely a family trait passed down from father to son along with all the other failings Bob Wheeler's mother had listed on many occasions, always with a smile. Wheeler's father would snort in reply and his son grin. His mother knew really that the hours spent discussing the latest leader in the newspaper were not wasted. After all, it had helped Bob to form an articulate argument.

Together they read under the dim light of the oil lamp in the cold front room of the small house, well away from the airing washing and the endless mashed tea. His mother might have swiped at his head with a towel when he was too lost in thought to shift himself to help her but it was as much her wish as his da's that their son, Bob Wheeler, should get some learning under his belt and go into the offices of the colliery not the darkness of below ground which had stifled his father's urge to improve their lot, and the lot of their fellow workers. He had been too physically broken within a few short years but from those offices they knew that their son would keep a clear head and a vision beyond the blank coal-face. Bob Wheeler frequently thought, though, that vision was one thing and progress quite another, for how could you get blood out of a stone? It was satisfying trying nonetheless.

And that was it, he was completely satisfied with his work to the extent that he never missed not having a wife or family of his own, even now with his parents dead. His mother had died of flu the doctor said, but Bob felt it was a broken heart after his father had died of black spit. What he did miss, though, were his conversations with his father and he wondered whether this man, Archie Manon, might prove to be something of a substitute. He looked as though he saw beyond the confines of the Wassingham streets.

'Business any better with Ramsay in power?' Bob Wheeler asked.

Archie stirred, about to speak but it was Albert who replied. 'Business would have been better if the mines had stayed under the eyes of the government,' he grunted, settling himself back in his chair. 'Bloody stupid handing them back to the owners with exports down. The wages come down and that makes my business difficult.' He pointed to Archie. 'We were saying as we came along that the owners did all right out of the war, not like the rest of us.'

Bob Wheeler caught Archie's eye and they exchanged nods.

'Where are these papers then?' Bob asked, and took them from Archie as he passed them over. 'Shall I stick my name under both of yours as witness? Is that the idea?'

'If you don't mind,' Archie pointed to the area with his finger. 'The owners have iron and steel interests as well, I think you'll find, Albert. They sell cheap to the plants and get even better profits from their iron companies as well as exploiting the miners. What do you think Bob?'

Bob twisted his pen round and round, his long face thoughtful. His hair which was greying at the temples had receded slightly giving him a broad forehead and an elderly air but Archie guessed that they were much the same age, about 40. His brown eyes matched exactly the colour of his hair but his moustache was more red than brown.

'I think you're right Archie.'

'How come the South is getting all the new industries? After all the unions supported Ramsay's campaign and most of the strong union men are up here. Why can't the chemicals and radios come North for a change?' Albert slapped the table. Scotch had spilt down his chin.

Archie had to admit to himself that Albert had a good point. Chemicals had come on greatly during and since the war and there was talk of the small companies merging to form Imperial Chemical Industries to make them more efficient but that would not take place up here, there was no doubt about that. If only they had brought the car industry up North. The steel works were up here after all and so were the men. It was crazy.

'I know why,' Albert cackled and answered his own question. 'They're afraid our lad's will get to like the feel of clean hands and light work, then they'd have no bloody coal or steel at all.'

His face was very red, his eyes now bloodshot and ugly. He breathed Scotch across the table at Archie. 'Ain't that right Archie? But then you never liked dirty hands did you? Had to keep 'em clean up in that hoity-toity office at the top of the heap. Didn't matter that I got mine dirty in that poky little shop, did it?'

He was beginning to slur his words and Archie felt his face flush with embarrassment at the scene that was developing. Embarrassment and guilt because it hadn't mattered to him that Albert got his hand's dirty, but for God's sake, he was not his brother's keeper.

Albert had not finished. It was as though a dam had burst and he could not haul the words out fast enough.

'Mr Wheeler's big too, you know, in the union. Works in the office of Bigham colliery but is rising faster in the union. Clever to juggle the two like that. But I was forgetting, you're not big any more, are you, Archie, you're just like me now. You and your bairns are just like me. Especially Don.'

At last Archie began to feel a stirring of unease. The children, he had forgotten the children when he had decided he could no longer be hurt. He tried to gather his thoughts but Wheeler coughed and looked at Archie.

'I quite enjoy the work you know, but it's the union side that matters. The men need more than they're getting on the dole.'

As he spoke, Archie let go of his children. He would return to them later, but now he would listen to this man who he felt held something he needed: a possibility of companionship.

'They need something more than soup kitchens, there's nothing for them to do, nothing to remind them that they are human beings.'

He accepted another tot of whisky from Archie.

'They need something else.' He tailed off in thought.

Archie was glad that Bob Wheeler had scooped the conversation out of the scene that had promised to develop and now Albert seemed to have lost his thread and was slumped quietly in the chair.

'I was thinking before you came of that problem,' he sucked at his pipe, prodded the tobacco with a match. 'I used to arrange football behind the lines – I wonder if . . . ' he looked out of the window. 'Yes, I wonder.'

Silence fell momentarily, Albert slurped the last of his drink, then slapped the glass back on the desk.

'Partners now, Archie.' His voice was slower and he was lisping. He thrust the papers over the desk to Archie.

Archie did not look at them, just longed for Albert to go now, but if he did, so would Bob and he didn't want an end to the discussion which seemed about to begin. The air in the room was heady with tobacco smoke which mixed with fumes from the oil lamp, whose wick had not been burning clean.

'You want to trim that you know,' Albert said. 'Get that lad of yours to do something to earn his keep.'

'Were those the children we passed as we came down the street?' Bob asked, as Archie eased open the lower sash-window. Immediately there was a breeze and the sound of the fair increased.

'That's right,' nodded Albert. 'Off to the fair, were they Archie?' He gave him no chance to reply but turned to Bob with a truculent face. 'What's the government doing then, you never said. Bloody Labour in and nothing's changed.'

Bob Wheeler appeared to be marshalling his thoughts for he said nothing for a moment, but his face became set in bitter lines.

'I'll admit Ramsay's been a disappointment. He's more set on joining the establishment than doing much for the likes of us but I suppose, in all fairness, he's sensible to take it steadily. Labour's a new party and after the revolution in Russia people are afraid of the same thing happening here. Perhaps he doesn't want the country to think that's what the Labour party is, a bunch of revolutionaries in disguise. Remember too, Albert, that his is a minority government so he needs to persuade the Liberals to support him if he wants to change things, and that's easier said than done. Remember they're a bosses' party.'

'It's hard to explain to the miners though, isn't it, Bob,' Archie said gently, 'especially when they threw their weight behind Labour in these elections?'

Bob nodded. 'You're right there. It's not too bad because some coal's still selling abroad at the moment so let's hope that goes on. It'll keep the job situation stable though it's pretty poor I grant you.

Archie nodded. Albert seemed to be asleep, thank God, his head was slumped on to his chest. 'Once the German and French fields are back in full production though, we're in trouble.'

'Exactly.'

'And if we go back on to the gold standard?'

Bob looked up in surprise. His face took on a look of respect. 'Then, my friend, the North is in deep trouble. If the external value of the pound is raised, exports will fall even further. Production will decrease, our men will be out of work in droves. We need customers for our coal. If there aren't any customers, why should the owners pay miners for coal they can't sell?'

'What about the modern pits?'

'They're not up here though. Nottingham should survive. They've the latest machinery and high production from good seams. Good seams and good conditions mean good working relations. They'll be all right down there but up here it'll be a different story.'

And so the talk swayed between them through another glass of Scotch until Albert woke.

'Wages still going down, aren't they,' he spluttered 'and talk of another strike an' all. Christ, if that happens . . .'

'Then,' said Archie slowly, 'perhaps we've done the right thing to come together at last Albert.' He felt the need to reconcile himself with this man.

'Clutching at bloody straws, I reckon,' grunted Albert, and Archie wondered if he meant the partnership or his own deeper meaning.

'It's new owners we need,' urged Bob, 'one's that'll put money in and stop shoestring mining that kills and maims.' He was still with his miners, Archie realised, a long way from the partnership he had just witnessed. 'Owners that will give a decent wage and invest to improve efficiency and safety. State control and ownership must come.'

He stopped himself and raised his hands. 'Sorry, my hobby-horse. I forget where I am somethimes.' He smiled at Archie. 'Well, I wish you luck with the shops. Who knows you could be founding a business which the children will take over and expand. End up employing some of the poor devils round here.'

He pushed himself out of his chair. 'I must get off to a meeting now. Are you coming, Albert?' He looked to see if he was ready to leave.

'Aye, we'll get off now.' Albert rose without looking at Archie. He lurched towards the door and was through it and on his way down the stairs without a backward glance.

Archie watched and bit his lip. Bob walked on ahead of him, stopping in the doorway. He smiled at Archie.

'I enjoyed our talk,' he said.

'And so did I,' agreed Archie. As the door closed, he said again, 'And so did I.' He smiled and cradled his amber glass. He felt as though he had touched something interesting for the first time in a long while tonight and because of that he pushed the unease that Albert had evoked into the background.

So much of the time he felt shut away, he mused, shut away to one side of the life that went on around him. But sometimes life almost touched him as it had done just now and during the meal when he had decided he would go to the fair with his family. But the children had seemed so preoccupied, he had felt an intruder. Lethargy had claimed him and it had all seemed pointless again. He felt invigorated now though, his horizons had widened. Just so long as the gold standard stayed a fiction, maybe they could still pull through. And how he had enjoyed meeting Bob Wheeler.

There was a further knock at the door. He finished his drink, savouring the heat of its passage. He wondered what on earth Bert would be offering as a pay-off for his debt this time. Surely not the pony again? From now on, he was determined that credit was not going to be extended beyond a repayable sum for anyone. After all, exports had improved slightly, as Bob had said, but maybe not for long.

Annie was gloriously weary, her skin was singing with pleasure and a good tiredness, the lights were busy behind the crowds of people who were still milling as Don and Georgie took Grace to the toffee-apple stall. She had met them at the entrance to the fair and Don had not spoken out of turn once. Annie and Tom had wedged themselves up against the edge of the firing-range, waiting. Annie flexed her spine on the sharp edge of the upright.

'Give us a scratch, Tom,' she said and squatted down as he was doing. 'Have you had a good time, bonny lad?'

'It's been the best day of my life, Annie,' he told her, his eyes solemn. 'And I didn't have no trouble with me coins, did you?'

She laughed. 'Not even a sideways look.'

They stayed on their hunkers, Annie drawing her skirt up so that it was squashed between her thighs and calves; better that it was creased than became too dirty sweeping the ground, she reasoned. They clasped their arms round their knees and waited for the others. The sounds were raucous and indistinct but if she relaxed she found that bits floated to her as people passed; private soppy love-words that sounded right on a night like this. The cracks from the rifle stall melted in with the general muddle and all she could see were legs; heavy-booted men's and stocking-covered or barelegged women. She had not noticed how much people moved their feet when they were supposed to be standing still. She nudged Tom and pointed to one pair which seemed to be wriggling like a pair of stung ducks.

'Reckon he needs a tiddle,' she whispered but Tom couldn't see past two sets of heavy ankles.

'As long as no dog comes along who needs one too,' groaned Tom and she laughed.

Annie peered at the barrier of mottled hefty hair-covered legs, grimacing at the bulging and knotted blue veins, then up at the face. Bye, if it wasn't Mrs Maby from Sophie's road, aye and with her eldest, Francy, and if she isn't a fast one I'd like to know who is, Sophie had always said. She was about to pull at the uneven hem but preferred to lean back and let her ears pick up their talk. There was little flow as yet but their heads bent forward.

'Hasn't he grown, that young Don,' Mrs Maby was

mouthing loudly to her companion. 'Eeh, he was nought but a bitty bairn when she did you know what.'

'I don't know what, Mam. Come on, tell us?'

'Well, you know, the mother. Mary Manon it was, did herself in she did. The baby died you know, soon as it drew breath. Well, some do, some don't and her in that posh nursing home an' all. They should have known better than to leave things like that unlocked.' She shrugged her head into her neck and clicked her tongue. 'They say she went off her head and took poison from the medicine cupboard. Burnt her guts out, they say, with acid. I mean, it's not right, is it, with those two bairns at home. That little Annie Manon was only a wee one. Sight too fanciful she was, that Mary. Should have thought of others. They say he's a ruined man now, taken to drink he has, but then he's lost his wife and all his money. I mean, look at that Don, looks like a ragamuffin, and them so posh once.' She sniffed. 'I hear he gives that Betsy a dog's life. Taken to drink she has an' all. Not right, is it? Still the mighty shall fall they say and bye, he's come a cropper.'

The legs shuffled away, mingling in with the stream of passing revellers, but Annie did not watch them go. She just sat with her eyes fixed on where they had been, sensing her mind floating high above her body and away, taking all her feelings with it and leaving her stuck in the ground amongst a world which seemed to have slowed and become silent. Tom had gripped her arm, his hand was stroking her face. She reached for it and held it tighter and tighter.

She looked up and saw Don there and knew he had heard it too because his face looked still and thoughtful. She tried to stand but couldn't and Tom pulled her up. She was stiff and her feet tingled and hurt with her weight. The toffee-apples dangled heavy in Don's hand and he did not notice as Grace took them from him.

'We'll go home now, shall we Annie,' Tom said and Georgie nodded at him and pushed Don before him. The lights had lost their colour and people their faces as they walked free of the place. The noise pursued them and she wanted to swat it away so that she could think but when they had moved out of its sphere no thoughts would stay in her head long enough for her to grasp and shape.

Their footsteps sounded hollow as they approached the back

and they did not notice Georgie and Grace leave. The only light in the street was from their kitchen; all else were back in the spinning light and frantic music. Annie felt a spurt of rage which tensed even her eyebrows; the bloody bugger couldn't even unbend enough to come out on a night like this, be a real father. Too afraid of getting his spats dirty. Well, she hated him, hated them all, hated her for dying, hated the legs with blue veins. Oh God, oh God, I want me mam, she wanted to shout, I want me own mam. She cried then, tears that raced hot and sharp and shook her body so that Tom was frightened. He kissed her hand, again and again.

'There now, there now,' he soothed. 'It's all right, I'm here, I'm here.'

And she knew she would always love him for those words but the pain peaked again and she tore from him, from Don who tried to stop her and ran, ran through the years, into the house past him and her and up to her room, way up across the rag rug into the high bed with its patchwork quilt. Her hands held her head and she rocked and moaned through the jagged slashing hurt and still there was no colour.

Archie had looked up with a start when the door banged open, as the latch snapped up and Annie hurtled through, her face contorted and her limbs swinging wildly. He started after her but turned, grabbing Tom's arm as he ran in behind her and made to follow. His face was white and drawn.

'For God's sake, boy, what's happened?' he demanded. Betsy had risen and rushed to turn Tom's face to her. His eyes were confused and he looked from one to the other, unable to speak. He shook his head.

'Donald, what's happened?' asked Archie urgently as Don came in, putting out a hand to stop Betsy following Annie until they knew more but she looked past him to Don who stood in the doorway. His face was pale too. Betsy shook free of Archie and gathering up her skirts ran after the child, her heart thumping with fear; Annie had never cried in all the time she had known her.

Her legs were heavy as she reached the top landing and she put out her hand to steady herself and draw breath. It was dark here and the wooden boards creaked beneath her feet as she placed one foot before the other, the dark unnerving her. She felt along the wall until she reached the oil lamp on the sill and, striking a match, lit it. She could hear the frantic sobs and putting her hand to the doorknob called to Annie.

'Can I come in, pet?' She waited but, receiving no answer, went in regardless. The landing light shed a dull glow into the room but it was not enough to pick out the girl. Perhaps it was as well, Betsy thought. Problems were sometimes better spoken out loud to a faceless shape. She sat on the edge of the bed, the quilt soft beneath her; she could feel its seams with the fingers which supported her as she leant over to Annie. Her own mother had made it before she died of the flu in '19 and she could picture the colours in her mind. Annie had it because she liked it so much and that had pleased Betsy.

'Now, my bonny lass, my little Annie, what's the matter?' She lifted the crumpled body on to her lap and sat crooning and stroking the damp hair away from the hot wet face. The sobs gradually stilled but Annie said nothing; her eyes felt heavy and it was as though she was almost asleep and then the wracking sobs began again. They seemed to have a life of their own and she was a small voice inside this strange frantic body, apart from it but linked to the noise and leaping shudders. She wanted to escape from it, to leave all the distress here, in a little heap, while she walked free, back to the allotment and this morning, back to the time before the lady with the ugliness of the blue-veined legs and loud words. Back she would go and then come this way again, remembering nothing of what had happened.

Archie came to the door and looked helplessly at Betsy as he came across and sat on the bed.

He sighed and shook his head. 'Annie, I'm sorry that you heard about your mother's death in the way that you did. I should have told you long, long ago but I couldn't bring myself to. There seemed no need, you never asked. But I should still have told you.'

His eyes met Betsy's across the head of his daughter and hers were narrowed in deep distress. She held Annie closer, wanting to berate him for his selfishness. He should have heeded her and Sophie earlier instead of putting the world to right in that study of his. And he was filled with guilt for neglecting such a task.

He reached across and took his daughter's hand, a gesture which seldom occurred. He had forgotten how soft and small the hand of a child was. He rubbed it between his thumb and forefinger, angry at himself.

'Your mother went away to have her baby, Annie, but it was poorly as many babies are and it died. It was another daughter. Your mother became ill. It was septicaemia which affects not just the body but makes the mind rage when it's in the throes of fever. One night, when the nurse was elsewhere, she found a cupboard and taking a bottle, drank it and died that night.' His voice struggled to keep steady as he relived what had happened – was it only eight years ago – it seemed an eternity, one long day following another.

'It could have been that she was thirsty and just wanted a drink. What is certain though, is that it was a mistake which was purely the staff's fault. I've hated nurses ever since.' He ended in a low voice.

He leant forward to stroke his daughter's face. She seemed so small, so defenceless that he lifted her from Betsy and held her close to his body. She smelt of today's sun. Don came to the door and Archie lifted his head and beckoned him, drawing his sturdy body to his side. There were tears on Don's face.

'I can remember her with her pretty face and her laugh; she was always laughing and singing. Then it ended, she went away and never came back.'

Tom had crept into the room and now stood by his mother, his eyes never leaving Annie.

'I know lad. I came home when it happened but once I was back I found the longer I stayed away, the more difficult it was to return.'

Annie stirred. 'But Fatlegs said she burned, Da, and if she didn't burn then, she will be burning now, won't she?'

Archie stiffened. 'What are you saying Annie?'

'Well, if she killed herself, she'll go to hell, won't she and if we want to see her again we'll have to do it too. All that light that was in her face will be clouded behind the fires of hell. I want her but I don't want hell.'

Annie was surprised at breakfast. The table was laid and Betsy and Tom were sitting quietly. The tea vapour was drifting lazily from the spout in the middle of the table and there was the humid richness of its flavour throughout the kitchen mingling with that of freshly baked bread. The loaf was on the table, crumbs scattered beyond the breadboard and the knife glinted as it lay half-on and half-off the smooth but scarred wooden platter.

'Sit down, pet,' Betsy said, a smile on her face. 'Your Da has slipped out for a moment, with Don. They'll be back in a minute. How are you this morning?'

Annie sat down. 'All right, Betsy.'

She didn't want to talk about last night. She had pushed it into the black box she kept in her head for thoughts that should not be seen again. She would just turn her head away if they crept out, or push the lid hard down. The sky looked blue across the yard; it was going to be another good day and the school holidays had just begun.

She winked at Tom. 'What shall we do then, Tom? How about finding some jars and catching the minnows down Bell's beck, or slinging a rope to the lamp-post and having a swing?' Her throat felt sore when she talked and she didn't feel quite the same as usual but it would get better. She would make it get better.

Tom's face lit up. 'Eeh, that'd be a grand idea, Annie, but you've got a . . .'

'That'll do now, Tom,' broke in Betsy sharply.

Annie looked from one to the other as she sank her teeth into the spongy whiteness of the bread. She had peeled off the crust, eaten that first and kept the best bit until last. Good thing her da wasn't here to see it or else there'd be a do. She sat back in her chair, feeling tired. There was no sound, not even the hissing of the range since Betsy had allowed the fire to die down. She used the gas cooker a lot now, did Betsy, but not for bread and that pleased her.

Don lifted the latch and called to her. She looked at Betsy who was grinning and Tom who was wriggling.

What's the matter with the daft great things she thought; the silly beggars are up to something. Warily she followed Don out into the shady cobbled yard where despite the cast shadows it was still much brighter than inside. She stood bemused just outside the door and her father led the pony to her.

'This is for you Annie, just for you. It can go in the stable when we've cleared the rubbish out. Bit smaller than a dray, I know, but come on,' he beckoned her, 'come and take him.'

Annie stretched out her hand and she felt the hot air from the pony's black, dry nostrils gust in short spurts into her palm and the softness of his lips as he nibbled sideways then backwards and forwards across her stretched fingers.

She looked at Don. 'But what about you?' she asked.

He held out the leather football and grinned.

She turned to Da, then to Betsy with a question clear in her eyes.

'Your da took it as payment for a debt,' she offered. 'He wanted you to have something special. It's a Shetland, that's why he's so small and he never was a pit pony so he's still got good eyes.'

'He's lovely,' Annie said burying her head in the hollow between his neck and shoulders, drinking in his musk.

Betsy and Archie nodded as they turned. The shop should be open by now. The pony's mane was long and coarse and Annie pulled Tom over and lifted him onto the felt saddle.

'I expect I'll look a right nellie with me legs dangling to the ground,' she muttered. 'But I'm right pleased with you, lass. Black Beauty, that's what I'll call you.'

Don stopped bouncing his ball. 'Don't be so daft, she's a he and it's black and white.'

'I'll do what I like,' she retorted. 'And what's more, I'll sell his doing's at the allotment for a penny a bucket. You and me'll go into business together, Tom, how'd you like that. Will you come in too, Don?' She looked at him.

'Not bloody likely, kid's stuff, that is.'

But Tom grinned, 'I'd like it right enough, Annie.' He was glad she was with them again, but he could still see the hurt at the back of her eyes and it made him want to hug her.

Don looked across at them and laughed, loving the seamed leather in his hands. He tossed it into the air, letting it bounce on the cobbles before he kicked it against the stable wall. Thank God the hysterics were over, he thought. She was like his ball, tough and always bouncing back.

Annie thought, maybe it won't matter one day, any of it and the hurt will go and let me forget.

'You and me will share her, Tom,' she whispered, leading the pony forward. It wasn't right that Tom should have nothing – again. After all, he had lost one of his parents too, but no one ever thought of that.

CHAPTER 5

The broom handle felt sweaty as Annie swept the corner of the kitchen, six weeks later.

'You'll knock up more dirt than you sweep away at that rate,' complained Betsy. 'Do it proper, girl, for God's sake.'

She pushed Annie to one side and took the broom.

'Here, like this, see.' She used long slow strokes. 'Don't slap it about.'

The trouble is, thought Annie, you've got great big arms with muscles like Christmas puddings and I can hardly raise a bump. She stood behind Betsy and jacked up her arm, prodding the raised muscle. It was hard but small. The best things come in little parcels, she consoled herself.

Betsy stood back to admire her handiwork. 'There you are, now try and do it like that. I know your da wants to make a lady of you, but I reckon he'll never do it with things as they are. It's best you learn how to clean; there's always a living there.'

Large circles of sweat were spreading underneath her armpits and it was not just her apron but her clothes that were grubby, Annie noticed. She looked down at her old flowered dress, cut down from one that Betsy had been given, and was grateful that at least Betsy made sure she was clean. She touched her arm lightly.

'It looks right good, Betsy,' she said and took the broom from her. It was heavy and she was tired but then she was still having dreams of fat blue-veined legs and flames that leapt higher than their house in a place of awful darkness. She shook herself and brought the broom towards her slowly. She didn't hear the knock at the door but felt the push as Don shoved past to reach the door.

'You two've got cloth ears, I reckon,' he said, and, as she

63

turned, Annie saw Betsy put the beer that she had been drinking behind her back and glare at him.

The door had been closed to stop the dust from swirling and, as it opened, the dirt lifted and caught in her throat. She coughed but needed water to clear her throat. Betsy poured it for her and passed it across before she could reach the sink. She doesn't want me to see her booze, she thought. They must be daft if the pair of them don't know I can see how much they tipple, and all day at that.

Georgie was at the door. She smiled at him.

'It's a right good day for mating,' Georgie said as he stood in the doorway. 'Let's go up the beck.'

Annie gawped, then spilt her water. It splashed on to her dress and she brushed at it with her hand, Betsy's jaw had dropped.

'What the bloody hell are you talking about?' Don gasped, looking back over his shoulder to see if the others had heard.

Annie smirked at him. We did and all, she thought.

Georgie laughed. 'Get the kids, Don. I promised Tom I'd take him to the hives and it's a real scorcher today. The queen might just take it into her head to be mated.' He called in, over Don's shoulder, to Betsy, 'I've never seen that, Mrs Manon, you know, and it might just happen today. It's bright enough.' He was swinging his da's bait-bag backwards and forwards in his hand.

Betsy nodded, suppressing a smile. 'Well, I can think of worse ways for a load of bairns to spend a summer day.' She looked at Annie and cocked an eyebrow. 'Worth a picnic anyway, lass.'

Annie looked from her to the sun which streamed in through the door. It was warmer out than in on a day like this and yes, to be out, away from the smell of boiling dishcloths and dust that puffed up into your mouth and nostrils, yes, that would be a belter. She looked at Don who was pulling Georgie towards him, speaking quietly in his ear. She knew he was about to get his ball and pile down to the end of the street with Georgie for a game. She held her breath but Georgie shook his head.

'Just call the bairns, Don. I promised Tom and we're meeting Grace at the end by Monkton's.' he turned as Don shrugged and slouched into the passage to call Tom.

'You've got some butties then, have you?' called Betsy after Georgie.

'Aye, Mrs Manon,' he called and settled himself on the edge of Beauty's water-trough to wait. He always looks comfortable thought Annie, even on that.

Annie held Beauty's reins loosely as they strolled along the street behind Georgie and Don. Chairs were set up outside front doors for the women to sit on later, whilst they did their mending and gossiping. The leather of the reins was hot and she wanted the air to get between it and her, to stop it going soggy. Tom rode and held their bread and dripping tied up in an old tea-towel and it didn't look that clean, thought Annie, but who cares. She looked up over her shoulder at Tom who beamed down at her.

'Ain't she grand, Annie. It's only taken her a few weeks to settle down, hasn't it?' He patted the pony's neck.

Grace looked over Beauty's head at Annie. She had been late and had run to catch them up. She was still panting slightly in the heat and her freckled cheeks were tinged with red, her auburn curls were damp.

'It's not as though she was a bundle of fire when she came though, is it, Annie? If she settled down any more I reckon she'd be asleep.'

Annie chuckled and ran her hand down Beauty's face to her nostrils which puffed and snuffled in her palm. 'Later you can have your apple because you're a right little cracker.' She crooned into her ear which twitched in response. 'Don't you take any notice of your nasty Aunty Grace. Just wants a ride, she does and it's too hot for us big 'uns on you little 'uns.' She heard the giggles of the other two. 'We'll just get one of Georgie Porgie's little bees to sting her backside, shall we, darling, then she really won't be able to sit on you.'

'Did you hear that, Georgie?' Tom shouted. 'Annie wants one of your bees to do a nasty on our Grace and there's no way I'll be putting bicarb on that sting!'

They were passing the last of the terraced houses which fronted directly on to the cobbled streets.

'Mind your head on the cage, Tom,' Annie shouted, and he ducked beneath the canary which Old Man Renton had put out to hang above his door. It was singing, though it stayed in the shade of the cover which was half over the cage.

'It must be grand for the birds not to have to go down in the pits any more,' said Tom. 'Do they miss it, do you think?'

'I don't know about that,' said Annie suddenly oppressed by the houses which seemed to press in on her, to trap her in the heat and dust, to make everything seem dark. The coal-dust covered the bricks and the cobbles, bringing gloom with it.

It was a relief to reach the wasteland with its space and grass-hillocked ground. Grace's uncle tethered his goats here, but there was only one today.

'Did the others go into the allotments once too often then and eat the prize marrows?' Tom asked, shifting in the saddle to look around. The clip of Beauty's hooves had changed to a soft thud as they crossed towards the lane which led through the trees to the meadow and then the beck. It was still some way off and shimmered in the heat.

Grace shook her head. 'Not this time, Tom. Me uncle's been laid off an' all. They've sold off the billies for meat. They need the nanny to feed the bairn. Me aunty's gone dry.'

'Anyway,' she added, 'the billies don't half pong.'

Annie grimaced at the memory. 'I know,' she said. 'I used to kick the ball up here with Don before he had his good one. If there was a wind . . .'

'And I always thought that was you, Annie,' chipped in Tom.

They laughed and let Beauty stop to crop at the grass. The noise of tearing grass and clinking bit added to Annie's growing sense of freedom. She turned to look back at the streets they had left, cut off from the world as though someone had sliced through them with a knife.

'You'd have thought someone would have curved 'em round a bit, or dotted a few to make it look nice, not just plonked 'em here.'

'It's to do with the owners of the pits, I reckon,' Grace said. They both looked round as they heard Don and Georgie call them from far ahead, then returned to looking at the town.

'They just stopped building when the miners had enough houses,' Grace continued. 'They didn't care what it looked like, didn't think the likes of us needed anything nice.'

The older boys were racing back towards them and Don panted up to Annie. He stopped and caught his breath.

'That stupid pony's supposed to make it quicker,' he gasped,

66

and began to bounce the ball at Annie's feet. The dry earth flew over her sandals. She kicked it away and as he scrambled after it, Tom said:

'No, she's supposed to make it better, and she does, Don.'

Don scooped the ball up, flicking it underarm to Georgie who fielded it with his hand and then dribbled it away from the others.

Don strolled back until he reached the pony, then glared at Tom. 'I've told you two that it's a boy, a bloody boy.' His thin face was screwed up.

Annie pulled up Beauty's head, clicking with her tongue to move on. 'She's what we want her to be and so she's a girl.' They were moving forward now at a leisurely pace. She tilted her chin and looked at him sideways. 'Anyway, clever clogs, tell us why they just stop the houses like that?' She waved her hand towards them.

Don turned back to look. 'I don't know what the hell you're talking about.'

'They just stop,' Grace said, 'that's what we're talking about.'

Tom was standing up in the stirrups to look, wobbling in time with Beauty's stride. 'They're so ugly. Someone's just dumped them there, in the middle of nowhere.'

Georgie was walking with them now. 'It's on top of a seam of coal and that ain't nowhere to the bosses,' he said softly. 'They'd get the workers here by giving them a roof, then the poor sods couldn't leave if the wages got bad because they'd lose their houses as well.'

'Good idea, that,' grunted Don and sidestepped round Annie to take the ball off Georgie. 'Come on Georgie, race you to the lane.'

Annie watched them go. She would have liked to run too, but Grace would have found it too much.

Tom called softly. 'That's not a good idea, is it, Annie?' His face was troubled.

'Nay, lad, you'd think some of them would go away now wouldn't you? They can call their homes their own these days you know.' She looked over her shoulder again. 'There's something that keeps them all together, I reckon.'

'Us all together, you mean,' Grace corrected her.

But Annie knew that was not what she meant. She looked back again and still she thought of the town and its people as them. She wished she did not. She wanted to feel that she belonged somewhere and then she looked at Tom and felt a surge of warmth; here was an us, she thought.

Even across the unbroken wasteland there was no wind, and there was a hush because the pit wheels were idle, over on the other side. They couldn't even hear the bleating of the sheep as they grazed on the grass-covered slopes of the older slag-heaps. Poppies sagged in the heat at the side of the grass track and Grace said she would pick some on the way back, but Tom said they would die and that he would paint her one instead. Annie saw that the boys had reached the lane now and were about to disappear into its darkness. Tom had seen too and wriggled free of the stirrups.

'I'll get down now, Annie, and give the old lady a break. I want to run a bit and Georgie said he'd show me how to blow on grass and make it whistle.'

He was already throwing his leg over the saddle and was on the ground and away before Beauty could stop. He flung the picnic over his shoulder as he ran.

'Crumbs for lunch,' Annie said, laughing, and slipped round the front of the pony so that she was walking with Grace. She slipped her arm through the other girl's. Grace always smelt nice and she let her look at her arithmetic in class. It saved her getting caned too often by that old witch Miss Henry. Old Dippy Denis had never hurt them and he'd let Grace come up a grade into his class even though she was a year younger than the rest. She'd be 9 now, thought Annie, but she's better than the rest of us. Quick at her work, but not a swot.

'It was a shame about old Dippy,' she said to Grace who nodded.

'I wonder why he did it.'

'Me da said it was the war.' Annie remembered her da's hands when he'd heard about it and how they had started shaking. 'When the lorry hit the playground wall and the bricks came down he must have thought it was a shell. That's what me da said anyway, and the boys who stood and watched must have looked like Germans.' She saw again how Dippy had thrown himself on the ground in the playground, screaming, then crawling towards the bricks, then on to the boys who stood rooted to the spot. He had grabbed at two but had not had time to kill them.

'He's still in the loony-bin, isn't he?' Grace asked, fanning herself with her hand. 'It's so hot.'

Annie thought of Dippy being locked in a dark room with bars away from the sun and the sky and the birds. He had been 26, her father had said. There were so many years to live, she thought, shut away.

She said. 'He looked so kind. When they took him away there were tears all down his face. It was raining but I know they were tears.'

She looked up at the sky. It was so blue with light white clouds. War could only happen when it was grey and wet. People could not fight on a day like this, no one could do anything but feel this feeling. She drew a deep breath. This feeling that she thought perhaps was joy. Sophie had always called her a joy and delight and a day like this sounded like those words.

She looked sideways at Grace to see if she felt it too but Grace looked uncomfortably hot. Some of her curls had stuck to her forehead and cheeks. She walked over on the sides of her feet as though they hurt. It was a shame she would never put on a swimsuit, otherwise they could have had a swim in the beck. Betsy had told Annie to put hers in with Tom's, but she had not. She knew Grace would be upset. She said it was because her skin was so fair that she wouldn't strip off, but Annie knew it was because she felt fat and ugly. But she wasn't, she was lovely. Grace pulled her blouse in and out trying to get cool and, as they entered the lane, Annie snapped off a beech twig from the hedge that ran along between them and the fields of corn. She found one with plenty of leaves and handed it to Grace.

'Fan yourself with that, bonny lass.' She dug into her pocket and fetched out a piece of apple. It was warm and covered in bits, but Beauty wouldn't care. It was cooler here with the branches locked into one another over their heads like fingers creating a church and steeple. The birds were louder than she had ever remembered, caught as they were in this tunnel of leaves. The boys had slowed and were not far ahead now and, as they approached, they heard the screech of Tom's grass whistle.

Georgie had stopped altogether and was peering into the hedge off to the left. Annie saw him beckon to Tom and together they bent down. She saw that Tom's face was still but his eyes were dark with concentration. She pulled Grace with her and they trod softly up behind.

'Get a look at this then, Tom,' Georgie was whispering. 'See the hind legs?'

It was a bee, its head deep into a cornflower and pollen stuck so thickly to its back legs that it seemed impossible that it could ever fly. But it did and soared out and up, past Tom, who flinched and then Georgie who did not move a muscle.

'It might have stung you,' hissed Annie, pulling at Georgie, frightened for them both.

He turned and shook his head. 'Suicide for them. They only sting if there's no alternative. They can't take their sting out again you see. It's a once and only weapon. Protection of the hive is what it's all about, deep inside their heads, I reckon.'

Annie had not heard death mentioned since the fair six weeks ago. How strange to think that it could be discussed so casually by other people.

Georgie strolled forward, on to the meadow with Tom. Annie and Grace brought Beauty, Don had gone before them. 'They fan themselves like you to keep cool you know, Grace,' Georgie said. 'With their wings, in the hive.'

'Clever, aren't they, Georgie?' marvelled Tom.

'Do the others miss them when they sting and you know . . .' Annie faltered.

Georgie dropped back to walk beside her. ' 'Spect so, but it's life really. It's happened, it had to happen.' He paused. Grace had walked on to be with Tom. Beauty was swishing her tail to be rid of the flies. 'A bit like your ma really. Perhaps she felt there was nothing else to do and the rest just have to go on. Just like the bees.' He coloured now, and took her hand in his as they walked, squeezed and was gone. She watched him catch up with Tom who was chasing Grace with a spider.

No one had spoken of her mother since that night and she was glad now that someone had. Her face was relaxing again and she allowed herself to notice the birds above her and the corn which waved in the slight breeze that had now appeared. Bees could die and still the sun came out. She wouldn't think about people yet but she could still feel the heat of Georgie's hand around hers.

The hives lay across the other side of the beck in Mr

Thompson's land. He owned the meadow too, the one in which they sat and which ran up to the beck. He had said Georgie could bring them all today.

'We come all the time anyway,' boasted Don. But Annie thought it was nice not to have to post a look-out for once.

She was sitting on the bank of the beck with her feet flopping in the water. Tom was in his swimsuit, the one that Betsy had knitted before her hands had slowed her up too much. He had brought a jam jar tied round the neck with string; it had made red marks on his hands where he had wound it round so that he could hang on tight as the water tried to tear the jar from him. The beck was not more than a foot deep here in this hot dry end of the summer but already his costume was sagging with the wet and he looked like a sack of potatoes.

'Caught any yet?' she called.

He shook his head but did not look up. His legs were so pale they could do with a good dose of sun and she wished she was in there too but down at the deep pool which lay beyond the willow that hung in the water just by Tom. Instead she pulled her dress up over her knees and lay back on the grass next to Grace. It was rich and warm and green. She turned over, pulling herself further on to the grass with her elbows, then lay on her face, breathing in the freshness.

Grace spoke lazily at her side. 'Me mam says that's what they get the consumptives to do. Pure oxygen, me mam says. The grass eats our breathings out and spews back good pure stuff. Gives you rosy cheeks, me mam says.'

'Someone should bottle it then,' said Annie, too lethargic to speak clearly. 'Give it to the miners with the black spit.'

'Me mam says they can do that, in the hospitals.'

Annie raised herself on her elbows so that she could peer out through the high grass across the meadow. There was a sheen of yellow from the buttercups; black-eyed daisies sat in wide clumps. She could hear the thud of Don and Georgie's boots as they kicked the balls and their shouts as they gave directions. The plop of Tom's jar sounded behind her as he scooped it out and back in again when he had checked on a catch.

'Your mam talks to you a lot,' she remarked to Grace as she turned on her back, flinging her arm over to shield her eyes. She saw red spots dart themselves across the inside of her lids and hoped Grace hadn't heard the note of irritation in her voice.

'She wants me to get on, see,' Grace said, stirring at Annie's side. Annie knew that Grace was too hot but could not imagine ever feeling that way herself. The heat oozed into her and she loved it.

'What will you do then, Gracie, when you're grown?'

'Me mam wants me to go into the library I reckon. It's clean and quiet with a nice sort of people.'

Annie laughed out loud. 'It's quiet right enough, Gracie. Remember being chucked out for giggling when Don got the hiccups.' They both lay back grinning. 'But what do you want, Grace?'

Grace flapped her beech twig, the air stirred over Annie too. 'Seems good enough to me,' she said. 'But what about you, Annie?'

There was a scrabble of stones and then a splash and Annie was up and over to the water before Tom could cry out his fear, but then she saw that he wasn't going to. He was sitting up grinning, water dripping from his hair into his face, his body drenched.

'I think I'll do a wee while I'm here, Annie,' he called and splashed her as she stood on the bank laughing. 'I should have brought the soap and saved meself the trouble of bath-night.'

Annie splashed him. 'Come on out for your bread when you've finished poisoning the fish, you little toad.' She turned and waved to the other two boys. 'Come on, you two. Or we'll eat the lot.' She was ravenous.

They all lay on the grass, close to the water looking over at the hives where there were a few bees hanging in the air. Tom had taken his pad from Beauty's saddle-bag and was drawing.

'So what about this mating you wanted me to see, Georgie.' Annie peered closer at the other bank.

Georgie pulled at the grass about him, throwing it up into the air and letting it float down. 'It's the queen, you see, she mates once in her life on a sunny day. I've never seen it happen.'

'But you've been coming for years to help here, haven't you?' Grace asked.

He nodded. 'But I've never seen it.'

'Well, you won't from here, will you,' mocked Annie. 'Their private and personals are a bit too small.'

Georgie laughed. 'It's not like that. Hardly anyone has seen it. She leaves the hive on just the right day, circles over it so

72

she'll recognise it again and flies way up.' He pointed with a grass stem. 'Then the drones come out after her and the lucky one does it there, right up in the air.'

Annie looked up into the sky above the hive. White-streaked clouds seemed miles above them.

'Lucky old drones,' Tom murmured.

Don said, 'Well, I hope he thinks it's worth all that flapping about, that's all I can say.'

Georgie looked at them sideways. 'Aye, it needs to be a bit special. It's a dance of death really because his gubbins breaks off inside her when he's done and she drops him off dead, on her way back down.'

'That's disgusting,' protested Grace, her face screwed up. She stood up and made her way down the shallow bank into the stream. She pulled up her skirt and paddled. Her thighs were dimpled and wobbled as she moved.

Annie pinched Don as he started to giggle and frowned at him. He turned his back on her.

'I'll tell you something,' Don leered at Georgie. 'She's got to be something for them to chase her around like that with the big black nothing at the end of it.'

Annie wondered at the way death seemed to poke its nose into everything, or did it just feel that way to her at the moment?

'Is she,' she asked at last, 'is she something special?'

'Aye, she is that,' answered Georgie. 'She's a whopper.'

Again Don looked at Grace and sniggered. Once more, thought Annie, and I'll pull your bleeding hair out.

Tom had put his pad down and was looking out across at the hives.

'How though,' he asked, 'does one of them get to be so special?'

'It's just luck, lad. The queen lays her eggs in small and big cells. The ones in the big cells are fed with royal jelly when they become larvae and the first to become a bee kills the others, the rival princesses, and becomes queen.'

He showed Tom how to make a daisy-chain.

'And so,' urged Annie, 'what about the old queen?'

Georgie looked up, 'The queen has to leave the hive and find another. That's when they swarm. She takes some of the bees with her.'

'That's what I like to see, the women doing well,' Annie

called to Grace who laughed and nodded. Her hair was wet from the water where she had been dipping in her hand and patting her forehead.

Georgie looked out from under his brows. He looked like the tailor of Gloucester, Annie thought, with his legs crossed and his fingers busy making slits in the daisy stems to thread through the next link in the chain. Tom was too clumsy to continue with his and turned instead to his drawing.

'I'll do something that takes a bit of skill,' he muttered putting his finger under his nose and thumbing it.

Georgie punched him lightly.

'It's only the queen, remember, who has a life of luxury. The workers are all females. They work their guts out in the hive, cleaning and feeding the growing kids and all the drones of course who have to be fit for their only use in life – to fly up to the sky for that big moment.'

'Quite right, too,' said Tom, 'they know their place,' and he braced himself for Annie's slap, which came.

'But don't they ever get out?' Annie persevered.

'Oh aye, they're off out after nectar or pollen, like the one we saw, then they rush back to roll their sleeves up to make the honey and wax.'

Annie was red with anger and flounced up to join Grace in the stream. The pebbles hurt and she wobbled. 'Just like Betsy it is. Work, and nothing else. It's a bloody disgrace.' She raised her voice so that the boys could hear. 'It's a bloody disgrace, I tell you.'

'Calm down, hinny, you'll stampede the pony,' drawled Georgie.

'Never,' called Don. 'Never will that pony stampede anywhere. Just look at her.'

'It's a him,' snapped Annie, and scrambled out of the water and marched away across the meadow, away from the hives. She picked a bunch of black-eyed daisies.

'Only take a few from each clump,' shouted Georgie. 'Helps them to make up their numbers.'

'Can't you think of anything but breeding?' she retorted and their laughter restored her humour.

She collected a few buttercups, then saw the smoke from a train as it appeared and ran along the track way off into the distance. She could hear it surprisingly well and wondered where it was going; what the world was like away from here. I had forgotten, she thought, that there was anything apart from the streets, from the pits. She looked around the meadow. I must come more often and perhaps one day I will get clean away from here.

'Come on, then,' called Tom. 'Let's see who likes it and who doesn't.'

Annie wondered what he meant and then remembered the buttercups hanging limply in her hand.

Yellow bounced off all their throats and they licked again at the remains of the bread and dripping and pretended it was butter. She threw the buttercups on to the water and watched them float out of sight.

Grace dried her legs as she sat down near Tom. Don had moved along the bank and was trying to play ducks and drakes with flat pebbles but the water was too fast-flowing. Tom was drawing a picture of the willow tree and Georgie had finished his daisy-chain.

Annie turned from them and looked across towards the train but it had gone. The oaks at the end were absolutely still, there was no breeze at all.

'Did you see any clover?' Georgie asked, as he rose to his feet. He came to her and tossed the chain over her head. It was so long that he looped it over her a second time.

'Better than pearls any day, lass,' he said and strolled away, head bent, searching. He stopped and called her over. Crouching he pulled out the clover petals from the plant between his thumb and forefinger and sucked the moist white ends. She moved over and watched as he did it. He pulled out some more and handed them to her but they loosened and showered to the ground as she reached for them.

'You do it,' she said.

She wanted to watch his strong brown fingers against the soft pink and white and see how he had not bruised them at all. He held it to her mouth and she sucked. She was not sure if she could taste the clover at all but she had felt his fingers against her lips and her tongue had caught the essence of his skin.

'It's nectar,' he said. 'The bees like it.'

By four the mating had still not burst into the air and Annie felt a disappointment as sharp as Georgie's. Don was restless and paced round Georgie who dug into his bait-bag and brought out a jar sealed with muslin.

'It's honey-comb,' he said and untied the string around the top, peeled back the muslin and, using a spoon from the bag, levered out a piece of honey-dripping comb. He gave it first to Annie and she felt her face flush. He smiled, then passed pieces round to Tom and Grace. Don and he shared the last. The white comb was waxy and stuck in her teeth. The honey was sweet and sticky. Some had dripped on to her leg and she scooped it up with her finger and licked it. Tom looked at a piece of comb he had saved. 'It's perfect,' he said. 'Look at that shape. It's quite perfect.'

Don took a mug of water from the flask, though it was luke-warm by now, and swallowed.

'There's got to be money in this,' he said and Annie sighed.

'Sorry, Don,' Georgie said disappointing him. 'It's too cold up here really. You'll have to make your fortune elsewhere. Try the horses.'

Don strutted about. 'I reckon I could be a jockey.'

'Well, you're small enough,' chipped in Grace, and Annie was glad that she had got her own back on him. She had thought Grace had seen his earlier sniggers. He was small enough an' all, she thought – that's a good idea of the lad's.

'There's money in riding,' he continued, ignoring Grace. 'You get to hear of all the best tips.'

'You've never ridden though, Don,' Annie pointed out. 'Would they take you d'you think and what'll Da say? He wants you to do something important or take over the shop when it's doing well again.'

'Well, it won't go well, will it, the pair of them drinking all the stock. And don't you or Tom go telling him before I'm ready.'

'As if we're likely to try and talk to him about anything.' She glanced at Tom and he shrugged. 'If it's what you want to do though, we're at your side, aren't we, Tom?'

Tom nodded. 'It'd be a grand life, Don, all that fresh air.'

Annie saw that he had, in his drawing, draped the willow fronds in the water, though they stopped just above in reality. His version was better.

'Hold it up a minute, Tom,' she instructed and put her head on one side and studied it.

'He'll be an artist when he's older,' Grace said. 'He can come and hang his pictures in the library when I'm in charge.'

Tom beamed and put his pad down, tearing out the sheet and giving it to Grace. 'You can put it on your wall if you like.'

'Queen bee then, is it, Annie?' Georgie teased.

She looked at him, then the others, then out over the stream, seeing the way the water eddied round the boulders and sucked at the bank as it went on round the lower bend. Then she grinned and twirled her daisy-chain at Georgie. 'With these pearls, what else could I be?' She let them drop. 'But I'm telling you, I'll be off to another hive and things will be a sight different there, just you wait and see.'

'A revolution,' grinned Georgie.

'And not before time,' breathed Annie. 'The women will live a little, just you wait and see.'

And then it happened.

Over beyond the beck, in the baking heat, the bees left the hive in a long meandering trail, round and round and then up. High into the air, towards the sun.

'Georgie,' screamed Tom, but he had already seen and in one lithe movement was up and on the bank, standing still, his head raised as he watched. Everyone watched, for what seemed like hours. Annie strained to distinguish the queen and her lover, who would soon be cast to the ground. She winced at the thought of dying at the peak of love, plunging to the ground, the children safely made but never to be seen by you. She stood with her hands clasped as the bees settled back into their hive and only the sentinels remained, buzzing like always above.

No one moved and still no one spoke until Georgie sighed and turned. 'That was something I shall never forget,' he said and his mind was on his face and that was something that she would never forget.

She moved her arm round Tom who had come to stand with her. The shadows were lengthening rapidly. The willow cast itself well over to the other bank. She squeezed him to her as Georgie and Grace packed up their picnics.

'Remember this,' she whispered fiercely. 'Remember that something happened here today that someone really wanted.'

She looked again at the hives. 'It shows that things can go right, bonny lad.' She felt wonderful, full to her throat with success.

'It's been the best day of my life, it has,' she said.

77

CHAPTER 6

Annie sat on her knees beneath the bedclothes pulling on her liberty bodice whilst trying to keep the blanket hooked on to her thin shoulders. Bye, it was freezing, the bodice felt cold, damp and prickly and too small which only added to her irritation. At 13 she was still wearing the same one she had worn at 11. Oh God, the thought, I shall have to stick me legs out to get me stockings on, but she was a suspender short.

Throwing on a blouse and wool jumper which had thinned at the elbows she wriggled into her skirt and, bracing herself against the chill, slipped out on to the rug, its knotted rags knobbly beneath her feet. More by feel than by sight she hunted, but it was no good; she lit the oil lamp and there beneath the bed it lay amongst dust which lifted and floated before her probing fingers. The rubber was dry and cracked. As perished as I am, thought Annie, as she clambered into her boots, fingers stiff with cold.

There was a heavy dust hanging all over the house these days; it seems as dead as the rest of us, she sighed, and peered out of the ice-frosted window. It was going to be a mite cold out on that football field she thought as she scratched and filled her nails with ice. Serve the silly beggars right!

She stamped downstairs to the bathroom, thankful as always that Joe had a bathroom put in when he was living here. It was cold but at least she didn't have to break the ice in the privvy, though the torn-up bits of paper were no silk stockings on her bum.

She was reluctant to start the day; another Saturday, another pie-day and Tom not even here. She kicked the bathmat. He was only supposed to be at his Aunty May's on Wednesdays but it looked as though it was creeping into Fridays too. She missed him. Missed him pushing past her to the basin in the morning, missed his chatter and his smiles.

He was thinner these days, so maybe it was as well that May, Betsy's sister, asked him more often. Poor bairn, at least his aunty fed him up good and proper, brought a bit of colour into his cheeks, and he liked being with May's boys, especially Davy. He was older than Tom but good with him. She bit her lip as she thought of the two more in his class who had gone down with consumption. She'd heard Betsy telling Ma Gillow in the shop last week and the anxiety she had felt then clutched at her again. She rubbed her face violently to chase the thought away. Yes, he must go more often to his aunty, much more often; she would make sure of it because Tom must be kept safe. She reached for the towel which was already damp after Betsy.

'Get down here, Annie, for God's sake,' she heard Betsy call and leant against the basin, glad of the interruption, a new train of thought.

Thank God it was for the last time; this match, these pies. Next Saturday she'd be able to go to Grace's to read her comics. She'd take Tom too and Grace would be sure to share her liquorice with them, she always did. Grace was lovely that way. Tom would buy some pink mice too, now that he'd taken over from her on the manure round. She was glad she'd passed it over; at 13 she was almost a woman and muck sales didn't fit in with that. She straightened herself and undid the plait that she now slept with every night. Yes, there were some waves, not many but a few. She put her shoulders back and looked at her chest but there were still only the smallest of bumps. Grace was enormous and even her shadow wobbled when she walked.

She hoped Tom wouldn't cram all the mice into one pocket again. They had come out in bits last time, all over Grace's floor. Her da had roared with laughter and given them money for another two pennyworth. He was never cross, Grace's da wasn't. Even when his stump was swollen and new after his leg had come off in the coal fall he had still smiled but there had been new deep lines round his mouth.

It was strange when he lost his leg, she thought. When the siren went Betsy and me were washing and never thought it was him. You're always frightened it will be someone you know but you never really think it will be. The siren had gone on and on that morning and they'd seen the women pass the door, shawls over their heads but without their usual faces. They were blank and empty and there had been Grace's ma but she hadn't seen them. The women never saw anything until they knew their man were safe, or not.

It was the week after they had been to the beck and seen the mating but it wasn't warm then, or did it just seem as though it wasn't. She tried to remember but could not.

'Will you get down here, girl.' Again she heard Bet call.

'Coming, Bet,' she shouted. 'Keep your 'air on,' she added but more quietly; no good looking for a clout she thought.

She rubbed her teeth with the flannel. Bye, they'd had some good laughs, her and Grace, even after Georgie and Don had become too old for the gang although it wasn't quite the same with just the three of them. She thought of the time her da had bought a load of manure off Sid at the allotment and come home tutting at the way some of the neighbourhood children earned themselves a few extra pence. Sid had been her muck man, selling it off for her but she was the one with the shovel heaving up steaming blobs from the road and Beauty's stable. Her da would have killed her if he'd known.

She squeezed the flannel dry and hung it over the edge of the basin, then tried to find a dry bit on the towel which was worn to a thread. It hurt her chapped hands. She envied Don away in Yorkshire, galloping across the wide moors he had told her about. It must be good to be a boy, to get away.

It was strange where her da found the money to drink so much, and Betsy too now, breathing heavy breath into her face all day. It made her repulsive and what's more she didn't half clout now. At least Da never became slobbery, just quiet, deathly quiet as though there was a wall drawn up around him. She sat on the edge of the bath, first putting the towel beneath her, the iron was cold enough for her to stick to, she grinned. What did he do in that study all day she wondered, except booze.

He had started going in there when 'Churchill's returned to the gold standard,' he had groaned. She remembered him coming in and saying that. It sounded so silly, what the hell was a gold standard? Let some silly old fool return to where ever he wanted, she thought, I'm making me tea if you don't mind. Then he had rushed off to see the glorious and good Mr Wheeler who she had shortened to God but that was no loss because he was never in the shop now, Annie thought, her right foot arching and stretching. Good for slim ankles Grace had said.

'For the last time, get down them stairs or I'll belt you.' The call came louder this time and she went down now, slamming the bathroom door behind her.

Archie heard her as she passed the study. He threw down the pen with trembling hands, his letter to Joe finished and took another drink, feeling the heat as it burned down his throat. The trembling improved. His shoulders hunched as he pored over the figures yet again but the answer was no different – he was finished.

Albert had been quite right to bow out of the partnership a year ago, no point in them both going down but it still grated, especially the look of supreme pleasure that had for one brief moment lighted Albert's face when he had sat back and listened as Archie told him he was near to ruin and needed the bolster of the partnership more than ever. Albert had shaken his head and said that he was sorry, he must think of himself and that he was sure Archie would not keep him to an arrangement which would destroy both their father's children. That would mean total shame for the family name.

Archie remembered wanting to put his hands round Albert's neck and squeezing until the veins bulged on his forehead and his bloodshot eyes blazed. But the man was right, of course; it was logical that one of them should survive.

This year, 1926, had been the crunch for the business, that and Churchill's gold standard budget of the year before. The General Strike, though, that was what had ended it for him. It might have been over in a few days for the rest of the workers but the miners stayed out for months. They starved, so he starved and it had been little better when they had returned to work, for wages had been even less, if indeed there had been a pit left open to take the men.

And Bob had said last night that this was a picnic compared to what was to come. What was it he had said? Archie gulped at his drink as he tried to organise his mind, it was difficult for him to hold the thread of his thoughts these days; he knew it was the drink but was glad because he did not want to be able to think coherently. Now, Bob had said that Europe, including Britain, would be in trouble if they had to repay their American war debts. That our economic well-being depended on America's economic stability. If that went, debts would be recalled, world trade would slump, industry would collapse and he seemed to sniff that this could be a possibility. He was usually right, but then it really wouldn't matter, would it? 'Would it?' he said aloud and smiled, cradling his glass in his hand, feeling the cut patterns in the crystal. He finished his drink, picked up the letter addressed to Joe and smiled again. He ran his finger round the rim of the empty glass and it rang, a low continuous note. He withdrew the stopper of the matching decanter and poured a large drink and pondered his success and failures.

A good thing to come out of the last few years had been the football team and through that had begun his friendship with Bob. Sport had worked as a morale booster during the war when, well behind the lines, on yellow gorze-flecked land, his platoon had kicked a ball and forgotten for a moment the hell and concentrated on a victory of smaller proportions. It had worked here too. He had approached Bob with a plan and the men Bob sent had warmed to the idea of victory also. The team had become important to them and had pushed the lack of a job into the background for an hour or two and the pies he provided had kept their hunger at bay for just as long.

His friendship with Bob had grown through their efforts to set up the matches and it had satisfied a hunger of his own. A hunger for conversation of a kind he had known before and during the war. Every week they met either here or at Bob's home the other side of Wassingham and discussed things other than the declining money in the till or what he wanted for tea, as Betsy increasingly insisted on calling it. Almost as though she was challenging him. Into the small hours they would talk about world affairs and matters which took him beyond the confines of his life. And so Bob had kept his starvation at bay, he thought wryly, but now he could no longer help the men with their's, for there was no money in the till to pay for the pies which were served at the end of each game and he, Archie Manon, felt that now was as good a time as any to hand over to someone else.

The whisky was slipping down smoothly now and his hands were quite steady. Might just as well drink the remaining stock as pour it down the drain he thought sourly, aware that his

thoughts were becoming increasingly disjointed, his movements more clumsy, but that was comforting.

He looked at his son's photograph set in a wooden frame
standing behind the decanter. I wanted so much for you, Don,
he thought. A racehorse owner, not a stable lad and so much
more for Annie. A better education, more opportunities to see
another life, to move from here and make something of herself.
It's all been such a waste of time. He saw that his glass was
empty again and refilled it and sat, elbows resting on the table
until even bitter thoughts became blurred and slipped away
before they could dig in and spiral into his brain.

Annie knocked on the door and, turning the handle, entered.
He was just sitting there, his face towards her, his eyes fixed on
where she was but not seeing her.

'Da,' she began, then louder, 'Da, Ted's come for you,
they're waiting outside to go to the field. Betsy called up to tell
you.'

He frowned with the effort of concentration and leaning
forward said clearly and distinctly:

'I can do nothing more for you, Annie. I have nothing that
will help you make your way in this world except to say, for
God's sake, girl, marry above you and get out of here. Never
marry down.'

Violence made him spit and Annie watched the bubble rest
on the shine of his desk and wondered how much he'd had and
it wasn't even breakfast.

They heard Betsy call up from the basement door and Annie
said, 'Come on, Da, let's find you a piece of bread before you
go.' She moved before him down the stairs, impatient with this
man and his never-ending misery, but knotted up inside
because of it.

Betsy stood by the brass fender which no longer shone, with
arms folded as Annie cut a hunk of bread and handed it to her
father. He passed out of the door, taking his coat off the hook as
he went, looking at neither of them, and Annie thought that
once he would rather have been seen dead than in clothes that
were as torn and dirty as that coat was. The tea was stewed and
coated her teeth with bitterness.

'He's been at it again,' she said and Betsy nodded but was too
tired to care. She pressed her hand to her breastbone, her
indigestion was bad again she thought.

'Come on girl, give us a hand with these pies or they'll never get cooked and hand me some of that magnesia while you're at it.'

She was mixing the pastry, and flour clouded the table as she pummelled, her sleeves rolled above her elbows. She pointed with a flour-covered finger. 'For God's sake, next to the salt.'

Annie reached up and passed it over, tying the apron round her waist. It was warm in here.

''Ere, take over from me while I get this down me.' Betsy moved to the sink with the magnesia.

Annie plunged her hands into the mixture. She hated the way the lard slipped through her fingers, then clung to her as it became pastry.

'Though God knows it's the wives and bairns who need it as much as the men but who are that lot to give a monkey's.' Betsy elbowed her to one side and the bitterness in her voice penetrated Annie's thoughts of Grace and the new dress, the one she'd worn to school on the last day of term. Must be nice to have men in the family who were in work. Grace's brothers were all in the same pit as Georgie, Grace said.

'Still,' Betsy continued. 'if they don't have the men to feed for one lunchtime at least it's one more helping for the kids.'

'But not a hot slice of meat and potatoe pie though,' replied Annie, as she washed the carrots and potatoes under freezing water, then chopped them. 'You're right, Betsy, it's a bloody disgrace.'

The clout knocked her to one side. 'Don't swear. You're nothing but a bairn and bairns don't swear.'

The back door opened and Tom walked in. Annie knew that he'd heard the crack as Betsy's hand had caught her head. 'Not growing another cauliflower, are we, Annie?' He was smiling but his eyes were angry as he turned her head, lifted her hair and checked. 'All right, bonny lass.' He turned and glared.

'You shouldn't do it, Mam.' But Betsy ignored him. Annie ruffled his hair, her ears ringing. He was nearly as tall as she was now.

'Go and sit by the fire and get warm. We'll be out taking these little bits of heaven to the men soon.'

He grinned and passed her the towel to dry her hands, then walked over to the table. His jacket was torn at the pocket and his scarf was too thin to be of much use. It was so discoloured that its stripes were indistinct. His boots clumped as he crossed the floor.

He stuck his fingers in the bowl and rubbed it round and licked it.

'Bring those tats here, pet,' Betsy called to Annie. It was her way of saying sorry, Annie knew. Tom winked at her. 'The women will make do with their smithering of dripping and be none the worse for it,' Betsy continued.

'But . . . ' Annie retorted.

'And take your jacket off, Tom,' Betsy called to him. 'You'll not feel the benefit when you go out. And you Annie just get done with your mithering, there's nought you and I can do about it.' She wiped her hands down her apron which was stretched taut round her body which seemed to get fatter by the day, Annie thought.

'I'll stoke the fire, Mam,' offered Tom.

'Right lad, we'll need the gas and the range today.' The rolling-pin crunched her swollen hands as it travelled beneath them, thinning the pastry. Annie saw the tears fill her eyes as she lined two tins with lard. She left Betsy to finish, to fold the pastry into the tins, load in the vegetables and a few scrag-ends of lamb and seal the edges. She held the oven door as Betsy put one in the range. The other was put into the gas oven.

Betsy stood up and sighed, stretching her back.

'I'm off to the shop now. Can't leave it locked all day,' Betsy called, as she left the room. And can't go on much longer without a beer, thought Annie, as she and Tom sat on by the fire.

'Did you have a good time, Tom? Was May good to you?'

Tom sat on her right, his legs splayed as he relaxed in the heat. He had hung his coat on the end of the fender but it was beginning to smell of burning.

'Move your coat, Tom. Keeping it warm is one thing but it'll be a puff of smoke in a minute.'

He nudged it off with his foot and kicked it on to Betsy's chair.

'Oh aye, May's right good to me. So much to eat. Here.' He struggled to bring from his pocket a piece of apple pie. 'It's a bit squashed, but good.'

Annie laughed and ate it. 'You should go there more often.'

She looked at the fire as she spoke, not at him. The heat thrown out made her shield her eyes.

'I'd rather be here with you, trying to keep your ears out of trouble.'

'Don't be daft, I've got too much to do without bothering with a scruffy little tyke like you.' She leant across and pinched his leg gently. 'You must go more often Tom. I'll see you do.'

Tom said nothing and neither did Annie. It was nice to sit here and have nothing to do for half an hour she thought, though she should really be washing the dishes; but she made no move to do so, just wriggled her toes and enjoyed the heat. We'll have to get up to the slag-heap again soon and try and sort out some bits of coal.

Betsy came in when Annie was feeling her lids drooping, her hands heavy. Her face was flushed and her lips slack from the drink. She tipped the pies from the oven on to the trays. Annie nudged Tom and pointed to his coat. She took hers from the peg.

'Get these off now and no messing mind.' Betsy threw the towel on the table and sank into her chair. 'And shut the door behind you,' she called as they left.

They carried the weighted trays out over the yard, past Beauty who stamped in her stall, and down the back alley; the steam was white in the colourless chill although the pies were covered by two layers of boiled white cloth to retain the heat.

Annie turned down Sanders Alley halfway down the street. They had passed no one yet this morning. It was too cold to go out unless you had to.

'Where are you going, Annie?' called Tom, as he stayed, uncertain, at the mouth of the alley. 'You're going the long way round.'

'We're going this way today, Tom,' Annie ordered, her voice tight.

He took a step forward, then stopped. 'But it's too cold,' he wailed.

'Just do as you're bliddy well told,' she shouted, her shoulders bent under the weight of the tray. 'We've got things to do today, Tom, important things you and I. It's time you learnt a few facts of life, a big boy like you.'

She continued, knowing that he would follow. His tray was

the smaller of the two and would not be too much for him on this longer route.

They moved through the alley into Sindon Street with Annie stopping at different doors while Tom's eyes widened in horror until Annie was finally ready for the field. Tom had not spoken at all. When they arrived they put the trays on the frost hard ground. A frost that had whitened and stiffened black smutted grass that crunched beneath their feet. There was no one else watching the game and there were no pitch marking but the men cheered and slapped when a goal was scored between two old coats. The final whistle was blown by Archie and Annie turned to Tom.

'Go home, Tom. Now.' The sky was grey and pressed down on them. They could hear the laughter of the men as they gathered together, shaking hands.

He hesitated, his eyes travelling from her to the men, who were now ambling across the field towards them. They looked big and were getting nearer. Fear made his legs feel weak. He should stay with her, he knew he should.

'Go home,' she repeated, shouting at him. She pushed him from her. He was crying now, silently. He turned and looked towards the football field then to her. He should stay, she looked so small here on the big field with men closer and closer looking like dragons breathing smoke as their breath met the cold air. God, he was scared, too scared.

'Go,' she said, turning from him to wait for her father and then he fled. His feet turned on the frozen ground but he didn't stop. He ran and ran, hating himself but not going back. She heard him but did not take her eyes off the men. Her feet were very cold but not numb yet. She wriggled her toes and transferred her weight from one foot to the other.

Her da was feeling the cold too, she thought, watching him walk towards her, rubbing his hands, his scarf wrapped up round his chin. She saw him stop and wait for the men, herding them towards the trays.

'We're ready for this, aren't we, lads?'

'Right enough, Captain,' the men laughed and blew on their hands.

Makes him feel big, Annie thought. Captain this and Captain that but I suppose he hasn't got much else so who can blame him. She could smell the booze on him and all around him and he was a good five feet away. The men stood round her now, their breath blowing white; they blocked out the light and hemmed her in. She stepped back, out of the circle.

'Come on then lads, take a slice and let it warm you.' Her da pulled aside the cloth.

The bits of bread and dripping were very dull, Annie thought. They didn't steam like the pies had, like the men as they turned to face her. They looked cold like the air and the ground; like her feet; like her father's voice as he said:

'What's the meaning of this?'

Annie set her feet and braced her shoulders, her small breasts sore in the chill wind. The men seemed larger now.

'The meaning is that it is just not fair,' she blurted. 'You run around chasing a little ball and having hot pies when the families have this muck while they're stuck inside four walls. They cook and wash and never get out of the rut. It's like a bliddy hive.'

She stepped back as her father moved. He stood still.

'If you don't like this, why should they?' she challenged.

There was a dog barking over by the coats which had made the goal. It pulled one along, tossing it, then barking again. The slag-heap in the distance was grey with frost. No one spoke.

Annie turned back to her father, her anger under control but her resentment still present. 'Who's thought to give the women anything like this? Don't you think they have longings too?'

He was looming above her. His face was red and there was sweat on his nose. He found his voice at last. 'That is enough, more than enough.' He had his hand up like a bloody policeman, she thought. 'Go home to my study and I shall see you there.'

She stood for a moment, there was more to say but she could no longer find the words. She pushed her head down into the bitter east wind and left, but twisting her head she called:

'I told them that you men had decided to do a swap. It wasn't their fault.' Her words were whipping back in her face; her face felt frozen with the cold.

'It wasn't their fault,' she shouted again.

'Go home,' her father replied and she knew then that he had heard.

Betsy was sitting at the table as she opened the door. Tom leapt to his feet from his chair by the fire and rushed to her;

putting his arms round her. His warmth pressed into her. She held him close.

'It's all right, bonny lad. It's fine, everything's fine.' She stroked his hair. He might be tall for 11 but he was all skin and bone.

Betsy had heaved herself out of the chair, her mouth working soundlessly, then she shrieked. 'You bloody little fool!'

Beer froth was lying on her lips. She slopped the jug she held in her hand and beer ran over the table.

'What did you want to go and do a thing like that for? When will you think before you act? You've made him look a fool and he'll lather you.'

Tom clung tighter to Annie. 'I'm sorry,' he wept. His voice muffled. 'I should never have left you.'

Annie took him by the shoulders, pushing him a little from her and looked into his face. 'I've told you everything's fine and when have I ever lied to you? He's not cross.' Her gaze was steady, she shook him slightly and looked over his head to Betsy. 'Tom should go to May's tonight, Betsy. He could do with a good meal after today.'

Betsy looked at her, her hand resting on the mug that now stood on the table. She looked confused and beer had splashed down her bodice; she dabbed at it. 'Oh, perhaps you're right,' she said abstractedly, her anger gone as fast as it had come, tiredness taking over and making her slump back into her chair. She didn't want him to go, he was her son but there was not enough food any more; she always felt hungry and if she did, he did.

She looked through bleary eyes at Annie and Tom standing there and saw the red welt on Annie's cheek that was still there from that backhander this afternoon. She knew she shouldn't do it, but Annie was his child – that bugger who lived up those stairs and had brought them all to this. She would have been better off with Joe; at least he knew how to run a shop and would Archie listen to her if she tried to help? Not bloody likely. She wanted to hit him, to slap his pompous face but she couldn't and all the time she had this anger inside. The drink helped, but it made her even more tired. Life was too much of an effort. The kids were too much of an effort, they got under her feet, they never stopped wanting, and when the rage got too bad she had to hit, had to shout, had to drink even though she could see that it made Annie cut off from her. She had loved her once, loved them all once. She supposed she still cared for Tom but inside there was only this anger.

'Can he go then, Betsy?' Annie's voice interrupted her.

She sipped at her beer and enjoyed the taste. She waved her hand at Tom. 'Get on over to May's then,' she said.

Tom looked up at Annie and she winked at him, wiping his wet cheeks with her hands. 'Go on, Tom, and bring me back some apple pie as a present in the morning.'

After wrapping him into his jacket and shooing him out of the door, she went on up the stairs to sit on the study chair for the two hours it took for him to come home.

She had tucked her feet beneath her and wrapped her coat around, glad of its extra layer in the bitter room. She realised that she had never just sat before in this place, which was essentially her father's den where stale tobacco had threaded into the curtains and lined the walls, and she felt an intruder. It made her sit upright in the chair, stiffly uncomfortable and nervous in case he should come in and find her lolling as though at her ease.

So little sunlight reached this spot and today was worse than usual with its grey cold cloud. She wanted to set up the oil lamp, to throw some of the shadows back into the deepest corner, but dare not. She felt she must make as little impression on this room as possible, rather like her attitude to her father over the last few years. He was there, around the place but not of it. She swallowed; never before had she directly involved herself with this man and she felt small and vulnerable and friendless. She sank her chin on to her chest and wondered what Don would say when he heard as he undoubtedly would, for in this neighbourhood it would be round like wildfire, and a letter would be sent. Maybe he would tell Georgie, but would he remember their day at the hives and understand? She didn't know because he was too busy with his grown-up life to see the kids who used to be the gang.

It was silent up here; there were no sounds drifting up from the alleys. It was not drifting weather, she thought with a sigh, and ran her hand along the top of the desk. The green leather square which slipped into the sharp edged mahogany top was warm in comparison with the cool shine of the desk. Papers were everywhere, some in piles, some just scattered as though abandoned. There were two photographs, one of her and one of Don but none of their mother. I wonder what she looked like, she pondered. There was nothing to give a clue to their father except his pipes and feather cleaners.

She looked more closely at the papers before her. They were a jumble of figures which held no interest for her since they did not speak to her of the man who was her father. Leaning forward she poked her finger under the corner of the nearest stack and laying her face sideways against the desk she could see spidery writing stalking across the paper. Lifting the top sheets she started a landslide and slapped her hand down on the top. The desk was damp where her breath had skated across the surface. She wondered why her father had been writing to Joe about coming back to take over in the event of 'my demise'. Demise was an odd word, she thought, and wondered what it meant.

When is the man coming? she sighed, then whistled tunelessly through her teeth. The waiting seemed endless. She wondered if they would go to the pantomime in Newcastle this year, probably not after today's little effort, she thought, especially with things being so bad. But it was such a delight, so bright and exciting, with Betsy in her hat, her stockings held up instead of rolled down round her ankles and Happy Harry in his spats and striped trousers.

Suddenly she longed for Tom to be downstairs waiting by the fire for her. She rubbed her nose harshly. No tears, she had promised herself long ago; they did no good.

Then she heard her father on the stairs and rising, she edged away from the chair to stand next to the wall, her hands pressed against the cold plaster and her chin lifting; she chewed the inside of her mouth. The door opened slowly. He said nothing to her as he entered the room and she wondered whether he had remembered her. He sat heavily in the chair looking only at the papers which he tidied absently, not acknowledging her presence in any way. She waited, fascinated by the small pale hands which first patted the papers into squared layers, then fingered a pipe, the wide-bowled one; and after he had drawn the pipe-cleaner through he prodded tobacco into it, lit a match and sucked until it glowed red. She had never seen this private ritual before and felt as though she was watching him clean his teeth. She fidgeted.

'So, you chose to make your own judgement and then to act on your decision.' He finally turned to her, leaning forwards, his elbows on his knees. His pipe hung from his right hand and glowed weakly. It was the only warmth in the room.

'If you ever interfere in my life or that of the neighbours again, I shall take strong remedial action. At thirteen years of age you know very little of the real world, so do not presume to act the adult. Is that fully understood?'

Annie nodded, one look at his face which was drawn tightly to a point made his meaning abundantly clear. And how could he say all that without drawing breath; she was amazed.

'You'd better come over here, take your coat off and bend over.'

Annie blinked. She really had not believed it would come to this and her cheeks burned. Stiffly she walked to where her father pointed, taking her coat off and letting it drop in a heap on the floor, a gesture of defiance which he ignored.

Archie took the wooden ruler from the drawer, his hand shaking in spite of the drinks he had taken throughout the day.

'Bend over,' he repeated, keeping his voice impersonal with an effort. She was so small, looking 9 not 13 and she was thin, her buttocks outlined against her skirt and her vertebrae ridged beneath her sweater. He took a sharp intake of breath and briskly delivered three strokes and Annie said nothing, just retrieved her coat and slouched into it, turning to face him. It was not the pain but the embarrassment. She hoped he had not seen her suspenders while she was hanging head down with her backside in the air.

'Have you anything to say to me, Annie?' Archie asked.

'I still think it's unfair to the women,' she said, determined that she was not going to apologise.

And at this Archie felt tired and his distress from the punishment churned deep inside.

'Maybe it is, but you are a child and it is not up to you to change patterns which have held good for generations. There is a great deal that is bitterly unfair but you, of all people, must know that we have enough to do to survive without you throwing pebbles in the pool. As it happens, this time the men were amused but maybe they would not be again and we need their custom. If you want to change things then change them for yourself, not for other people. And Annie,' and here he paused 'you must make sure you do change things for yourself. Get out, get up that ladder. Now go and have some tea.'

He would have liked to draw up the corner chair for her and really talk to this child who saw beyond the confines of her world to things that should not be, but felt constrained. She would sooner be away downstairs, warmed by the fire.

She started to speak and he leant back and looked at her quizzically.

'Are we going to the pantomime this year, Da?' she asked, wanting to talk about patterns and life and themselves but knowing that here was a man who had no use for her chatter and none of the need she had for company. She wanted a reason for not turning to the door and stepping out into the gloom of the landing that led to no one she wanted to be with and nowhere she felt at home. But she had only been allowed into this room for punishment and she knew that here there was no place for her either.

Oh Annie, my little love, Archie thought, thank God you have no thoughts to torment you, no loneliness to plague you, just your wonderful zest for life, the love of tomorrow and he desperately wanted the brightness of her youth, now and in the future; the nearness of her small warmth and her interest. But he tried to restrain this intrusion into his daughter's life and merely nodded at her request and again when she pleaded that they should all be together for the trip, Don too.

There was a silence between them, her hazel eyes looked up into his.

He could bear it no longer. 'I love you, darling child,' he murmured, so softly that Annie could only guess at what he had said. She leant forward to try to hear again and he reached out to her and kissed her soft cold cheek. Annie wondered again what he had said.

He dropped his arm from around her. As he had feared, the time had passed when he could expect love from his family and he knew that the blame was only with himself.

'Off you go now,' he said, patting her. 'Find Betsy for some tea.'

Annie went, feeling that something had slipped from her, something important and she couldn't quite see what it was. Silly old fool, she hissed, hurt and angry as the door shut behind her leaving her cold and alone. He doesn't care whether I'm alive or dead; all he cares about is his bloody shop and his booze. Well I just don't give a damn. He can drink himself sodden. I just don't care about you any more, she hurled silently at the door. You and she's just as bad as one another, her with her beer in her tea mug. You with yours in that posh glass. You must think I'm daft, the pair of you, if you think I don't know what's going on and she flung herself down into the kitchen to find it deserted with practically no fire left.

It'll be me to make the tea again, she thought. Bet's in the shop and she'll be too sozzled to turn a hand to anything. She opened the door into the passage that led up through the basement into the shop. Bet was sitting behind the counter on the high stool, her hand resting limply round her mug, the earthenware jug to one side. Annie saw the jug was nearly empty and thought of the clumsy evening ahead of them as Betsy slipped and slumped around the kitchen.

'Shall I do the tea then?' she asked, her voice indifferent and hollow in the deserted shop.

'Aye lass, I'll be a while yet.' She did not look round and Annie did not expect her to. What closeness there had been had become submerged somehow during the long grey weary days, weeks and months of depression and despair.

'May doesn't mind having Tom, does she?' she asked over her shoulder as she began to leave.

'No, God bless her,' murmured Betsy, her lips so stiff with beer that some trickled from the corner of her mouth and she lifted a distorted hand and wiped it back on to her tongue. 'It's the best for him, I reckon, with things as they are.'

She half turned, tears brimming, her breaking heart clear in her eyes but Annie refused to notice. She forced herself to feel revulsion since it did not hurt as much as pity. She thought, as she left, of Betsy's buttocks and sagging thighs planted on top of her seat, her legs wide apart, her feet lolling on their sides, straining against dirty brown shoes. At least her da kept himself a bit neater, she thought.

It'd be one pennyworth of chips tonight and a piece of fish, no one else would be in a fit state to eat. She felt weary and had a pain and that night Annie had her first period. She came down from her room, her cardigan wrapped round her shoulders, held together with a hand small with cold and touched Betsy who was slumped face forward on the table, her snores rattling her gaping lips and blowing across the pool of saliva that had oozed casually from beneath her tongue.

Annie shook her again, shivering in the cold of dead embers. It was no good. She stood, frightened and in pain, not wanting to go upstairs again to the smell of the oil lamp. For a moment she held her cardigan together with her chin, the knitted rows scraping her skin and awkwardly piled some kindling on top of paper and began the range for the kettle. The gas stove would be quicker but did not give the same warmth and it smelt funny so she put some coal on and knelt as it took hold. Somewhere she knew there was a hot-water bottle and that, pressed to her stomach, would ease the ache.

The kettle was singing gently now as she looked round the room. The dresser was bare of all but a few plates and the door dragged as she opened the cupboard which was full of old sheeting but right at the rear of the pantry she found it. She scraped her knuckle on the stopper but, as she filled it, the heat became a balm. Betsy stirred and Annie called to her.

'Betsy, I've come on, what do I do?'

'What's that you say?' Betsy reared up, her eyes glazed and heavy. 'What's that you say, my pet?'

She reached for Annie who stepped back out of reach of the flailing hand.

'It's me, Betsy, I've come on and I don't know what to do.'

She hated it, every bit of it, having to expose herself to this woman, to anyone, in this most secret of things and her face was hot with humiliation.

Betsy shambled to her feet, leaning her weight on one hand and pushing off from the table towards Annie.

'It's a bloody shame, that's what it is, and you such a bit of a bairn.' She crossed her arms. 'Now don't you go mucking in the lanes with any of them boys. Just you keep yourself to yourself or it'll be trouble and this house has enough of that as it is.'

Annie backed away towards the sink.

'I just need something to wear, Betsy, that's all.'

'Well, you'll have to make do, same as me.' She staggered to the linen cupboard and pointed. 'There, see that pile of old rags, not the sheets, those at the back. Take 'em, use 'em, wash and boil 'em then use them again. Now, I'm off to bed. I suppose he isn't in?'

Annie shook her head as Betsy nodded towards the door.

'Put the guard up and some ash on that fire,' she slurred heavily towards the end and left the room.

Annie looked at the rags bunched in her hand. Da might come in at any moment and she crept out of the door, her boots slopping at her bare ankles, up the dark stairs and into a bed grown cold. Safe, clutching the stone bottle, her head beneath the blanket, it seemed very lonely up on the top floor. It wasn't fair that Tom had an Aunt who loved him. She felt for the Australian Christmas card which had arrived this morning and told of the baby Eric and Sophie were so proud of and which they had named Annie.

She beat the mattress, crumpling the card and hating the child who had taken her place and her name. She thought of her body, bleeding and sticky and railed at it for taking the child's body from around her thoughts and feelings and replacing it with one which would soon be really adult, not just pretend. She lay quiet, hearing her own breathing. Tom would be here tomorrow and maybe Don and she thought of the scarves she had knitted. It was Christmas Day in the morning.

Archie sat in Bob Wheeler's front room. It was a long walk across town but he had felt the need to stretch his legs and see his friend. Bob lived near to the Bigham colliery because, he said, he liked the sound of the pit wheel.

The two men had been silent for some time. Bob had found the suspension of the seven-hour shift and less pay a poor Christmas present, he had said. It was a poor reward for a strike which started as a general one and ended yet again as a miners 'down tools'. His face was set and he looked back over his years in the union and despaired. Archie asked:

'Why didn't you go ahead and strike in 1919 when coal was booming and they desperately needed you? With unemployment so high you had no bargaining power this time. It seems all wrong.'

Bob shook his head. This is what he had been awake thinking about for the last three nights. He had moved the clock on to the landing in the end because the ticking had drummed '1919' again and again. He had feared all along the General Strike would fail. It was the wrong time. 'You don't need to tell me that, man. We thought we'd get the support of all the workers, but the essential services continued. The country kept going in other areas with the volunteers and the government did well with their propaganda.'

'Didn't the TUC support you properly?'

Bob laughed. 'As much as anyone could do in conditions of such low employment. But it was more than that. They were worried, Archie, I think, especially after the *Mail* published a leader saying that a general strike was almost the same as revolution. The Council want respectability in order to be able to negotiate with government in the long term. They don't want a revolution, I don't know anyone that does. Changes, yes.' They both nodded and Bob leaned forward and poured whisky into Archie's glass and added more to his own. He must put back that clock, when he was sleeping better. It had been his mother's.

'Anyway, after a few days, Samuels arranged a meeting with the TUC to end the General Strike and they arranged terms, but they were bad terms. The workers came out with nothing, just less pay. And you know what, Archie?' He leant forward and pointed with each word. 'There were no miners' leaders there. The Council wanted the strike ended because they knew nothing was to be gained by it so we were on a hiding to nothing, but the miners were bloody livid. They'd been baton-charged by the police in Newcastle and all they were getting for their pains was another hiding, so they stayed out for another seven months, not that it did them any good. They came out with less pay, just like the others, only they'd starved for seven months to earn it. The whole thing was bloody stupid.' He was talking to clear his own mind, running through the events of the past few months, trying to make sense of it all.

Archie held his glass up to the fire, tilting it so that he was looking through the liquid at the flames. The fire was set in a blue-tiled surround which was matched by the curtains and chairs. It was a plain room but spotless. Bob had good neighbours, he had told Archie, and the wife came in to run a duster round from time to time.

'So why did they decide to strike now not in '19 when there was full employment and the country needed coal? There were stockpiles this time Bob.'

Bob nodded, throwing his hands up in despair. 'I know, I know, but the government were withdrawing their subsidy and the miners were told they'd have a drop in pay and longer working hours again. It was desperation and anger I suppose, anger over 1919.' He stopped.

Archie said again, 'But you didn't strike then and got better conditions.'

Bob took a deep breath. He remembered those times vividly. He'd come back from the war and his da was ill but not too ill to take an interest in what was going on and they'd sat up late talking, hoping for public ownership of the mines. His da would have died happy then, but it didn't work out that way. 'Yes, we got better hours and wages but we did not get public ownership, which was the main demand. Look Archie, Lloyd George arranged to set up a commission under Sankey if the miners postponed their strike which they did.' He was speaking clearly and slowly as though to a schoolroom of children, thought Archie, but he felt it was Bob's way of controlling his feelings.

'The Federation and the owners agreed to a compromise at an interim stage of the inquiry, hence the hours and pay and then public ownership or state control, whatever you want to call it, was considered and – glory be – Sankey came out in favour. But, and it's the biggest "but" you'll find, the government betrayed the miners and refused to accept the recommendation.

'Under the owners, you see, the profits are not ploughed back into the industry to increase efficiency and safety. There is no security. There is no attempt to set up other industries now that coal and steel are in decline.'

Archie knew all this but he let his friend continue. He seldom spoke as such and it would do him good.

'The men are bitter, Archie. It's something they'll never forget, never forgive. Betrayal ruins trust forever, it will affect relations between the government and the miners for a long while yet.'

'And how do they feel about the unions now? Surely they'll feel let down. First it's the government, then the TUC, or maybe that's how it will look in their eyes?'

Bob rose and walked to the window. It was snowing. He drew the curtains and returned to his seat and smiled at Archie.

'You're right. They'll see that in conditions of high unemployment there is little the unions can do. Membership will fall off, dues will lessen so there will be a decrease in financial support and even weaker unions. It's a vicious circle.'

He saw that Archie's glass was empty and refilled it. 'It'll be a white Christmas anyway, the sledges will be out tomorrow.'

Archie nodded absently. 'Will the government leave it at that? Allowing prevailing conditions to curtail your power?'

Bob smiled. 'That's the interesting one of course. They're preparing another bloody Disputes Bill, trying to stop us striking, supporting each other. We shall just have to wait and see whether it leaves us toothless. Labour will not be able to oppose it in the Commons with its small party.' He sipped his drink. His throat felt dry from the long discussion. 'I would like to see the day when even the middle classes will have unions. That and better employment figures. That will give us conditions for a concerted push, a better world.'

Opposite him, Archie nodded his agreement, his mind dwelling on Bob's last words, and then he felt the familiar feeling of panic come to him here, in this safe front room. He made his movements slow and careful as he raised his glass and took a drink. He tried to stop the words which were forcing themselves out into the room but it was no good.

'I was once in a concerted push, you know,' and he laughed, but it was not a humorous noise, 'or rather should have been.'

Bob Wheeler had been deep in the problems of the unemployed, chasing them round in his mind and he took a moment to grasp what Archie was saying. He sensed then the giving of a confidence, one that he feared might ruin the tenor of their friendship based on a comfortable, somewhat detached atmosphere of political discussion which never grew intimate. He looked at Archie rather more closely; he was drunk but that was nothing unusual. There was something else though now, something which darkened his eyes, pulling him back to another time and place.

Bob was attempting to defuse the situation. 'I was always at the back of the big push you know. The transport columns never got to the front. They were shelled though.'

Archie seemed not to have heard and Bob knew that he had lost him for now. He had seen it and listened before to those who had never quite left the war behind. The fire leapt in the grate as he leant forward and put on a log. He liked log fires and had one every Christmas Eve. There was a small Christmas tree by the window, lit by the glow from the gas lamp. The pine smell filled the room and presents for his neighbours lay amongst its branches until tomorrow when he would take them next door in time for Christmas lunch.

He waited.

Archie said again, 'Or I should have been.' He looked up as Bob pushed a log further on. The flames curled round and began to blacken the wood.

'It was all a bugger. Best forgotten,' Bob soothed quietly.

But Archie was not to be dissuaded.

'The barrage had started in the evening. We were to attack the next day. You see, they liked to soften up the Germans first, but all it did was warn them we were coming and shake the ground so the trenches began to crumble. I was sent with my platoon to replace the sandbags and shore up the trenches. We worked all night.' His voice was measured and too slow. He was not seeing the fire but the wet earth. 'It had been raining you see, raining for days and Ypres is heavy clay. We couldn't dig deep trenches because of that so we had had to build up the traverses and lay duckboards because of the mud and if you fell off you drowned. The water couldn't run away you see, it just went on making mud, inches, then feet, and they wanted us to go for a big push.' His laugh was sudden and harsh. 'Bloody mad they were. You couldn't walk in that mud, let alone storm the bloody huns. No man's land was a marsh by then.'

Bob handed him a drink. 'Come on, Archie, have this and where's your pipe?' But Archie couldn't hear him, couldn't see the drink.

All he could hear was the noise of the whizz-bangs, the machine-gun fire. He felt his hands beginning to shake and he put them between his thighs. He did not have time to breathe deeply, there was too much to say.

'I was to take my men over in the first push at dawn. The sun rises in the east, but of course you know that. Just for a few moments as dawn came up we could see the Germans before they saw us, and in those few precious minutes we could get out and over the top and maybe not get killed.'

Bob took a swallow of his Scotch. Archie was rocking backwards and forwards, but Bob was not alarmed; it was a familiar pattern with other friends, other survivors. He waited, hoping that when it was over Archie would not regret his confession because Bob now knew that this is what he was about to hear.

'Gas is dirty soldiering, you know.' Archie was talking in a conversational tone now. 'Dirty soldiering. The noise was getting worse. It was still dark but there wasn't long to go until daylight, until we went over. I was by the signal dug-out. If I hadn't been there, it would all have been different. Captain Mollins called out: "Manon, get down to the gas company, they've lost their officer. Shot through the head. Let off the gas. It's got to go before dawn. We want it on the Germans and clear of no man's land by the time we get over. Get on with it, man."'

Archie's voice was no longer calm, its pitch was higher, the strain was in every word.

'I slipped as I turned to him. My sergeant held me up. The mud was greasy beneath my hand and I was on my knees. A shell hit the trench further down, the barrage was still blasting away, the noise was horrendous. Mud flew over us. "But sir," I said "there's no wind."'

Archie was shaking, he was wiping his hands as though to free them of mud, but they were shaking too much so he put them between his thighs again.

' "Do as you're bloody well told, Manon. We need that gas. It's five of clock already, man. We're going over at six." He was shouting, his face pushed towards me but I could only just hear him against the crash and scream of the shells. I pushed back towards the gas enclave, climbed over the collapsed trench to get there. There were bits of men in it. I trod on a leg. The gas team were waiting. The shells from our battery were falling short, landing around us. There was flying mud everywhere. It was impossible to think.

'The sergeant was struggling with the valve on the gas cylinder. "Give me that," I said, and took the spanner, it was icy. The rain had stopped and there was a mist so I knew there was definitely no wind. I sent a runner back, Bob. "Tell him there's no wind," I said. We were pushing back the sandbags all the time. They were being shaken down as fast as we replaced them. My sergeant was killed by a sniper, shot through the eye. The runner came back. The captain had said, "Get it off now," so I did.' Archie was quieter now.

'The cylinder discharged all right, but the gas fell back into

101

the trench. It's heavier than air you see and there was no wind to blow it across.'

Bob nodded but Archie did not see.

'It fell back and the company stampeded, struggling to get their gas masks on. Why didn't they put them on before? Why hadn't I ordered them to? God knows.'

He was shaking and rocking. 'They stampeded over the top but they weren't the only ones. The push had started too soon, we had lost our advantage of the light and the Germans put flares up and could see us all.

'The wire wasn't cut in front of us. My mask was on, I don't know how. I was alright but those who had survived the gas were being cut to ribbons on the wire, shot to bits and hanging like rag dolls a few feet in front of the trench. I was cutting it, trying to cut it, tear a way through when I felt a hand on my leg, pulling at me. It was my corporal drowning, yellow-faced in the gas, his buttons already tarnished green.

' "Murderer, murderer," he bubbled. Someone from further down the line was screaming. I trod on him, Bob, ground him into the mud, anything to get him away from me, and then a shell exploded, it must have been near. Knocked me out but didn't kill me. God damn it, it didn't kill me.'

All he could hear were the screams and the guns. He looked at his hands and rubbed the palms and Bob could see that they were crossed with white scars. He reached across and held Archie's wrist. Forced him to take a drink, guided it to his mouth. The frenzied shaking had ceased.

Bob looked keenly at Archie. 'It happened all the time, old friend. It was a nightmare and no one was to blame in that chaos.'

Archie smiled but it was without humour. 'I've said that a thousand times, Bob, and it just doesn't bloody help. I killed a lot of people that day and I wonder every night, I wonder, if it wasn't because I just wanted to kill myself. I'd just returned from burying Mary and wanted to die, so did I let off that gas deliberately?'

There was silence in the room except for the ticking of the clock on the mantelpiece and the crackle of the fire.

'No,' Bob said gently. 'No, you didn't, and it's best not to think about it. Life is very strange and we do the best we can.

That's all, we just muddle through.'

Archie seemed exhausted, perhaps a little more at peace with himself, but Bob was not sure. He watched him as he slowly collected himself.

'Anyway,' Archie said in a voice which betrayed his tiredness, 'it's over with now, and yes, maybe one day we will get middle-class unions. Baldwin really would go demented if he thought that was on the cards. Who knows, Bob, maybe one day you'll have Labour back in. You should think of that, think of big-time politics for yourself.'

Bob silently applauded Archie's attempt to regain the thread of their earlier conversation. 'No, Archie, I'm too old for that particular game. Not enough fire in the belly. I've too much to do here anyway, too much everyday trouble in the area.'

A silence fell, a companionable silence, and Bob was relieved that, if anything, the relationship had been improved by the glimpse into a private hell.

Their glasses were empty and the fire was dying. Archie looked at the clock. 'It's very late. You must get some rest.' He looked at Bob earnestly. 'It's good that you have much to do. That's the way it should be, my friend. Thoughts of tomorrow.' As he rose he nodded. 'Yes, that's as it should be.'

They moved from the front room into the hall which was lit by a solitary gas lamp. Archie took his worn coat and hat; Bob helped him into it. His scarf was still hanging on the hook and Archie took it and wound it round his neck while Bob opened the door.

The snow had stopped and there was only a light sprinkling on the ground. The night air stabbed at their lungs and Archie lifted his scarf across his face.

'Have a good sleep, Archie,' said Bob, touching his elbow.

Archie stood looking out across the street. 'It's the dreams though, Bob, the faces, the voices. They make strange bedfellows these days and there's too much noise in my head to find answers to them or the problems of the shop.'

He shrugged and began to walk down the street, his feet unsteady on the slippery cobbles. He turned back to Bob. 'Today, my little Annie did what I should have done; did as she thought right, and I punished her.' He paused, 'Thank God these children at least won't know the feel of a war.'

He moved away, lifting his hat to Bob.

'Merry Christmas,' Bob called after him and watched until he reached the corner. He closed the door. He did not know what else to do.

CHAPTER 7

The tram-stop was a bare one hundred yards from their shop and the morning was crisp and most houses were quiet. It was Boxing Day. The tram rattled to a stop and Archie pushed Annie and Don, then Tom and Betsy before him on to the platform. He might be without his watch, but who cared. Today was special. Today his family was going to Newcastle, to the pantomime, and Donald could redeem the damned watch any damn time he wished. He, personally, had no need of a watch any more. He felt euphoric, as though the decision he had made had drawn every line stronger, every colour brighter and the years were shed and the minutes savoured.

His gaiety was infectious and the children scrambled on to the bench laughing, pushing and poking. Betsy and Archie settled themselves opposite. Betsy had borrowed powder from Ma Gillow to hide the meandering red veins in her cheeks and nose. She'd begged a coat for the day also though she still had no gloves that would fit over her knuckles, so instead she kept them bunched in her pockets.

Annie was wedged between Don and a stranger whose heat penetrated and touched her. She tensed, stiffening against the sway and lurch and fought away from the pressure of the unknown body which pressed closer to her than her closest friend Grace would ever dare. The woman had thighs that should have been hanging in the butcher's but which instead nudged against her and her floppy bosom pulled at the buttons fastening her coat. She had a sweaty face and perspiration lay along the line of her scarlet lipstick which was sticky and had gathered into a lump at the corner of her mouth. Annie wondered how she ate without clogging up her innards.

She laughed inside, grinning up at Don, winking at Tom. It was so wonderful to be actually going to the city, going to the

Empire to see Peter Pan just when she had thought that nothing bright would ever break the long grey winter.

She dug her hands deep into her pockets, regretting that Don's Christmas present of pear-drops had split their bag and seemed fluffy to the touch, but then who would see in the dark of the theatre?

Don was quiet, she thought. He had changed since he had left home. It wasn't just that his hair was short or his voice deep. He seemed further from them than ever now that he was away so much, even when he was this close, and she felt she hardly knew him. She had noticed Betsy and Da sitting either side of the basket so as not to squash themselves buttock to buttock. She bit her lip; her father was so neat today and small beside Betsy who was doughlike and spreading. Jack Sprat had nothing on this little lot she thought.

She looked past Don to Tom.

'Stop picking your nose, Tom,' she whispered, reaching across to slap his hand. 'Don't think you're too far away for me to get at you.'

'Weren't picking,' he mouthed as he leaned forwards. 'Just itching it, that's all.' He tucked his hand beneath his legs and hunched his shoulders. 'It's good, isn't it, Annie, altogether like this.' His eyes were alight and his grin was broad.

Annie wanted to put her arm across and toss his hair and press him to her. He was such a bonny lad with his smile that always seemed to be waiting to plaster itself all over his face, if it wasn't already there.

She nodded. 'Yes, lad, that it is.'

He looked so much better for having wrapped himself round Aunt May's Christmas pud and had brought her back a bit an' all. It had hardened as the suet set but had been rich and sticky.

The tram windows were steamed behind their heads but she could sense the darkness of the station terminal as they arrived. It had blotted out the midday sun. The bustle and noise of the station, as they stepped down, confused her; it seemed to be all around, swirling in a senseless pattern, opening and closing around them as they stood while their father decided which way to go.

'Come along,' he called, sweeping foward into the mêlée, and she reached for Tom's sleeve, tugging at him and running along behind her father's hurrying back. If they missed the train, oh,

106

she couldn't bear to think of it. Instead of swanking in the new school term, there would be nothing to tell.

'I'm not going to disappear in a puff of smoke,' he panted. 'Let go of me arm, Annie, I'm all at an angle.'

But she wouldn't, she was too excited to hear him.

Archie turned, still walking, his face red. He looked again at the chalked boards. 'Come on, Annie,' he called and took her hand. 'You must keep up with us, we haven't time to wait for you both.'

They all broke into a run as a train steamed and roared to a spark-spitting halt and the steps were a blur as they raced up over the bridge, then down the other side. The hoarse smell was everywhere. As they approached, the train doors lurched open and swung, slapping against the sides. Annie saw her father and Betsy climb aboard. She sucked more breath into her lungs.

'Come on, Tom,' she shrieked. Don was urging them on. He stood with one foot on the platform, one on the train.

'For God's sake, get a move on,' he bawled and, as they arrived, he heaved at her elbow. 'Bloody girls,' he hissed. She shut her eyes over the yawning gap between platform and train.

'Get Tom, too,' she cried, her voice high and seeming to come from the top of her head. Doors were being slammed the length of the train and finally they were all in.

Their carriage was empty but for them and Annie threw herself on to the seat, heaving a sigh of relief. She pulled Tom down beside her and they laughed and couldn't stop. The seats were prickly and dark red and the paintings of the seaside which were screwed to the wall above them looked dull and uninviting. She tucked her coat beneath her, gasping at the lurch and stagger as the train set out for the city.

There were arms with ashtrays between each place and Annie screwed her nose up against the smell. Black-tipped matches were piled up in the dead ash. A lipstick-tinged cigarette-end had been ground out on the floor. She had heard Georgie telling Don about women like that, it was a sure sign, he had said. If one of them girls up the market is standing smoking in broad daylight with thick red lips, you can lay a penny to a pound she's on the game. Common as muck they are, he'd said. She'd asked what 'game' was and they told her to wait until she was grown up, then they'd tell her. They never had.

The countryside had a smattering of snow but most of it had thawed yesterday. There had been so little anyway and she was rather glad because Tom would have wanted to go sledging and she couldn't bear the cold. It seemed to be racing past; the cattle in the fields looked unreal. In the distance she could see a farmer as he laid down straw by a water-trough. He seemed from another world and she wondered if people in the train had felt the same when, or if, they had seen a group of children in the meadow by the beck that day so long ago.

The picnic buns were still warm from this morning's baking and, long before they drew into the yawning Newcastle station, Betsy passed round chicken which oozed and hung out of tangy rolls. Even Don looked wide-eyed at such luxury and Annie thought the world had gone mad.

'Thought black pudding would be the height of it,' Tom murmured as he held his and just looked.

She looked at her da who smiled and Betsy who nodded and then she sank her teeth into the soft white meat and lifted up her shoulders and hugged her elbows to her sides. She could hardly breathe through the pleasure.

The taxi her da pushed them into, when they came out through Newcastle Station, was so tall they could almost walk into it. There were three small seats which flipped down behind the driver and she and Tom sat on those while Don tried to choose between sitting high up between Betsy and Da or low down with them. Annie knew it was no contest and was not surprised when he squashed in next to Betsy and smiled down on them as though he was Lord Muck.

The Empire was bright and like Christmas had always seemed as though it should be. They stood across the road and watched the crowds as they spilled into the foyer. Annie could not believe that she was actually going through the front and could look the red-uniformed commissionaire in the eye. She nudged Tom and he winked, his shoulder bracing back as he moved closer in the noise of the traffic, the smell of exhaust and the clatter of horse-drawn carts. There was not one pony as small as Beauty, he thought.

'It'll be great to go in the front way, bonny lass,' he whispered and Annie laughed, glad that his thoughts had found their way through to hers. She could feel in her mind the weight of the exit bar at the flea-pit which she had so often heaved up to let the others in. Six for the price of one was good going. Georgie, Grace, Tom and Don and whoever had tagged along that day. Today though, there was to be no ducking as the usherette came down the aisle. Maisie had known who had passed her torch as she stood in the doorway into the cinema and who had just appeared but she had only found them once. Today they could forget it all and just be there, maybe even have some chocolates.

Inside the shell-shaped lamps were pink, the curtains were a vivid red that soaked up the light in patches and was dark and bright in turn. Excitement hummed and was echoed deep within Annie and her hands felt limp with satisfaction. She turned to her father and smiled.

'Thank you, Da,' she said.

He nodded, handing her the binoculars, but with these she could only see parts of the whole and she preferred to be without detail and soak in the buzz and laughter. The chocolate was passed. It was already soft and stuck to the roof of her mouth. She sat perfectly still to let it last. There was its stickiness around her mouth and on her hands until Betsy licked her handkerchief and wiped around her lips and it smelt of her breath until Annie dragged her sleeve harshly across her face. She grimaced at Tom who tried to jerk his head back but Betsy scrunched his hair in her hand until she was done. He shuddered at Annie and leaned nearer.

'We need one of those, then she won't do it.' He pointed to Don's straggly moustache. 'That means they've dropped, you know.'

'Shut up you little –' Don growled, not daring to call him names so close to his da.

'I'd rather have me mouth wiped,' answered Annie. 'They'd stick me in the circus if I had one of those.'

Archie ignored these exchanges. He was training his glasses on the boxes which held calm ordered well-dressed families. All the excitement seemed to come from the well of the theatre and the cheap seats where they were sitting. The orchestra were in the pit, tuning their instruments. It wouldn't be long now.

The heat beat against Betsy and she ignored the bickering between Don and the others. Her dress was too faded and stained to remove her coat so she had to endure the next few hours in it. She opened the collar and let her hands hang as far from her body as the seating would allow. It was good to be away from the shop and Wassingham and Archie looked young again and eager. That was it, she thought, he looked eager as though he knew of a secret joy. He was still such a strange man, so stiff and alone. Her head felt heavy as the lights dimmed and her thoughts trailed away. Her hands were eased by the warmth and she was comforted by the lack of pain. Her chin dropped to her chest.

Annie looked at Betsy. As long as she doesn't snore, she thought. Please God, don't let her snore. She looked along the row beyond her father to Don and saw him unwrap the muffler she had knitted for his present. She had noticed how he had run his fingers between it and his skin a thousand times since he had wrapped it round his neck but hadn't removed it until now and that was kind.

She knew the wool was rough because she had pulled out one of her sweaters to make them and they were all like wire wool. She had thought boys skin was hard and they wouldn't feel the prickling as she did. After all, they were always going on about being so tough.

Tom still wore his but outside his coat. He said he liked to be able to swing it up over his nose and let it hang down his back to keep out the cold air. He had given her a bag of pink mice when he had returned from May's late last night but he had painted her a Christmas card earlier and she had put it on the mantelpiece with the ones from Grace and Sophie on Christmas morning. Sarah Beeston's had arrived the week before and Betsy had put it away for her to open on Christmas day. The package had been soft and it was gloves again, as she knew it would be and they fitted too, they always did. They were dangling on the end of her elastic and she stroked them. The wool was so soft. Bet had stayed in the shop all Christmas Day, empty of trade though it was, and her da had stayed in his study, unspeaking. Both had been drunk.

But now the music was heaving and barking as Mrs Darling settled the children into bed and Annie watched them in their warm bright bedroom being kissed by their parents, tucked in by the dog, Nana. She soared with them when they followed Peter out through the window to Never Never Land and clapped, clapped, clapped to save Tinkerbell's light and life.

She booed the crocodile, screaming with laughter when Tom stood up and shouted his warnings.

At the end she hated the lost boys for returning to real life and called, 'Don't go, don't go,' when Peter asked her, for it was her he was asking, not really the whole audience. Asking whether he should return or stay with Tinkerbell and the treehouse and his freedom. She clutched Da's arm. 'Don't let him go,' she beseeched and he put his hand over hers and said, 'I won't my love. Everyone has a right to be free.' And he had kept his promise.

The trip home was full with quiet and the smog held the pantomine close to Annie where she hugged tight the thought that Peter had stayed. She looked at her da through lids heavy with sleep as the train thundered away from the glowing clouds back to the shadows of home and was glad that he had saved Peter for her. Tom had fallen asleep against her and she moved him slightly to ease her arm.

Don had waved them goodbye at the station to catch the Yorkshire train and Annie had seen Archie grip his arm but had not heard him say, 'Happy New Year, my boy. I have always loved you both, look after my little girl.' She had seen him turn and then Don was gone but not before Annie caught his expression of contempt. Too much booze making the old fool maudlin, it had said.

Betsy woke, her legs stretched out across the bed. No Archie as usual, she thought. He'd be still asleep over his desk in the study. She stretched, her hands playing with the brass bedstead and thought how she loved this bed when it was hers alone. Her limbs could sprawl and her body lie loose on its back unlike the nights when Archie was here. Then she was rigid, careful not to cross the empty space between them, her head motionless on the hardening pillow, tense in case she should irritate her meticulous husband. It wasn't so bad when she'd had a wee drink, then she slept and the more she drank the more she slept. Softened the edges it did, gave her a sort of pleasure. She felt good this morning, no headache, no sour taste from too many gills of beer. She had energy, she was new. Bye, they'd have to go into town more often.

She dressed briskly. In the bathroom, the water was crisp, too cold to wash. She tapped on the study door as she passed but there was no reply. Up and off early on some business no doubt and she was relieved. She thought of the cleaning up she would do this morning, then later she could take the two bairns out for a change. Last night had made her feel excited and energetic and she smiled to see that Archie had laid the fire and the table was ready for breakfast. He must be feeling good too, she thought, and wondered if this could be a new beginning.

The hose that was attached to the gas cooker ran past her up the stairs and she looked at it, her hand still on the doorknob. Her feet felt heavy as she turned for the stairs noticing now how neatly it was laid against them. Up, up she went, seeing the fibres of the carpet clearly but not seeing them at all.

There was a gap under the study door as there had always been and the hose fitted beneath with no noticeable flattening. How could she not have seen when she passed, was it just a moment ago? Her breathing was shallow, rapid.

'Archie,' she called. 'Archie!'

She rattled the door. 'For God's sake, answer. Let me in.'

But there was silence as she knew there would be. She hammered on the door and then it opened at a mere turn of the knob and the ugliness of the gas filled her face in a rolling wave. She shut it again and leant on the door, rubbing her forehead backwards and forwards against the panel. It was cool; so cool. You bloody bugger. Oh my God, you bloody bugger, how bloody could you. She beat her fists on the door, her mouth working and her rage growing but she did go in again and she did open the windows, her hand across her nose, gagging against the drowning mist and she did look at his body, upright in the chair except for his head which hung on his chest but she did not touch him. The gas was still writhing out of the grey flaccid hose but it was silent which was how his death had been, she thought bitterly.

Upstairs Annie half lay on Tom's warm body. She was glad he had crept in as he usually did when the cold had sucked the warmth from his feet. She slept better when he was here; when he wasn't at his Aunt's. She pulled the blanket over her head and sank back into the underground treehouse and the lost boys. It had been the most wonderful Christmas of her life and she still felt the thrill of a world she seldom saw. The lights, the size, the gaiety, and she wondered if the people there knew of the world the sparkle did not reach. Tom had said he would shout loud enough one day so that everyone would know; paint it on canvas for them to see. Good with his hands Tom was. She drifted, seeing daubs of yellow, red and green slashing from dark to light.

Through the warmth she felt the clumsiness of Betsy's feet as they banged against the stairs, heard her shout and the hair on the back of her neck rippled. Betsy could not run! The landing was cold when she reached it and she stood looking at Betsy as she came towards her and saw the words slowly fall from the working mouth and she wondered if she could push them back, stream after stream, hand after hand but she knew they would just keep escaping though they would not reach her ears. She would not let them do that. Betsy pulled her hands away from her ears, jerked her, held her between strong hands and then Annie could no longer escape.

'Finally gone and done it, he has. Joined your bloody mother,' shrieked Betsy. 'Bloody well stuffed himself with gas, d'you hear. Didn't care a bloody monkey's did he?'

'What do you mean,' Annie shouted, wanting to be heard above the noise.

'Bloody killed himself, hasn't he.'

Annie's scream was loud and went on and on. Tom was there now, pulling at her, pushing at his mother. He had heard what Betsy said and it couldn't, no it couldn't be true. Annie's face was ugly, her mouth was open. This wasn't happening. It couldn't be happening. 'Look at Annie's face!' he shouted at his mother, 'What's happening to her face?'

Annie held him back. 'Get away from me, you bitch. He wouldn't do it. He wouldn't do anything so ugly. He was too neat. He wouldn't leave me for her.' She screamed again and could see herself from a great height; she was as ugly and distorted as he must be and she wondered if she would ever fit together again. And she saw and remembered throbbing bulging veins and heard the grinding fairground music. She refused to see the body and so did Tom.

Don came home the day after it had happened. He walked in the door and came to her. She was sitting by the fire, her hair was uncombed, she didn't speak, just looked up as the door opened and he walked in.

'So, the old fool left us all sitting in the middle of a right bloody mess, didn't he,' he said, sitting down beside her. He had red eyes, Annie saw, but hers weren't red. The pain still wouldn't explode into tears, just sat in her body and tore her apart. She reached for his hand and he held hers. He had put his bag down by the chair but had kept his jacket on.

'Where's Betsy?' he asked.

'Round with Ma Gillow. She said she needs a good cry and someone to read the tea leaves for her.' Annie laughed, then shook her head. 'Poor Betsy. There's no money but there is a ticket for you to get his watch back. It paid for the pantomime.'

Don stood up letting her hand drop. He walked to the sink and poured himself some water, then threw the mug back into the sink.

'No money at all?' he asked, turning to face her, his face dark with anger.

'None. He wrote to Joe suggesting that he came back and took on the shop, using Betsy as housekeeper.'

'Well?' Don said, walking to and fro behind her, still thin-lipped, still raging, she knew, because he hit the back of the chair every time he passed with his fist.

'Joe says yes, but not me and Tom.'

Don came and sat with her. 'Well, I can't have you,' he said. 'I've got me job to think of.' He stood up again and this time walked through to the shop and poured some beer. His voice was distant but she heard him say. 'Can't you go to Albert's?'

And Annie felt more anger to go on top of that which was already filling her to the brim. 'I am going to Albert's so Betsy says. Apparently he's the nearest relative. Sarah Beeston wanted me but Albert said I was to go to him. Betsy said she'd trained me well enough to suit him.' She tried to stroke through her hair with her fingers. It was like rats' tails.

The door opened again and Tom came in carrying a tray, 'May sent you this, Annie.'

She looked up at him and smiled as he took off the cloth covering a steaming bowl of broth and brought it to her.

'You're like a little old man, Tom.' Her voice sounded strange to her, thin and flat.

'Remind me to put me shawl on next time,' he said, passing her a spoon. He sounded tired and sad.

'Don's back.' She took a sip though she was not hungry. She felt she would never want to eat again. The spoon felt heavy.

Tom looked up as Don came through. 'Glad to see you, Don.'

He smiled but looked at Annie in query as Don glowered back.

'He's just heard there's no money,' she offered.

Don came and propped himself up on the fender. 'So where are you going, Tom? Your Auntie May, I suppose?'

Tom nodded. 'I wanted to go with Annie.'

'I told him May would do a better job of looking after him. He wouldn't want to go to Albert's.'

Don drank his beer. 'He's all right you know. Don't know what you all go on about. He knows how to make money, not like . . .'

He stopped, aware that Tom and Annie were looking at him. He leant over and took the spoon off Annie. 'Let's have a bit of that,' he demanded.

'Only a bit,' said Tom. 'She hasn't eaten for ages.' Why did Don always come and shove his weight around? Couldn't he see Annie wasn't right. He was almost as tall at 11 as Don was at 15 but he was no match in weight. Don looked him over as he spooned another mouthful. Annie felt the tension between them.

'Let her have it,' Tom said, squaring his shoulders.

Annie's hand felt heavy as she reached forward and touched Tom's arm. 'Do you think May could run to a bit more for Don? He's had a long journey remember, he's tired and upset. Just pop round the corner to her, there's a good lad.'

She smiled at him and he looked at her, nodded and left. It was what she wanted but he was also scared.

Don grunted as he left.

She ate what she could before she passed it over to Don to finish up. 'I'm going to bed,' she said and did not come down again except for bread and dripping until the day of the funeral, though she did go into Tom's room whenever she heard him crying and she hugged him and told him everything would be all right. Think of the day at the beck – wonderful things do happen, she would say wishing she could believe this herself.

But he was the only da I had, Annie, he had wept, and she had almost felt the pain burst out of her into tears but it had not done so. Still there was this harsh blackness which choked her and which was shot through with great gusts of rage. She had patted him, hoping that, in May's husband, Tom would find a father who would treat him like a real son. She sent him over there after that.

She did not see Don until the funeral. He stayed with Albert and earned himself a bit of money helping in the shop, and she would not think of that.

Betsy called her down on the morning of the funeral. She polished the sideboard, dusted the table, flapped the curtains a little free of dust. Tom helped her put in the middle leaf of the table and they carried through the food and it looked like a feast. But the smell and sight did not tempt her to eat. She felt as though she wasn't really here, as though she was floating above it all but couldn't escape.

CHAPTER 8

The funeral was simple. It was cold and wet and Annie knew her feet were soaked and frozen standing in the earth at the edge of the coal-black hole and she felt grief give way to anger yet again. The graves looked pathetic, she thought viciously, just the two of them side by side in this poky corner to one side of the consecrated ground. Well, she hoped they were happy now, the two of them, wherever they were, because they'd sneaked themselves out of this beggar of a life very nicely thank you.

What about us, her mind challenged the yawning darkness as the coffin was sunk deep into the ground but she was suddenly too tired to work out any answers. She stood apart from the others, shoulders hunched and heard words solemn and deep-spoken by a vicar who could not say God, only Gond. Fancy choosing a man who stumbled over that word, she thought. His words went on and were licked away by the wind before they could settle. She preferred the silence which fell as they turned from the grave, from her parents and walked back through the narrow streets past neighbours who took off their caps and lowered their eyes. Another victim of the bosses, they thought and looked to the pit wheel in the distance which was still and quiet and had been since the owners had closed down the mine. They squatted down oblivious of the drizzle as the mourners arrived at the shrouded house. The ham tea was laid out in the dining-room.

Coats had been hung in the hall by Annie, and dripped on to the black and white tiles. Umbrellas, the few that there were, had been shaken and set in the stand. Sarah Beeston's was grey and stood out against the black of the others, and the clock just went on ticking, thought Annie, as she moved past it and through into the dining-room. A room she had never sat in before.

She slid into a chair, set round the polished dark table. The

117

clink of glasses and murmur of voices washed over her. Tom squeezed her leg and she covered his hand with hers. Albert sat across from her, his face satisfied and for once not dour and bitter. Like the cat with the bleeding cream, she thought.

There were people she didn't know. God was there, of course, in the shape of Bob Wheeler who looked pale and stroked his moustache continually. Grief was on his face and Annie was strangely pleased that he mourned his friend. Next to him was Sarah Beeston. Annie had not known her as she climbed out of the taxi. She had arrived just in time for the service and had slipped into the back of the church and Betsy had nudged her. Thank your da's cousin for the gloves before she leaves, she'd said. She was tucking into the ham all right, saving herself a dinner when she got home, thought Annie, and my word, gets on well with God doesn't she. Sat at his right hand too. The vicar would like that, sat at the right hand of Gond the Father.

She put Tom's hand from her gently. 'Get on with your food,' she said quietly and rose. He was pale and shaken but wanted to stay next to her, so he rose also but she put out her hand to stop him, so he sat again and saw that the laughter, the smiles were growing now that the sherry was out. Annie could see Don swigging his back. He had been quiet at the graveside but now he was laughing with Albert and she wanted to bang their heads together but moved instead to the musty faded brocade curtains which had once been green, she knew, but now had no colour. Like the streets outside and the slag-heaps beyond and the distant laughter behind her. She gripped the curtain, dug her nails deep into it. How could the lost boys have come back to a world like this when they could have been free forever?

'Annie, bring the decanter over, pet, let your Uncle Albert have some of your father's whisky. Been a bit of a shock for the poor dear, hasn't it?'

Automatically Annie turned to fetch the whisky. Betsy looked flushed, her eyes were still red-rimmed. She had cried and howled and Annie had been surprised at her grief. It had a fierceness about it which was almost savage, more like a rage that had burst and could only be forced back bit by bit. Perhaps it was an overpowering anger and who could blame her. She had borrowed a dress from her friend, Ma Gillow, who lived on the corner and was here, stuffing her face as a reward. Bet's hands were permanent claw sausages in this weather and she was struggling to cut her ham. Annie moved across and did it for her. Poor bloody woman, she thought.

'And what about you, Joe dear? Will you have a sup of Scotch?'

Annie stood straight again, putting the knife on to Betsy's side-plate. She felt the anger stir again.

Yes, what about you, Joe dear, thought Annie. Coming back to get your feet under the table again are you, just as he planned. Nice and neat, Da, you were always nice and neat. Little letters to little people, but it's gone wrong and we are to go to places we don't like. There are some things you can't organise you know and other people's lives are one of them. One day I'll pay you back for what you've done, just you wait and see.

Betsy slapped her. 'For God's sake, hinny. Pass the decanter.'

It had been moved down here from his study and stood on the newly dusted and polished sideboard. The rich clean smell of polish lingered. Annie still had it on her hands from the waxed cloth. Not beeswax, Georgie Porgie, but it still looks good.

'It's all that's left of his good stuff,' minced Betsy to Ma Gillow. 'Wedding present, not ours of course, his first.' She pursed her lips and pressed her breasts up with her arms.

Annie felt the weight of the crystal solid in her hands and observed with mild interest the speed at which it dropped on to the floorboards. The nuggets of shattered glass exploded about her feet and were pretty as they reached the corners of the room. A room which was so beautifully silent now that she was able to watch the spreading stain loose it's amber tone and merge into the darkness of the floorboards in perfect peace. Tom flung down his napkin and left the table which was now beginning to seethe with outraged mutters.

'Don't worry, Annie.' He took her hands and understood her look of satisfaction as she stepped over the remains. He squeezed her hands.

There Da, she shaped. There is nothing left of you but a mucky floor and you never liked mess did you?

Her eyes were dry as they had been since his death and left Tom and looked beyond him at the table as she moved towards the door. Ma Gillow's mouth had fallen open. Albert was

119

taking more sherry. Don was glowering at the loss of the family heirloom, she realised. God was still stroking his moustache and Sarah Beeston met her eyes and nodded her approval.

She started up the stairs. No loose ends now, Da, eh. There's even the redemption ticket for Don to reclaim the watch, but what about the running sore that twisted and clung throughout her body and wept with no sound. She walked along the passageway to the bathroom, looking curiously in the mirror at a face which had not changed. It was the same as last week and it should be so different.

Next morning her limbs were still heavy and her face was still stiff as though it had never been used. Even speech was an effort. Annie stood in the yard and heard no sounds beyond the yard gate, not the laughter that was pitched high by the crisp snow which she had watched falling throughout the night nor the scrunch of boots as they packed soft whiteness beneath their concerted march. She heard only the snuffling breath of the pony and saw the white vapour disperse gradually into the vast space beyond their two figures. The sun was bright and sharply etched the gables and the water tub, like one of Tom's charcoal drawings. The ice was loud in its breaking and reared sharp-pointed before settling in patterns around the rim. There were several shards, clear as diamond splinters, in the tin which was used to ladle water into Beauty's trough.

It had been difficult to pass from the crook of warmth against the pony's side not because of the cold but because her feet would only move if dragged forward by a demand she found she was reluctant to form, but the restless shift of Beauty's weight forced her.

His coat was dry but not unyielding and she stood again with her arm along his mane, her face pressed into his smell and his snorting and bubbling filled her world and she found a satisfaction in the sweep of his neck, the stretch of his throat as the water protested and swirled but was drawn in nevertheless. Even the ice was gone and all that remained was a long slick of saliva which hung from the left side of his mouth as he raised his head but this too lengthened and snapped as he coughed and shook.

'Bit cold was it, my pet?' she murmured. 'Sorry, lass.'

And she felt her voice begin to shake and at last there were tears in her eyes, then coursing down her cheeks. She should have warmed the water and she hadn't and now she wept, racking sobs which she knew were only partly for the pony and mainly for that lonely, wretched man who had been her father. In spite of herself she could feel his despair as it must have been, his hopelessness, but to leave her, to leave them all as he had done was not a clean death. She could not grieve for him properly because it was ruined by anger at his wanting to go and leave them all behind to continue a life he had found unbearable. She gripped Beauty's mane, gulping in air. Trying to stop. I am in despair too, she cried, but I want to go on living, fighting, getting out of here to something better. I just don't understand how you could do it. The pony pawed the ground and moved backwards, unsettled now, and Annie lifted her head from his neck, sniffing hard, forcing herself to smile, taking in a deep breath until the shuddering ceased. It seemed to take forever. She rubbed the pony's nose.

'I'm going today, Beauty, going to Albert. Tom'll take care of you. Probably do him good, give him something of his own. His Aunt'll let him come on his way to school. He'll want to see Betsy anyway.' Her lip trembled again as she remembered how Betsy had wept when Tom had left; she had leant on the door and sobbed a moaning sort of crying that went on and on until Annie had left the room. She knew that Tom had been crying too, from the set of his shoulders as he passed down the street, walking next to the cart that took his bed and mattress and a bundle of clothes. May's was only two streets away but to Betsy it must have seemed like the end of the world.

Again Annie felt the confusion of feeling, the pain that gave way again to rage this time because her da had killed himself and she and Tom had nowhere to live. He should have made sure Joe would have them before he did it. Then Tom wouldn't have to leave Betsy and she wouldn't have to go to Albert who couldn't wait for her to start, which filled her with foreboding because she had always felt he loathed her guts.

She heard the knocking on the gate and hid her face against Beauty as it opened. She did not want anyone to see that she had been crying.

'What are you doing there, lass? It's your death of cold you'll be catching.' Ma Gillow hurried on past. 'Come on in, for the love of God.' The kitchen door slammed behind her and her footprints were clouded by the scuffing of her long black skirt.

'Silly old fool. She's a witch you know, Beauty. Wears long skirts and reads tea leaves. I reckon the greedy old fag just fancies food and drink she hasn't paid for.'

She felt shaky still but more in control.

The back door opened again. 'Will you get in here now, Annie. Albert doesn't want no germs in his house and that's all you'll be taking him if you stay out there much longer.'

Annie heard the words but let them carry past her and disappear into a sky she now saw was blue. How strange to see that she thought. It was like seeing Grace's mam's primroses in the window-box telling you that spring had come. The streets wouldn't tell you in any other way.

'If you don't come in here, lass, I'll come out there and belt your hoity-toity backside. Thirteen and she thinks she's a bloody princess. It'll be the Prince of bleeding Wales she'll be escorting to the races next.' Raucous laughter greeted this sally and Betsy slammed the door again. There'd been more in Betsy's mug than tea this morning, Annie realised.

The long mane hairs caught round her fingers as she moved away and Annie was glad at their resistance to her going.

'I'll be back one day, my love,' she whispered.

They were bunched over the table as she had known they would be. Elbows planted and hands possessing steaming cups which they dropped their heads down to in a way which would have tightened her da's mouth but here her thoughts snapped shut and she fought against the sweat which seemed to swamp her body and the trembling which laid her open. Why couldn't Tom be here? Why couldn't Don have stayed a little longer? Don't think, don't think of anything except this minute. Look, there's Betsy staring at Ma Gillow.

She had passed her cup across and now her lower lip hung red and full and looked as though it would drool as it often did and Annie hoped it would not since the bread was just beneath her and she had not eaten yet. Quickly she slid on to the chair opposite Betsy and moved the bread but Ma Gillow was too close so she moved the chair further to the end, bringing the loaf with her. There was no hunger in her but it was important to prove she was untouched by sorrow. The bread was dry and her throat small but no one was watching anyway.

'What do you see, then?' Betsy breathed. Ma Gillow rotated

the cup, tilting it away, then setting it down. She pursed her mouth.

'Times is hard,' she announced and glanced at Betsy who sat back in her chair.

'You don't need to see that in the tea leaves, just step outside that door.' Betsy shifted with irritation. 'What about something special?'

'Nothing special today, Betsy lass,' she said flatly, pouring herself another cup.

Betsy pulled at her lip and wiped away a streak of ooze. She looked round the table. 'Well, what about Annie here? What about the skivvy job with Albert. Keen to have her he was, thank God. That Sarah Beeston didn't like it but he's family, you see. Is she going to do well? Tell you what, see if the School Board'll find out she's left before time. Should have done another two terms by rights but she's a big strong girl, ain't you, lass? Here, take another piece of bread.'

She broke off a piece of crust and pressed it into Annie's mouth. Annie felt sick.

'Give the lass a mug of tea, then we'll see.'

It was just half a cup and easily finished. Anything to be left in peace, Annie thought.

Ma Gillow looked at the leaves, turned the cup about and checked again. Her face was puzzled.

'Oh aye, she'll do well,' Ma Gillow murmured. 'Won't be with Albert mind. It'll be with your Tom, it will.'

But it was to Albert that Annie first went. Into the kitchen with its rank odour of damp and unwashed dishes and then systematically through the rest of his house which was behind and over the sweet-shop, for that was all he sold now, that and cigarettes. It was a shop that smelt of nice things. Liquorice that could be unwound from its shoelace packet and rewound round fingers. Good for bowels, Betsy would have said and nodded her approval. Sherbet which frothed and stung the tongue on lazy allotment afternoons. Victory cough-drops which burnt out the back of your throat making it impossible to cough or even breathe. No wonder they worked, Georgie had gasped one winter. They clear out the cough by burning out the whole of your inside. Nothing left to make a cough, is there?

The smells did not creep beyond the thick oak door which divided the shop from the house. Here there was a parlour along from the kitchen. It would only need a quick flick since the curtains stayed drawn to keep out the cold and Albert grunted that he never used it anyway. The outside privy was quite another matter though and the torn newspaper strung on an upturned hook broke through the grey apathy.

Skinflint, that's what you are, she seethed inwardly. Black ink on me bum as well as chilblains! He was no longer with her but had passed back through the kitchen without a word and then on through the door which opened on to cupboard stairs which wound up to the next floor. There was no light and no carpet and Annie felt her way up following the squeak and creak of his boots. We'll be a pair of Wee Willie Winkies up and down these stairs, holding a bloody candle, for there was no gas up here and she hadn't yet seen an oil lamp.

'Here's where I sleep and I likes it clean,' he wheezed.

It was a bare room looking out over the street with yellowed net curtains suspended halfway up on a horizontal wire. Nothing much else, just a bed and a chest with an oil lamp, thank goodness, and a hairbrush on top, though from the look of his thatch he wouldn't be needing that much longer.

Annie wondered how long the long-stroked strands would stay swept over the balding patch once a wind got up. She was standing close to him and disliked the old man smell which lingered wherever he was.

'Your room's up those stairs. I'll have tea at six when locking up's done, me supper's at nine and breakfast is half past six. I like it in a warm kitchen, mind.' His stare was hard and then he was gone.

There was another door on the half landing which, when opened, showed a further set of stairs. The plaster was crumbly beneath her touch and damp with spots of green and black mould, thicker at the bottom than the top. Tom would think this was one of his abstract masterpieces, she thought.

Annie quite liked the room with its small window which overlooked the street and a ceiling which followed the line of the eaves and ended halfway down the walls. Like her uncle's room, there was little in it, not even a net curtain or a chest. Not that anyone would be peeping in up here unless they were very desperate, she thought, or blind. The bed was small and not made up, but so what, she shrugged. Her bag took little room and she could put her da's watch on the floor. She had not wanted it but Don had left it in her room. It'll get nicked at the stables, he had said. She wanted nothing of her father's she had raged, but its usefulness overrode her anger and she was ashamed that pain could accommodate practicalities with such ease.

He was waiting for her in the kitchen, sprawled out in front of the fire in a chair. He kicked with his foot towards the coal-bucket. 'Put some more coal on and then fill the bucket.'

She leant over and dug the rusty shovel into the coal and tipped it on to the fire. She was aware of him watching, grinning. His lips drawn in a hard line which slightly opened over long yellow teeth. Like one of those pub dogs, she thought, but there was no smell of booze on Albert. So that makes a change, she thought. She began to pick the bucket up but Albert said:

'I'll have a cup of tea first.' She washed her hands, which were still winter raw, in the sink that had green slime beneath the tap where it dripped.

'There'll be no pay for you of course.' He was tapping his knee. 'Your keep and sixpence every two weeks. That's more than enough spending money for a bairn of your age.'

She wouldn't look round, she told herself and set her shoulders in a straight line.

Albert watched her. 'You'll get used to being a skivvy, looked down on wherever you go.' He licked his lips. 'Look at me when I'm talking to you.' His voice was rough, violent suddenly, and Annie turned, making herself do it slowly.

He was looking at her with a look of satisfaction.

'Looked down on all me life I was, by the likes of you and your da. And look where he ended up. Down the bloody spout leaving everyone to sweep up his messes.'

'I'm not one of his messes. I'm me own person,' Annie retorted hotly, her back to the sink. He surged forward in his chair, his face ugly. A strand of his long hair slipped off his pate. She gripped the draining board, determined not to flinch. Bloody old fool, she said to herself, trying to control her fear. He was so big.

'You listen to me girl. You're my person now. I bloody own you. And what would he think of that, the blue-eyed boy, the father's pet.' His voice was grinding the words out. His finger was stabbing the air but he had come no closer.

125

'He had brown eyes, and I'm me own person,' Annie repeated, not understanding his hatred. He's barmy, she thought. She rushed on, 'I can go into service anywhere I like. I don't have to stay here. I'd have a starched pinny an' all.'

He laughed at her then and sank back into his chair. The room seemed lighter all of a sudden.

'Oh no, you slaggy little bitch. That you can't. Not at your age. You should be in school, so no one would touch you with a barge-pole. You'd better wake up to the fact that no one wants you. Joe don't and Sarah bloody Beeston can't. I won't let her, you're mine, see. You're mine to clean up me mess. At last it's my turn, you see, and I've waited a long time for it too, one of his brats skivvying for me.' He was shouting now, leaning forward with his hands between his knees. They hung down with big knuckles.

'You wait then, just wait until . . .'

'Just get me tea, for God's sake,' he interrupted, and pulled himself out of his chair. She braced herself for a blow but he pushed passed her and opened the door into the shop.

'Bring me tea out to the shop,' he grunted, 'and remember to keep your mouth shut. You've got more wind than sense and you'll have to learn to keep your place like the rest of us had to, all but your bleeding da.' He slammed the door behind him.

'I'll make good and sure none of me precious sixpence goes into your till, anyway, you miserable old bugger,' she hissed, but not loud enough for him to hear. She felt better for fighting him but there was no doubt who had been the winner. So, she thought as she filled the kettle, her da had rattled the old misery's cage good and proper and it looked as though she was going to have to pay the price. Her stomach tightened and she was afraid.

That night, when she was in bed and the chores were finished, she let the tears come again. She had decided, before she left for Albert's, that she would only cry in bed at night. That she would live her life in sections until the pain had eased and was not a constant ache which covered everything in a dull grey. She would keep her da in the black box with the blue-veined legs, tight shut it would be, right at the back of her mind.

She had been pleased to fight her uncle. She had been pleased to feel frightened because it meant that she was not dead inside. The house was quiet, there was no rustle from a bedroom that had been Tom's, no hug goodnight from him. She drew the bedclothes over her head and thought how, on her Sunday off, she would go to Grace's and they would fetch Tom and walk and talk, but not about her da. They would walk past the church along the graveyard and listen to the bells as the ringers practised. Annie forced herself to think of the sound which was one that she loved, but which Grace said drove her da mad, which was a shame because they lived just round the back of the church.

She felt her limbs going loose and stretched her legs down into the cold part of the bed. If I live from Sunday to Sunday it will be all right. As long as I see them Sunday, it will be something to hang on for.

Her jaw was slackening now and sleep would not be far off and she wondered whether they would see Don again soon. He had said not to bank on it, he had a lot of rides coming up. He might write.

CHAPTER 9

'I'm off now, Uncle,' she called behind her, expecting no answer and receiving none. The spring evening was fresh but milder than it had been for what seemed like years. It was Sally's party and she hoped her hands were not too red and chapped, but in any case her cardigan was too big and the cuffs sat low on her hands hiding her wrists. She liked it better loose than tight and the stars were making her feel good to be free but how would it be meeting the others after all this time? She had seen Grace of course but no one else. She had not wanted to see them after the funeral and even less when she was up to her elbows in Albert's dirty drains but Sally had seen her in the corner shop and insisted she come. Nice that was, Annie thought. She'd always been a bit flighty at school but she had been kind.

Come over Friday, Annie, she'd said, we haven't seen you for, what is it, four months. Most of the lads will be there but not too many girls. Scared, I expect, or their mums are anyway, can't think of what, she'd giggled and nudged. Anyway, no one sitting at home to make a prig of you, is there, Annie, and Annie had smiled at the bobbing yellow curls as they minced away but wondered at the ache the words had caused.

Sally lived a mile away and the evening was fading fast as she walked through the streets. She could hear the shouts of children in the back alley and had to dodge a group of boys as they kicked a ball.

There was noise but not much light coming into the yard from Sally's kitchen window. Annie dropped behind the privy, changing her boots for the sandals she had carried in newspaper. She stuck the boots in the corner where they were hidden by the shadow and walked on feet that felt as though they were bulging grotesquely between taut straps. Her feet and legs were bare and she hoped no one would notice feet that were puffing out of shoes a size too small and being rubbed red by the straps.

She had not noticed she had grown so since last year. She certainly hadn't got much of a bosom or a bum yet. From the back or front she still looked like an errand-boy, or so Ma Gillow had said when she came into the shop for two pennyworth of glucose drops the other week. For the indigestion, she had offered, as she poked her nose further into everything.

At her knock, the door opened. 'Come in, lass.' Sally pulled her in and shut the door. Her long ear-rings were dangling nearly to her shoulders, Annie thought, and matched her red dress and red shoes. Sally was laughing to someone over her shoulder and pointed Annie to the table which held some beer and lime cordial. 'All right, I'm coming,' she called to the boy who was tugging at her arm. She raised her eyebrows at Annie and giggled, 'He's so impatient,' and turned from her and was gone into the bobbing shapes which circled and flowed and filled the room.

The room was lit only by a low oil lamp but the heat was oppressive. Her feet throbbed and her eyes took in no one person but filled themselves with the hissing phonograph, and the movement which had swallowed Sally completely.

She edged sideways to the table wanting to choose the lime but the jug was full so no one else had. She poured a beer. She stood with her back against the wall which ran on from the sink and smiled, feeling her face widening and stiffening. She held the glass with both hands to stop the trembling and still it was as though she had not entered, for the movement continued unchecked and bodies flowed amongst it, their mouths working but the sound milling with the greater noise through which laughter threaded like the pink silk borders on Auntie Sophie's antimacassars. Annie fixed and held her smile while she brought the glass to her lips. Aunt Sophie; why had she not thought of her for so long? But here was warmth like those days which were now blurred and distant.

It wasn't so bad at Albert's now, she thought. He had stopped his shouting and seemed to have accepted that he couldn't make her cry so he just made her work harder instead and that seemed to satisfy him. He didn't hit her now, just took away her sixpence if she cheeked him, so she didn't. Just kept her mouth shut and hated him. She did not cry every night now, either. It still swept over her like a storm but far less often and she had worked out how she could snatch an extra moment with Tom when she was supposed to be fetching a drop of dripping from the corner shop. She'd rush to the school and they would walk home to May's together, her arm would rest on his shoulders, but only just, for he seemed to have sprouted and thickened since he had been there. It was amazing what six months could do, she thought. They would laugh or be silent together and she would tell him she was all right, as happy as he was at May's.

When they arrived at May's he would plead for her to come in and May too, but she never did. It looked too warm, too happy and she was afraid that if she saw what life could be like then she would cry in front of him.

She looked down at the beer, away from the circling laughter, and took a sip. It was sour and harsh and stung her throat and she felt the retch begin but pressed the cold glass hard to her lips and forced it down, feeling the sweat break out under her arms. She pressed her elbows to her sides. For God's sake, don't lift your arms, bairn, she ordered herself, mimicking Don, you'll bring down the wallpaper. It made her laugh and the tightness at the base of her neck softened and she felt her body ease. The music seemed louder now and the sink she leant against was cold and her smile became easy and meant but still at no face which sought her out.

Figures whirled past, some very close together, but still moving in time to the music. Snatches of conversation escaped to float past her.

'They'll get in this time. There'll be a Labour government, you mark my words,' merged with soft dance-time. 'They'd better, things won't improve under this little lot. We need improved dole if more bloody pits are closing and the shipyards.'

She hummed to herself to drown the talk which was the same, day and night, on every street corner where men squatted on their hunkers or stamped from foot to foot in the cold. 'Nothing else would matter in the world today, we would go on loving in the same old way,' she mouthed the words now. Not tonight, no politics tonight.

'Burns your tonsils out, Don used to say.'

The boy was broad and shut out the dancers from her. In the dim light she saw large black eyes with lines which deepened as he smiled at her. He was tall now for a Geordie, not as wiry as most, and his voice had deepened, but not changed. His smile still turned up on one side.

'You've grown, lad. I would hardly have recognised you.' It was Georgie. He reached forward and stroked her cheek with one finger. She wanted to be like a cat and wind herself round his hand.

'I'd have recognised you anywhere, hinny. You've barely grown at all.'

Try telling that to me feet she thought and forced more beer down to prove that she was nearly 14 and was glad when the noise hid the explosion and Georgie's handkerchief dried her eyes and dress. Then she could breathe again.

She laughed before he could, but he did not. People danced to a quickened tempo, they jostled closer to her. Georgie moved to shield her.

'Takes time to get used to, beer does. Come and have a dance.'

He smelt of the mines. It was a hard smell and Annie was surprised since it was all that was strong and big and adult to her. His hand was hard, unlike the hand that had beaten coins and created daisy-chains when summers were hot and Annie knew that time had passed, years had passed, but inside she felt just the same, just as far away from everyone. His arm was loosely round her waist and his breath was faintly beery on her forehead and she could think of nothing to say.

She had not danced before but she had watched and now followed his slight sidesteps tensely. He had hairs on his upper lip which were downy and his neck was thick and she liked his collar with its top button undone. She could feel that his chest was warm beneath his shirt and she was proud to be dancing with Georgie and felt her flesh melt in a way which was peculiar to her. She wanted to flow all over and into him but that was just plain daft. Still Georgie had not spoken but his head dropped on to the top of her hair gently, and he pulled her closer.

'You're such a bonny lass,' he murmured and she felt the tingle through each of her limbs. Should she say something?

131

She did not know. She could see and hear the other dancers but they did not intrude.

'It's been a long time since you were in the gang, bonny lad,' she replied and shook her head when he asked if she had seen Don. 'I see Grace and Tom every week though,' she said. 'Don has a lot of rides and rides are money.' She raised her eyebrows and they both laughed. She barely noticed the pain in her feet when he walked her home still in her sandals because she felt too ashamed to collect the boots from their hiding-place.

The bed was cold but she could still feel his head on hers and you're a bonny lass, he had said. On the way home they had held hands and she would not wash that hand just yet in case it removed the feel of him. Georgie had kissed her softly and gone, his face wet from the drizzle and until then she had not realised there was any. He had said nothing about seeing her again but she wondered what had filled her thoughts before the shape of his face and the sound of his voice had soaked into every space of her being.

In the morning, the sun was shining though it was a bitter grey dawn and Albert wanted his egg.

'We'll be needing some more coal soon, Uncle,' she said as she poured his second mug of tea. He did not look up from spooning out the runny yolk with a jagged piece of crust. It dripped on to the plate, hardened and darkened.

'I'll need to go out later for a bit of sugar, Uncle.'

'Don't be long about it. I want me dinner on time and there's work you can be doing. Take a walk up to the slag later. Pick out some coal.' He threw down his spoon. 'Just hope this new idea of that flabby fool Baldwin will stop the strikes now. Business is bad.' He pointed his toast at her. 'Longer hours and less pay, that's all they got for their troubles last time and when their money goes down, so does mine.' He pushed his chair back. 'High time they brought in something to stop their nonsense and thank God they've done it. Trade Disputes Act, they call it. High-faluting name but it'll stop sympathy strikes and reduce picketing. That'll sort the buggers out.'

As he rose he said, 'Can't beat the owners, you remember that. And what am I?'

Annie said as she had done many times before:

'You're an owner, Uncle.'

'And what's an owner?'

'An owner is a boss.'

'And what do bosses do?'

'Hire and fire, Uncle.' And stuff their bloody faces with eggs that'd be a bloody banquet for most of them round here. Her face was set. She would never look at him because she knew it made him feel as though he wasn't winning.

'Just you remember that. If you want a job, you have to do as you're told. That's one lesson we should all 'ave learnt by now.' He pulled out his handkerchief and wiped his nose. He dropped it on the floor, watching it as it fell. 'Boil that up today.'

He pushed past her to the door. 'You're lucky to have such a tolerant boss, Annie. Work, that's how you survive these days.'

She shook her hand at his back as he shut the door. And lending money out and adding on a power of interest, you bloody old skinflint. Don't think I don't know all about it. You're a blood-sucking scrooge. She picked up the handkerchief with the shovel and poker and heaved it on to the fire. It might mean a clout but it would be worth it, to show him he didn't treat her like that. Today it didn't matter anyway.

The boots were still there in the corner, the newspaper was soggy from the thawed early spring frost and fell away as she lifted them but she did not put them on although her toes were numb, neither did she hurry as she walked back from Andover Street and shopped at the corner near Wilson Terrace. Georgie lived near here and just maybe she might see him when he came off the midday shift.

The walk home was long because he was not to be seen although the whistle had blown at the pit for the shift end. The sandals found new areas to rub and she tottered into the yard, the sugar heavy in her hand and he was there, leaning against the shed rolling a Woodbine, his face black from the pit, his cap on the back of his head. Annie knew her nose was red and her legs mottled by now without stockings. She was joyous and ashamed.

The yard broom had slipped down the wall by the corner of the privy and she set it back in its place. The mortar was crumbling between the bricks and flakes fell where she had disturbed it.

'The pit needed pudding and pie today, then,' she called and marvelled at these words which came from herself and sounded quite calm.

133

He moved from the wall, settling his cap more firmly on his head.

'Never change, our little Annie, do you?' he drawled.

This time she could not answer because the words would have found no way to squeeze through the swelling in her throat. Our Annie he had called her.

'Here, try this then.'

The finished cigarette was thin and flopped in the middle with tobacco straggling from either end. It was still damp from his lick down one side and smelt like her father's pipe. The taste though of the dark brown shreds was sharp and bitter and when he lit it the paper flared, her mouth opened and it dangled helplessly from her lower lip quite unalight. He reached out and between strong square thumb and forefinger gently peeled it off her lip without tearing the skin.

'Like this, pet,' he said and placed it between his lips which were pink on the inside but otherwise dust-covered to blend with his face. He lit it with a match picked from amongst others, red-tipped and pale-stalked. The sulphur scent lingered long after the hiss of striking until the mellow breath of lit tobacco replaced its odour. He was the most beautiful creature Annie had ever seen.

'Now breathe this in as though you are sucking them corn stalks we used to pick up peas.'

Sharp and burning was the drawn breath but his lips had held it as hers were now doing so heaven was in every puff.

'Where's me bloody lunch and put that fag out of your mouth or I'll belt your behind, you lazy little strumpet.'

The door slammed behind Albert as he withdrew his head and the noise of the back alleyway came alive and the yard looked small again.

He grinned and lazily pushed his bike to the gate.

'See you, bonny lass, and don't burn his bread and cheese.'

How had she never noticed his eyes were brown and his lashes as thick as the hedgerows along by the beck?

Before he rode away, he turned. His face no longer smiling. 'You tell me if he ever hurts you, Annie.' He hesitated, his foot on the cobbles, steadying the bike. 'I won't have anyone hurt you.'

The days passed in a rapid pulse of waiting and being with him. The summer evenings were lazy and long and the fish shop had a lamp-post which had known Tom's swing-rope and now knew their shoulders well. Around their feet the crumpled paper blew and she failed to notice when a scattered sheet would catch against her legs until tugged further by the breeze. Until nine at night she was Albert's, after that she was Georgie's and the gang's. Albert had said she could do whatever she liked and Annie had been deflated; she had expected a battle but he had merely shrugged. Your da wouldn't have liked it, he had grunted and turned again to his paper.

When Georgie was on late shift she still passed along Mainline Terrace on shoes bought from Garrod's used goods shop and lolled and laughed but did not soar and felt tired when she was the last to be dropped at home because no parent would be breathing fire and threatening damnation of bairns of 14 walking home late with lads of 16 at well past the time decent folk were in their beds. Aye, but when the lad was there, then was the time for flights of pleasure as rough hands held hers and arms which thickened daily with twisting muscle lightly pulled her to him and she was special.

The hours merged into softly breathed air and mirth which melted one girl into one boy and they strolled with occasional words the longest way to the door, then long, closed-mouth, breath-held kisses left her yearning and bereft to see him go. Annie knew he was her summer sun and the only reason she drew breath and that no one in the entire world had felt as she did.

On Sundays, they would collect Tom and Grace and stroll to the beck with Beauty. She was too small for any of them now but still kept Tom in liquorice and pink mice with her manure and nuzzled Annie as she lounged on the bank. Sometimes Georgie would have some honeycomb and they would lick and suck the honey. They watched one day as Georgie and Mr Thompson smoked out the bees to lift the combs and Annie had never known such fear for another person as when the bees attacked their covered figures. Later she had dabbed bicarbonate of soda on Georgie's arms where he had red stings up to the elbows. He had brought it in a screw of paper and she used the hem of her skirt, dampened in the beck to whiten the lumps. The swellings were large and angry but he had never referred to them again that day.

135

Life's too short, he would always say, it's for enjoying, Annie. There's so much to look at, to find out. And he would kiss her and Tom would look at Grace and they would raise their eyes and pull a face.

Tom always brought his pad and would sketch and draw the changing season or the fly agaric toadstool which grew under the birches, marking in the white warts on the scarlet cap, and which Georgie explained he must never eat because of the poisons it contained. Or the speckled wood butterfly which Georgie showed him on a sun-spotted leaf. Or the foxglove with its tuber-shaped flowers drooping on one side of the stem only and which Georgie told him contained digitalis which doctors used to heal hearts. Tom had said that Georgie and Annie should have a bit of that since their hearts seemed to be all over the place.

Grace pulled a face when he picked her feverfew for her headache and made her eat it. Her headache disappeared.

Summer turned to autumn and winter sharpened the air. Grey overlaid blue warmth but Annie saw only sun and butterflies dancing. She answered an advertisement for a housemaid now that she was 14 but was refused because Albert would not give her a reference. She would go on trying always though, in spite of his rantings. You're mine, I've told you once, he had growled, and she did not tell Georgie what had been said but instead allowed her thoughts to fly high above the cracked ice of the lavatory pan and the soda fumes as she prodded and plunged with the long-handled brush.

I bet he even looks a cracker with his trousers round his ankles and sheets of newspaper in his hand she thought and pulled her sleeves down as far as she could to stop the chapping as the wind tore into every crevice.

But winter passed, then spring and summer waned into a gentle August and she was pleased when he rolled up, with quick deft fingers, his shirt sleeves and she saw his strength. The movement of his muscles held her eyes and quickened her breath and tears seemed close but why they should hover and return she could not understand.

'Tell you what,' he said, as they walked home late one night. 'On your birthday we'll go as far from here as we can and not come back until the end of the day. How's that then?'

Annie had forgotten there was anything else apart from these streets.

'Will we walk then or go by train?' she asked. 'Shall we take Tom?'

He squeezed her to him and she fitted in with his stride.

'No, this time we won't take Tom,' he said. 'And you just wait and see where we go and how we go. That's part of the surprise.'

'Great God almighty,' she gawped. 'There's no way, no way, my lad, I'm getting on that.'

He laughed as he pushed the cycle at her, propping his own against the wall of the yard. They were standing in the alleyway at the back of the shop. 'You'll get on and bloody well like it. I'll hold the saddle, you just peddle and steer.' He put down his bait-bag because he had brought the picnic with him.

'Peddle and bloody steer,' she panted, as they went down the alley for the fifth time, rushing past back gates, dodging the central gulley. It was coming but he had to start her on the saddle and push her fast or it was without hope. One hour later, they were ready to go.

'Just follow me and do what I do,' he told her, bringing his bike alongside. 'And don't fall off because the beer's in your basket and I'll tan you proper if you break it!'

They laughed and he bent forward and kissed her cheek and was off. She followed. It was good but the cobbles rattled her teeth and made the beer chatter. His jacket was flying wide as he turned yet another corner and jumped off, putting out a hand to steady her halt. They were surrounded by piles of coal waiting for shipment to the ports.

'Into the station now, we'll put the bikes in the van.'

Annie remembered the steaming of that other train, but here the sun was shining and the gap between platform and train held no fear for her. She held his arm, pulling him to a stop as they walked down the platform to a carriage.

'Tell us where we're going, Georgie.'

'We are going to the seaside.' He grinned and kissed her face and loved her.

She remembered the colourless pictures on that other train and her heart sank.

The train jerked and spat and roared and pulled and stopped and left them on the quiet Northumbrian coast. The bikes beat into the wind and her hair whipped across her face and she saw

137

more sky than she had dreamed existed and forgot the pictures.

The pale white sand ran out from the creeping blackness of the coal-spoilt beaches and swept round the endless sea in a curve that was clean and quiet. The waves left bubbles as they ran away from her feet which clenched at the sand; the sea, determined in its greed, plucked and sucked from beneath her. Her legs stung as the salt dried and Georgie stood smoking back at the couch-grass-tipped dunes. She knew no haste because this moment had been here for ever for the sea and would be here long after she had left. Waiting, always waiting; the sea, the wind, and the shriek of the gulls too, proved how little anything mattered as it rolled and swept away every imprint.

'Look, Georgie,' she called, trailing and pulling through soft shifting sand until her calfs dragged and her breath rose in pants. 'There's no sign of me down there and I've only just turned me back.'

He was down on his hunkers now and his eyebrows were raised.

'They throw the tiddlers back, you know. Just not enough meat on you, lass, to do more than just tickle it a bit.'

She was nearing the dune now. 'I'll show you I have grown enormously since last year.' She drew herself up in the wind which dragged her clothes tight against her form. Her nipples challenged by the cold stood proud on small firm breasts and she laughed down into his eyes, her hands on narrow hips, half child, half woman and Georgie felt a thickening in his throat.

He turned to watch the white caps behind her and pulled on the Woodbine which burnt fast as the wind rushed in gusts around them. Annie could smell the smoke but not see it. It was snatched and thrown into nothingness and she tipped her head back.

'Wouldn't it be wonderful, Georgie, to be like the wind. It's just as it is, no memories to carry with it, no rules to heed. Just free.'

'Come and sit down, you daft fool. Wrap yourself round this ham roll, it'll do you more good than standing there catching your death. Some memories are good. I need mine.'

The hollow-sided dune was quiet after the buffeting wind and surging water and Annie felt the tightening of her skin as her feet dried. Holding the roll in one hand, she scooped sand up in the other and let it fall through her fingers and then lay back on one elbow.

'But what about the bad things, how do you stop them creeping back?'

'You don't. You just clobber them, see them for what they are and throw them out again. You don't run away from them. Have some beer.' He passed her the bottle and she took just a sip. He was watching her.

'What if you can't do that?' The beer had left a thick warm taste.

He tilted his head back and took a drink. His throat was bulging up and down. He wiped his mouth with the back of his hand, then looked at her.

'Then you learn to do it.' He dug the bottle into the sand to hold it firm, then leaned forward and rubbed her feet until there was warmth. He was never cold. In all the time she'd known him he had never felt cold, she thought. She watched him as he lay on his side like her, propped up on his elbow.

'Does your mam scrub your back, Georgie, when you get home from the pit?' She couldn't look at him while she asked, she was too conscious of the line of his body, the way his leg lay partly on hers.

'Aye, and me brothers an' all, them that's in work that is.'

'Do you like the pit then, Georgie? Don said he'd never go down but that was me da telling him.'

The gulls were wheeling above and Georgie threw the remains of his roll far down the beach and they shrieked and clustered around it.

'I don't remember me ma or da ever talking to me about it. The pits are there, the slags are there, getting higher every year, slipping further down towards the houses in the wet. Each day me da went to the pit, me brothers went and so now I go and every evening so far we've come back. We've been lucky. It's all just there, Annie.'

He reached over and stroked her arm and her softness amazed him yet again.

Annie persisted. 'Well, do you like the pit then, Georgie?'

And he said all he could for the moment. 'What's liking got to do with anything, our Annie? The pit's there, me da was a pitman, I'll be a pitman, our kid'll be a pitman. There's nothing else round here.'

Annie felt the thudding shock in her stomach. Georgie looked at her with his smile hooked up at one side but his eyes anxious.

'How'd you like to scrub me back in front of our own fire then, bonny lass?' He ran his finger slowly round her lips.

She caught his hand and pressed it to her mouth.

'When?' she said, her voice muffled.

'When you're 16, if the old skinflint'll let you go, but then I'll just have to make him.'

His voice was soft, he was laughing, his brown hair was lifting in the slips of wind which dropped before being forced upward and through the pale dry green grasses on the encircling sand-solid slope and then his eyes became dark and the laughter left them. His mouth was still, his hands were gripping hers.

'I love you, little Annie. Shall we be together, you and me?'

'Yes,' she said and sat within the curve of his arm.

The day sped by in thoughts and words and skin held close together and his hands were firm not rough as he stroked the length of her body and she was not cold without clothes and there was no mark of coal on his. But there were scars where jutting rock had torn and sliced into the hard muscle of his back or the rounded curve of his shoulder and she kissed the raised and shining wounds.

His scent was sweet and strong in the curve of neck and shoulder and grew stronger as beads of sweat pricked up through his skin and his breath grew short and rapid. She had never seen a naked man before and the sense of his power made her pull him closer, ever closer, feeling him against her, his heat, his strength, until he threw himself away. And Annie lay alone and cold, his weight pinioning her arm into the shifting sand while the other chilled without the warmth of his body. Her body, so unhidden, lay open to the sky. She wanted to moan because it was unfinished, incomplete. She curled up to watch his stillness.

'Put your clothes on, hinny.' His back was to her, his voice was strained.

She pulled her arm free and still with no words pulled on first her pants, then her stockings which were warm with the same hole in from this morning and her dress whose button-holes seemed clearer than before. The third one had frayed so that the stitching hung limp and useless from the bottom end and finally her cardigan which was smooth and wrapped her away into herself again.

She sat with her hands clasping her knees, her face pressed hard down against them and they tasted salty, not of herself as they should. Her mind would hold no thoughts and her mouth no words and all she could hear was the roaring and threshing of waves which followed no pattern.

He was beside her now, his arm around her shoulders, his head on hers and their tears came quickly as her face pressed into his neck.

'We don't want a bairn yet, you're no more than one yourself, my little Annie. We must wait.'

The sun lowered itself enormously into the sea, red with effort, as they pushed the bikes on to the road and the uncertain dusk helped them to see each other's presence but not their eyes or mouths which still trembled. The train was crowded with last-minute returners so still they had time to pause and fit each fragment of themselves into a whole that felt something like it had once done, only better.

'Race you home, our Annie,' Georgie called as they left the station and, closeted by the street lamps, they laughed again and sang again and then lapsed silent for the lights were on in Albert's kitchen and they stood still, for he was always asleep when they returned.

'I'll come in with you,' he said and took her arm but before they reached the door it opened.

'And what time do you both call this for coming home?' It was a woman's voice. 'Come in this minute, Annie, and I will see your friend here at ten o'clock sharp.'

Annie hung back. She could picture the grey umbrella in the hall-stand on that wet funeral day. Georgie looked at her, confusion in his eyes.

'It's Sarah Beeston,' Annie said. 'She gives me gloves.'

He reached past her and took the handlebars. 'I'll come in with you, pet.' He spoke firmly.

'No need for that,' Sarah's strong voice answered. 'I've never been known to eat people and I doubt whether I shall start now. It would probably give me fearful indigestion at this time of night.' She had appeared full in the doorway now, standing quite still. They could not make out her face because she was standing with her back to the light.

Georgie touched Annie's hair with his fingers, then cradled her head against his hand. She leant into the caress. 'Will I see

141

you tomorrow?' she asked, not wanting him to move from her side. This he sensed and turned back to the figure in the doorway.

'I'll be coming in with her, if that's all right with you.' He was already taking the bikes and propping them against the side wall.

'Very well,' Sarah said. 'Come in both of you.'

She spun back into the house and light fell out into the yard. Annie took Georgie's hand, lifting her eyebrows and shrugging at his silent question.

The fire was banked up in the kitchen and Sarah Beeston pointed to the chairs around the table and sat in one at the head. Georgie took his cap off and stuffed it in his pocket, steered Annie to a chair and took one himself.

'Now,' said Sarah. 'Here's tea. I was just pouring one for myself. Your uncle, Annie, I am pleased to say, is now in bed, though there will be more to discuss in the morning, I am quite sure.'

She sat back, her calm eyes watching them as they watched her. Her suit was black with a straight skirt and she had a white blouse on that had no frills but she was not pretty, neither was she ugly. She was strong, decided Annie and her apprehension grew. The mug was hot between her hands. She took a sip.

'It won't do, you know, Annie, all this running riot until the early hours. In fact none of this will do.' She swept her hand round the kitchen.

It looked clean enough to Annie. She had a clout if it wasn't. The fender was shiny, the sink was clean with no trace of slime. The table was scrubbed. There was mould on the walls at the bottom but that was because Albert would not pay for any whitewash.

'It won't have to for long,' Annie answered, adding to herself – and what business is it of yours anyway? The steam wafted into her face as she sipped. She looked over her mug at Georgie and smiled.

Sarah's eyes were steady as she looked at them both. They seemed painfully young, as of course they were. Annie was just 15 and Georgie, for that was the name her informant had given her, could not be more than 17. Well, she thought, I wonder what our Annie has decided she's going to do with her life, because she was very sure it was not what she, Sarah, intended and so she asked her.

'And why is that, might I ask?'

'Because we shall marry when I am 16 and leave anyway.'

Sarah watched her sit back, pleasure at her statement evident on every line of her face and body. She knew it was not unusual for early marriages up here and in the mining communities of Wales, just as the areas bred young militants, but this girl was not going to be one of those young brides. She, Sarah Beeston, who had watched from a distance her childhood turn into youth and her youth into blossoming womanhood was not going to be held back from putting this girl into an arena where she could choose what sort of a life she wanted rather than one which seemed the better of two evils. Thank God for Bob Wheeler who had written to her, as she had asked him to, at the funeral. Tell me if there seems to be a problem she had said, when she was baulked yet again of taking custody of her cousin's child. Don, she had decided, was well able to look after himself. He had seemed to know precisely where his future lay when she had spoken to him at Archie's funeral. With himself in the main, she thought, and everybody else could go hang. She shook her head again at the suspicion that he and Albert were pretty much alike.

She had always thought that Albert was as he was because of the favouritism shown to Archie but Don had had two parents who doted on him and it appeared that still his God was himself and damn the rest. Perhaps therefore it was after all a family trait that reared its head whatever the circumstances. She wondered if it was inherent in Annie. It would be interesting to find out because, if it was, she felt sure it was in a form that would encourage survival of the spirit, but not at the expense of others.

She had called in on Betsy before she came here. She had been sitting by the fire sewing whilst Joe had been doing the books at the kitchen table. It had seemed that at last that poor unfortunate woman had a modicum of contentment, but was the loss of a son too high a price she wondered? Betsy had made her a cup of tea. Sarah looked down at the one which was in her hand; she felt full with the liquid and longed for the Earl Grey which Val made at home in Gosforn.

She had explained to Betsy what she intended for Annie and

143

Betsy had nodded. Annie deserves better than Albert, she had said, with a hard look at Joe who was oblivious as he reckoned up his day's takings. Take her away she had said to Sarah. I couldn't do anything for her, maybe you can.

So here she was now, she thought, and focussed again on Annie. Marry, indeed. Not yet, not while she still had breath in her body.

'I think not, Annie. I would like you to come and live with me in Gosforn, go back to school and have the opportunity to make something of yourself.'

There was a stricken pause and Sarah saw shock in both their faces.

'I'm bloody not coming with you.'

Georgie sat and waited.

'Albert and I have decided that you are to come and live with me and somehow I shall produce something that your poor father would have been proud of.' Sarah poured herself another cup of tea, not because she wanted one but because the scene she had had with Albert still made her want to castrate the man.

He had allowed her in, though he had recognised her immediately and no doubt remembered that she had been against him taking Annie after Archie's death. She had bowed then to the fact that he was a closer relative and that it might be better for Annie to remain in an environment she was familiar with after such a bereavement. And indeed Annie did seem inordinately attached to her step-brother which Sarah could understand. She herself was no advocate of blood ties automatically ensuring compatibility and the fact that Tom and Annie had chosen to cement a close step-relationship through choice not expectation was altogether laudible. That relationship, Sarah had felt, would help her more than anything. The fact that she now had a boyfriend did not bode so well, especially as Albert was allowing the child to run riot as well as mistreating her.

Bob Wheeler, God bless his upright soul, had discovered all this for her. He had been attached to Archie and had always felt in some way responsible for his death, though why, Sarah could not imagine. He had taken it upon himself to write with regular reports of Annie's well-being and had become concerned at gossip and rumour which seemed to indicate neglect and perhaps violence. Sarah had received the last of these yesterday, had arranged leave from her job in the solicitor's office where she worked and driven over.

Albert of course had blustered and created but Sarah had seen his type before. Out of my way, she had said, as he tried to prevent her coming further into the house, or I shall get the law on to you.

His mouth had fallen open, she recalled, and what a mouth it had been. Very few teeth and what there were would not invite closer examination.

This child that you have living with you, she had begun, stripping her gloves off and sitting by the fire, in his chair, she hoped. I shall take her with me tomorrow, you have done quite enough damage.

She remembered his mouth, opening and shutting and the abuse which had been hurled from it had been quite entertaining.

That's quite enough of that, she had said. Annie is to come with me now.

She can't, he had said, moving in towards her. She had learnt self-defence years ago and had been totally unperturbed. Albert was a bully and would not attempt any violence on a grown person she had been quite sure, and if he did, she would make short work of him. He had quite a beer paunch on him and looked flabby.

She had allowed the tirade to go on for quite some time; it so often defused a situation, she felt. It was amazing how many aggressive husbands, being sued for divorce, entered the office and then left, mild as lambs, after expelling a great deal of hot air.

Albert, of course, had not wanted Annie to leave. She's mine, she remembered he had kept saying. But, Sarah Beeston had said, she is nobody's but her own. She is old enough to leave you and if you make a fuss I shall call the police and explain to them that you initially employed Annie as an under-age servant, and what is more, subjected her to considerable abuse, is that clear? She had stood up at that point and he had actually stepped back.

In fact she was not too sure of her rights in the case but how was he to know that. She would check when she arrived back at the office.

He had told her to get out and she had said certainly not, not until Annie was home, then they would both remove themselves in the morning. It would be an uncomfortable night on a chair for her, but she had known worse. But now, back to the matter in hand, she thought.

Annie had been looking at Georgie, drinking him in and he had kissed her hand and smiled.

'Me da gave me nought to be proud of,' she said. 'He was a bloody fool who stuffed himself with gas to save getting on with it.' Annie was fighting for her life now, her fists were clenched and she was standing, leaning forward, her chin tilted, spitting out the words at Sarah.

Sarah applauded her courage, aware that, inside that rigid body, a heart thought it was breaking and who knows, it might have been.

'Sit down, Annie, let me talk to you both.' Sarah stirred her tea and her voice was gentle; she was moved by this child more than she cared to show.

Georgie was waching her closely, she saw, and he put out his hand and held Annie's arm. 'Sit down Annie, let's hear what –' she saw him hesitate. 'I'm sorry, what do I call you?'

'Sarah,' she said. 'I am Sarah Beeston.'

'Let's just hear what Sarah has to say, Annie.' His voice was soothing. Sarah felt the atmosphere become calmer and was aware of Georgie's power.

'Now listen to me. You have no choice but to come, Annie, because Albert has agreed. You could, I suppose, go and find a job elsewhere but I doubt whether Albert would give you a reference.' She knew that she would have to convince Georgie if she was to succeed, so she continued. 'Naturally, if you still want to marry when you are of age, we shall reconsider. In the meantime, I am offering you the opportunity to be free to make a choice about your future. Here there is no choice.'

'But there is . . . ' cried Annie.

'Hush now, pet.' Georgie turned back to Sarah. She could see the fear in his eyes, the pain. His voice was still steady but it was only through a desperate effort, this she could tell.

'Things are going to get worse in the pits.' Her eyes were steady as she talked directly to Georgie. 'You know as well as I do that coal is not being sold as it once was, that more pits must close; that you can no longer strike effectively for better conditions, with the Trades Disputes Act in force. You are in

146

work today, Georgie, but your pit might close tomorrow. Unemployment benefit is low. MacDonald's Labour government won't do anything to improve that.' She held up her hand to forestall his protest and silently thanked Bob for his political information. 'They might want to but they can't. It's obvious. The Liberals and Conservatives will combine against them to thwart it.'

It was what was being said in every pub, on every street corner and Georgie could only nod and affirm the truth of what she said.

'There's a depression coming that will make the others look like a picnic. The North will suffer as it always does. With luck you would both manage. But is that what you want? Just to manage? I want to get Annie out. I do not want her to breed children with rickets and consumption, and neither do you, I am quite sure.'

Georgie was hurting, probably more than he had ever done before, but she had to go on.

'Neither do you, Georgie.'

Annie broke in. 'I love him, I want him as he is. That is the life I want for myself,' but already she was remembering that train at the beck and the life outside and hated herself for the glimmering of wanting, of needing to go.

'Just for a while, Annie,' Georgie was saying, 'just for a while.' He was raising his voice to get through to her. Shout at me, Georgie, she was thinking. Shout at me so I don't hear this other half of myself. She gripped him, afraid that he would see her conflict, afraid that he wouldn't.

Sarah was watching them keenly and saw Annie's face and knew that it would be all right. The talk went on, back and forth, loud then soft, until Georgie said, 'I'll come at ten o'clock.' Georgie was speaking now to Sarah and she nodded, placing her tea mug down. She did not enjoy another's pain.

His voice was deathly tired and Annie wanted to stop the clock, stop everything because it was going too fast. Too fast to think. Too fast to go back to the beginning and start again. She rose as he kissed her and told her he would be here in the morning and that what was said made sense. He said that it was time he left Wassingham to sort something out for himself and that he would come back for her when he was ready, and she was ready. He seemed not to care that Sarah was there and kissed her hard and held her close to him. Then he turned and left without saying goodbye to Sarah, desperate to be gone before he could change his mind and drag Annie with him.

Annie walked to the door but did not open it, just stood facing it.

'I belong to him,' she said.

Sarah sat silent for some moments, not trusting her voice because she remembered the sparkling wedding of cousin Archie and Mary. The christening of this lovely child, for she was lovely, just like her mother; and intelligent. And for that reason she had to give her all that she could.

She finally said: 'I want to provide you with the opportunity to be free to make a choice of belonging with someone, but never to someone else. Perhaps one day you will be glad and now we shall wash up the mugs and we shall leave at 10.15 in the morning.' Her voice was firm. 'You must say your farewell to George when he arrives at ten, but before that perhaps it would be an idea to see Tom and Betsy, and perhaps Grace.'

Annie was too tired to wonder how Sarah knew so much about her.

She still stood facing the door.

'We belong together you know. I will marry him. I'll make something of myself and then I'll marry him.' She half wanted to go to that world out there; she knew that now and knew also that Georgie had known and had made it easy for her, but still she could hardly breathe for the love of him, and the pain of separation would be another ache to put into the black box. Was there no end to being torn apart? she wanted to cry.

Sarah nodded to herself. She had depended on a short sharp action. It had proved successful.

CHAPTER 10

Tom sat in the corridor outside the headmaster's study. His legs were set firmly on the floor and his hands lay in his lap, just touching. He felt the damp heat where finger met finger and put them instead on either thigh. At 13 he felt too large for the chairs which were short-legged and small-seated and, since this morning, he felt too old for school. The brown of the corridor paint was unrelieved by even a timetable and would look a good deal better for a few of me paintings, he thought. You could get a good run of them down there, though the light was poor. He found that he could think like this, just as he would ordinarily, but all the while, underneath, there was the great deep gouge of Annie's going running like a silent groan. He felt tired and unreal as he allowed those few minutes to rise to the surface; it was as though he could not leave the memory alone.

He heard again her call to him as he turned the corner to cross into school, just a few hours ago. Tom, Tom, she had called, and it sounded torn down the middle with jagged edges and he had felt the hairs lift on the back of his neck. She was at the head of the alley, off to the left of the gates, standing with one hand against the wall as though she needed its support and he had been unable to move towards her.

His feet had stuck to the ground as though they had taken root like the gnarled oaks up on the start of the hills behind the town. He had thought of their brown-sinewed strength because he could not bear to look across at her standing there with such pain running down her face in streams of tears. His breath had beaten in and out through his mouth as everything around him stopped. Her tears were rolling down her cheeks past a mouth which was white like May's dough as it lay in the bowl and Annie never let him see her cry. He had stood and watched her and her eyes were on his as she walked slowly over the road, her hair lying in unkempt strands, unkinked by overnight plaits.

She had begun to run when she was halfway across and he watched as she favoured one foot.

He had let her come right up to him, still not moving because of the great weight which was settling in him. He had felt her breath on his face as she said she was leaving today.

He looked at her boots then, not at her eyes, not at her mouth which was saying the words again and again. Slowly, as though they hurt her throat, the words kept coming but he would not look at her. Would not listen. It was her boots which had held him; cracked and scuffed.

You should tie your boots better he had said, stooping and grasping the flapping ends. You should tie your bloody boots better, then you won't get blisters. He had pulled the laces savagely until they cut into his hands, telling her again and again that she should tie them, while she told him each time that she was leaving in a voice that stabbed and twisted in his chest so that he could hardly breathe.

Don't keep saying that, he had shouted in the end, but she did. She told him that she was leaving for Sarah's in Gosforn this morning. That she did not want to go but that a piece of her did and she hated herself for that. He heard her but he would not listen. He had felt her pulling at his jacket until it lifted taut from his shoulders; he heard his bait-tin fall to the ground.

He had tugged and tied a bow, then a double and then he had felt her hands in his hair and she pulled until he could stand the pain no longer and lifted his head as Don had done in the allotment that day and he smelt again the leeks and saw the sunshine and the lead coins. And could not bear that she should leave him here. Then finally he had stood.

You've never come to see me at this time before, he shouted, blaming her, hating her. His voice had been loud and fierce and she had taken his head between her hands and there were still tears running off her face on to her faded dress but no sound of crying from her and finally he listened as the bell sounded in the yard and the children filed one by one into the school. She told him that she was going and with whom and when.

He watched the rope left swinging on the lamppost as it ground slowly to a halt. He saw the women come out of the open-doored houses with brooms, sweeping the dust into the road. He saw the cages emptying at the top of the slag, churning up the black slope behind the streets, up and up just as they had done yesterday and the day before and he wondered how they could when Annie was leaving.

He had looked at her then, her dark hair and thin face with dark patches beneath her hazel eyes, hazel like the nuts which lay on the ground on the paths leading to the beck, and knew that nothing could be the same again if she left him, but he lifted his arms which felt heavy and clumsy and pulled her to him and the wet of her tears and her warm breath were against his skin as she told him everything. He rocked her and himself and his tears were gulping gasps whilst hers were still silent.

It's this big black gaping hole in me belly, he had said, to think of you gone from here and he saw that the women had finished their sweeping but that the cages were still travelling and dumping the slag.

He stroked her tangled hair and soon there were no more words from her and he brought out his handkerchief, tugging at her hair as she had done, but gently.

Lift up, bonny lass, he had said, or you'll be going to school with a bald head and you'd need to polish that every day and she had laughed and wiped her face in the white linen as she swung from him and leaned back against the wall.

She had looked up at him and smiled saying that it was the choice. Yesterday it was all so certain; she was staying here, each day was the same and, in time, she would marry Georgie.

He had stood sideways to her, his shoulder rubbing the wall, listening as she explained how suddenly last night nothing was sure, there was this chance and she wanted it but wanted to stay here too, to stay here with everyone.

Sitting in the school passageway Tom felt again the warmth of the two pennies he had jingled in his pockets and the heat of his legs through the trousers. He had asked what Georgie said and she had looked at him then with all the pain he had ever seen in her face, as much as on her father's death, or the day of the fair. Georgie, Annie had replied, made it easy for me but I could still have fought but I didn't and her voice cracked and her lips trembled too much for her to say more and then he had gripped her chin and made her look at him, telling her that she was brave to go and that the world did not stop at Wassingham; he and Georgie would come to her at Sarah's. She was to go, to get out and he meant it, however much it hurt, he meant it. He had not cried as she had pulled him to her, kissed his eyes, his cheeks, his lips then torn away, running from him back up the alley, still favouring her foot.

He shifted on his chair and pressed hard down with his hands. He must not cry here, in the corridor. He focussed on the cracked linoleum, covered in smeared mud, stabbed with studded boots. The headmaster had still not called him in and he wanted to be back in the classroom, busy, not sitting with time to think. The chair was digging into his thighs where the wooden frame stood above the sunken cane. He sat on his hands, trying to lift himself level so that he was more comfortable.

What did the old man want, he thought, pushing Annie slowly back to a manageable depth. The Head, Wainwright, couldn't know he'd been late because Mr Green had cornered him the moment he entered the school and sent him to the art room to do the pictures for him. He smiled wryly at the term 'art room', for it was an old store-room with poor light and a few tables and paints.

It couldn't be the lateness then because Mr Green would not have told on him. He liked Tom too much. He sighed as the bell rang in the playground to call in the others for afternoon school. It went on and on, like it was the start of the second coming. That Nobby Jenkins loved his bit of power and leant into the bell like a miner leant into a rock-face and bye, he was giving a good shake today, thought Tom, and that was because Nobby knew there was someone outside the Head's study. Other people's trouble gave that lad strength in his elbow. It'd be the same when he started in pubs. He'd throw his beer back at the first spot of scandal and still be licking his chops for more.

Tom stirred. He'd make no pitman, that grubby little misery, and he looked at his own hands and nodded. Maybe he did like to handle a paintbrush but he was good and strong an' all. No nancy boy like Nobby liked to make out; his voice had broken already, hadn't it?

They were coming in from outside, slipping into the classrooms lying either side of the corridor. He nodded at those who waved and those who glanced at him furtively, crossing his arms and extending his legs. He wasn't nervous, not after this morning.

One boy slipped out of the line leading into Mr Thomas's room.

'You all right, man?' It was his friend Ben. They were to start in the pits together in February. 'Has he seen you yet?' His blond hair had a centre parting and was cut very short.

'Awa' with you Ben. If I'm held up here, tell me Auntie May I'm at the library.' It was a lie she would easily believe. His aunt was used to him catching the worms in that book place, as she would say, and he would laugh as he always did and say that one day he'd bring her one home, a book worm that is. And she'd shriek and say he'd get a dose of liquorice if he ever did that and Davy, his cousin, would wink and grin.

Ben nodded. 'What've you done, man?' he asked.

Tom shook his head. The corridor was empty now. 'Nothing, I've been painting all morning. Get along with you Ben or you'll be here next.'

'Take care now, lad, he's already thrashed Sam today,' Ben said and scooted back into his classroom.

The headmaster was a cruel bastard, Tom thought. It was no wonder some had looked sideways at him as he sat here. It was said he'd been sent back from India after he'd lost his position at a mission school or that's how Green had put it to another teacher when Tom had been busy in the art cupboard. The sun had addled his brains which was why he was so short-tempered. The man hated it in the North, Green had said, the cold, the squalor, and blamed everyone but himself for having to be here.

It was quite silent in the corridor now, not even the murmur of the teachers' voices from behind the doors and then the headmaster's door opened and Mr Wainwright called, 'Get in here, boy,' in a voice as cold as the wind that whistled through the town when it was coming in from the east.

All Tom could see was a yellowed hand on the door and a starched cuff. Well, our Mr Wainwright, he thought, you'll need to soak that hand in vinegar for a while if you're ever going down the pit, but then you'll never do that like the rest of us, will you?

He stood up and walked into the study, his boots clumping on the wooden boards, until he reached the square of patterned carpet, and then becoming silent. The headmaster was sitting behind the desk now, and his paintings were spread out before him. He said nothing to Tom, just sat there looking at him.

Tom stood still. Yes, he thought, even this way up they're good. It's the colour. Maybe he wanted to put them up in here? The room was certainly dull and needed some brightening. Even the carpet which had once been many-coloured was a mixture of browns except for the beige thread which broke through to the surface where feet had worn a path. The walls and the wooden filing-cabinet were brown also and there was not even a brass fitting to relieve the monotony, only a wooden handle.

Tom looked back to the pictures, then to the man behind the desk. He sat back in his chair, his hands steepled under his chin. His eyes were a pale slate-grey from which it seemed all feeling had been washed long ago. They were sunken in dark hollows. There were deep lines that ran from his nose to the corners of his mouth and his lips were set in a thin line. Behind him, Tom could see the deserted playground through the window. A ball was caught in the corner where the tall wall ended and the railing began. The sky was clouding over, making it look colder than it was. He looked back again to the headmaster, waiting for him to speak, but he just sat on, looking Tom up and down, his face twisted with distaste and Tom wondered again why he was here. And then the man moved. He pointed a long finger at one of the paintings.

'What have you to say about this then, boy?' His voice was cold and his face barely moved as he spoke.

Tom thought, the man's gone daft, can't he see it's a bloody painting. He cleared his throat. 'It's a painting. Mr Green asked me to do two for the class wall.'

'And this is what you produced, is it?' He paused. 'How dare you.'

Tom felt confusion stir within him, overriding the churning darkness of Annie.

'Don't you like it, sir?' He looked at the painting again. It had been done from the heart, for her, and he thought it was the best he had ever produced.

He saw the headmaster rise and lean forward, resting his weight on his hands. 'Don't take that attitude with me, boy.' Pink was beginning to tinge the sallowness of his cheeks, spittle settled on the desk.

154

Tom kept his face still. Thank God he missed the painting, Tom thought, but these silent words were just a device to gain time for some understanding and he found none. He looked at the man who stood across from him and did not know what he meant.

'I don't understand you, sir. Is something wrong?'

The man picked up the painting, shaking it at Tom. The paint had dried hard and thick and a flake fell off. Tom jerked forward, his hand outstretched but the headmaster pulled away from him. All Tom could see was what he had painted. A small child on a freezing cold playing-field holding its hand towards a girl with a tray of steaming pies. She was holding back a pack of men, their breaths clouding the air, whilst she gave them to the child.

'This is what is wrong, Thomas Ryan.' The headmaster was holding the painting with one hand and pointing with the other.

Tom felt his thoughts become disjointed, broken up. There was nothing wrong with the picture that he could see, the colour was good, the perspective correct.

Wainwright's face was jutting towards him, ugly in its anger.

'Don't think I've forgotten I had your cousin Davy Moore here at school before you and had nothing but trouble from him and now I see it rearing its ugly little head from your direction.' His eyes had narrowed and his forehead was etched with deep horizontal lines.

Davy, thought Tom, he's been in the pits for four years now, what's he got to do with anything?

'What is, sir, what's rearing its head?' Tom was confused. Davy didn't paint, never had done. He was good at his work though but even better as a union man. But he wasn't a painter.

Wainwright was talking as though he was a river in full flood. '. . . I shall stamp it out boy. I shall stamp it out.'

Tom watched the reddening face of the headmaster and felt at a loss.

'You and your kind will try to bring the country down to your level if you can. Marx, Engels, don't think I don't know what you rant about in your lodges and your halls. Kier Hardy is your idol and it should be God! God!' He was shouting now. 'God and Empire!'

Tom just stood there, listening but not following, his mind a

155

maze of images that wouldn't stand still. The man was moving too fast and Tom did not know in what direction he was going.

'Well I hear your cousin has just been thrown out of another pit for his rabble-rousing and so now you think you can try it here, do you? Well, not in this school, you don't, not in this school.'

The headmaster was still shaking the painting and minute flakes of paint were lying on his desk, on his papers; one had fallen on the covered inkwell. Tom saw that the man's fingers were grey from the paint where he was holding the paper.

'I can see what you're trying to say, boy, say all over my walls. Well, you won't, see. This is seditious propaganda, a dirty bolshevik slur.'

Tom looked at his painting again; he could only see Annie on a cold bleak day.

'It's people like you that have driven people to ruin, driven people like me to ruin. Given natives ideas above their station. Louts, that's what you all are, louts.' His voice was vicious now and his eyes were staring and then he stopped abruptly, breathing heavily. He wiped his hand across his face leaving a grey trail. 'I demand an apology from you.' His face was hard, his words clipped and loud.

Tom stood quietly, he looked again at the painting and wondered how far Annie was from Wassingham now and how far Wainwright was from bursting all over the room. He was pulsing with rage and Tom still did not know why. He shook his head at the man.

'I can't apologise for painting that,' he said, feeling tired and miles from this room.

Wainwright seemed to stop breathing as he looked straight at him and slowly tore the painting through once, then twice, then again.

Tom swung back to this room as the pieces scattered on to the desk and one fluttered to the floor at his feet. Blood filled his face, his eyes, his ears. That was Annie who had been torn and she had been torn enough. He moved one step forward.

'That was my sister you tore,' he said, his breathing rapid now and his hands bunched. He wanted to smash his fist into that yellow face, into his ribs and belly. 'It was only a picture about sharing, about something that happened a long time ago.'

Wainwright moved round the desk towards him. He was bigger than Tom and he was shaking.

'That picture,' he snarled, 'was of a seditious nature, an encouragement to revolution which I will not have in my school. I've heard your cousin's call for redistribution of wealth and he's put you up to this. I know your type, Tom Ryan, and I don't like them. I've been watching you, waiting for you to start, like he did.' His breath was sour in Tom's face.

Tom drew back but Wainwright held him fast.

'It's about a girl and a few bloody pies, man. That's all,' he hissed.

And now the headmaster pushed him over towards the chair in the corner.

'It's about far more than that, don't take me for a fool. But I'll sort it out, don't you worry, like I wanted to do with David. Bend over that chair.'

The headmaster was rolling up his sleeves now, grunting as he did so, grinding out these words, 'You can tell Davy Moore from me that I don't want his bolshevik propaganda in this school. There is no room for anything but the Empire here, boy, and I want you to remember that.'

Tom gripped the back of the chair as he felt the first searing stroke across his back; up high, near to his shoulder blades.

Christ, he thought, what the hell is happening here? What the hell has happened today?

Tom felt the next and the next. 'I still don't know what the bloody hell you're talking about,' he hissed, turning his head.

'Another five for lying and another five for swearing.'

The pain was like a knife slicing across Tom's back. He could hear the stroke land and feel it through to his belly. And then the fury came again, pushing aside the shock and he rose and wrenched the cane from Wainwright's hand. The headmaster was red in the face and sweating. His sleeve had half rolled down.

'If I knew what you meant I could answer you, man,' said Tom, his voice not much more than a whisper. 'But I'll find out what it is that is ranting through your crazy mind and tearing up my pictures. I'll find out and then I'll do something about it.'

They were both panting, facing one another. Tom broke the cane over his knee and threw it into the corner, then moved to

157

the door. He heard his feet clump as they hit the wooden boards after the silence of the carpet. He could feel his shirt sticking to his back and knew he was bleeding. He left the room and shut the door quietly. He didn't know whether Wainwright had tried to stop him, he couldn't hear him, or anyone. He walked to the art room and painted the scene again. He would need it when he arrived home and asked Davy to explain to him what there was to a painting about a girl giving a child a pie.

The front door of Aunt May's house was open as it always was when the weather was mild but Tom slipped down the back alley and in through the yard gate. He could hear Davy in the wash-house and knew that Wainwright had spoken the truth when he said Davy was out of the pit again. The afternoon shift was still underground.

He hesitated by the door; he could hear the water run off Davy's body and on to the floor and the clang as he put the empty bucket down.

Then he saw May standing in the scullery.

'Come in here, lad, and have a piece of bread.' She waved him into the kitchen where there was bread on the table and blackberry jam which she had made from the overflowing buckets that he and Grace had picked with Annie and Georgie.

The fire was blazing in the hearth, cooking the stew for tea and heating the irons for May. She had moved to the far end of the table by the pile of linen and her face was red from the heat of the fire. She spat on the iron and thudded it into the stiff white clothes, rubbing backwards and forwards with all her weight.

He loved the smell of heat on linen and sat down, careful not to lean back against the chair while he spread the jam straight on to the bread. It had set something splendid this time, he thought, and wiped a drip off the jar with his finger and sucked it, not thinking of the pain; easing himself back into this room which he loved.

It was naturally dark in here with the small window and the stairs which spiralled straight up from the corner to the three bedrooms upstairs but it was dotted about with vivid patchwork cushions and rag rugs. Brass reflected the fire which shone warm on the fender and on the horse brasses which hung down the walls. The cat was sleeping on Uncle Henry's chair and some of its ginger and white hairs had already settled on his trousers.

May changed the irons on the hot plate, holding them in a thick white cloth. She looked at him as he poured a mug of tea.

'One for me, boy,' she said, 'or don't you think ironing's hot work?' She threw the cloth at him and he caught it with one hand but the pain from his back snagged as he began to laugh so he just poured the rich stewed tea and added a drop of milk. There were no brown sugar crystals today, which definitely meant Davy was out of the pit again. Sugar always went back into the cupboard when they were one pay-packet less; to make sure there was some for Christmas, May would always say.

He looked up at her and she pointed with her head to the sideboard. 'Put it on there, bonny lad.' She watched as he rose and walked with care round the table and put the mug on the wooden mat he had painted for her.

He knew that she was watching him and wanted her to ask, not to have to tell. He always thought May should have been a farmer's wife. She was as big as his mother, her sister, but not pale and flaccid as she was. May was firm and pink with the same blue eyes as his, the same eyes as Davy, though the other boys, Sam and Edward were brown-haired and brown-eyed like their da. May's hair was like the corn, but with white shot through it. He had once said how pretty she was, how few lines she had, not like his mother and that was the only time she'd slapped him. It had been a real slap too. I would have them if I'd had your poor mother's life, she had said. But Tom had turned away from her. His ma had given him and Annie away so she wasn't his ma any more.

He turned back to the table and sat down and then she said: 'Trouble is it, you've been having with your back?'

She spat and the iron sizzled. She leaned into her work again, backwards and forwards.

'I was thrashed today,' Tom said. He felt tired. 'She's gone, you know.' But he knew she would already know, word went round like a slag fire that hit the surface. 'She's gone and I did a painting and the bloody man thrashed me for it.'

May folded the clothes carefully, making a neat square of the tablecloth she had finished.

'I know she's gone, lad, but you'll see her soon.' Her voice was full of kindness. 'Now lift up that shirt, lad, let's be seeing it.'

He felt a flood of relief. She would soothe the hurt, which did not pain him like that black hole which had grown since this morning, but the soothing would help that too and make him feel less alone.

He hung his jacket on the hook and then tried to ease the shirt from his back. It was stuck to the flesh. May tugged her apron straight as she moved round the table towards him.

'Give it to me,' she said and turned him round. She just held his shoulders, didn't lift his shirt or even tut.

'Get sat down again,' she ordered and her voice was carefully flat. 'I'll get Davy in here.'

She bustled past him, not looking at him, out into the yard, banging on the wash-house door.

Tom lay his head down on the table. He was so tired, so bloody tired and the pain from his back seemed to go up to the top of his head and down to his legs and the ache for Annie was everywhere that the thrashing wasn't.

Suddenly Davy was there before him, crouching down and lifting up his head. Tom felt as though he had been asleep but his eyes had not been closed.

'That's a rare old belting you've had, my bonny lad.' Davy's eyes were smiling but there was a blackness behind them. He stood and took the bowl of lukewarm water from his mother and the cloth and sponged the shirt free. Blood reddened the water darkly and Tom tasted the blood in his mouth from the lip he was biting. He must not cry out in front of a pitman and he forced the sheet of pain to lift by talking.

'So you're out of the pit now, Davy?'

There was a soft laugh from Davy, whose lean dark face was transformed. He was a miserable-looking devil, May always said, until he smiles and then the sun comes out from where it's hiding and we all have a bathe in it.

'Well lad, how word gets around.'

May snorted as she piled up the linen and carried it to the cupboard. 'Less talk and more work and this wouldn't happen my lad. More money than sense it is. More mouth than sense if you ask me. What's the point of setting the world alight if we have to put the sugar back in the cupboard?'

Davy dug Tom in the ribs. 'The kettle's boiling again,' he said, 'rattling its top off.' And they both laughed.

'We'll find out how you got your lugs on to that news later, our Tom, but I want to find out how you picked up this little masterpiece.' He was wrapping round greased clean flannel and the heat was taken out of his back and he felt the tension ease in his neck. He liked the feel of Davy's hands, quick and firm, as they passed the strip of sheeting round and round his body. It made him feel like a bitty bairn again.

Davy stood up. He groaned and Tom wished he had thought to stand up. Pitmen hated to crouch; they spent all day doing it and their backs were creased for life.

'You'd like the pattern on your back, Tom,' joked Davy. 'Stick it up on the wall, you would, boy, but I'd like to know the name of the artist if you don't mind.' He was carrying the bowl back out to the scullery and May called for a sprig of thyme to be put in the stew.

Tom watched him as he lifted the lid and followed the steam as it puffed out up the chimney. He took a sip of tea and poured some into Davy's cup as he sat down. The smell of thyme wafted now, faint to begin with but increasing to a pungent thickness.

'It was that bugger Wainwright,' he said and saw May return to the room and stand with her hands on her hips. She had taken down a string of onions from the hook by the pantry and they rocked across her full thighs. He went over the scene for them; it was vivid still but full of colour and there had been none in that room apart from his pictures.

'He said that, did he,' remarked Davy at length. 'I think you've just been thrashed for another man's work, Tom lad. He's wanted to belt me often enough and never found the excuse. Called me a guttersnipe radical.' He patted Tom's knee. 'Me mam's right, I've more mouth than sense.' He sat back in his chair.

'It was a good painting was it, lad? Worth the cane-work?' he asked.

'The best I've done,' said Tom. 'It's in me jacket.'

At their look of surprise, he added: 'I painted another before I came home.'

Davy laughed and signalled for him to stay put and fetched it himself, raising his eyebrows as he studied the painting. Tom felt again the cold of the field, the fear of the panting men, his own breath rasping in his chest as he ran and left her. Now he'd had his beating too and the aching felt a little better.

161

Aunt May took the picture from Davy and said: 'Redistribution of wealth, isn't that what Wainwright said?'

Tom protested. 'It was Annie sharing out the pies.'

Davy laughed and slapped him on the back before he remembered, 'Sorry lad, I forgot. I wouldn't mind taking this for a poster though because that's what it is right enough. It's a good one boy. Your Annie had the right idea.'

'Davy, lad,' warned May, 'don't start the boy off on your ideas. See where it's got you, on the blacklist. No pit'll have you now.'

Davy shrugged, his face closed and no longer smiling. 'Someone's got to say something.'

'Leave it to the unions, Davy,' his mother said as she cleared the jam from the table and gave him the knives and forks to put round. She waved Tom back into his seat. 'You,' she commanded, 'sit down and don't listen to this man. Eighteen and he thinks he knows everything.'

She flounced out to the kitchen and began to chop up the leeks.

'Why are you out then, Davy?' Tom asked.

'Oh, the overman kept giving the best seam to his mates. It's piece-work in these pits you see, Tom, or if you don't, you soon will when you go down. And those in the better seams get pickings; more money. Should be done by ballot, by luck, not by favours. I told the overman, see, and he had me out.'

Tom looked at him as he finished laying the places and perched himself on the fender.

'Why didn't you leave it to the union then, Davy, like your mam said? You're a union man.'

'Because since the General Strike, the unions have no teeth, man. Now the owners can use the workers to get rich and get away with it more than ever before, and the overman can flex his muscles and do us rabble-rousers down, as your Mr Wainwright called us.'

Tom narrowed his eyes as he remembered the headmaster. 'I don't want to go back, Davy. He's a bully.'

Davy looked at him firmly beneath his brows. 'You'll go back and stay until you leave to go to work. You don't let bullies chase you away. Look at your Annie, she stayed with that bloody old bully Albert and now she's free of him, thank God. I wonder if she'll go on giving away pies to people?' And he laughed.

Tom smiled and wanted to put the ache back where it had been, well below the surface.

'What did Wainwright really mean by redistribution?' He forced himself to listen to the answer, to keep his mind on things outside himself.

'Sharing boy, that's all it means.'

'But why did he belt me?'

'Because, I suppose, one way of doing it is to tax everyone harder on their incomes, that would take more from the rich, spread it about a bit. Makes those with money right mad to think of it. It's sharing, like I said.'

'And who were Marx and that other one then?'

Davy laughed. 'No more questions, get on with your tea. You'll learn soon enough when you're working.' He lounged out to the kitchen. 'I'm just off to see someone about a heavy right arm, Mam,' he said and May just nodded.

'A warning, that's all my Davy.' Tom saw him nod.

He took a sip of his tea but it was cold.

May called through the door. 'What about going to see your mam, tell her about Annie?'

'She'll already know,' he replied and May shook her head.

'She'll like to hear it from you.'

He shook himself into his shirt and then his jacket. 'Maybe I will, Aunt May, but I've to go and tell Grace first.'

'Putting your girlfriend before your mother then is it?' She stood in the doorway and grinned, shaking a spoon at him. He dodged round her.

'I'll be in for tea,' he called, avoiding her blow which never landed.

He walked down the back alley, his hands in his pockets since it looked more grown up and did not jog his back so much. His girlfriend, Aunt May had said, and he wondered how Grace would take to that, her in higher school and him a year younger. But soon he would be a working man and she would like that. He felt as though he had changed today, grown up. He would not see Betsy, of that he was more sure than anything, because it was her fault that Annie had gone and he hated her even more now. If she had fought Joe and made him take them both he would not have gone to May's and she would not have gone to Albert's. They would have stayed together and Sarah would not have needed to come . . .

CHAPTER 11

At ten-thirty prompt, Sarah edged the bull-nosed Morris away from the front of Albert's blank-faced shop, leaving the chattering groups to disperse once the novelty of a car like this, driven by a woman, for goodness sake, had been talked to death. Georgie was not there to wave to Annie.

He had arrived at ten and had stood quite still, in the doorway of the kitchen, his cap held loosely between slack hands. He had looked at Annie steadily and her eyes had held his and had answered the question they held from the deepness of her life.

Worldlessly he had turned and leant against the wall, one foot wedged against his bike. He had taken out his cigarette paper, rolled it round tobacco teased along its centre while she had stood close enough to touch the length of her body against his as he licked and lit the cigarette. She breathed in the scent of sulphur as he sucked in the smoke. She opened her lips as he slipped it from his mouth to hers and she felt his moisture as she had done before, so long ago and they remembered without words those months and weeks and every minute between then and now.

He had not kissed her but had cupped his hand about her cheek and laid his face against hers. I've still to teach you to hang by your arms on that bar, he had said, and she had whispered, I'll love you all my life, my love.

And now she was gone from him, leaving him and while Sarah peered through the windscreen, steering the car clear of tram-lines, she looked back as the juddering cobbles changed to asphalt and the car climbed the hill out of the town. She could see the slag creeping ever nearer to the houses which looked as though they were banked against the black advance. She could hear in her memory the whine of the cages which were swaying as they lurched and climbed steadily higher up the coal-dust mountains to discharge at the peak a dense choking black cloud.

She looked to the front, to the hill which was unfolding as they, in turn, climbed and wanted to wrench at the door handle and fling herself back down to Wassingham while she still had the time because, once you left, you never came back, never truly came back. The crest was drawing nearer, the car engine was groaning, then it hesitated, as Sarah changed into a lower gear. Now, her mind screamed, now, but the crest was here and they were over and the world was in front of her in a burst of light. Sweeping fields and trees flicked past faster and faster and her knuckles were white on the door handle. She turned and looked back but now could only see the hill, not the town which clutched Georgie and Tom in its grip. It's too late, she told herself, and the tearing inside seemed quieter. It's too late now, she repeated to herself.

It took two hours to travel to Gosforn through rolling countryside that was dotted with pit villages and ironworks that belched foul smoke onto sprawling mean streets. Sarah pointed over to Newcastle on the left but Annie could see nothing of the city with its bright lights and theatre drapes, just grey smoke bulging from pencil chimneys into a late August sky. She could not yet speak to this woman who had stirred her into betraying Georgie, betraying Tom.

Sarah's house was not joined to another, none of the houses were, Annie saw, and the light seemed to pour through the gaps lightening the whole road.

There were gated front gardens which ran down to the pavement and Sarah's was shielded by a clipped privet hedge. The car jumped as the engine died.

Sarah set her hat straight and gathered up her bag.

'Take your things then, Ann, and you do not need those sandals any more, they are far too small.'

'I'm keeping them,' replied Annie as she clutched them to her and slammed the car door. She lifted the latch on the wooden gate and walked up the path to the front door past the privet hedge which sported pollen-heavy flowers and separated this house from the neighbours.

Inside, the brown and white tiles looked crisp and cold and

her boots clicked loudly as she walked along behind Sarah, past the hall table. She stopped to look at the large gong which stood by it. There was a brush on the table and a few letters stacked in a neat pile. She put her cardboard suitcase down and brushed her hair in the mirror. It was still the tangled mess it had been this morning.

'I usually brush my coat with that,' said Sarah gently. 'You might find it full of fluff.' She stood in the doorway to another room and Annie hurriedly put the brush back.

Sarah spoke again. 'That table is walnut, it has a nice grain hasn't it? Incidentally we ring that gong twice for meal times. It's a bit like a race and goes back to my father, I suppose. Once means on your marks, twice means it's on the table and things are going to get a bit frosty if you are not waiting for it.'

Annie looked along the passageway which went on past Sarah, down to a closed door. She looked back again at the brush and felt the heat from her reddened cheeks. It all seemed very strange and she felt so alone.

'Come along, my dear,' Sarah beckoned to her. Once inside the room, it seemed slightly darker than the hall but not much because the windows were large and stepped out from the room. The air was heavy with beeswax and the dark red chairs were like train seats, but not quite so prickly. Annie sat upright, her skirt tucked under her knees to stop the irritation.

'I remember using a dog's brush once to do my hair, when I was in a strange house,' Sarah said, removing her hat and putting it on the table next to her fireside chair.

Annie did not answer. She watched as Sarah smoothed stray hairs back into place. Her hair looked smooth enough now, she thought, and shining as though it was a copper that had been burnished. It was short with crisp waves. Sarah sighed and sat back.

'It's so nice to get home . . .' And then she stopped and frowned. 'I am sorry, Ann, that was tactless.'

Annie sat as she had been doing. She was not going to show this woman that she had felt a flush of longing, a loosening of tears; that she wanted to run back down this light street, down the miles of road and then over the hill that led back to the pits, to the streets, to the people she knew.

'Me name's Annie, not Ann,' she said.

'But I think Ann is more mature,' Sarah replied and walked

to the window. 'Tomorrow,' she continued, 'we have an interview at a school nearby. It is one of my choice since I know the Reverend Mother quite well, we play bridge together and, of course, it was my old school. She is prepared to accept you and coach you for your examination, old though you are. There is a bicycle in the shed for your journey to and from school and school uniform can be obtained from a shop in the centre of town. We will equip you there if there is a successful conclusion to the interview.'

There was an anger growing in Annie.

'I'm not living with a gaggle of bloody left-footed penguins.'

The prints on the wall were of the sea. Grey and blue they were, not a drop of colour anywhere. Georgie would look for birds, Tom would check the perspective and Don would wonder how much they would fetch. There was a white marble clock on the mantelpiece with a gold slave hanging all over the top of it. Bet he had a shock everytime it chimed, thought Annie, and pictured their father's clock which had made her jump but she was not going to think of Wassingham until tonight.

'You are quite correct,' Sarah was saying. 'You are not. You will be living with me and leaving any excess of religious zeal that you may acquire within the walls of the convent when you depart at the end of the day.' She paused as she looked at Annie who was watching the clock creep towards one o'clock; anger was mixed with helplessness now.

'It's a strange clock isn't it, Ann?' She did not wait for an answer but went straight on. 'It's one my father brought home one day, quite why my mother and I could never understand. It's perfectly hideous, don't you think, but it keeps excellent time.'

Annie looked at her, then back at the clock.

Sarah spoke again. 'My father was a shopkeeper too, you know, so it runs in the family.'

Again Annie just looked at her and then back to the clock. She would wait for it to chime and then she would not be able to run out of the house, back to Georgie. Once it chimed she had to stay here, as long as it chimed before she could count to one hundred. As she finished fifty, the clock reached one and a chime rang out, and she sat back in her chair, on her hands to lift her clear of the bristles. She had to stay now, she thought.

She had to stay because the clock had chimed before one hundred and it was not her fault that she was still here, it was the clock's; but was the clock enough? She felt herself begin to sweat.

She looked again at Sarah, who was watching her closely. Through her confusion Annie saw that it was a nice face, quite old though, she must be in her middle thirties.

'These nuns, Ann,' Sarah resumed, 'are neither penguins nor left-footers but are a protestant order with an excellent academic record and reputation.'

'I've not understood a word you've said.' Annie moved only her lips as she spoke, her voice was terse.

'That, my girl, is precisely why you are here,' Sarah riposted and enjoyed Annie's fleeting grin. 'Any other points you wish to discuss?'

'Can I have me dinner?' Perhaps if she was rude enough, Sarah would send her back. If she did not, then she, together with the clock, had decided for her.

She felt the sandals on her lap, the cracked straps that had dug in at Sally's party, that she had not worn since but that she would always keep because they brought every minute back sharply the moment she saw them.

'You may have your lunch. If you insist on asking for dinner when I'm quite sure your father explained the difference to you, you will, presumably, be quite happy to wait until eight this evening.'

Her hands sat in her lap and her face stayed still round her eyes and all Annie heard was the deep tick of the clock.

'You'd better show me the kitchen then,' she said, unable to think of a retort. 'I'd better get on with it.'

Sarah looked at her more closely then and there was movement across the brow.

'Come with me, Ann, there are some things I must show you and others I must explain to you.'

Annie followed her through the tiled hall to the door at the bottom which led into the kitchen. An elderly plump woman in a red apron was putting some cold meat and hard-boiled eggs on to plates. The white was blue next to the yolk and she could smell it as she entered. The meat safe was tightly shut, its cream paint was chipped and one piece was hanging. Annie pulled it off as she stood next to it.

'Ann, this is Val who helps me to run the house. Val, this is Ann, my ward, who will be living here as I've already explained to you, from today. We have prepared the back bedroom for her, haven't we? It gets so much sun we thought you'd prefer it, my dear.' Sarah looked at Annie and smiled. She turned back again to Val. 'Lunch in half an hour, I think.'

Val smiled at Annie and her eyes squeezed to slits above round cheeks. Her arms were pink and dimpled and there was no sign of any bones. Annie followed Sarah from the kitchen to the bedrooms, up a staircase with a turned banister and more prints on the walls. So, thought Annie, she hasn't sent me home, and she didn't know if she was relieved or not.

Sarah turned towards the back of the house and opened a dark panelled door on the left of the landing. She did not go in but stepped back and urged Annie forward. She was still clutching the sandals and her hands tightened as she walked into the room.

'This is your room, Ann. You will hear the gong in just under half an hour. We will be ready to sit when we hear it the second time. The bathroom is next door to your room. You will find a few things in the drawers. I bought them for a fifteen-year-old but a few sizes smaller would have been more apt. A clean pair of knickers every day please and also a bath. There is a linen-basket in the bathroom. I know little about godliness but cleanliness is just plain commonsense.' She pointed to the bathroom.

'Incidentally, in this house there are no servants. I work as a legal secretary at Waring and James, Solicitors, in order to keep myself. Val works in order to keep herself. Ann Manon will work in order to one day provide for herself. In this house we are all members of a household which will only thrive if we all play our parts. We are all people in our own right, no one should have to suffer another.'

Sarah shut the door quietly and perhaps went downstairs but the carpet was so thick Annie could not hear.

She had not understood the last part of Sarah's speech, for that was what it was, Annie decided. She talked as though she ate a book for breakfast every day.

The sun had filled the room with warm light, her suitcase was on the carpet by the bed. It was a carpet which ran to the walls and her feet sunk in with each step and when she removed her boots she felt the softness beneath her soles and the tufts which rose up between her toes. She traced the swirling pale blue pattern with pointed foot and ran her hand along the smooth sleek quilt. She had not known such comfort existed.

There were no gas lights, just a switch on the wall. She flicked it and the light came on and she knew that this was electricity because it was so quiet.

She stroked the quilt again and wondered if this was what silk was like and sat on top of the bed which sank effortlessly beneath her weight. The curtains were pulled back and the polished window-sill held a vase with just one white rose.

Annie walked across and the rose smelt thick and rich, caught against the leaded window. She looked closer at the tight corners; they must be a pig to clean she thought.

The garden was grassed with rose-bushes edging a lawn that looked smooth enough to lie on and she stretched herself instead full length along the carpet, her hands running to meet one another, collecting carpet fluff which lifted before her passage. The bed was high and beneath was an enamel potty.

She felt a surge of excitement and then, as quickly, it was overtaken by a despairing panic, an encompassing sense of loss, of guilt. She wished she could cut it out of her mind and just enjoy all this but she could not, so sprang to her feet, anxious to move, to push back feelings with action and slipped on to the landing and into the bathroom.

The bath was encased in rich mahogany with a step in the side. The basin had a mahogany cupboard underneath and there were toilet rolls on the shelf. She touched the bath taps. They were brass and heavy and beautiful and the water gushed out steamy hot. The toilet flushed at the first pull. There was dried lavender in a bowl on the window-sill and she picked some out with her fingers and smelt the long-ago scent of Aunt Sophie.

She had scattered lavender heads on the window-sill and picked them up in a fever of anxiety in case Sarah should come in, then smoothed the bowl over but could not remember whether it had been flat or heaped and felt her face flush and tears come to her eyes. Then the gong sounded. The better-get-going gong and she splashed water on her face and was glad that she had not let the tears really come and redden her eyes;

so that they would see. She dried herself on the white towel that was so full of pile she could have slept on it.

The table was not laid with a cloth but with table-mats backed by cork. She sat down where Val showed her and they waited for Sarah who, by rights, thought Annie should be frozen to the marrow since the second gong had gone and Val had brought the food to the table already.

'Did you like the room, my love?' asked Val as she unrolled her napkin from its ring and pointed to Annie to do the same.

'It's the most lovely room I have ever seen and the carpet is so thick and enormous. There's no wood around the edge at all.'

She heard Sarah's laugh as she entered and sat at the end of the table and knew that if she had known Sarah was there she would never have said what she had. Here was someone stronger than her, who had power over her like Albert and Annie found herself thinking that at Albert's at least she had worked and received some small payment which was different to here. Here there was all this just given to her which took away her right to anger, to argue. She was beholden now and it felt all wrong. She couldn't fight back and this would have to be changed if she was to stay. Her name was Annie, not Ann.

Sarah was dishing up the thinly sliced meat; pink ham and something else but she didn't know what.

'Ham and beef for you, Ann?' Sarah asked and Annie nodded. She had no idea what beef tasted like but it had to be good for only the wealthy ate it.

'You must be very rich,' she said, as Sarah passed her the potatoes.

'No, and one does not discuss financial matters at the table and I should leave the parsley on the potatoes, Ann; it's rather nice. Potatoes, Val?'

Annie put back the spoon and looked at the green bits which were spread all over the waxy white of the vegetable.

'Where do you sleep, Val? Up in the attic?' she asked as she picked up her knife and fork.

'Val does most certainly not sleep in the attic,' Sarah broke in. 'Her room is opposite yours and just the same, and your knife would really be more comfortable if you don't use it like a pen.'

Annie altered her grip. Albert had eaten like that and she had forgotten what her father had always said.

'I didn't have a nice room at Albert's.'

'Look, Ann, you really must accept that we are all equal in this house, it is just that our tasks vary. One day you will be an adult earning money and you will find that equality is not usual for women but it should be. It's something worth fighting for. Last year we were at last given the vote at 21, something to thank Baldwin for but it took far too long.' She paused to wipe her mouth and Annie wondered whether she ate a book for lunch as well? Perhaps that's where she had been when they were sitting waiting for her, stuffing herself with the latest book from the library. She grinned to herself. She must tell Grace that, she thought, when she comes to see me and she felt happier at the thought. Wassingham was not too far after all.

Sarah had put down her knife and fork, and was leaning forward on her elbows. 'Just remember that you might need to stand up and say, this is not what I want, but you must know what it is that you wish to put in its place. It is not enough just to be dissatisfied. You have to have an aim. Can't stand woolly thinking.'

After dinner Annie left the house through the kitchen door to check on the bicycle as Sarah had suggested. Down past the roses with their warm heavy scent to the shed which stood behind the green waxed laurel. The garden was bordered by a red brick wall which beat back the afternoon heat and sheltered the garden from the wind. The latch was stiff and it was dark inside. The smell was of dust and old sacking, of creosote. The bike leaned up against the wall, black with spokes that were slightly rusted.

She moved towards it over floorboards that were springy and creaked and touched the handlebars. The rubber grips were worn through to the metal either side. She felt safe in here, with the same smell that had been in her da's shed, the same creosote thickness around it. It made her remember that she was still in the same world as Georgie and Tom, as her old life. That some things stayed the same; that she was still Annie, not Ann. She moved to the window which was sectioned into four panes. Val had said the shed was ash, like the greenhouse on the other side of the garden. Seasoned ash she had said and Annie had pictured the trees with their pale grey bark and late leaves and remembered Georgie as he had pointed to the ashes past the hives and she saw again the purple flowers which came before the leaves.

She ran her finger along the frame. The creosote had stained the grey to dark brown. She could miss him here, in private. She could let the pain come and think of his laugh as he held her on the bike, his hands as he stroked her body on the sand, miss his voice, his eyes.

The glass pane was dirty where dust had collected at the base and her finger came away grey, not greasy-black from the pit dust. She peered through the window out to the wall and above it there was sky, pale blue sky with clouds streaked and still. There was no slag mountain, just clear air. She felt a racing panic, an urge to run, to get free, to be back again in Wassingham.

She moved past the bike, past the window to the door then back again, to the end where there were dry dusty sacks stacked one on top of the other then sat on the floor, her arms clutched round her knees and she rocked herself, her head down, remembering Grace and her dimpled legs and her soft arm which was good to hold. Remembering Don when he had given her Da's watch, remembering Tom when he fell in the beck and did a wee. Yes, she would remember that and Georgie, looking up into the sky at his precious mating bees which no one could see but which everyone could picture.

She put her mouth to her knee and smelt her skin. She would think of that day when things got bad. She would think of holding Tom and making him believe that sometimes things would work out. She lifted her head to the window, shrugging her hair back out of her eyes. Yes, that's what she would do and what's more she'd make bloody sure they worked out and what wasn't going to was being given everything for free; it made her a prisoner here, it tied her tighter than rope would have done. She leant back against the wall, her hands clasped loosely now and watched a tortoiseshell butterfly at the window, caught in the square beams of light. The dust was tumbling around it, caught too, and she pushed herself suddenly from the floor and quietly cupped the tortoiseshell in her hands, edged open the door with her arm and threw it gently into the air which was bright and hurt her eyes, then walked along the path leading to the greenhouse and opened the door.

The humid heat made her flinch, it seemed to spray out at her as she moved amongst the tall staked tomato plants and felt the weight of the red fruit in her hands as she crouched and sucked in the fresh smell. They were so glossy red, with dew caught on the leaves. Condensation streamed down the inside of the glass although it had been whitewashed against the heat.

'Lovely, aren't they,' said Val behind her.

Annie spun round and up, knocking a tomato off and watching as it fell and split and the pips oozed out on to the dark rich peat.

'I didn't mean to,' she said, backing off.

Val smiled. 'It doesn't matter, my dear, they're so ripe they are ready to drop on their own. Pick me some, there's a love and I'll get on with the lettuce. Bring me the basket when you've done, dear.'

The basket was large and Annie did not know how many to pick; whether to pick them with the green bits or not. So she did four with, four without.

Val was over by the vegetable patch. One row of lettuce had gone to seed and she was bent over feeling the hearts of the rest.

Annie waited beside her while she pulled up one, then another. Rich dark soil clung to the roots, even when Val shook them. Even have better soil than we do, Annie thought. It's not bloody fair and she remembered the dry thin soil of Wassingham that baked as soon as the sun shone.

She watched as Val threw the roots into a wooden-sided bunker which had no top and stood next to the vegetable patch.

'That's my compost,' explained Val. 'Must have a compost or you don't get the goodness. Mustn't waste anything in a garden you know. If you take out, you must put back.'

She smiled as she put the lettuce into the wicker basket that Annie still carried. 'A few radishes now, I think.'

She stooped and pulled up several red orbs and laid them on top of the lettuce.

'I used to sell me pony's plops,' said Annie. 'Manure's good for the garden too, you know.'

She stood as Val moved along to the chives and knelt by the bed. 'I like to be able to pay me way, you know. Makes me feel better.' She waited to see if Val would understand.

Val looked up, her face was red now from the heat, then

down again as she picked a few more thin chive shoots. At last she said:

'Why don't you go in and talk to Sarah, Ann. She'll understand. I promise you she'll understand. Give us a hand up now.'

Annie moved and grasped her elbow; her fingers sank into the warm flesh as she tugged. Val took the basket from her and Annie did not want to let go of that arm but she turned and walked from Val to the house, her chin up, her fists clenched, looking for words which would tell Sarah she was strangling her, not setting her free.

Sarah was reading the paper in the sitting-room and Annie did not knock but walked straight in, her boots loud on the wooden surround.

'I need to talk to you,' she said.

Sarah looked up and over the paper, then laid it on her lap. 'Yes, Ann.'

'That's just it, you see,' Annie blurted out. 'Me name's Annie but you can call me Ann because I haven't got any choice. You keep me, pay for me food and school and I don't earn it so you can tell me what to do, even change me name if you want. I can't let that happen. Me name's Annie and I want to earn me keep or I can't say what I think, I can only say what you think.'

Her hands were down by her side and her chin was jutting. Her eyes had not left Sarah's face while she had spoken but in the silence that followed she looked away; at the fireplace, at the lamp with a shade made of coloured glass sections, at the photograph beside it of women wearing hats and veils and men in funny trousers. They all wore long slats on their feet and it was snowing. She hadn't said all that she had meant and it had come out badly. She had wanted to be calm and talk as Sarah did but she didn't know how.

Sarah had her finger to her mouth, she was frowning and Annie clenched her hands but stayed standing still.

'Please sit down.' Sarah pointed to the chair opposite. 'We're both tired you know, we've been on the road for quite a long time this morning and your uncle, I'm afraid, is a most difficult man.'

Annie did so. 'He's all right but I worked me way there and

got sixpence as well. I never felt beholden to him.' She was leaning forward, her elbows on her knees.

Sarah smiled ruefully. 'Oh dear, Annie. You are quite right of course, but I am your godmother you see and so I do have a certain right to act *in loco parentis.*'

And what the hell does that mean thought Annie and was about to say as much when Sarah laughed.

'I'm sorry, you must make allowances, Annie. I'm not used to children you see. What I mean is that I can undertake, in your case, the role of parent but,' and she put her hand up as she saw Annie about to interrupt, 'you are quite right. I am not your parent. Therefore, if you feel as you do, we must remedy the situation.'

'Do you mean I can earn me keep then?'

'I consider that you will earn your keep if you work hard and find a career that is worthwhile.'

'Or marry Georgie,' challenged Annie.

Sarah paused. 'Yes, we did agree to that, did we not, but marriage does not necessarily mean you do not have a career.'

'But I still need to earn me keep for me own sense of being me.'

Sarah sat back and looked steadily at Annie, then to the window. She nodded. 'Very well, I accept your point but I shall have to sort something out. Can you give me a bit of time?'

Annie sat back, her hands under her legs against the prickles. 'As long as it's not too long,' she insisted.

'I promise,' Sarah said and smiled.

Success surged through Annie. She would be a person who had rights and that was what she had wanted. She breathed a deep sigh and smiled at Sarah. It was the first one that they had exchanged. The clock was approaching four o'clock, the fire was laid for this evening.

'Is that you?' she asked, pointing to the photograph. 'What are those things on your feet?' she asked when Sarah nodded.

'Skis for sliding upright down snow slopes. You must try it some day, you'd enjoy it, I'm sure. It would present a challenge.' Sarah moved over and picked it up and passed it to Annie, who noticed for the first time that there were lines under her eyes, grey in her brown hair.

'How old are you, Sarah?'

Sarah looked at her and laughed as she turned to sit down.

'I'm 38 and Val is 45 but you mustn't ask anyone else their age. It is considered rather rude.'

Annie nodded and looked again at the photograph. 'You look young here, but very thin.' She looked more closely at the photograph. 'So very thin. Were you ill?' She was thinking of the boys in Tom's class with consumption, but not him, thank God.

'No, not ill. Shall we just say that I had been having trouble eating. It was called the cat and mouse game, Annie, and one day I shall tell you more about it but now, now I think it is time I sat and thought carefully about what we should sort out to solve our problem. Can you for now go and help Val with the salad, Annie?'

Annie nodded, rose and left the room. She stopped outside the door and went back in.

'Thank you, Sarah,' she said and Sarah smiled. 'I'll ring the gong from now on, shall I? That'll be a start.'

And Sarah nodded.

That night, Sarah lay in bed too tired to sleep, too full of the change in her life. The curtains were not drawn since there was a full moon and she could never bring herself to waste the strong colourless light which lit the bedroom, bringing no detail but an awareness of shape.

She shook her head slightly at what must be almost an obsession with waste, much like Val's with her compost but then she'd been with the family for thirty years so was as imbued with tradition as she was. It was her father of course. Waste, I cannot abide waste, she heard him say with a clarity of remembered sound that startled her. And the vividness of that particular scene that was so long ago took her unawares.

Her father had entered the sitting-room, the same one that Annie had stormed into today in those dreadful boots. Must do something about those tomorrow, Sarah reminded herself. Yes, he had entered the sitting-room rather later than usual dressed as always in his black suit and starched collar which was his uniform as manager of the hardware store. Hardware was an understatement since Mr Mainton, as the town always called her father, never Martin Mainton, had built up the store into more of an emporium for the owners, a complacent and rich family called the Stoners.

Sarah frowned as she fought to remember what she and her mother had been doing and then sighed with recognition. Embroidery. Her mother was explaining that embroidery should be as neat at the back as at the front since it was somewhat like underwear. Seldom seen but always clean and tidy, and they were laughing gently together.

Waste, I cannot abide waste, he had said as he had come rushing in. She had never known her father to walk, it was beyond his capabilities. They had looked up, not startled because they were used to his fads but a little wary, especially her mother who had suffered recently under the burden of producing meals which her father had decided would stimulate their 'flushing systems' as he had called it.

What now, her mother had said in that voice. With a flourish, her father had produced two bicycles. Exercise and freedom, freedom to enjoy the countryside, the beauties of which are being wasted by you. You have energies which are being wasted, he had finished and had stood there beaming.

The next day, she remembered they had obtained split skirts and were soon traversing the country lanes and indeed they found freedom. She and her mother had travelled for miles stopping for picnics and talking. Talking about the dreams and aspirations of her mother, her frustration at wanting to do so much and not being able to within the confines of a provincial society and marriage, though her father had been an enlightened husband. Sarah had spoken of the suffragettes; it was 1910 and she was 19 and her mother had applauded their efforts, their bravery.

Her father had relished their adventures and was proud of their independence though their neighbours were somewhat shocked especially the Thom sisters next door who played the piano at the picture house in Gosforn. But Sarah had always thought they were, in reality, envious. What would they think now about this girl living with her, because they were still next door, though no longer at the cinema.

That summer, her parents had determined that their daughter should be equipped with skills which would enable her to weather the rest of her life, good or bad. All they could afford was a secretarial course but it was the best. Sarah sighed with satisfaction and pushed herself up on to her pillows. The moon was half obscured by fast-moving clouds, much as it had been so often when she was driving ambulances during the war. That was another of her father's fads. Both his women should learn to drive. A waste of potential he had roared and pushed his wife into the driving-seat. She had hated it but Sarah loved the feeling of power.

She had taken a job in London, staying with Aunt Jesse, her father's sister, and it was there she had become involved with female suffrage. She had worn green and purple rosettes; marched and spoken at rallies, been punched and pushed by hecklers for her pains as she left the halls. There had been spit down the front of her jacket when she had returned from one meeting. She had thrown it away and cried in her room, unable to bring herself to wipe it away.

When she was a member of a group blocking a road near Trafalgar Square, she had been arrested. The cobbles they were sitting on had been cold in that winter of 1912 and she remembered how they had been told by their leader to go slack when the police picked them up and threw them into the van but she hadn't expected the pain and the bruising as she hit the studded floor of the vehicle.

Aunt Jesse had come for her in the morning but she was charged with causing an obstruction and breaking the peace. The sentence was three months in prison. She had gone on hunger-strike like the rest, like her friend Norah, but they had been kept in separate cells and Sarah moved in the bed as she remembered the fear of dying, the hunger, being alone and then after days or was it weeks they had come and pushed the tube into her nostril and down her throat. She thought her nose, her throat, her chest would burst and then finally it entered her stomach. Each day they had done that, pouring liquid, not much but enough to keep her alive and each time, when they had left her and she had still not screamed and struggled, she had been proud of herself but had lain in fear hour after hour until they came again.

They had released her early to build up her strength. Her father had collected her and taken her to Aunt Jesse. He had been pale but still bustled. Val had fed her up and said she would sit in the streets with her if she didn't stop. No, they need you, Val; if I'm not here, you must be, she had said. They had wanted her to come back but she had to stay in the district and would not have run away anyway, or would she? When she was fitter, the police came for her to finish the sentence and her father did not ask her not to go on hunger-strike again, nor did her mother. He had kissed her and said that freedom must be worth a great deal and he couldn't ask her to go against that but he had aged, and his mouth was trembling and she had turned from him to the policeman frightened that she would cry and beg to stay. Look after me, Papa, she wanted to cry, hold me, send them away.

She had starved again and the tube had come again and the pain and weakness until her sentence was finished. Until the next time she was arrested and the cat and mouse resumed. It was a very effective form of fear, she reasoned now from the safety of age, that cat and mouse game of the government's, but it didn't break them, just killed a few, like her dearest Norah. She felt a thickening of her throat at the thought of the tube going into her friend's lung instead of her stomach.

At last in the early spring of 1914, her father and mother had sent her to Austria, skiing, for fresh air and good food and to keep her from the streets too she suspected. There had been relief at boarding the ship, then the train, leaving the battle because they had asked her to, just for a while. That way it was less like desertion.

Then war had come and the campaign had ceased for the duration and women were given jobs, useful jobs and she drove an ambulance and was glad it had come and she no longer had to suffer.

Annie should be told one day because, throughout it all, her father had supported her financially and had not regretted one penny. He told her so when he and her mother caught flu after the war, just before they died. After she had sorted out the little matter of Mr Beeston her life had settled into its tranquil lines and again she settled herself more comfortably on the pillows.

And now she had Annie, a child who had burst in on her life when she had spun into Wassingham to sort things out after Bob's letter. She had not known definitely whether she would be bringing her back but what she had found in Wassingham was waste and the well ordered life in Gosforn would just have to accommodate this awkward spirit, this child who was not a child. It would be interesting, to say the least.

She was sorry that Archie would not be able to see his daughter develop but in her heart of hearts she also knew that she was supremely relieved. For if he were here, she would not have this repeat of her relationship with her parents. A repeat of the knowledge and caring that would be passed on again. A repeat of love, for that is what she was already feeling for this child.

CHAPTER 12

Annie felt strange in her stomach two days later when August had changed to September and Sarah drove through the large wrought-iron gates, past dark full-leafed bushes, which lined the gravel drive, and up to the entrance of the convent school. Sarah told her that the grey stone building had once been a hunting lodge in the days when Gosforn was a small hamlet, before it had grown up into a market town and a dormitory for Newcastle.

She looked at the sloping gardens beyond the shrubs which Sarah said were rhododendrons from the foothills of the Himalayas, wherever they were, thought Annie. She made her hands lie still in her lap as the car crunched to a halt though she felt as though she was trembling all over and she had a tightness in her chest. The engine died and the car jumped.

'Out you come then,' Sarah instructed and they stood together at the bottom of the three wide steps which led up to the studded double wooden doors. The building seemed to be falling over and would crush them at any moment, Annie thought as she looked up to the turrets which lined the roof, but at least that would mean she would not have to go through the next few minutes.

'Of course, rhododendrons are at their best in early summer,' Sarah continued as she took her arm and nudged her up the steps. 'Large glorious blooms, so much better than the original purple of the wild ones.'

Her gloved hand reached for and pulled the bell chain and Annie's legs felt uncertain. She turned to look out over the drive, down through the yew hedges set in squares which lay in front of the school. They were cut as sharp as Val's bacon when she scissored off the rind. There were flower-beds within their squares with a path running from the drive right through them

183

down to the empty playing field which Annie could see at the bottom.

It looks like a bloody mansion, she thought, not a nunnery. And where were all the girls, because that's all there were. Boys were not allowed through the gates, Sarah had said.

They could hear the bell peeling deep inside the building and Sarah turned and stood looking across the grounds with Annie.

'It is rather lovely isn't it?' she said. 'I was here as a girl and very little has changed, only the length of the hems.' She laughed. 'Mine was down to my ankles and just look at yours. Mother Superior would have had the vapours.'

Annie looked down at her grey pleated skirt, ending well above the ankles and smoothed it over her hips. It was so soft and light, but warm too. The vest she wore did not itch at all. She had not known you could be warm but comfortable. She ran her finger round her neck, chafing against the collar but she liked the grey and red of the tie against the white of the shirt. She wasn't sure about the red cardigan since it seemed to drain her of colour but Val had said that a few games of hockey would soon bring the roses into her cheeks.

She had not known what hockey was and Sarah had shown her an old stick, told her that the object of the game was to get the ball into the other team's goal and that you bullied off for possession of this ball when the referee started the game. You'll enjoy it, she had said, but Annie had thought it sounded ridiculous.

Sarah rang the bell again and Annie half hoped that no one would hear and they could go back to the house again. She could not say home, not yet, not ever, she determined. Home was Georgie. But she would not think of him now, he was for the darkness and her bedroom.

'It is nice, Sarah,' she replied, waving her hand at the gardens, looking again at her shirt, feeling that everything matched, even the grey blazer with its red piping. This had never happened before and she grinned in spite of herself. She'd have to change out of them when she arrived back this evening. Sarah had decided that they would keep hens and that it would be her job to feed, clean and collect the eggs. They should be there, at the house by four and the men were erecting the coop and wire run this morning. If Val had anything to do with it, it would be done in record time. Bye, thought Annie, I bet she could pack a punch.

The door swung open and Annie spun round. A nun in a dark blue habit and a white wimple stood there smiling, just like a penguin, Annie thought.

'So nice to see you, Sarah, let me take Ann in with me, shall I, and we'll meet you at four o'clock.' She had a pink and white face with full lips and a wide brow over pale blue eyes and looked as though she had washed with a scrubbing brush, she was so fresh. Annie smiled at such a neat dismissal of Sarah. That's one in the eye for her she thought, for getting them to call me Ann and opened her mouth to correct the nun. There was no need.

'My ward's name is Annie, Sister Maria. We do so much prefer it to Ann. It was my mistake, I'm afraid.'

She was smiling at Annie, her blue hat set at an angle on her head, matching the coat which had a silver brooch set in a leaf on her lapel and Annie felt her shoulders relax, her stomach feel better. She stroked her hair which she had plaited this morning and adjusted her school hat. It would be good to see Sarah at four o'clock.

Sister Maria stood with her on the top step as the Morris swung round and crunched back down the drive. Sarah tooted and the sound was out of place in the quiet of St Ursula's and Annie knew that it was Sarah's response to Sister Maria and she grinned.

The nun led the way into the high-ceilinged entrance hall. She didn't walk, she glided, Annie decided. It was as though she was one of those little wind-up fat people that rolled along a table with no feet, just wheels. She cocked her head to check that black shoes appeared at the front of the habit and they did. Perhaps it was the wimple that made them move like that; it was so starched it looked as though it would crack if it was jogged at all.

Sister Maria turned, her smile kind and reaching her eyes. 'We'll have a quick look round the school, Annie, and then we'll slip you into your class. Is that all right?'

'Yes, thank you,' Annie replied, looking round the hall which was wood-panelled except for a mural of the crucifixion with drops of blood falling from Christ's hands. Below, on a walnut table, larger than Sarah's, was a vase of russet chrysanthemums. She moved over to touch the petals and could smell their scent all round.

Sister Maria touched her arm and brought her to a halt.

'You must address the nuns as Sister, Annie, and as a sign of courtesy the girls never turn their back on us.'

Annie swung round to her, her face flushing red. She bit back a retort and said, 'Yes, Sister,' but thought, I'm the Queen of the Nile, because it was just like royalty. What would Tom say to this then? She had received a letter from him this morning telling of the Wainwright episode. I'll be a right little bolshie next time I see you, he had said, and she put her hand in her blazer pocket and touched the lined paper which held his pencilled news.

They moved down to the corridor which led from the entrance hall and she had to quicken her pace to keep up with Sister Maria's glide. Her patent leather shoes were catching the light from the windows which ran down one side of this end of the corridor. They were the first shoes she had worn and were so much lighter than boots that she felt as though she had bare feet and they didn't rub anywhere. On the other side of the corridor she saw that there were notices pinned on to cork boards. Hockey and drama stood out in bold red print but then Sister Maria spoke as they rushed on.

'We have put you in with the younger children since you are a little behind, Annie, but never fear, you will improve and at the end of three years you will undoubtedly have your school certificate.'

Annie stopped, her shoes forgotten, her face twisting, her eyes suddenly full. Sister Maria stopped and turned, her hands clasped together under the sleeves of her habit.

'But, my dear,' she said, 'there is no need for the other girls to know. You are so lucky, oh so lucky to be *petite*, so delicate. How they would envy you if they knew.'

But it was not that which had taken the breath from her chest and brought blood to her face. Three years, three years echoed round her head and she wanted to rip the clothes from her, throw them to the ground and run back to the caustic air and noise of Wassingham, back to Tom and Georgie. She had not asked Sarah how long all this would take and now she knew she felt that it was not bearable.

Sister Maria took her arm and they walked together down

the corridor which had lost its windows now and merged into a large dark area which was criss-crossed with stands spiked with pegs, covered now in blazers and hats.

'You will leave your hat and blazer here when you arrive each morning.' She shook Annie slightly as though she were aware Annie wanted to run, to leave here. 'You will come, won't you, Annie?' She looked closely into her face and Annie stared blankly back, deep inside herself. But hadn't she decided that first day that she would stay, Annie told herself, so stop making such a bloody fuss. If she shouted at herself loud enough, it might stop the panic which seemed to swoop and drench her with ice, then fire and leave her so much alone. Sister Maria shook her again.

'You are going to come, Annie?'

And this time Annie nodded, her chin tilted. 'This is my peg is it?' she asked hanging her things on the blunted hook, and was surprised to find that her voice sounded quite normal.

The Sister smiled and patted her arm, then showed her which one to hang her shoe-bag on and also mentioned that she would need a hockey stick, skirt and boots.

Well, thought Annie, that means more work from Sarah or I shall be playing in me bare feet.

'And along here, Annie, is the chapel.' Sister Maria still held her arm as though she was afraid that Annie would turn and run but she wouldn't, not for three years anyway.

'Services are held in the chapel daily. I gather you are not confirmed so we shall have to arrange that.'

Annie raised her eyebrows. We will, will we? she thought. I'll have to think about that.

The chapel was painted cream and there were wooden beams up into the roof and thick long ones that spanned the width of the chapel and held the lights which hung down on black metal rods. It was so light and calm, Annie thought, not like the one which had buried her da. Here the windows were large and light streamed in. The pews were light wood and smelled of beeswax. The altar was simple with a white altar cloth and a metal cross, which shone green and red from the light which dropped through the stained-glass window.

Sister Maria was ahead of her now, pointing to the choir stalls, the pulpit and the lectern which was a gold eagle with a beak which could catch someone a nasty nip if they fell asleep during the sermon, Annie thought.

'We embroider the hassocks ourselves, with the help of you girls of course. Do you sew?' Sister Maria was moving back towards her now. The air was heavy with more chrysanthemums. They were in every window and either side of the altar; orange, purple and yellow.

'No, just a few buttons and repairs,' Annie said, touching the back of the pew. She had not moved down the aisle yet. She had seen Sister Maria cross herself and she could not remember which way round she had done it.

'Well, you'll learn quickly enough. We have a competition coming up which you would enjoy.' Her voice was not Geordie but more like her father's and Sarah. It sounded pleasant, not high or low, and if she sang it would be a comforting sound.

Sister Maria stopped halfway up the aisle. 'Shall I teach you to genuflect, Annie? Would that make things easier for you in here?'

Annie stood still, confusion clouding her thoughts.

'The sign of the cross,' Sister Maria added.

Annie sighed with relief. It was not going to be too bad here and she copied, with her right hand, Sister Maria's movements.

They left the chapel and passed along polished floors and gleaming cream-painted corridors which murmured with muted voices as a door opened and closed and another was left ajar. Three doors on, they stopped.

'This is your class, Annie. I'm sure you will be very happy but, when you see Mrs Beeston, please ask her to buy you another pair of shoes. Patent leather is not permitted in this school, but, for this week only, we will make an exception.'

As they entered the classroom which Annie had noticed was opposite a conservatory, the lesson stopped and the girls rose in unison and Annie wondered how much another pair of shoes would cost.

'Slip into that place, Annie.'

She pointed to a space at the end of a long bench which was attached to a desk of the same length. Annie was aware of turning heads as she passed between the rows and slid into place. It was indented with Christine loves John and Sandy loves Sister Nicole. The girl next to her passed a sideways look and smiled. She did not look very much younger, none of them did, thought Annie, and why did the Sisters object to patent leather shoes? They were so beautiful.

'Shows your knickers it does. The patent leather reflects them, or so they think,' Sandy told her at break. 'Gives the old girls a thrill and they get palpitations.'

'Do you love Sister Nicole?' Annie asked her. The milk tasted thick and made her thirsty. Val had given her a flapjack for break and she shared it with Sandy. They sat in the playground on a wall which was wedged thick with other girls. The crumbs fell on to her skirt and she brushed them clear, anxious about grease. She did not want to have to ask Sarah for another one, there'd be enough jobs to do after today as it was.

Sandy's cheek bulged with flapjack and she waved her hands and pointed to her mouth and Annie grinned. 'Don't rush,' she soothed and was glad that Sandy was red-haired and had freckles because she reminded her of Grace except that she was skinny and her hair was more orange than red.

'Oh, I loved old Nicole last term. This term it's the gardener, he's glorious. Watch out for Batty, she's after break and squeaks the chalk and makes your teeth ache, then throws the board-rubber if you daydream. So you keep your head up and go to sleep with your eyes open or it's the conservatory for you. That's the punishment block you know.' Sandy picked at a tooth with her tongue. 'Lovely grub. Did your mother make it?'

'No, I live with my guardian and the housekeeper. She made it.'

'Oh, I live with my ma and pa, deadly dull and Ma will fuss so. Much more exciting to be different like you. Are your folks dead, then?'

'Yes,' Annie said, not wanting to open the black box by speaking of them. 'How old are you?'

'Dreadfully old for the class. I'm nearly 15 but we've been abroad and I got frightfully behind.'

'Yes, I've lost some time too.' Annie paused, then rushed on, not wanting to explain further, 'I'm 15.'

Sandy grinned and squeezed her arm. 'Good, someone to talk to at last. Jenn is another girl who's older but she's away at the moment. Got a bit of a tongue on her but she's all right, I suppose. When we go for the garden walk, which we do every day after lunch, we can make up a three.'

'A three?'

'Oh yes.' Sandy tapped her heels against the wall. 'Have to go in threes, pairs create unhealthy friendships or so the old girls think. Wish they'd let us have a few healthy ones instead like a stroll with the gardener or something.' She roared with laughter and dragged Annie up. 'Come on, the bell's going to go. Let's get to the front of the line then we can grab a desk at the back. Batty's aim isn't so good then.'

It's a different world, thought Annie, as she moved across the playground. It's so easy and most of her would love it in time but there was still the sharp ache for lost alleyways and windswept dunes.

She felt in her pocket for Tom's letter and wished there had been one from Georgie too.

That evening, Annie stood by the chicken-run, her fingers hooked into the wire. The hens were jerking about the run and already the ground was scratched near their coop but she loved the noise of the clucking, the glossiness of their feathers, the shine of the cock's tail.

Sarah stood by her, with her arms crossed, her brown cardigan matching her skirt.

'I thought we should get the cock, then you can hatch some chicks and sell them, or keep a few more layers, whichever you prefer.'

Annie felt a rush of relief; she had not been able to tell Sarah about the shoes or the sports kit and this would make it easier. Sarah went on:

'I've been thinking about the shoes we bought, Annie. I do feel that it would be more economic to keep those for home and buy some sturdy ones for school. Your feet have practically stopped growing so they should last for ages. Would you mind very much if I asked you to help me in this way?'

Annie kept on looking at the chickens and nodded, her back to Sarah. Thank God, thank God, she thought but there was still hockey to sort out and if Sarah was economising? She chewed her lip.

Sarah continued. 'I have some hockey clothes which a friend of mine has given to me. They used to belong to her daughter. You will no doubt be needing some this term.' She was looking down at her and Annie felt her gaze. 'And there's my old hockey stick.'

'You must be a witch,' she said as she turned to look at her.

Sarah laughed with her head right back and put her hand on Annie's shoulder where she allowed it to lie. Annie wanted it to, for a while.

'No.' Sarah shook her head. 'Not guilty, Annie, but I had a look at the uniform list when I arrived at the office and realised we had made some mistakes.'

'So, is it true then, about the economising?' Annie asked, ready to draw back from her hand, to think of more work she could do. She wanted no charity.

Sarah felt the movement and said, with no hint of laughter now. 'Absolutely, Annie. Good strong shoes as they suggest will be far more appropriate and last so much longer and I really have been given the sports kit. Now get those chickens fed and come in and settle down to some homework before dinner.'

'Where's Mr Beeston?' Annie asked. 'Sister Maria called you Mrs today.'

Sarah looked surprised, then amused. 'Let's just say I lost him, shall we?' She stroked Annie's hair and turned to go but stopped. 'I wonder what Tom would think of these?' she murmured. 'Shall we ask him over and Georgie?'

Annie gripped the wire tighter. She kept her voice level as she replied. 'Oh yes, and Tom will come but Georgie won't, not until he's ready.' She pressed her lips together in a straight line and turned again to the chickens.

'Well, what about Don?' persisted Sarah.

'That's an idea. I've written to him telling him where I am but he's very busy. When men leave home they build other lives, don't they?' Sarah nodded at her. 'But I'll write again and ask him. It'll be good to see him, after so long. Hope he hasn't grown too much.'

At Sarah's quizzical look she explained that he needed to keep small for riding and Sarah nodded, laughing at the hen which was pecking near their feet. Then she walked down the cinder path, stopping to pull at a few stray weeds, then a lettuce.

'Make it two,' Annie heard Val call from the kitchen window. The Thoms next door were bringing in their washing from the line and called good evening to Sarah. There were birds in the apple trees down by the greenhouse and the sound of bees as they snuffled the fallen apples. Georgie had always said fallen fruit made them drunk and lazy and that's when they would sting you more easily, forgetting that they would die.

She opened the gate to the run. It felt wobbly but was safe enough; it swung shut behind her and the bowl was half full of feed. The hens were pecking at the ground, brown and plump, lifting their feet as though they were about to burst into a dance with their eyes beady and swivelling. She threw corn to them and watched as they chatted about and chanted in excitement and one came jerking across while she squatted. She held the hen round the neck and stroked it and was surprised and disappointed that it was not soft all through but hard as though there was a brittle cage just beneath the feathers.

'Never mind, bonny lass,' she breathed. 'Just you do a good job laying and we'll get along fine. Who knows, you might get a bairn of your own.'

It was nice to talk in the words she had used in Wassingham because slowly but surely she already felt herself sliding over to the language of Sarah and the people who lived in this tree-strewn town.

She let the hen go as it pecked her and rubbed her finger and laughed. 'Any more of that and you'll be in the pot,' and waved her hand at Sarah as she called her in for homework.

'Ruddy slave-driver she is,' called Annie to the cock and threw him the last of the corn as she headed back to the house.

The smell of sponge pudding wafted from the kitchen window and her mouth watered. It was still strange to have meals cooked for her, it made her feel guilty but pleased. The house had a paved area by the dining-room, under her bedroom and held wrought iron chairs and a table on which lay Val's book from this afternoon. Annie stooped and picked it up as she passed. It was *The Modern Compost Guide*.

'Annie, do come along,' called Sarah. 'Val has some ginger beer and cake here for you and then you must do some work.'

It was going to be hard to be unhappy here but she felt that the others should be sharing all this, that laughter should not come without Georgie, but it would, she knew that now and she also knew he would understand.

CHAPTER 13

Tom's hands were cold. It was November. Annie had been gone for nearly three months and, this Sunday, Grace and he were walking out of Wassingham, along the road to Bell's farm. It was a walk they had often taken when the four of them were together but now, just two of them remained. Georgie had left last month and Tom still did not know how to tell Annie.

He had come round to May's last week when Tom was having his tea, knocked at the door and while Tom stood on the backstep wiping his mouth on the back of his hand he had said he was off. He had a suitcase which was bruised at the corner and ripped where the cardboard had softened too much. Tom had grabbed his arm and stepped out into the yard, shutting the door behind him and the light went with it, so that he had been unable to see Georgie's face.

Are you going to her, man? he had asked, but Georgie had shaken his head. Not yet, our Tom, I'm off to see if there's something better away from here and you'd do well to think on that too, Tom. The pit's hard, Annie doesn't want it for you, you know that, but Tom had shaken off words about himself, it was Georgie who was going, Georgie he would miss.

What about going to Don? he had said. You and he was mates, he'd get you a job in the stable.

Georgie had laughed and picked up his suitcase. I'm going further than that lad and higher. Down south, I think, that's where the jobs are. May had called through the door that his tea was getting cold and Davy had come out then, the light had shone too bright and they turned away. The tin bath was propped up on one side of the wash-house and threw a long shadow down the yard. Come away in Georgie, Davy had said, there's enough for you too, but Georgie had said no and punched Tom lightly on the arm. Take care, bonny lad, and then he'd turned and walked in his measured stride to the gate and was gone. They'd listened to his boots on the cobbles and Tom had pictured the sparks striking from them.

As he and Grace walked round the bend the wind was blowing from the east, harder now than it had been and he grasped his sketch-book more securely under his arm and hunched his shoulders, turning up his collar.

'Oh, so you're back with me then,' Grace said from his side, poking at his arm. 'If I had a penny, I'd give you one for 'em.'

'For what, bonny lass?' he said, grinning at her.

'Just for your thoughts, so that's quite enough of that.'

They laughed and he pointed to the path leading off the road up over the sparse farmland where sheep grazed.

'Come on,' he said. 'Let's go over the top of the hill. It's a better view and we'll sit in the usual place while we have our picnic.'

And I can help you over that too, he thought, as she nodded and they turned towards the wooden stile.

'Give us your bag.' He took it and put it with his by the end of the hawthorn hedge. 'For God's sake, mind yourself on the thorns,' he called, as he grasped her arm. The hedge was stripped of leaves now and the thorns were eager to snag their skin.

'Don't know about keeping in the sheep,' Grace said, as she stepped up, 'but there's no way I'd try and get through that lot.'

She was still plump, our Grace was, thought Tom, as he watched her teeter on the first bar, and he gripped her harder. But she'd grown, bye, she'd grown and had breasts like any he'd seen in Botticelli's pictures, or he thought she would have beneath her clothes anyway. Her body must be creamy and dimpled and that hair, free of its plait could curl all about her shoulders and her back and he would paint her one day with one strand between those breasts. She was so nice too, was Gracie, like Aunt May. Plump and kind with blue eyes like cornflowers that grew in the meadow down by the beck. And teeth that were even and white. Her freckles were soft beige.

'Give us a hand then, you daft dollop,' Grace called, one leg half over the top bar. There was no step up this side, the wood had fallen clear. He kicked it to one side then came behind her and levered up her buttocks and she shrieked and tried to slap him but he dodged and said:

'For God's sake girl, I'm doing you a favour. Get yourself over, will you, before you break me bloody back.'

But he grinned as she scrambled over and jumped down the other side. She was flushed and panting and pulled her dress down where it had hitched up above her knee.

'You can get yourself over, and the bags,' she stormed and stalked across the grass, her head up, her hands busy trying to tuck stray curls back into the curves and hollows of her plait.

Aunt May had packed bread and cheese and a flask of tea and the bag banged against his side and against Grace's which hung over his shoulder too as he caught up with her. As he took her arm, she sniffed then glanced sideways at him. He grinned, then so did she.

The farm was half a mile away now, he reckoned. It was strange coming here on their own. It had always been a race to the top with the other two. Georgie always won, he was second, though Annie had beaten him twice and Grace had insisted on walking with the bags. She said it was undignified but they all knew that she didn't like the wobble of her body and loved her for it.

The oaks near the road were the only trees on which leaves remained, though even they clung in shrivelled clusters and would come down if the wind increased. The sheep grazed all around them as they walked and those in front moved away as they approached. Tom liked the farm, liked the walk to it, the picnic in the hollow on the far side of the hill and the view from there which he had sketched again and again. Each time it varied; the cart was not there or had a different load and the sky behind was blue or grey or flecked with rain. He patted his pocket. Yes, they were still there; the pencils Annie had sent with her last letter. She'd been to Woolworth's, she'd said, where everything was under sixpence.

They were breasting the hill now and the wind snatched at their breath as it whirled across from the sea over to their right, but too far for them to see. There were no sheep up here on the top but rocks showed through the scant soil and the wind tugged at what grass there was and pulled and pushed at the dark spiked gorse-bushes that almost, but not quite, reached the crest. The farm lay at the bottom.

Tom looked at Grace, at her hair with its escaped curls leaping and flicking about her face and reached across and pulled the collar of her thick cardigan up round her neck. They dug heavily into the ground with their heels as they began the descent.

He took her hand loosely, wondering if she would pull away but she did not. He tightened his grip and she did also and then they looked at one another and smiled. It was not so bad after all, thought Tom, coming back here without Annie and he whooped into the air, scattering the sheep and making Grace laugh.

He pulled her faster and faster until they were running and she was with him and laughing and not pulling him to stop. Leaping from hillock to hillock, avoiding the molehills and the sheep which thudded away from their path until the breath bounced in him and they were taking great gulps of air and laughter. He lost his footing half way down and dropped her hand as he rolled over and over, seeing the grass, the sky, his sketch-book as it flew from his hand, his bait-bag as it leapt as he rolled. Over and over he went until he fetched up on the flattened area that was theirs. He lay flat, his arm out, his bag and Grace's flung over his chest, laughing and panting until gradually he was able to heave himself up on his elbow and look for her.

She was running along the hill, not down it, chasing the loose pages from his pad which the wind was sucking and blowing into the air, turning them about and letting them swoop, but always too far for Grace to reach.

'Leave them, Gracie,' he called. 'Leave them and come on down.'

He watched as she turned and cupped her hand to her ear. Her skirt was blowing up over her knees and tight against her legs.

'Leave them,' he called again, then beckoned her with exaggerated hand movements and she saw and came down but not running now, though she was laughing. He could see that and hear her.

'Oh, you great daft thing,' she said. 'No wonder Wainwright gave you a belting. I'm surprised he didn't expel you for breaking his cane.'

She sat down next to him and they edged up so that their backs were against the slope.

The sheep were tearing at the grass all around them, calm again.

'Our Davy had a word with him, or so May said, so he only stopped me from painting, but Mr Green lets me take paints home with me so it doesn't matter that much.'

Grace shook her head and reached for her bag. 'It's as well you've got Davy now. He's taken over from Annie.' She brought out some bread and dripping.

'He'll not do that, nobody'll take over from Annie.' His voice was devoid of laughter now. It was hard and firm. Grace looked at him sideways, sinking her teeth into the crust, it was tough and with her fingers she tore a piece and chewed it.

'Not even me?' she asked, looking down at the farm this time.

'Don't talk with your mouth full. It's common.' He slapped her leg and pulled a face. 'You're not me sister, are you? I feel something different for you.'

He felt the ground cold through his trousers and brought out from his bag an old knitted baby blanket. 'Lift your backside and stop being daft.'

He put the blanket beneath her and she handed him what was left of his book. The pages were askew and out of order. 'All that's left after the wind had a look.'

'Never mind lass,' he said leafing through them, straightening the pages. 'I'll do the farm again. They were just sketches of the yard.'

'Have something to eat, for God's sake,' she said. He looked at her bread and dripping and handed her some of his cheese that he had dug out of May's parcel. The wind was far less raucous where they sat sheltered by the slope behind and it seemed unnaturally quiet. Even the rooks settled along the branches of the elms around the farm were silent as though bowed in sleep.

'You're on dripping then? Are the boys out of work again?'

Grace nodded. 'All but young Frank and he brings in a pittance. Me da's getting right fed up and me mam wants to know how she can feed a family on a few shillings a week. That's why I'm starting at the library next week. At least I'll bring in a little.'

'Do you mind?' asked Tom, taking some bread from her and laying some of his cheese on it before passing it back.

She shook her head. 'It's what I want. It's stupid staying on when I know what I want.'

Tom nodded and lay back, his arms over his head, listening to the sounds of the sheep; there were no insects to buzz and click in his ear at this time of year.

What was it Davy had said last night when he had sneaked him into the snug with his mates? He frowned as he went over the scene, trying to capture the flow which had rolled round and across the table.

He could still taste the beer which had bulged down his throat and the excitement of being included and what Davy said had made sense, all that about families needing an extra allowance from the state to make sure that no one starved. Frank, Davy's mate, had been right too when he'd said that would be a chance for the owners to drop the pay again.

Tom sat up and stared down at the farm, not seeing it, not hearing Grace as she told him to sit still, for God's sake, she was trying to have a sleep. She settled down again, pulling her cardigan tighter round herself. He took off his jacket and put it over her.

Aye, it had been interesting right enough and it had been grand to see Davy's face when he'd suggested that along with the allowance the unions should press for a decent basic minimum wage so that the bosses couldn't try that trick. Tom grinned to himself as he recaptured the look of surprise on Davy's face, surprise which changed to respect but after all they were only ideas which Davy himself had taught him. Davy had gone along with that but had come up with an even better idea himself; that the allowance should be paid to the women so there was no way the bosses could carp that it was supplementing the men's wage packet. Tom looked across at Grace. It wouldn't half help her ma, an idea like that, help everyone, especially up here, whether they were in work or not.

Davy still had no job but he was talking about taking one at Lutters Pit. There was talk of the owners opening it to get what they could out of the bottom seam. It was better than nothing, Davy had said, when May protested and Uncle Henry had banged the table. It was danger money Uncle Henry had shouted. That pit's been closed too long, there's too much water to weaken the props and loosen the coal.

Tom had said to him later that night that he should go away

198

like Georgie, like his brothers, but he wouldn't. Who would help with the union if he went, he had replied? He was in line for union representative and someone had to stay.

Tom turned now and looked down at Grace. 'Our Davy says, if you start at the library, get 'em not to black out the racing in the papers will you?'

She laughed. 'Tell him I'll bring round the dailies after work if you like but I can't stop them blacking the runners. Can't have men on the dole finding a bit of pleasure in gambling, can they! Anyway, your Davy likes coming into the library. It gets him out of the house and he can find more facts to cause trouble with.' She poked her tongue out at him and grinned. Aye, the lad liked the library right enough, and tinkering with his old motor bike which he refused to sell however much he needed to.

The farmhouse was bordered by outbuildings and today there was washing on the line and a dog lying over the back doorstep. The cart was slewed at right angles to the barn, half full of sawn logs; its wheels looked as though they were growing out of the mud which covered the yard. There was an old plough rusted in the lee of the barn, almost grown over with nettles. He took out his pad and drew in sweeping lines.

'I had a letter from Annie today,' he said.

'Another,' replied Grace. 'I had one too last week.'

'Aye, she told me. She sent me the pencils and another pad. The hens are laying well and now she sells some off to the old sisters who live next door. Their cat got stuck up the monkey-puzzle tree further down the road and they had to get the fire service out. Caused quite a stir.'

Grace smiled and moved her arm arcoss her eyes as she lay back, almost asleep.

He still missed Annie, he thought, though it wasn't such a raw ache and it helped have Grace to walk with on a Sunday, though she hadn't let him kiss her mouth yet. He chewed his lip as he wondered how he was going to tell Annie that Georgie had left.

'Does she know Don's back?' Grace asked through lips heavy with sleep.

'I wrote and told her,' he replied. 'I dropped into Albert's the other day to see him. He looks well enough and has taken to the shop like a duck to water.'

199

Grace clambered on to one elbow. 'Can you pass us the tea then, Tom?'

He unhooked the cup from the top and poured the brown milky liquid, took a sip first, then handed it across. 'There's no sugar, Grace.'

She shrugged and sipped.

'I had a letter from Annie.'

Grace laughed. 'You've just told me that.'

He put his pencil down and balanced his pad on his knee whilst he dug the blue paper from his pocket. It was written in pen and the ink was black. 'She talks about Betsy. I'll read you that bit if you like?'

Grace was looking at him quizzically and nodded when he looked at her. She tucked her hair behind her ear and adjusted his jacket over her legs.

He smoothed the pages and looked through the first one, then put it to the back and stopped halfway down the second page.

'Here it is,' he said. ' "I've been thinking about your mam, Tom. Just imagine how it must have been having to slave away for me da, putting up with all the work, the booze and the misery. Looking after Don and me as well as her own bairn and it wasn't until the end that she belted me, when her hands were like balloons and the booze had got to her.

'She must have felt so beholden to Da because he had taken you too. That's why she could never say what she felt, never stand up for herself, so she got drunk and angry. Then he killed himself and left her with the mess and nowhere to go. At least Joe gave her a job and some money so she can pay May for your keep. She couldn't keep us, you must see that. How could we have lived in some poky room on a pittance she picked up skivvying?

'I feel bad about the way we didn't go to her. We should have done and I'm going to write to her. I think you should go and see her Tom, I really do. She loves you and what else could she do?

'See you when you come next week. Is Grace coming too? Thanks for telling me Don is back. I've written to him at Albert's. I hope he's all right there. It worries me to think of him with that man but he always seemed to like him.

'All my love to you, Tom." '

He handed the letter over to Grace and looked again at the farm. The farmer was out now, loading more logs from a pile by the cart. He used his hands and never seemed to pause between swinging the logs through the air and picking up more.

'Will you then?' Grace asked, when she had finished reading through it again.

Tom shrugged. 'Maybe, maybe not.'

He took up his pencil again and shaded in the side of the barn.

'Did you know she paid towards your keep?'

'Oh yes, me Aunt May told me when I was going on one day, just after I moved in.'

He tore the page out and handed it to Grace. 'What do you think of that?'

He was drawing again, this time trying to capture the farmer in action. It wasn't working and he threw himself back and watched the clouds as they scudded darkly against the grey sky. It wouldn't rain though, the clouds were too high.

'I wonder what me da was like,' he mused. 'Poor old Barney.' It was hardly his fault he'd been killed in the war but what would he have thought of Betsy palming off his son. He thought of his mother, blowsy and overblown and he could not imagine, did not want to imagine, her locked in passion with a man; that gross body all panting and eager. He shuddered and flopped over on to his side, pulling at the grass.

He remembered her clouting Annie, shouting at her and at him, again and again. She was ugly, in the same way that the woman with the veins at the fair had been ugly. Her hands bulged and he didn't want to go and see her, didn't want to go and have to be touched by her. Annie didn't understand. Betsy was not her mother, she was his and had given him away. He wasn't interested in whether she felt beholden, she should have kept him.

Had Annie, he wondered, forgiven her father yet for killing himself? He, Tom, had because Archie had not been his real father. Oh yes, he had been upset, he had grieved but he had forgiven him, but he doubted whether Annie had, whether she ever would. He remembered her saying that she hated him and could never forgive him. Well, he wasn't about to forgive his ma. It was the same thing, he would write and tell her or perhaps he would keep it all inside. It was better there.

He felt Grace's hand on his shoulder. 'Me da knows who your father was, you know. Barney Grant he was, their family came up from the Welsh mines years ago. He had a lovely singing voice me da says. Blue eyes and black hair.'

Tom saw the breath from the nostrils of the sheep grazing nearby. He turned over and said sharply.

'Is that all he knows?' So his surname should have been Grant should it. He had often wanted to know his name.

'That's all he'll tell you.' She sighed and stroked his face. 'He thinks you should go and make it up with Betsy too. He says it's not right for a boy to hate his mam.'

Tom stood up, brushing his trousers free of grass. The farmer was hitching the cart to his horse now, urging him to the track which led eventually to Wassingham. Tom stooped and packed the flask away, offering it wordlessly to Grace before he did so. She shook her head, watching him anxiously. His mouth was set in a thin line, his brow was furrowed in a scowl and his movements were rapid and sharp, almost violent. He was seldom angry and she felt the tears come to her eyes.

She stood up and he snatched the blanket from beneath her, shaking it. The grass flew up and into her eyes; she buried her head in her hands and tried to blink the dust from them. Tom saw and dropped the blanket, brought her hands from her face and lifted her eyes.

'In your eyes is it, Gracie? I'm sorry, lass.' He dug into his pocket and with the corner of his handkerchief slipped out a piece of grass which was in her eye, then lowered her lid over the bottom one until at last it was clear and the tears had stopped. His face was close, his eyes concentrated on hers as he searched for stray grass and dust. Then, satisfied, he said:

'I'm not a boy any more, Grace. I feel a man and I'll be doing a man's job in two months. I can't change how I feel.'

He dropped down and secured the clasp of his bag.

'Won't change,' Grace corrected.

He stood up now and took her by the shoulders. The wind was whipping the hair across her face, he felt the cold through his jumper.

'Can't,' he shouted. 'If I could, I would but I bloody can't. I love me Auntie May but me mam broke me heart when she sent me away and then Annie went and that was her fault too.'

202

Grace pushed him away from her and slapped him then, hard across the face and red marks came almost immediately.

'Annie, Annie, Annie. All I ever hear is bloody Annie. I'm here too but for all you care I could be one of them sheep cropping the bloody grass.'

She was red in the face with rage and he felt the heat and the pain from the slap and kissed her hard on the mouth, pulled her against him so that her warm soft body was pressed to his. It was his first kiss and he had not known that lips were so soft and he wondered whether he should breathe or not. He did not.

At last they drew apart but he held on to her arms.

'I'm telling you for the last time Grace, you and Annie's different. She's me sister just as much as if Barney had been her father. We're part of one another. I love her, she loves me but when she's not here I feel as though half me bloody heart's gone too. If you went, I would probably feel that the other half had gone. But don't bring Annie up again like that. It's different, what I feel for you both.' He was shaking her now and she nodded and then smiled.

'Don't forget your book,' she said as a page began to blow away again.

He raised his arms and galloped after it, stamping his foot hard down on it.

'I'll take you out for some chips in February, when I'm working,' he shouted as he came back with it bunched into his pocket. 'Until then, you can take me.' He grabbed her to him and kissed her cheek, then picked up the bags and made her wear his jacket as they set off back up the hill.

'I never did get the farmer right,' he murmured as they turned and watched the cart disappear round the hill. 'I can't get me figures to come alive somehow.'

'Annie wants you to go to art school you know. She's frightened of the pit for you and so am I. Look what it did to me da.'

'It's not going to get me, bonny lass. Maybe one day I'll go but it'll take money you see. Anyway, there's time enough.'

'And you'll see your ma, will you?'

She felt him tense and saw the muscle in his cheek jump.

'Maybe,' is all he said. 'Maybe.'

CHAPTER 14

Annie was smoothing down her new blue dress which slid over her skin and hung soft from her shoulders. She turned before the long mirror which was screwed to the inside of the mahogany wardrobe in her room and then she heard Tom's voice.

'I should stay here in the hall,' replied Sarah. 'It is somewhat improper to visit a young lady in her bedroom.'

But his steps were nearer and she faced the door, hiding her laugh in her hands.

'You lovely boy,' she cried and ran to him. His dark jacket was prickly and his chin rough as he held her tight and swung her clear off the ground.

'Aye, but you've grown,' Tom laughed. 'In three months you've grown, bonny lass. And in quite the right ways too.'

She held him from her and grinned.

'Don't be improper,' she mimicked Sarah and minced from him with one hand on her hip. 'Come on, is Don downstairs?'

She grabbed his hand and moved towards the door but he pulled her back. 'On me back then,' and her laugh jogged in her throat as he reared towards the stairs with her on his back and then on down, past the prints. She leant her head on the back of his and felt his warmth as he spun to a halt on the bottom step. Don was waiting, his elbow on the banister, his eyebrows raised.

'Not made a lady of you yet, then?' he drawled and she flung her arm round his neck and kissed his cheek. His moustache was very bushy now and she wondered how he ate without it getting in the way.

'I sometimes feel that day will never arrive, Donald,' called Sarah as she came through from the kitchen with an apron on.

She had been cutting egg sandwiches for tea and Annie could smell them from here.

'She hasn't got ears, you know,' Annie whispered to Tom. He hitched her further up his back. 'She's just one big flap that picks up everything.'

Don frowned and Tom laughed. Annie knew it would be all right. Sarah liked to be teased.

'I don't think we wish to go into my anatomy just yet awhile, Annie. Why don't you go into the garden and see the hens?' Sarah smiled and walked back to the kitchen and Annie winked over at Val who had come to the door and was laughing.

She dug her heels into Tom. 'Come on then, get a move on.' Tom edged out through the back door, still with her on his back and then he galloped down the garden, past the rose-bushes which were stunted with pruning and Annie felt the air jogged from her and the garden tipped and lurched. She waved wildly to the Thoms across the fence and turned to look back, beckoning to Don.

'Hurry up,' she called and her voice sounded as though she was rolling over cobbles.

He didn't see her as he talked through the window to Sarah in the kitchen. Tom dumped her by the wire but still kept an arm round her waist as he struggled to regain his breath. She held on to his shoulder and he kissed her cheek. Her hair was loose and kinked, almost curly and he touched it.

She grinned. 'I put it in lots of plaits at night. Sandy, one of the girls at school, taught me that little trick. It's better than just a few. Do you like it? She's nice; red-haired and blue-eyed but not plump like Grace. Couldn't she come, Tom?'

She'd said it all in one breath and her face was wistful as he shook his head.

'She's working tomorrow, bonny lass, and her Frank was in a fall in the pit, so she's home nursing him.'

Annie gripped his arm. 'Not bad is he, not like his da?'

Tom smiled and squeezed her to him. 'Just a bit of a knock. The coal fell behind him and he had to be dug out so he was bloody lucky. She sends her love.'

Annie bit her nail. Suddenly she was back in Grace's kitchen, laughing as Tom spilt his pink mice all over the floor, back in the dark streets, the beck and on the moors. Back where the wind tore through her hair on the beach, back where slag-heaps loomed wherever you looked and coal-dust coated the trees. Then Tom slapped her hand from her mouth, lightly, but enough to bring her back to the light and the cleanliness of the garden and the hens, but part of her still called for the past while the other sank back into the space and light of the present.

'Don't bite your nails, hinny. It's a disgusting habit, or that's what our Gracie would say.' He was smiling at her, his blue eyes deep into hers and she knew she would be all right if she could still feel his arm round her, see his pictures as the years went by. All right if the pit didn't get him and fear clutched at her and she banged the wire to attract the hens towards them.

'We'll feed them in a moment,' she said, 'when Don gets here.' Anything to put that image from her mind. She looked round for Don again.

He seemed to have been a man for years and years she thought. Above and away from the two of them, always busy with his own plans, never needing them, seldom writing when he moved away. She felt like a fly Beauty's tail would want to swat when she was around him. He was old, he'd been old for a long time and she couldn't find ground between them that she could walk on and reach him. But she loved him. He was her brother.

She watched Tom as he squatted by the wire and stuck his finger through, waggling it to attract a hen. 'She'll think it's a worm and nip you,' she laughed, pushing him so that he nearly fell over.

He stood up again, taking his cap from his pocket and slipping it on to the back of his head. He moved his shoulders as though his back ached and suddenly she remembered.

'Your back,' she gasped. 'I must have hurt you when I was having me ride. Here, let me have a look.'

She darted behind him and held up his jacket and the shirt with it and her skin went cold as she saw the raised red scars. She heard Don strolling up the garden behind her and turned.

'Look at this will you, Don. I'd have bloody killed him if I'd been there.' Her lips tightened with rage and she touched Tom's back with her fingertips.

Don had walked on past and was clucking through the wire at the hens.

'Teachers have a job to do,' he said. 'Tom's like you, all mouth. He probably asked for it.' He twanged the wire with his finger and moved further down to see the cock which was pecking at corn left over from this morning.

Annie felt the old irritations rise up as she tucked Tom's shirt back. She wanted to slap Don's face, push it into the wire so that he had red marks and then tell him he had too much of a mouth on him and begged for it. But Tom winked at her. Albertitis, he mouthed, his hand up and she nodded and shrugged. Nothing had changed, she thought, between them all, but wished that it had. She pulled a face at Don behind his back.

'If the wind changes, you'll stay like that,' Don said without turning his head and her eyes widened at Tom and then they started to laugh and she moved up to Don and put her hand on his shoulder, hoping he would stay next to her and talk. Tom nodded quietly at her and she showed Don her best layer. He moved from her to take some corn and flicked it through the wire. Her stomach tightened and she looked away, not at Tom, not at Don, but at nothing until she was able to smile again through lips that were stiff.

She gave them bowls and watched as they took in the corn and spread it about, laughing at the hens that pecked and chattered and pushed to reach the choice piles, leaning on the wire while the weak sun fell on her back. Don had let her touch him for a while at least. She would not tell them yet of the card she had received this morning from Georgie saying that he had left Wassingham and was in the Army now. That he would come for her later and that he loved her and always would. She had left it under her pillow and would allow herself to look at it and feel it again tonight and until then would not think of him being where she could not imagine him, not see him sitting or standing in a place she recognised.

The wire lurched as Tom slammed the gate behind them and screwed the wire shut. He stood next to her and looked back at the house. The winter sun was low and he pulled his cap further down over his eyes and took out his pad while Don walked over to the greenhouse. He sketched in the french windows of the sitting room, the flagstones and rose bush in the tub which was pulled close to the house for frost protection.

'I need colour really,' he murmured and Annie looked over his pad, shading her eyes as she studied the house again. He had caught the essence of the place.

'It's lovely here,' Tom remarked. 'Are you happy?' Looking at the house not at her.

Annie moved to the laurel tree and picked at a dark leaf. 'It's too early to answer that. I love the comfort, the ease. It's electricity here.' She heard the pride in her voice. 'But it's still strange, still as though I'm not really here.' She was going to continue but Don called over.

'How much do you make on the eggs then?' The cinders were wet from yesterday's rain and did not move beneath his feet but stuck to the soles of his boots as he came towards them.

'Enough,' replied Annie and waved to Val as she came to beckon them in to tea. 'Coming,' Annie called. 'Race you in, Don.' She grinned at him, willing him to run with her, but he shook his head and walked with his hands deep in his pockets towards the house so she walked beside him, pointing to the vegetables and the shed which was full of garden furniture, as well as her bike.

'Well, you have done well for yourself then, haven't you,' he murmured before they reached the kitchen and she wanted to tell him that she would, somehow, make it up to him one day. She would give him his share of her good luck.

As they entered, Sarah handed Don the tray of cups to carry through to the sitting-room and Tom left the sketch of the house on the table and pushed the trolley, taking over from Val and making her go before him into the room. It clattered as he pushed it and the smell of scones was strong because Sarah had covered over the egg sandwiches with a bowl.

'Annie's eggs are beautiful but they are rather ripe when hardboiled, don't you think?' Sarah asked as she settled down by the teapot.

Annie watched as the boys took a sip of tea and had to bite her lip to stop laughing out loud. 'It's Earl Grey,' she explained. 'I like it now.'

Sarah looked up from her sandwich. 'I'm so sorry, would you prefer Indian?' She had flushed with embarrassment and Annie wished she had said nothing because underneath Sarah's poise there was an uncertainty at times, one that was usually to do with her. She wondered, not for the first time, how she would cope if her home was invaded by a girl from a different background who endlessly upset the routine.

208

Tom had shaken his head but Don nodded. 'Tastes like soap.' He pulled a face.

'I said you'll get to like it,' Annie snapped and took his cup to the kitchen and made another pot of tea.

'How did you manage to leave the horses then, Don?' she asked on her return, her voice friendly, her face stretched in a smile which was too broad. She was sorry for snapping, sorry for Sarah, annoyed with herself.

'Just take a look at me, Annie. I've grown you daft thing. Too big for the horses now.'

'So how long are you at Albert's?'

She noticed how he poked his scone into his mouth all in one whilst she had cut hers into quarters. The butter dripped out of the corner of his mouth and ran in a greasy trail to his chin. There were crumbs in his moustache. She passed him a napkin to wipe his mouth but he opened it and tucked it in the open collar of his shirt and the butter ran under his chin. He wiped it with the back of his hand.

'He's going to make me a partner. I'm in your old room.'

'But how could you go in with him?' Annie protested. 'How could you even think of it? He's a money-lender and he charges the earth.'

'So what?' He reached for another scone. 'There's more out of work, so more'll need to pawn or borrow. We'll do both.'

Tom put down his knife. 'Well, you set your rates too high for the likes of Grace, you know; the likes of anyone round our way. We're struggling with things as they are. They're our people you know, Don. We grew up with them and you're making mint out of their bad luck. We should be working together to try to sort it out, not gaining from it. They don't like it, Don. It'll lead to trouble.'

'We run the shop as well,' Don was sitting back now, sipping his tea, smiling as he savoured the rich brown brew. 'Don't forget that. And how is our Gracie these days? Still a wobble a minute, is she?'

Annie put her hand up to stop Tom who jerked forward. Tension had leapt into the air, sparking between the three of them as it had always done, but louder now, more serious than just the squabbles of children and Annie did not want his anger growing and souring her family. She loved them both.

Silence fell whilst Don sipped, his eyes cold on Tom, who glared.

Sarah cut in, her voice crisp and clear. 'So things are bad, are they, Tom?' And Annie settled back in her chair though she knew that trouble had only sunk to just below the surface and was ready to rear out, spitting, at any moment.

Tom explained that work was more difficult to come by because coal was just not selling; that poverty was increasing; that Grace's family was finding it harder, like all the others and that the miners couldn't do anything, they had no power now. Annie looked at the scones dripping with butter on the doily-covered plates, the sandwiches and the cakes, at the two pots of tea, and the dark streets seemed far away. It was easy to forget that Wassingham had rickets and consumption, bare feet and starvation.

Sarah had lit the fire when the tea had been poured and the heat was reddening Val's cheeks as she sat with her hands on her lap near the hearth. Her eyes were nodding shut and Annie let the conversation wash past her now, thinking that soon, as it was every day, Val's head would be on her chest. She knew also that later she would sit with her sewing-box darning over the wooden mushroom or altering dresses or making napkins out of old tablecloths and that Sarah would read the paper until nine-thirty when she would make the cocoa and call Annie from her homework.

Life had a gentle pattern these days. School with Sandy and Jenn and the walks round the gardens, then Val and Sarah. It was as though she had been ill and was slowly recovering, slowly finding herself whole again, but she must not forget what life was really like.

The sharpness of anger broke in on her thoughts and there were her two brothers clashing again. Don sat upright and stabbed his finger at Tom, speaking with scone in his mouth.

'Albert's got a right to make a living like everyone else. He's all right. You just want a revolution, you and that Davy of yours. He's always stirring things, he is. What's wrong with making a profit?'

'You shouldn't make a profit at the expense of your neighbours, that's all I'm saying. Don't do it, man, don't follow that old bugger and go against your own. You're too good for that.'

'He's not an old bugger,' Don stormed and Annie looked to Sarah who was not remonstrating, just listening. Val had her head up now.

Don continued. 'He's giving a service you know and if you treat him proper he's all right to be with. He's me uncle after all, me da's brother. He's family, isn't he?' There was a hard set to his face now.

'Our Annie treated him proper,' Tom was shouting now, 'and look what happened to her and it was because he was your da's brother he did that. He told her that an' all. You're on the wrong side, Don.'

Annie felt a knot tightening in her stomach again, her hands gripped the arm of the chair as the voices went through her.

Don leant forward. 'Our Annie rubbed him up the wrong way if I know anything about her. He didn't have to take her on, did he?' He jerked his thumb at her and Sarah went white. Val was poking the fire loudly.

'For Christ's sake,' hissed Tom and put his hand on Annie's arm.

Don stabbed at Tom again. 'If you don't like the facts of life, boy, why don't you get out, like she's done, like Georgie, and have your revolution somewhere else? You've got no one to keep you in Wassingham. I've got me uncle.'

Don turned to Annie now, ignoring Tom's sudden silence. 'Gone in the Army, Georgie has, did you know? I heard from his mam when she came in.' He put up his hand as Tom began again. 'To buy some fags it was, not to borrow, so keep your holier than thou shirt on.'

Annie nodded, angry at him for throwing Tom's family in his face, angry at him for throwing Albert at her as though he was a saint, wanting him to stop making her feel as though she deserved to be belted and screamed at, wanting them both to think the same way, to stop quarrelling, to stop what she feared had become hate. Wanting most of all for him to stop talking about Georgie, but needing to hear more.

'He'll be all right, will Georgie. Uniforms bring in the girls, they do, and he'll be all for getting his leg over if I know him.'

Tom was on his feet now, his face white. 'Well, you don't know him do you, so that's enough.' But Annie pulled him back down although she felt cold with shock and everything seemed impossibly far away. Don did not know about her and Georgie, so it was not his fault, none of this was his fault. It was because of Albert that he was like this and was it, she wondered, something about her that inflamed him?

She watched as Sarah patted her mouth with her napkin with a hand which shook. How strange, Annie noted with detached surprise; she had never seen that before.

'That's quite enough of that language please, Don,' said Sarah in a voice as cold as ice. 'You've obviously been around horses too long.'

Annie stroked butter on to a teacake, then cut it carefully in half, then quarters, watching as the butter flowed over the knife. Tom was sitting stiffly in the chair beside her; she saw that his fists were clenched, that he was breathing quickly. No one was speaking. The fire was crackling though and Val used the brass tongs to put two logs either side of the grate.

'Could you help me with my embroidery, Tom?' asked Annie desperate to break the tension. She put down her plate and looked across at Val. 'Could you pass it from there please, Val?' Her voice sounded strained, high-pitched but it was better than the silence.

Strung across a frame was the hassock material. Annie nudged Tom. 'I have to enter this competition.'

'What's the prize?' asked Don, drinking his tea again.

She ignored him. Tom rose and took the frame from Val.

'I can't bear the flowers as they are. I want something different, Tom, but it must be easy.' She laughed and slowly felt as though she was more in touch with the room. Sarah was looking at her, smiling her approval.

'Something Art Deco do you think?' suggested Tom, sitting down again, keeping his eyes on her work, away from Don.

'Art what?' queried Annie and Sarah cocked an eye at Tom.

'What do you think of Art Deco then, Tom? I'm not sure myself.'

'It's different right enough, but I like the geometric lines.' He turned to Annie, his face less red, his eyes concentrating on his thoughts, not flashing with frustration as they had been. 'Makes me glad I did a bit of geometry at school. It grew out of the Art Nouveau movement which showed that art could be used in an industrial age and Art Deco tries to unite design and industry. They say that it can enter into the design of anything, even a cinema. So why not a hassock?'

212

'A hassock's not industrial,' objected Annie.

Sarah laughed. 'But why not borrow the idea? It would shake Sister Maria up a bit.'

So, guessed Annie, you still haven't forgotten the first day of school, and laughed, but made sure that Sarah thought it was at the idea of Art Deco hassocks, not at her in this instance.

Tom had taken out his pad and was drawing a rising sun design but Annie told him it had to be a flower motif, so he altered it to a sunflower. She passed it to Sarah.

'Could I do that in satin-stitch and cross stitch?' She grinned at Tom and then, stiffly, at Don. 'It's all I can do.'

Sarah passed it to Val for her opinion.

'Should be fine,' agreed Val. 'As long as she keeps it tidy at the back, she won't disgrace herself.'

Annie heard Don grunt and showed it to him but he did not react. She took back the design and heard Sarah ask Tom why he didn't go into textile design. 'It would combine art with manufacturing.'

And bring him out of the pits, Annie thought, and watched the lad as he leant back and looked at Sarah, his expression thoughtful.

She looked around the room, then at the curtains and then the wallpaper. 'Hey, what if the curtains and the wallpaper matched. That'd look good. What do you think Tom?' She felt a stirring of excitement.

Tom grinned. 'It's a good idea. Does anyone make them like that?'

'No one round here anyway,' Val commented.

Sarah leant forward. 'Make them yourself then, Tom.'

Suddenly the room was alive again, full of ideas and thoughts and words, though Don would still only sit and drink his tea. The fire died down as the time strode past and Tom said, 'What do you think, Don? Would you want to come in too, if we could get it off the ground?'

'It's funny,' said Don, 'bloody funny. There you are, shouting your mouth off at me because I lend money and here you are, you and Annie, talking of setting up a little capitalist empire.'

'No, Don, that's just what we've been saying,' Tom enthused. 'We're thinking about a cooperative. Then the men share the profits; if productivity rises, so does their money.'

213

Annie took his arm and pulled him back into his chair.

'Just a minute, Tom, remember that day at the beck when I said I'd lead me swarm out? Well, if I came in with you I'd want half the work-force to be female.'

She looked at him in triumph as Sarah and Val laughed and nodded. Don settled himself against the back of his chair and said, 'That's the end of that idea then, Tom.'

Annie lifted her chin. 'Just why is that?' she asked.

'The men wouldn't wear the lower wages. If you employ women, the wages would have to come down to match theirs.' Tom was tapping his fingers on his knees.

'That's no problem,' said Annie airily. 'You bring the women's up and they have same share of the profits.'

Tom and Don burst out laughing. 'There'd be a riot from firms elsewhere,' Don argued.

Tom nodded. 'We'd be setting a precedent. The unions wouldn't like it.'

Annie would not give in. She was determined now. Here was something she could build up. It would get Tom out of the pit eventually and maybe Don would come in and get away from Albert, be closer to them. There would be a place for Georgie and for Grace and for all those women.

'Then they'd have to lump it. Look at Sarah, why should she be paid less for doing her job than a man would? She has to keep a house. If I don't marry, I would have to. It's not fair, is it, Sarah? Surely you can see that Tom.'

His face was thoughtful and she could see that he was trying to sort it out. 'You can't be a socialist and not care about the women too,' she insisted, and listened as the talk swirled round the room again and soon the scones were finished and the cakes too.

Then he nodded. 'You're right. Of course you're right. We'll make the women equal.'

And he took a cup of warm tea from Sarah and gulped it down, his mind busy, and Annie was thinking that she would find Georgie and bring him back. They could go to the Lancashire mills for the cotton. Then Don said, 'You'd need to go to Art College, wouldn't you?'

The words cut across the excitement, the thoughts of the future, and the dreams disappeared, but then Sarah said, 'That's no problem. I will fund the Art College training.' Annie looked up at her and Tom spun round. His face had fallen into hopelessness but now was alight with hope. He looked at Annie, then back at Sarah. She leant forward and switched her table lamp on and it threw the light on to her face and showed her enthusiasm.

'Oh, so it's a paintbrush you need, to get anything round here, is it?' Don sneered. His eyes were on his cup and Sarah kept her face still as she turned it to him in the hush that had fallen again. Annie felt the sweat break out as she heard his words.

'No, Don, you do not need a paintbrush. I was intending of course to give you the same start as I would give Tom. In that way, all three of you will be equal.' Her voice was carefully expressionless and Annie flushed with shame for her brother and despair for herself.

Sarah rose. 'Come with me now to the study. I'll sort something out for you now. It might make the partnership you speak of with Albert that much more businesslike.' She smiled at Annie. 'It will be two years at least before Tom is able to go to College and we have plenty of time to sort his affairs out.'

Annie sat on as they left the room. Val and Tom cleared the tea things and rattled them out on the trolley and tray. The fire flickered lower and she did not think to replenish the logs. It was right of course that Don should have the same from Sarah as she had had, but now her task would be to find the money to repay her guardian for all that she was to give to her brothers or there would be no freedom for her. It would be like Betsy all over again.

Later, long after they had left and she was in bed, with Georgie's card in her hand, held against her body, she cried for him, wept for his strength. Georgie was her rock, the only one stronger than her. He had taught her, loved her, shown her a world that she had not known existed. Taken her by the hand to see the marsh marigold, the rowan berries ripening in late August. Made her look beyond her mere existence; to push thoughts from her head so that they did not absorb her energies, to enjoy the moment. What was it he had said? Push those black memories away, they don't have to stay inside your skull unless you want 'em to.

She needed him, needed his body, needed his strength that

had steadied her and then coaxed heights of passion from her. She knew he would be back, but only when he had brought himself up to the level that Sarah had determined for Annie. Only then, when he could match her, not need to take from her, would he be back. That was the love she missed, the love of someone she did not feel responsible for.

Don's whispered request, as he left, made her writhe again; the feel of her da's watch as she had given it back to him, as he had asked, made her feel a repeat of the anger she had felt.

It wouldn't get nicked from Albert's, he had said, pocketing the watch, so there was no longer any need for her to hang on to it, and now she forced the anger she felt away from him across to her da because it was a watch he should still have been wearing but he had killed himself, hadn't he. He would not make her angry at her brother for something which was his fault and she cried again as she tried to push the black memories back into the box, but it was too late now, they were out again and she wondered if they would ever give her any peace and go away completely.

CHAPTER 15

The marigolds were growing spindly in the beds and their bulging green seeds pulled the long stems down into the path; their acrid smell would be stronger as the sun rose. Annie dead-headed them as she went past, then segmented one in her pocket using her thumbnail and, pushing her bike, bumped down the steps through the gate and out into the road.

She was early for school today, deliberately so, and she did not ride the bike but pushed it along until she reached the lamp-post beyond the Miss Thoms; then she propped it up by the kerb and leant against the street lamp, unfolding Georgie's letter which she had already read twice since it had arrived after breakfast.

Here, on the pavement, with people walking past and lorries braking and revving as they came round the corner she reread every word, slowly savouring the shapes and lines, seeing in them his face as he bent over the paper, his hands as they fashioned these words, hearing his voice, even though he was so far away. It was two years since she had seen him. Two years since she had left Wassingham.

April 1931

My dearest Annie,

I never thought I would be writing to you from the North West frontier of India when I last wrote. It will take a good few months for this to reach you because letters from here travel by foot, mule, train before they reach the sea. Is your summer nearly over?

217

I am hunched round the fire with the snow falling all around. It is freezing hard and we have been marching all day in the column out from the fort to keep an eye on the Pathans. These are mountain people who enjoy a bit of fisticuffs between themselves and the odd raid into the lower farmlands. We are supposed to keep them in order. Some hope!

They like our guns so will be trying to take them fairly soon but they won't be successful.

We are also here to check the passes and make sure that Russia is not about to invade India but the officer here says that the bolshies are probably too busy with their own problems to be starting any nonsense like that. I expect Tom could tell us all what he means by that.

I'm a lance-corporal now which isn't bad for 19. I got me first stripe soon after we landed in India, so have just helped our lads to build a stone wall, which is called a sangar out here, before reporting to the sergeant. He's set up a machine-gun inside it and of course ourselves.

The hill we have climbed today is rather higher than the one we used to race up to get to Bell's Farm and you would need all the vests you could find to survive. I can't see you climbing in our gear. The brown woollen shirts would prickle you to death and on top of that the jerseys scratch through them. Our shorts go as far as our knees and the footless hosetops, socks, puttees and the boots would drive you mad, they're so tight.

We sleep out in the open, though some sit up round the fires, preferring the warmth to a good night's kip. I don't mind it too much, Wassingham could be pretty bad – remember? But if I were here with you neither of us would notice the snow, even if it fell for a million years. I've missed you so, my bonny lass, my darling. I think of you every night, every day. Think of you with Val and Sarah, think of you sitting on your wall with Jenn and Sandy. Think of you lying in bed and I want you so much it hurts. I can picture your friends but wonder how wrong I am. It must be grand to have a break from the hard graft of life and you must enjoy it, you must try not to spoil it by worry over the boys or missing me.

Tom is right, you know, when he says that Don is asking for trouble with his money-lending. His interest rates are far too high from what Tom says when he writes, but he'll talk some sense into the man so don't let it get to you. The idea of your own business still seems to excite Tom and at least it will get your bonny lad out of the pits won't it, which is what you want more than anything, isn't it?

I wonder, though, whether the business is what you really want. You sound so interested in your work at the hospital but Sarah's right to say it's too much for you. Little hinny, you must take care. Don't work your guts out just to pay her back for Don's money. She doesn't want it and even if you feel you must make it up to her there's all the time in the world to do it.

You mustn't worry about me out here either. We are really sent out from the fort to push off boredom and it is just a bit of a ramble so you can imagine that it suits me grand. The hills are covered with the holly-oak scrub with leaves that barely rot when they fall, so we march through inches of them. Their acorns don't ripen for eighteen months either so new growth is slow here. I want to get down to the Himalayas which should be our next posting and will then see the rhododendrons you talk of having at the convent. It will make me feel nearer to you, my little lass.

I think if it was warmer you would find it good here. The views take the breath from your chest and the wild life is the sort you only read about in books. Yesterday I saw a leopard and we hear the wolves at night. The Hindu Kush mountains are too large to be real. I will bring you to India one day, but not here; I will find a place I love and that is warm and clear and it will be there that we will have our honeymoon.

It will make the time go more quickly to think of

that day, but I don't know how long it will be; there's quite a way for me to go before I have a chance of becoming an officer because that is what I intend to be; for you and for me.

I thank God, the real God not Bob, that Sarah took you out of Wassingham when she did. The depression, what we hear of it, sounds bad. Tom tells me a bit, but not all. He's in work, he says, but not Davy yet, though they're both up on soap-boxes shouting their mouths off most of the time from what he tells me. If we had married and still been there, what would have become of us?

I have to write these long letters my darling, there is so much spilling out of me, so much I want to say to you, but what I want more than anything is to see your face, feel you in my arms, kiss your lips. But it will be a long time yet and I will say what I always say to you; you must be free my love, free to make other friends, take other lovers, because life is too short to be wasted and to turn down love.

Just remember my sweetest darling that I love you more than life itself and that, in the end, I will be there to teach you how to hang by your arms from the bar. I didn't on that day of the fair, did I? I will always regret that.

Sweet dreams, my bonny lass. Thank you for your precious letters which I keep with me all the time, though some are so well read that they are in pieces.

I will write again, my love,
Georgie.

Annie smoothed the letter in half, then quarters and put it in her inside pocket. She was still in the stinging snow, amongst scrub holly-oak, still standing dwarfed by the mountain range as she pushed her bike out into the road and on towards school. She rode up the drive past the rhododendrons which had been beautiful in June, a month ago.

She would like to see them growing at the foot of a mountain, but only if it was with him, with her love, and the ache which his letters always brought burned through her and she wanted to walk and run anywhere so long as it was without people. She wanted to lie on a warm meadow bank or on a windswept dune and think of him, urge him to come home, will him to come back to her. But today was Wednesday and she was here, at school, and it was piano with Miss Hardy. She shrugged Georgie up into a corner of her mind, pushed him until he could barely be seen, be felt, until she was in bed tonight, free of interference and climbed back into the convent and her life today.

The music room was across from the main building in what used to be the old hay loft above the stables. Marjorie Phelps was in before her and the notes flowed melodically through the brown door behind which the old bag would be sitting, smiling like the Cheshire Cat because some little nimbled-fingered princess of the keyboard was putting pianissimo where it belonged.

Her leather music-case flopped along her thighs as she sat on one of the two chairs which lined the small waiting-room. She was tired today, she always was on a Wednesday because Tuesday evening she was at the cottage hospital. It had been Sundays only at first but Sister Newsome had asked her if she could come in on one evening as well to read to the patients. It calmed them before their operations Sister Newsome had explained, her purple sister's uniform crisp and her buckle large and glinting.

Annie had been pleased because her duties should have been just tea-making and plate-washing in this part-time job she had seen advertised in the local paper. This small sister though, with her laughing eyes and brisk, but kind efficiency, had begun to ask her to roll bandages, sit with ill patients, play with sick children with shorn deliced heads. And Annie loved it; loved to watch the nurses as they changed dressings, fought for a life. Loved to watch Sister Newsome take charge of a crisis or just run her ward from day to day. She envied her authority, her competence. Yes, she had been pleased but it made her tired. She would not stop though because, as well as loving it, she needed to be able to give Sarah those few shillings each week.

She looked at the door opposite and a pulse flickered in her throat at the thought of the next half hour. That Sarah should think piano-playing a useful asset in later life was absurd. Even Jenn's mother had let her stop and she was very much a drawing-room devotee.

There was no noise now, no flowing scales, no fluid arpeggios. The door opened.

'Oh dear, come along in, Ann, and very well done, Marjorie. One would wish all one's pupils were such a joy.'

You're no violet yourself, you know, thought Annie as she squeezed passed the small round woman with gold-rimmed glasses and moles on her pale dry skin.

She slid on to the stool and pumped away at the scale of 'C' as Miss Hardy first stood behind her, then moved to sit down on the chair at her side. The metronome gained on her as usual and the sharp pencil jabs began.

'Evenly, Ann. How often do I have to say it? Have you practised at all?' The metronome continued to tick.

Annie yawned; it was slow and deliberate because one knuckle was oozing blood slowly and it hurt but she would not show that she was affected.

'I suppose you have been out gallivanting with all and sundry and paying no attention to your work.' Miss Hardy was sitting bolt upright on a chair next to Annie. She could see the movement of her plump thighs each time her rhythm broke but it was the fidgeting broke it. The piano had a dark glossy varnish and was wedged across the corner of the small room. The window was to the right of Miss Hardy and through it Annie could see the girls as they walked from the tennis courts to the changing-rooms in the school. They trailed their tennis rackets in loose hands and clouds hung motionless in the pale blue sky beyond the school vegetable garden. A row of runner beans was beginning to sport heavy red flowers and she smelt the scent of leeks from long ago and felt Don's hair as she tugged his head up to hers and wondered yet again why he went on provoking the neighbourhood and knew that it was because there was more money in it for him. He was a fool, a bloody fool and he wouldn't listen to her but Tom had said he would make sure he got through to that thick skull before an iron bar did. Tom was growing up fast, she thought, older than his 15 years but the pits did that to a man, so did a woman and as she stumbled over 'Sunshine after Rain' she grinned to think of him and Grace and was pleased.

'This won't do, you know, Ann.' The pencil jabbed again into the back of her hand. 'Two mistakes in that piece and no heart at all.'

Miss Hardy flicked over the pages of the book, her gold charm bracelet rattling as she did so.

'Try this one and remember the "F" sharp.' She pencilled round the note with a flourish.

Annie stumbled over the 'F' sharp as she always did; somehow her fingers just did not make that lift to the black note cleanly. Miss Hardy's voice was rising nicely, she thought, a little earlier than usual perhaps and she braced herself for the tirade. Annie knew she provoked this woman, always had done and she felt it was something to do with Sarah but did not know what.

'I blame the home of course.' Miss Hardy was rocking in sharp movements and Annie was ready for the jab when it came. The kettle was boiling on the small table in the corner and Annie noted that the outburst was rather more powerful than usual. She lurched into an arpeggio, also in 'C' and the kettle was allowed to continue boiling; the lid rattled and Annie could see the cup out of the corner of her eye and wished Miss Hardy would have her usual tea-break. It always calmed her down.

'I suppose,' Miss Hardy went on with her voice like a coiled spring, 'it's boys, making you tired, making you rude and obstinate.' She jabbed again and Annie felt the first stirrings of anger.

'Now "The Skater's Waltz", if you please.' She reset the metronome. The tick was faster.

Still the kettle rattled. 'Shall I turn off the kettle, Miss Hardy?' The steam was drifting across the ceiling now.

'You see, I do not go out at night.' Miss Hardy was staring at her, her glasses glinting and her face screwed up as though she was about to cry.

'I live with my friend, hardly ideal, is it? We don't really get on but it's better than being alone. No men left you see, all killed you see. It's not that we were unattractive, you know, it's just that there was no one left from the trenches.' Her voice was shrill and unpleasant. 'It's not out of choice that I'm teaching, spending hours with girls like you who do not wish to be here.' She was shaking now and Annie left her seat and turned off the kettle. 'We're all wasted women aren't we, dried up, all wasted.' Miss Hardy was ranting now.

'Well most of them are nuns,' Annie replied.

'Not just here, you obdurate girl,' she raged on. Her face red now, her breathing rapid almost as though she was choking. Jenn said she got like this when she'd had a row with her friend.

'Stupid, stupid girl, get out of here. I refuse to teach such impertinence, such appalling lack of talent.' She sat straight-backed, her lips pursed. 'And there are those that throw marriage out of the window as though it were of no value. Trollops and scarlet women as you know only too well.'

Annie looked at the woman, at the sweat that lay in a sheen on her top lip. This was a new line, she thought.

'Divorce is a sin, and to think that she was once at this school and now sends you here. It's a disgrace. I saw her fetch you yesterday in her smart little car. I hadn't seen her for years until then and she looks so young still; it's not fair.'

Annie felt her jaw set and picked up her music book and placed it in her case; anchored the metronome so that there was silence in the room and left. She was sure that she would never touch a piano again.

'How was your day?' Val asked her over dinner.

'Is Georgie well?' Sarah spoke before Annie could reply.

'Yes, he is, Sarah,' replied Annie as she cut up the beef which she had come to accept as normal. 'And yes, Val, it was interesting.' She kept her voice carefully neutral. 'Miss Hardy went barmy.'

The runner beans were stringy; Val must have cooked the edges again. Keeps you regular, all this roughage is what she would say if you dared complain.

Val looked up, then laughed while Sarah wiped her mouth carefully with her napkin. 'Would you care to improve on that remark?' she asked.

'After she started to prick my hands she went off into hysterics about not being married and those that were pushed it out of the window and became scarlet women. That divorce was a disgrace.' Annie drew a deep breath and grinned. 'And that she would never teach me again.'

Val banged down her knife and fork. 'Well, I never did, and

224

she was at school with you as well, Sarah; always a mouse though, never any admirers.'

Sarah rang the school after dinner and said that Annie would no longer be continuing with the piano since it would appear that she had no appetite for the subject. Another victim of the war, she had sighed, and Annie half knew what she meant. She would write to Georgie tonight, he would be glad her piano lessons were over.

'Should I know about divorce, Sarah?' she asked as her cousin poured the after-dinner tea with a steady hand. The cups were the white bone china which made the tea taste quite different.

'I was married during the war but my husband left me two years after the armistice.'

It was simply said and there was no tremble as she passed Annie her cup. Her face was quite calm, though her voice was very careful.

'Why did he leave you?'

'I suspect because I failed him. Now finish up your tea and do your homework or is it time for another letter to Georgie?' Her smile was gentle as Annie nodded and told Sarah all his news.

The drive out to the country was unexpected and so had been Annie's excellent end-of-term school report. She had felt a smile grow and stay as Sarah read it to her.

'We both deserve a treat, especially as the conservatory has seen you only once this term,' she announced. 'Look, one punishment mark, that's all. Come on, put your jacket on, we're off for some lunch.'

They pulled into a country inn with a sweeping drive and a garden at the rear with a small patio on which tables were set; more spilled on to the lawns. Red and white cotton umbrellas shaded diners from the sun. As they sat down, Sarah pointed to the river running slowly past the bottom of the terraced lawn.

'I'm told they catch trout here, but so far I've never seen any signs of success.'

Annie sat back. They had no umbrella and the sun was hot. She raised her face and all she could see through closed lids was a blaze of yellow which distanced all sound. She thought of Georgie showing Tom how to tickle trout and how Tom had told her that the beck was now so dead with black sludge that the fish were gone.

A man's voice said 'Good afternoon, Sarah. How are you?'

Annie shaded her eyes and looked in the direction of the voice. The back of the inn was a glaring white, with dark beams sharply exposed and much nearer, standing by their table was a well-built man, rather like Georgie except that he was fair and had a pale moustache. Georgie was clean-shaven, or had been when she last saw him; she must ask him whether he still was.

'Very well, thank you, Harold,' Sarah was replying. 'You haven't met my ward, Annie Manon, have you? Mary's child, of course.'

Annie felt a quietness sitting on Sarah who turned to Annie.

'This is Mr Beeston, Annie. Shall we order?'

The tables were filling up now and Annie looked at Sarah as she sat against the sun.

'May I have chicken salad, please?' Annie asked. It sounded quite normal and Sarah ordered the same. The man smiled tightly and left.

Sarah said nothing as they waited for their meal, just smiled with her mouth until Annie asked, 'Why did you come?'

Sarah did not answer immediately but sat thinking quietly, then said, 'Oh Annie, I don't know really. A need to beard the lion in his den perhaps. To assure myself that I have a full life which gives me great pleasure, especially now that I have you. I suppose it's a laying of ghosts and besides, my dear, they do have such excellent food.' She turned and thanked the waitress as she brought their meal.

They both sat back in their chairs and Annie did not taste her food, she was too busy with her thoughts. A laying of ghosts, Sarah had said, and she envisaged her own ghosts as they trampled through her room at night. Don who seemed intent on stirring up hatred, Tom who sank down into the pits each day and had so far come up each time, but for how much longer? She almost hoped he would lose his job like the rest of the poor buggers. She thought of Georgie and wondered if he had moved to the Himalayas yet, of her father who had begun all this. She stirred restlessly. She was still not free of memories and fears and remembered how she had clung to Betsy and told her that she would be free, would not be like her. Annie rubbed her eyes; thank God she had written to poor Betsy, but she had not heard back because Grace said she could no longer write with her hands as they were.

Sarah spoke again. 'I rather fear I emasculated poor Harold. I had changed you see from the girl I was before the war when he knew me through my family. I had wanted female suffrage and I fought for it. I then drove an ambulance during the war. I was financially independent even before my father and mother died. I was a person in my own right and I thought we married on that basis. What I did not realise was that he had in his mind this picture of me as I was when I was your age and living in Gosforn; an age when I did not even know he existed other than as a friend of the family.' She sighed and then continued. 'He, poor man, had a vision of me soft and malleable. He'd had the bad war that everyone had and came home to a wife that he soon found threatening.'

Annie looked at her. 'Threatening, what do you mean?'

Sarah laughed. 'I mean that I was independent in thought as well as means. I didn't need him in those ways but what he could not understand was that I loved him dearly and needed him emotionally. I was distraught when he left and I lost the child I was carrying.'

Annie felt a flood of feeling; she wanted to rush round and hold this woman tight and instead she covered her hand with hers and looked at the face which seemed softer now than when she had first known her, her hair was in gentle waves round her face, her clothes were less severe.

'Did he know about the baby?'

Sarah nodded. 'Oh yes, he knew, but he didn't care. I repulsed him with my personality, I suppose, and that is something that I hope will never happen to you.'

She gripped Annie's hand and looked hard at her.

Annie smiled, her face was older she knew, more mature and her hair suited her cut shorter. Her eyes were more considered in their glances. She felt absolutely sure, as she said:

'Georgie would never treat me like that. He would know I needed to be free.'

'But it might not be Georgie, Annie. It could be so long before he is back that you find someone else.'

Annie shrugged. 'It might be a long time and there might be others before he comes but it will always be him in the end.'

'Oh my dear, don't be too set on that. You should always

remember that choice is going to be there for you. It is a great freedom.'

'Freedom to me is leaving all the darkness behind, forgetting everything you want to forget, releasing yourself from responsibility for others being, oh, I don't know, unmarked, I suppose.' Annie leant forward, a frown drawing up between her eyes. She could talk to Sarah now, trust her because with her job, with her hens, she felt almost without debt to her; almost but not absolutely, but that would come. But here she sighed. There was still the business course after her exams to be paid for and she felt a flash of frustration as Sarah laughed and tapped her hands. A slight wind was drifting up from the river and the frill of the umbrella on the next table was wafting in the breeze.

'That freedom is a dream, Annie.' She gathered up her handbag and smoothed down her skirt where it had creased as she sat. 'Come along, it's time we were on our way. I do so enjoy tipping that pretty little blonde thing at the till.'

They walked arm in arm in the weakening sun to the counter, the breeze chilling the coffee of those who still remained.

'Thank you so much, Mrs Beeston.'

Sarah smiled sweetly. 'Another culinary delight. Do give my compliments to the chef, Mr Beeston.' And she walked past, her eyes full of something which looked like defiance, Annie thought.

CHAPTER 16

Tom shut the backyard gate behind him and joined the stream of men walking down to the pit. It was a warm morning and would be a fine day, not that he would know about it until this afternoon when his shift was finished. He sank his hands deep down into his pockets, his boots making the same noise as those walking in front and behind. Uncle Henry was on the afternoon shift at the same pit and was still asleep and Davy had started work at Lutters Pit yesterday; he too was on the late shift but if Tom and Henry had been able to do anything about it he would still be going to the library and kicking a ball around with his mates.

It wasn't that they didn't want him to work; they did, anywhere but bloody Lutters. Tom kicked a stone hard against the wall as he turned into the cobbled street that led down the hill to the pit. That Lutters wasn't safe, he knew it wasn't safe. It had been unworked for far too long but Davy had insisted. It was the only pit that would take him with his reputation and the means test that the government had just introduced to try and cut down money given to the long-term unemployed had made him take the risk.

Tom nodded to two of his mates, shambling on past him.

'See you tonight then, Tom, at the meeting.'

He nodded. He would be there because they needed to talk more about this new test but before he went there he had Don to sort out.

He pulled his scarf round his throat and stuffed it down inside his jacket. He didn't need the warmth of either now but he would when he came up out of the heat and dark when the hooter blew for the end of the shift.

There were too many curtains still drawn on the houses he passed, too many men still in bed, still without jobs. Too many starving bairns and again he thought of Don. He'd have to go and try and knock some sense into the bugger. Annie had spoken to him but he just called her a bloody bolshie. Tom scowled as he passed through the colliery gates and rubbed the back of his head. If what he'd heard in the pub was anything to go by, our Don was going to get told good and proper about overcharging on loans but it wouldn't be with words.

He'd been with his back to the next table with Davy arranging the meeting for tonight since it was no good leaving it to the union rep; he was a flaccid little tyke who kept out of everyone's way. Even if there was an accident you had to chase round after the little bleeder to make sure he got to the hospital to deal with the owners' offer of compensation, if there was one.

Tom waited by the cage door, his head down. He didn't want to talk, he wanted to think. But it wouldn't do any good, he had said to Davy about the meeting. There could be no strike; they had no clout with the unemployment and low union funds. But at least the men could talk and that was better than nothing, Davy had argued.

They'd heard the men behind them then in the snug, saying that they were going to get Don. Bad as a blackleg, one of them had said. The sort of bloody bugger that'd do our job when we were out on strike. We'll get him, we'll beat his bloody head in for leeching the blood out of his own people with his bloody rates. Tom had not been surprised; he had been expecting something of the sort. The cage was up now and it was no easier today than when he had started to go down two years ago. It was still the same iron cage lined with wooden planks blackened by inches of dust that stank raw and filthy even before you plunged down into the black heart of the pit.

Don was forgotten, Davy too, as he crushed up against the next man, his bait-tin digging into his hip. He clenched his nostrils against the smell of coal and looked away from the last sight of the sky to the back of the man in front and waited, his mouth dry with a fear he could never conquer, a hate he could never master.

Then down they went, screaming through pitch-black cold rushing air and his legs felt as though they would never catch up with the base of the cage but stay forever two inches above it as it plummeted down the shaft. The cold made his skin crawl and always he wondered if they would not slow but instead hurl against the shaft end in a tangle of wreckage and shattered bodies but, at last, there was a slowing, a stopping and his legs felt firm again as though they were at last bearing the weight of his body.

Dimly lit by lights every few yards, the main seam throbbed with men, the smell of coal, the rumble of the trams as they were pushed back with coal from the headings to be taken to the surface. There was the hammering of the picks as they heaved and tore at the face. In each tunnel, in each hole, miners attacked the face.

Millions of tons of coal pressed close on top of the workings and Tom removed his jacket in the heat. Their boots clumped and they edged sideways where the heading narrowed, careful always of the tram-lines and their cargo which could take off a foot. The men pushing the trams did not look up, their heads were down into their shoulders, their bodies streaked in black sweat. In the narrow entrance to their heading, away from the lights, they felt their way along, their lamps scything through the darkness, cutting a beam in which the black dust danced.

Tom was bent double now as the seam reduced in size and then he crawled, with Frank, Davy's marrer, who had been put with him today, going on ahead, until they reached the face.

Frank was quick with his pick, hammering with short sharp blows while Tom heaved the broken lumps. They worked in silence changing jobs to ease the tearing muscles of shoulders, back and stomach, lying down and throwing the pick-head deep into the coal and, when straining thighs could take no more, they squatted. And however much coal was moved, more was always there, waiting.

It was there above him too, Tom knew. Hanging there with its miles of height and weight. It grew grass on the top and grazed sheep but hung waiting over the ants of men which picked and irritated its great bulk here below. It had chosen not to fall yet, not on him but he was reminded each day that it was only waiting as a fine coal-dust spewed down all the time and lay in every crease of skin, every pore; filling nostrils, mouth and lungs. Oh yes, Tom ground out, as he heaved at his pick and pushed back the coal to Frank, kicking the slag to the sides as he worked, you remind me you're there, you bugger. Even when I eat me bait, when I drink me tea, you're there crunching in me teeth, reddening me eyes, falling in me cuts.

231

He never counted the hours, just lay, crawled, squatted and picked at the coal, grabbing a sip of tea now and then; smelling the coal, the excrement, hearing the rats and he longed for the end of the shift, longed for the end of fear and screaming muscles. He tore his shoulder as they edged and crawled back towards the main seam when they had no more strength and it was, thank God, the end of the shift. He felt the tear but could not see the blood; it ran down his back and dripped on to the ground as black as the sweat which joined it.

His legs always shook as they walked down the main heading which was brick-arched and busy. But there was soon to be air, air and light and the coolness of a breeze. The clean, clean air; until tomorrow of course. He breathed and coughed, breathed and coughed as he slumped towards home, towards the water which would sluice him clean; his body and his mind.

May had set the buckets out in the wash-house as Tom had done for Davy and Uncle Henry, and Frank and Edward before they had gone to the Midlands and the factories.

Inside the wash-house, he could feel the stiffness of his clothes as he dropped them on to the floor. He leant against the inside of the door, the trembling still in his limbs, his arms too tired to raise the buckets. Let me be for a minute, he moaned to himself. Just let me be, I'm so bloody tired, so bloody scared. He stood naked, his head thrust back on the door and felt the roughness of the wood against his shoulders and buttocks. He fingered the raised untreated grain, traced it up and down and slowly the panic subsided, slowly the steam from the buckets looked inviting, looked normal. He took the first and poured it over his head, his body; gasping as it covered his face and then on down his chest and back. He lathered the soap and, still standing, ran it over his face, the whole of his body, eager now to remove the taint of the coal. Another bucket, another soap and then another so that the water slopped over his feet before running across the floor into the gutter which ran to a drain in the corner.

He scrubbed until his flesh felt raw and at last the coal was nearly gone. He could see his own colour, his own flesh and now he stepped into the bathtub, easing himself down into and under the water, his hair floating, his muscles easing into looseness.

'I'm ready, May,' he called and waited as she came from the

kitchen. Much thinner now she was, but still a smile, though with Davy at Lutters it didn't reach her eyes. Her scrubbing was hard across the back and shoulders, as it had to be, and the knots between his shoulders eased and he saw the blackness float past his hips and cover the water right up to the edge of the bath.

'There you are, bonny lad. A bit of a soak and then a cup of tea.'

She shook her wet hands at him and he dodged and ducked and laughed. He was always surprised when he laughed because he felt sure that just one more day in the pits would dry all the joy into a black dust.

The water still had some warmth and he ducked himself down for one more minute then he would sluice himself and climb into the clothes that May had brought and put on the chair which no one would sit on because it was rotten.

He wondered what it would be like to have Grace scrub his back, her plump soft arms holding one shoulder so that she could have purchase with the brush and the thought of her hand on his body made him flush with heat. They had kissed of course and he had felt the weight of her full breasts in his hands but always through clothes. He had never felt her flesh, her blue-veined flesh, never run his finger from her throat to her nipple and kissed that luscious softness. He dreamt of it more and more because soon he would go to College in Newcastle and then on down to London for three years. Would she come too?

He stepped out of the bath and held his breath as he poured the last bucket over himself. It would be cold by now and perhaps it was a good thing, he thought grinning.

And then he stopped. Oh God, he had to go to Don and his face set and he was glad his body had thickened with muscle.

He walked from May's, through Beckworth Alley, up past the school and down the alley where Annie had stood when she had come to say goodbye. His boots were noisy in the streets and alleys where children hung about at the back of yards, too thin and tired to play, some just squatting as they copied their fathers, doing nothing. Men were on street corners, propped up against lampposts and Tom walked past quickly, nodding as they said they'd see him tonight at the meeting. He kept his eyes lowered, ashamed of their redness which showed he'd had a day's work and they hadn't.

It made him angry and his jaw was clenched when he came through Don's backyard. He moved past the privy and into the kitchen. Don would be there doing his books; he was always there in the afternoon while Albert took over the shop. People slipped in the backyard; men with their caps drawn low over their heads, women with their shawls across their faces, barely able to repay the interest let alone the loan.

He realised that he hadn't locked the gate and he wanted no interruption for what he had to do this afternoon so he turned as Don looked up, turned without a word and walked back sliding the lock across and entering the kitchen again.

Don had half risen from his chair. 'What the bloody hell do you think you're doing? I've a business to run, Tom.'

He was resting on his hands which had gone white where the wrists had creased with his weight but his face was tanned by the sun and Tom felt a further spurt of anger that his own had the pallor of a pitman. He stood there facing Don, his cap folded in his hand, then took a chair from the hearth and set it opposite. The kitchen was dirty; there were dishes piled up in the sink and green slime where the tap had dripped. He sat down. Albert had not allowed Annie to have visitors so this was all new to him. There was a low fire in the grate and a kettle was on the hob but not boiling yet, a broom was propped against the wall but the floor was dirty with bits of paper screwed up and scattered around.

Don was watching him. He had a wooden box and a ledger written up in pencil on the table. His hair was too long and falling in his eyes, his mouth was pinched and he turned a pencil round and round between his two hands.

'Well, what d'you want? A bit short, are you?' Don laughed.

Tom felt the heat rising in him, the heat of an anger which was years old.

'No, I'm not, bonny lad, but you're about to be.'

Don looked at him and put the pencil down. 'What d'you mean by that?' His face was wary.

Tom told him then about the conversation he had heard in the pub. Explained that the men were in an angry mood, that the means test was pinching and they wanted to get back at

234

someone and that Don would be that person and it looked as though it would be soon.

Don flicked a pencil across the table and lounged back in his chair.

'Don't be so bloody daft,' he sneered. 'If they were after anyone, they'd be after Albert.'

But Tom shook his head. 'Nay lad, it's you they want. You grew up with them, remember. You're young and greedy and that's what they don't like.'

His words had become hard; he realised that he wasn't afraid of Don any more. He had always been, he knew suddenly, and had let Annie do the fighting, but not any more. She was worried about Don and so was he.

Don said nothing, just tapped the table and then rose and propped himself up against the fender.

'You're asking me to drop the interest rate, is that it?'

Tom nodded. 'If you drop by quite a bit, Don, word would get round by the end of the day and you'd be safe. I could spread it about at the meeting tonight too, if you like.'

Don was pacing in front of the fire now. 'Well, I don't like. I don't believe a word of it,' he said. 'I think you're making every bloody bit up. You just can't stand me getting on, that's it, isn't it? Annie's been rabbiting on as well and I reckon you're both jealous because I'm going up you see. You've come to put the dampers on; that's what Albert's been saying and I reckon he's right.'

Tom leant forward. 'For God's sake, man. I've come to warn you. I'd get a good belting if anyone knew. I don't want to see you getting hurt, that's all. I want to see you doing the right thing by everyone and I want to see you getting on, of course I do, but not like this.'

Don moved to the door, holding it open.

'I told you, I don't believe you so you can get out and leave me to get on with my life and you get on with yours and your bloody stupid politics. Just stop siding against me, the pair of you. It's like Albert says, you both hate me.'

Tom rose, his cap was still in his hand and he stuffed it in his pocket. Don looked tired he saw, tanned but tired.

'Don't be bloody stupid, no one hates you and I'm not going Don, not until you bring your rates down. I'm not having you beaten up by anyone but me and I'll do it if you don't give in any other way. That way you'll still have your head on your shoulders, not a bloody smashed eggshell to hold in your hands.' He moved towards Don now. 'For God's sake,' he ground out, 'don't be so stubborn. Annie's right worried about you, you know she is.'

Don was still holding the door. 'The pair of you can sod off together. You always were together weren't you, always. You on the inside, me out there somewhere.' He flung his hand wide. 'Now bugger off home, Tom.'

He moved out into the yard, towards the gate. The shadows were thick today in the light of the sun and Tom took off his jacket and flung it on the ground.

'Don,' he said softly. 'We care about you. We don't want you to be hurt. For God's sake, you're family, man.'

Don turned, his face red and hands bunched. 'You don't care, you and she don't care. Thick as thieves you've always been. Haven't wanted me around.'

Tom walked towards him. 'That's not true.'

He searched in his mind, looked back at the years which had gone. 'That's not true, man. You were older, had your own friends; you had Georgie and then you went to Yorkshire and, by the time you came back, there was no home left. We were all on our own. Think about it, man. We both care for you. I keep telling you, that's why I'm here.' He stopped and drew a deep breath. 'But you're not that easy to love, Don. You shrug us off. You're a bit like Albert, you know. He's made you like this. He did his best to get back at Archie through hurting Annie and now it's you. You're going to get hurt now. For God's sake, I wouldn't be here if you weren't me brother and I cared.'

There was a pause and then Don said slowly and clearly, his mouth thin-lipped. 'But you're not me brother, are you? You're a bastard.'

Tom knew he would say it, knew that Don would throw it in his face at some stage but he did not move, just looked and said quietly:

'I'm your brother and I'm not going to have someone come and bash your bleeding head in, so are you going to lower your rates?'

Don shook his head and they stared at one another and then Tom moved quickly but Don was quicker and the blow caught

Tom on the side of the head. Here was another, hard into the stomach and Tom felt the breath go from his body and was surprised at Don's strength; at his speed. He stepped back quickly. It was not going to be as easy as he had thought to stop the bloody fool from meeting a few men on a dark night.

He closed and they slugged punch for punch, their breath mixed in harsh pants and the yard reeled round them as they pushed and punched from wall to wall. Tom's lip was bleeding and he had blood on his shirt but Don's was worse. His nose was pumping blood and Tom backed off.

'Come away now, man. That's enough.' But Don came after him and the fury that was in both of them exploded and they knew nothing but darkness and blows and grunts. They went down, their arms round one another, their fists still punching into sides and backs.

Tom's knuckles were bruised and one hand was caught between Don and the ground and he feared for his painting and reared up with his body, punching Don to the jaw, until he rolled over and then was able to snatch out his arm, then he grabbed Don's hair and pulled him back to lie flat beneath him.

'Lower your bloody rates will you, man,' he shouted, his breath coming in gasps.

Don just looked at him through swollen eyes and Tom's heart broke for this man who had always been his brother and the heat left him. He released his hair and instead gripped Don's shoulders and shook him.

'For God's sake, Don lad, I don't want you bloody killed. Can't you see that? We care, of course we care, that's why I'm here.'

He sighed at the blank look in Don's face, the lack of response and he clambered off him, dusting his trousers down with hands that trembled. His legs were weak and his lip was swelling. He ran his hands through his hair and looked again at Don, then reached down with his hand. There was no movement from Don, he just looked back up at him and then, as Tom dropped his hand he raised his.

'Give us a hand up then, lad,' he said through lips that were swollen. His clasp was strange to Tom. He had never held Don's hand in his before and he pulled him up, helped him back inside to the darkness of the kitchen and his chair. Neither of them spoke and the air was loud with laboured breath as he moved to the sink and poured them both a drink and hoped to God that Annie never heard about this.

'Don't tell Annie about this, Tom,' said Don, mirroring his thoughts. 'She'd give us both hell.' He looked at Tom and winked, if that swollen lid could wink and Tom tried to laugh but his chest hurt too much so he just slumped down in the chair and they sat for minutes in silence.

'What'll you do Don, lad?'

Don sat hunched forward, his hands between his knees and said nothing for a while. The fire was out now, grey and lifeless in the grate and Tom was too winded to riddle it back.

'Since you've asked me so nicely, I reckon I'll lower the interest rate.'

Don's voice was thick and Tom smiled, then stopped. His lip was too painful.

'And I'm right sorry about what I said,' Don went on. 'I get clumsy, living here. I forget about people.' His movements were slow and painful and Tom nodded.

'I know, it's all right, but we didn't want you to get hurt, see. We're all family, aren't we?' They looked at one another and at their own bruises, shrugged and laughed. Tom could not remember the last time they had laughed together.

Don rose stiffly and took a towel from the fender. 'Come here then, lad, and I'll do your face, then you do mine. We'd best get a bit of cold on these before we both look like footballs.' He dabbed at Tom's lip and his cut brow, then handed the towel to Tom who did the same to him.

The afternoon turned into evening and they sat at the table, cold cloths pressed against their faces, talking of the years gone by; the horses on the moors which galloped so smoothly that you did not know you were on one, the early morning exercise, the feeling when a race was won. They talked of growing up, of Betsy who Tom had still not seen. They talked of Archie and his death, of Annie's continuing bitterness. Of Sarah and Georgie and now Don knew and would never again talk of him as he had. They also discussed Albert and Don said he liked the old bugger and thought he could turn the business round and the old boy at the same time. It was worth a try.

He wouldn't come to the pub with Tom.

'Another night,' he said as Tom opened the gate. 'You'll not get me involved in your crazy ideas,' and as Tom left he called: 'Thanks, lad, and how about you doing as Annie wants and make up with Betsy?'

Tom waved back but did not go to the pub because, as he approached from Enderby Terrace, the disaster siren rose above the town, wailed and tore through the early evening air and he ran, ran back down the street, his ribs hurting but he did not notice. He ran and the breath jogged in his chest like a knife but he knew he must keep on because it was Lutters Pit, Davy's pit, and he could see the coal which was above him this morning piling down on top of the men, on top of soft flesh, grunting and grinding the life from them.

It had been Davy of course, it had to be him, May kept saying as they carried him back to the house much later when the bodies had been dug out. She washed him, wiping the dead blood from his ears and nose and mouth. Henry had straightened him out while Tom stood at the side of the front room watching and felt the fear and grief building up as though he were a dam. He remembered Annie screaming and shouting when her da had died and he wanted to hang back his head and do as she had done.

He turned from the house, walking at first, past the drawn windows that lined the streets like dead eyes. The town was in mourning but that wouldn't bring him back, bring his young body back, whole and strong, bring back the light in those blank eyes that looked just like houses. He walked quicker now; he wanted to reach her, to feel her hold him, to cry and weep and have her make it better.

His boots struck sparks as he moved over the cobbles; his feet were heavy and the night seemed black as pitch but when he lifted his head it was a deep blue and the stars were out alongside the moon.

He was nearly there now and he began to run, thrusting open the yard gate, past the stable and in through the door, his hands finding the latch as though it was yesterday. And she was there, gazing into the fire, her arms plump where the sleeves had been rolled up, her hands motionless on her lap. He stood in the doorway and the tears were coming now, loud shaking sobs.

She had turned at the noise of his entrance and moved to take him in her arms.

'Oh Mam,' he wept. 'Our Davy's dead,' and felt her hold him close and he sank into her warmth.

CHAPTER 17

Tom changed gear as he roared Davy's motorbike, which May had said he could take, up and over the hill as he left Wassingham that same night. It was midnight but he had to get to Gosforn to see Annie and tell her about Davy, tell her that things had changed now, that the future was to be different. He pushed up the goggles and wiped his cheek with his finger where the sweat and grime from the road had started to chafe the cut that he had received in his fight with Don.

The villages he rode through were dark and quiet and the hedges of the road and the fields beyond stood out black against the navy of the sky.

He thought of his mam whom he had left just a few moments ago; of the feel of her arms as she drew him into the kitchen when he was desolate and in pain. The room had been brighter somehow than he remembered and he could not think why until he noticed the patchwork cushions on the hard wooden chairs, the bright tablecloth. Even his cut-down chair had a cushion and he had been surprised that Betsy had kept it.

She had taken him across to the fire, sitting him in her chair, stroking his hair. She had heard of course but listened as he told her again and again, in short bursts. It had all come out. Davy who was so quiet and dead and black, and later there had been Annie who had gone, a mother who had given him away. It all came out, bursting and stopping then coming again and his head had lain against her body and she had held him to her, rocking him, her apron smelling of clean boiling, not the greasy staleness of the days gone by.

He had said how he had wanted to come before but could never do it and she nodded, understanding him better than he did himself. Her hair was grey now and there were lines around her eyes and down to her mouth, deep as though carved with a

241

chisel but the blotchiness of the booze was gone, there was no smell on her but that of baking.

She had made tea; thick and brown and they talked of Joe who was in bed and she had smiled at him as she told him of Annie's room which was now hers. Done up with me own money, she had said, and he had reached over and taken her hands, gently because he could feel the throbbing heat of their pain.

He had asked her not to give May money for him any more because he was earning now but she had shaken her head and explained how she wanted to, needed to, because she could not forgive herself for not keeping him and Annie.

Over cheese and bread he had told her how he liked the room and she had laughed and he had no recollection of hearing that sound from her before. As he leant into the bike to take the sharp bend which meant he was halfway to Annie's, he shook his head at the thought. But she had laughed and said that she had finished the patchwork before her fingers packed up for good.

They had talked of Davy again, so young, so much to give and he had felt lightheaded and restless, unable to sit, unable to eat and had put his plate down on the table and paced the room, touching the dresser, free of dust now, moving to the back door and looking out, up at the sky. He had heard Beauty in her stable, shuffling and stamping and had walked out into the warm night air and leant in, running his hand down her neck, stroking her soft nose.

His mam had been sitting as he had left her when he returned and asked her if she was happy. He sat at her knee on the floor with his legs crossed, his hands playing with the rag rug beneath him which was a mixture of blues and red worked into a soothing design. She nodded. The fire was hissing as a damp coal dried out and she explained that she was happy because she was her own woman now.

Is it enough for you though? he had asked. You're a young woman still and she had laughed in a great peal that made him smile even as he remembered it and told him that 33 wasn't young round their way and that, aye, it was enough for her since she had not known a man's touch since his father.

Tom had said nothing but had felt the shock run through him as he thought of Archie and the years of their marriage. She had gazed calmly into the fire, her hair neat in its bun, her floral frock spotless with its small round-edged collar.

She explained how Archie had not wanted a wife and that she was pleased now because it enabled her to remember Barney more clearly. He was a good man, your da, she had said, and had gone on to tell that he was a face-worker in the pits until the war and she would be eternally grateful that, when he'd died, he hadn't been the same as poor Davy stuck like a rat in a trap but in the open air though it had been raining and he hadn't liked the rain. She had stroked Tom's hair with the back of her hand. So like him you are, she had said, and, thank God, soon there'll be no more pit for you my lad and never another war.

She had sounded distant as though she was remembering things long gone which were still clear but only for her to see. He was a real bonny lad he was, Tom, strong but not tall; I wish you'd known him.

He had not asked her more then but he would another time because he was hungry now to know and see and feel his father. To know what he sounded like, know what he painted, what he drew because, as he had his father's body, he would also have his talent.

As he passed the first houses of Gosforn he throttled back to quieten the bike. His arms were shaking now from the vibration and from tiredness but his mind was racing still with thoughts and feeling and decisions he must make.

Annie woke to the sound of knocking but couldn't for a moment think what the noise meant, then she heard Val and Sarah calling.

'Who is it? Just a moment.' Then Sarah spoke more quietly to Val. 'Better fetch the poker.'

Annie leapt from bed into her dressing-gown and slippers, then on down the stairs. When Sarah opened the door, Tom stood there.

His face was grimy from the road dust with white patches where his goggles had been, his lip was swollen and his cheek cut. He wore his dark jacket only and she knew he must be cold. Pushing past Sarah who stood speechless in the hallway, her hair tucked up in a net, she pulled him in, feeling the trembling in his body as he clung to her.

'Davy's dead,' he said and Sarah gasped and Val moved up behind them.

'Shut the door, Sarah,' said Annie with one arm round Tom. She moved with him into the sitting-room as she would have done with one of the patients in the ward. 'Can we have some tea, Val, or perhaps cocoa would be better.'

She put on the light and sat him in the chair near the fire which had been banked up for the night and still gave off a little heat. Sarah sat down looking frail suddenly, while Val disappeared into the kitchen. Annie was calm as she sat on the arm of Tom's chair, one hand on his shoulder.

'I've been to Mam's,' he said. 'We talked and she helped but he was too young to die, Annie. It was that bloody pit; it had been closed too long and the maintenance had just not been done. God, if he were here now, he'd be slanging the bloody owner something shocking.' His voice broke but there were no tears. He punched one hand to the other then winced and Annie saw his bruised knuckle.

Val brought him cocoa and he held it between both those hands and sipped and talked while they listened and watched but said little until he was talked out, until he was tired, finally tired.

Annie still sat on the arm of his chair with a hand on his shoulder. The photograph of Sarah skiing shone in the light from the lamp next to it and outside the birds were beginning to stir as the dawn threatened to bring a weak sun to the early morning. It was four o'clock and she leant over him and gently touched his face.

'And how did you manage these cuts? Were you in on the rescue then?' He looked up at her, his lids heavy, his face drawn with exhaustion. God, he was so tired now, so bloody tired and still hadn't told her of his decision.

'Annie, I won't be going into business with you now. I shall have to take over from Davy,' he sagged back in the chair, unable any more to keep awake, to cope with the voices that were jumping in his head, clamouring to be heard.

Annie and Sarah fetched blankets down from the chest and pillows and together they made him walk to the settee, removed his jacket and boots and he was asleep before they closed the door. Annie went with Sarah to her bedroom, crossing to the window and looking out through the open curtains. The sky was lifting into a paler shade and against it the trees were grey not black any more and soon colour would be flooding into the garden, into the road which she overlooked.

She turned. 'It's a pig's ear, isn't it, Sarah?'

Sarah was sitting in the cane chair near the bed, her pink wool dressing-gown folded round her and the satin quilted collar turned up at the back. She reached to her neck and flattened it.

'That's one way of putting it, my dear.'

Annie moved to the bed and sat on the thick blue blanket which was still crumpled and thrown back just as it had been by Sarah when Tom had knocked. The floral bedspread was folded neatly at the foot of the bed as it was every night before Sarah went to bed; as hers was too.

'Of course it is the grief talking,' Sarah went on. 'He won't give up his art so easily.'

Annie had meant Davy's death but she pulled herself round to Tom's words. 'He won't give up his art, you can bank on that, but he means what he says. Our Tom always means what he says. It'll be his way of paying back I reckon, if he takes over Davy's activities.' She nodded because she understood.

'Oh I can see that, he was so very fond of the boy and it is such a waste, such a tragedy, but Annie, what about you, the business course you had decided to do?' Her voice was concerned.

Annie looked down at her hands as she drew the dressing-gown around her. She had made it at school during needlework and the seams were puckered and it did not hang straight but the colour suited her; a pale green which made her look a bit fatter, rather more of a woman. But what about her future, she thought, and felt a sense of release now, a release which would always be tinged by fear though. Fear for Tom working in the pit because she could not bear to lose the bonny lad, could not bear it if he died under that stinking mass of coal.

Sarah was frowning at her, her eyes concerned, her hands pressed tightly together.

'I'd like to nurse, Sarah.' Annie knew now that she had wanted this ever since she started work at the hospital. She picked some fluff from the blanket and rolled it into a ball between her thumb and finger which sprang back when she released it.

245

'But Annie,' Sarah protested. 'My dear, it is such hard work, so little money and you would need to leave us, to live in the hospital.' Her face had paled and her hand was across her mouth. Annie looked at the ball of fluff, she would not look at the face that went with that voice.

'I know all these things, Sarah, but I need hard work, it makes me feel myself somehow. It's all I've known up to now, you see. This has been a holiday for me, a rest to sort myself out. It's time I got back into the real world, a bit like Tom, I suppose.'

She looked at Sarah then. She was sitting back in her chair, her hand away from her mouth and lying casually on her lap and her expression calm. Annie knew the effort that it took and was more grateful than she had ever been to Sarah before.

'I don't want Tom to go back down the pits but I can't stop him. He must be free to make his choice.' Annie was picking her words extremely carefully. 'Davy's death has given me the freedom to choose too and nursing is really all that I want to do, at this time. I don't want to start the business yet.' She would not say that nursing would give her freedom from Sarah, from the burden of taking from her all the time. This would hurt the woman she had grown to love.

To be earning, instead of enrolling on a course which would cost Sarah money, was a luxury she craved. She was determined to lift herself up, to be somebody, as Sarah wished, but it had to be done on her own and nursing would pay her, give her lodgings and the responsibility for other people's well-being in a professional sense. She wanted to be Sister Manon, a person in her own right, and that was a kind of freedom.

Sarah had risen and come to sit next to her on the bed. She took her hand and smiled. 'If that is what you want, my dear child, then of course we shall pursue it.'

Her voice sounded almost as usual and any tremor could have been put down to tiredness. Annie put her arm round her.

'Thank you, Sarah.'

They understood one another and sat quietly thinking and remembering the calm of their time together, the ties which now held them. Sarah stirred herself at last.

'I think that it might be an idea however to keep something of an eye on our young Tom. What we don't want is a bad seam coming his way because of his socialist activities. I rather feel he could become a little extreme under the circumstances.'

'I know,' replied Annie. 'That's what I can't bear to think of. Imagine if he was hurt.' But she could not go on. Sarah patted her hand.

'I think I shall mention it when I write to Bob Wheeler,' she mused.

Annie jerked up her head. 'God. You write to God.'

Sarah burst out laughing. 'We correspond from time to time, my dear. But I'm not sure that he'd appreciate the promotion you've heaped upon him; he's an atheist after all.'

'But why do you write to him?' Annie protested. 'He's old and dry and Da's friend anyway.'

Sarah sighed. 'Don't be silly, Annie. He's been a good friend to you. How else do you think I knew that things were not as they should be when I came for you. Poor Bob thinks he was in some way to blame for your father's death; he feels he could have done more to stop it happening and we talked at the funeral, before and after the crystal decanter episode.' She nudged Annie who blushed but said nothing. 'I asked him to check up on things and he did. He's a good man.'

So Da, thought Annie, you've left someone else with a packet of grief too have you, a burden of responsibility and she remembered how her father had hated nurses and it made her decision even sounder.

'Please write to him then, Sarah,' she said. 'Tom'll need all the help he can get, one way and another.'

As Tom left for Wassingham that morning he dug in his pocket and brought out Da's watch. 'It's from Don,' he said. 'He wanted you to have it, to keep.'

Annie felt the cold of the silver in her hand and the chain flopped over her hand and swung to and fro. She looked at Tom who shuffled his feet and climbed on to the bike, his head away from her.

'We had a bit of a talk yesterday and he's seen sense about the loans and one or two other things.'

She looked at his hands again, at his split lip and cheek.

'He's all right, is he?' she asked.

Tom lifted his leg and brought it down on the kick-start; the engine roared into life. He nodded.

'He's fine,' he shouted. 'We're going for a drink next week.' He looked suddenly bleak and she cupped his face in her hands.

'I love you, Tom. You must be careful, bonny lad. Careful in that pit and with your mouth at the meetings.' She was shouting to make herself heard above the noise of the bike and he nodded as he leant forward and kissed her cheek.

'You're sure about the nursing then, are you?' he asked in her ear. Sarah was on the step watching.

She nodded. 'I'll get me school certificate and then I'll go to Newcastle but you must keep on painting though you'll need a teacher. Somehow we must get you a teacher.'

He grinned and pulled at her hair and before he could go she pulled his hands to her lips. 'You must be careful,' she insisted as he slipped the clutch and pulled away from her.

'Be careful,' she called after him as he turned to wave and the smell of exhaust lingered where he had been.

CHAPTER 18

Tom clutched Grace's arm and pulled her through the back gate into the yard. Betsy had daffodils growing in a tub by the edge of Beauty's stable and they were bright with only a light covering of black smut. She was cool and her mouth tasted soft and clear and her lips pressed back and her body was hard against him.

'That's enough of that, you two, it's Sunday,' laughed Betsy from the kitchen door and they turned and waved to her.

'I know it's Sunday, that's why I'm only kissing her once, before lunch anyway.' Tom tilted his cap on to the back of his head and leaned over Beauty's stall, stroking her and bringing out the apple which had been stored in crumpled newspaper along with the rest since last autumn in May's cupboard. It was wrinkled and soft, a murky yellow, but Beauty ate it dripping juice into his hand which he kept beneath her mouth, letting her nibble and kiss him with her warm blackness.

Grace leant against his side, her head on his shoulder. 'We'll take her for a walk this afternoon, shall we?' she asked, stroking the pony's ear so that she twitched away from her. 'Up the beck. It's warm enough.'

Tom slipped his arm around her, pulled her even closer against him, moving his hand upwards until he could stroke her breast. Her nipple hardened and she moaned softly. 'I'd like that,' he murmured. 'It'll take me mind off tonight.'

Grace pulled away, her head up and her curls spinning as she stalked from him to the kitchen, her buttocks jumping beneath her yellow dress. Tom laughed and called:

'I'd like that even if I didn't have the meeting tonight.'

He watched as she shook her fist at him before disappearing in to Betsy.

He was nervous and leant on the stall with both arms, letting

Beauty lift her head and blow hot breath into his chest. Annie had said it was time he did it, time he gave the talk that Davy should have done six months ago but which his death had prevented. Betsy had agreed with Annie and promised him a lamb roast to put some iron in his blood.

He sighed and smoothed Beauty's fringe. The days in the pit stretched endlessly now that there was no stopping-point any more, no art school to make the minutes and hours seem an irritation to be endured temporarily. That fact had clouded his grief for Davy and made his anger sharper for, if he was to stay here and take Davy's place, he wanted the men to feel anger along with him, to fight for something better, to work in the bloody pits and be able to afford food for hungry bellies. He wanted those out of work to feel that they should be employed and, if they weren't, to have, as a right, enough to live on without losing their dignity. Davy had been right to make them want to talk, make them want to think and he owed it to the lad to take his notes and make them into words.

He felt soft hands slide round his waist and her breasts and belly press into his back and buttocks. 'Come away in, bonny lad,' Grace said. 'Your mam's ready to see your ugly mug, you know.'

Betsy was pouring out steaming water from the greens into the sink. She held the lid on and kept the gap to half an inch and Tom felt the damp heat as he kissed her and took the pan from her.

'Don't let them fall out, like you did last week,' Betsy scolded and he grinned.

'Taken the gravy water out first then, have you?' he replied with a wink to Grace.

'Teach your grandmother to suck eggs, would you?' Betsy sniffed and went back to stirring the thick liquid on the top of the oven.

Grace was laying out the knives and forks and Tom saw that there were spoons too.

'Having a pud today then, are we?' He tipped the greens out into the bowl.

'Aye, lad, thought you'd need a lining to your stomach if you're to be telling the lads what they should be thinking tonight.'

Tom sat down; there were three places laid, so Joe was out at

Newcastle again then. He was glad; he wanted his mother to himself. Joe was all right really but he was her boss, wasn't he, so it made for a funny feeling. Funny-looking bloke and all, he was, long and thin and jerked his head a bit like that cock of Annie's but at least he didn't crow. Just sat there looking as though he should have a drip on the end of his nose and always with a worried look on his face. Maybe it was his age, 50 was getting on a bit.

He smoothed the cloth with his hands, there was black dirt under his fingernails and a flick of green paint on his cuff. May would grizzle when she saw that but Tom guessed that she liked it really for it gave her something to do, something to pound at in the tub; take out her rage at the pits which had sent two of her boys away to the factories and crushed the breath out of the other.

'I'm not trying to tell the men how to think, Mam.' She brought the meat to the table and the juice of the lamb oozed from beneath the joint and the fat was cooked to a crisp. She smiled at him and passed the carvers.

'You do it, bonny lad, and get yourself sat down, Grace.' She pointed to the chair opposite Tom and sat down herself. She looked pleased, her mouth lifted in a smile and her blue eyes relaxed. Her hands were not so swollen today Tom noticed as he took the knife from her.

'Better are they?' he asked. Grace was putting the plates in front of him and, as his ma nodded, he cut the meat and lifted two slices on to each plate. It was pink in the centre and his mouth watered. He wondered if the rich aroma would float through the window and out past the back doors of the other houses in the street and the thought made him feel uncomfortable. There'd be no meat for most of the buggers today, he thought, or the next day or the next. The carvers had bone handles and they were well balanced.

The light of the fresh spring day and the sound of the birds as they came after Beauty's oats came in through the window.

'I thought Don might come,' Betsy said as she passed the mint sauce to Grace along with an extra potato, waving aside her protests. 'You've gone thin lass and you suit a bit of flesh, don't she, Tom?'

'Oh aye,' Tom said, but thought she's bloody marvellous whether she's thin or fat and remembered the first time they

251

made love, up on the hill by Bell's Farm when it was so cold the grass had been like dry bracken but they'd not noticed. He felt the warmth of his longing rise in him and looked across the table, his eyes heavy with thoughts of her, and she kicked him and his ma asked:

'So where's Don then, lad?'

Tom swallowed past his throat which felt swollen, then forced down some lamb. 'He's off to Annie's, today. He said he'd like to come next week if that was all right. He's borrowed the motor bike and will be back tonight. If he's got a strong enough stomach he said he'd come on to the meeting, if only to give me a bloody good heckle.'

Grace laughed. 'I bet old Albert's right livid at his going across to Gosforn again.' She passed Tom some more greens and Tom helped Betsy to cut her meat.

She nodded her thanks and held her fork awkwardly as she ate her meal. 'There was bad blood between him and Archie. He won't want them two to be friends, I reckon.' Her lip began to tremble. 'I never realised how he was though or I never would have . . . '

'Hush now, Mam,' Tom interrupted.

'I never would have sent her there if I'd known he was so bad. I reckon he wanted them kids ruined to spite Archie, you know, and I should have seen.'

'Now, Betsy,' soothed Grace, 'eat your meal and forget all about it.'

'I can't really remember much about them days you see, it's all a bit of a blur, what went before and what went after.' Her cheeks were red and her eyes darted from one to the other.

'Mam,' said Tom firmly, shaking her arm and feeling its softness beneath his fingers. 'Mam, it's gone now. We're all fine and you should have seen the lad on the bike.' He was speaking loudly now making her listen and he saw her eyes focus on him and knew that he had her attention.

'He's bought himself a helmet and goggles and looks like something out of a horror story.' He laughed and Betsy did too. He felt Grace stroke his leg with her foot and caught her eye which was gentle on his.

'So it's working out, is it, sharing Davy's bike?' Tom nodded and wiped his mouth on his sleeve.

Betsy slapped his hand. 'Use your napkin and don't be a pig,

252

lad.' He raised his eyebrows at Grace and was glad that he had pulled his mam back to today.

'Them eggs you brought back from Annie's were beautiful and fresh. They're in the pudding you know.' Betsy cleared the table and gave Tom the cloth to carry the sponge from the oven to the table. 'She sounds keen in her letters about this nursing, but worried, lad; worried about the pits. She wants you to go on painting.'

'We all do,' agreed Grace, frowning at Tom.

He showed her his cuff. 'See, I've done some this morning already.'

'But Annie says you need a teacher and we reckon a correspondence course is the best idea.'

Betsy sat back at the table heavily and handed the spoon for Grace to dish up. 'Don't we, Grace? You, me and Annie.'

Grace grinned and nodded.

'And I've got the money,' said Betsy.

Tom shook his head. 'No Mam, I've some money from the pits.'

'I've got the money, I said,' insisted Betsy. 'Annie says there's one for six pounds. You send away to London and I'll pay.'

'No, Mam,' said Tom, his mouth full of custard and sponge, his words indistinct.

He winced as Grace kicked him. 'Let her, she wants to,' mouthed Grace. 'Or I'll not go to the beck with you.'

He finished his mouthful, the laughter welling up. Now there was a threat to be reckoned with. Betsy ate on, not looking up as Grace pulled the kettle on to the hob.

'Can you manage it then, Mam?' he said at last when his plate was scraped clean. 'Maybe a couple of bob.' He knew she'd be disappointed but he didn't want to ask her for too much.

She nodded and sat back in the chair with her arms folded. Tom grinned to himself to see her in Archie's chair. She was a strong woman now, his mam was.

'It's not right that you've gone into the pits for good. You should have gone to College and then on to this business with Annie. It's bad you know, the life down there. Your da wouldn't have wanted it for you.'

Tom sighed and pushed back his chair, carrying the pile of

plates that Grace handed to him. 'I know, Mam, but it's just something I've got to do. Maybe later Annie and I'll get together.'

Betsy nodded as she moved over to her seat by the fire.

'Aye, that you will. Ma Gillow always said it would be you and Annie together and so it will be; if not now, later.'

She tucked her head into her neck and smiled as Tom stoked the fire for her and sat down while Grace made a pot of tea.

'So me da wouldn't have wanted me to go into the pit, then?'

Betsy shook her head. 'Nay, lad, he didn't like it himself you know. His da was killed when a cage fell and my Barney couldn't forget that. He didn't like the dark either, or the rain.'

'So tell me more about him, Mam.' Tom was leaning forward, his hands resting between his knees. Grace turned and watched him, then brought tea to him and Betsy.

'How old was he when he died then, Betsy?' she asked gently.

'Nineteen he would have been, lass. Nineteen, that's all. He was the only one, you know. There were no other children.'

'So what was me grandma like then, Ma? Did she visit us?'

Betsy shook her head and sipped her tea, holding the cup between two hands as she had always done. Grace sat down next to Tom, lifting the cushion from his cut down chair as she did so, tracing with her finger the hexagonal lines of stitching. Tom watched the line of her face, her cheek, her chin and he reached out and touched her softly. Betsy nodded as she watched them.

'No,' she answered quietly, blowing the steam from the top of her cup. 'No, she never saw you, lad. She died not so long ago but didn't want to know me. I was a slag, you see. I'd had a bairn out of wedlock and nice girls don't. You were her grandson and she didn't want to know you even though both her men had gone.' Her face was sad but she smiled gently at him. 'But my mam thought you were a right cracker, she did, and then she died too, of the flu, you know.' She sighed and Grace put the cushion back in the chair. 'Joe cut that chair down, you know, lad. He's a good man in his way. Took me in, paid me he did, when lots wouldn't have done.'

'Aye, Mam, I know.' Tom replaced his empty cup on the table. The dresser against the wall was catching the sun, the blue and white plates looked fresh and clean. 'So didn't me da ever think of doing painting then?'

Betsy looked over her cup at him, her face puzzled. She stretched out her legs and leaned back in the chair.

'Now why would he want to do a thing like that, then?' she asked.

'Well, look at me. I'm like him, you said.'

Betsy rose from her chair, then sat down again. 'Tell you what, lad, take your young legs up them stairs, into your Annie's old room. Bring me down the picture that's on the side of me bed. Off you go now. Grace can hop up with you or stay here and keep me company.'

She smiled at the girl, at her copper curls and soft blue eyes and Grace said, 'We'll have another cup of tea, shall we, Betsy?'

Tom had not been up into the house since the day he left and it all seemed smaller somehow, the black-patterned hall floor, the turned banister which led on up to the study where it had happened. He opened the door and the room was empty. The old dark desk was gone, the prints were no longer on the wall. It was an empty room which did not even hold a ghost, just a vague memory of the man who had locked himself up in here so often, until the last time. The walls had been whitewashed as though to wash away the stains of the past and the northern light made his breathing quicken. He walked on into the room, stood in the centre, turned around judging the size, judging the feel. It was right, you know, just right, he walked swiftly to the door, and down the stairs before he remembered that it was to Annie's bedroom he had been going.

He walked on up as he had done for all those years. The stairs seemed dark when he was a child and his footsteps had always sounded sharp and cold but now there was a carpet on the stairs and at the top a large oil lamp which glowed as the old one had never done. He did not go into Annie's room yet, but opened the door into his own and there were the drawings he had done, still pinned to the walls as he had left them. His old cardigan was on the chest which had been at the bottom of the bed, but now of course there was no bed, for he had taken that with him, the day he had left. There was just a square section of black-painted floorboards surrounded by cracked linoleum. The little table which had held his oil lamp was spotless and there lay his jacks which he had left because he could not believe he was never coming back. He moved to pick up the stones, the hard ball, but then stopped, leaving the room as he had found it; as his ma wanted it.

He crossed the landing into Annie's room and this too had been whitewashed. The bed was draped in a new patchwork quilt in muted beige and purple colours, ones that picked up the rag rug exactly. There were flowers on the dressing-chest and he felt a tightness because Annie had never had it like this and thanked God that his mam now had some beauty, some peace.

There was a picture of a man's face on the bedside table. It was in pencil and he knew it was his da. It was his own face he was seeing but with darker hair. The face of a young man who had only been three years older than him, for God's sake, when he had died.

He picked the drawing up, brought it to the window. It was good, there was life in the face, in the eyes. It was easy for portraits to look like death-masks, the colour too heavy, the eyes blocked in, but this was good.

He took it down to Betsy. 'He was a lovely man, Mam.'

She held it carefully in her swollen hands. 'He said he'd buy me rings for me pretty fingers, called me the Queen of Sheba and afterwards I drew this.' She sat still, looking at the drawing, framed in glass, the mahogany polished until it shone vivid in the firelight.

Tom was still, quite still, watching her, watching her hands, hands that had once drawn this and could now barely hold the frame.

He gripped his own hands tight together, seeing again the design of the rug he had his feet on, the colours of the patchwork and he knew he should have guessed before. His mother, he knew now, had the soul of an artist, his soul and that she must have felt as he did when it was stifled, when life took over and snatched the dream away. One day, he decided, one day when he had done enough here, he would be an artist, then come back, he and Annie together, because they had much to do.

'It's good, Mam, so very good.' He said, 'Look, Mam, if I'm to get on, if I'm to be a painter I'll need another pound towards me postal course. Can you give it to me?' He wanted her to feel that she was making art possible for him.

Grace reached over and took his hand, squeezed it and nodded at Betsy.

'Aye, lad, I reckon I could.' Betsy looked again at the picture. 'D'you really think it's good?' Her voice was tentative.

'It's the best, Mam. It's the best I've seen.' He looked again at the face of his da and knew that here was the real man.

He took Grace's hand and pulled her to her feet.

'We'll go now, Mam, take Beauty for her walk.' But Betsy did not look up. She was gazing at Barney, running her swollen finger over the outline of his face.

As Tom left the room he stopped and turned. 'Mam, d'you think Joe would let me use the study for me studio? It's the light you see; the light is right and if I do the course, I'll need to get a folio together.'

He thought she hadn't heard because she sat so still and then she lifted her face to his and looked hard at him and said nothing.

'D'you think Joe would let me?' he repeated. It was as though she was making a hard decision and thoughts chased across her face too quickly to grasp and then she nodded.

'Oh aye, he'll let you.' But there was a strangeness about her and he turned to go back but Grace called him on.

'I'll pay him, Mam,' he offered as he stepped out into the light.

'No, bonny lad,' Betsy said quietly. 'I'll be the one doing the paying.'

The Lodge Meeting Hall was crowded and Tom slipped through the men, nodding to some, not recognising others. Smoke from cigarettes held in cupped hands rose into the air and stung his eyes. He edged between two groups and forced his way through to the platform, nodding to Davy's mates who were setting up the lectern. Frank patted his shoulder and he nodded, his mouth suddenly dry, his hands shaking and he put his notes down on the sloping stand as the men slowly noticed he was there and the talking became a murmur, then the murmur slipped off into silence.

The only light was on the platform now and he turned to Frank who nodded. 'Get on with it, lad,' Frank whispered, 'they'll not stay quiet for long, the bar's open.'

He turned again to the floor and felt too young for this. It should have been Davy; he was the one the men had come to hear and that was why they were suffering him, so he'd better do a bloody good job, he told himself.

'Davy,' he began tentatively, fingering his notes. 'Davy died just before he was going to talk about the means test; about what it means and his thoughts on where we should be going, what we should be asking our union to do for us. I have,' and he held up pencilled pages, 'his notes here.' His voice was stronger now. He put down the papers and leant on the lectern.

'We all know,' he said, 'that, because of the world depression, there is long-term unemployment and God knows when it is going to end, whilst here we are, up the bloody swanee without a paddle.' He waited for the whistles to die down, the calls and cheers to fall.

'What this has meant to us up here in the North is pit closures, no work for two thirds of us. That means that families cannot buy newspapers, or a stamp to post a letter, can't help a neighbour any more, join a sick club, pay subs to the union. People feel helpless.'

He was in his stride now, the words were coming quicker without any need to look at the notes. His voice was stronger and the trembling in his legs and hands was gone. It was still dark on the floor but he could see shapes, the glow of cigarette ends, the stillness of men listening and felt a surge of power, of enjoyment. The lectern edge was cool and hard as he gripped it again.

'Bairns have no spending money; we have nothing to give them. Their das have no tobacco or beer money; mothers have no dresses. There's not enough food to keep the family healthy or free from hunger that keeps us awake at night. There is not enough coal to keep us warm in winter and we are living on top of a bloody heap of the stuff.' He banged his hand in his fist and nodded at the calls from the hall, the agreement in their tone encouraging him to continue.

'So what have the National Government done, a government which I might add, brothers, is led by a Labour Prime Minister? Why, they have brought in the means test.' He bowed ironically and the catcalls were loud and he held up his hand to quieten the hall.

'The means test is a grand way of lowering the money paid out by the government and at the same time does a bloody good job of lowering the dignity of the unemployed. Who likes snoopers coming in, poking their noses into cupboards, telling us we have to sell grandma's best teapot? Nobody.

'The means test must go, Parliament must be lobbied, we must make our complaints loud and long. Get your unions to make them for you.'

He stood back and let the calls and the talk between the men on the floor continue while he took some water from Frank and sipped at it, asking him over the top of the glass how it was going.

'Good, man,' said Frank. 'You've got them thinking, got them talking. Just give 'em a burst of Davy's allowance idea and call it a night.'

'Aye,' agreed Tom and picked up the gavel. The knocking brought a hush to the hall again.

'But, lads, as we all know and as Davy knew, there is another problem. What about the low wages when we're in work? Work does not bring fresh milk. It does not bring butter. It will bring one egg if you're lucky and that doesn't keep our bairns well. So, you will ask, what do we do?'

'Aye, that's a question could do with some answering right enough,' called a deep voice from the well of the hall and was taken up by others, loud and long.

'Well,' shouted Tom, forcing his voice through the uproar. 'Well; we can stop having bairns but the bosses would like that less than a wage rise because their future workers wouldn't be produced.' He pulled a face and the men laughed. 'We need a decent minimum wage; we need state control of the mines so that our men are on the board and can make sure of safety, reinvestment, a decent return for our work. But, more than that, men.' He held up his hand for silence.

'We need an allowance, not just for the miners but for all the workers in the land above and beyond wages. An allowance that is paid out by the state to the families, a certain amount for each child. That would mean that, low wages or no wages, there would always be enough to feed your bairns.'

There were cheers now and he could feel the sweat running down his back and sides, running down his face and on to his open shirt-collar.

'What about the unions though?' a voice cried from the back of the hall. 'They won't back that idea, it might make owners pay less in wages if they thought we was all getting extra anyway?'

Tom smiled; this'll get them going he thought. 'Then it should be paid direct to the women, that'd settle that argument and give the lasses their own income.'

He watched as men turned to one another and the volume of argument and discussion grew louder and louder. They were talking and that is what Davy had wanted and, bye, he wished Annie had been here to clip back her ears at what he had said about giving it to the women. She'd have been right surprised, right glad, but it wasn't just for her he had said it; he'd done it because it made sense.

He turned and moved over to the chairs where Davy's mates were sitting. They were leaning forward and talking amongst themselves and he listened as he heard Frank say, 'I'd forgotten Davy said that.'

'Well he did,' Tom replied pocketing his notes and standing with his hands in his pockets. 'It makes sense you know. It'll be hard enough to get union backing for the idea but if you make it payable to the women it's different somehow. It doesn't affect their bargaining position so much, does it, when they come to negotiating wages.'

He looked as a smile slowly spread itself over Frank's face. 'Come over to the bar for a drink, lad.' He rose and took Tom's arm but Tom looked over at the men, milling towards the bar which had opened at the end of the hall, at the smoke and the dim lights which had now been lit and his legs felt heavy with tiredness. His head ached with the noise and it was as though a band was being drawn tighter and tighter and he shook his head.

'I'll get on back now, Frank.' He shook his hand, then the others. The grips were firm, the faces friendly. 'I'm tired now and me feet is killing me.' They joined in his laughter and he pushed down the steps, through the men, his back stinging with slaps and his head full of their arguments until at last he was out, into the cool air. He drank in the spring-laden coolness, felt the fine drizzle, relished the quiet once the door swung shut behind him.

He dug in his pocket for his cap, stuck it on his head and sauntered down the street which was dark with many windows boarded up and houses deserted, their tenants gone from them to the South, to anywhere which might give them a living. Yes, the men were arguing, talking; they would have more to think about tonight than how hungry they were, how they were going to last until the end of the week. His boots slipped slightly on the wet cobbles and he hunched his collar up against the increasing wetness.

He was not going home but to the pub where he and Davy had sat the night before he had died. Don had not been there at the meeting and he was glad really. He wanted to be quiet for a moment, to think back over this evening, to think back over Davy's words and check that he had said all that he had wanted the men to hear. Bye, it was a powerful feeling, that it was, standing there knowing that they were listening, knowing that they were chasing around in their minds for questions, answers and arguments. It was a bit like looking at a painting; sizing up the texture, the light, whether the artist had caught the moment, what he was trying to say. He shouldered his way through the doorway of the pub, undoing his jacket and easing the white muffler until it hung loosely.

'Just half a pint,' he said to the barmaid. His voice was hoarse and his throat slightly sore. He took the glass from her, sucking at the froth and taking a mouthful of rich brown beer, feeling it slip down his throat and soothe the rawness.

'You'd better watch yourself, young man. Speaking out like that could see you out of work. One of the Socialist League, are you?'

Tom knew the voice, low and measured and thoughtful but it was a long time since he had last heard it. He did not turn his head, just took a sip before saying. 'I belong to nothing, Mr Wheeler, and my business is none of yours.'

Bob Wheeler laughed. 'Two half pints, please. You'll have another, won't you, Tom? Revolution is thirsty work.'

Tom turned. 'Hardly revolution, Mr Wheeler, and aye, I'll have another drink.' The man had aged, he thought. His hair was now quite grey, his face thinner and his skin was dry and deeply lined.

'Let's sit down?' Bob waved towards a booth in the corner.

The pub was quiet but then there weren't many with money for beer these days, as I've just been saying, thought Tom ironically. The lights were muted and the curtains at the

261

windows were drab and uneven though the table they moved to was spotless. Tom's glass left a wet ring.

'You remember me then, do you?' Bob Wheeler said.

'I remember when you used to visit Archie Manon.'

Bob nodded and brought out his pipe, filling and lighting it while they sat in silence. He had been waiting to speak to Tom, waiting since he had received Sarah's letter asking him to keep an eye. There had been little for him to do so far but if tonight was anything to go by this lad would need a bit of a rein on him, a bit of steering or no pit would touch him. He would be marked down as an agitator, a trouble-maker as his cousin had been. He sucked at his pipe looking over at the lad as he drew on his pint. Maybe he would side-track him with union business. Tom was a good-looking boy, heavy set with intelligent blue eyes and a manner much older than his 16 years. Oh yes, Tom Ryan, there's not much I don't know about you, my lad, he thought, and I daresay rather more than you know yourself.

He smiled to himself at the tone of Sarah's letter; it had been urgent and worried. Well, let's see what we can do about it all, eh? And he shifted in his seat, pleased to be involved again with Archie's family, pleased to be able to pay off his debt but perhaps it was more than that. Perhaps it was because he was lonely that he was prepared to become interested in this young man with the jutting chin. He had spoken well, there was no doubting that and he had caught the men in his hands, something that was hard to achieve.

'So, how many points did you make tonight, then?' Bob asked.

Tom looked confused; he had been thinking of Davy and the night they had sat here and had overheard the group who were going to duff up Don. It seemed an age ago.

'Oh, I don't know. Two main ones, I suppose.' He sat back on the seat and looked at Bob.

'That's what I reckon, lad.' He acknowledged Tom's look of surprise. 'Oh yes, I was there, a union official should know what the members are getting up to! It was good, lad, but leave it at one point each meeting and only up it to two if you must. People don't remember a great deal, you know.'

Tom leaned forward, his brows lowering, his face interested. He was going to learn from this man tonight and they talked then until closing-time and on some more in Bob's house.

It was strange, Tom felt, walking into the small two up two down that Archie used to visit; that he had visited the night before he had killed himself. He wondered whether Archie had sat here as they were doing, round the kitchen table with the fire glowing in the grate, the kettle heating on the range. The table was covered with a heavy wool cloth with darker tassels which caught on Tom's thighs as he sat down. A jug of beer frothed between them and Bob poured them each a mug.

'It'll keep us going until the kettle's boiled,' Bob laughed and Tom nodded and looked at the photographs on the wall to the right of the dresser which had only a few plates propped on the shelves. A man and a woman looking stiff in Victorian dress peered down at them and Tom could see the likeness between Bob and the man.

He pointed and asked, 'Is that your da then?'

Bob craned round and nodded. 'Yes, it is. He was a good man. Bought this house, though it took a lot to do it. He was a pitman, Tom, though I never was; I went into the office.'

'Me da was a pitman an' all,' Tom said tracing the weave of the wool cloth on the table. Bob knew already. He had done some ferreting about, as he had told Sarah, and found out quite a bit about Tom's background, about Barney Grant.

'I know, lad,' he said. 'I know that Barney Grant was a good face-worker, a good pitman.'

Tom sat up, his eyes eager. 'You knew me da then, did you?'

'No, not exactly but I knew of him.' He had found some of Barney's mates, those who had been in the pits with him; joined up with him. He'd found them through the union records and they had wanted to talk but mostly about the war and so he had let them, listening as they spoke of Ypres, which they called Wipers. They told him of the salient which guzzled up lives like a bloody great pig and the waterlogged trenches that never moved forwards. They told him too of the tunnels, one hundred or so feet deep, which the big nobs, as they called the Generals as they spat into the gutter, had thought were a good idea.

One of Barney's friends explained that the idea was to blow the Germans up. He was a cripple of 35 who had broken his back in the pits in '25. Survived that bloody mess, he had hissed, to lose me back in the pits; like that Barney, you know, but Bob did not know and had said so looking along the mean streets which converged on to the corner where they were all

263

standing. The man had shaken his head in disgust. They needed miners, you see, he had sneered, miners to carve out the tunnels, build up the shafts and then lay the charges beneath the German front-lines so what did they do, they took us off the surface, didn't they, brought us down into the clay and put us to work, like bloody rats in a trap again.

They wanted to shift the Germans back off the salient, the man had grunted as Bob frowned, and they couldn't do it from the top so we crept along beneath them, quiet as bloody mice because they were tunnelling too. We lived down there, one of the other men explained. I can still hear the pumps as they kept the water out he had said with a shudder, but not the dampness, so you still coughed and your skin looked white in the lights but at least they had light and electric they were too. The other men nodded and one said that it was grand what could be done when the nobs wanted it enough, while the other cursed and became restless.

Bob had passed round Woodbines and brought them back on to the subject and learned how the men had lived and worked down there until the tunnels were long enough and deep enough and the poor buggers above them had been blown to bits. Went up like a bairn's mud pie kicked by a horse, the cripple had said, but Barney Grant didn't see it, did he. He was killed when the bloody ceiling fell in two weeks before. The man had hunched himself forward in his wooden wheelchair and stabbed a finger at Bob. Gone all the way from our pits, he had said, to die in a bloody frog's. They hadn't told Barney's missus, of course, not that she was his real missus but you know what we mean and Bob had nodded and he remembered their faces even now as they had walked away from him, not wanting a drink, just wanting a job. He had watched them as they walked down the street, all but the one who had told him the most. He was being pushed by his mates. They had all been at Ypres together; they were all out of work together.

He sighed and put his beer down, moving past Tom to the bread-tin, bringing out a loaf and some cheese from the dresser.

'Have a Scotch,' he said to Tom, hoping that he would not ask but knowing that he would.

'No thanks, I never touch it,' replied Tom. 'Tell me about me da.' His face was serious, his eyes steady.

'Have some cheese.' Bob cut some bread and passed it over

on the point of the knife. He moved a plate to the lad and some cheese. 'Tell me, when are you going to start your painting again?'

But Tom did not eat his cheese, did not answer Bob, so, in the end, the older man sat back in his chair and told Tom about his da. About his life as a pitman, about his marrers who had been with him until his death. Tom sat quietly while the fire dwindled and the kettle puffed its lid gently up and down. Silence fell between the men and Tom thought of his mother and knew that he would never tell her that Barney had not seen the sky when he died.

The hours passed as they sat at the table, the older man and the young one talking of Barney, of Betsy, Annie and Grace. Of Don and Albert, of the pits and what could be done. Bob had known Davy, known his thoughts and he grew now to know Tom's.

Tom heaped his bread with cheese as early morning came; some crumbled and fell and he picked each bit up, pressing it against his finger then sucking. It was a sharp salty taste and went well with the beer, and then the tea which they made an hour later. His muscles felt loose and he was leaning easily back in his chair. He must remember to tell Don how God had been made man; he would appreciate that, would that canny lad.

It was three when he reached for his jacket and shrugged himself into it. The next day he'd be for it with Grace; she'd be cold at his hangover when he came into the library after the shift to read up on Van Gogh.

'It's his colour, his fragmented impressionism,' he explained to Bob as he left his house. 'That's what I like. The life in his brushwork.' And Bob told him that he should not be wielding a putter's shovel alongside a palette knife.

'Grace says that he paints as though he has one of her migraines,' replied Tom as he waved to Bob from the street. 'I've got to stay in the pits. It's just something I've got to do for now but me mam's sorting out a studio so that's going to make it grand.'

As he walked back through the streets to May's, Tom pulled his jacket round him and shivered but it was not the cold, it was the thought of the black pit waiting for him.

Betsy lay beside Joe in the double bed that she had shared with

Archie. She was naked beside him, his hand lay on her breast, it felt cold and damp. She could still feel his weight on her as he had thrust his body into hers, kissed her with thin lips, his breath on her face, his tongue probing her mouth. She had closed her eyes and thought of her clean white room above, her patchwork quilt which would be too small for this bed and about her son who needed a studio; which he would now have.

CHAPTER 19

Annie was relieved that Sarah was coming with her to Newcastle Hospital for her first day. They drove in on roads lined with fields and copses which slowly merged into the spacious houses of the suburbs and then into streets lined with terraces clenched tight against clumps of factories which belched black smoke. Gulls wheeled over the hospital as they approached, flying in from the docks. The sky was lighter over there, as it always was by the sea, Annie thought, remembering the call of the gulls and the cold of the sea as it had dragged the sand from beneath her feet.

Sarah stopped the car at the entrance to the tall redbrick building. A statue of Queen Victoria looked over them to the town and the bedding plants had been cleared from around the plinth as it was September.

'So,' said Sarah as the engine jumped, then died. 'So one day they will put up a plaque saying that on September 1932 at two-thirty in the afternoon Nurse Manon began her career.' She laughed and laid her leather-gloved hand on Annie's arm.

Annie sat back, feeling the leather-seamed seat, seeing the dark brown wood of the dashboard, the pot-pourri that hung in muslin from a knob and which Sarah said would trick you into thinking the Morris was a new car with new smells. She remembered picking the oily lavender and the rose petals which they had then dried, together with the herbs.

'You'll feed the hens then, Sarah?'

'Of course,' Sarah nodded. 'And sell the eggs, taking the money towards Don. But I'd far rather send it to you, my dear. Remember that you get no pay for the first quarter and then it's only thirty shillings a month.' She was pulling her gloves from her hands, finger by finger.

'I'm fine. I've saved enough from the job and the patients' collection means that I can manage.'

'Come on, then,' urged Sarah.

The side entrance, where they had been instructed to assemble was signposted and Sarah's footsteps were brisk as they walked quickly past the trimmed lawns, down the path alongside the long-windowed building until they were there. The door was closed and Annie felt the same trembling, the same tightness in her stomach that had come on her first day of school. She looked at Sarah.

'Does this remind you of something?' Their eyes met and they smiled. But it was not the same, Annie knew. Today she was to begin her freedom.

'I'll be home on my first day off then, Sarah, if that's all right.' She leant forward and kissed her and Sarah's hand came up to her shoulder and held her close for just a moment and then she was gone.

Inside, the hall was lined with white tiles and there was a smell of disinfectant. Eight girls sat on a bench in the corridor and there was space for two more. Annie sat down and smiled at the girl next to her.

'I'm Annie Manon,' she said. 'From Wassingham.'

The girl, who was sallow-skinned and thin, returned her smile. 'I'm Julie Briggs from Whitley Bay and I'm scared to death.'

The girls laughed, all along the line, and leaned forward; words came slowly and then laughter joined them. Julie was 18 too, she told Annie, and had come over by train. She was the last of her family to leave home and the only girl. Her brothers were fishermen and married.

Sarah pulled on her gloves as she walked back to the car, skirting the lawns she did not really see and people who nodded and she did not acknowledge. The drive home seemed too quiet and too long whereas the three years with Annie had disappeared with a speed she would not have thought possible. She would not cry, could not cry while she was driving, but the loss of the child who had filled her life would always be hard to bear, too hard to speak of, even to Val. She wondered how she would fill her evenings, her weekends until that day off, the day Annie came home.

There would be no more hot cocoa at the end of each day with Annie, no more of her friends home for tea. Would Tom still come with Grace, or Don, now that Annie was not here?

She put the car into third gear to take the corner which led out from Newcastle. Her ward, her child was free now and she must be on her guard never to restrict that freedom.

Julie and Annie shared a room in the nurses' home and they prodded the beds and felt the stiffness of the blankets, then walked down green-painted corridors and stairs until they found Sister Tutor as they had been instructed. She was in a dark navy uniform and cap and wore a frown which looked as though it was never wiped away.

They wrote for the next two hours in a classroom cramped with desks and other girls until Annie's hand and mind were as jumbled as the room. There was an overwhelming smell of beeswax and the desks were sticky with it and a blackness formed on her cardigan.

The next day they were issued with pale blue uniforms and starched aprons and caps which crackled when they walked, but she did not glide as Sister Maria had done. Her heavy black shoes felt like boats and her feet at the end of that day were swollen and throbbing. Together she and Julie dabbed methylated spirits and talcum powder over the toes, the feet and up to the ankles before they crawled into bed, unaware of the heavy blankets, unaware of anything but the white-tiled corridors, the rows of beds, the sisters and nurses, the doctors and students, the dining hall, the mortuary, the Children's Ward. Unaware of anything until the call at five-thirty the next day.

For six weeks, they wrote and watched and listened in the classroom but did not see the wards again. Annie wondered if she would die of cold in her short-sleeved uniform, but each morning she hugged to herself the thought of the future, of the present, of her freedom.

She learned of leeches and smiled to think that Don could have used them after his discussion with Tom over the interest rates. Sister Tutor asked her to share her joke with the others and when she could not, she had to write out the lesson twice.

She learned about enemas, bedsores; about dangerous drugs which must always be locked. Suddenly through the open window the sound of the gulls seemed much louder and the whistle of the butcher's boy, the grinding of gears as a lorry struggled up the hill past the hospital. So simple really, she thought, a pin anchoring a few keys in a nurse's pocket could have saved a woman's life, not any woman but my mother. She had to copy up the notes she missed during that lecture from Julie that night.

They had no days off for those first six weeks or for the next four when they were on the wards at last.

The wards were large and white and smelled of disinfectant. Her feet swelled every night and did not go down by the next morning. She was in casualty when twelve miners came in and the enamel bowl shook in her hands as she washed and washed until the blackness was gone, leaving white flesh and red eyes.

She could see the blood then, but Sister drove her on to the next for washing and she smiled and talked soft words and pushed the thought to the back of her head that this could be Tom; this could be Tom. And so on to the next and the next and the next. Her apron was black and her hands too and later she scrubbed until they were red raw, until the smell of the coal and the sight of it was gone. But she could still smell it, see it as she cut clothes from a child who had hurt his arm, still smell it above the vegetable soup she served for lunch and that night she dreamed of dark tight streets, of pitwheels and slag-heaps, of allotments, of a shop, of a room with a snake which writhed and vomited gas. When she woke, in that moment before Julie's breathing was heard and the day had really begun, she knew that memory was still hers, that hate still remained. She was tired all that day and made sure that the black box in her mind was pushed tightly shut.

The week before her first day off she was moved to the Women's Ward. At six-thirty she took tea round, at seven she bathed and washed and combed hair. At eight she made beds, folding corners and putting on clean pillowcases with their openings away from the door. At nine she had a cup of tea and poured one in the small kitchen off the corridor for Julie who was on Men's further down.

'Guess,' Julie said, as she walked in, her hands behind her back. 'Guess what I have here.' Her eyes were dark with bags beneath and Annie knew that hers were the same.

Annie sat back in her chair, her legs up on the table, her ears pricked for Sister. 'Guess you're an idiot. Come and have some tea, we've only another seven minutes.' She checked the time against the watch that Sarah had given her when she was accepted for training by the hospital. 'Another eight minutes,' she corrected.

Then she saw the crumpled letter that Julie brought from behind her back but dropped and they watched as it floated to the ground, blue against the white of the tiles and the green of the linoleum.

It was from Georgie. Annie knew before she saw the writing, before she held it in her hands and saw the creases and stains from miles of travel. She tore at the envelope, ripping it open.

'Where did you get it?' she asked, not listening as Julie told her Sarah had brought it into the hall porter.

She searched now for his words of love.

June 1932

My dearest darling love,

You will be 18 by the time you read this and probably bossing everyone around in the hospital but I want you to know that I don't miss you any less with time, I just love you more and more. It is deeper and tucked down inside me but I am still seeing everything new here with your eyes as well as me own. I wonder, I do, if you would like the mountains which sometimes I can see as clear as day but which can get hidden by the thick clouds that clump together all of a sudden, here in the Himalayas.

How are you, my bonny lass, my darling girl? How are your feet? Tom says you soak them in vinegar like the miners do. He says it's a voluntary hospital supported by contributions from the miners mostly; have you had any in yet? If you have, try not to worry about Tom. Push it away, it can't happen, you love him too much.

It's hot here, the rains haven't come yet so it is a wet heat and I'm drinking lime juice until it comes out of me ear holes.

We've been down to the plains to Lahore which is

in a right mess. There's been a lot of fighting between the Muslims and the Sikhs and we're supposed to stand in the middle and calm it down, which I suppose is what we did. It's all a bit difficult, you know, here with the Indians. They want their freedom from us, (and I can't say I blame them) and I reckon there's going to be some fighting before too long; against us and one another. Anyway, I got me corporal's stripe out of it all, so now I'm waiting for me sergeant's but that could take a while.

Will you wait, my love? I don't mean miss out on things, just want me when I come, because I will come but it is all taking so long and I worry that you'll get tired and find someone else; a permanent someone else.

You would like it here today, my love. The geese and ducks have just flown over, heading for the water on the plains, and the bullock carts have been plodding by the station all day, but they always do. We have musk-roses which are white with a scent that your Sarah could put in her pot-pourri and make the Morris smell as sweet as a baby's bum. The whitebeams are trees which I really like. They are everywhere and have huge leaves which are dark green above and furry white below. There's a bitty fruit which changes to English autumn colours and the birds make right little pigs of themselves.

It was grand that the boys have sorted themselves out and that Don is back with you all. Who'd have thought that Bob was Sarah's flappy ears in Wassingham but I'm right glad he's keeping an eye on the lad. He needs a bit of controlling, you know.

I'll write again, my darling. I'm hoping to go to Kashmir because I'm told that it's beautiful, but before that we're off on exercises which will mean marches of ten or fifteen miles a day, so we'll both have sore feet.

I'll love you forever, want you forever, your soft skin, your beautiful face; my dearest darling, I miss you so.

Georgie.

Annie looked up at Julie. 'He still loves me.'

Julie smiled and took their cups to the sink. 'Sister won't love you if you don't get back, you know. It's the nit-round after the doctors.'

The medical students were crowding round the small man in a dark suit as he walked swiftly down the corridor and Annie pushed the letter into her pocket and slipped into the ward ahead of them and took up her place beside the senior nurse at Sister's desk. Mr Morton, the small physician, marched past, three of the medical students with him but the fourth stopped to tie his shoe lace in front of her. His blond hair was cut short and his neck bristled with shaved hair. He turned and winked and she blushed; his shoelace had not needed tying, she could see that now.

'Such nice legs, nurse,' he murmured, his wide mouth barely moving but his voice carrying beyond Annie to the senior nurse.

Annie flushed and he grinned, walking away now to catch up, his white coat flapping, a stethoscope dangling round his neck. Senior Nurse Wilson, her lips pulled into a thin line, pointed to the screens around the bed at the top of the ward near Sister's table.

'Try and leave your love-life outside the ward, nurse. There's a septicaemia case just come in. Doctor's already seen her so get on and delouse her and better stay with her for a bit. She's very poorly.'

Annie felt her hands grow damp. How poorly was poorly, she wondered.

The woman was lying still when Annie moved the screen gently, slipping through and pulling it closed behind her. She was yellow and thin, her face ravaged by illness, her eyes bright but not with health, with fever. Annie longed for the day when she would be able to take pulses and temperatures, give medication instead of dragging a steel comb through nit-infested hair.

She smiled at the woman. 'Hallo,' she whispered. 'I'm Nurse Manon, I have to check your hair, I'm afraid.' She wanted to think of Georgie's letter but knew that it must wait until tonight.

She hated it, hated the humiliation that they must feel. The

273

lice she found were big and black and full of blood and Annie touched the woman's hand.

'What's your name?' she asked and had to lean forward to catch the faint words.

'Well, Mrs Turner, you're fine here, nothing at all on your hair, but I'll just run me comb through and put a bit of this stuff on just as a precaution.' She held up the brown bottle. 'We don't want you picking up anything while you're in here, do we?' It was a very small lie, she thought.

Mrs Turner's hair was dry and split, shot through with grey. She moaned as the comb pulled through.

Annie stroked her face with one hand. 'There now,' she soothed. 'This won't take long.' She squashed the lice between the bowl and her fingernail, hating them, wanting them to die for sucking what little blood this woman had and for forcing her to do this to an already ill patient. At last it was done and Annie smoothed back Mrs Turner's hair, wiping the tears from her cheeks where they had smeared as she had tried to brush them away before Annie saw.

'Oh, lass,' she whispered 'It's no job for a young girl. I'm right ashamed, you know.' She turned her face away from Annie, towards the tiled wall but the glare was too bright and she shut her eyes.

'There was nothing there, I promise, Mrs Turner. Nothing.' She put the bowl on the locker, covered with a cloth.

'Let's get you comfortable now.' She smoothed the sheets down and gently plumped the pillows, then sat. The woman was hot, very hot and Annie remembered that when she had been feverish with a heavy cold every touch had felt like a needle on her skin, so what must this woman have gone through just now.

'You'll soon begin to feel better you know, now you're here.'

Mrs Turner turned, her eyes were sunken and the lines around them were so deep it was as though they were coloured in with soot.

'Aye, lass, maybe I will. I lost the bairn see, lost the wee thing and now I've got the poisoning.' She coughed slightly and Annie held a glass of barley-water to her lips, holding her as she took a sip.

'I'm sorry about the baby, Mrs Turner.'

The woman smiled weakly. 'Thank God, you should say, lass. One less to worry about.' Annie laid her back on the pillow. She did not try to argue with the woman because she had not forgotten Wassingham; the cold, the hunger, the men on street corners.

Mrs Turner died at the end of her shift.

'Died just like that,' Annie told Julie as they ate their supper in the dining-room. 'There was this funny breath outwards; it went on and on and then she was dead.'

The cabbage was soggy and the fish dry and tough. It had been left too long in the oven again.

'No talking shop,' called a senior nurse from the other side.

Annie stood up and walked out of the dining-room, out of the hospital to stand by the grass. There was a rich smell of grass cuttings; it must be the last cut of the season she thought. For God's sake, it's the end of October already. She walked on past Queen Victoria who had her nose in the air. Well, it can't be the lobelia, they're not here any more, it's got to be me feet and she looked up at the plump shape and out through the gate over the town where the lights made the sky seem black above it. She stood with her arms crossed. That woman was starved before she came in, she thought. She died because she was poor, not because she had septicaemia. You don't die from septicaemia without a fight unless you take bloody poison or are starved. She said it again, challenging herself to shrink from the thought of her mother. She walked up and down and she felt the tears come down her cheeks and the heat of Mrs Turner as she had held her hand, the moan as she had torn the metal comb through her hair. There shouldn't be bloody nits, she shouldn't have had to go through that. She breathed in deeply and looked up at the sky wondering if she would be able to take the suffering that she was going to have to see over the next few years, but knew that she would. Above the glow of the town the sky was black and the stars were vivid. She wiped her cheeks and shook her head, angry now. These women needed work, needed money and one day she would do something about that, she and Tom together would make it a little better between them but not now because Tom had other things to do and so had she.

Annie caught the train to Sarah's on her first day off. The walk from the station was cold but the sky was a bright blue and the light seemed to fill the streets again, just as it had done when she had first come here from Wassingham.

She walked up the path, breaking off a leaf from the privet hedge, bending it over, hearing it crack clean, free from sap. Sarah held her close in her arms and Val hugged her and she took the bowl of corn that Sarah gave her and walked down the garden past the pruned roses, opened the wire gate and threw the corn to the hens, watching as they jerked, watching as the cock strutted.

The shed door opened easily and the smell of creosote was slight without the hot sun and she edged in past the bike, past the worn rubber grips to the window. She rubbed the glass, looking out into the open sky and leaned against the wooden frame. She loved it, she loved nursing. Loved the work, the girls, the being on her own, but she was glad to be back.

Lunch was calm until the doorbell rang and there were Tom and Grace, Don with a girl. Tom held her close, looked at her feet and said they were like bloody battleships. Grace kissed her and said how she'd grown. Don hugged her and gave her a bag of victory drops to keep away the germs and introduced Maud who was little with very curly hair and had Don right under her thumb.

Val laid more places at the table and Sarah laughed. They ate well and laughed and talked, then sat in front of the fire and Tom told them about Bob; how he had met him, how he was teaching him all about the unions and Sarah and Annie did not look at one another but at him and acted surprised. Don held Maud's hand and Tom winked at Annie. Grace asked about her work, about the food and they all laughed, Don too.

She told them about the Sister Tutor who had dragged them over the coals for the first six weeks, about the doctors who thought they were God but not about the blond medical student, William. She told them about the boy who had come into casualty with his head stuck in the potty but not about the child who had died of a congenital deformity and who she had carried in her arms, wrapped in a cloak, to the mortuary; you did not let the little ones take that last cold journey on their own, on a trolley. She told them about the woman who had produced a bairn when she thought she was suffering from indigestion, but not about Mrs Turner.

The train ride back was quiet after the talking and the

laughing and the hugs and kisses. They had asked after Georgie and she had told them about Lahore, about the heat, the fighting. She had not told them that he had said she was to live her life until he was back. The train pulled into the station. It was dark and the sparks flew up until they died and disappeared. She took the eggs and cakes that Val had made, the toffee that she and the others had boiled up in pans, then rolled and thrown at a nail Don had hammered into the door. Again and again they had taken the slack and thrown it and stretched it until it was ready. They had left it to harden while they had taken a last look at the hens, at the garden, then Tom had hammered it into pieces and they had taken some home with them but the rest was here, in this white box, for her patients in the morning.

The platform was empty by the time she had collected her parcels and climbed down from the step. She walked to the domed exit, through the dim lighting and the smell and huff of the trains and there was William, as he had said he would be.

He took her parcels but she kept one so that they each had a hand free to hold loosely. The night was fine and papers flew about their feet. Taxis waited in the ranks and they saw the glow of cigarettes in the cabs.

They walked back to the nurses' home and now everything was close to her after a day of distance, of waiting. They stopped at the pork stall on the corner and William ate a dripping sandwich which oozed and ran down his chin and Annie wiped it with her handkerchief. His laugh was light and easy and that was what she wanted. He took a piece of his bread and put it in her mouth, his hands were small and pale; he was going to be a surgeon.

He kissed her lips at the gates, away from the lights and she could taste the pork as his lips opened over hers. The parcels were in the way and she laughed and pushed him away knowing that she would see him again when they were on nights next week.

She was on duty at Christmas and sang carols round the tree and kept her hand in her pocket clutched tightly round Georgie's letter, the one that she had received in October. She smiled across at Julie, at William and knew that Georgie was safe deep inside her, quite safe from William or any other man.

Night duty was tiring because they had to work at lectures as and when they could during the day. As winter turned to spring, Annie took pulses, gave enemas, read temperature charts and spent two months in theatre. She took the severed legs to the chutes, mopped the surgeon's brows, watched William watching the specialists.

Tom and Don came to Newcastle with the girls and they went to the Empire, to the pantomime. Julie and Trevor, another medical student, came too, and William. The lights were still the same shell-pink, the curtains the same rich red. The binoculars were released from their stand on the back of the seat for the same sixpence. The seat prickled and Annie sat back and tried to forget her da. Tom pressed his arm to hers.

'All right, bonny lass?' he whispered and she nodded and most of her was, but still there lurked that dark hate that would not leave her in peace.

Tom wrote to her that week, wrote and asked her if she was all right now, asked about Georgie, about William, and she smiled and replied that she loved Georgie, she liked William because he made her laugh. She said that she wanted Tom to behave himself, keep out of trouble and sent him love for Grace and Don and Maud; for Don was still with this pale small girl.

Every other day off, she went to Sarah's but the others were for her and William. They walked in the parks, went to the cinema and sat on seats which flicked up the minute they were left. She screamed at King Kong and laughed at the silent movies that were still being shown.

In the summer, they went on holiday with Julie and Trevor to the Lake District and she shared a room with William. It was a small private hotel which lay on the banks of Windermere and had chalets which lay some distance from the hotel.

The hills across the lakes were not as high as the hills that Georgie wrote of and were seldom hidden by cloud. She was shy when William had locked the door, it was the afternoon of their arrival and the sun was hot. He turned to her, his hands stroking her face and she could feel the tremble in them.

He had blue eyes not brown like Georgie and soft hands, not hard like Georgie's and then she stopped herself. This was William and Annie and was quite different, quite separate from Georgie. He kissed her then, his lips soft, his eyes shut, his eyelashes casting a shadow on his cheeks. He was a good boy, Annie thought, as her lips pressed into his, from the South and different, but a good boy.

He undid her blouse and stroked her breasts as her nipples hardened: his breath was quicker now and he picked her up and took her to the bed.

'I'm a virgin,' she said as he sat down on the bed. He looked at her, traced the line of her cheek then her throat and her breasts and promised to be gentle. And he was, and afterwards she lay on the bed, wet with his sweat and her legs overlaid with his, looking out through the window at the water. There was a boat which seemed to be barely moving, the curtains were flowered and puffed out in the breeze. She turned and stroked his face and he kissed her hand.

She needed him, needed a man and a love that was light and happy and did not dig too deep.

They walked the next day, Julie and Trevor behind them, Julie's voice fading as they marched on higher and higher, avoiding the scree and laughing as Trevor slid down until he reached a rocky outcrop. Home Sister was a million miles away, Sarah was in Brighton with Val on holiday, and Wordsworth travelled with them as William shouted his verse and they hiked down to the lake and paddled in the cold clear water.

At the pubs where they stopped on their outings, the beer was heavy, the cheese flaky and it fell from their mouths as they threw back their heads and whooped with glee and Annie dug her hands deep into her pockets and let the wind whip her hair and swung into William's arms as he wished it, or she wished it.

They boated or made love as bees flirted with the heather and ladybirds plopped on to springy turf and hustled in and out of the shadows in a rush to find their way home before their houses burned and their children were all gone. Annie lay on her back and listened as William spoke of his home with its tennis court and the girl he would one day marry, the girl he had grown up with, and she felt a freedom which made her want to sing and shout from the mountain top because he wanted nothing more from her.

He told her about his mother who rinsed her hair blue and his father who was a stockbroker and had survived the crash of '29. She did not tell him of her father who had not survived, of the streets which were cruel and hard because these things were her memories, her problems and one day she would solve them.

She chewed the fleshy stalk of the long grasses and showed

William how to suck clover and flood his mouth with nectar and then wished that she had not for that was Georgie and she would not make love when he pulled her to him, the clover discarded in the grass.

The holiday was a release for them all, from the 67 hours she and Julie worked each week. The sun shone each day and they laughed on the train back to Newcastle.

Interim exams were just after the following Christmas in the January of 1934. Annie passed near the top though Julie only managed a scrape.

Annie spent some time in Male Surgical, nursing damaged miners, not just washing then. She checked for the redness of bedsores, eased dressings off burns and knew before she began each one that it would stick and cause the man to turn from her to hide his face. Once it was over there was no relaxation for they would go through the same process the next day. Then there was the shipyard worker who had fallen from twenty feet up and broken his back and the man with ingrowing toenails.

In Men's Medical, she nursed miners with black spit but most were sent home to die because their condition was too advanced. She would look into the sputum mugs and want to scream that it wasn't bloody fair.

Maternity was always busy with malnourished mothers at risk and underweight babies. The Children's Ward was full of bairns with shaved deloused heads who missed their mams and cried for them because the doctors would not allow more than a rare visit in case the child became upset. They called her Nurse and she liked the sound of it and of her feet as she bustled from bed to bed, knowing now that she was capable of caring for these people.

Georgie wrote in the early spring and she received the letter on the first day of June, just as she was leaving for Windermere again and perhaps fields and slopes full of daffodils.

March 1934

My darling love,
    I've done it my love, I've made sergeant! We had a real party, about as good as Christmas but then it

was better because the sergeants waited on us and the officers on them.

It is still quite cool here, the rhododendrons are in full flower, purple not red like the ones at your old school. You would love to see them, have you any at the hospital?

The lakes you wrote about sound like the ones in Kashmir but much smaller. I managed to get there on my leave, darling, and it's where we'll spend our honeymoon. We'll take a houseboat and spend two weeks just being together. Would you like that? Please say you would.

We've been very busy here, on exercises. It's so hot and the dust gets everywhere and your feet get rubbed raw. I'm right surprised the vultures don't come and have a go at us; they hover around though wherever we go, they're buggers and I hate the bloody things.

The trees are so lovely now. The leaves are sprouting on the oak, chestnut and walnut. Do you remember that walnut hall table you told me about at Sarah's? Well, it probably came from here.

My bearer is having a high old time because the snakes are always getting into the ghuslkhana, or privy to you, so when he sweeps out the excrement, and don't pull that face, they usually come wriggling out too. I'm very careful before I use it, I can tell you, hinny.

Now, my darling, listen to me. I'm worried about Tom. He's getting very het up about this Mosley and his blackshirts. Try and stop him taking it so seriously, won't you. I know there's trouble in Germany but I don't want our Tom in any bother in England. He tells me he wants to go to one of their meetings in London to tell the other side of the story. They'll be rough on him, bonny lass, if that happens. A mate of mine who's just come out from Blighty says that the blackshirts are buggers who like to put the boot in and his da says Mosley's trying to be another Hitler. Stop him, hinny, tell him to stay clear. I hope he'll listen to you and maybe Don. Get Sarah to ask Bob.

You work so hard at the hospital. I hope you're not too tired. I lie awake when we're on exercise looking up and thinking that somewhere you are under the same sky. I feel better now, pet, better because I can see an end to it all. It should be possible to become an officer, especially if I transfer to the Engineers. It's easier to come up from the ranks in that set up, me old sergeant says. I'll be applying and if I'm taken on I will be home to take my commission at Woolwich.

Don't hold your breath though because it will still be some time yet. Please don't write to me again telling me that you want me home. It is too hard to read that out here, when all I want is to be with you. I love you so much but you must see that I have to make it in my own way.

Please enjoy yourself and remember that I love you.

Georgie.

Sitting on the bed, Annie read it through again. Julie finished her packing and looked across.

'Still loves you, does he?'

Annie nodded. 'Oh yes.' I will never ask you that again my bonny lad, she thought, because she understood exactly what he meant.

'Does William know anything about Georgie?'

She shook her head. 'He knows precious little about me at all, that's the way I want it. I like him, I'm fond of him, but that's all.'

Julie shrugged. 'You could have him if you want him, you know. Marry a doctor, Annie, wouldn't it be great?'

Annie stood up and put on her coat before locking Don's watch in the wardrobe. She did not want it stolen while she was away. 'No thanks.'

'Why not though, Annie? You'd be comfortable for the rest of

282

your life. I reckon Trevor's going to ask me if he passes his finals. He'll hear when we get back.'

Annie smiled at Julie, at her face which was still tired but fuller now; the sallowness gone and her cheeks pink. 'So you'll miss your finals will you? Just rush off and marry the boy?'

'Without a backward glance,' Julie said as they carried their cases down the stairs.

Annie wondered whether she would if Georgie came home, but knew she wouldn't. Knew she wanted to finish, to have that buckle on her belt and the full salary to finish paying Sarah, and then it would be time to force Tom into a college. She would be able to afford it herself then.

On the train they talked about the blackshirts, about the Nazis and William said that his father thought it might be a good idea if Mosley did well. It might get the trains running on time and sort out some of the slackers.

The train was passing through fields rich with green corn and the banks leading to the railway lines were sprouting green again through blackened stubble where sparks had set the grass alight the previous year. There was a farmer driving a team of horses which were turning over the earth. Rain had been forecast for the end of the week.

She looked at William as he sat back, his head rolling in time to the train's movements. 'What do you mean, slackers?' Her voice tightly controlled, she was aware that Julie had tensed and was looking at her. Trevor laughed.

'These buggers on the dole. You can always find work if you want it.'

Annie looked at him, at his curly black hair and red lips then turned back to William. 'You've seen them in the hospital, William. These people are hungry. They want work but there is none. It's not easy to move out of your area to find it either, you know that, and if they do go who's to say there'll be a job at the end of it. It's a big depression. These people are ill because they haven't any work.' Her voice was too loud, her words too slow.

William looked at her, his brow contracted with irritation. 'Don't shout at me, Annie. I know work is difficult to come by, but perhaps if someone like Mosley came in there'd be work. People would have to do as they were told. Look at Germany. There's full employment there or as good as. This Hitler's getting them all organised.'

Annie remembered last Sunday and Sarah sitting by the fire reading the paper, passing it to her and shaking her head over the brawling in the streets, the camps for the Communists and the Jews.

'What about their camps, what about the Jews? That can't be right. You can't think that is right?' protested Annie.

'That's only temporary,' William laughed, reaching for her hand kissing each finger. 'Once he's got things organised, all that will die down and the movement will become respectable.' She wanted to pull away from him, slap his face until it burned red but she caught Julie's eye, the fear and the pleading, so she said nothing more but wrote to Tom from the hotel repeating what she had said to him before but doubtful that it would make any difference. Then she walked in boots up the hillsides and drank beer and made love to William without enjoyment. She thought too often of the patients that these men thought were shirkers, of the people her brothers were and their friends. It was not warm this summer and she felt the breeze through her cardigan, felt William's hands cold on her flesh and no surge of wanting. She lay with him and beneath him noting when his passion spent itself inside her and that the lampshade and the cobwebs that hung from the ceiling and wafted in the breeze were not there last year. She saw the cracks which ran to the corners and the mirror that was not screwed on straight to the wardrobe door.

The weather broke on Thursday and storms lashed the hills and turned the lake into a stormy sea. They packed their rucksacks and took the train to Newcastle. William and Trevor found that they had passed their exams and Annie was glad for she wanted William gone from her. Trevor asked Julie to marry him and Annie was sad at the waste of a career.

There was also a letter from Bob to say that Tom was leaving on 6 June for London to attend a blackshirt rally at Olympia. She was on duty and could not intercept him at the station and she knew that it would have done no good if she had.

CHAPTER 20

Tom arrived too early for the train from Wassingham on Thursday and Bob waited with him. Frank had told Tom about the rally in London the week before. He'd said it would be a big one and they had arranged to go with two more from Frank's street.

Tom had told Grace while he sketched her by the beck where the wild honeysuckle was out and the shadows were sharp in the sun and the air was thick with scent. She had said he was a trouble-maker and all mouth, like Annie, only she had the sense to get out and stay out. She'll not come back, Tom, so don't go on expecting her too. She'd meant to hurt, wanted to hurt but he'd drawn her to him, kissed her, pulled up her blouse, stroking and kissing her breasts until she'd pulled away saying that she wouldn't love him any longer if he went down to London, but he knew that this was something she would never do.

'It's a matter of principle,' he explained to Bob as they waited for the train. Frank was over on the seats, playing cards with his marrers. 'No one objects to this man Mosley, they think he will bring good roads and trains that run on time.' Bob looked at his watch then and Tom punched him on the arm. 'Aye, Bob, we can put up with a bit of lateness, you know.' And they laughed. 'He's a bloody fascist. He's drilling his men and marching them through the East End. He's Hitler in England and look at what's happening over there in Germany. We could go that way, you know. Anyone who disagrees with the bugger would be squashed.'

Bob sighed. 'For God's sake, man, he's a nutter. No one will take him seriously, and besides, it's not your fight.'

Tom looked down the line but there was still no sign of the train. He moved from foot to foot. 'Look, Bob. This bugger dresses up his goons in black uniforms, then sets 'em on anyone who gets in his way and what happens? Sweet nothing. The cops just hold back the hecklers while he marches past or finishes his speech. He's got the support of the establishment, or some of them. It's bloody disgraceful, man.'

'So what are you four going to do then? Take the Fascist Union on single-handed?' Bob had a pink tinge to his cheeks, his voice was rising. There were very few people on the platform at five in the morning. The slag trolleys were tipping their loads behind them.

'I'm going to speak out, Bob, that's all, bonny lad, just speak out along with a lot of others.' He turned and whistled to Frank and jerked his head and then Bob also saw the train as it came round the bend, its smoke thrusting up into the fresh early morning air. He felt very old.

'So they're going to listen to a lad of 18 are they?' Bob called into Tom's face as the train steamed and screeched passed them to a halt.

Tom looked at him and laughed. 'I'm the one with the good lungs, aren't I, too young for the damage to have been done yet, no black lung for me, but ask Annie about the others.' He slapped Bob's arm. 'Thanks for coming, Bob, and for trying. It's just something I have to do. You understand eh, man? Annie does.'

Bob nodded as the door slammed shut and the train jerked out of the station. 'No one will hear, Tom,' he said quietly and waved as they passed round the bend.

Tom kept his eye on Frank as they left the train in London and headed for the underground; he was afraid of getting lost. The loudspeaker boomed across the concourse but he could not distinguish the words. At the top of each stairway there were men in blackshirts waving copies of their paper and calling 'Action! Action' and Frank grabbed Tom as he moved towards them, his cap low over his eyes.

'Nay lad, it's the meeting we're here for, leave it a while.'

They rushed down the steps past posters and toward the noise of trains. Litter blew round their ankles and up into the air when a train roared from the tunnel and it felt as though he was being sucked into its path.

There were over 15,000 people there, the papers said the next day, it was hot in the auditorium and they stuffed their caps into their pockets and shouldered through the crowds until they were halfway down the hall where they separated. Frank and he to one side, the other two, Jack and Sam, pushing their way through to the opposite wall.

Tom felt the sweat break out on his face and undid his jacket. The noise was so loud that he could not hear Frank when he spoke so the man leant forward and mouthed into his ear. 'Let's wait and see what the man in black has to say, shall we?' and Tom nodded but his mouth was dry as he watched the stewards in their black uniforms circling the hall, beating truncheons into the palms of their hands.

The stage was dark until the lights were dimmed in the hall and silence fell. Spotlights prodded the side of the stage then picked up the slim dark-moustached figure in a neat black shirt and suddenly the noise was deafening and Tom felt the mass of feeling sweep from behind, in front and all around him and felt a fear that drenched him, that was different to the pits because it rolled over him in sharp waves in time with the rhythm of the cheers and then the man spoke and it was as if he had waved a wand for silence.

He spoke for ten minutes until the first heckler interrupted, but a spotlight found him and the blackshirts moved in. There were more and more disturbances and more spotlights, more men in black and Tom set his shoulders as Frank tensed by his side.

'Sings like a bloody canary, doesn't he, this little man. What do you say to breaking his rhythm, Tom lad?'

Tom nodded but he wanted to run away far from the men who looked and listened all around him, their faces turned to the stage as though it was a god who spoke from the platform. He felt suddenly the cold of that football field, saw the trays which he and Annie carried, watched as the men came closer with steaming breath and then there was his own breath jogging in his chest as he had run, run as far from the field as he could go, leaving her, his Annie, there alone.

It was easy now in this hall and he drew himself up.

'What about democracy in this corporate state of yours, then? What about liberty, man?' His voice was loud into the blackness and he heard Frank's echo of his words and then the murmuring men around him moved as the spotlight found him, blinding him so that he held his arm across his eyes. He did not move or try to twist out of the beam. 'What about freedom?' he called and the stewards found him then, gripped him on either side and though he resisted there was no chance because there were four of them and thousands more besides and they were dragging him so that his feet could find no purchase.

There were faces and fists shaking at him, spit hit him on the face and still Mosley talked on and on until the sound stopped as the doors swung shut and he was in the passageway. Dark it was as they flung him first to one wall and then the other. The light from the solitary lamp which hung at the end of the corridor wall did not reach them here except for a stray glint on the large belt buckles and the gold tooth of the man who faced him. He was smiling.

It was the smile that crystallised his fear; he wrestled hard now against arm-locks which held him almost immobile. 'Oh Christ,' he groaned, as a truncheon broke his nose and pain exploded like a great noise. He could see nothing, not even the smile now as his eyes filled with the tears of pain, and so, as the fists and truncheons drove into his ribs and stomach, and grunts thudded against his ears, he reached back and brought out Annie standing in the cold, standing facing her da and the steaming breathing dragons of men. A boot caught his thigh and twisted him half round, knocking him free of the clasp which had held him upright.

The floor seemed no distance away but he hit it hard. He dragged himself up on his arms until they were kicked away and he tasted the blood pumping from his nose and mouth and again he hung on to Annie. The floor was linoleum, he knew that because of the feel and the smell and he curled up against it as the kicks developed a pattern of pain which swallowed him, leaving only his fear, and Annie. He knew he was weeping, he could hear himself, but he curled up round his hands and they were unhurt and that was his victory, you buggers. Me bloody victory and then he heard them laugh and then he didn't. Away and back they came and the light at the end of the corridor was there and then not and he was here and then not. On and on it went until he felt the hands as they lifted him by his coat and the sudden draught as the door opened and he was rolled on to the sun warmed pavement into the light June evening. It was over.

It was bloody over and then the boot crunched into his back and it was too bad even to scream.

Frank and the others found him after searching round the building inside and out where the police were arresting the demonstrators, not the blackshirts. They half carried him to the station and the train and laid him on a seat and Frank sat with him and held his hand and cleaned his face but the blood still came from his nose and mouth but not so much now. Tom smiled at Annie on the field, smiled at her as she stood and held out her arms to him. I knew you'd stay, she said. I knew you'd stay and face them with me, my bonny lad.

'We should have taken him to a London hospital,' hissed Jack to Frank but he shook his head.

'Nay lad, he wanted to get home, get to his sister's hospital so that's where he'll go.'

They sat hunched on the long journey back. They were bruised only, they'd been lucky. Tom moaned now as the train lurched round bends and scrambled over the points. His foot was burning inside his boot. He wanted it off, oh God, he wanted his boot off and his chest hurt. It hurt when he breathed as though knives were slicing through his lungs but it was his back that swamped him, that chased Annie away and then allowed her back as it eased. He held on to her face, held on to her voice and the feel of her hands as she stroked his hair and told him she would make the pain go away, but how could she do that, out here on this field with all these men around? He struggled to tell her, to push them back but then the pain came again.

Annie was asleep in the room she had shared with Julie before she had gone straight back with Trevor, back to the South to meet his parents and make sure he didn't trip over a Southern lily, Annie had thought wryly as she had waved them off and William too. She had kissed him, remembering the good times but unable to forget the things he had said.

She woke at the first shake. It was Staff Nurse Norris, her finger to her lips. 'Come to casualty, Annie. We have your brother in. Quick now, he won't settle until he sees you.'

It was Tom, she knew it must be Tom and her hands trembled as she put on her uniform, checked her belt and her shoes and ran down the stairs. Running is only for fire and haemorrhage, she chanted to herself; and Tom, and Tom. The wards were dark with just dim lights at the sisters' desks and she trod quietly past but still ran down the corridors and more stairs until she was in the glare of the white tiles, stretchers, screened examination-beds, drunks who lolled on benches.

It was Frank she saw first, his jacket creased and his boots loud as he paced up and down, his face grey with tiredness. He was large here and stood out strongly in the unsparing light. His jacket was rough as she gripped him, pulling him round, shaking him, saying:

'What's the matter with him, Frank, what's happened to him?'

Before he could answer, Staff came through from the screened-off bed. Her face was thin and she was older than Annie, nearly 30 someone had said and still unmarried.

'Nurse Manon,' she called softly, 'the doctor hasn't been yet, he's on his way. Your brother's conscious, on and off and he wants to see you. Keep him calm until doctor comes, there's a good girl. He's in great pain.' She smiled and patted her arm as Annie moved towards the screen, noticing where the red material was pulled slightly to one side of the frame and stopping to adjust the top. The trembling was back in her hands. She turned and Staff Norris smiled. 'Go on,' she said. 'He needs you,' but Annie was too afraid of what she might find.

The screen frame was cold in her hand and she held it as she slipped through and walked to the bed. He was still dressed but his boot had been sliced off with a razor and his foot was swollen and bruised and she could tell that it was broken, badly. His eyes were closed and his nose was also broken and his lips were swollen and bloody. She slipped open his shirt, checked his ribs and knew there was damage. She ran her hands along his legs and left his hands to last and they were untouched.

She held one and kissed it, stroking his hair, smelling the sweet scent of shock and knew that Tom was hurt, badly hurt and she leant over and whispered in his ear.

'Well, I leave you for a minute, bonny lad, and look at the mess.'

She watched as he struggled to open his lids and took a swab from the enamel bowl on the trolley and wiped away the trickle of blood from his split lip.

His eyes were on her now and she moved herself above him so that he would not have to turn his head.

'You're all right now, bonny lad. I'll make you better.'

He smiled.

'They were buggers, Annie,' he whispered.

'Aye, and you were all mouth, as usual.'

His eyes creased fractionally. 'Aye, like you.'

Then the doctor was there and Annie was sent away. She boiled the kettle in the small kitchen and gave Frank a cup of tea, then sent him back to Wassingham to tell Bob and Betsy. Then on to Grace and Don.

So this is respectability is it, William, she said to herself and was glad again that he had gone.

Tom was operated on immediately. His kidney was damaged and there was internal bleeding. It was removed. His foot was set and his ribs strapped. He was in Men's Surgical and Annie asked for and received a transfer to nurse him.

He was white against the pillowcase and was in the bed nearest Sister's desk. There were screens around and Annie sat with him checking his pulse every fifteen minutes and his blood pressure. His drip was set up at the head of his bed and she held his hand, talking to him, coaxing him back, telling him Grace would come. Betsy and Bob would be here. Don would bring Maud. Sarah and Val would bring toffee. She had to leave to dish out the lunches but his hand closed on hers and he whispered, 'Don't.'

'I'll be back,' she assured him and was, to sit with him through the afternoon.

Bob came with Betsy and they were asked to wait in the corridor. Annie left him again and again he said, 'Don't.'

Sister Grant waited by the ward door. 'I've spoken to them, Annie.' And Annie was grateful for the use of her name. 'But you have a word. They may see him briefly. He is very poorly, you know, my dear.' Her eyes were kind and Annie nodded.

Her head felt light and she was one step removed from everything, from all of them but Tom and was impatient to return to him; after all, she had said she would.

She pushed the door and Betsy was sitting on the bench with Bob beside her. Annie heard her shoes on the floor; they sounded brisk. There was a clatter from the sluice and she sat down by Betsy.

She had aged, had Betsy. Her hair was a little grey but there was something that wasn't to do with age in her face. It was fuller, somehow more complete. Annie took her hand. 'He'll be all right Bet, he's a fighter.'

Betsy nodded, 'Aye, lass.' She could not say more, her throat was too full and Annie put her arm round her and let her cry, looking over her shoulder to Bob.

His face was drawn, his eyes deep and he fingered his hat, round and round. 'It's his kidney, you see,' Annie told him as she patted Betsy. 'A broken foot and ribs and his nose.'

She smiled at Bob. 'That'll teach him to poke it in where it's not wanted.' She patted Betsy again as he nodded and tried to smile back.

'He'll be all right though, I promise you, Bet. I'll make sure he is.'

Grace came later that night and she and Annie sat by the bed but still Tom didn't really wake. All night they sat and next day Grace had to work or she could lose her job. Sarah came in the afternoon with Val and they stayed as Annie took round the tea. Don sat with him in the evening.

It was the next day when he rallied and took some liquid, but not much because of his kidney. Bob came and brought in papers which protested at the violence of the fascists at Olympia.

'At last,' he said and, in the weeks that followed, support waned for the blackshirts.

Tom was in hospital for ten weeks and they talked each day and each evening. Talked of the future and Annie told him she had had enough worry over him, that he was to go to art school now, do textile design and, if he didn't, she would break his other foot. He laughed at her and told that he had already decided he must do something of the sort.

She spoke to Sarah that evening, while Grace and Tom kissed quietly and sat together talking of bairns and art.

'He's agreed to go, Sarah. In fact he had already decided, so all our nagging won't be needed.' They laughed together. 'But it's the money.' Annie heard the strain she had been feeling transmit itself to her voice.

Sarah tapped her sharply on the arm. 'It's no problem, you know that. Tom hasn't had his share yet, has he, so that's that.'

Annie sighed. 'I know that, Sarah, but I can't begin to pay

292

you back for Tom until I'm qualified in 1935 and I still haven't finished Don's money yet.'

Sarah shook her head. 'It's no use me saying don't, so what I will say is that you can pay me back when you are able to. There's no hurry because we'll be jogging along for years yet.' Annie looked down the corridor, at the nurses who pushed trolleys or backed into kitchens and sluices, at a world that she felt a part of and turned to Sarah. 'If it wasn't for you, I wouldn't have had all this.' She leaned forward and kissed her.

'Nonsense. You would have made it happen somehow. And how's Georgie, while I remember?' She was embarrassed and tucked her arm into Annie's and listened to the news that he had been on exercises and had also written about the walnut trees and Sarah's hall table.

When Tom was close to going home in August and the ward was quiet with the lights low above the beds, Annie straightened his sheets and then they sat for a while, listening to the sounds of the ward, the coughs and muted conversations, the laughter. It was then that he told her of a conversation he had held earlier with Bob. He told her of her father, of the man who dragged at his leg, of the still air that made the gas fall, of his heartbreak over her mother and Annie felt her skin grow cold and she took her hand from his but he took it back.

'You must forgive him some time, Annie, for your own sake. Try and understand.'

But she could not because the hate was too strong. After all, her father had killed himself and left them as though they were nothing, but she didn't tell Tom that, just nodded and said that she would be qualified in two years, he would be finished in four, which took them to the back end of 1938.

'So you see,' she said. '1939 will be our year. We'll give you a year to produce some designs and earn a bit of money for capital. I'll probably be a Sister by then and will have saved a bit and in the meantime I'll keep my eyes on the administrative procedures and see how things are run.'

She put the thermometer in his mouth to stop him bringing up her father again.

'It'll be grand, lad, to do something for the people here. Give them an alternative to coal or steel. It's exciting, isn't it, Tom?' He shook his head and pointed at the thermometer and she laughed, taking and checking it. 'The rudest of health, my lad.'

She put it back in its container.

'And what about Georgie?' he asked.

She leant over him and tucked the sheets in around him. 'He'll be here when he's ready and I'll be waiting for him. He's the man I love, the man I'll always love.'

She reached over to turn off the light. He was looking better these days, the pallor was gone but he'd be weak for a while yet. London would do him good and Grace would go with him, though they neither wanted to marry yet and Grace's da didn't seem to mind. She pictured him laughing at the pink mice all over the floor.

'So, 1939 it is, then,' Tom whispered and she nodded.

'The back end,' she said. 'When the summer has gone and the nights are drawing in. It's my favourite time of year.'

Tom laughed. 'See you in September, Annie Manon.'

CHAPTER 21

Annie remembered Miss Hardy and piano lessons today. It was August 1939 and newspapers spoke of war over the Polish crisis but she could not believe it. There had not been war over Czechoslovakia last year so why should there be one this year? She shrugged the thought aside and walked towards the bus-stop which would take her from the Manchester Cancer Hospital where she now worked to the restaurant where she was meeting Sarah.

Don was to be married this afternoon in Wassingham and Sarah had promised to buy her an early lunch on her way back from the Lake District where she had been holidaying. They could then travel up to Wassingham together.

She took the lift up from the bottom floor of the department store and was shown to Sarah's table.

'My dear,' said Sarah, kissing her and patting the chair next to her. 'You look so well and I do like your hat.'

Annie smiled and touched the net with her fingers. 'And you're looking pretty grand yourself, Sarah. It takes a wedding to bring the smart ones out of the cupboard, doesn't it? I hope mine doesn't smell of moth-balls.' Sarah looked better for her holiday. She had come to the nurses' home when she travelled through, two weeks ago, and Annie had thought she looked tired. Her hair was now very grey and her skin was pale and translucent but she'll be 50 in two years' time, Annie thought, and wondered where the years had gone because, as she had reminded herself just last week on her twenty fifth birthday, she was no chicken any more. Sarah had sent her a five pound note and Georgie had enclosed a piece of Indian silver in his letter. She showed it now to Sarah, her face alive and full of hope. She knew it off by heart.

Central Provinces.

My darling lass,

Well, it looks as though it could be any day now. My transfer to the Engineers has been accepted and my C.O. is supporting my application for a commission. By the way, did I tell you his daughter is nursing in England?

Now it is finally happening, my commission that is, I can hardly believe it. The sergeants' mess is celebrating every night but I wish they wouldn't. My head won't take it and they might be in for a disappointment.

I'll talk of other things, it might be unlucky to go on too much about what I've dreamt of all these years which is coming home to you. If I get it, I'll be sent to Woolwich for my training, see.

I'm pleased to hear that Don has finally popped the question to Maud. She looks a bit like him from the photo you sent me; fairly small the pair of them but his hair looks as though it's getting a wee bit thin whereas hers is good and curly. I've sent them a silver tea-caddy.

Got a letter from Tom last month. He's loved his time in London, hasn't he; living the life of an artist and Grace with him too. A bit bohemian isn't it, not being married? Bet Wassingham had something to say about that. Grace seems to have liked her job in the library and feels good at sending her ma and da some money each week. Tom says he's about ready to start on the business but he has to finish this commission to paint a mural at a restaurant in Piccadilly first. Well, that sounds grand doesn't it. He says it will give him a bit of capital to go with the money you've saved. I've a bit too, remember, which can help you get started.

It makes sense to start in the small way you've planned and the idea of it has kept him at his art instead of blasting off to Spain or anything daft like that.

Bob must have missed him badly all these years but Tom says he's been right busy with the union, pushing for state ownership of the pits. There's still not a lot of work up there, he tells me.

It's grand to hear that things have settled down a bit in Germany but there's talk here in the mess that Hitler won't stop with Czechoslovakia. Will there be another war, Annie? It seems so far away here though we keep an eye on the Japs who seem to be pushing their way into China in the war they've started there.

We're exercising down in the jungles of the Central Provinces since Burma would be the way into India for the Japs and this is similar terrain, but maybe they're just game-playing.

There's a great deal of trouble in India. They want us out, though Gandhi is doing his bit to make it a peaceful independence movement. I guess that Tom would approve.

The butterflies here in the jungle are beautiful, very different to the Camberwell Beauties that used to settle by your da's shed, do you remember them, my bonny lass? There is one we call the Cruiser which is very fast and high-flying, it's a sort of yellow brown and there is a really beautiful one called the Swallowtail which has a flash of blue across its wings. It seems very nervous and hovers over the petals of the lush flowers you get in this steamy climate. It's bloody hot, sticky and humid and we go up to the hill-stations for a break. Darjeeling is the best. We ride horses up the trails and cool off a bit. I'll take you there one day.

Well, my dearest little lass. I will close now and will write again as soon as I have any news. I have kept all your letters, there seem to be so many but then years have gone by since I last saw you. I can't bear to think of that. I will love you always with all my heart.

Georgie.

Sarah passed it back, took out her compact and patted her nose with the powder-puff. She looked at Annie over the mirror, the back of which was studded with seed pearls.

'I've watched you all these years, my dear, laughing and flirting and learning. By the way, how is Dr Jones, such a nice Welshman?' But she did not wait for Annie to answer. 'You were always waiting for Georgie though, weren't you? How can you be so sure, my darling, that you are still right for one another, that he will ever come? I know he says he will, but after all this time, can it work?'

Annie picked up a knife and set it absolutely straight against the mat which was a view of the Manchester Ship Canal. The handle must be solid, it was so heavy, but surely it was silver plate? She listened to the strains of the Blue Danube and watched the cellist lean back and ease her shoulders. The mock palms were bright green.

'He'll come and we'll be right for one another, don't you fret.' She tapped Sarah's hand with her finger. 'He knows me, knows my family, the streets, the pits. He knows that you have a walnut hall table, that your bathroom is posh. That Tom lost a kidney, that Don loves Maud and is the only one who can handle Albert. I don't have to explain myself, that I'm not the posh person I sound now.' She lifted an eyebrow at Sarah who laughed. 'He knows me and I've never had to look after him, he looks after himself and I'm right proud of the lad.' Her voice was soft now and she had slipped back into Geordie and she didn't care.

Sarah beckoned the waiter and asked for wine. It had to be white and chilled and he brought the ice bucket and set the bottle back in the crushed ice after he had poured them each a glass.

'I'm just wondering, Annie, whether you love him because it's safe to love someone who's so far away, someone who won't try and get too close? I wonder if you're running away from anything?' Her face was quizzical.

Annie looked puzzled, her thoughts slowed down and she watched the bubbles in her wine break through to the surface.

'I don't know what you mean, Sarah.' She would not dig deeper into herself to try and understand her guardian; she did not want to disturb the black box.

Sarah smiled absently. There was a pause then. 'Did I do the right thing, Annie, taking you away from Wassingham, from him?' Her face was sad and tense.

Annie ran her fingers up and down the stem of her glass, then carved stripes down through the mist of the bowl. 'You've not taken me away, Sarah. No one will take me away, that's where I'm going now, back there for the wedding, back there with Tom, soon, to start my business. I couldn't have done that without you and I would not have known you, had you not come, and that would have been intolerable.'

She leant back as the sole arrived. It was fresh but the sauce was not as good as Val's. The mannequins were parading round the tables now, their backs arched and their legs going on forever. Sarah's face had relaxed and she was flushed after Annie's remarks. They smiled at one another.

'What about the war if it comes? Your business? Georgie?'

Annie took a sip of wine, it was dry and light. 'There won't be a war surely, Sarah? Chamberlain's sorting it out, isn't he?'

She thought of Dippy Denis who had been led away and locked up in a place she had always imagined would not have windows. Would he still be there, she wondered? No, there could not be another war, not after the last one. The lettuce that accompanied the sole was crisp, the tomatoes fresh. And besides it was the summer and she could never imagine war on a summer's day, with the sun out. It should always be wet and cold. Grey. There would be no war; no one wanted war. There were still too many damaged people from the last one, but she would not think of her da and his gas. She lifted her glass again.

Sarah had finished her meal and was studying her glass. 'But if Chamberlain should fail, Annie,' she persisted, 'would Georgie come back? What about the business?'

Annie frowned. 'I just don't know Sarah. I really don't. Georgie would still come home, surely, and I would stay in nursing, I suppose. They'd need nurses but it wouldn't last long, would it, Sarah, so we could start the business when it was over.'

Sarah was pleating the thick starched napkin that lay beside her plate. Her fingers were steady, her eyes on her work. 'We said that about the last one.'

'But it's different now, we have planes. It would be quick.' Annie did not want to think any more about it.

Sarah continued however. 'God forbid there is one but you

could travel with a war, Annie, you could join the military nurses, even pick up ideas for fabrics from other countries and give Tom a run for his money on design.' She smiled. 'It's got to be better than nursing here with that dreadful radium stuff dripping from needles stuck in those poor patients. Why you every transferred here in the first place, I can't imagine.

'Thank you,' she said to the waiter as he poured her more wine.

Annie laughed. 'Hardly dripping, Sarah, and we do manage to save some of them you know. But only some,' and her voice tailed away. She had moved to gain more experience and the pay was better which made Tom's fees easier, but she was tired of suffering now, too tired to stay in for much longer. She was ready to start on the next stage and Tom was ready too. There must not be a war, not when they had people to help and a firm to set up.

They took a taxi to the station. Doors slammed and whistles shrieked and the compartment was full with people as they left the city and the low cloud which seemed to hang motionless sucking all the light from the city.

'How can you live here, Annie? It's always so wet and gloomy.'

'I hope you're not becoming imprecise in your old age, Sarah. It is often wet but not always.' They leant into one another and laughed and then their hours were their own and Sarah slept while Annie felt the effects of the wine make her limbs easy and she watched cities merge into country. The noise of the train must be the same as any other but it seemed to rush and lurch and she could not sleep and then they were there and it was the same station they had flown across with Da to find the Newcastle train, but now it was small and she was helping Sarah as she stepped from the carriage to the platform over no gap at all. Sour coal was heaped high in the sidings outside the station as it had been when she last saw it, as it had been the day she and Georgie rode their bikes here for their day by the sea. The slag-heaps were bigger. Oh God yes, they were bigger and still the cables churned the carts up until they tipped more slag on to the top.

They took another taxi, this time to the church which was darkened by soot though the windows were lit by the lights inside. Their heels made sharp sounds as they walked to the front and Don turned and smiled. He was sitting with Albert who was best man and whose face hung even more than usual from his brows. Always the same ray of sunshine, thought Annie, and squeezed Don's shoulder. He turned and grinned but he was nervous and had bunched his handkerchief in his hand and was kneading it.

'Like your hat, bonny lass, and like seeing you even better,' whispered Don and she was back again amongst the life they had lived together, one that she had avoided until now, but why, she wondered? She glanced at Sarah who nodded.

'Nice to be back, is it, little Annie?' she asked and squeezed her hand. Yes, thought Annie, and realised that the veneer of speech and polish was thin indeed. Sarah was looking along the pews searching for Val who had come up from Gosforn separately. There was a wave across the other side and there she was, in pale blue with her handkerchief out, sitting with Bob who was smiling.

'Oh dear, she'll cry,' she whispered to Annie who giggled and waved across to the plump woman.

'Tom couldn't make it after all, then,' Annie breathed into Don's ear.

'They're still in London. Tom's mural is almost finished but not quite.' He pulled a face. 'He'll see us when he gets back.'

The pews were dark brown and the hymn books wobbled in their binding. The blue stamp of St Mark's Church was faded on the flyleaf and she was glad that Don had chosen 'Eternal Father'; it was Da's favourite. She had not been inside a church since the convent and here, today, there were no chrysanthemums but dahlias; red, yellow and purple. There was no incense either to laden the air but Albert's stale smell was just the same. Thank God for Sarah's Chanel. Maud was late and Don fidgeted.

The vicar came out from the side chapel. God almighty, she thought, it's the same vicar who buried me da but without the dewdrop this time and then the organ stirred them and Maud arrived. The vicar still said 'Gond' and Annie wanted to laugh.

The reception was at Merthyr Terrace, at Maud's home, but the neighbours would have their doors open for the overflow as always. They walked along the streets and Annie talked to Bob about Tom and thought how much older he looked. 'It's the men,' he explained to Annie, 'still no work and now perhaps the war.' She talked to him of Grace and whether she and Tom would every marry; she did not want to talk of that subject, the one which the papers ran as headlines. It was the wrong time for war. This was to be her time; Tom's time.

The ham was pale pink on the table which was stacked high with plates and salad bowls and punch. Betsy stood near with Joe, hand in hand, and Annie kissed her and shook Joe's hand.

'Are you well, Betsy?' Annie knew that she was. Her face was relaxed and her eyes were soft and Joe laughed as Annie said, 'And your lad's coming back soon, then.'

'Oh aye,' said Joe. 'He's always got a room with us, they both have, Grace and him.'

Annie nodded. 'And how's May?'

Betsy smiled. 'Her other boys are back so she's happy. Made me a patchwork quilt for our bedroom. It's lovely, isn't it, pet?' Joe nodded his reply.

Betsy looked over towards the table with the drinks, then handed her glass to Joe. 'Get me a barley-water would you, pet?' He smiled and moved away.

Betsy looked up at Annie, almost shyly. 'I'd never have thought I'd be this happy, you know.'

Annie looked after Joe. 'Is it because of him, Betsy?'

'Aye it is, lass.' She paused and searched for words. 'I had to do something a long while ago that I thought would make me unhappy, but it hasn't. It was gradual, see, very gradual but I love him now. But I still keeps me own name and he still pays me for doing the housekeeping. I don't want to get back to being a skivvy, see.' She looked confused and defensive and Annie held her arm and looked into her eyes.

'You're right, Betsy, absolutely right.' The people were pressing round them and Joe was back with Betsy's drink and Annie thought of the way her father had treated Betsy and the old anger was back again, though it had never really gone and she swallowed it down as she always seemed to be doing.

'I tell you what, Betsy,' she said taking herself in hand telling herself that she would think about it some other time because, try as she might, it was something she could not throw out completely as Georgie had said she should. It just wouldn't go but lodged inside the black box, waiting. She shook herself. 'I tell you what,' she repeated. 'Tom and I will make you some matching curtains for your bedroom when we're in business, how about that?'

Joe shook his head. 'I reckon that might have to wait, lass. We'll maybe have a war.'

Sarah had found Albert over by the food. He was drinking beer by himself.

'Well, Albert,' she said planting herself in front of him. 'You didn't destroy Don, then, like you promised you would. It was the destruction of Annie though to begin with wasn't it, but they've both escaped. So Archie wasn't destroyed either, was he?' She hated this man for what he'd done to Annie.

Albert sipped his beer. 'Just an old dried-up prune you are, Sarah Beeston.'

She wanted to tip his beer out all down the front of his suit but just smiled.

Albert turned from her and looked at Don. 'He's a good boy, that one. He's not like his da, not a high-flier like the girl. He's been all right to me and I'll be all right to him, so let's leave it at that.' He moved from her, into the other guests, his eyes hooded and she heard him say into his beer. 'Like me own son he is. A good boy that one.'

And she felt moved and saw him as he really was, lonely and unsure.

Annie had moved on from Joe and Betsy, waved to May, talked to Bob and then saw Ma Gillow peering into her cup of punch. Good God, she's trying to read the bloody fruit, she thought, and felt the laughter well inside.

'She's trying to read the fruit then, is she?' and he was there, just like that, a glass of beer in his hand and her breath caught in her throat. 'You've changed a bit, bonny lass.' Georgie was so close she should have been able to sense him there, should have known he was within a mile of the place, and then he turned her to him. Tears were caught on the lids of her eyes and her lips were tight together and she could not see him unless she blinked and if she blinked the tears would loosen and weave downwards like the rain on the train windows.

'And where the hell have you been, you little bugger?' she said and he wiped his thumbs beneath her eyes and held her

303

head between hands which were still the same only broader, stronger.

'Waiting for today, bonny lass,' he said and kissed her lips and eyes and hair and she heard no one, saw no one, just him as he held her and drank her in.

Then Don was there, standing in front of them. 'I see you remember one another,' grinned Don. 'About time too, lad. She was turning into an old maid before our very eyes. Like the khaki, like the pips.'

She saw then the Sam Browne belt, the pips not stripes and felt his arm tighten round her and the hardness of his straps against her.

'Took too long getting them though, Don,' Georgie said, but Don was away again and his eyes were the same brown as he asked. 'Did I, hinny, did I take too long?' His skin was brown and his smile white and one-sided as it had always been.

'Never too long to wait, not for you.' She stroked his face and then the speeches began and the toasts were drunk in sparkling wine and beer was pulled as afternoon turned to evening and the dancing began but all she noticed were his hands as he held her, his arms round her strong and certain; his voice as he talked and his eyes as he listened, his lips as he kissed her. All she felt was her body wanting his, because her love was the same, only stronger.

Ma Gillow bumped into them as she wove her way through to the punch again. 'Told you you'd do well,' she smirked, 'but it should be with Tom. You mark my words, it will be with Tom.'

Annie laughed and Georgie grinned. 'It will too Mrs Gillow, just wait until the lad gets back up here.'

'But there's the war, isn't there?' And Georgie's face grew still.

Then Sarah came and smiled at Annie. She shook Georgie's hand and he leaned forward and kissed her.

'Thanks for looking after my bonny lass, Sarah. And for your letters.'

Annie felt her jaw drop and she turned to Sarah who had blushed.

'Yes, I just thought a few letters might help keep you both in touch. I do so hope I didn't interfere.' Annie laughed and kissed her cheek. 'You really are the most extraordinary woman and I love you so much.'

Sarah turned to Val who had come up behind them. She could not speak, just nodded and turned away. Val sighed and looked at Annie. 'She's waited a long time to hear you say that and I'm right glad you have but we'll get off home now. We won't be seeing you tonight, I dare say.' She patted Annie's cheek and they were gone.

Annie ran her hands over his uniform. It prickled her and his shoes were so shiny, Mother Superior would have had him straight in the conservatory, she thought, as they left two minutes later.

The streets were empty but still lit and they found his hotel room without ever feeling the pavements change to cobbles and the dry night to drizzle.

This time there was no fear of bairns, of passions which frightened and confused. They were not two children beyond their experiences but two people who talked and kissed and remembered their youth together; who spoke of their times apart.

The room was whitewashed and the curtains were soft pink. The light came from two bedside lights and the double bed was soft. He undressed her and kissed her shoulders as he slid the clothes from her body, kissed her breasts and her stomach, her thighs and she lay and watched as he unbuckled his belts and threw his clothes over the armchair which stood in the corner. His body had hardened since that day on the beach and he was tanned except for his buttocks which remained stark white. There were still the blue-ridged mining scars down his back that he would never lose.

'I've missed you so much,' she breathed as he walked towards her and his eyes crinkled as he stood by the bed and looked from her face down the length of her body.

'You are so beautiful. I hope, bonny lass, that you have been loved?' His eyes found hers and there was a question in them that demanded an answer.

Her voice was level and strong when she answered, 'Yes.' Because none of her men had touched the place she kept for him.

Her hands felt loose with relief as he smiled and nodded and said:

305

'As I have too, bonny lass, but it never touched you at all.'

There need be no lies with Georgie and that was something she had always known. He sat down on the bed and his weight made the bed lower and she slid towards him.

'How long will you be in Woolwich?' That was where he had told her he was posted.

'Not long, my darling. There could well be war.' She pulled him to her then, covering his mouth with hers, not wanting to hear that word here, in this room with his body so close to hers. She could smell his skin and it was the same as it had always been. His mouth grew demanding, his hands were feeling her breasts, her thighs and she stroked his back, his legs, his arms as they moved along her body and she loved his strength, his power.

'I want to leave the light on, my love. The missing has been so hard and I must see and feel every second of tonight because that's all we have for now.'

His voice was deep against her mouth and his breathing fast as she rose to meet him and she knew only the dark rush of years without him and his touch which was the same today as it had been so long ago. Evening turned to night and still they clung together, still their passion remained and had to be satisfied once more.

They did not sleep all night. His arms were round her, stroking her hair, telling her of the heat and dust, the beauty and filth. The memsahibs who drank tea and were fanned by bunka wallahs and looked down their noses at pitmen who became sergeants and sergeants who became officers. She told him of Manchester and Tom's progress, his limp and his tiredness. His talent and her determination that they would provide work so that her patients, or some of them at least, would recover from illnesses which should not kill but did.

'Will you be here, in England, for a while, my darling?' she asked as she kissed his fingers which had just teased her to such heights.

'I should be, if the war doesn't happen. I'm with the Engineers now, bomb disposal but there aren't any bombs, thank God, so we build bridges instead, or blow 'em up.' He pulled her close to him, breathing in her scent. 'If there's a war, God knows where I'll be. Maybe it will be back to India but it won't be for long and we can get married, my love, you can come back with me.'

Her stomach tensed, her back stiffened and she felt every breath.

'There won't be a war,' she said. 'There can't be war, not after the last one.' She turned to him, kissing him fiercely. 'No, we need not marry, not yet. There's no need.'

His eyes were closed and she kissed them. 'We are together now, there's time to make plans later.' She kissed him again and again and slowly his arms closed round her.

The next day he left on the early train which would take him back to Woolwich until he could see her again.

'If we were married,' he urged, 'you could come with me.'

But she shook her head. 'There's time for that,' she repeated.

Annie walked to the station two hours later and, apart from the click of footsteps which were her own, a Sunday silence cloaked the streets. The glazed lightless shop fronts seemed to hang and the scent of her home town was all around, the black dust lay on each sill, in each gutter. Suddenly the sky brought darkness and lightning clawed the clouds which rolled thick and black and the wind sucked air in great gulps and hurled harsh rain which poured down drains and swirled in the alleys. On and on it came, soaking through her coat. Her tongue tasted the savage cut of water and she could neither see nor hear until suddenly it was over and she was frightened and alone and calling for Georgie deep inside but he had gone and she had not left with him.

She transferred back to Newcastle on 1 September, wanting general nursing now. Evacuation had begun in the hospital of all patients who were not at death's door to make way for possible war casualities. Gas masks were to be carried at all times for all people and air-raid shelters which had been started at the time of the Czechoslovakian crisis in 1938 were finished. The parks were dug over with trenches. Light bulbs in the ward were painted and sandbags at the windows cut down the light. Sarah asked her for lunch on Sunday but all leave had been cancelled.

War was declared on 3 September and soon barrage balloons were flying over the Tyne. Annie nodded as the matron at the War Office building in the city asked her if she was prepared to give up her independence for the duration and two weeks later she was accepted into the Queen Alexandra's Imperial Military Nursing Service.

Georgie was still in England and they met in London before she received her posting.

His eyes were veiled as he talked about his movements. He had lines which cut deep round his eyes but they forgot the war, forgot their faded hopes as they lay together and drew closer than ever. They talked of Tom's marriage, the day after war was announced. They had called into Annie before they took the connection for Wassingham. Grace had clung to her and Tom had stood back and their eyes had met. Georgie saw her off on the train back to Newcastle. He did not know when he would see her again but he was meeting his CO in London and would give him her name because his daughter was joining the QA's too. Maybe the boss could wangle the same posting for you both, he'd said, and get you into a safe zone.

They had kissed and hugged and promised they would see one another soon, that each moment until then would be an ache.

CHAPTER 22

Annie's first posting was to a girls' boarding school in Oxfordshire which had been converted into a small military hospital.

As she was driven up the long drive by the army car that had picked her up at the station she saw that tents had been pitched on the sweeping lawns that led down to the line of oaks which designated the boundary of the school where it met the road. Oaks also lined the drive and there were two rows of drab military ambulances parked where the horses had once paraded outside the stables. There were steps which led to the hall and she returned the driver's salute wondering if he could see her hand tremble. It was the same feeling in her stomach and legs that she had experienced at the convent and the hospital on her first day but this time there was no Sarah and she missed her.

The hallway smelt of wax with overtones of disinfectant. Was there ever a hall that did not, she thought? There were Daily Orders pinned where timetables should have been and she followed the lance-corporal as he clumped on ahead of her up the wide stairs, his boots clattering where lightfooted girls had previously trod. She smiled to think of the army descending on the convent. Jenn and Sandy would have been in heaven. Where were they both now, she wondered? Sarah had heard that they were both married though she had not received letters from either for years now.

Her room was on the top floor; it had previously been a teacher's study, the lance-corporal explained as he clicked his heels and left her to unpack. There was another bed in the room but so far it was unoccupied. The window overlooked the side garden and beyond was the playing-field, just so long as there was no Miss Hardy they'd be all right, she grinned to herself.

There were flowered curtains at the window though the beds had plain blue covers. There were photos of old school hockey teams on the walls. The faces were blank as they stared at the camera with hockey sticks held to the right of the knees. It was all very proper.

Matron gathered the new arrivals into her office which was light and faced south. She was dressed as they would be when they were on duty, in a grey dress with a cape trimmed with scarlet and a white veil which fluttered in the breeze coming in through the window. Annie pulled down the jacket of her grey QA uniform.

'You'll have your inoculations today and your medicals,' Matron explained in a relaxed voice that was hard to accept after years of civilian hospitals. 'You are all here, bar one; a late arrival, I'm afraid.'

The medicals took an hour each and the inoculations were painless but made Annie wonder where she might be sent eventually.

They toured the wards; the orthopaedic with Balkan Beams already installed; the operating theatre, surgical and medical, and the burns unit. It was strange to see no flowers by the beds, just the statutory towel correctly folded for commanding officer's rounds each morning and the shaving kits.

'No nighties here anyway.' Annie murmured to the dark girl next to her.

The girl grinned. 'Cheer the men up no end if there were!'

Her name was Monica and she came from Birmingham but Annie already knew that from her accent. They had tea together in the Sisters' mess. Toast with butter and jam and thick brown tea. All the rooms were high-ceilinged with ornate coving. Grey cobwebs hung down and floated in long strands on the breeze. Well, as long as I don't have to get up there and waggle a duster about, it's not my problem, Annie thought and ate another piece of toast. She looked at the oil painting that Monica pointed out. It was of a woman and child and was badly in need of a clean.

Halfway through tea, Pruscilla Briggs arrived. Monica nudged her and pointed to the door. 'Your room-mate has finally arrived. Lucky, lucky you,' she murmured.

A blonde girl stood in the doorway, her suit straining over a large bust, her eyes wide and her lashes fluttering.

'Oh dear, I'm so dreadfully late,' she gushed to Matron who had risen to meet her. 'I'm so frightfully sorry but we lost our way,' she simpered, 'so daddy's adjutant and I decided to stop for tea in this dear little café to ask the way.'

'Well, you won't need any more, will you?' replied Matron crisply. 'Go to your room and perhaps your room-mate, Sister Manon, will be so kind as to show you round the wards. Your medical and inoculations will just have to wait now until tomorrow. The doctor will not be pleased.' She moved swiftly past Pruscilla who giggled helplessly and smiled at Annie as she groaned at Monica and moved towards the girl.

'Come along then, I'll show you your room first. Then we'll have a look around, shall we?'

Pruscilla chatted her way up the stairs but was quieter by the time they reached the fourth flight. She was plump and panting and her footsteps were quick and short, a bit like Mrs Tittlemouse's, Annie thought, not like Grace and Val who walked in tune with their size.

Her luggage was already there, all six cases of it. And I bet the corporal loved that, thought Annie.

'What will you do if we're posted, for goodness sake?' and then wished she hadn't asked as Pruscilla told her how Daddy would surely send someone to help if it couldn't all go on the train.

That night at dinner, a piper played in the gallery and there were candles on the table. Oak panels lined the dining-room and chandeliers hung above. Cutlery gleamed and wine accompanied each course. Pruscilla sat with Annie and dabbed her lips with her napkin as she finished her melon. 'Of course, I'm used to this sort of thing with Daddy being in the Army. CO of a station in India actually. I schooled in Devon but popped home for the hols.'

Annie laid her spoon and fork down as Pruscilla had done, neatly at one side of the melon shell, and was silently grateful for her unconscious guidance.

'You must find it a bit cold in England after that heat. I know someone who has been in India for years and finds it freezing.' She smiled at Pruscilla and Monica, pleased to be talking about Georgie. 'And you haven't a tan.'

Pruscilla fluttered her eyelashes at Annie, her eyes really

were remarkably blue she thought and moved slightly to allow the steward to remove her plate.

'But one doesn't allow oneself to become tanned. It's all too frightfully common, don't you know. And yes, it does get a trifle chill but one just has to bear this sort of thing for one's country, doesn't one?'

Annie took another sip of wine; trust her to be sharing with Pruscilla, and she sighed to herself. The piper had begun a lament.

'Mark you,' Pruscilla went on. 'Daddy's station is in the Himalayas so it never becomes as hot as the plains. They've been exercising in the jungles over the last year though where it's been humid enough to sprout orchids out of nothing, Daddy says.'

Annie fingered her glass. So she thought, the CO managed it, did he? Good God almighty. There was a steady murmur of conversation on each of the three long tables and the stewards in white jackets refilled glasses as soon as they were empty.

'My friend's name is Georgie Armstrong,' she said.

Pruscilla leant back in her chair and looked up towards the piper. 'I do wish he'd stop soon, I've such a headache. Yes,' she turned to Annie. 'I know Georgie Armstrong. A sergeant made up into an officer. Good man Daddy says, good body the wives say.' She tittered and thanked the steward as he placed fish before her and held the silver platter whilst she took carrots and small potatoes.

Annie wanted to tip it into her lap and turned to talk to Monica instead but Prue's voice continued. 'Georgie is being posted back, so the adjutant says. He's been seconded to Daddy's regiment from the Engineers. They'll need a bomb expert out there and someone to blow bridges if the Japanese come in through Burma.' She was eating her fish now, daintily.

Annie took just a few carrots and one potato as the steward stood on her left, waiting. She was no longer hungry. The candles were flickering along the table and the Sisters all looked alike in their grey suits with Matron at the head of the table. All at once the piper's wail was irritating and she felt alone and only wanted him, Georgie.

She began to eat her fish. 'I didn't know he was leaving,' she said.

'Oh, but neither does he, Annie. Not yet anyway.' Pruscilla

stopped and looked at Annie and her face sobered. 'Oh I say, is he rather more than a friend. I'm so dreadfully sorry. I would never have said. I never should have said anyway. It was a secret and I never know when to stop talking.' Pruscilla was red now, her eyes distressed. She seemed young, Annie thought and smiled.

'I'm always the one being told to stop talking, you know. Don't worry about it, Pruscilla, it will be fine.'

They talked in bed that night or Pruscilla talked and Annie listened. Prue had led a life that seemed identical to that which Georgie had described for the memsahibs over the years. There were the bearers who served food, dressed and fanned you, saddled horses, brushed hair, but Prue's mother had died when she was 16, six years ago, Prue had mused, and that had cast a shadow. I don't really miss her, she had said, because I didn't know her awfully well but one misses the guidance, you know. Daddy is a sweetie of course but fathers aren't the same. Annie did not reply but looked out through the gap between the wall and the black-out curtain at the moon which was large. The harvest would be in now and the winter would be here soon. Would she see him before he went back, she wondered? She didn't want to talk of her father.

Georgie came for two hours, three weeks later. She met him in the town and they had tea in the small café on the main street and he smiled when Annie said she'd met Prue. He was to go away, he said, but they would meet again soon, that the war couldn't last forever. That he would write, but then he fell silent and they couldn't eat but just sat with hands clasped and then walked through the town not noticing its black-beamed prettiness, just wondering and longing.

'I'd like to marry, my darling,' he said, stroking her cheek holding her close to him and his dark eyes were looking deeply into hers and again she felt the tension grip her body.

'Not now, my love,' she said. 'It's not the right time now.' Her words were strained and he said nothing but continued to look and his eyelashes cast a shadow on his cheeks. He bent his head and kissed her lips gently and held her head in his strong hands.

She felt a longing for him but something else as well and the pain which flooded through her showed on her face. He pulled out his cigarettes and lit one passing it to her and they stayed in the shadow of the overhung houses as they shared it. He kept his arm around her, holding her gently to him and kissing her hair and cheeks and she felt his breath on her skin and the tension slowly faded and she pulled in close so that she moulded into his body.

'I love you, bonny lass. I'll always love you and one day you'll be ready to come with me.'

She waved him away on his train, half an hour later. He leaned out, his broad shoulders stretching his uniform.

'I love you, Annie,' he shouted again and again as the train gathered speed and she replied, 'I love you, my darling.' And her tears were those of anger and despair and were directed at herself.

Pruscilla and she were assigned to the burns unit and there was still no way of removing a dressing painlessly or waving a magic wand and regrowing noses, faces and hands but there was plastic surgery, she told her patients, and when they were stronger they would go to a specialist hospital for treatment.

In the meantime she arranged with the manager of the local cinema that they should all go to see a film once a week but, he insisted, they must come in after the lights went out and leave before they rose. He didn't want to scare away his regular customers.

Annie felt Prue's hand on her arm as she made to protest.

'So kind of you, dear man. We, of course, do not want our patients upset by other people's ignorance,' Prue had replied and swept out with Annie in tow.

And so through the winter months they went to the cinema every Thursday evening, even when Annie was transferred to surgical and nursed soldiers without legs or checked the drains and drips on those internally injured. The black-out slits on cars were also reaping their reward and traffic accidents were high and many lives were lost that winter.

In the spring she received a letter from Georgie.

Central Provinces.

My darling love,

Well, I'm back here, bonny lass, back in the jungle and I can tell you this because I'm sending the letter back with a friend returning to England on sick-leave. Malaria is the curse out here.

Things are different this time, my darling. More serious. We seem to be learning a new craft and travel miles with heavy packs, track through jungles, lay charges and that's where I come in – I teach the others.

It's right noisy here, you know. There is always something moving above you or alongside and the monkey's chatter must sound like Prue from what you say.

We're living off the land and roast monkey is very tasty and the blood right good for quenching your thirst.

Burma looks as though it could be a ripe plum for the Japs with their oil refineries at Rangoon, and the CO (Mr Prue to you) says that if the Nips decide to take Burma, they're likely to come on into India across the border expecting the Indians to turn on us from this side and who knows, maybe they will.

Tom shouldn't be in the pits, you know, he should be checking on the surface. I know he's a good pitman and that's what they need but it's not right, I agree with you, not with his injuries. Good old Don getting a cushy number. That lad has the luck of the devil, clerk in a supply depot, well I'm buggered. Maud sounds well from what Tom says and Grace has taken to munitions work like a duck to water. There's more money there too, he says.

Sarah has written and says she liked the hospital when she visited you. She's a game old bird, isn't she, and loves you so much but it can't be as much as I do.

I must stop now, my darling. We will be together when this is over, won't we, my darling lass, and

then I'll bring you to Kashmir. I must go, the plane
is flying my mate out now. I love you. I always have
and I always will, my own precious Annie. I miss
you.

Georgie.

In May, Dunkirk fell and their days were long with a steady
stream of shocked men with war wounds that gaped and
maimed, and they worked until their eyes were black with
tiredness but still Prue fluttered her eyelashes, but not at Annie
any more because she had threatened to trim them while she
was asleep if she continued to create that sort of draught around
her. Prue called the British Expeditionary Force the Back
Every Fridays and had her backside pinched by a major who
could no longer walk.

It was their way of dealing with the horror.

In June, France fell and Prue was relieved that Paris had not
been bombed, such a lovely city, darling, she had breathed as
they sat in the mess. The art galleries are like no other. Annie
had written this to Sarah who had replied that they must
arrange for Tom to go after the war, which they would win of
course.

July was busy in the wards. The Battle of Britain had begun
and they saw the dogfights above and then the burns unit was
busier than ever. Annie was transferred back to comfort the raw
red heads which had once been young faces and took too many
gins in the evening with shaking hands. Day after day there
were new patients and the hours they worked were long and she
grew thin but Prue did not. 'I never lose weight, darling. I never
lose my appetite, that's the problem.' And they laughed
together.

And then there was the blitz and the bombing of the
provinces and the ports and Annie heard from Tom that they
were tired but still all right, though the bombers came every
night and sometimes during the day.

Prue and Annie took a train to London on their day off in the
autumn when things were quieter and passed Peter Robinson's
which looked strange with such a large chunk missing. There
were gaping holes wherever they looked but still people worked

and talked and laughed and there were lunchtime concerts in church halls and they went down into a crypt and sat with Londoners and listened to Chopin and Annie wished that Sarah could have been here. She would have sat, her head moving slightly with each stanza.

Georgie wrote from India. He could say little and there were great sections blacked out by the censor but she could tell where he was from his description of the cruiser butterfly and she thanked God that the Japanese were not involved in the war.

She worked on through the winter, thinking of the times they had been together, the love she felt for him, the ache that was always with her now he was gone.

Now there was extensive rationing but Pruscilla still did not lose weight and the Sisters' mess had a bet on that, by the end of the war, she would still be the same plump blonde, and made Annie promise to write to them and tell them all, wherever they were if they had won.

And so winter turned to spring, and May to June 1941, and they played tennis on the old school courts and Dr Smith taught Annie the backhand and pinched her bottom at the net. Prue threatened to tell Georgie and Annie laughed and chased her until they fell in an exhausted heap under the budding oaks.

The grounds were sweeping and bordered at the back of the house by magnolia trees which were tranquil in the winter and bore white waxed blossom in the spring and, lying beneath the largest in June, Annie could see patches of blue through the fresh green canopy of leaves which had taken the place of the flowers. She could hear the drone of planes and could never imagine a time when she would grow disenchanted by the sun. It drove the thoughts of the wards and injury to the back of her mind. It made Georgie seem nearer and Tom and Don safe and Sarah had written to say that, after seeing the blossoms of the trees when she was down last month, she would try to obtain one after the war.

But Sarah died while she was lying there, while she was relaxing and thinking of nothing, one arm over her eyes and her hand picking at the grass. There was an air raid as Sarah shopped in Newcastle, but she was unmarked and beautiful, Val said in the letter the orderly brought over to her as she lay there. It was another blast death to the rescuers but to Annie it brought the world to a stop.

The letter lay on the grass, discarded. She gripped a handul of grass, it was young and taut in her hands. Sarah couldn't be dead. She would not allow her to be dead. She needed her, needed her voice rolling out words as though she was a book, needed her kindness, her sharpness. Needed her visits as she passed to or from her holidays, needed her letters which told of Gosforn and the hens, told of Val and the Miss Thoms, told of herself. She had been her mother, so how could she die too, like the others?

The magnolia leaves were rustling above her, the sun played fleetingly over her hands which clutched the grass. No, she could not be dead; they had sat here together and enjoyed the sun just a few weeks ago, she could still hear her voice, see her smile. No, she could not be dead, not be cold, Annie loved her too much for that to have happened and what the hell was she doing shopping in Newcastle when the bombs dropped? What the hell was she doing taking risks for a yard of cloth? What did she want a yard of cloth for? Annie looked at the grass she had torn up, grass which hung from fists which were lifted to the sky. Oh God, if only she didn't know what a dead body looked like.

Sarah, don't leave now, not now, not ever.

There was another letter too, from the solicitor, and the envelope was stiff vellum; its edge cut her thumb and it bled but she did not feel it, just brushed the drops to a smear as she focussed on the typewritten words which must be read, Val had said in her letter, but which were an irritation, an intrusion. She wanted to think, to remember, but not to either, because how could she bear this loss? Why die over a bloody piece of cloth? Oh Sarah, why? Grass lay discarded on her lap now dark against her uniform, against Val's letter.

The solicitor informed her in black detached perfect lettering that she now owned the house and also a large capital sum including an account which had been set aside to receive her repayments for the loans Don and Tom had received. This was also hers now. Sarah had assumed that she would continue to maintain a position for Val, who had been comfortably provided for. Annie would not have thought to do otherwise but money was not what she wanted to clutter her mind up with now; it was Sarah who must fill it, who must stay with her, tight

318

inside her, safe, well, devoid of a yard of cloth, devoid of dust on her dear cold face.

She went back on duty and changed the dressing which was overdue on the amputation and read aloud the letter that the blind pilot's wife had written, made tea for Pruscilla and herself in the ward kitchen, drank it while Pruscilla remained silent and watchful. She could not taste it and her hand trembled only slightly as she replaced the cup in its saucer, right in the middle, so that it fitted perfectly or was it a bit too much to the right. There, that was perfect, or was it too much to the left?

'Leave it, Annie,' Prue said gently.

Only that night when the moon was brilliant in the sky and had blazoned the stars into nothingness did she cry, standing at the window and gripping the frame, silently at first until Prue led her back to bed and then the sobs rasped deep in her chest and her fists beat the pillow which was wet from her mouth and eyes and the missing was deep and dark and she could now believe that she was never going to see her again.

Georgie's letters eased her pain a little over the next days and weeks and months, but only a very little. She filled in ward forms, ate at mealtimes, played tennis again but could not remember doing it. She never lay beneath the magnolia tree again because her comfort was gone and that is where she had last been. Sarah was gone and life would never be quite the same again.

They knew that they were soon to be posted overseas because they had been instructed to buy tropical kit and Annie was glad. Glad to leave England, to be nearer Georgie because she needed him more than ever now that Sarah was gone.

Annie took the train to Gosforn for her embarkation leave. The privet hedge still smelt of dusty yellow pollen and she took a leaf and bent it between her fingers and it snapped into segments; so autumn is with us, she thought.

The key slid easily into the lock and the brass doorknob shone as it had always done and the hallway was empty as it often was but it was an emptiness now which rolled off into the sitting-room because Sarah was not in the winged chair with her glasses low on her nose as she looked towards the door and rattled her paper.

Then the kitchen door opened and Val bustled through, her

arms pink and plump and warm as they held her close.

'I've put the tea on for you, my dear.'

But first Annie climbed the stairs, took off her grey suit, looked under the bed and there was the potty. She moved to the window, slipped the latch and leaned out. One last cut would do the lawn, the roses could be pruned and the air was still heavy with the scent of honeysuckle and baked bread. The hens were still in their runs and she smiled as the cock strutted backwards and forwards. Nothing has changed, she marvelled. But everything has changed.

There was boiled egg for tea, the warm brown shell of which peeled off to expose a fresh white and then a vivid yolk which welled orange and rich.

Annie leaned back. 'Are you able to give the Miss Thoms a few too, Val?' She dug her toast soldier into the yolk and chewed at it.

Val nodded. 'And they give me honey because their gardener has a hive.'

And there it was suddenly, vivid in her mind; the hive across from the beck, the black-eyed daisies in the meadow and the train that steamed away to God knows where. 'I wrote to Tom and Don and they are going to come over, Val, if they can manage it. Don's been called up and has landed up as a clerical private in the supply depot. Tom's in the mines again. Did they tell you?' She raised her eyes as Val nodded.

'They pop in from time to time,' she smiled. 'Worried that I might be lonely, I think. They're good boys. Did you know that the Miss Thoms have lent me their gardener as well, Annie? Kind of them but he drives me mad. Rake, rake, until I could scream. Why doesn't he just bung in a few seeds, that's what I'd like to know? I don't let him feed your hens, don't trust him to do too much. Bit old, bit dense, if you know what I mean.'

She touched her finger to her head and pulled a face.

'He says a girl like you should be tucked up in a little house with a few bairns hanging off your skirt but I say to him that, if I had to decide between that and being waited on hand, foot and finger, I know what I'd choose.'

Annie laughed. 'I do a bit of work too you know, Val.'

'Oh, I know that but you're an officer and officers don't do much, do they?'

Annie just shook her head and smiled. Her egg was finished

320

now and she took a sip of tea. 'Do you miss her very much, Val?'

Val sat down, easing her legs round and under the table.

'It feels as though she's still alive. I think I hear her coming down in the morning.' She reached over and cut some more bread. It was fresh and fell on to the board as the knife sawed through. Annie picked up some moist crumbs pressing them together and wondered if there would ever be a time when simple gestures did not take her rushing back to the past.

'Aye, I miss her, every day I miss her,' Val said in a calm voice. 'But it's not an aching. It happened and it was quick and everything is the same except she's not here but there again, she is, if you know what I mean. Life goes on, lass. I think of her and it pleases me. It doesn't pain.'

Later in the darkness of the sitting-room Annie felt the sameness and was comforted. She lay her head back in her chair opposite Sarah's and was grateful for the table at its side which held the same lamp, the same photograph of the skiers. The only difference to the room was the black-out and the empty chair, but otherwise so little was disturbed and Sarah's essence was everywhere bringing good memories. Death did not mean the end of everything as it had done before. It did not have to be ugly and wounding but calm and part of natural life.

Time passed and she rested her head on the back of the chair. Well, Sarah, she thought, tropical kit, iron kettle and a tent pole. What do you think it means? Where will I be going now? I'm a bit old for camping at 27, aren't I?

First though, the lawn had to be cut and as she rose the boys were there; Tom limping towards her and Don grinning as he came along behind.

'Had to come now, bonny lass,' Tom said as he hugged her. 'Got an early shift tomorrow and Don's on night duty. Grace sends her love and so does Maud but they're both working at the munitions factory so can't get away.' He held her at arm's length and smoothed back her hair. 'You look tired, bonny lass.' Then Don pushed him out of the way.

'Let me have a kiss then. She doesn't look so bad.' He hugged her and she liked the feel of their familiar arms around her.

She led them into the garden and watched as they took turns to push the lawn-mower. They talked and fell silent, laughed and were serious as the late afternoon sun stayed high in the sky. She knotted her cardigan round her waist by its arms and the secateurs felt warm in her hands as she pruned the roses right back. They began the bonfire as the sun started to go down and burnt the dead roses, the old wood from the lilac and the lavender clippings that Don had cut. They laid down the grass cuttings as a mulch and then after tea they were on their way again, sweating from their work, sleeves rolled up and hair in their eyes, eager to be back before the black-out but not wanting to leave.

'It won't be long now,' they said as they put on their motor cycle helmets. Tom looked hard at her. 'Get some ideas for design then, bonny lass. Sarah told me it would be a good idea. Then, when it's over, we'll get on.' He kissed her again and pointed to Don. 'That miserable old bugger doesn't want to come in with us.'

Don shook his fist at them both. 'I've got me own business and it'll do very well, thank you, now that I've got Albert doing the right things. He actually smiles at the customers, makes a right nice face an' all he does.'

She heard their laugh well into the night when she lay in bed and watched the stars and smelt the grass clippings and fastened her brothers in her mind as they had been this afternoon because she did not know when she would see them again.

She arrived back at the hospital two days later in the evening, after Pruscilla. The wards were nearly empty and there were crates in the hall. She met Prue on the stairs and she was panting.

'The stairs are really too steep for this rushing about, darling. It's so undignified.' There were shouts from downstairs and the revving of lorries in the drive.

'You're just too fat,' Annie grinned.

'Now don't be cross,' Prue pouted. 'Now come along, back down with me. Matron wants us all assembled.' She pulled her towards the next flight down. The oil paintings which lined the stairs were shrouded in white sheeting and Annie paused to peer at the last picture, lifting the corner of the cover.

There were only dim lights on the stairs and none in the hallway below them. 'Oh, come on, darling,' urged Prue. 'We've got to get down now and strictly no lights allowed so put your torch away and stop poking about looking at pictures that are not yours anyway.'

She was flustered, Annie could see that now. Her forehead was furrowed and her face was flushed.

'So what's the hurry, I thought we had another half an hour?' She put her torch in her pocket and started down the stairs.

'Our transport is arriving then and the old dragon is having a heart attack every five minutes.'

'Matron is very nice,' Annie said quietly.

'To you maybe,' whispered Prue as they approached the hall. There were other nurses there now and orderlies were moving amongst them with lists in their hands which they played their torches over.

Annie stood with Prue over by the corridor. 'All right,' she gave in, 'tell me what's happened.' She leant back against the door jamb and hitched up her gas mask.

'All so terribly trivial, darling.' Prue's eyes would be wide, Annie knew that from the tone of voice. 'I put down her list, that's all, and I can't remember where and before that the corporal in charge of the baggage was heard to say that he was buggered if he'd herd a bunch of camels like this again. When Matron said she'd take down his number if she heard language like that again, some wag said Corp wasn't on the phone but he'd take her on instead. Well, you can imagine, darling.'

Annie was laughing now, so hard that her stomach hurt and Monica, who was standing further down, hissed, 'Shut up, for God's sake, she'll have your head on a platter.'

The train was unlit, unheated and there were no seats left and Annie came to the conclusion as she sat on her kit in the dark corridor and pushed Pruscilla upright that this was no way to fight a war. She wore her tin hat as orders were orders but it was noisy when dropped which it did with every lurch of the train. It was so cold that she could no longer feel her feet and her hands were stuck deep into her greatcoat pockets. The corridor smelt of stale tobacco and dirty bodies. Pruscilla snored but there was no rhythm to it, just a series of disjointed grunts and gurgles.

'Can't you stop that bleedin' din, Sister?' called a man's voice but Annie ignored it. Nothing but a cork would do that or a pinched nose and there was no way she was about to do that and provoke Prue's hysterics. The Thermos was still full and she unscrewed the cap and took a drink as the train rattled over the points. The hot tea was tangy but warming; the steam made her nose run. It was midnight.

The black-out blind banged against the frame and it seemed lighter outside than in and she could see that they were passing through the edge of a town, then the train began to slow. It lurched and Pruscilla flopped forward and they had arrived. It was cold and dark and noise was still forbidden but this was Lime Street Station in Liverpool. Pruscilla had docked here before and recognised the station.

'I want to hear nothing, not even the clink of a hat, not even a snort.' The sergeant-major was very red in the face and Prue blinked.

Searchlights stabbed the sky and an air raid was on. They stayed in the station, listening to the crump, crump of the bombs and the reply of the ack-ack as they pounded the planes.

Annie's head ached with tiredness and the bombs were too far away to be real so there was no fear. But it was still so cold. At last they were able to drag their kitbags over to the transport when the all-clear sounded and she could smell the brine of the sea and feel its stickiness in her hair.

They were still bound to silence as they approached their ship. The gangplank was steep and the non-slip strips were too wide for Annie's stride and the water gurgled beneath them, oily and dirty. Hands gripped her as she reached the top and handed her down to the deck which was vibrating as the engines idled. It was pitch-dark still and she and Prue were passed along to where Monica and two others stood.

'You five Sisters follow me,' said a male voice in scarcely more than a whisper.

Once inside the hatchway, dim lights showed narrow steel-riveted corridors and the tremor beneath their feet was more noticeable and there was a heavy smell of diesel.

They were led along narrow companionways until the sailor stopped, checked his list and opened the door.

'This is your cabin.' He still spoke in a whisper. 'Water twice a day at oh-six hundred hours and eighteen hundred hours. Sea soap is provided for washing. No noise until we're under way.' It was an order and his face told them so.

They moved into the cabin. There were six bunks and one

nurse already in the cabin. Prue sidled up to Annie. 'They look awfully small, darling,' she whispered and they all laughed.

Monica was with them but the rest were strangers. Prue looked tired and frightened and Annie said, 'Have the bottom bunk, lass. It's less far to fall in a rough sea and I'll get you some tea from the flask.' She steered her towards the bunk and patted her arm.

Monica was stowing her kit in the space at the end of the bunks and Annie put hers and Prue's on top. She grinned at the other three Sisters and one with a faint moustache smiled back.

'Would you like some tea?' breathed Annie, remembering the noise regulation.

The other Sister nodded her head. 'I've something which will make it taste a little better,' and she drew out a small hip flask. 'Tea and whisky. Best thing for sea-sickness.'

But it wasn't and they were. They still did not know where they were going but Annie knew it would be nearer Georgie though further from Tom.

CHAPTER 23

Grace stood by the kitchen table, impatient at the time the tea was taking to cool. She wanted to pour it into Tom's morning flask and get to bed before the air-raid siren sounded. It was nearly eleven and in half an hour the bombers would start. The Germans were always on time, had been for months now. Aiming for the docks they were, the papers said, but you could have fooled Wassingham.

After the first week of it, Bob had explained that the Germans were a mechanical people who liked a timetable; his face was serious and his tone that of a teacher and Tom had slapped his back and told him he'd buy him a German watch with a bloody great cuckoo leaping out every hour.

Grace dipped her finger into the tea again. 'Strange how they grabbed you the minute we arrived back up here, isn't it?' she said. 'A disabled agitator one minute, too crippled for the army and an essential worker the next. What a difference a war makes, eh Tom? Two years now and how many more to go, bonny lad?'

Tom grunted and moved the picture frame he was pinning to catch more light from the single bulb which dangled above him. There were a pile of gleaming steel pins on the scrubbed table and a small hammer which lay near them. The room was cheerful in spite of the gloom with scattered patchwork cushions given to them by May and Betsy creating colour, but the heavy smell of size and stove-black from the make-shift black-out curtains permeated the whole house. The furniture was sparse but familiar since it came from Joe and Betsy.

He was glad to be working like this, busy with his art after the shift, but his hands were not as dextrous as they used to be, he had noticed recently, because they were stiff from muscles knotted with manual work and damaged by dust-saturated cuts. His nails were stained black again too as they had been in the old days but he still had the energy, just, to take a painting class once a week at the library, so long as it didn't coincide with his firewatch duty.

He held the last pin in his mouth, scored a small hole in the joint and then tapped it in. He slid his painting of the unfinished air-raid shelter, roofless and stark, into the back and secured it. He felt a sense of continuing exasperation at his situation; painting scenes which depicted the lack of care for the local population when all he really wanted was to be out there fighting the Nazis. But no, it was the pit he was stuck in, with a bit of daubing on the side to make him feel he could still say something about the things that angered him.

'That'll do,' he said to Grace as he arched his back and ran his hands round his neck. 'I'm getting old, lass, creaking and groaning like the pit-props, an old man at 25.' He put a quaver in his voice and pulled her to him, running his hands down her back and over her buttocks. There was not much spare weight on his bonny lass these days but at least rationing had made things fairer and no one starved, like they used to. Everyone was just bloody hungry. Grace bent over and kissed the top of his head, full of the smell of coal again after being clean for four years. She sighed and tested the tea again. It was ready.

'It's a bloody disgrace about that shelter you know,' Tom went on, watching her as she poured the tea into the flask and secured the top. She had nice hands still, had our Gracie, in spite of working in that factory. 'Fancy telling people to go and shelter in the cupboard under the stairs until they find money from somewhere to finish it. We've said we'll do it if they can produce the materials but even that doesn't speed things up. The bloody war will be over before they get round to it or I hope to God it is.' He brushed the pins into his hand and put them back in the old tobacco tin which held them, opening the drawer beneath the table and throwing in the hammer, then the pins. God, he hoped it was over soon but how could it be without help from the US and there was no hope of that at the moment. As it was, it looked as though Hitler could be over here any time and he shuddered, then hoped that Grace hadn't seen.

'Are you glad I dragged you back up here then, hinny, and didn't make you go through the blitz in London?' He was grinning now as he tried to talk away his forebodings. Grace was tipping ash gently on to the fire and she finished before straightening up and tucking a red curl behind her ear.

'Oh aye, lad,' she laughed. 'Much more cosy to be bombed in me own home.' She came over and sat on his lap. It would be time for bed in five minutes, he thought as he stroked her face and laid his head on her shoulder, but they wouldn't go earlier than ten past eleven or they would have more time to think of the bombs that would soon start. They sayed in bed now, didn't rush to the dark tight cupboard. It hadn't saved Ma Gillow's friend or the children who had been crushed just the same. It seemed so pointless somehow to rush like rats into a hole and die anyway; it was too much like the pit.

He remembered Chamberlain's message to the nation at 11.15 a.m. on 3 September as he breathed in Grace's scent and heard the beating of her heart beneath the green jumper that had gone felty in the wash. And how, now a state of war existed, they, like the rest of the population, had headed for home, like animals in a storm. Married they'd been though, the day before, and had stood together in the corridor for the length of the journey because the seats were packed full. It was the children he remembered most, that and the feel of Grace as she had stood close to him and pressed against him as they swung with the train.

To begin with, the bairns had run past them shouting and laughing but had soon subsided into bored lethargy and tearful boredom, sprawled all over their parents and one another, their gas masks sticking into them, making for more tears, more discomfort.

A few hours out of London the guard had come along and insisted on a drill and Tom remembered the smell of the gas mask rubber which was choking, and the misting of the glass which cut down his vision. The train had still been swinging and lurching and the children were crying now except for one red-haired boy who kept his on when others had gratefully dragged the mask from their faces and sucked at the stale train air. The boy had blown out hard and the raspberry was loud enough for the old lady with her luxury gas-mask container in the first-class compartment to tut and wonder how she was to survive the war if she was to rub shoulders with the likes of these. Did she have any evacuees now? Tom wondered, and grinned at the thought. That should knock her delicate sensibilities out of the window.

He had sketched the boy quickly and in pencil while Grace looked over his shoulder. It was good, she had said and then sat down on the suitcase propped against the compartment door. It was splitting with age and she had set her feet apart and hunched herself over her knees.

She had asked whether the Germans would really use gas and he had laughed and said of course they wouldn't, hoping that she would not hear that Mussolini had used it in 1935 against the Abyssinians. So far though, the Germans had not used it, they used bombs instead. He lifted his head from the warmth of her shoulder and checked the wall clock. Fifteen minutes past eleven.

'Come on, lass, up you go. I'll get me boots out and me clothes for the morning.' He laid his pit-clothes over the fender so that the early winter chill would be kept at bay by the small ash-banked fire.

They had called in to see Annie when they had reached Newcastle, then continued on to Wassingham and it seemed as though they had never been away; the slag-carts still churned upwards and there was that smell in the air. But as they walked on to Grace's home, they passed white-painted kerbs and lampposts and heaps of sand which some children had spread on the pavement and turned into a soft shoe shuffle stage. It stank of dogs' pee, he could smell it now, and so did the sandbags which were stacked in front of the library windows and shops as blast protection.

They had gone from Grace's house to Bob's and he had shown them the two up two down he had found for them to rent with a privy out at the back. He looked well, less drawn, and Tom had taken him and Don for a drink while Grace and Maud sorted out the house. She'd stuck her tongue out at him and called that she would tell Annie he was a pig.

It was because there was full employment Bob had gloated as he supped at his beer and the froth stayed on his upper lip until he wiped it away with his handkerchief. There's a munitions factory opening up down the road, he'd gone on, and it'll take our lads and they won't have to care if the pit's open or not. Tom laughed with Don and winced as the lad kicked him under the table. War's done you proud has it, Bob? Don had said, and

329

Bob had blushed and admitted that, to some extent, Don was right, explaining that the lads would be able to get away from Wassingham now into the services or, if they stayed, they had the chance of better conditions in the factories, not the bloody pits. And of course, Tom thought, as he shut the kitchen door and climbed the stairs, he'd been right.

He boarded up the bedroom windows with the cut-down doors which Bob had unscrewed from his unused bedrooms and was in bed before the nightly raid began but the crump crump and shudder of the house made his mouth run dry as it always did and he soothed Grace who clung to him. The thudding of the ack-ack as it replied did not help his fear. He was glad that Maud was with her parents in Merthyr Terrace while Don was at the supply depot outside Manchester. She wouldn't come to them, felt too much of a gooseberry, she had laughed, and Albert scared her and Tom could understand that. It was better to be where you felt at ease.

'Tell you what, bonny lass,' he breathed into Grace's ear, making her listen. 'We'll take Val's Christmas presents on Sunday shall we, take Maud and clear the garden, now that the old boy can't cope any longer. You tell Maud in the morning.' He pulled her hair slightly and there was a louder nearer explosion and a tremor ran through the bed and the mirror on the dressing-table rattled. 'Listen to me, Grace,' he had to raise his voice to be heard. 'You go and tell her after work tomorrow.' And then she nodded but she was like a rigid board in his arms and he stroked and kissed her but they were too frightened for passion.

He left the house at five in the morning having dozed for what seemed like a few minutes. It was still dark as he joined his Uncle Henry further down the street.

'Everyone all right?' he asked. 'May, Betsy?'

'Aye, lad, and Maud's area's clear an' all but the library got it.'

'God damn it, now where'll I find for me bloody class?' Tom grumbled. The dust was still falling from the bomb damage. It was in their eyes and hair but the fires were mainly under control though the glow was still bright enough to show the smoke rising in a pall from Gladburn Street where the library had been and further over, nearer the slag-heaps on the north side of town.

'That's your problem,' grunted his uncle and they nodded as they passed more miners coming out from doors and alleys to start the shift. Henry was rubbing his eyes, dragging his hands down his face though his eyes were no more red-rimmed than everyone else's, the dust and coal took their toll and the tiredness just came on top of all that. 'Bloody shattered I am. This fire-watch is too much at my age. We'll need some more young 'uns in the pits too, soon. I'm 55 lad.'

Tom gripped his shoulder. 'You're all right, Henry. Good and strong.' But decided he would take more of the face-work. He knew he was a fool to still be in the pits himself but somehow he couldn't make himself take an easy option. It would be bad luck somehow and after all Annie must come back safely.

Their boots were loud on the cobbles as they walked along to the pit-yard. The buildings crowded in on them and the dawn had yet to break though there was a lightening of the sky.

'I hear there's talk of striking,' said his uncle quietly as they waited in the queue for the cage. Men were murmuring all around them. There was the noise of boot against cobble, bait-tin against bait-tin. A miner spat.

Tom nodded. 'So Bob says.' His muffler was tight up round his throat and his foot was hurting as it always did but it did not swell quite so much these days. He knew he was thinner, his face was drawn and etched with sharp lines that were not there before the pain. A pain which was with him every day, every minute since Olympia.

His uncle was close up to him now, his head near him. 'It'll not do us any good in the country, lad. The press'll have a ruddy field-day and I don't know as I'd blame them, it's wartime, lad, and I don't hold with striking.'

'Aye, I reckon you're right but you can't blame the men. The pay's lousy, the hours are longer and longer along with poorer maintenance and now there's talk of drafting pitmen and their lads back here into the pits, just when the poor buggers thought they'd a chance for some to get away. Why should they be drafted back is what the miners feel, drafted back out of the factories and the war to be killed by coal and for a bloody pittance too? They've still got to support a family, Henry, for God's sake.' His voice was rising and his uncle pushed him along as the queue moved.

'Keep your bloody voice down, lad, or you'll end up being locked up like your pal Mosley and how would you like that?'

Tom pulled at his lip and submitted to the match search before squatting on the floor of the cage. 'Piece-work should be abolished an' all.'

His uncle glared as the men squashed close up to them laughed.

As the cage sank, Tom was quiet. The stench was always the same, the thick dust on the floor of the cage, the dropping, the scream of displaced air and then the crunching of the cockroaches beneath their boots as they wound their way along the main seam, hearing the rats darting away as they approached. They turned off into the tunnel to the face they had been allocated.

There was more than two inches of water today and, as they bent over to squeeze further into the flattening seam, his uncle cursed. 'Picked a right one for us today, haven't they, lad. Might do well to keep your mouth shut, if you ever could, that is.'

The heat was stifling and Tom took the hewing this time with his uncle on the shovel. He lay down stiffly and angled his pick but work was slow and difficult. There were not going to be many trollies pushed down the seam today and it meant his pay would be down again and they'd not enough to cope as it was.

He tugged and tore at a lump which had wedged itself. Thank God, Grace worked in the factory and could pass some over to her da. It was bloody good of Don to have put him in the shop while he was away, it gave him a bit of dignity as well as some wages, and between that and Grace, her parents would survive. He'd write and tell Annie about that, she'd be right pleased.

He groaned as he shifted his weight off his back and his foot and hoped to God he didn't get a chill through lying in the water. It gave that remaining kidney too much to do, said the doctor, but there was a fat lot he could do about it with an overman like his. He heard Henry ease up a pit-prop.

'How many today then, Uncle?' he panted, straining his head round to see.

'Just the two again, lad, for each section.'

Tom swore and went back to work listening to the sounds the props made, listening for a rush of dust, a creak and groan that would mean the coal had finally got him. They needed three props, three bloody props, not two. He turned on his side and heaved at the coal again. There had been two men killed yesterday and that had been less than the same day last week and it would go on if basic safety was ignored.

Thank God, Annie was out of all this and the bombs, the cold and the hunger. She'd written that Singapore was out of this world with just the right temperature and just maybe she'd get to see Georgie. It was pretty close to India wasn't it, he'd asked Grace, and she looked it up in the library and said he was right. Well, at least the bonny lass was in the sun, living like a bloody duchess and looking at the fabrics. Just as long as she was enjoying herself, that was the thing; she'd earned it, every bloody minute.

CHAPTER 24

Durban had been glorious with its surging and plummeting surf. Sun, sea and everything that England had been without for two years but Singapore was incomparably better, Annie thought as she and Prue sat at Robinson's Hotel for coffee as usual on their day off. It was a pattern that had been quickly established in the three weeks they had been here, though it seemed longer because she had become so used to the life of ease and splendour.

It was all so beautiful, so different to Wassingham that it was hard to believe the cold dark hardness of the mining town still existed when life could be as it was here. It was early December now and the sun was still so hot that Christmas seemed an impossibility. She and Prue would have tea at Raffles this afternoon and look for presents until then in the crooked streets which were full of shops and arcades and yellow or blue-white houses splashed with red Chinese lettering. Full of the noise of trading, of birds and fowls that squawked and fluttered in wooden cages, of motor horns and rickshaws and the revving of cars. There was colour everywhere, material which would have made Tom's mouth water and silk which hung in bales in small shops and invited touching.

What on earth would he think of the cathedral which they passed on their way into the centre from the nurses' home? It was like some icing-sugar sculpture. He'd either like it or loathe it and she was pretty sure it would be the latter.

In the narrow streets, washing hung out, not on washing lines but on bamboo poles hoisted across from window to window and fish dried on pavements amongst fowl that scattered as cars thrashed by; flies swarmed over everything. The odour and noise were always present.

Annie smiled as she thought of the first time they had driven out to the suburbs. It was like her first view of Gosforn. A sense of space, of light, only far more so as the palatial white houses of the Europeans blasted back the light. Bougainvillaea, calla lilies and frangipani clustered in the grounds and were repeated in all the parks and their lushness made her want to stop and touch, bury her face in their colour and their warmth.

The early mornings were the best though, she had decided, with the breeze flicking in off an ocean which was even bluer than Prue's eyes. She stood each morning in the hospital grounds listening to the rattle of the palm fronds as they were disturbed by the freshness and again in the evening watching the birds as they settled on the telephone wires and wondered how she could be in amongst this and still have an emptiness, an ache which only Georgie could fill.

She and Prue had only been out into the countryside once, and that was with a couple Prue had known in India, the Andertons, who were now happily settled in Singapore where he, who was moustached, neat and correct, held a post in Government House, and she, Mavis, wore head-hugging hats and presided at receptions. They had climbed into his open car last week and Prue had held firmly on to her hat but Annie had removed hers and let the wind rush through her hair, tumbling it around her face and cooling her.

They had driven past mangrove swamps and coconut groves and she had seen again the coconut shies at the fair where they had slipped the lead coins and heard the lady with the varicosed legs. She had screwed her hands in the car and watched as though from a distance the rubber plantations with their latex smell and the jungle scrub which lay all around.

They had driven past two reservoirs which were as large as lakes and then on past the Causeway before she had pushed her memories back into the box and nodded as Mavis pointed out the villages which were called kampongs. Changi jail was on their route and Annie wondered how anyone could bear to be locked away from all this sun, this life. Was Dippy Denis still in his cold dark prison?

The port was chaotic when they drove through, horn sounding at the Tamil labourers who were everywhere around them, carrying goods into and out of the go downs which loomed high along the docks full of different wares. These warehouses were cheek by jowl with fuel tanks, offices and customs sheds and it had been a relief to relax on the verandah at the Anderton's home that evening drinking pink gin brought by servants and talking of the war in Europe, talking of their good fortune at being where they were, in the peace of Singapore. But that was not what Georgie's letter had said, Annie thought as she sat here in the sun with Prue and moved uneasily in her chair. That's not what he had said at all. Get out, he'd insisted.

Prue interrupted her train of thought.

'Annie, these strawberries are scrumptious, absolute heaven.'

She was licking her spoon and Annie saw strawberries against her white teeth. Her gold charm bracelet clinked as she put the spoon back into the crystal bowl and scooped out some cream. Prue closed her eyes as she swallowed and there were faint freckles across her nose.

Annie grinned. 'Not more strawberries surely, Prue? You'll burst and I am not, definitely not, going to clear up the mess.'

Prue opened her eyes languidly and looked about them at the other tables, then back at Annie. 'Do stop being boring, darling. The fly boys bring them in fresh every day just for us and I should hate them to feel that we did not appreciate their efforts; and who is that gorgeous man over there with Monica?'

Annie didn't need to look; she knew it was Martin Edge who had come over with his battalion four days ago.

'Nice, isn't he?' she grinned. 'And I warn you that I shall remind you of the convoy's zig-zagging and the storms if you eat very many more helpings. You've put all that weight on, you clot, and you were just talking of the new slim you the day before yesterday.'

'That was then. I met the most divine man last night, darling, who said he likes a real armful, so much more womanly.'

Annie grinned as Prue finished the bowl and poured another coffee. She ran the cream over the back of the teaspoon which she held against the inner edge of the cup. It spread thickly over the surface and, when she drank, it left a white moustache on her upper lip until she dabbed at it with her napkin. Prue looked over at Annie, her eyes widely innocent as she set the napkin back beside her coffee cup.

'Talking about self-indulgence, Miss Goody-Twoshoes, I

noticed you tucking into the salmon at Raffles last night and who was that major anyway?'

Touché, Annie thought as she lit another cigarette, drawing the smoke deep into her lungs. She pushed away the silver cigarette-case, seeing the misting left by her finger.

Yes, she thought dryly and lifted her cup to Prue who smiled. Yes, who was the major? Someone she vaguely knew, someone to talk to and dance with. She had not liked the feel of his body as they danced past the Palm Court Orchestra and had missed Georgie and wondered where he was, if he was safe? And if he was safe, would he be so next week, next month? She narrowed her eyes against the sun and looked across as a car narrowly missed a rickshaw while a Chinese child ignored the ruction and offered to passers-by a chicken which flapped hopelessly as he held it upside down by the feet.

Sam Short had brought the letter. He had called in at the QA's mess early this morning, suntanned and in shorts and had given her the white creased envelope which was soft and warm as she took it. Sam explained that Georgie had asked him to deliver the letter as she took it from him, eager and grateful; trying to think where she could take him for a coffee, a drink, but Australians were not allowed in the clubs because they were colonials, not Europeans. She burned with shame because she had not defied the rules and invited him anyway.

He had stood there in his hat with the strap beneath his chin, his eyes wry with amusement. He was off up-country anyway, he had said, making the clubs safe for you people to enjoy and she had put her hand on his arm. We'll meet by the harbour, she replied, have a walk, then you can tell me how he really is, but he had shaken his head and smiled and his eyes had crinkled more on the left than the right where there was a healing scar.

He told that Georgie was fair dinkum and that they had been training together but that she must do what he says in the letter. I'm off to Penang he had said and the Japs are sure to come, Annie. He had stood there, his face in shade from his hat, his webbing and equipment hitched over his shoulder. His voice had grown suddenly urgent. Just do what he says, there's a good girl.

She had watched as he sauntered down the steps then and merged into the bustle of the city and without waiting to reach her room had peeled the flap of the letter back and she could see fingermarks on the envelope and hoped they were Georgie's.

'Penny for them, darling?' Prue was shaking sugar on to another bowlful of strawberries and looking at her at the same time. Annie stubbed out the cigarette and caught Pruscilla's look of distaste.

'I've told you that I'll stop smoking while you are eating as soon as you cut down on this appalling guzzling.'

Prue ignored her and took the letter which Annie handed over.

'See what you think of this,' Annie said.

November 1941
Central Provinces.

My darling love,
    I'm writing this quickly and then sending it with Sam. I'm off to Burma. The Japs are getting active and we think they'll go for Rangoon and maybe into India.
    But I think they'll also go for Malaya and Java and you too. Get out now. Go sick if you must but get to India. They treat prisoners badly. We've heard about them in China.
    Come out my love, bring Prue. The C.O. is working on it too. I'll keep you safe here. I love you. Just come out on the first ship.
    I have to go. We're moving out. My love always.
                                                Georgie.

Annie watched as Prue scanned the letter once, then again and finally handed it back. Her hand was on the table, the sun glinted on the gold bracelet.

'Well?' asked Annie.

'Look around you, darling. Does it look as though we're in

338

any danger? Has anyone even hinted that we might not be safe and besides the fleet came in last night, just in case there should be any trouble. There's a difference between us and the Chinese anyway. Europeans would not be treated in the same way, would they, should the impossible happen, which it won't.'

Her plucked eyebrows were raised and there was a faint smile on her lips. Annie looked round at the elegant Europeans who sat as they had done for the last hundred years and would continue, it seemed, to do so for the next one hundred with not a hair out of place. But they were flesh and blood weren't they, they would still bleed, just as the Chinese were doing? She shook her head to clear it of these thoughts, her irritation at Prue's snobbery.

Singapore was taking precautions, she reasoned as she drew out another cigarette. The air-raid sirens went off each Saturday morning and searchlights still danced over the harbour at night but anyway everyone knew that the Japanese could not fly planes with their slant eyes, or so Mavis had said a few nights ago at the dance they had held; she had worn full evening dress and sipped champagne. It had been dry and delicious. Should slanted eyes prohibit flying, she wondered and rather doubted the sense of that sort of reasoning.

'Why has he written it, then?' she mused aloud.

Prue put down her spoon, her bowl empty. She rubbed her hands together. 'That's easy. He can't get you to marry him any other way.'

Annie watched the rickshaw drivers and traders, coins glinting and clicking with each transaction and pencils waving as each chit for goods was signed.

'Thought royalty were the only ones not to soil their hands with filthy ackers,' she said to Prue who answered:

'Let's face it, darling. Here we are almost royalty. Look around, ducky: an awful lot of Indians and not many chiefs.'

Thank God that just this once Annie Manon is out there on top, Annie thought, trying to push Prue's remark about Georgie away. How long was it since she had done any washing for herself or an evening without dancing until the early hours under crystal chandeliers?

'So,' Prue persisted. 'So, why didn't you marry Georgie after all the years of waiting, of missing? Then, when you could have married and stayed together, you didn't.'

Annie collected her cigarette-case and lighter together, putting them into her bag. The lighter smelt of petrol and there was a smudge on the silver.

'Annie, are you scared to commit yourself to anyone? Does it suit you to have him at arms length, there in the background to love and miss but not too close in case he manages to touch something inside you?'

She wouldn't think about what Prue was saying. She talked too much, always she talked too much. She breathed deeply to release the tension in her stomach, in her shoulders.

'Come on, Prue, shift yourself. Let's go and admire the good old *Prince of Wales*, everyone else seems to be.' Prue shook her head.

'You'll have to face it sometime, Annie Manon, whatever it is that comes between the two of you, because he'll ask you again.' Prue groaned as she pulled herself to her feet.

The sun was hot on Annie's feet and the harbour was crowded and she pushed Georgie out of her mind, and Sarah too because the pain of her death had surfaced suddenly.

The *Prince of Wales* looked glamorous against the blue sky, strong and firm and all that was good about the Royal Navy. There was a buzz of well-being at the arrival of the Far East Fleet and the woman on Annie's right was explaining breathlessly to her neighbour, 'Nice to think she's here, even though Singapore is invincible.'

'Will you be at the dance tonight?' Prue asked as she waved her gloved hand in front of her face to ward off the persistent flies.

Annie shook her head, she felt irritated now, off balance and confused. She could not forget his letter and she opened her bag and fingered it. Where was he, she thought again, was he safe and how could she leave when no one else was worried?

The air-raid sirens woke Annie four nights later, on Sunday. She heard the wail through her sleep; Don's watch said it was four in the morning, for God's sake, had the ARP wardens gone mad practising at this time of night? She walked across the cold tiled floor and looked from the window at the street lamps lighting the road below and at the searchlights sweeping the sky. She was tired and walked back towards the bed, then heard the guns thump and the dull drone of aeroplanes. Then there were the crashes and bangs of bombs and her room shook as she

340

clutched at the bed. She threw herself to the floor, her hands pressed to her ears but the vibrations shook the building and she felt and heard the explosions even though she was trying not to. Nothing was stable and she could smell the smoke and feel the rug beneath her where it was damp from her dribble of fear.

Oh God, oh God, my love, you were right, she moaned and she knew she was talking aloud because her lips were opening and shutting against the rug and her breath was puffing back up into her face.

She pulled herself upright, switched on the radio but it was only playing dance music, then she crawled to the wardrobe, pulled on her uniform and staggered into Monica's room where together they watched the flames from the go downs as they burst into the air and the smoke and noise and dust as Singapore exploded into small pieces.

When the all-clear sounded they stumbled across to the wards. Prue was on night duty and her hair was damp from sweat, her face tense from the effort of calming the patients. Matron sent Annie to the Resuscitation Ward and, all day, casualties were brought in and it was as though Tom was here again, smelling of shock. She washed them down as she had done the pitmen, cleared them of dust and black grease, smelling the smoke in their hair and on their clothes along with the shock. They worked for the next thirty-six hours with six hours off in small bursts and at the end they picked their way over the rubble past Robinson's, which had been hit, to Raffles where they were to meet the Andertons to celebrate the entry of America into the war.

They sipped drinks from glasses that were chilled and misty just as always, as though there had been no bombing, no death, no dust, no fear. Servants replenished their drinks and the talk was gentle and not concerned with war. Annie ran her finger up and down the glass and heard but did not listen to Prue's chatter as she watched the big red sun go down and wondered how Americans could help hold the Japs back when they were not here.

She had learnt Georgie's letter by heart now and knew he had been right, knew by the fear stirring in her body, making her hands go cold but she could not leave now, not with the patients coming in every minute, including military casualties

341

dribbling in from up-country. Casualties in khaki with drawn secret faces. And this must be only the beginning.

She eased back her head and rubbed her neck, looking round at the women in smart hats and immaculate make-up. She and Prue should return soon, Matron would need them. She listened for a moment more to talk of the tennis draw and how inconvenient this unpleasantness was and why didn't the boys clear it up at once. So, she thought, talk had veered over to the problem and that was at least a start.

Mavis said, 'The boys are fighting the Japs up-country and they are obviously not trying hard enough, they should have been pushed into the sea by now. They are such small people.'

Annie rose and walked back to the ward, leaving Prue to follow in her own time. She did not belong to those people, did not belong to their irritation over tennis niceties. She belonged here: taking blood pressures, checking drips, soothing Chinese who could speak a little English, Tamils who had burns from the dock fires and never complained when the dressings stuck, Europeans who were stoic. She was busy and glad of it.

The black-out was in force now, she wrote to Georgie, wondering if the letter would get out on any boat and if it did, whether it would find him.

The *Prince of Wales* was sunk and the mess fell quiet at the news. Nurses prepared more bandages and cut tattered clothes from damaged bodies as the bombing continued that night and every night.

She was too tired to feel shock but the fear was still there, fear which made her feel sick and weak because they were hearing the stories which came back with the men. And what about Georgie, was he tattered too like one of these men that she nursed?

Air-raid practices went on when the bombing paused, but were not supported because they clashed with the tennis tournament. Tension together with tiredness drew deep lines around her mouth and hammered pain across her forehead. The stench from bomb-damaged drains hung amongst the dust and made her want to vomit as she gave inoculations against typhoid.

She took Prue to coffee at Robinson's when Matron gave them an hour off, two weeks after the bombing had begun, but Penang had fallen and refugees sat at all the tables so they walked back to the hospital past a team that were digging for bodies, past trenches that were dug in parks, on sports grounds, past crashed aircraft and a school which they could hear rehearsing for the nativity play which was to be held on Christmas Eve at the end of the week.

Sam Short came in by field ambulance, his leg blasted away below the knee and tourniqueted, his liver gone. He died while she held his hand.

'Get out,' he whispered before he died but no nurses were leaving yet, only civilians. She closed his eyes and wished she had taken him to the club while she could.

The rains were sheeting down one day here and one day there and it was humid beyond belief. Prue's roots were showing and Annie had not known she was a bottle blonde. It was better to concentrate on bleach than the queues stretching past the go downs, past the customs houses to the boats which daily took people away to safety but not them. I wish I was going, my love, she called to Georgie as she sponged another body with shaking hands and tried not to listen to the cries and groans from all around.

Hong Kong fell on Christmas Day but the nurses had a turkey and champagne since food was still plentiful. Dancing took place every night in the Centre.

Three nurses were killed when they were caught in a raid down by the docks. The sun was not visible now during the day; it was hidden behind the smoke which hung over the city. Mavis Anderton hosted a garden party on her lawn but it was spoilt by the rumble of guns all around Singapore. Finally trenches were dug at the cricket club but not the golf greens.

The Palm Court Orchestra continued to play and, one night, she and Prue danced at Raffles but not on New Year's Eve for, while the Fancy Dress Ball was held into the early hours, they bathed injured troops who were covered in layers of black grime from the bombed oil dumps they had tried but failed to save over by the Causeway.

The Chinese shopkeepers refused European chits now and would only accept cash and at this the rush for the boats became intense because traders always knew the truth.

The Causeway was blown on the last day of January, Sarah's birthday, but Annie was too tired to do more than nod as she handed a scalpel to the doctor. Neither of them jumped as a

343

plane crashed near the cathedral and made the operating-theatre shake. Her uniform was never clean now, her hands never still. When they were at rest there was still the trembling, still the blood, still the boats, the ships leaving without them. Prue cried all through her three hours off one night and Annie held her and told her it would be all right, she would make sure it was, bonny lass. Her headache was too bad to think, her veins stood out on her hands and Prue felt thinner in her arms.

The humid heat dragged at her feet and each new day the injured increased, uniforms were everywhere. Matron sent Prue, Monica and Annie to the cathedral which was taking the overflow and they went from stretcher to stretcher soothing, calming but unable to do much without facilities. A sip, bonny lad, she would say and pour a little water past split and swollen lips.

'How much longer?' groaned Prue as she staggered to her feet and handed a soiled bandage to Annie and then, in February, she had her answer. Malaya was lost and so was Singapore. On 15 February, the surrender was signed and Annie walked amongst the men and wondered what in God's name would become of her patients now, what would become of the women and what had all this been about anyway?

Two days after Valentine's Day, Raffles Place was crowded with British, Australian and Indian troops, heads hung with weary confusion. It was strange not to hear the sound of gunfire.

In the cathedral, dust lay thick on the pews. The stretcher cases continued to arrive and lay inside and outside the building. Smoke still hung over the city. Small Rising Sun flags had appeared overnight and more were hung even as she looked from windows. Japanese staff cars roared past, their klaxons sounding raw in the square, soldiers in small tanks ground their way past. The flame trees still glittered and the breeze still rattled the palm trees and her fear was still stark. The troops were given until the next day to assemble at Changi prison and Annie cried as she remembered the building they had passed with the Andertons. And where were the Andertons now?

Annie and Prue with Monica and their contingent of nurses picked their way back to the nurses' home, packed up what belongings they could carry and returned to find their wounded moving out.

Later it was dark and cool in the cathedral and Annie stood by the altar, watching the sun as it came in through the window and caught the dust which was leaping in its beam, as it had done when she was last in the shed at Gosforn.

She touched the wooden altar rail and thought for a moment she could smell chrysanthemums and feel the coolness of the convent chapel. Prue was kneeling in the front pew and Monica was down at the font. Three other nurses were sitting quietly behind Prue.

Fear was making her breathing difficult and tiredness was making her head feel apart from her body. Her hands were wet and she wanted to cry, to run and hide, go to Georgie and make him hold her and not let them get her but she could hear their feet outside the big doors coming closer and closer and then they were there, framed in the doorway, their bayonets fixed and their language harsh. Annie made herself move from the rail to Prue who would not look up as the Japanese moved down the aisle towards them, their bayonets catching the sun as they passed each window.

'Come on, bonny lass,' she said as she reached down for Prue's hand. 'It's time for us to go.' Her voice was trembling so much she wondered if Prue could understand.

CHAPTER 25

Tom received the letter from Georgie on Monday, when he came in from the pit.

November 1942

India.

Dear Tom,

I was there when the Japs took Rangoon but got away with my platoon and some stragglers. We walked back through the jungle. Thirty started, ten got back.

It was bloody, Tom. Kraits, the shoelace snake, got some of the men and the cobras too. Then there were the Japs, but worst were the flies and the butterflies which ate their bodies. I can't bear butterflies now, they were like a moving tablecloth on my men. It was so hard, lad.

She didn't get out you know. Where is she, Tom? Is she alive? Have you heard anything? Oh God, she must be alive.

I'm back in the Central Provinces. We'll be going back to retake the Burma Road when we're ready. God help us.

Georgie.

Tom replied that night.

Dear Georgie,

She'll be all right, bonny lad. Don't you fret. I know she'll be all right. If anyone comes through, it will be her. If I hear, I'll let you know straight away but you concentrate on keeping your head down and staying alive until she comes back.

We're all well here. The rationing is keeping us fit. Don is still at the depot and Maud is living with her ma and da. I'm still in the pits so nothing changes. I'll write again but look after yourself and get through to the end. She'll need you then.

Tom.

Tom told Grace he meant every word he had written about Annie but sometimes in the dark of the night he would clench his fists and be unable to sleep.

The miners had gone on strike as they had threatened and very soon after that the government had agreed to introduce a ballot system to give pitmen a chance to get out of the mines and fight in the services. Reluctantly a minimum wage was also agreed which would enable the miners to have sufficient money to keep up their strength for six working days each week.

Tom liked the boy who was seconded to their team. He was from Surrey and had been to public school and was called Martin St John. He wrote poetry and hummed to himself on the first day as he helped to push the trolley. None of the boys were pleased that their number had been picked and that they were to spend their war as Bevin Boys and the miners thought they would probably be more trouble than they were worth but it was better than their sons automatically taking the pityard walk.

In the summer, Martin kept his head when Tom's uncle stumbled while shovelling the coal into the trolley and had two fingers shorn off at the root when the trolley was pushed forward on to his hand. He'll do, his uncle had said as he was taken to the surface. Production had been good that day.

347

Martin had been quieter than usual as he and Tom had walked back through the main seam after they had watched the cage screech up the shaft but had retrieved the short putter's shovel and laboured on with no outward sign of disturbance.

The boy had really wanted to go into the air force, Tom had told Grace that evening as they ate Woolton Pie, which they knew as potato and pastry. His back still stung from the scrubbing Grace had given it because she had not seen the graze down the length of it until it was too late.

Tom was too tired to go to the allotment again that night, like so many other nights. His foot and back hurt so much each day that his face was always white and drawn once the coal-dust had been washed away and there was grey hair at his temples. He was 26.

His days were blurred. He rose at four in the morning on six days a week, freezing in winter and still chilled in summer as he walked down past the same terraced houses each day until the seventh when he limped to the allotment with Bob and pulled some carrots or whatever had been coaxed out of the soil and then called in for a watered beer at the pub. Sometimes he and Grace went to Betsy for lunch, sometimes Bob came to them and would tell them of the *Daily Worker* which had been banned for the reportage of the air raids or that attitudes to trade union negotiations would be different after the war because Russia was in on our side and people no longer feared the Bolshevik menace.

As 1943 changed to 1944, he would struggle home and lie on the bed, too tired to paint, too tired to talk politics with Bob, too tired to notice that Grace was dark beneath the eyes and feeling sick. She was four months pregnant before she told him and that was only because a tip and run raid had scored close to their house and the floor had felt as though it was about to tilt them down into rubble and dust. My baby, she had screamed, and he had wanted the bombs to stop for just a minute to grasp what had just been said.

He had then wanted them to stop forever, more than he had done before or for Grace to stop work at the munitions factory and go to the country or to Val's but she would not leave him or her parents. They need the money, she had said, and anyway the raids are very few now. He wished now that he had taken the money that Annie had wanted to give him before she went, but he hadn't, so that was that.

He would look at Grace. Quiet nights and restful days, was that too much to ask, were the thoughts that spun in his head, and he knew that it was. He would turn on the radio and listen to familiar voices while he waited for the fire to take and the kettle to boil. Listening to the news made him feel that they had come through another day and so had the rest of the world.

He kept chickens in the yard, foregoing his dried egg ration in return for some chicken meal so that she had at least one egg every two days and Val gave them eggs and honey when he took Maud and Grace over to Gosforn having managed to get some petrol. Sometimes Don would meet them there when he could arrange leave from the depot and they would sit in the living-room while Val sat in Sarah's chair pouring tea.

Tom would sit back and smooth down the arm covers, listening to the fire as it crackled. They would talk of victory in Africa, the Russians fighting hard and the need for a second front. They talked of days gone by, of the old cock they had eaten last Christmas and how cross Annie would have been to miss it, but he would never let the silence fall, the faces tense, because she was alive, he would say. And coming back. One day she will be back.

In February 1944, he worked on the pit face with a new mechanical cutter which the government had thought would increase production and it looked as though they were right. It also increased the dust and his eyes became raw much earlier and his throat dry as though it had been rubbed with sandpaper. As he worked, he remembered the fair, the hammer you could whack down and ring a bell. He thought of Annie's mother and the legs near the stall and the voice that had destroyed Annie's smile that evening and for so long after. He remembered her father and how he had done much more than remove her smile. That man had bitten as deeply as the cutter was doing and the jagged sore was still there. Tom knew it was there, because Annie hadn't married Georgie.

This week the team was still on the bad seams and he was still crouched and angled while his uncle and Martin shovelled and pushed the trolley back through the dark damp tunnel which was too meandering to install an automatic conveyor.

The owners had planned the route to avoid Squire Turner's

land and the royalties he demanded for mining beneath the surface of his land. And so it was, bugger the workers, Tom cursed, but think of the profits, you bastards. He attacked the coal, his eyes almost shut as the dust exploded into his face while his uncle worked close to him, still one-handed because the pain lingered in his damaged hand. The noise of the cutter tore at his head and he could no longer listen for falling dust or creaking pit-props and it made him anxious. He knew that the coal was there pressing down above him, each day denser somehow. Martin was thin now and no longer hummed and it wasn't just because the machine cloaked all speech; it was because the noise and the dark choked all thought, all the poetry in his head.

His uncle's sinews gleamed with black sweat in the light from Martin's lamp as he pushed the trolley to the end of the tunnel and returned with another that was empty and the lad shovelled again. Henry's hand seemed easier today, his lips were not drawn so thin. Tom eased his back as he looked at them over his shoulder and stopped the cutter; he could taste the dust between his teeth and he was thirsty.

He pointed to the flasks; his hand was still shaking from the vibrations of the cutter and his ears were ringing. He shook his head to clear it as Henry nodded, but the boy continued shovelling for a while longer since he wanted to get this last load done. Tom sank on his haunches. The tea was refreshingly cold and he spat into the darkness where the slag was heaped against the sides. Coal-dust swirled in the beam from their lamps and his uncle squatted next to him while Martin flopped to the ground.

'D'you hear that Ma Gillow's been killed in the black-out? Run over by an ambulance.'

Tom shook his head. 'Bet she didn't read that in the tea leaves.'

'Bet she didn't read that the Yanks would come either,' moaned Martin gloomily.

Tom and Henry laughed and Tom nudged the boy with his boot. 'Don't you worry, your Penelope will stick by you. One look at the muscles you've developed and she'll throw the nylons back at them.'

Martin grinned wanly and Tom felt pity for the lad. Penelope sounded too nice to leave him in the lurch and he said so.

Martin looked up. 'Anyway, it'll soon be over, won't it, and then we can all go home.' His voice sounded weary. 'Now Italy's given in and there was Alamein in '42, it's got to be over soon.'

'There speaks the sweet bird of youth,' yawned Tom. '1944 and it's all over, is it? We shall see, my brave young poet, but in the meantime let's be getting on with this here.' But they stayed sitting for a while longer, listening to the sounds of the mine, thinking their own thoughts until Tom finally made a move.

'How's Grace?' asked his uncle as they scrambled to their feet.

'Due next month,' said Tom and suddenly felt impatient to be out of the blackness and up with her as she rested after lunch, now that she had finished work in the factory. He loved to crouch by the chair, his hand across her swollen belly feeling the baby kick and then he would stroke her full breasts with their blue veins and want her and she would pull him to her.

'Come on, let's get on with it,' he ground out as he hauled himself back into the narrow space.

His uncle winked at Martin. 'Wants a big load today, aiming to wet the baby's head with champagne.' But the noise of the cutter drowned out Martin's reply and the creak from the pit-props, the warning fall of dust. Henry just felt a blast of air and was knocked off his feet as the trolley shifted beneath the rushing air and coal which roared down and spilled outwards towards his feet. It settled as he lurched back against the side, coughing in the flurry of grit and the smell of raw angry coal.

It was minutes before he could find his breath and move, before he could tear with his hands at the pile of blackness. His Tom was in there and he couldn't hear a bloody thing. He had called, he told the first rescuers but there had been no answer from Tom or the lad, no tapping, no nothing.

His head was ringing from the waves of noise that had come with the fall and his stumps were bleeding on to the ground and he welcomed the throb of pain since it made him think of something other than the two who had been with him just a moment before. His foot kicked Tom's bait-tin and he shoved it back into the slag.

The rescue team were working methodically now, passing the coal back then listening for a tap or a cry but there was still

351

nothing. He moved in to find a space to work but was gently turned away to one side.

'Stay over there then, Henry, we'll get at them quicker this way.' A trolley was shoved passed him, taking the first load back and out of the way.

And then the overman was there, edging along, bowed over, irritated at the lost production. He stood next to Henry, his mouth pursed.

'No point in setting up the siren if there's only two men involved.'

The man at the rear turned, blocking Henry's fist as he swung.

'No, don't waste your bleeding siren, any more than you waste your bleeding pit-props. Not enough props, not enough rest and you expect more bloody coal.' The man spat at the ground. 'This is the second accident today.' His headlamp caught the overman in its beam, his face was too black to distinguish any features. 'Aye, save your bloody siren, man. You should be sick of yourself and them out there. How many deaths, how many legs, hands, feet do you want?'

'Leave it out, man,' called the leader, his voice strained from wrenching and heaving his pick. The miner stared and Henry moved in closer until the overman backed away. Then they both ignored him as the struggle continued well into the night.

Grace knew it had happened when Tom was not home and the bath water was getting cold by the kitchen fire. She pulled her coat around her and would have run to Betsy's but she could only walk with her hands holding her laden body.

Betsy was at the kitchen window and saw Grace come in past Beauty's stable and when she did not stop to hand in a quartered apple she felt her mouth go dry and she turned to Joe. 'It's my bairn Joe, it's my Tom.'

He put her coat around her and took each of the women by the arm, making them walk at a gentle pace, for it had snowed during the day and was slippery.

It was so quiet, thought Betsy, with the snow. There was no sound of striking boots, no wind to buffet them as they passed the alleys. It was a clear night and the stars and the moon were sharp and she felt as though she could reach out and draw them to her.

352

As they walked down the hill, she could see the men clustered round the pit-head. More women were coming out of their houses now, their shawls drawn round their heads and no words were spoken as they slipped in the gates to the head. There were no lights because of the black-out but the moon was so bright and the snow so fresh it did not matter. Joe forced his way through to the Manager's Office and shouted above the clamour of women's voices as they called to find out who it was that was trapped.

'Tom Ryan and Martin St John,' Betsy heard and held on to Grace as she moved to run to the cage. She was moaning and pulling from Betsy, her face drawn apart with anguish and Betsy saw May and together they held her back and Bet stroked her hair as Grace said, again and again, 'He should never have been a pitman, he should have been painting. He should have been painting.' And she was screaming now, her mouth stretched wide as though it would tear across her face. Betsy held her close, her arms tight around the girl.

'There now, hinny, he'll be all right. The lad'll be all right.' She looked up at the sky and couldn't see the stars and moon because of the blur in her eyes and hadn't realised until then that her own pain had turned into tears.

They waited by the office. Grace would not go in but stood shivering in the cold and Betsy chafed first her hands, then her arms and kept it up until Grace jacked over and her labour began. Bob was here by now, standing quietly with Joe, his face calm but his eyes watching every movement of the cage, every change of rescue team.

An ambulance came for Grace and Betsy went with her but she wanted to stay to wait for her son.

It was late that night when the team reached them. The air was fetid behind the coal wall and Tom was half buried. He had been unable to call because of the weight across his chest and had lain there in the pitch-dark, his fear catching him and the cold seeping into every part of him. I hate you, I hate you he had sworn with every breath at the coal which hung above him. It creaked and groaned and tormented him with its hanging weight. He couldn't see or hear Martin or Henry but they would be on the other side, clawing at the fall as the rescuers were.

As the pain in his foot increased and the cold made his kidney grip and send him into fever he looked at the girl who came running across the beck towards him, her hair kinked by overnight plaits, as he sat in the water on a summer's day. Annie, Annie, his mind called and she laughed and said, 'Hang on, bonny lad, I'll come for you. Just hang on, Tom,' and so he did.

It was late that night when they reached him. Martin was dead and looked as Davy had done, with blood from his nose and ears and mouth. He was never going home again.

Tom went to the hospital and was washed and his leg was set. His ribs were bruised but not broken. He thought she was Annie until his fever subsided and the nurse was blonde with blue eyes and then he wept.

Grace had a baby one hour after Tom was sent into surgery and she called him Robert.

Bob sat with Tom while he lay in traction the next day and plumped his pillows and poured him lemon barley-water.

'This is getting to be a habit, lad.'

Tom turned and looked at him. 'Poor little bugger, poor Penelope.' He could say no more for minutes, then, 'Thank God, Grace is fine. He's a bonny lad, is our wee Bobby then?'

Bob nodded, his face breaking into a smile, his eyes shadowed and dark through lack of sleep. There had been air raids the night before and plaster from the ceiling lay in the corner. He moved over and picked it up, throwing it into the bin before he sat down again.

'You'll take the checker job I got you, lad.' It was not a question but a statement and Tom nodded. He'd been offered the surface job in '42 but he had not taken it because he had to trade off for Annie's survival.

'Aye, Bob, I'll take that now. She'll be coming back, will our Annie. I know she will.'

CHAPTER 26

So far during this roll-call, there had been no beatings. The numbers though still did not tally with this morning but then they could not, could they? Annie's hands hung open by her side, still raw from digging three shallow graves which would receive rigid bodies but no coffins. The gods had not been smiling, had they, for there were no boxes of adequate length yet again.

Sweat dripped slowly from her bowed head on to the dusty earth, enlarging the already darkened patch and in the submissive silence her hair hung limp, her neck was raw and she felt and saw her feet swell and crack in the pounding heat. Feet really should have shoes, she thought. Shoes as clean as Sister Maria had always ordered for chapel. But not too shiny, Tom had laughed. Yes, she heard his laugh deep inside her head and she grinned in spite of sun-tightened lips. You'll never improve if you don't obey rules, she had been ordered to chant after one service, head bowed over dull shoes, breath visible in the autumnal cold of the conservatory.

She eased her neck as much as she dared. Her hands were throbbing now and one foot was hidden by the collapsed body of Prue. How strange, she thought, I hadn't noticed. She felt no pity, just relief for its shelter since Prue was no great weight any more. Cold, she pondered, daytime cold was quite beyond imagination and as for rebellion, that seemed merely a way of sapping energy already drained and wrung out like the sparse rice around which their lives revolved.

Would you be proud of me now, Sister Maria? Would you write home to Sarah that I was a credit to myself, the school and my guardian as you did at the end of my first year? Don't you worry though, I shall revive my friend as I did yesterday and she for me the day before but I can't promise for tomorrow because she is a little under the weather, dear Sister Maria and your God seems to be busy elsewhere. Perhaps you could write on his report: Could do better if he tried?

She listened to the count of the Japanese guard begin again. She did not dare to flick at the flies that were crawling over her lips and eyes for she would be beaten if she was seen.

'Ichi, ni, san, yong.'

One, two, three, four, she echoed in her head. Look at me now, Sarah. I'm learning a new language, experiencing new things, or isn't this quite what you meant? God all bloody mighty, how much longer would this go on, the stupid fool has been told by the doctor that three died before lunch so, unless there's been a few immaculate conceptions since then, how could the numbers bloody well tally?

They always did this before a move, dragged them out into the compound three times a day instead of the morning and evening delight. Was it their way of saying sweet farewell she wondered? Along her row, a child cried out and was quickly muffled. She felt the tension that the noise created ease as the guard continued his walk, his boots clumping and throwing dust into the cracks which meandered in the baked ground. At her da's allotment, ants had wriggled in and out of the summer-dried cracks that she had thought led to Australia; deep down and out of the other end. She must tell the doctor about that. How would she like her home town to be at the end of a Wassingham crack?

She lifted her head slightly to ease the stiffness. He was in the row behind now and the commandant still stood rigid on his platform, pale lavender gloves immaculate, eyes straight ahead as though he found them too distasteful to set eyes upon. Likewise, you bugger, Annie thought. The guard was returning now to the front and then it was over. They were dismissed.

She and Monica grasped Prue beneath the armpits and dragged her back to their hut, her heels bumping and kicking up clouds. Annie tightened her grip because Prue was slippery with sweat. They propped her up on the verandah against the wall of the hut. Monica was on duty at the hospital hut and wiped her arm across her face, pulled down the hat she had made from a pair of old shorts.

'All right then, Annie, I'll be off.' Annie nodded and reached for the old tin can which held the water that she and Prue had earlier strained through muslin before the heat of the day had really begun to bite. There were always a few worms left wriggling in spite of the filtering and she dipped her fingers into the brackish water and scooped out the two that she could see, squeezing them between her thumb and finger before grinding them beneath her clompers. Her skin crawled; she hated them.

'Here, hinny, take this.' She held Pruscilla against her and trickled some water into her mouth and over her breasts to take the heat out. She poured some on to her own hand and dabbed at Prue's forehead, then waved the fan she had made from *atap*. She had split the bamboo and folded palm leaves round it, then fastened this together with pieces of *rotan*. It was a small copy of the tiles they had made to roof their huts when they arrived at their first camp after the march from Singapore. Nearly three years ago now, she mused, as she rubbed Prue's hands then resumed her fanning, which made a welcome breeze. Dr Jones had asked her to make more for the hospital hut and it had kept her busy during the first long weeks of their internment when they did not know whether they were to be killed like the people they had seen as they passed a village. Weaving the *rotan*, pushing it down and threading back again, helped her not to wonder about death, about where they were, not wonder how long the war would take to end and who would win when that happened and if Georgie was still alive.

They had been marched for two weeks after leaving Singapore. At first they'd been able to buy food from the natives in the kampongs but soon their money had run out and they lived on rice that the Japanese dug out of sacks and handed them, glutinous and stinking. They had stumbled and dragged one another along and been kicked when they fell and when they cried; killed when they would not bow their heads. Two elderly women had died like that, not shot but bayonetted. The children had been made to watch and had become quiet and Annie had sold Don's watch to the headman of a village for four chickens and that night they had cooked them and the children had eaten a piece each and had walked better the next day.

Natives had stoned them at one village, stoned the memsahibs and Mavis Anderton had cried then and said that nothing would ever be the same again.

The hardship had not been as difficult for her as for most of the others. She had thought of Albert and Wassingham and told herself that she had always liked the heat and she should be grateful for that at least. It was different for Prue.

Annie shifted Prue's weight on her shoulder. 'Come on lass,' she murmured. 'Three years in the camps and you've still got a punka wallah fanning you so open those eyes and throw me a rupee.'

She eased her back. There was no one in the hut with its moist panting heat; they were outside as she was, sitting in the shade or hoeing the vegetable patch; teaching the surviving children over in the hut by the commandant's office. Annie stroked Prue's hair.

'Come on, my wee lass,' she whispered. 'Don't give up now, don't leave me here on my own.' Louder she said, 'One of the Dutch has some peroxide, we need most of it for the hospital but I've earned enough with the washing I did for Van Eydon to dye that streak in front. Give old bandy legs a thrill, eh, make him faint on parade for a change.'

She felt a stir from the girl and smiled as Prue slowly straightened.

'That, darling, is quite the best idea you've had in a long time.' It was faint but it was good.

'What a vain bitch you are,' Annie laughed. 'I'll tell you one thing. We must write to the girls in Oxford, when this is all over, and tell them they've lost their bet. There is a new slimline you with a fetching streak in your fringe as well.'

Prue pushed herself from Annie and sat up against the wall. Her eyes were dull and heavy-lidded and she had a sore at the corner of her mouth. 'This will never be over, it's nearly three years now and we won't be alive much longer. It's too hard and not worth the effort.' Her head sagged on to her chest and Annie scrambled to her knees. A pebble cut into her leg, then scraped her ulcer as she shoved it to one side. The pain made her feel sick.

She took Prue's chin in her hand but she would not lift her head, so she took her hair and gently pulled until she could see her face, then shook her until she opened her eyes.

'We'll survive and it will be over. Lorna told us that "D" Day happened in June, you remember? They'll come for us, you see. Just hang on, Prue. We must hang on. There's India waiting for you and your da. Think of your da. How would he feel if you left him alone?' Prue's eyes were closing again and Annie took her chin in her hands, smoothed back the hair from her face.

'What about me if you let go? Who's going to drive me mad, keep me going? What would Georgie say if you let me die, because you weren't here any more?'

Prue's eyes were open again now, but her mouth was slack with weariness. She was worn out with dysentery and malnutrition like them all but there was no way this girl was going to die. She was too young and it would be a waste, as Sarah would have said. And Annie would miss her too much.

'We'll survive,' she said through gritted teeth. 'If it bloody well kills me, we'll survive.' And suddenly Prue's eyes were not dull any more but alive with laughter, and Annie grinned, her body limp with relief. She rose, then dusted off her knees and entered the dark heat of the hut to fetch the scissors.

She cut Prue's hair as she had been asking all week and told her she looked like Veronica Lake but piebald. Monica called then from the hospital hut next to them and Annie patted Prue's shoulder, feeling her bones through her flesh.

'Tea-break over.' She picked up the tin can and checked that some water remained. 'Take a bit. It's clear of worms. Just stay in the shade and I'll do your shift.'

They had built the hospital hut large enough to take twenty patients and it was always full. She went from bed to bed with the doctor, checking pulses and bathing foreheads, easing discomfort if possible.

At five she had supper, the last meal before the long night. The rice grain had been spread and sorted all through the day, she had seen the team busy over by the kitchen hut. There were a few vegetable scraps today which was good but nonetheless her throat closed as it did now against the meal which had not varied since they had been interned. She pushed rice deep into her mouth with her fingers, forcing herself to swallow.

Monica was sitting next to her. 'Prue all right now?'

Annie nodded. 'I saw her come across for first sitting earlier so she's eating anyway.'

It was dusk outside. It had come quickly as it always did and the evening felt cooler after the heat of the day but still sticky and Annie walked back to their hut while Monica went over to the Dutch to cut hair for cigarettes.

Prue was waiting on the verandah, propped against a

359

doorpost, her eyes half-closed, her mosquito-net pulled about her. She smiled as Annie sat down next to her and took the blanket that she passed, wearing it as the pit women wore their shawls only this was for protection against mosquitoes, not the cold. There were groups of women all along the verandah talking in low voices, and in the huts. She took a piece of bible paper from her pocket and rolled it round the shredded leaves they had dried in the sun during the day. Pruscilla hugged her knees.

'Feeling better?' Annie asked as she put the cigarette in her mouth and lit it. She had packed the leaves tightly so that they would burn slowly. Prue nodded.

'I don't fancy the idea of the move tomorrow,' she said.

Annie drew in the smoke. 'I'm 30 tomorrow and don't feel like that kind of a party either. Don't worry though, you'll be feeling better by then.' She swatted at a mosquito that buzzed close to her. It was never silent here; there was always the noise of the jungle, the murmur of insects. She had seen the flash of colour as butterflies wove in and out of the undergrowth around the camp and she had thought how Georgie would love it. Then there were the moans and restless turning of the patients which they could hear easily from here and the children who cried out in the dark, especially those who no longer had a mother living. One hundred human beings here now she reckoned, minus three of course. No wonder there was always noise.

Prue reached in under her net and held out her hand to Annie. 'If we hadn't been on the move tomorrow, I would have given you this in the morning. But since you're 21 again I thought I'd push the boat out for you.'

There was a chilli in her hand. 'More precious than bloody gold,' breathed Annie. 'All those vitamins.' She fingered its shiny smoothness and leant back against the hut.

'Thanks, bonny lass. The best present I've ever had. We'll have a party when we arrive. Chilli con carne but without the con carne.' She paused. 'Do you remember the strawberries and salmon, Prue, and how we thought it would last until the end of time? We were wrong and Georgie was right.'

'I know and I said some things I should never have said to you then, about you and Georgie. I've always wanted to say I was sorry.' Prue's face was in shadow. They were talking quietly as everyone was doing in these moments before they crawled on to their beds.

Annie drew on the last of her cigarette, feeling the heat near her fingertips. 'I don't remember you saying anything,' she replied, but she did, every word and suddenly she could not wait to be on her pallet and able to think of him. Of the coldness of the beach as they had lain together the first time, of the feel of his skin, the scars that ridged down his back, of his arms as they held her and of later, when they met again and loved again. This is what she thought of each night, what she saved up through the day using it as a prize which beckoned her on through every hour. Georgie kept her sane, kept her alive. That was how she thought of Georgie and all the questions were kept in that little black box in her mind where dark things belonged.

On the third day of the march, it rained and Annie's clompers stuck in the mud with each dragging step, wrenching her toes and rubbing further raw patches. It swept over struggling bodies as they toiled along the tracks which seemed to lead nowhere. It was still hot, in spite of the rain, and the humidity sucked away their strength. Four died on that day, and a child. The guards threw the bodies into the swamp and would not allow time for burial.

Annie watched Monica's back and counted to fifty and then again and again. They kept in step because it helped them to keep going and made the stretcher they carried less bumpy for the patient who was bloated with beri beri and should not last the night, or so the doctor thought.

The camp was reached on the seventh day at noon and the woman only died when they laid her down inside the wire. Annie's hands were bleeding and her shoulders felt as though hot wires were strung from shoulder to shoulder.

The doctor organised the burials and explained that the smell which was strong was latex and that this was a work-camp. The rubber plantation was all around.

'There'll be more work for us, more injuries to the women Sisters,' the doctor said, her face drawn and looking older than her 40 years. Her auburn hair was now almost completely white though she had once been a beautiful woman. 'Now come on over, we're to be addressed by the commandant.'

He spoke through an interpreter while the rain beat down

and it dripped down Annie's bowed neck and face and off the end of her nose.

'Nippon number one,' he said. 'And the war finish in one hundred years. You work well, you be treated well. Remember that.'

They stood up straight as he picked his way through the mud to his car and roared away, klaxon sounding.

'Thank you and goodnight,' murmured Prue as she walked painfully with Annie over to the hospital hut. Their legs were trembling and so were their arms. The bamboo slats laid down for mattresses glittered with bugs which scattered and scuttled across and down the cracks where each cane met the other, so when the rain had ceased they lit fires with a lighter made of plaited cotton dipped in coconut oil and a flint. Annie felt the heat as they passed the slats quickly through but they knew that still some would survive and that the night for the patients would be one of torment as the bugs bit and the smell of bad burnt almonds rose as they tossed and crushed, and not just for the patients of course.

There was more rain again the next day and it poured through the *atap* tiles which were too few to create a proper roof on the bamboo huts. They had to move the patients so that rain dripped only on their bodies not their faces. Then they heard shouting in the compound and a woman's screams, loud and long and despairing. Annie felt cold rush through her body.

Guards burst through into their huts then, their boots clumping and kicking at the platforms, tipping patients on to the floor, emptying out the doctor's bag where they kept what little medicine they had, smashing bottles with their rifle butts. Her mouth went dry. She should stop this but she was too afraid. The guards came towards them, their bayonets fixed, their faces bulging with rage, words spitting from their mouths.

They were pushed, patients and nurses, out of the doorway. Prue stumbled and Annie caught her and held her upright as they were slapped down the steps. She turned and helped two patients and Prue took another across the compound to where the other prisoners were waiting in silence in three long rows. They were not to bow their head, the interpreter said. They were to watch what happened to those who disobeyed.

Lorna Briggs's radio had been found. She was 24, still with her Scots accent and covered in freckles from the heat of

362

Malaya. Now she was beheaded quite silently in the centre of the compound and the blood that shot two yards was washed away in the deluge before it had settled.

And Annie drew in her head beige and pink flowers, any sort of flowers that might do for wallpaper, for curtains, as she had done before in the camps when her friends had been swatted and destroyed and she had been unable to bear it. Why not have matching lampshades and crockery? While the rain sheeted down and they all stood there she closed her mind to the pain, the body and the blood, pushing it into that black box at the back of her head.

Later she rolled her cigarette on the verandah with Prue and they listened to the cicada and she thought of Sarah's house, her house now and decided she would start with the bedroom. Tom could help. They would design that first, see how it worked before they went into production. Yes, they would do that and now she must think of a design, a design that would keep today out of her thoughts tonight. She drew on the cigarette and lit Prue's from the stub.

Not lush flowers but small gentle pink and beige with an indefinite outline for wallpaper and larger flowers for the bedspread and the curtains. Slowly she cut, pasted and papered the bedroom up to the picture rail and brought soft beige emulsion across the ceiling and down to meet the paper. The lighting was a problem and she turned to Prue.

'Right,' she challenged. 'I've decided on the wallpaper and curtains, the bedspread too, but what about lighting?'

Prue flicked away her cigarette stub into the compound and it was doused by the rain before it hit the ground.

'Is this your business idea you're on about?' she asked, smiling slightly.

And Annie nodded. It always worked and made them turn from the present when it became too cruel.

'Yes, but first I've decided to do the house and I'm stuck on the light fitting.' Their voices weren't quite right yet but by the end of the long night they were sounding normal and they had not had to bother with the agony of sleep.

It took weeks of arguing through their off-duty hours while they discarded Prue's chandelier and Annie's ruche material but finally Annie decided on a glass bowl with bamboo etched on as a centre light with duplicated bedside lamps.

The monsoons were over and it was not quite so humid though the latex still permeated every corner. 'How can you want anything that reminds you of this place? You're inhuman,' Prue flung at her as they scooped Mrs Glanville's ulcer. 'Bamboos, how can you choose bamboos?'

'Come on, Prue,' retorted Annie as she dropped the final swab into the tin that Prue was holding. 'Just because we're in the wrong place at the wrong time doesn't mean that ugliness is everywhere; the flame trees still flame and the sun still sets.'

'It does that,' said Mrs Glanville. 'Right over good old Blighty.'

They both stopped glaring at one another and turned to the emaciated woman who lay beneath an old torn sheet. Annie ran her hands down her torn, dirty uniform and looked at Prue's which was the same.

She laughed then. 'None of that talk, Mrs Glanville, or I'll have to talk with the doctor,' she scolded, 'and then there'll be no more grapes at visiting time.' She took the woman's pulse and touched her cheek and was glad that she also smiled. They moved on to the next patient.

'God, my legs,' Prue groaned. Their periods had stopped long ago along with most of the women and their legs had swollen and permanently throbbed but whether it was as a result of this or just the diet and the work no one really knew.

Not exactly the place for research the doctor had said as they had talked it over in the early days of their captivity. She had worked in a children's hospital in Sydney and had come to Singapore in 1939.

Annie stood with Prue at the side of the beri-beri case who was dropsical and exhausted.

'The doctor has asked Cricket Chops for some Vitamin B again but he made her wait two hours in the sun, then sent her back speedo to look after the sick she was neglecting. Without the vitamins of course. No red cross parcels again, he said.' Annie was angry as they moved away to sit at the end of the hut until they made another round in half an hour.

'Did you do Van Weidens's washing?' Annie asked.

'Only half before roll-call. Can you finish when you get off?'

Annie nodded. 'It might buy us a banana from the guard, but don't for God's sake try with the big one. He belted Monica last week and took her money anyway.'

364

Prue raised her eyebrows. 'Sounds pretty par for the course. Anyway, Annie, you really can't have that glass bowl. It's unpatriotic.' She was looking down the hut towards the other door which corresponded with the one behind them. There was sometimes a slight draught but not today.

Annie picked up the fan from the desk and rose.

'Well, I'm going to anyway. I like the lines of the bamboo. Tom would too.'

She stood waiting for Prue to join her in fanning the patients and she did pull herself to her feet but would not look at Annie as she started alone for the first bed.

'Then you'll have to sort out your own damn sitting-room, because that's next on your list isn't it, darling. I want no part of it.' Her voice was full of bitterness.

Annie turned her back on her friend and tried to decide on colours for Sarah's room as her stomach tightened. These rows were breaking out all over the camp as people became as taut as over-stretched elastic about to snap. She soothed Mrs Glanville then moved to the next bed, fanning the woman who lay unconscious on the pallet. Annie wondered if the sitting-room was always empty now or whether the boys were there from time to time to see Val and had anyone heard from Georgie? She knew from the radio – she would not think of Lorna, just the radio – that Rangoon had fallen long ago but that did not mean he was dead. She must not think of him being dead. That would make it impossible to live. So she thought instead of Tom reading letters from Georgie, sitting by the fire with Maud and Grace and Don, eating hot buttered toast while Val poured tea. Were the girls pregnant yet, she wondered? Was Tom safe in the pits and Don in his supply depot? But she would not think of these questions, only of scenes; of people sitting as they had always done; of Georgie watching the sun setting over the lakes and the ducks against the sky.

A patient called and she moved towards the bed. Her hair hung limp and irritated her neck; she'd have to cut it again although Georgie liked it long. She rubbed the back of her hand across her forehead.

'Nurse, go and wash that hand. Septicaemia we definitely do not want.' The doctor was watching her from the end of the hut, then stooped again to her patient.

Annie stood still, her legs trembling as she saw again the

365

varicosed veins at the fair, so vividly that she was startled. She washed at the basin and wondered whether plain white paper would suit the sitting-room.

At lunch Prue sat on the Dutch table and did not look up as Annie came in, so she sat with Mavis Anderton who smiled. Her face was drawn and her teeth had rotted into black stumps; her hair was quite white and cut very short.

'Had a row, my dear?'

Annie murmured. 'It's the heat, it gets us all down.' She felt so tired today, even more so than she had done yesterday but not inside her head, not where she planned the sitting-room and, when that was finished, there was the kitchen and then the greenhouse to plant out.

'Wallpaper can be so dull, can't it?' she said as she swallowed the last of her rice. A piece fell on to the *atap* table and was lost between the weave. The women either side of her stopped eating. Mavis shoved her fingers in her mouth and sucked hungrily at the rice water while her eyebrows lifted. Monica looked round at the walls of the hut.

'Yes, I have to agree, palm and bamboo do become a trifle tedious. Let in the the draught too.' Mavis waved her hands to the walls. 'Should we complain to the management, do you think?' The whole table was laughing now and Annie glanced at Prue but she had turned her back to them and was busy eating.

'What are you up to now, Annie?' someone called from another table. More rice was pushed into open mouths again.

'Just thinking of doing up my house when I get back.' And that sounded good.

'You'll use your own firm, will you, the one you keep talking about?' Mavis was wiping her mouth with the back of her hand.

'I thought so, my brother and I together.' The sound of running feet broke into the conversation.

Camp leader stood panting in the doorway, holding on to the frame. 'Roll-call, *tenko*, quickly now everyone.' Her hair was falling over her face and she flicked it aside with an impatient hand. The women pushed the remains of the rice into their mouths as they ran towards the door knocking over stools in their haste. Mavis was in front of Annie and gripped the leader's arm. 'Not another Lorna, is it?'

'No,' she gasped, still trying to catch her breath. 'They've decided on three a day that's all, but they're creating merry hell

366

anyway.' Then she ran back to the compound past Annie who had begun to run to the hospital. There would be a beating if they were late but she was on duty and needed for the stretcher-cases. She pushed through the running women and struggled up the steps. She could not run for more than a few paces now, she was just too tired and the heat was beating on her head. Oh God, she'd left her hat in the dining-hut.

The doctor was just leaving. 'It's all right, Sister, stretcher-cases can remain inside today. For God's sake, hurry. He's in a rage, just look at him stamping.' The doctor took her arm and they stumbled down the steps and ran again for parade. The others were already lined up and bowing and Dr Jones's hand tightened on her arm and Annie felt her bowels loosen with fear.

They reached the lines and bowed and barely breathed as feet slopped along in boots which seemed too large always and had to be held on with binding. It was frayed Annie saw and the boots were dirty and scuffed up small clouds of dust as they approached and stopped. The blow knocked her across the doctor on to the ground and the sand was gritty in her mouth, blood trickled from the corner; she lay motionless.

'You come speedo, you bad woman.' The boot kicked and hands dragged her upright and Annie felt the stickiness of his spit as words were hurled. 'You stand here all day. Look at sun, all day.'

Her face was rigid with animal fear, she felt urine escape and stain her shorts. The bamboo caught her across her midriff cutting into the flesh where her uniform was torn. She was silent. It struck across her hands and she screamed and though her eyes were open she could see no faces and then they filed away as the pain covered her.

'Ichi, ni, san, yong,' kept leaping and snarling in amongst the pain which coiled tight now around her broken finger. The guard smelt and beige roses merged into glaring white suns which wrung the sweat from her body. Her tongue grew large in her mouth, her lips cracked and burst and her throat was too swollen to swallow.

'Look at sun.' The guard kicked and turned her body, but her eyes stayed shut and he could not force them open. She fell and large boots kicked her up. She partially opened her eyes and fixed them on the tear in his trousers, then the verandah in the distance and then at Prue standing on the steps and she did not fall again.

'Chin up, darling.'

Not bloody likely, sang her mind, and dehydration wrung her miles away and she heard the wind on the dunes and felt the sharp sting of the sand and the waves as they rushed and swirled and she felt his hands and drank his tears. Look at the boots, she thought, look at the huts. What can I put on the white curtains? And finally dusk came and Prue and Monica carried her to her bed, away from the mumbles of the hospital. They pushed her in from the end of the pallet since there was no space between the platforms. Prue slowly poured a little tepid water into her half-open mouth and Monica held a soaking cloth to her head and the doctor strapped her hand.

'That'll teach you to be late, you silly clot,' Prue said and pressed her hand to Annie's cheek. 'For God's sake, I'll get you there on time if I have to drag you tomorrow.'

Annie spoke and Prue leant close.

'Glass bowl with bamboo, OK.'

During the next five months Annie finished all the bedrooms and the sitting-room and her finger was beginning not to hurt and her eyes to see clearly again. One Monday in June, the guards issued postcards and Prue had the only pencil in the hut. It was short and an HB which smudged in their sweat-drenched hands. They filled in the blanks. 'I am quite . . . . ., what should we put?' asked Annie.

'Quite well, if you value your other hand,' responded Prue. So she did. Flies were crawling over her face and the corners of her mouth. She was too tired to move them, only to have them resettle in the next breath.

'I'm sending mine to Daddy. What about you Annie?'

Annie had been looking at the work-party breaking up dried lumps of soil with emaciated fingers, shorts stained with dysentery. It seemed a betrayal to name a survivor for surely, if she pointed a finger, God would find them and they would be killed. Georgie or Tom or Don, who should she send it to?

She watched as the working women fingered the small segments to dust and moved, crouching, along the line to bang another large piece on to rock-hard ground, then again and again. Vegetables were to be growing for the 1945 September inspection, so they would be showing if they wanted to live. It was her turn tomorrow when she had finished her duty.

'I'll send it to Georgie,' she challenged. 'He'll think I've turned senile looking at this writing though.' Her hands had shaken since the beating. They were improving but not much.

Doctor Jones came out on to the verandah and looked down at them. Her face was set and she held her finger to her lips.

'Number three bed has diphtheria,' she whispered, and Annie broke out in a rush of sweat as she scrambled to her feet, pulling Prue.

Doctor Jones stood with her hand in the pockets of her linen coat. 'It could go round the camp like wildfire. Absolute rest for her and isolation; my room at the end.' She walked out into the heat of the square. 'I'm going to see the commandant. They don't like epidemics in case they catch it. Perhaps we'll get some disinfectant from the old devil.'

She turned. 'Write her postcard for her Annie please and we'll steam her pallet when I get back. For now, strain her water through the last of the disinfectant. The two beri-beri cases are in the last stages. Both of you pretend to write their cards please.'

The disinfectant came while they were dragging the large oilcan from the cookhouse to the bricks which the commandant had given them for the sterilization of the bedding. Their legs shook but the can had to be back for lunch and they could not bear the thought of the mid-day sun as they worked. They worked up the fire inside the bricks and boiled up the can; the steam began to rise and they stood either side on old buckets and held the pallet over the top. The steam billowed out at their faces and their hands and Annie's arms shook and her hand ached.

'Frightfully good for the pores, darling,' breathed Prue. Finally it was done. They damped the fire with earth and tipped the water out of the can before stumbling back to the cookhouse balancing the pallet on the top of the can.

As they placed it down there was a shudder and Annie staggered slightly, grabbing at the verandah for support but that was shaking also. There was another shudder and a distant rumble and Annie remembered the tiled floor in the nurses' home and the crash of falling bombs, searchlights which stabbed the sky and knew that it was here again.

369

'Air raid, Prue. It's a damned air raid.' The doctor was calling them back to the hut and they ran with the pallet, past guards whose neckcloths flapped as they rushed across to the prisoners and herded them inside, standing guard outside the closed doors.

The hospital door was also slammed shut and in the dark they each went from bed to bed soothing until Doctor Jones sent Prue into the diphtheria case and Monica to the two with beri-beri.

'It's the allied planes,' Annie soothed as she passed between patients. 'Yes, it must be getting near the end.'

Near the bloody end, she sang to herself. Can it really be near the end? Was there still a world out there beyond the wire and, if so, would their guards let them live to see it?

The guards pinned up black-outs and the beatings became more savage and Annie's finger was broken again. Prue had a bad sore throat and couldn't eat her rice. It was diphtheria.

Annie nursed her in the doctor's room, swabbing and sponging, straining the water until she could smell nothing but disinfectant, but still the disease ravished what little was left of Prue's body. For weeks the bombs came but never hit the camp. The ground shuddered, not every day or night but enough to make the guards more cruel and the women more frightened, for now they all asked the question; would they be allowed to live if Japan was defeated? Long into the night Annie sat and held Prue's hand and somehow she lived but lost her mind and sat winding her hair round and round her middle finger and smiling and doing as she was asked but only for Annie.

Annie cut her hair and streaked the fringe and took her to *tenko* and made her bow when she should and stand when she should so she was not beaten. She made her eat her rice but Prue whimpered unless the rabbit was made to find its hole.

'She could pick up, Annie,' the doctor told her as they wound the bandages in the evenings. The smell of the coconut oil lamp was not unpleasant. It was the same as it had been for three and a half years and perhaps it kept the mosquitoes away.

'It's not exactly a world anyone in their right mind would rush back to, is it?' Annie replied. 'So perhaps she is the only sane person here.' She put her hands on the table; they were trembling badly again. 'Do you think the Allies will ever come and, if they do, will we be alive to see them?'

Doctor Jones patted her hand. 'I don't know. Sometimes I dare to hope that we'll survive but at others . . . ' She shrugged. 'I just don't understand these people.'

'At least they've broken the sahibs' rule, haven't they? They've pricked the bubble now. We've been coolies too and we bleed like the Malays do. We've spoilt it for the ladies who danced at Raffles, spoilt their image haven't we?'

'Perhaps not before time?' the doctor murmured and Annie was surprised.

'I worked in Liverpool in the thirties, before I went back to Sydney. Those bloated little bellies were not so very different to these in the camp.'

They sat in silence for a while. Moths flew at the flame and one was caught.

'Will you go back to England or Australia?' Annie asked.

'I'm not sure yet. What about you?'

'I have a house and I'm going to decorate it but I want the sea as well. I want to walk by the sea again where the wind can clean me and my eyes can stretch forever. I want to run my business and to live with Georgie.' She said it quietly, rolling the bandages again, feeling the creases and smoothing them out.

'In that order?' the doctor asked.

Annie could not answer.

CHAPTER 27

Bob and Tom sank yet another beer. It was still watered down but it tasted like ambrosia and, bugger me, thought Tom, if I don't feel like a bloody God. VE day had been grand with lights blazing from windows out into the streets for the first time in years but this was even better.

'July 5th and Labour's in.' Tom drummed his fingers on the table. 'Hitler would turn in his bunker if he knew, eh Bob. Socialism in England when he wanted to kill 'em all. Bye, makes you feel grand doesn't it, man?'

Bob chuckled. 'Aye lad, it does, that it does. No depression after this war and if there is, no one will starve anyway.' The pub was full of men, sun streamed in through windows and there were banners on all the sills.

'Have another drink, Bob.' Tom wiped his mouth with his hand. A toast to Clem Attlee, eh, and how about one for Wainwright, wherever he may be.'

Bob laughed 'We've had enough, Tom. Let's get back to see Bobby before Grace takes him to bed.'

Tom sprang to his feet, his face breaking into a grin. He shoved his change into his pocket. 'It's all been worth it then, Bob. War's over and Labour's in and Don's bloody livid.' He showed Bob Don's postcard. He would be demobbed by August.

The pub had filled since they came in and they pushed their way through the groups of excited miners, slapping backs and grinning, until they reached the door. The sun was still hot and the light creased their eyes until they adjusted to the glare. The streets they walked down were humming with activity. Women hung around their front doors, aprons on and sleeves rolled up, some with bairns on their hips. Men laughed over cigarettes, dark from the pit still, unwilling to go home until the victory was talked into manageable size.

Tom and Bob turned into the back alley and then through the yard gate. The kitchen door was open with Bobby sitting on the step. Grace turned from the wall; Mrs Fenney was leaning over and they were laughing.

'Now you're here, Tom Ryan, you can wind down this line for me,' ordered Grace and collected together the last of the washing. 'Staying for a bite are you, Bob?'

As she carried the basket into the house, Tom slipped up behind her and kissed her neck. Mrs Fenney laughed and Grace squealed.

'Tom, I can smell beer on you. You can just behave yourself.'

But by now Bobby was pulling at his trousers and laughing. He weighed nothing at all as Tom swung him into the air, then back close into his arms. He blew gently down his neck and nuzzled his son, who had skin which was almost too soft to feel.

Working as a checker gave him more time for the lad and it pleased him. The committee work at the pit consumed one evening a week and was as interesting as Bob had promised it would be and still gave him time for his painting class with the lads.

'Come on Bob, get sat down.' He steered him into his usual chair to the left of the fire which was a dull glow on this hot day. The irons were already heating on the hot plate. He slapped his cap on the table and, still carrying Bobby, sat down and stroked his brown hair as they gathered their thoughts in silence. The beer had made his body loose and he kissed his son's head. The clock was ticking on the mantelpiece.

'It was the bombers really, wasn't it?' Tom said eventually. 'That's what won the election. It dragged lice and smelly kids into posh homes all over the country. Bye, I bet some noses had a shock. The old 'uns too, bombed out and nowhere to go. Made a few people think, I reckon. Think about how the posh lived, how the poor lived.'

'The press certainly splashed it all over the papers,' agreed Bob.

'Free milk, free school dinners, they'll be keeping those on, I reckon, and Davy should have been here since I dare say they'll be extending that Family Allowance the evacuees had.'

'Archie will be the one turning in his grave if you're not

careful, Tom. Can't you hear him saying, "Lunch, if you don't mind, Thomas."'

They both chuckled now but their eyes were thoughtful at a picture of a man defeated by a life that would not be allowed to happen now.

'Tough on Winnie, though. Must feel like a kick in the teeth,' mused Tom, watching as Grace brought the washing in and then wiped a flannel over Bobby's face, which was sticky with toffee Betsy had made. He was asleep now on Tom's lap and Tom kissed Grace's arm below the elbow as she reached across.

'Nationalisation must feel that way to him anyway. Poor old soldier and now it'll come, thick and fast.' Bob patted his lip with his forefinger.

Grace nodded. 'It doesn't seem fair somehow.' She was folding the clothes into a neat pile, ready for ironing, then smiled at them. 'Come on, you two, get up the allotment, the pair of you, while I do a spot of ironing and then put the bairn to bed and fix a bit to eat. You can sort out the world up there. The birds will appreciate a few crumbs of wisdom.'

Bob and Tom raised their eyebrows at one another.

'We've had a better audience than this when we've been canvassing. Cheered I was, on the waste land,' puffed Tom.

'Out!' Grace laughed.

So they linked arms, bowed and ducked the cloth that Grace aimed towards them. Tom curtailed his limping stride to fit in with Bob's frail step as they walked up the hill. They did not hurry but nodded to Sam Walker, as they passed, before continuing in a contented silence until they reached the allotment bench, which Tom had angled in between the shed and the wall so that Bob could have a windless patch when he joined Tom here on Sundays.

The bench was warm from the sun and they leaned back against the wall. Bob filled his pipe, still with tea leaves. He had said he'd only use tobacco again when nationalisation had taken place and Tom was right glad that it looked as though it was on the way; the smell was dreadful. There were still a few hearted lettuces but the cabbages were young yet and the beans were beginning to hang heavy on the poles.

'I suppose the government will have to buy the owners out?' Bob nodded. 'Yes, they'll be offered compensation. It'll be better than the way you once proposed. A revolution with a temporary dictatorship?' He looked at Tom sideways.

'Aye, and you could say the war had one and look at what was achieved.' But he put his hands up as Bob started to argue. 'I know, I know, I was only mithering. Wish to God the buggers would put some of their compensation into newer industries up here though, Bob. That's always going to be the trouble in coal you know. Heavy industry is vulnerable. Even if mining is nationalised it will always be vulnerable. It's a declining industry.'

'I know, lad, but one thing the men'll have to do is to have a national union, not the various groups making up the Federation.'

Tom nodded. 'That'll be more work for you, Bob. Can you handle it? The campaign took it out of you.'

He looked with concern at Bob who had door-knocked and spoken on street corners alongside Tom and that had tired him enough, damn it. The man couldn't be far off 60.

'I'll do a bit, lad, but what about you? Could be a great opening for you. You'd make a grand union man.'

The sun had dipped almost out of sight behind the slag but it was still light and the honeysuckle which climbed the wall to their right made the air heavy with its fragrance. A sparrow was busy where the chicken meal was kept. Tom stopped and threw a pebble towards it. As it flew off in a flurry of fear, he said, 'No Bob. It's time I was off out of it now. Me foot hurts, me mind goes round in circles. I want to get on with our own ideas now.'

Bob stopped sucking on his pipe and turned to look at Tom.

'Your Annie's not been found yet, Tom. They've opened a few camps, found such dreadful things. You must not be so sure of the future.'

Grace had spoken to him, asked him to make Tom consider that Annie was probably dead, try to get him to think of life without her. He patted Tom's knee. 'You must think in terms of yourself, not ourselves, lad.'

Tom shook his head. 'Don't you fret, Bob. She'll be back. There's a lot for us to do. Houses will be rebuilt, they'll need decorating and it will give a great deal of work, half of it to women. She knows that. She'll be back, I tell you.' It was now the half-light of a summer's evening and the birds were still swooping over the allotment and, in the honeysuckle, a finch was fluttering.

'Georgie's going when Japan is finished and he won't stop until he finds her. I can't live without her. I couldn't work at the business unless she's with me.'

Bob felt a cold shaft cut down through his body.

Tom tapped his arm. 'Let's get back, shall we? Grace will mither us for letting the food get cold.' He took Bob's arm as they walked out of the allotment, past the alley that led to Betsy, on down the darkening streets which could now be lit with street lamps.

He saw again the girl standing by the school, saw her run towards him with her shoelace undone; felt again the coal squeeze his breath and kill Martin, heard her voice.

A dog barked and children ran out of one street and on to the pavement behind them, laughing and kicking at a ball. She'd come back, he nodded to himself. Annie would always come back.

Bob rubbed the back of his left hand. There were age spots on the translucent skin now and his knuckles ached much of the time. He felt immensely weary. What would happen if Annie did not come home again?

CHAPTER 28

It was morning and Annie woke and undid the rope which tied Prue to her wrist for the night, since she had been found wandering in the compound one night and was lucky not to have been shot. Annie sat her up and washed her hands and face. The sore at the corner of her mouth was larger now.

'Come on, lass, it'll be roll-call in a moment and then it's time for the rabbit again.'

She took her hand and Monica stood with Prue while Annie straightened their pallets and put Prue's net under the blanket to hide it from the guards. They turned as the leader came into the hut.

'They've gone,' she said, her voice full and tears running down her face. 'The gates are open and they've gone. It's over. It must be over.'

Annie caught at Prue's hand and pulled her to the doorway then out on to the verandah. It seemed so quiet. Women were walking slowly out of their huts and into the compound, their clompers causing dust to rise. There was no cheering. The gates hung open and the guard-towers were empty. The plantation began just outside the wire and women were at the gate but not going through.

She took Prue down the steps slowly at first and then faster, edging sideways through the others, easing her way to the front. There it was, the open gate and the dark tumbling trees beyond.

They were free, at last they were free but the air was still that of a prison, the wire still stretched around the camp and they must pass beyond it and so she walked with Prue out into freedom. She held her hand and slowly they passed from the baked earth to the undergrowth of the rubber trees. Others now followed, taking different paths. She felt tired as she stepped over a fallen tree; she was free but she still felt tired. How strange.

'Mind the undergrowth,' she warned Prue. It had tangled and woven itself up and over the trunks of once-tapped trees and the musky smell overrode the latex. She stood still and lifted her head high and watched the branches link overhead like a steeple and for a moment she was back in the lane leading to the beck, back listening to Beauty's hooves and watching Georgie as he showed the bee to Tom. But here there was really only the chatter of the monkeys, the crackle of other feet now, on other paths. Voices which had at first whispered were now shouting because there was no one any more to crash a rifle butt into your head.

'Come on, hinny,' she said gently and Prue smiled and stumbled alongside her. Annie could no longer find some of the graves which were now hidden completely beneath the fast-reclaiming jungle. Prue's hand lay in hers and, when Annie finally stopped, she did also.

'I want to be able to tell Mr Anderton where Mavis was buried, but I can't find the place.' Her stomach was tightening again. Prue's face screwed up into tears because Annie was sad.

'Don't cry,' said Annie gently and so she stopped.

The jungle had come down into the plantation. There were creepers as thick as ropes hanging from the trees and green moss everywhere. Annie ran her finger down a rubber tree and looked at the green lichen on her finger and then at the smear on the bark which would be overgrown by tomorrow.

'We'll go home now,' she told Prue who obediently followed her back to the cookhouse where they were queueing for rice.

The doctor was counting packets in the hospital when they had finished. 'We've broken into the store. Camp leader brought these over, marmite tonight for everyone please, Sister. Monica is already giving some to the beri-beri cases. One way of getting Vitamin B into them anyway. The fluid will pour out of the dropsy cases.' Her voice broke. 'The Red Cross parcels were here all the time. We could have saved so many.'

Annie felt her own eyes blur. 'Shall I tell everyone to eat only a little, they'll be ill if they dig into the parcels straight away, won't they?' The doctor nodded.

There were boxes stacked in the middle of the compound as they stepped out into the sun. 'What are those?' Annie asked.

'Our postcards,' replied the doctor. 'They were never sent.'

The allied trucks arrived seven days later. It was strange to hear English spoken by male voices, to hear rounded vowels which rolled off the tongue rather than harsh words that spat at you from the conqueror. It was strange to see khaki and if they weren't all so ill and tired they would have minded being dressed only in bras and shorts or torn dresses held together by the merest of threads.

There was nowhere for them to go, they were told, so would they mind awfully staying here until repatriation could be arranged. They did in fact mind awfully, but there was no strength left in anyone to complain. Clothing and food were trucked in and the sick taken to hospital.

The doctor insisted that Prue should go, though she screamed and cried when she was taken from Annie, who kissed her and said it wouldn't be for long. She must go home now, to her da.

Annie lay that night beneath Prue's mosquito net which was so much cooler after the blanket that she had used for the last three years. The real cigarette tasted wonderful and kept the mosquitoes away better than the leaf tobacco. She could not hear them buzzing all around now but her head was swimming with the pungent inhalation. Her wrist felt strange without its tether and she felt frightened now that she was quite alone.

With no duties, they all had little to do and Annie's mind was full of thoughts and dreams and shadows that darkened with each day, leaping from the black box and then disappearing before she could keep them long enough to examine.

Early in September, the heat of the day was rising and her sweat dripped on to the verandah floor. Monica was bartering for bananas from a native down by the gate. More jeeps were driving into the compound, racing up to the Union Jack which now flew where the Rising Sun had done. Georgie climbed out of one and the doctor spoke to him, touched his arm and pointed. He was tanned in his shorts but dust lay on him in a light layer and only her eyes moved as she watched him walk towards her through the heat. She felt the verandah sag as he climbed each step but she sat quite still; so tired, so very tired. He sat beside her and took her hand. It was the same hand that it had always been. After this time, it was still quite the same.

'You never change, do you, bonny lass?' He held her head

between his hands and his eyes were as brown as they had ever been, though lines dug deep. His eyelashes were as thick as hedgerows, if hedgerows still existed. His smile was still one-sided.

'Yes, I do,' she replied. 'I do change, my love.' It took time to form the words, her mouth felt stiff these days and her voice sounded as though it came from someone else.

'Not to me, my bonny lass,' and he kissed her tired thin old face and rested his head on hers so that she should not see how his eyes had filled and his mouth trembled.

Annie sat just as she had been but rested her head in his hands and breathed him in and wanted to sit like this until she died and the dreams that were so dark went away.

She didn't look back at the camp as she left. It was her home and she was leaving her friends but this had happened before, hadn't it, long ago, and Georgie had said that she would see them again anyway, so she would, wouldn't she?

In the Raffles Hotel she lowered herself into a full bath; her legs lifted and floated, her arms did the same and her body sank into the warmth while the water blackened. She rinsed herself again and again but still she felt unclean. In the mirror the face that was reflected was an old skull with yellow skin and eyes that were sunk too deep, and there was no life in them.

She lay that night with Georgie on a bed too soft for sleep but she did not want to sleep for then the darkness came and the black box bulged and struggled to open. She lay beneath the net and he held her hand but on the other wrist she could still feel the tether and hear the noise of the hospital hut and smell bad burnt almonds. He took her in his arms and held her close and her love for him was in every part of her body but she was dead to his touch because passion was a luxury and she had no strength for luxuries. No strength to do more than see and feel him from a distance. She heard his voice, felt his touch, watched his lips as he talked softly to her, but he could not come inside her head and help her with the black box and that was what she must concentrate on, all the time, keeping the black box closed.

The next day, the jeep took them to the blackened airfield past platoons of Japanese soldiers who guarded buildings, directed natives, dug at bombed buildings.

'We haven't enough soldiers, my love, so we are using the

Japs for now to keep things ticking over.' She nodded and looked straight ahead. She would not look at these men who had kept their marmite from them and stolen Lorna's head.

Bombay burst in on her as she stepped out of the aeroplane, the heat surged against her face and the smell of the continent was all around. Diphtheria did not creep up gently on her but suddenly with violence, that first day in India. It closed her throat and hurled darts of pain to every nerve-end and here, in this strange clean white hospital, dry fingers held her and gave her injections of something called penicillin. Soft hands bathed her and there were no insects, no moans from other huts, no guttural screams from booted guards, no lover. Just a fan that purred.

She ran her fingers softly round and over the raised embroidered laundry mark. The fan moved round, her arm was brown against the turned-down crisp sheet and only her eyes played with the branched shadows which flickered and rushed silently across the pristine white tiles, and she wondered what tree it was that so silently teased the everlasting sun and denied its passage to her room.

Four weeks it had been, the nurse had said. Four weeks of gentle hands, four weeks with no need to speak, with sips taken from cool glasses and a head which was held up by another's efforts. Four weeks of protection and now there was a world out there forcing its way in. Along the corridor she could feel it march, hear the ringing of its heels and then feel finally the click and rush of sound. Holding the door open, Georgie smiled. How brown he is, all brown, she thought. His uniform was khaki, his belt was brown but no, she was wrong. His shoes were coal-black, his buttons were icy yellow. So, she smiled, he's not just brown, nobody's just anything. But what does it matter anyway.

'You're coming home, my love,' he said, his mouth buried in the palm of her hand.

'Yes,' she replied. 'I want to go home.' She touched the bleached streaks of his hair. I'm coming, Tom, she called silently. I'm coming at last.

'Next week, the doctors say, and I have arranged the ceremony here and we will spend two weeks in Kashmir. Do you remember me telling you about it and how you'd love it? The waters go on forever, Annie, but never seem to flow. The mountains lie and wait and when you are there you will wait with them and recover.'

She stroked his face and it was rough. 'I'd like that and then I must go home.'

He kissed each finger. 'Yes, I've found a nice bungalow. It's all ready and Prue is back on station with her father. She's so well, Annie, and young Sanders seems to have taken quite a shine to her. He's a good sort and she's blooming again. A bit quiet perhaps. A bit strange but well. She's coming to the wedding, blonde hair and all.' He laughed, his face was close to hers. He held her hand tightly to his chest. 'I'm so happy that at last we're to be together. Each day has been an agony, not knowing if you were alive or hurt. I shall never let you go again, my darling Annie. I shall look after you from now on and nothing will hurt you ever again.' He laid his head against hers and she felt his breath and wondered why he could not hear her screaming. Why no one could hear her screaming.

She wanted to go home, to have space around her to breathe. Could no one hear her screaming?

Kashmir was high above the plain of India, nearer to the sky than she had ever been. The houseboat nestled quietly and gently in its berth. Georgie wore a white shirt, the sleeves of which he rolled up above his elbows and she watched his sinews, his strong familiar arms and clung to him as he carried her over the threshold.

'Kiss me, darling,' she pleaded desperately and he did, his lips soft at first and then hard and urgent and he carried her to the bedroom, past the bearer who stood to one side. He laid her on the bed and she watched as he dragged his clothes from his body and, gently then, removed hers. He kissed her and stroked her, licked her breasts which were fuller now. Kissed her thighs and she ran her hands down his back, his stomach until she held him in her hands, large and hot and he groaned and entered her and she cried out to him, 'Deeper my love,' but he was still not far enough into her. He could not push back the heat of the compound, cast off the tether from her wrist or the blood that shot two yards from Lorna's body. She wept as he came inside her and he held her and tears were on his cheeks too as he cradled her in his arms and kissed her hair as they lay together.

'You've made me so happy, my darling,' he whispered and she smiled and looked at the curtains which hung round the walls of the bedroom. Yes, she still had the dining-room to sort out. Still the wallpaper in there.

That evening, they sat out on the verandah and the bearer brought them gin. The glass was heavy and cool. Georgie's wicker chair creaked as he reached forward to take her hand. He turned the plain gold ring which he had placed on her right hand. He reached over and touched her broken finger gently with his. His wrist was strong and she wondered if he would like to take the tether for a while but did not want to trouble him.

That night, she did not want to close her eyes, so lay there planning a pale green cool dining-room but her lids were heavy and soon there were shapes which squeezed out of the box because she couldn't keep the lid down. She pushed and pushed and cried for Georgie but he was on the outside of her head and could not hear. They were tumbling out now, secrets which slithered out and over the floor of her mind. She pushed them back: Lorna, varicose legs, broken fingers, Albert's hands which lunged at her, panting men on a playing-field, a hose-pipe which writhed out gas and her da, mostly her da, his face yellow, his mouth gaping. She pushed them back, her screams so loud that it made her head ache. Slowly, steadily, she pushed them back with her hands inside her head but now her hands were slimy.

The bungalow was square, its edges cut through the parched bleached air. White stones marked the pathway.

'Welcome, memsahib,' bowed the bearer, bearded and dark.

'Thank you,' she replied and entered Georgie's home wiping her hands down her skirt.

Prue was on the station, rounded now, with a bloom to her cheeks.

The days were long, movements were slow and the plains seldom varied. The heat rolled across the earth and Georgie was often late because he was in bomb disposal again and busy with the troubles.

The bungalow was painted plain white and the floors were tiled black and white and her feet left damp impressions as she walked.

'What would the memsahibs say, darling?' Prue asked as

they sat one morning in floral-covered chairs with cane tables scattered between each one. 'One really does not bare the feet in front of the servants,' she mimicked.

'Well this one does,' Annie rejoined. Her voice was quieter these days and each morning she woke unrefreshed, but Prue was the golden girl again though she would never be without the extra lines. She was better for them, Annie decided. They sat opposite one another. Fans disturbed the air and made the heat bearable.

Prue tapped her half-full glass of lime juice. 'You will come to the club for tiffin, darling, won't you?'

'Must I?' asked Annie, her legs curled up beneath her. She wiped her hands down her skirt and then rose.

Prue said, 'Yes, you must, and where are you off to now?'

'To wash my hands.' They were slimy again.

The water was not cool. Prue called from the sitting-room.

'You must come, Annie. It will do you good. Your mind is obviously on Georgie and there's no need. They're not using too many explosives in this area. The troubles are further from the border. Come on.' There was a smile in her voice. 'They are dying to have a proper look at you.'

Annie dried her hands and walked back. She liked the cool of the tiles.

'That's not much of an incentive.' She felt better when she was with Prue somehow. The tether had slipped from her wrist now that Prue was well but she wouldn't think of the rest because they would be here again tonight as always.

'Very well.' Prue sat forward, her finger pointing. 'I suggest a trade. You want to ride? I shall take you. You will come to the mess – and before you object – I have some jodhpurs but wear your topee. It's cracking down outside.'

The plain shimmered in the distance, the scrub clung in parts to the wide-cracked surface and the pony shambled beside Prue's. The palace on the hilltop brooded as they passed. Their escort stayed behind them at a suitable distance, the stirrup leather pinched her inside leg and the sound of their shifting harness was all that disturbed their progress. Annie wondered if Tom still had Beauty. She had written to him but had not heard back yet and would not try and picture him because the missing was too much.

'The maharajah hardly ever comes now,' said Prue, lifting her crop to the palace. 'He lives in Bombay and sends his sons to school in England.'

'Crazy, isn't it,' mused Annie. 'While the British sent their daughters to live in India to find a husband. How is Lt. Sanders by the way? You haven't mentioned him yet today, or perhaps only a hundred times!' She smiled as Prue blushed.

'Just maybe, Annie, maybe this is it. I do love him and I think he loves me. I'm so glad you've decided to stay here with Georgie. We can all be together now.'

Annie rubbed her hands together then down her trousers. She couldn't get them clean, couldn't breathe; everyone was too close. She urged her pony forward, taking in gulps of air.

'Though how long any of us will be here is a moot point,' Prue continued, keeping up with her. 'Georgie was telling Daddy that in a couple of years he'll take you back to start the business because he doesn't give the English any longer than that anyway.'

Annie nodded.

'Is that what you want? We must settle close to one another Annie, when we do all go back.'

They were moving along the edge of a gully now and the earth scudded down into it. Annie nodded again. It would be nice to have Prue close and yes, she wanted to go back but two years had a great many long days inside it.

'We should all have left before the troubles became so bad. All such an undignified scramble, darling. So much tension everywhere, you can feel it even before the shouts and riots break out. Suddenly India isn't home any more.'

Annie dragged herself back.

'You must be the only insider who thinks so.' She wound the reins round her hand. It had healed quite well.

Prue shrugged as her pony pawed the ground and they began to move again. 'They must know, deep down, but if they admit it to themselves, let alone anyone else, it is too real. But there'll be a few more years anyway though it won't be the same as it was. I so longed for it in that dump as well. Shall we ride back now, nearly time for tiffin remember?'

Annie pushed the thought of home aside, the thought of cool sea-breezes and followed Prue back down the wadi. The palace seemed very empty and vast. What will happen to you, she wondered, when we've gone and the country is free?

The party sitting around the table was languid in the mahogany-darkened room. Conversation was desultory, tea-cups rattled softly and always there was the hum of the fans. The brightness seen through draped windows and shaded verandahs seemed distant.

Annie shook her head at the cake. There was dark panelling on each wall and oil paintings with heavy gilt frames.

'Surely not slimming, my dear?' Tea was laid on a walnut table.

'No, it's still rather too rich for me, thank you.'

'Not for me either, thank you, Mrs Bearing.' Prue waved the plate away.

'Slimming too?'

Annie glanced at Prue.

'We're not slimming, Mrs Bearing.' Prue raised her voice and spoke slowly, each word clearer than the last. 'We can't digest rich food yet. We've only been back in India about two months.'

The woman shifted her gaze to the spot between the two. She had white hair and spectacles and wore a blouse that was ruffled at the neck. Her lips were thin.

'Quite so, my dear. Did you have a pleasant ride?'

'Lt. Sanders was asking after you, Prue dear. He has just come in from up-country. He's a good boy and has rather a soft spot for you, I think.' An elderly woman was speaking, her skin was sallow and lined, her grey hair short and crinkle-permed. She had a nice face, Annie decided. The bearer stood in the corner, ready to renew the teapot. 'And it's so nice to see you looking so well,' the woman continued.

'Yes, yes, indeed,' Mrs Bearing called across the table. 'One heard such frightful stories. Such bad form, don't you know, women in coolie hats and rags. I mean, how can one be expected to keep the Empire intact with that sort of thing being allowed to happen? Can't have been our sort. Others brought in for the duration most likely.'

The elderly woman laid her hand on Annie's arm. A sapphire stone was set in plain gold and her skin hung loose beneath her arm.

'More tea, my dear.'

Annie shook her head. She must strip the dining-room wallpaper; she must pull large sodden strips and drop them into piles until her feet were covered. Then it would be green stripes, pale green and cream stripes. It would be so cool.

'I think, Prue, I shall have to make the curtains, they don't seem to match material to wallpaper, do they?' She rubbed her hands on her napkin, again and again.

Prue sat quite still in the silence that drifted outwards across the table; faces looked blank, then embarrassed. Mrs Bearing fingered her pearls.

'Do have some more tea, Mrs Cantor,' she offered the elderly woman who kept her hand on Annie's arm. She smoothed her collar as she asked the other women too.

Prue leaned forward, making room for her cup and taking Annie's from her. 'I think it is time we left.' She spoke carefully and equally carefully, she said, 'Thank you so much for an enlightening afternoon, Mrs Bearing, but now we have letters to write, to our coolie friends.'

She rose, touching Annie's arm. 'Yes, I rather think you will have to match them up yourself or perhaps it would be easier just to paint.' She led Annie from the table.

Mrs Cantor also rose, taking Annie's other arm. Annie liked the older woman's eyes, they were deep and they smiled.

'Come on, Annie, let's go home,' Prue said gently.

'Yes, I'd like that,' and the brightness of the window seemed further away than ever and the darkness of the heavy mess furniture with its cold silver loomed larger than ever.

'Make her rest, Pruscilla, and do not overdo it yourself.' Mrs Cantor spoke softly and watched as they walked out into the heat. It was pre-monsoon and their lungs expanded with effort.

'When is Georgie coming home?'

Annie wondered why Prue was so careful, her voice so tightly pitched.

'Perhaps not until tomorrow but probably tonight.' She stopped. A thought had flickered past her eyes and gone but here it was again.

'Why does he do this, Prue? Does he want to die? Every time be probes for the fuse he must think, this time may be the time. It's a bit like suicide, another suicide. Such a lot of suicides.' She walked on. The bungalow was not far now. It would be cool there. She could wash her hands, tear off these clothes, lie on the bed. She ran her fingers round her collar, rolled up her sleeves. They stood on the verandah.

Prue said, 'Father says the best at the job are those who want to live most. Georgie's the best.'

'But he shouldn't be doing it, not now the war is over.' The verandah rail was smooth and painted white but she could see a knot slightly raised. 'There is no need for anyone else to die.'

'He won't die, Annie.' Prue frowned. 'You're very tired, I'll come and see you later.'

'It's the bedside lamp that is the problem. Shall I match it to the light or to the paper?' Annie shook her head. Everything flashed through too quickly for her to hold all her thoughts. She watched Prue leave but she turned at the bottom of the step.

'I'll hang on for a bit I think, Annie.'

But Annie shook her head. 'Don't be silly Prue, I'm fine. Just want a bit of peace, that's all, just a bit of peace.' She waved. The square shimmered and the lines of quarters broke down into heat-fragmented images. It seemed the same, day after day, week after week. She fanned herself and held the rail. Oh for a cold sea-breeze. She smiled at Kassim as she entered the bungalow.

'I'm lying down for a while. Please don't disturb me unless it's an emergency.'

Beneath the mosquito net, she heard the monsoon begin and saw it suck the light from the day. She lay in a cotton nightdress but still the sweat ran from her body in the stifling heat. The rains plunged, water ran off ground too hard-baked to absorb its ferocity. It seemed hotter still and the noise drummed, punctuated by a shutter that banged, and Annie watched the black box. Even with her eyes wide open, she saw it. It was bulging and, unless the lid was opened, it was going to explode in little pieces all over the room, all over her brain and then she would never gather all the pieces together and back into the box and they would creep and slither around her forever and so she lifted the catch and let the secrets out. The moans came first and then Lorna and Albert's hand which grabbed for her and the vicar who could not say God. They were crawling across the floor and she could not catch them all. They were nearer now, the boots which kicked at her hands were stamping up dust and varicose legs were dancing round and the moans were mixed

388

with music from the fair and then Da came out and across the room towards her and Georgie wasn't here to help. He was out there trying to die like her da and she had always known that the man she loved would leave her if she let him close to her. He would die like her mother, like Sarah, like her da.

There was pain in her head now. It was bursting as it beat in time with the noise of the rain, the fair, the shutters, the screams and she took pills for the pain. They were sour and the water was warm. Her hair rubbed her neck; the pillow was too full. She pushed it to the bed edge and over it fell and was forgotten. The rain still drummed and the music went round and Albert's hands were nearly at her and the pipe which wriggled with gas was closer still. More pills but they were sour again and the pain was still with her. The fan was drumming now in time with the rain. And still there was the throbbing in her head and the blood from Lorna's head began to lap closer even than the gas-filled hose and then there was her da coming closer with his mouth wide open. The pills were not sour the next time and the noise was fading at last and the pain was easing. The black box was empty and everybody was leaving now in a spiral through the top of her head.

Her body was quiet, there was just her mouth that breathed and even that was slipping. She smiled at the peace. There was no heat, no noise and now the deep darkness was near. The peace.

Prue shook her hair as she arrived. It was wet and the water dripped off her mackintosh. The house was quiet.

'Thank you, Kassim. Is Memsahib awake?'

'She still sleeping. No want to be disturbed.' He took her coat and watched as she walked to the bedroom door. There was no answer to her knock. She turned the handle and entered. The shutters banged, they were unlatched and there was no light.

'Annie, are you awake?' she called but only the shutters crashed.

'Come on, darling, Georgie's with Father, then he's coming straight over.' She felt for the light, it was dim yellow and she saw the pillow half under the bed. Annie's hand was hanging not far above it, her arm half-hidden by the mosquito net. Prue's scalp tightened. She walked quietly across and pulled back the net.

389

She was too pale, too sound asleep.

'Wake up, Annie, let's clear this place up a bit.'

Her wrist was still warm but the pulse was faint. The brown bottle lay on the bed; it was only half full. Pruscilla pressed her lips together, her pulse was hurting in her throat. She heard steps on the verandah and the door opening.

'Shut it quickly, George. Do not let Kassim in. No one must know.' Her voice was low but steady and she did not look at him but at Annie.

He stood in the doorway. Pruscilla gestured sharply and he shut it behind him.

'What's wrong with Annie?' His voice was loud.

'Come over here and for God's sake keep your voice down. Let's get her up. She must walk, walk it off.'

He threw his hat to the corner of the room and caught Prue's arm. His face was suddenly anxious.

'Is she drunk?'

'Don't be so bloody ridiculous. She's taken an overdose.'

His arms felt slow at first but he reached her at last, his Annie, his love. Her shoulders were so fragile, her head lolled back. He looked at Prue.

'Will she live?' It was a desperate question, a whisper.

'If she doesn't sleep.'

'I'll get her to the hospital.' He was on his feet striding to the door.

'No time for that my lad and do you want the whole station to know? Do you want her to face criminal charges if she lives?'

'Can we do it, just the two of us?' He had turned helplessly to face her.

'I rather think we should, it will be much kinder.' She moved to the other side, regretting already the sharpness of her tone. They heaved Annie upright, the net caught on her hair and Prue pulled it away.

'Come on darling. Let's get those legs moving. Come on now.' Her voice was urgent. Nothing happened.

'Drag her, come on, drag her,' she hissed. The shutters still crashed against the frame, the rain was heavier.

'It's no good,' Georgie groaned. 'We're not getting through.'

'Hold her,' Prue snapped. She slapped Annie's face again and again, harder each time and still the shutter banged.

'Sahib, do you need me?' called Kassim.

'Go to your quarters!' roared Georgie, sweat rolling down his face, his hair wet with it.

'Shout at her, Georgie, shout ichi, ni, san, yong,' and he did.

'Speedo, speedo,' urged Prue roughly and again and again they shouted and dragged and her feet began to move and soon she started to retch and dawn made the lamp redundant. She was sitting in a chair with Georgie at her feet, his head buried in her lap, his shoulder shaking as he wept his pain.

'I'm going now,' Prue said, her voice soft and weary. 'Tell him, Annie, you must tell him you want to go home. How can he help if he doesn't know?' She touched his shoulder and wondered if either had heard her.

It was later, much later that Georgie opened his eyes. Her hand was on his head. He stirred and his movement lifted Annie's heavy lids. He rose and took her in his arms, carried her to the window.

'The rains are lighter now, my love,' he said softly and she nodded.

'I want to go home, Georgie. I must go away from the heat, back to my house, back to walls that are solid, pictures I know. I want to breathe again. I want space to breathe, that's all.'

'Aren't I enough for you, Annie?'

Her mouth was dry and she touched his hands which had pulled clover and held it to her lips, stroked his arms which she had bathed when they were stung. Touched his mouth which had smiled when she turned somersaults on the bar and she smelt again the leeks wilting in the heat on that summer day.

'You are too much for me.' And she did not know what she meant. 'I'm in small pieces and I want to go home.'

His eyes were reddened and pain was drawn into every corner of his face and she knew that all she wanted now was to be away from anyone who had ever pulled at her. And as he had done before, so long ago in Albert's kitchen, Georgie made it easy for her.

CHAPTER 29

The gangplank was gone, the sprawl of India was retreating; the smell was of the sea and for six weeks she sat or walked the deck, breathing easily now for the first time since she left the camp. Her hair was thick with salt and her skin was white-smudged with it too.

It was winter as they docked, and crisp. The bare-branched trees and darkened green fields first filled the train windows as she travelled towards the North and then fell away in the face of ploughed fields lying fallow.

The train embankments were blackened from sparks and stubble fires. Small fields and small horizons, Annie thought. The seats were the same; they still prickled. The pictures behind glass above the seats were faded as they had always been.

As she walked up the path to the Gosforn house, the privet leaf snapped as she bent it between thumb and forefinger, and then there was Val. She came down the path, her arms outstretched and Annie stood quite still as she laid her head on that familiar shoulder. She did not weep but stood silent as Val rocked her, then walked to the door and into the sitting-room. It was so very much the same and she put her case down and held on to Val's arm.

'I'm so glad I'm home.' The fire was in the grate, red and crackling but Sarah was not there.

'Let me take your coat, my dear,' said Val and kissed her cheek as Annie handed over the Harrods mackintosh that Prue had given her to brave the English winter. Her hands were cold and her cheeks too but it was a good feeling.

She woke the next morning and there was no sweat-drenched sheet, just a slow awakening. The black box had stayed shut when she had pushed the lid down. Was it over? Was the darkness over now that she was alone and at Gosforn? But she knew it wasn't; it was just waiting.

She lay with her hands beneath her head and looked up at Val's knock. The blue cup on the breakfast tray was the same as she remembered. She traced its scalloped lines with her thumb and sipped slowly. Val turned on the electric fire and drew back the curtains.

'Misty again,' she said and walked across to smooth the sheet down. 'Why don't you stay in bed today? You look so pale.' She had her hair drawn back in a bun and it was very white now, but she was still rounded, still as soft.

'Val, I love you. I'm as brown or yellow as a bunka wallah. No one could possibly call me pale.'

'Well, I do and Sarah would too, if she could see you now.' She folded her arms across her bosom. 'You are pale.'

Annie shook her head and leant back on the pillows. 'We've a great deal to do, Val. I want to start on the house, get the business going. You don't mind, do you, if I change things here?' She was restless and fingered the sheet. She wanted to be busy, not to have to think. 'It's not that I want to forget Sarah, I'll never do that. It's just something that I'd like to do.'

Val smiled and walked to the fire, flicking on the second bar.

'Do what you think best, lass. It would look good with a bit of paint.'

'Paper mostly.' Annie said firmly.

Val was standing by the window, rubbing at the condensation.

'Has it changed you very much; this dreadful business, I mean?'

Annie picked up her toast. 'I don't know, Val. I don't know about anything very much, any more.' The marmalade was tart, the toast crisp and the butter hard. That was enough to be getting on with and she would feed the hens soon.

Tom read the letter which arrived in the morning as he was cleaning his boots. It was his day off from the pit.

India.

Dear Tom,

It will be early December when you receive this.
Annie will be in England now. Look after her for me.
She thinks I don't understand but I do now. I love
her you see, I always have and I always will. I want
to come to her but won't unless she decides she wants
me. Her da comes between us, Tom. Makes her
scared of loving me. Help me, Tom. Help her.
Georgie.

Tom put on his boots half cleaned and threw the letter on the
table. Grace looked across from the sink, her sleeves rolled up,
her hands red from washing.

'We'll not be going to Betsy's for lunch,' he told her as he took
down his crash helmet and goggles. 'Read the letter, bonny
lass, then go and tell me mam we'll be there this evening, Don
too and that I'll be bringing Annie round in the afternoon. I
want to show her a few things.' Bobby was playing by the table
with bricks Bob had made and Tom had painted. He looked up
at Tom and laughed as a pile fell over. Grace put the letter
down again.

'Be careful, Tom. You can't go interfering in people's lives.'

He turned as he went out of the door, his face firm and set.
'It's about time someone did,' he said.

Annie stood by the wire. This new cock was as arrogant as the
last had been. It strutted backwards and forwards just as the
camp commandant had done. The wire dug into her hands and
she made herself loosen her grip, rubbing at the deep red
grooves it had made on her fingers. She didn't hear Tom until
he was almost by her side and then she turned and his face was
grimy where the goggles had been.

It felt so good, so very good to have his arms round her, his
blue eyes smiling down into hers. He was grey at the temples
and he had far more lines than when she had last seen him. His

394

leather coat was cold against her cheek and she felt a calmness, a coming home. The hens were clustering at the gate and the cock was preening and flapping.

'I was just going to feed the hens.' She stood back and smiled at him. 'You have always been such a bonny lad, Tom.' She felt her voice begin to break so stooped and picked up the bowl, passing it to him.

He laughed. 'I knew I shouldn't have come.' He held open the run gate and stood with her and they threw corn from the bowl. He saw that she used her right hand, that her left had a finger which was crooked and misshapen.

'So someone didn't like your Ruby Red then, eh bonny lass? You and me is gimpy together.' He tapped her hand gently and she smiled. The hens were pecking at the ground which was bare of grass now and hummocked like a bomb-blasted moor which had been rounded in the wind.

'Is Don home yet?' she asked.

'Aye, we'll be seeing him later.'

Tom lifted his head and tilted back his cap. He looked steadily at her but she turned from him, throwing the last of the corn to the furthest corner of the run.

'Let's go to the shed,' he said softly and she nodded. They walked together past the laurel, its waxed leaves moving in the wind. She looked at her watch, it was nearly midday. The rice would be . . . She stopped herself and shook her head. Tom opened the door. Creosote still stained the wood but the smell was only there if you brushed close. The bike was rusted and the rubber grips had perished right through and lay on the floor. She moved to the window and rubbed at the glass and her finger came away grey. She looked out over the Thoms' garden up into the sky.

'So, my bonny lass, you came back. I always knew you would.' Tom was squatting near the pile of sacks and dust rose in clouds as he picked at the frayed edges.

She nodded. 'I wanted to come home. We have lots to do, Tom. I thought we could start on the house first. Try out some ideas, then go into production.' Her breath was misting the glass and she rubbed at it but the moisture smeared so she pulled her sleeve over her hand and wiped it dry.

Tom said nothing. Just sat on his haunches picking at the hessian and the smell was acrid.

She turned and his eyes were still looking at her steadily and this time she knew she had to answer the question he was asking her.

'I had to come home without him. I needed to think, to get things sorted out.'

Tom still looked at her. 'Get your coat on, lass,' he said. His face was calm but firm. 'We've some places to visit, you and me. It's time we nailed this shadow, time you faced things once and for all. You can't go on hiding.'

Annie stood rigid, gripping the cold steel handlebars of the bike. She squeezed the brake and it hurt her finger. She squeezed it again. She wanted the pain. It stopped her sinking beneath the fear which crept through her and lodged in her chest. Her stomach was tight and her shoulders rigid. She wouldn't go. There was no way she would go back, even with Tom.

'I'm not coming with you, I have too much to do here. The walls to strip.' She thought of the cool green stripes for the dining-room but suddenly he was up off his haunches and standing before her. 'Get your mac, hinny, you're coming with me. We'll take the Morris. You might as well come back as you left.' He did not touch her, just looked and his eyes were dark and they saw right through her to the box and she knew there was no hiding from him.

The Morris breasted the hill and Tom drove it down towards Wassingham and there were the slag-heaps, bigger now but still with carts churning up the slopes showering dust on to the mountain which was growing each year. He drove her down into the streets which pressed together and shut out the pale December sun. There were no daffodils on window-sills to relieve the black-coated red brick and the windows were blank without the lights of evening shining out on the cobbled streets.

Down through the town, past Mainline Terrace and the bombed-out Garrods used goods shop. She and Tom had not spoken since they had left Gosforn. She did not want to. She was busy wallpapering the hall, but now as they rattled over the cobbles she could not hold the striped paper in her head. Could not hold the walnut table and the gong tightly to her. Women were walking with shawls over their heads, children were playing football in the street and Tom stopped near the school, close to Wassingham Terrace, Sophie's old street.

He switched off the engine and it jumped before falling silent. They sat and she rubbed her hands together. They were slimy and she ran them down her mac until Tom leant over and took them in his.

'Don't do that, bonny lass. You'll wear out that posh mac of yours.'

She focussed on him then, on his warm hands as they held hers, on his eyes as they creased in his gentle smile, on her mac which Prue had given her. 'I'm so very tired, you see, Tom.' Her lids were heavy, she wanted to sleep, not to climb out in this place.

'I know you are but this has to be done, my little lass. Out you get now. I'll come with you.'

He took her to where she had first seen her father. She turned and looked down the street, bunching herself deeper into her mac, leaning back against the railings and their chill sank into her back as it had done that day all those years ago. It had been misty then and Don and a small man in a brown coat had come down the road, out of the mist. She saw them again, the boy and the man with his thin face and his hazel eyes; drawn and tired he had been, so tired. She held the railing behind her and it was so cold it hurt, but not as much as it had done on that cold winter day. There was no wind to chap licked lips today. She looked at Tom, her bonny wee bairn, but he was a man now, standing taller than her and holding her arm as the day turned dark and she saw the man and boy coming closer and closer through the mist.

'It's a fine day today, Annie,' Tom murmured, and she saw the boy and the man stop and slowly go back into the mist which lifted as shadows of lampposts took their place and lay long across the cobbles and were crossed by the colours of the women who passed by them. She saw that two children were sitting on the kerb playing marbles; she heard the click as two collided. Tom looked at her and she nodded though she knew he had not yet finished.

The Morris started on the second try and Tom's boots seemed too large on the pedals; she saw that one was shiny and one was dull.

'Is this the new way of wearing boots these days, bonny lad?'

she asked, her voice strained, but he laughed as he steered the car away from the school and that misty day.

They stopped outside the front door. There were no railings now.

'Gone for the war effort.' Tom explained.

So Don and she would never know now whether they were sharp enough to pass right through someone. She sat still, wiping her hands, feeling the seat at her back hard along the seams where the leather was pulled into panels. Tom was out now and coming round to her door but she would not leave the car and go into her da's house. No, that was too much of him to expect. He opened the door and the cold struck. She shook her head and he leaned in.

'Come with me, we're not going in yet, Annie. I have something else to show you.' He smiled and his face was so dear that she pushed herself from the seat and held out her hand to him. He did not take it though, but took instead her arm since her distorted finger broke his heart almost as much as her eyes set so deep in her strained thin face.

They walked down the back alleys and although there was no frost it was almost the same as before but they were not carrying trays which stretched their arms and froze their hands. The smell of coal was in the air and decrepit back-gates hung in frames at the back of yards. Down they went, on through the lane which led out to the field, but it seemed so small now and there were only boys playing football in bright red shirts and they aimed at proper goals. She stood silent.

'I ran away when we brought the bread and cheese. Do you remember, little Annie?' Tom stood next to her and looked across the field to the slag beyond. His cap was pulled down and his scarf was tied in a knot at his neck.

'I found it hard to forgive meself for leaving you here. It was something I kept feeling I had to wipe away, but I couldn't. I just had to grow into it somehow.'

He put his arm through hers and she gripped his hand. How strange, there were no large men walking towards them with dragons' breath, not any longer. There were just boys and white marked lines. No dog pulling at the coat which marked the goal, no Da standing before her, just green grass and so much more sky than she remembered. More light.

'You have always been so brave, my bonny lass, and I cannot

go on without you.' Tom said. 'Your da is dead. He's found some peace. You must too, Annie Manon.'

She tried to pull away now, tried to push the picture to the back of her mind, into the box, but Tom was hanging on, making it all come back, making her see her da.

'You must have wanted peace, Annie.' He had swung her round to face him now. There were the shouts of boys in the background. 'You must know how he felt. For God's sake, Annie, you must understand the man.' He held her chin so that she must look at him.

But she shook her head free. She wouldn't listen to him. She would carry on stripping the paper, pulling it down strip by strip, piece by piece. She would not let him into her head, would not let him pull out her box, lift the lid, take her secrets out and make her see them. She wouldn't see the field, only the hallway that needed stripping, but he kept on pulling her back to the black box. He kept on, his voice was pulling the box closer, pushing aside the hall at Gosforn until she could stand no more and screamed until the sound filled her head and she could not hear him any longer but his mouth was opening again and this time she tore from him and his words and ran from the field as he had once done, down the lanes, the alleys but he was still behind her but she couldn't hear his words, thank God she couldn't hear his words, but there was his voice as he called:

'Annie, wait.'

But she couldn't, not for what he had to say. She could hear his feet, his uneven tread closer now. She ran and ran, her breath hard in her chest, in through the gate past the stable and then Tom reached the yard gate, gasping and clinging to the upright, watching as she checked at the door.

The door was ajar and she stood there, her head on the wall, her breath quick and heavy in her chest. She rolled her head against the brick and felt him come to her. She was home but she could not go in.

'Beauty's here,' Tom panted, and led her over to the stable and Beauty was so small. Her mane was still coarse and she wound it round her fingers and couldn't see clearly because her eyes were full and the tears might fall and she was not going to cry over him, over her da. He had left her. He had killed himself and left her and it hurt too much to love and then be left. She could not bear it again, ever again, even with Georgie, and she hated her da for making her as she was.

'I hate him,' she shouted, turning to Tom. 'I hate him. He left me and I hate him for it.'

Tom watched her lips draw back. Her skin was almost transparent, her cheekbones seemed to be breaking through.

'You don't. You loved him and he hurt you. You must understand how he could do it. You of all people should understand now.' He was shouting too. 'After all you've been through, you should understand.'

He was holding her shoulders, shaking her and her hair fell down and across her eyes. She brushed it aside. Anger was forcing its way up through her stomach which tightened against it but still it came, up and through and into her chest and then her head and there was the box again.

'He filled himself up with gas, didn't he? And yes, I understand the need for peace, but how am I to have any from him? He's dead, he can't hear me when I ask him to leave me alone.'

Tom was still holding her. His lips were as stiff as hers were, his throat felt as though it was swelling.

'You must just tell him, Annie. It's up to you,' he cried. 'Tell him and then yourself. If you don't, there is nothing for you but to run away for ever, for the rest of your life. Free but alone.'

'We've always been together, you and me. Why can't it go on like that?' She was holding his arm now, her lips were still drawn back as she shouted and her eyes were so dark that they were hazel no longer.

'That is not enough for you. I don't ask anything of you and ours is not that sort of love. You need Georgie, you bloody fool. You need the man you've always loved. You must let yourself love, Annie, if you are going to be any sort of a person, have a life which means anything. Don't let your da spoil that.'

His voice was filling the yard, her head. He would not let her think of green stripes, of lamps that must match. His voice was bringing the box closer and closer to the front of her mind. Her da would come soon.

'Come in with me.' He was still shouting and she pulled back.

'No, I can't face that.' She held on to the stable door. She would rather be alone, free and alone. She had already decided.

400

He turned and wrenched her hand away. It was her broken finger but he didn't care. 'Get in here with me.'

He pulled her now, took her hand and put his arm round her and forced her to the door which now opened fully.

'There'll be no need for that,' Betsy said, and came to Annie and took her and held her against clothes that smelt of freshness and arms that were soft. Annie tried to find air to breathe as she walked into her father's house with the wife whom he had despised.

On through a kitchen which was no longer bleak and bare but full of light and colour with Tom's old cut-down chair still by the fire. Patchwork cushions lay everywhere. On through they went, she and Betsy, up to the hallway and past the clock which had chimed so loudly that first day. She did not want to go further but Betsy would not stop. On up the stairs which were gently lit until they came to the room. The door was shut and the box in her head was opening now. The lid was coming up and he would be here soon, in her head. She would see him coming out with his gaping yellow face if she went into the room which he had filled with gas rather than live with her.

Betsy opened the door and Annie would not look but then she did. The study was gone; the dark table, the prints so faded that there was no picture; all were gone. His chair where he had lolled, yellow and dead was gone.

Tom slipped past them into the room holding out his hand to her. 'Come into our studio, Annie.' He would not come and fetch her this time and she had to walk in by herself. And she could not.

Tom watched her, then turned to the easel. 'This is Bobby,' he said. 'I'm doing it for Gracie.' The smell of linseed oil was strong and from the window he could see the washing hanging out in the yards. He moved on then. 'Here are the designs I've done for the first batch of wallpaper. I thought we could work from here to begin with.'

He was over by the table that stood against the wall, flicking through the paper. It was cool because the room was unheated. His hands felt cold and his foot hurt. His ears strained to catch the sound of her entry and he did not know what more he could do if she did not come in. How else could he bring her back to them?

But then, at last, there she was, next to him and she reached across and took the top design.

'It's good, bonny lad,' she said and there was a shaking in her voice.

He leant over and did not take the paper but held her hand so that it was steady enough for them to look together. 'Aye, better up the right way though, lass.' They laughed and it was a gentle sound and Betsy walked back down the stairs. She had a meal to cook for them all this evening.

They stayed in the studio, for that is what it is now, Annie thought, and felt the shadows lift and her stomach was no longer tight and the black box was growing fainter. Her da was not in this room, he was dead and gone. She said it twice and finally believed it.

Slowly, haltingly, they talked about fear, about pain and anger and it was like a river which washed through them both carrying away the debris of years and, as the light waned, it was time for the planning of their future, their dream which they had held for so long. They talked until the sun moved lower in the sky and the shadows were longer, casting themselves across the yard and then she knew it was time for the place she had still to visit, the peace that she still had to make.

There was no barbed wire along the miles of beach and Tom walked with her along the track that she and Georgie had once cycled down, beating against the wind. It still roared and blustered and she gripped Tom's arm and he held his cap on with his other hand. When the sand met the foreshore she left him and lifted her head into the North-East bite, letting it whip past and round her.

Down through the sand she walked, pulling free as it clutched at her shoes and ran in over the sides. She removed them and felt the sand beneath her feet, felt it run over her as she dug in and took another stride. It was white as far as the eye could see as it had never been in those days of her childhood.

It was cool, so cool and the sky was full of battling clouds and the sea full of buffeting waves which arched, hung, then crashed frothing before sliding back into oblivion with just a few surf remnants fast bursting on the sand. The wind tore at her hair and the gulls screeched but, beyond them, all she could still hear was the crashing sucking waves. She was home now and there was no anger left in her at da and there was no need for the box ever again. He could stay inside her with the good memories, with Beauty and Peter Pan. He had only wanted peace and she could admit that she knew all about that now. She had tasted the sour pills and the noise and shapes of horrors she could not escape until now. He was not to blame any more.

She sat down near the sea where the sand was not yet wet from the incoming tide. The years had passed quickly but now she allowed herself time to remember every moment tracing her way back from that misty evening to the salt wind of today.

At length she saw that the sky was darkening and the wind began tearing at her body, plucking at her hair and snatching it across her face, stinging her with sand. Her back was stiff and her hands were numb with the lost minutes, or was it hours, that had passed.

The wind lifted her hair again. You're lucky, she thought. That's all you carry isn't it, sand and the scent of brine. We have to carry everything that touches us and sometimes it is too heavy. She picked up a pebble and threw it hard across the waves but it was caught by a crest and dragged under, and now she was shouting to the wind: 'I'm glad, at last I'm glad that I have something more to carry than grains of sand and the smell of salt.'

She looked round at the hollow curves of the dunes which lay behind her. Memories can be good, Georgie had said and he was right. The wind tugged at her cuffs as she lifted her hands to her hair which was tangled and sticky. She tucked away the flaying strands.

He had stroked her body, but left her whole. He had let her go with Sarah, let her return to England. It was all so simple really but she had not allowed herself to see it; all these years it had been hidden behind dark shadows. She could trust him. For God's sake, she could trust him and love him safely.

She wanted to hurry now and the wind was behind her as she turned and ran back through the sand. It helped her now, pushing back towards Tom. She ran and her breath was struggling in her chest and her legs were thrusting into the dunes and then Tom was there, helping her, pulling her along. The time for peace was over, there was so much to do, but first she needed Georgie.

The Post Office was closed when they reached it but that didn't matter; she would break the door down if she had to.

Tom watched as she beat on the door. It was almost dark and lights shone out into the street from the surrounding houses. He was smiling and seeing again the lass who shared out pies. The lights came on in the shop and Mrs Norris opened the door.

'We're closed,' she said.

Annie looked at her. 'I've just come home from the war. I've watched my friend have her head cut off. My husband is still in India defusing bombs. I need to send him a telegram. Are you still shut?' Her voice was fierce. Annie Manon was back, Tom knew that now.

The woman sighed and stood aside, tugging at her grey cardigan which was done up on the wrong buttons so that one side hung below the other. 'Get yourself in then. I'll find you a form and then a cup of tea. I know you now, Annie Manon. So like your da you are.' Her smile was kind now. She shuffled back behind the counter and Annie grinned at Tom.

'Aye, maybe I am, but I'm Annie Armstrong now.'

Mrs Norris was reaching down into the cupboard behind the counter.

'I know I have some somewhere,' she mumbled.

Annie looked round, tapping her foot, wondering why everything was so slow. She was in a hurry, didn't anyone understand? She looked at the brown wrapping-paper that stood in rolls in the wooden bin to one side of the shop, at the birthday cards that were stacked in the rack to the left of the door, at Tom who was still grinning.

'Hold your bleeding horses, Annie,' he whispered. 'He'll wait until she finds the form, don't you fret. Then we can begin again, all of us.' As she stood there she heard the clink of lead coins, the boy who took her hand, smelt the sun-sweated leeks, saw the red flowers of the setting beans.

In the heat of the midday sun, Georgie opened the telegram which Prue had brought him. His hands were shaking so much that he could barely read the words.

The wallpaper business is safer than bombs Stop I love you darling Stop You never did teach me how to swing from the bar Stop Come home my love and show me Stop Annie

Prue held him as he cried and she smiled. He would be in England soon and not long after she would too with Dick Sanders.

It was time the British went home.

Annie's Promise

For Sue

Acknowledgements

My eleven-year-old daughter, Annie, whose birth spurred me to write my first novel *Only the Wind is Free*, has long been trying to persuade me to write a sequel – so that at last she can know the fate of her namesake Annie Manon when she returns to Britain after the Second World War. *Annie's Promise* is due entirely to her nagging! But I'm immensely grateful to her because it was a great pleasure to become involved with Annie Manon again, a character imbued with the essence of my mother – another Annie.

My thanks to my Aunt Doris who spent twenty years in India and was so generous with her memories and memoirs and – as always – Sue Bramble and her staff at Martock Library. Also, my thanks to Chatterley Whitfield Mining Museum, Stoke-on-Trent and their splendid guides – all retired miners – and to Beamish, The North of England Open Air Museum.

I especially want to thank certain friends (who wish to remain anonymous) for their help with drug experiences in the 1960s.

CHAPTER 1

Young Sarah Armstrong felt the sun on her face. The heat had caused the lettuces in the allotment to look limp and parched. She hugged her knees, resting her chin on them, laughing as her cousin Rob Ryan flicked grass at his brother Davy, and groaning when her other cousin, Teresa Manon, tightened her mouth and said, 'When Davy smiles like that his face creases and it looks as though his freckles meet. You die when that happens.'

Sarah looked at her and wanted to punch her nose. 'Still a bundle of laughs then, Terry.'

'My mother doesn't like you to call me Terry, especially now I'm ten, but then you wouldn't care about that. My mum said you'd lower the tone when you came home.'

'That's why Davy's smiling, because I'm back and I'm lowering the tone, but then we're only nine – we've got another year to improve.' Sarah pulled a face at Davy. 'It's a grand smile, look, it's made the sun come out, or has it come out because I'm here?' She gave a regal wave and ducked as the boys bombed her with grass darts, then chased her round the raspberry canes, netted against the birds. Davy caught her and pulled her to the ground, tickling her until she screamed. Then Rob stuffed grass down his shirt. Teresa had not joined in, but she never did. She just pursed her lips together like a prune and sniffed.

Sarah lay on the ground, laughter still in her throat, closing her eyes against the sun. She was so glad to be back here in the north east, in Wassingham with its slag heaps

1

and back to backs, and Grandma Betsy, Uncle Tom, Aunt Gracie and the boys. It was July 1956, her father Georgie was out of the Army, and her mother Annie was starting her textile business. They had come home and would live in her mother's house in Gosforn an hour's drive away. Unfortunately Teresa's family lived in that town too, but you couldn't win them all.

'Give us a swig of water, Rob,' Davy called.

Sarah rolled on to her side and watched as he flapped his shirt and the grass scattered to the ground. She loved Davy, he was three months younger than her and they'd always fitted somehow.

'Give us a minute.' Rob was dragging the bottle from the bag.

Davy sprawled on the ground beside her, and she watched him flick back his auburn hair. 'Your mum said we could go for picnics, now I'm back,' Sarah said.

Rob tossed them the water bottle and Davy drank from it, throwing his head back. His throat moved and suddenly Sarah felt as parched as the lettuces, and hungry. When would lunch be ready? She looked towards the entrance to the allotment but there was still no sign of her mother.

She sat up to take the bottle from Davy, and put it to her lips. The water was warm. Then she passed it to Teresa who wiped the neck carefully with her handkerchief before sipping once, twice. She patted her mouth and replaced her handkerchief. Only then did she hand it back to Rob who looked as though he could kill for a drink.

No, Teresa, you haven't changed a bit, have you, Sarah thought, hugging her knees again, looking down at the cracks in the ground which her mother, as a child, had thought went all the way to Australia. Sarah liked the idea of sitting where her mother had once sat. She looked up again at the old shed which smelt of creosote and the nettles which her dad said attracted butterflies. He had sat here too, when he was her age.

She closed her eyes and saw the shape of the shed against

her lids. Would it be roast beef for dinner? Her mum said no one cooked Yorkshire pudding like Grandma Betsy and she was right. She looked towards the lane again. No one was coming. A growing girl could die of hunger. It was all right for the grown ups, they'd all be there, sitting round Betsy's table drinking beer or tea and dipping crusts into the fat before Betsy made the gravy. 'You'll want to play,' her mum had said as she clattered them out of Betsy's kitchen, 'and the grown ups will want to chat.' Davy had said, 'No, we want to eat.'

Rob was standing up now, looking towards the lane too. 'I'm so hungry I could eat a horse. Where's your mam then, Sarah?'

Davy aimed a grass dart at him. 'Sit down, it's only been half an hour, it'll be a while yet. Let's have a gang, what d'you think? A gang for the summer now that Sarah's back.'

Teresa said, 'Gangs are common, they're for council school children. We're not allowed them at the convent.'

Sarah remembered her mum's words as they'd driven over that morning. 'Be nice to Teresa, we're back with the family and she might feel put out, you know, jealous. She's been the only girl for so long and if we're coming back to the north for good we don't want to spoil it. I'm being serious, Sarah. I know you don't get on with her very well but you've got to try. Families must stick together.'

Sarah dug her chin down hard on to her knees, swallowing the words 'toffee nose' and saying instead, 'But this would be a gang of cousins.'

'Teresa's got a point, but it's not common, it's just child-ish,' Rob said, looking bored and playing jacks with the pebbles he carried everywhere.

Davy held his nose and pulled an imaginary chain. 'You're only eleven and it'd be real good so stop that click-clicking.'

Sarah smiled. 'There you are, Terry, it'd be a way of getting together . . .'

3

Teresa was standing up, dusting off her dress. 'Anyway, they're not really family. My father says their dad's not really his brother, he's Grandma Betsy's bastard.'

Sarah watched Teresa's face screw up against the sun, she saw the redness on her forearms where the sun had caught her skin, the green stains on her bum from the dock leaves which her cousin had so carefully placed between her and the ground.

She didn't watch Davy's face, or Rob's, she just felt the silence all around and the anger which was choking her. She moved towards that smug cruel face, but then Rob sprang to his feet, hauling up Davy, grabbing Sarah's arm.

'Davy's right. It's a canny idea to have a gang and if Teresa doesn't want to join us she can go and get stuffed. Who needs a convent snob anyway?'

'That's right,' Davy shouted at Teresa. 'And we know our dad's a bastard, everyone does, thank you very much, and it doesn't matter to anyone except you. And anyway, Barney Ryan was brave, he was killed in the trenches and he loved our grandma, Da told us and he would have married her, he would, so there.'

Sarah stood with them, watching Teresa, hating her, but then she saw the uncertainty in the other girl's face, the flush in her cheeks, the shame. Perhaps her mother was right and Teresa was jealous? Perhaps she was just hitting out because she was frightened of being pushed out. Sarah had felt like that sometimes when her da had been posted to another area and she had had to leave her friends behind. She had hated the letters they'd written talking of new friends, it made her feel alone, angry, frightened. Sarah touched the other girl's arm.

'Look Teresa, be part of this, we're family, we really are and anyway Betsy's really kind to be our grandma too. She needn't be. She really only belongs to the boys but she treats us all the same. You know she does. Come on. Our parents wouldn't like it if we weren't friends.'

Sarah saw Davy shake his head at her, his eyes still angry but she said again, 'Come on, Teresa, they sent us here to play.' She looked towards Davy again and now he nodded and so did Rob.

'Yes, come on, Teresa, Sarah's right,' Rob's voice was tight.

Davy was looking towards the shed, the fence with its spare tyres, its old doors, then at the bar at the entrance to the allotment. 'OK, we'll all be in it, but first we'll have to pass a test to prove we're good enough. That's fair, isn't it?'

Sarah nodded, looking at Teresa, who paused, then said, 'I suppose so.'

'Right,' Davy said, pointing to the allotment entrance. 'We all need to swing three times over the bar without putting our feet to the ground.'

Sarah grinned. Her da had taught her when they'd been back on one of their holidays. It'd be easy.

Teresa was looking down at her dress.

Sarah pitied the girl. Uncle Don would never swing over a bar let alone teach anyone how.

'I'll help you. I'll keep your feet off the ground.' Sarah volunteered, touching Teresa's shoulder.

Teresa looked at her, her eyes travelling over the dungarees that Sarah wore. 'It's all right for you. It's always all right for you, you're wearing those stupid dungarees your mother makes.'

'Come on, let's get on with it,' Rob called, ambling over towards the bar. Sarah watched as Davy followed and saw Teresa look at them with a tremble to her lips.

'I'll get you some sacking from the shed,' she offered. 'You go on. I'll catch you up.'

The shed was dark and dusty and smelt good. She could see the runner beans through the window and as she picked up the frayed hessian she wondered how long her mother would be. She was hungry and fed up and she wanted to punch Terry on the nose again.

5

Annie and Betsy walked through the narrow streets, black grimed from the coal. The doors were closed on the ritual of Sunday lunch. Annie smiled. 'You didn't have to come, Betsy, those kids won't need any dragging you know, my Sarah especially.'

Betsy laughed quietly, her arm tucked in Annie's. 'That they won't but I just wanted to be with you, bonny lass. I can hardly believe you're back, see. It seems just yesterday to me that you were getting scruffy round the runner beans yourself.' She became serious again. 'Sometimes I wondered if you'd ever want to come back again after all you've been through.'

Annie felt the cobbles uneven beneath her feet as they crossed over, away from the shadows. Oh yes, she'd always wanted to come home again. But Betsy, she thought, squeezing the other woman's arm, it doesn't seem like yesterday to me. She dug her other hand deep into her pocket, smelling the coal which pervaded every inch of this small town as it had always done.

Annie had been fifteen when Sarah Beeston, her godmother, had taken her away from here driving over these same cobbles to middle-class Gosforn and a different life. Georgie had left Wassingham too then, feeling the loss of Annie as much as she had felt the loss of him, leaving the darkness of the pit for the hardships of the Army. But soon everyone had felt some hardship as war had erupted.

What was it Sarah Beeston had said as she had driven her from Wassingham? Ah yes. 'I'll educate you, so that you can make choices about your future, it's the least I can do now your father is dead.' Annie had chosen nursing. She smiled wryly, looking up at the cloudless sky. 'You can travel with nursing my dear,' Sarah had said. 'You can expand your horizons – decide whether you do still truly want to marry Georgie.' Well, her horizons had expanded all right, right up to the wire of a Japanese prisoner of war camp. Thank God her beloved Sarah Beeston had died by then.

They were approaching the allotment now and Annie could hear the children's whoops of laughter. They stopped, listening, smiling, relishing the moment.

'You're giving your Sarah what you didn't have, my dear,' Betsy said. 'A steady homelife and a good mother.'

'I won't have that talk, Betsy,' Annie's voice was fierce. 'I mean, look how you stuck it out with Da in that Godforsaken shop, hauling those barrels of booze around. You were as good a mother as anyone could have been, living like that. You never treated Don and me differently to your Tom, and I don't know how you did it.

'We love you, all of us and we're back now, for good. Georgie's out of bomb disposal, I'm up to my ears in plans for the new business, the *family* business, and it's all going to be great.' Annie kissed Betsy's soft warm cheek and together they walked down the lane, both of them comforted, seeing the children now, swinging over the bar.

Betsy laughed. 'Well, wonders will never cease, it looks as though they're all getting on. I thought Teresa might be a bit prickly.'

Annie nodded. 'Yes, it was more than a possibility. She's just so like her father. Why's *he* so tense today.' They paused again and Annie brushed her hair back from her face. 'I mean, he's my brother but I feel as though I'm more part of Tom, not him.'

Betsy nodded. 'It's his nature. He's always been the same. You have your da's depth, he has your Uncle Albert's – oh, what's the word I'm looking for?'

'Tight arse, I think,' Annie whispered, looking at her stepmother and now they laughed.

'I should clip your ear for using language like that but maybe you're right, lass,' Betsy said at last, wiping her eyes with her handkerchief. 'No wonder the old skinflint left him his pawn business – and lord knows what else. But I reckon it's the fact that you're back that's bothering Don today. He's liked being the only Manon around and of course, you're taking back Sarah Beeston's house. He won't think

7

you've been right kind to let him have it free all these years, he'll just be sour because he can't go on having it.'

Annie nodded then looked up as she heard Sarah calling to her, beckoning her forward. 'We've made a gang, all of us and we could eat a horse.'

Annie heard Betsy's chuckle and felt a surge of relief at the laughter of the four children. At least there was no tension here.

'Come on then,' she called to them. 'The Yorkshire pud will be just right by the time we get back.' Annie turned to Betsy. 'Don'll be all right after Tom and I tell him about our business ideas. I haven't explained anything properly to him yet. I thought I'd leave it until after lunch. We wanted to ask him face to face to be the financial director, then it'll be all of us in it, just like I've always planned. Everything will be all right, Bet. I know it will.'

Betsy was laughing as the children came running up to them, their faces eager, pulling at them to hurry. 'Nothing can go wrong now that you're back, Annie. It's all going to be just wonderful,' Betsy said.

The Yorkshire pudding *was* wonderful, the gravy rich and smooth, the beef tender and there had been little conversation from the children, from any of them as they ate. There had just been the sound of knife against plate, laughter as Sarah's carrot had skidded from beneath her fork and landed on the table. Don's wife Maud had tutted, but then she'd tutted when she'd seen Teresa's dusty dress.

There had been banana custard for pudding and Annie had wanted to kiss Betsy when she'd sprinkled a sheen of sugar on Sarah's to prevent the formation of skin.

They drank tea when the meal was finished and nodded when the children begged to go and play in the allotment again, though Maud would not allow Teresa to swing on the bar. 'Let her wear a pair of Sarah's dungarees,' Annie had suggested and had thought Maud would faint at the mere thought.

8

Annie stood at the sink now, her arms covered in suds as she waited for Tom to bring the last of the dirty dishes from the table. She looked out across the yard where geraniums lolled in cut down rain-butts. The stable was empty now, Black Beauty was long gone.

'Do you remember Beauty, darling?' she called to Georgie who was putting the bowls in the dresser over against the wall. She heard him laugh, heard Tom and Grace laugh too.

'Remember?' Tom called. 'Bye, she kept us in sweet money with her plops. "Does wonders for your rhubarb," you'd say to people. "Better than custard." Your da would have died if he'd known.'

'She was a bonny pony,' Betsy said, leaning across Annie, refilling the kettle. 'Just one more cup, eh, lass?' She smiled at Annie, who kissed her cheek.

'I told you then and I'll tell you now, that was a bloody silly name for a gelding. God knows what Da was thinking of, giving it to you. He should have sold it and put the cash into the shop. But then he didn't know what he was thinking of most of the time – bloody dead loss he turned out to be.' Don's voice was loud, terse and Annie felt her shoulders tighten.

'Don't let them get you down, Don lad,' Georgie laughed. 'They've got an idea they can change the world, so what's a pony's sex? And they will change it, you know, or Wassingham anyway, just you wait and see. This business is really going to take off.'

Annie felt her shoulders relax. Only she and Tom would have recognised the anger in Georgie's voice, but he had saved her from exploding. She looked out into the yard again. God damn you, Don Manon, you always were a miserable little tyke, never comfortable, never understanding, always pinching my wintergreen when we were kids, always spoiling things, always belly-aching. You're still belly-aching, misunderstanding. But then she hadn't understood either for a long while, had she? She watched a sparrow perch on the gutter of the stable.

Poor Da, how had he felt, coming back from the trenches, having to start all over again with his off-licence business destroyed, his fine house gone, the mother of his kids dead? He'd felt hopeless, that's what he'd felt but she hadn't understood that then. None of them had – or his suicide. She had realised though, after her own war. In fact she had very nearly followed him.

She looked back, round the kitchen they'd grown up in, smelling boiled tea towels, imagining the round shine-splashed boiler. Thank God they were all wiser now, tested somehow, more able to make the future work.

'Where are those plates then, Tom Ryan?' she called, turning round, seeing Maud still sitting at the table, polishing her long red nails, and she remembered that Don had been easier for a while but it hadn't lasted. Perhaps Maud was the reason why. You'd never think she'd come from a back to back in Wassingham too.

'Hang on, Gracie needs another tea towel and then I'll be there. Work, work, work, but worth it. That was a canny lunch, Mam.' Tom threw a tea cloth to his wife and then brought the plates to Annie who called to Maud. 'We'll bring gloves next time shall we, then you can help?'

Tom grinned at Annie and muttered, 'You'll be lucky, can't be breaking a nail, can we?'

'I'll break something of hers soon and it won't be a nail, bonny lad,' she murmured back.

Betsy called from the stove. 'Tea's brewed, Annie. Leave those to drip, you as well, Gracie. Come and sit down and have a last cup. Those bairns will be glad of a bit more time.'

Betsy smoothed her apron with hands that were still gnarled from shifting Da's kegs, but they were not as swollen as they had been.

'Are you happy Bet?' Annie asked quietly, sitting down beside her.

'Aye lass, I was before, you know with my bairn living in the top of the house and his bairns rushing through my kitchen to get to the yard but now it's even better – there's your Sarah with them too, and you.'

Annie touched the elderly woman's hand. 'I know what you mean. There's a continuity, isn't there?' She watched Georgie bring the teapot to the table, then looked round, seeing her brothers, their wives, Betsy pouring the tea, pushing the mugs out to each of them. Where had the years gone – did she really have as many lines as Gracie? She knew she had.

'Could have given us more notice of course.' Don's voice was cold. 'Had to get out of the house in a bit of a hurry didn't we?'

Annie looked at him. Here it comes – wind him up, let him go. Not many lines on your visage my lad are there, but then you weren't down the mine like Tom, in the jungles like Georgie, in the camps like me. Oh no, you were in the Supply Depot, building up your contacts, lining your pockets, not your face. She clamped her mind shut against these thoughts, put down her mug and answered calmly.

'You've had my house for nine years, without charge Don. Please remember that I wrote to you telling you of Georgie's discharge months ago. I think I made it clear that we would want to come home.'

Maud put down her tea which she had been drinking left-handed. Annie knew it was because their lips had used the other side. She caught Tom's eye and grinned – they were back, what did all this matter?

'That's all very well, Annie,' Maud said. 'But we've put a lot of work into Sarah Beeston's house. We've hung a chandelier and redecorated you know, got rid of all that dreadful bamboo.'

Annie breathed deeply as tension clenched every muscle of her face. She forced herself to look steadily at Betsy's patchwork cushions.

Think of the stitches, the thread. Please God, let me be

11

angry and not afraid – let the past be over. She felt Georgie's hand on her thigh, she felt its warmth, his nearness and she waited and could now hardly breathe because she feared so much that she would smell the stench of the camp hospital, the pleading of the patients, the helplessness of the nurses. She feared she would see Lorna's execution, feel the pain of the guard's boot thudding into her own body, or the rope around her wrist which had tethered poor mindless Prue.

She waited, barely breathing, feeling the silence, the grip of Georgie's hand but there was no pain, no darkness, there was just irritation, just the words 'Stupid bitch' in her mind, just a normal reaction to a silly woman. At last she relaxed, even as Tom leaned forward, slopping his tea, banging his mug down.

'You did what, after all Annie went through with those bloody nips. For Christ's sake, the thought of decorating Sarah's house kept her going, you bloody knew that. It helped her to actually do it when she returned.'

Annie reached out to him, shaking her head, relishing her own response but not his. 'Maud's right you know, think about it. That design wouldn't appeal to others, it was personal, it grew out of me, it was therapeutic. Business people have got to produce the goods the market wants, not just what we like, or what comes from our past.'

She looked from Tom to Georgie but their faces were set. She spoke again. 'Look, please, all of you stop worrying about me. I'm much better – I keep telling you. Yes, the bamboos might have been a trigger – I was unprepared but I'm fine, Maud's done us a favour. It's proved to you that it's all behind me, just as I've been saying all these months.'

Annie took her husband's hand in hers and kissed it but though he smiled when she looked into his eyes she saw only anxiety.

She said softly, 'I promise you, my darling, it's over. This just helps to prove it. Please listen.'

She looked from one to another. Oh God, would they never understand that the past was gone, finished? Yes, she'd had a breakdown in India, where Georgie had taken her after the war. Yes, she'd tried to kill herself there too, but they had come home and slowly she had recovered, couldn't they accept this? What more proof did they need?

'So, you're still going ahead with this business idea then?' Don asked.

Annie smiled, grateful for once that her brother had no heart. There was no concern in his eyes, or those of his wife. There was only a flicker of interest at the thought of the business they were embarking upon and she replied calmly, holding Georgie's hand tightly as she did so, willing him to believe.

'Absolutely, Don. It's the textile business we've always talked about, even when we were kids. Tom's designs, my practical knowledge, Georgie's management expertise . . .'

'Cosy, just the three of you, again.' His voice was hard.

'You didn't let me finish. You're a businessman, doing well from your property development, we'll need a financial director. You could fit it in with your other work.' She was glad to be back in the present, glad to be talking of the future and she wanted to grab the others out of the past too.

She looked at them all, smiling, listening as Don grunted then pulled out a cigar. Betsy rose, walked to the window and opened it, then pulled the door right back. Don knew Bet hated the smell soaking into her patchwork cushions, her curtains, her rag-rugs so why did he do it?

Annie watched her brother, and wanted to rip the cigar from his mouth and stub it out in Maud's mug. That really would be something for her to turn her nose up at.

'Tell me more about it,' Don said, blowing smoke across the table, leaning back, putting his finger in his waistcoat pocket.

'We'll operate it, as Tom and I have always said, in

Wassingham with facilities for those who are mothers. There'll be a nursery, childbirth leave and so on. There will be a bonus twice a year, a sharing of the profits.'

'That's it then,' Don said, his finger still hitched in his pocket, the smoke from his cigar spiralling up into the air.

He'll blow a smoke ring in a minute Annie thought and then I'll slap him and ruin all my good intentions.

'What do you mean, that's it?' she asked, trying to keep her voice level as he blew a smoke ring and Tom caught her eye.

'Crazy. It's your old half-baked nonsense, isn't it? It's the "life must be fair" rubbish again,' Don said, stabbing the air with his cigar. 'It's like Albert and I always said, the bottom line is profit – you need to drive your workers, not nursemaid them. What about your union work, Tom, are you coming out of the mine?'

Tom shook his head. 'Not right away, we've got to get it up and running first. Gracie and Annie are getting the garments made up working from home, then Annie's got some outlets set up to see which lines go best. Betsy's helping with the sewing, just so long as her hands cope, isn't that right, Mam?'

Betsy nodded. 'I wasn't much good to you in the early days pet, it was all so difficult with the shop and everything,' she said quietly. 'I want to be useful now.'

'I've told you, you were wonderful to us, and yes, we couldn't do without you but only for as long as it suits you.' Annie turned back to Don. 'Just listen. It's founded on sound sense. Workers will respond to fair treatment. You see, Don, you don't have to deal with workers in your line of business but because of Tom's pit work, Georgie's time with his men, and mine in the wards, we think we know how to treat people.'

'Meaning I don't.' Don blew another smoke ring.

'No, not meaning that at all, meaning that in property development you are not producing a product and so haven't

14

had that kind of experience but you do have financial know-how.'

'Sounds like amateur night to me,' Don said.

Annie saw Maud produce a nail file. Good God, how do you improve on perfection?

Georgie said, 'Tell him how experienced you are, Annie.'

'Yes, Annie,' Gracie called. 'Tell him about Mr Isaacs in Camberley and the shocked wives.'

Annie laughed as Maud looked up, her nails forgotten.

'Relax, Maudie, no scandal.'

'Better not be either,' Georgie grinned.

Don was scowling, looking at his watch, the gold plate glinting in the sunlight streaming through the open window.

'Sorry, Don, I'll get on with it. Right, I worked for Mr Isaacs in his rag trade business while Georgie was at Staff College at Sandhurst. The other wives were shocked, not the thing at all, though I probably made the bras they bought.'

'Bras,' Maud was shocked.

'Oh yes, Maud, they are made, they do not just arrive under gooseberry bushes.' Annie fingered her cigarettes but knew better than to smoke in Betsy's kitchen. She'd probably have her ear clipped. 'I learned to calculate how many rolls of cloth would be needed, how to use rotary cutters and sewing machines, how to pack and invoice. I learned business management really. Then I set up my market stall.'

'Market stall,' Maud murmured faintly. 'Not with an apron and things, not shouting out.'

'Oh yes, d'you want to hear me.' Annie stood up while Tom and Georgie began to laugh.

'No, I do not.' Maud was tapping her nail file on the table.

'So, how did it go, did you sell much?' Don asked, stubbing his cigar out on one of the clean sideplates, ignoring the ashtray.

Annie emptied the cigar in the bin, washed the plate and called back, 'Oh yes, we used the money to buy a machine and supplied other stall holders, but it's best to keep the middleman out really.'

'What did you make?'

'Knickers.'

'How common,' Maud said as Annie came back to the table. 'I mean, Annie, you won't be making those round here. Surely you could go into something, less, well less . . .'

'Essential?' Georgie asked, leaning forward, his hand on Annie's thigh again, squeezing gently.

'Or don't you wear them?' Tom leaned forward, his eyebrows raised.

Maud blushed, the nail file tapping even faster. 'Don't be absurd.'

Annie said quickly now, before the laughter got out of control and alienated these two completely, 'We will make knickers Maud, because they are essential but also because I can make them out of offcuts. It's much cheaper and while we're trying to get a toe hold in the market we don't want to invest too much capital in stock. We need to see which lines work well, then once we've realised our assets we can set up premises. Do it step by step.'

Don asked them about the forward planning of the business and Annie explained that to begin with they would produce only garments but as soon as possible they would go on to designing and printing their own fabrics, extending into home furnishings and wallpaper in due course.

'We'll need premises of at least two thousand square feet to begin with, and once we're into the textile side we'll need more space and must be near a sewage works.'

'I beg your pardon?' Maud said.

'Effluent,' Annie explained. 'You know the chemicals, the pongs.'

'Oh dear.'

'Quite,' Annie said.

'All of this to take place in Wassingham?' Don asked.

'Oh yes, it must be for the women of this town. It must,' Annie said, because it was a promise she had made to herself many years ago before she had left Wassingham. She reached across and grasped Don's hand. It was thin and cold. 'Join us, it would be the old gang again.'

Don looked at her. 'No, it's not my kind of business. It doesn't stand a cat in hell's chance. Just think about it all of you, it's daft, the whole damn thing.'

Annie sat back and looked at him and wanted to pummel him, make him see that he was wrong, make him see that he was standing aside from the family, as he had always done.

'We must go. Get your coat on Maud. We've cocktails at six and we'll be late. We'll pick up Teresa on the way.'

Georgie stood up. 'Hang on, Don. We need to talk to you about the money Sarah Beeston left Annie. Have you converted the investments you've been handling for her? We thought you'd have the figures for us today. Even if you don't want to be involved you should realise we need to get the show on the road.' Georgie's voice was loud, angry and Annie pulled him down beside her.

Don shrugged himself into his jacket as he answered. 'I'll see you about it tonight. I'll drop round to the Gosforn house. No time now.' He waved to them and followed Maud out into the yard, calling back, 'About nine tonight then, Annie.'

Annie didn't reply, just looked at the others. 'I thought he was going to join us after he showed so much interest in the premises and our plans. I just don't understand the man.'

'You tried,' Georgie said. 'He's just so difficult. You've done all you can, more than you should.'

Tom said, 'He's just different to us. He always was.'

17

Sarah stayed at Gracie's that night and Annie made scrambled eggs on toast back at the Gosforn house, which she and Georgie ate with champagne, toasting one another, toasting their future and Wassingham Textiles. They handed a glass to Don when he arrived, then sat at the dining table beneath the plastic chandelier which Maud had left. Don drew out a cigar. What the hell Annie thought, it's a celebration.

She reached behind her for an ashtray from the sideboard, placing it in front of her elder brother, and held her hands tightly together, hardly able to sit still.

'Come on then Don, stop shuffling through those papers, I can't stand this waiting.' She looked from Don to Georgie and winked. 'He's enjoying his moment of glory. He's dying to show off about how much he's increased Sarah's legacy.' She felt the pressure of Georgie's feet as they squeezed hers, the love in the look he gave her, the pleasure he too was feeling.

Don cleared his throat, tapping his cigar gently on the side of the ashtray, put it to his mouth again, blew a smoke ring and then picked up the top piece of paper. He looked at it again and replaced it.

He looked at her now. 'I didn't tell you this this afternoon because I was still hoping against hope that I could sort something out but I couldn't. There's no easy way of saying this.' Don looked at Georgie, then back to Annie. 'There is no money, Annie, none at all.'

Annie tried to laugh. She hadn't known him to have a sense of humour before. Perhaps he was learning after today's fiasco, but it wasn't amusing.

'Come on, Don, get on with it,' she said, prodding his arm.

He looked at her again, and then at Georgie before looking back at her. 'Don't be stupid, Annie. This is hard enough for me as it is. I'm not joking. I have to tell you that there is no money. I invested it but the stocks have crashed. You have nothing, nothing at all. I'm so sorry.'

18

Annie felt first the cold shock of his words, and then a searing panic.

CHAPTER 2

Breakfast was a silent affair. Annie's lids were heavy as she watched Georgie put one, two, three, four, sugars in his tea.

'Too many my love,' she said.

'Ichi, ni, san, yong,' he replied, stirring, stirring again and again.

Her hand tightened on her cup. Yes, all right, she'd dreamed of the camps, of roll call, of the terror, the camp hospital, but for heaven's sake their future had gone, in a few short words, it had gone and it was her own fault. She felt despair rise in her as it had done again and again throughout the night, but there was no time for it, she must keep telling herself that.

'I know I dreamt, it does me good. It's not serious, Georgie.'

'I'd call it a nightmare not a dream and when I hear my wife scream and chant in her sleep I call it serious.' He wouldn't look at her, couldn't look at her because she had been hurt in Singapore and he hadn't been able to stop it, she had been hurt again in India and he had allowed that to happen. She had been hurt last night, they had all been hurt and he could murder that bloody brother of hers.

Annie sipped her tea. She didn't want it, how could she want it after Don had told them his news? She sipped again, then looked at Georgie, how could so much have changed in such a short time?

'I could have smashed his face in, Annie, sitting there

with his cigar, apologising, simpering. God, he almost bloody wept.'

'We all nearly wept didn't we, and it wasn't his fault, it was mine. I signed the form he sent me, didn't I?' The cup slipped and fell, chipping the saucer, spilling tea. She ignored it. 'It was me. He was trying to please me by investing in a local firm, putting all my eggs in one basket because I'd prattled on about supporting the community. He knew it was what I'd want.'

The tea was dripping on to the floor, she watched it, heard it, counting one two three, ichi, ni, san – no, not that, there was no time for that. She turned from it. 'It was me. He wanted to be sure it was what I meant, which is why he sent me the letter explaining it all, and the form to sign. He knew there was a risk, he told us this last night, for God's sake. I read it, signed it, sent it back and was so damn busy sewing knickers I didn't think about it, and now I can't even remember doing it.'

She picked up the spoon and saucer, cutting her hand. Georgie came towards her and she pushed him aside, grabbing the cloth from the sink, wiping the table, throwing the saucer into the bin. 'I'm just so damn stupid, so stupid – I mean, just look at this mess. We're having a crisis so I spill the tea.' Her voice was rising, tears were near and she stopped.

'He shouldn't have done it. He should have had more sense. Tom Mallet for God's sake. He's one of his black market friends. I'm sure it sounded good, rebuilding the bomb sites, but he should have known he'd scarper and his mates with him.' Georgie wrung the dishcloth tighter and tighter. 'He should have known.'

Annie sat down. What was the point of talking about it any more, they'd gone round and round it last night and at midnight and at two, and at four in the morning until at last they'd slept, if you could call it sleep. She leaned back in the chair, stretching her neck, her eyes throbbing. No, there was no point in talking about it any more, it was gone, finished,

21

or their original plans were but she was damned if she'd let it all go, not after all the years of waiting, and in the long hours of the night she'd thought, planned, made decisions.

'Georgie, I want you to listen to me carefully, hear me out.' Her mouth was still, her hand hurting, she wrapped her handkerchief round it.

'Whatever way you look at it I agreed, sanctioned the investment. I was stupid, clumsy, careless.'

'Don't say that. You're not careless. So you muffed a paper, what's that? It doesn't do any good to keep on blaming yourself.'

'Then stop blaming Don,' she flared at him.

Georgie leaned back now against the window, his jaw set, his eyes cold, then he looked away from her out into the garden where the house martins were swooping and Annie wanted to take back the anger, take back last night, the form, Tom Mallet, but all she could say was, 'I'm sorry, but you see I'm not a leader, I get muddled, confused, I allow myself to shout and scream, I allow myself to make mistakes.'

Georgie started to speak but she shook her head. 'Please let me finish. I decided last night that I want you to run the business. You're trained for it. You can organise, you're methodical. You weren't born to fiddle about in Gosforn doing any piddling little job, you were trained as an officer, you know how to manage.'

He turned now, leaning back against the sill. 'Don't be so daft, darling.' His voice was gentle now, all coldness gone. 'I can't sew, or cut, or talk design with Tom and aren't you forgetting something rather crucial? A small matter of capital? We're broke.'

'Please – just listen.' Annie sat quite still. She could hear the ticking of the clock they had brought back from Cyprus. 'OK, so we haven't any capital, or very little anyway. We will sell the house – as we decided last night. We'll buy a smaller one.'

Georgie scratched his chin and took a packet of Kensitas from his pocket. He looked across at Annie then brought the packet over, lit hers, lit his own, and returned to his seat drawing in the nicotine, blowing smoke up above his head.

The first of the day always tasted good she thought as she spun the ashtray in front of her, even on a day like this.

'You see, my love, we can still start the business, but in a different way that won't depend on capital. We'll work from home, extend our list of customers, then set up homeworkers as the business expands, always ploughing profits back in, taking just enough to live on and making sure we build up a capital reserve as we go along. That way we can set up premises eventually.' He was listening to her, nodding, and she drew on her cigarette then continued. 'It will take longer but there's a market for our stuff – we know that. It can be done, should be done, for the sake of us all, for Wassingham. They need our sort of industry. We mustn't let this hiccup crush us.'

'Sounds good in theory, my love,' he said, flicking his ash out of the window, catching her eye as he did so. 'Good for the roses, they like a bit of potash.'

She laughed and was surprised – she'd thought that today she would not hear that sound.

'But there's no way we can both do it. I'll keep on looking for work, you do all this,' Georgie said.

'No, that's the point. I can't, not any more.' Annie stubbed her cigarette, squashing and grinding it until there were only shreds. 'You wouldn't have made that mistake. You wouldn't have signed. You've got to take it over. The army trained you to take control.'

Georgie was laughing now. 'Oh yes, I'll cut out, shall I, or sew on flowers? Give me a break, Annie, you're being daft. Of course you can do it.'

Annie shook her head, she knew she couldn't, she knew she'd been ridiculous to think she could. Oh yes, she could cut out, sew, come up with ideas, but manage – forget it, Don had shown her that.

'I rang Don first thing, he's buying the house.'

Annie paused, rubbed the table, it was still damp. 'I also

rang the local hospital. I worked there in the holidays while I was at school. They're taking me – I'm going back to nursing, Georgie.'

He said nothing, then straightened, moved and came towards her, his body tense, his shoulders set, his mouth hard. 'You're bloody not. You're not going back. It'll kill you. It'll all start . . .'

He was at her side now, gripping her arms, pulling her up, 'It'll all start, it'll kill you. This time it'll kill you.' His face was contorted, he shook her. 'This was why you had that dream, you'd got nursing in your mind and it all came back. For God's sake, if the thought of it does that to you, what about the reality? It'll be the end.'

'Of course it won't, I keep telling you it's over, this will show you that it is. I'll do the cutting out when I'm off shift, I'll help, I've worked it all out. Look, you were born to *lead*, for goodness sake, it makes sense, you've got to see that it makes sense. You're hurting, Georgie.' His fingers were too tight, he was shaking her harder. His face was too close, too angry.

'Georgie, listen to me.' She wrenched free, shoving the chair out of her way, backing from him, putting the table between them. 'Listen. I'm going back to nursing. I'm going to prove to you that I'm all right, I'm going to earn the money while you get the business going. It's the only sensible thing.'

He was walking away, out into the hall, his feet clicking against the tiles. 'Don't turn your back on me,' she shouted. 'Come back here. You've got to let me do this, it's the only way.'

He stopped, turned. 'You were nursing when the Japs came to Singapore. You were nursing when they cut off Lorna Briggs' head, and smashed your finger, when you buried – how many of your friends, breaking their bodies so that they'd fit into the boxes? What do you think it will do to you, to go back. It'll flip you over again.' He wasn't

24

shouting, he was speaking so softly she had to move into the hall to hear him.

'I'm nursing. You are setting up the business because I can't – I'm no good at that. You're so much better suited.' She put her hand out to him but he had turned from her, was walking away again.

'Georgie, come back,' she called as he opened the front door.

'I'm going to Tom's to tell him we've lost the money.'

Annie ran after him. '*I* lost the money. I lost the bloody money, not we, Georgie. That's the point. It was me.'

He was opening the car door. 'Are you coming?' His face was cold.

'Of course I'm coming.'

'I thought it was the market this morning.'

'Damn the market.'

They drove in silence, through villages and ironworks that belched foul smoke. She could see the chimneys of Newcastle in the distance. There were sweeps of fields too, darkening and lightening as clouds scudded between the earth and the sun. The barley waved as the wind caught it and all the time Annie's stomach was taut and her head ached with the tension of their row, with the strain of the silence which hung between them and she wanted to reach out and touch his hand which was tanned and powerful on the gear stick, but she must not give in. Once and for all, she must show him that she was strong, that the shadows of the past had gone, and that, since yesterday, she realised that the future was best in his hands.

Georgie pulled in for petrol, not looking at her. He stood with the attendant, chatting about the weather, about the north east.

'Born round here, were you?' the man asked.

'Aye, born a *pitman*,' Georgie said, and she knew that that was for her ears too and the row was not over yet.

They drove on, through a pit village with mean dark streets where children played or lounged. George drove carefully, meticulously for mile after mile until at last he was changing gear for the long climb up the hill which overlooked Wassingham. At the top he pulled in, stopped, opened his window, and rested his arm on it but said nothing.

Annie looked out across their birthplace, seeing the bombed site which had been Garrods Used Goods, the gap where Gracie's library had once stood, seeing the school where they had all sat at desks and where Davy, Rob and Paul now sat. She could see the football pitch where Da had led out his team of unemployed miners, and way over in the distance she could see the lightening of the sky where the sea washed the shore.

They sat and out of the silence came the voices of the past, the images, the laughter and tears and now she remembered the warmth of Aunt Sophie's arms as she held her in that small warm house in Wassingham Terrace, consoling her after her mother's death, putting aside her own grief at the death of her sister, taking her into her home to live, Don too – baking scones and making toast, rubbing wintergreen on her toes, loving her with every breath she took.

She remembered leaving Aunt Sophie and Uncle Eric to live with her father and Bet, but at the shop there had been Tom and love and laughter again to soothe the darker days. There had been the heat of the sun in the allotment, the smell of leeks, the sound of metal coins being banged out for the fair, the sound of the bees in the nettles, Georgie's daisy chains around her neck at the beck, the gangs, Georgie's kisses as they grew, and such love had grown between them.

Then there were the tears when Sarah Beeston came and Annie had run to Tom in the morning as he stood outside school, her misery jagged in her chest. She had held him, told him she was leaving but he wouldn't listen, instead he had pulled at her undone bootlace, shouting at her that she'd get blisters. The tears ran down their cheeks and all the time the cables were grinding up the slag heap, clanging and tipping. 'It's like a big black gaping hole in me belly,' he had said, 'to think of you gone from here.'

There had been agony when Georgie had come to the yard to say goodbye. He had leant against the wall, taken out his cigarette paper, rolled it round the tobacco teased along its centre while she had stood close enough to touch the length of her body against his as he licked and lit the cigarette. She had breathed in the scent of sulphur as he sucked in the smoke. She had opened her lips as he slipped it from his mouth to hers and she felt his moisture. They stood and remembered without words those months, weeks and every minute they had spent together.

He hadn't kissed her, he had cupped his hand about her cheek and laid his face against hers. 'I've still to teach you to swing on that bar,' he had said, and she had replied, 'I'll love you all my life, my love.' He had smiled and made it easy for her to go, and she had driven away with Sarah up the hill that she and Georgie now looked down from but how her heart had been breaking, and his too.

She felt Georgie's hand now on hers. It was warm, he was always warm and now she couldn't see Wassingham for the tears which hadn't yet spilled from her eyes.

Georgie lifted her hand to his lips, she felt his kiss, and his tongue running between her fingers, and then his arms which drew her to him. He kissed her eyes. She heard his voice. 'We need some fish 'n' chips to go with all that salt, bonny lass.'

Then his mouth was on hers, his scent was close. 'I'd like to come back here, lass. I want to come home,' he said against her mouth.

'Yes,' she said. 'It's been so obvious, how could we not see it?' Now her daughter could tread the same paths, the same fields, the same streets. She could hear the same sounds, smell the coal, feel the kindness of Wassingham's people.

'So we're going for it are we, darling?' she said softly, her hand stroking his head, his neck, his lips, kissing lashes which she had thought were as thick as hedgerows when she had first seen him, and still thought so. 'You'll do it then – Wassingham Textiles is on the way?'

'Yes, it's really on the way, this time.' He kissed her cheeks, her eyes, her nose, her mouth. 'I love you for what you've offered me today. I love you for your courage.'

There was a light in his eyes, a zest in his voice which had been missing since the Army and she was at peace because now they both had challenges to face and that was as it should be.

Georgie started the engine. 'We'll go home, shall we, bonny lass?'

She nodded, and they started down the hill to Wassingham.

Tom shouted, swore, banged Bet's table with his fist in his rage at Don. He fell silent when Annie said she was going to nurse, that Georgie was going to run the business. He stared at her, then began to speak but Sarah and Davy ran through the yard from the back alley, hurling themselves amongst the adults, Sarah hugging Georgie and then Annie.

'We're going fishing for minnows, Bet's tied us up some jam jars. Are you coming?' She looked from one to the other.

'Not now, darling. Not just yet, this afternoon perhaps,' Annie said, twisting Sarah's plaits round one another. 'Off you go now, see you soon.'

Sarah grabbed Davy's arm. 'Come on, Bet left them in the stable.' They ran out again.

'I could kill that bloody sod, he's just cocked everything up. And stop being so daft, Annie, it's not your fault. You're crazy to even think it is, crazy to think of going back.' Tom was speaking quietly now, slumping down into the carver chair that Bet used as her own. 'Don Manon's as much a crook as that crony of his. By God, I remember Tom Mallet all right, Don's got air between his ears, must have to trust that bugger.'

Annie went round to Tom, gripping his shoulders, telling him Don had only tried to help, that it would be better with Georgie and he in charge.

She felt his hand on hers now, gripping it, then holding it

28

more gently as he rubbed his cheek against her broken finger. 'You can't nurse, bonny lass. You can't, not after the camps.'

Sarah called through the door, 'What camps?'

Georgie, Tom and Annie looked round.

Davy peered over her shoulder into the kitchen, at his father, his uncle and aunt. 'When're Bet and Mum back, Dad? Can we go now? We'll be back for tea.'

'Aye, lad, hop it, and leave a few in the stream.' Tom was smiling, his shoulders relaxing slowly beneath Annie's hand.

Sarah still stood there. 'What camps though?'

Davy jerked her round. 'Don't be daft, camps are the things Scouts have.'

Sarah looked back into the kitchen. 'Scouts with toggles you mean, wobbling about? Did you have a toggle, Mum?'

Rob came up behind Davy now. 'No, only boys have toggles, don't you know anything?'

Annie laughed but the men were quiet. 'Now that's enough from you, Rob Ryan. Get yourselves off to the beck and no falling in.'

She watched them as they left. Tom's hand was still on hers. She clasped it, then went towards the door. 'We didn't tell them we would be living here.'

'Keep that until later. Don't think there'll be any complaints from anyone, do you?' Tom was smiling now, but then he dropped his head, picking at the grain of the deal table. 'Talk her out of it, Georgie, for God's sake, man.'

Annie stood with her back to the room, looking out at Black Beauty's stable, remembering the snuffles which used to greet her when she opened the door. There was only the sound of the back alley now, the clanking of tubs, then the sound of Georgie's voice.

'We've discussed it as much as we're going to, Tom lad. But I've a few things to do. Come on, she's said we're partners so let's get on with it.'

She heard him move towards her, sensed him stop and then felt his lips on the back of her neck. 'We'll be back

29

soon,' he murmured, slipping past her with Tom, taking his cap from his jacket pocket.

'Have a beer for me then,' she called and Tom grimaced. 'You're a bloody mindreader, woman. Bad as Ma Gillow and her tea leaves, but Ma was prettier.' He ducked as she grabbed a tea towel and threw it at them. Georgie caught it, flicked it up on to Bet's washing line and walked out with that crispness to his walk again.

When Bet arrived ten minutes later she argued and so did Grace when they heard of her plans but Bet, in the end, rang Matron, a friend of hers from the WI.

'You can go straight there,' she said to Annie, coming back into the room. 'But I wish you wouldn't, bonny lass, and I can't believe your Georgie agreed.'

Annie brushed her hair, smoothed her skirt, kissed Bet and pretended she hadn't seen the look her stepmother exchanged with Gracie. 'He did you know.'

The walk through Wassingham was hot and the climb up the hill to the posh end was hotter still. Her hands were sweaty but not slimy as they had been in India when the darkness in her head had gathered. She touched the palm with her finger. Yes, definitely only sweaty.

She could see the small hospital in the distance. She looked to the right, at the grand stone houses which lined the streets in this part of Wassingham. This is where she had spent the first three years of her life, before her mother's death.

Annie stopped now, drew a deep breath, then another. The hospital was closer. It was where her mother had died. She ran her hand along the picket fence where once there had been wrought-iron railings.

'Gone for the war,' she murmured, running her hand along the newly painted wood. Poor Mam. Poor Da.

Matron's house was built of stone too, but much smaller than her da's had been. She stopped to smell the Peace roses which lined the garden. They had greenfly, she began to wipe them off but then the door opened.

'Annie Manon, or I should say Armstrong.' A small

stooped elderly woman came out on to the grass holding out her hand.

Annie looked at the greenfly smeared on her own, wiped her hand quickly, and looked down into piercing blue eyes which held laughter and smiled herself as she shook the proffered hand.

'Well my dear, that's one way of dealing with pests. I often feel I would like to do that with some of my patients.' Mrs Antrop took her arm, walked her into the cool of her sitting room and served her barley water.

'Thought it more appropriate than coffee, just too hot m'dear.'

Annie sat stiffly. She was nervous, tense, frightened that the camps might come back. She might be wrong. She might not be offered the job. She might be offered it. But then Mrs Antrop began to speak.

'Betsy tells me you wish to work nights at this hospital. I placed a call to the Newcastle Infirmary.' She lifted her hand as Annie started with surprise. 'Oh yes, I know all about you, my dear. Betsy and I often talk and I do have tentacles in lots of pies – mixed metaphor but who cares. Newcastle think very highly of you, but much has happened since those days as we both know and it is of this that we must speak because obviously it might have affected your aptitude for the work.'

They talked first though of Annie's mother who had taken her own life, drinking poison from an unlocked cupboard whilst in the care of the hospital.

'There are no unlocked cupboards in my hospital. There is no unrecognised despair,' Mrs Antrop said.

They talked then of the war, of the camps, and of Annie's despair. Mrs Antrop nodded as Annie told of the nightmares, of the depression which had slowly eased, of the concern of her relatives that she might regress and attempt again to take her own life as her mother and father had done before her.

'I won't though,' Annie said, clenching her hands. 'I won't

31

and I have to prove to them that I won't. I need the job for that reason, but I also need it so that the business can begin.'

Mrs Antrop reached over, touched her hands. 'Relax, I'm not an ogre, believe it or not. We have to talk of these things because I have patients to consider and I must satisfy myself that you are capable also of considering them.'

Annie reached forward, drank her lemon barley. It was cool, fresh.

Mrs Antrop went on. 'I assume you need the night shifts because of your daughter.'

Annie smiled up at Mrs Antrop, then replaced her glass carefully on the lace coaster. Her hand smeared the polished rosewood table.

'Yes, I must have as much time as possible with her. There are always Bet and Grace, but I love her, I want to be with her as much as I can and I want to be able to help my husband by doing the . . .' She had been going to say sewing, but Matron might feel an extra work load would be to the detriment of her patients so instead she said. 'By being there as a sounding board.'

'So, we have discussed your well-being and your family's but what about my patients?' Mrs Antrop was sitting back, resting her head on an antimacassar, her arms resting quietly on her lap.

'If, when I start, I do not feel for them what I have always felt I will resign, immediately. If, when I start I feel that I am sliding, I will also resign, immediately.'

Mrs Antrop nodded, tapped her thin fingers but said nothing. Finally, peaking her fingers in front of her chin she said, 'My sister was in China as a missionary. She was beheaded by the Japanese. Even though I was not there I also dream and rage and I feel it saves my reason. I think what you are about to do is extremely sensible. I have a husband. Sometimes they get in the way of a full recovery, do they not, though we are fortunate their claustrophobic care is informed by love, and not by jealousy.' She put her hands on her lap again and leant forward. 'Yes, Annie, I think you would be an asset to the hospital. You will begin when you move here?'

Annie walked back down the hill and felt a smile on her face, a lightness in her step. One problem to cross off the list, now she just had to make sure it did not unearth a bigger one.

She passed the church without a tower, the space where Garrods Used Goods shop had been. She had bought her shoes there for the party at which Georgie had first danced with her when she was what? Fourteen, so many years ago. Was she really forty-two?

She moved on, walking from light to shade, crossing the cobbles, smiling to the women who were sweeping the pavements or washing coal dust from their sills. Yes, they were coming home, it was working out, they were moving forward again and not before time, Annie Armstrong, she thought. Good grief, you're almost an old boiler, and suddenly she was impatient to move, to watch Georgie's eyes brighten even more as he brought the business into being and saw that she needed no more protection.

She was crossing the road alongside the railway line when she heard the sound of running feet behind her and Tom's laughter, Georgie's shout of 'What's a pretty girl like you doing in a place like this?'

Then she felt them each grab an arm, march her between them, panting, laughing. They were too fast, the women in the streets gaped and laughed, leaning on their brooms whilst she struggled and told them to pull themselves together, asking how many pints they'd downed, laughing with them as Georgie kissed her mouth – but there was no smell of beer.

They walked down street after street and they wouldn't even stop when she called out to them that she had news for them, they could really get on now. Georgie just turned and kissed her again, saying that he knew they could. They were turning a corner into a street with compact terraces either side. She heard the sound of a train, close by, behind the terraces on the left. She strained to see the name, but they were past. It was all so familiar.

'Slow down,' she pleaded, panting.

'No time,' Tom said, clamping his hand across her eyes. 'No looking either.'

'Then slow down or I'll break my damn neck, you idiots.' Annie was giggling, laughing just as they were.

They slowed but their grip was so firm, her trust in them so complete she knew that even if they ran with her she would never fall and in the darkness she revelled in the firm touch of the two adults she loved most.

Georgie stopped, she felt him pulling her to the right, she felt the cobbles beneath her shoes. He turned her round, stopped. Tom took his hands from her eyes and in front of her was a terraced house with a For Sale sign screwed to its front wall. She looked to the right and left, then back at the house. Now she knew where they were. She searched down the street again looking for the name – Wassingham Terrace.

She moved towards the front door. It was Aunt Sophie's house and inside would be a sitting room which had once had a neat parlour, a kitchen where wintergreen had been kept on the mantel and, in the yard, a pigeon loft. She shut her eyes and could hear the soft coo and flutter of Eric's birds, she could smell the lavender water which Sophie used, she could feel arms lifting her tight and close.

She opened them, looked from one to the other. 'How did you know it was for sale?'

Georgie put his arm round her telling her that everyone had known but no one had mentioned it because they had been going to live in Gosforn.

'Do we want it?' he asked.

Annie looked at Sophie's and Eric's house again. 'Do we want it? Don't be daft.' Her voice was restrained, quiet or else she would weep her pleasure. She peered in through the front room window. Where were Sophie and Eric now? They had left for Australia immediately Da had taken the children from them, unable to bear the loss of Annie in particular,

Bet had said. There had been Christmas cards from Australia then nothing. But Annie knew that had been her fault. She had never replied, wounded at their leaving, jealous at the news of a daughter they had named after her. She had felt that they had replaced her. How cruel children could be.

She turned to Tom but he was backing off, shrugging at Georgie. He saw her looking at him, grinned, then looked again at Georgie. 'Well, it's up to you now, man. I'm not going to be here when the bomb goes off. Be gentle with him, Annie.' Tom was smiling at her. He looked pleased but nervous, as he used to when he'd pinched one of Bet's scones and knew he'd get a walloping.

'What's going on?' she asked, looking from one to the other, then calling after Tom. 'What's going on?'

'I'll tell you in a minute – have another look,' Georgie said.

She smiled, shook her head, tugged at his arm and drew him back to the window, peering in, telling him how wonderful he was, how clever, telling him it looked so clean, but would need painting, wondering if the old oven was still in the back room, deciding where they would put the walnut table, their pictures, hearing his voice as he told her that he hadn't known how much he'd missed Wassingham until he'd talked to the bloke at the garage. And now she looked at his reflection in the window, his eyes, his face, his happiness – but there was something else too – there was nervousness and she felt his hand steer her round now to face the street.

She listened to his voice, now so quiet as he cupped her cheek with his hand. 'Look at this, Annie, hear it, smell it.' He paused, then continued. 'It's me roots see. All this, even though Mam's taken the boys to the pits at Nottingham, all this is still me home, me roots, your home, your roots.'

She listened closely now, hearing the Geordie back in his voice as though the years away had not existed, hearing something else as well and now fear took hold.

'Tell me what you've done, Georgie. Just tell me.' She was no longer looking at the street, no longer listening to its sounds. She could see Tom, standing by the corner of the street, just standing, waiting.

'Just tell me what you've done,' she repeated.

'You heard me say I was born a pitman, Annie. You were going to marry one, remember, you were going to scrub me back for me as me mam did for me da. Well, I'm going back down the pit, you're running the business, that's what we've been fixing up this morning.'

Annie watched Tom, still standing, waiting. She looked at the woman who was polishing her letter box, a boy who was riding his bike over the cobbles, his cheeks juddering, just as her heart was doing, and her mind. Where were the words she needed, and the breath to speak them?

'Are you mad?' she asked quietly at last. 'Or just stupid?' She stopped, the boy was turning the corner, the sun was shining on the slag, the filthy dirty slag. 'Don't you remember Gracie's da, and Tom's marrer?' She was no longer quiet, she was shouting, gripping his arm, pointing to the winding gear, the steam house, the slag heap. 'It kills, it takes arms, legs. You're joking or irresponsible, I said I'd nurse didn't I, what are you talking about?'

'Yes, you said you'd nurse. I didn't say I agreed. Neither did Tom.'

Annie couldn't speak, what could she say to this man who had given her Sophie's house and then taken her nursing and perhaps his life from her? There were no words of her own in her brain, or in her mouth. She could only roll his around and around, trying to absorb them, trying to grasp them as more came and now he was holding her hand and telling her that he'd been to Bigham Colliery with Tom, smelt it, seen it, heard the shift going down, the other coming up.

'It's a club. They need one another to survive. They're a team, like the Army. I know the life, it's in me bones. It's what I want, I know that now. I knew it when I stopped the car but I think I've always felt it.'

Annie found words at last, pointing to the slag, asking why anyone should want to go down some bloody great hole, asking what was the matter with him, telling him he would go down the mine over her dead body and didn't anybody care what she wanted?

She felt his kisses on her face, his breath as he said, 'But you see, I do want to go down that bloody great hole, bonny lass, so you don't need to nurse.'

She pushed herself from him. 'Don't you call me bonny lass, Georgie Armstrong. You're just messing up our lives so don't you dare call me that.' The words were quiet, strained, they hurt her throat, she was gasping for breath and she ran from him then, wanting to catch Tom, wanting to drag him back, make him talk to Georgie, down street after street, it felt like miles. The breath was catching in her throat as she pounded up the back alley, into the yard, into the kitchen. 'Bet, Tom, Gracie,' she shouted, leaning on the table, panting hard. She heard Georgie coming in behind her.

She turned, there were so many words now, tumbling out, hurling themselves at him, 'How could you. I thought you'd accepted the change. How can you be so stupid, how can you do this to us and what about my plans, how dare you just push them aside when they make so much more sense?'

Georgie was leaning against the doorpost grinning, breathing easily and she couldn't bear the thought of the dust and the grime, the weight of the coal above his body. She couldn't bear it and so she went to him then, leant into him pleaded with him, wanting him to be safe, wanting him to be as far from the pit as possible.

He pulled her back out into the sunshine, the smell of geraniums strong as the early afternoon sun beat against the brick wall, and told her that she was to start off the business and forget the letter. Everyone was allowed a mistake.

'Not in the pit, Georgie. Mistakes kill you – they are not allowed, for God's sake.' She was shouting so loud that her throat ached.

He asked her to remember that they had promised one another a future and now they were there, in that future and he needed to earn his place back here in Wassingham, he needed to prove that he hadn't run away from the pit, only from life without her. He'd had the ears and eyes of a pitman, he wanted to know he still had and that he could still read the old sow like a book. He wanted their neighbours to know that they were the same as them, that they weren't just piling back into the area on the side of the bosses.

He was stroking her hair and the words made sense, in some ways they made so much sense but what about the danger for him, what about the days and nights of worry she and Sarah thought they'd left behind? What about her nursing?

She looked into his face, his eyes and there was so much love, always there was love, but there was need too, now, just as there was in her own.

She leant back on the wall, closing her eyes, feeling the heat on her face.

'It's got the edge I had in bomb disposal. I miss that, I know now that I need it,' Georgie said quietly. He said nothing more as Annie heard the humming of the bees, the distant sound of children and the pigeons fluttering in the loft in the next yard. He had let her go when Sarah Beeston came, it had broken his heart but he had let her go, just as he had let her leave India, so what could she do? She could only agree and pretend that she was not afraid.

CHAPTER 3

The next month passed quickly. Annie sold most of the Gosforn furniture to Don because there was so little room in Wassingham Terrace.

'Don't let him have it,' Georgie said on their last night but she shook her head.

'No, he's so sorry, you can see he can't even look us in the eye. If we don't let him have it we're being petty and vindictive and it will only lead to a real breach between us all.'

As well as the walnut hall table she kept the small tables, the pictures, all the things that were Sarah Beeston. She arranged to keep on the Gosforn stall, and took on two others on the route to Wassingham, talking another stallholder into trying her goods, sale or return. Soon there would be more, there must be more.

'It's too much,' Georgie murmured into her neck as the moonlight played on his body, on his scars.

'No, not enough,' she whispered, holding him close, touching his skin, wondering how much more torn it would become when he started in the pit on Monday. He had passed his medical which she had prayed he would fail. He did not need to retrain because of the apprenticeship he had already served. She must see to it that the business thrived because he must get out of that pit and stop playing these stupid games.

In the morning Annie did not look back at the Jaguar which was pulling in behind them. She did not look back at

39

the home which she had shared with Sarah and Val but reached across and held Sarah's hand.

'We're going home then, bonny lass.' She felt her daughter's hand tighten on hers.

'It's going to be so good, Mum.'

When they were scrubbing the kitchen floor the next morning Annie looked across at Sarah, hearing Georgie's hammering, his curse, a crash.

'Bet you didn't think it was going to be as good as this, did you?' she laughed, settling back on her heels, dragging the hair from her eyes.

Sarah's hands were red from the water, her dungarees were splashed and dirty. 'This isn't good, this is awful. Davy's out playing, Mum, it isn't fair. They're going up to the farm after lunch, said we could go too.' Sarah dropped the brush back into the water. 'I bet you didn't have to do this when you lived here.'

Annie nodded. 'It's as well we didn't have money on that, my girl. I scrubbed, brushed, washed dishes, fed the pigeons . . .'

There was another crash from upstairs. Annie raised her eyebrows. 'You'd better go up and see if you can hold something. He's trying to put up a shelf in your room. You can put my father's paper knife on it.' She smiled as Sarah leapt to her feet, throwing the brush back into the pail, dodging the spray. 'I hope you thanked Betsy for it too.'

'I did, Mum. She's going to the farm too, please can we go, please?' Sarah was hanging on the door, her face flushed and then there was another crash. 'Goddamn this bloody thing,' they heard again.

'Perhaps we'd better if the house is going to survive. Go and tell him he has only another half an hour.'

Annie finished the floor, carried the pail into the yard, tipped the water down the drain, sat on the step feeling the sun on her face as she looked at the pigeon loft, remembering Uncle Eric banging, crashing, cursing as he repaired it one year, remembering the cooing of the birds, the gentleness of

40

his hands, his leg which had been irreparably damaged in the trenches.

'That dreadful war,' Aunt Sophie had said. 'It ruined so much.'

Annie leaned forward now and touched the lavender plant she had dug up and brought with her from Gosforn. So, Sophie, has Eric got a smithy at some mine or in an outback town, or are you in Melbourne, or Sydney? Oh God, I wish I'd kept in touch, I wish I'd written back.

She remembered the old railway prints on the wall, the best white table cloth, and then the tears Sophie had cried as Annie left to go to the shop with Da.

Annie's shoulders tightened at the memory. She had never seen an adult cry before and it was as though the ground had lurched beneath her feet, as though there was no safety, no certainty left in the world, and she shook off the memory, watered the lavender, swept the step, polished the mantelpiece and the fireguard which was still as it had been when Sophie had hung her tea towels on it to dry.

When she and Betsy were walking together past the oaks later that day, she asked her if she had heard anything of Sophie, but Bet had not.

'You could try and find her though, lass. Not all that many people in Australia you know. Mind, she'd be getting on a bit, in her seventies, and Eric too. Lovely they were, kind to me, kind to you.'

The sheep grazed around them as they walked up the hill and the wind took their breath as they breasted the rise. The sky was light in the distance, over the sea, the rocks cut through the scant soil, the gorse-bushes, yellow spiked, jigged in the breeze. Yes, she would try when she had more time but this week there were garments to make up, deliver, sell, there were the days to get through while Georgie was down beneath the ground they were standing on.

'Varies each time you know,' Tom said in her ear, his arm creeping round her waist, his finger pointing to the broken-down cart in the farm-yard beneath the hill, the tractor

41

splashing its colour on the scene, the slipped tiles on the farmhouse showing up dark.

'You should know, you've painted it often enough.' Annie's voice was cold.

His grip tightened. 'Don't be cross, bonny lass. He wanted it.'

'You needn't have talked them into taking him, you needn't have vouched for him, wriggled him in.' Annie shrugged herself away from him and stood, watching the children playing tag on the hill, hearing Tom coming up behind her again.

'No, I didn't have to, but it's what he wants. Stop sulking, if the wind changes you'll stay looking like that and it's not a pretty sight, Annie Manon.'

Annie turned now, gripping Tom's arms. 'I remember you being smashed up beneath coal, I remember the lads in the hospital. You're a bunch of kids, all of you, just a bunch of stupid kids but without the sense of that lot down there.'

They both turned and looked at their children and again Tom put his arm around her and this time she leant into him. 'Remember us, Annie, at their age, always together, always up to something, always just managing to rescue the situation. If you don't, I do. I remember how you always looked after me so d'you think I'd not make it as safe as I can for him if he's set on it – and he is you know. I've put Frank on with him and he'll have the good seams, the easy seams. I took him into the lamp room, down the shaft to try and put him off but he just breathed in the air and said "Ambrosia". Trust me, and for God's sake put a smile on your face.'

Annie watched Sarah being chased by Davy, was she going to get back to the stump, was she? Yes, she'd made it and Annie kissed her brother's cheek. 'You're a good boy, Tom Ryan, and my daughter can run faster than your son, just like her mother.'

She grinned at Tom because he was right, she must smile, she must rise at five, pack Georgie's bait tin, watch him leave, wait for his return, and smile, just like every other woman in Wassingham had always done and always would do. But more than that, she must work.

Sarah and Davy sat panting on the stump while Rob blew on blades of grass, his cheeks straining with the effort, the sheep nearby moving away as he did so.

'Just look at your mam run,' Davy said, coughing and pointing.

Sarah shaded her eyes, holding her throat as her breath rasped in and out, in and out, she nodded but couldn't speak, not yet. She had beaten Davy but she'd thought her lungs would burst out of her while she did so.

'She's faster than you, Sarah,' Rob said, then blew the grass again.

'Not as fast as Da though, look at him go,' Davy was standing now, laughing. 'Look he's almost caught her. Your dad's chasing them now, and Mam.'

'Blimey, it'll be Bet next,' Rob said, standing too, no longer whistling, just shaking his head. 'Parents are embarrassing. I mean, they're too old.' He looked around. 'No one can see them anyway or you lot would never hear the end of it. Doesn't matter to me. They wouldn't hear about it at the grammar.'

Sarah laughed now, her breathing easier. 'Unless we told them.'

Rob turned on her. 'Don't you dare. Don't you bloody dare, it's going to be bad enough without that.'

'You worried then?' Davy was sitting on the ground now, flicking grass at a stone.

'Course not, it's just new, that's all.'

Rob walked off, up to the crest of the hill, his hands in his pockets, his head down.

'Spect your da feels the same too,' Davy said watching his brother, then the adults still chasing one another.

Sarah squatted at his side, rubbing the dry soil with her fingers, forcing it into the cracks. 'Don't know why he's going into the pit, Terry said Mum should have nursed, said no

43

one would really want to go down the pit. It's dirty and smelly. She says there are no lavs, that's horrid.'

Davy looked at her, then up at their parents. 'He wants to though, he said that.'

'Terry said her mum said he would say that. I don't want him to go down. How could anyone want to go down under this.' She pushed more soil into a crack. An ant ran over her finger. She cupped it in her hands, letting it run, but not escape. 'She says Mum should have nursed.'

'Since when have you listened to Terry or her mum. I told you, he wants to go down and it's daft, but then, grown ups are daft, look at them.'

Sarah watched her mother trip and fall, watched Tom and Georgie stop, pick her up, one by the shoulders, one by the feet and give her the bumps.

They both looked round now to see that there was no one from town to see it. Yes, they are daft, she thought, stupid and daft and she put her hands on the ground, letting the ant run on to the ground.

'People die though, don't they Davy? It's like Dad's bombs. You never know which one it will be that's going to get you.' She squashed the ant, rubbing her finger over and over it until there was nothing left.

'Well, my da was in the pit for ages and he looks all right and Frank, his marrer, still goes down. All the Wassingham men do, seems right somehow. They do get cut and the scars go blue, but I don't think it's like the bombs. No, not the bombs.'

'But people do die?' Sarah was looking at him now, holding his arm.

Davy was quiet, then he nodded. 'Yes, they die.'

There was a silence between them and then Sarah felt his hand holding her arm, his fingers tight, his skin warm, his eyes troubled but only for a moment because then they heard the shouts, the laughter, felt the pounding feet and her father scooped her up as Tom grabbed Davy, and swirled them around until they gasped, set them on their feet, held their hands and ran them down to the bottom. It felt as though she was flying, as though she would never stop and at the bottom she hugged her father.

'I love you Da, I love you,' she shouted.

Annie was up before Georgie, stoking the range, cooking him bacon, eggs, sausage, not thinking, just doing. She checked the clock. Five a.m. She heard him in the hall, padding through in his socks. She held out his boots as he came through the doorway.

'There's no need to get up, Annie, you've a busy day.' He took the boots, sat down, shoved his feet into them and ate his breakfast, pulling a face at the milk she gave him.

'Drink it, it'll line your stomach against the dust.'

She packed his bait tin, filled his water bottle, his cold tea flask. She stood behind him as he drank, wanting to hold him, press his strong body against hers, wanting to run her hands down his chest, his thighs, wanting to make him forget all this and stay here. But she did nothing except hand him his tin, his old clothes stuffed into a holdall and his flask. She kissed his mouth, touched his face and smiled, opening the door into the yard at Frank's whistle, walking with them to the gate, watching as they walked together towards the pit, joining others as they came from their yards. Georgie did not walk as they walked, he did not hold himself as they did. Couldn't he see he wasn't one of them any more?

Their boots were loud on the cobbles as they walked to the pit-yard, the buildings crowded in on them and Georgie and Frank nodded to each man as they joined the group. There was no talk, it was too early, too grey, these were not men on a ramble, they were workers facing a full day, heavy with sleep. There was no surprise in their faces at his presence, word spun round quickly in a pit town. There was wariness though as he had known there would be and he was glad that he was here, proving himself to them, proving that his

45

family had the right to come back into their midst but more importantly, proving something to himself.

Once inside the entrance they passed the canteen, then clattered into the locker rooms and Frank pointed out the one that would be his from now on. He changed into old clothes, locked up, then walked with the others to the supply room, collecting his helmet, kneepads, steel-capped boots, gloves, belts. It was like the Army again, it was like coming back into the team.

'Come on man, let's get your lamp.' Frank shouldered past the other men, leading the way into the lamp room. Tom had shown him this last week but he still felt the same surge, the same sense of being a boy again. He handed in his metal tag to old Jock who exchanged it for a lamp.

'Good to see you, lad. You keep your bleeding head and back down, and your feet up and your wits about you. I don't want to be left with a spare tag at the end of the shift, your Annie'll have me guts for garters.'

Georgie grinned. 'No she won't, bra straps perhaps. You've not aged at all, you old devil.'

'You have, you were a boy last time, just you remember that, Georgie Armstrong. Reckon you need your head examined, what d'you think, Frank?'

Georgie was moving along now, being pushed from behind.

'Too right, Jock, but I reckon he thinks it's good for the soul, or maybe he thinks he can talk us into buying Annie's bras for ourselves.'

The men were laughing and Georgie stood at the cage while he was frisked for matches, lighters, cigarettes. He'd left his Kensitas in his trousers and the checker flung them in the bin and growled. Georgie flushed and Frank dug him in the ribs. 'Nice one, lad. Don't happen to have a bomb in the other one, do you?'

There was more laughter but it was good humoured and Georgie relaxed. Bloody fool, don't do that again, he told himself, knowing he'd have had more to say if it had been one of his bomb team.

He waited with Frank whilst the miners queued for the cage. There was the low hum of the dynamos running the air pumps, he'd forgotten that, but not the feeling in his stomach as he waited to plunge into the darkness.

'You OK, lad?' Frank murmured, shifting his weight from one foot to the other waiting for the banksman to get the men in, the wire guard shut. Georgie nodded, his arms hanging loose, emptying his head as he had taught his men to do. They were all in now, the gates were closed, the cage dropped. Jesus Christ, he'd forgotten how your heart lifted, how silence fell, how the faint surface light faded, how quickly you travelled, how the light from the helmet lamps flickered on the surface of the shaft, the cables, the pipes, how your mind persuaded you the earth was closing over you, how the ground bounced beneath you as the cage stopped, how you breathed out as the cage door opened. Jesus Christ, he'd forgotten and now he was grinning, stepping out with the others, their bait tins clanking against one another, their batteries too.

He breathed in the air, sensing its motion, its warm lifelessness. Yes, it was the same. He blinked, then narrowed his eyes in the brightness of the light. He'd forgotten how like a tube station it was.

'Need a few advertisements, Frank lad,' he said quietly as they headed for the paddy train.

'None of this comfort when you were down last, eh Georgie? Shanks's pony then,' Frank grinned, squashing himself into a seat, pulling Georgie in.

'Shove over, let a tiddler in,' Bernie Walters grunted, sinking back as the train started. 'Bloody Ritz for you, isn't it, Georgie?' He stuck out his hand, shook Georgie's. 'Worked in the old seam with your brothers. Like Nottingham, do they? Good thing you came back down, lad, they'll open up to you now, would've been difficult otherwise.'

Georgie nodded, smiled. He knew he'd been right. He looked to the sides, electricity still lit their way, they passed stores of fire-fighting equipment and first-aid stations. He

47

moved with the motion of the train knowing that any minute they would be plunged into darkness and now they were and their lamps picked out steel pit girders and unpainted brickwork.

'You'll be working with wood props at the pit face,' Frank said.

Gorgie nodded. Tom had told him. He saw traces of coal on the walls, the roof. There was already stone dust on his lips, in his throat. Thank God for that, flash fires were less likely. The train stopped, they eased themselves out, their feet kicking up the dust, tasting it in their mouths.

He moved along the roadway, his lamp picking out Frank's back, the roof, the walls. 'Pick your feet up, man,' Bernie hissed behind him, 'it's like a sandstorm back here, and keep up.'

He moved more quickly now, remembering to feel with his feet, bending as the roof lowered to four foot, remembering the pain that dug into his back and legs. His lamp was picking up the roof and the floor and the sides, but in front there was nothing but a wall of blackness because Frank had left him behind. Bernie turned off down another roadway. God, he was alone. He moved more quickly, carelessly, caught his back on the roof, felt the jagged slash, the sharpness, the dampness of blood, black blood. He moved even faster, straining his back as he kept low, straining his thighs. Come on, come on, keep moving until his lamp at last picked up Frank and now the roof was higher, they were upright, but it was so hot.

'We'll strip off here, gets too bloody hot, d'you remember?' Frank asked.

'Aye.' He could do do more than grunt in the heat and tiredness and he hadn't even lifted a shovel yet.

He felt the blood on his shirt, sweat in his eyes, the taste of it in his mouth. He wanted a drink but not before Frank took one.

They walked on inbye until there it was, the old sow's black face, scarred and blasted by the night shift who'd cut it and now, together with others, they shovelled the coal on to the clanking rasping conveyor but it wasn't until ten o'clock that Georgie at last managed to maintain the ceaseless steady rhythm of the others. His throat was dry and his head splitting with the noise of the conveyor but he knew that the cutter would be much worse.

The broken coal came away quickly, leaving the jagged roof exposed. He and Frank propped it, sawing, heaving, banging and it was easier than Sarah's shelf. It really was, and he laughed and Frank shook his head, then called 'snap' which was picked up by Bernie further down, who called it too, and so it was echoed down the line and at last they sat in amongst the coal dust, listening to the creaking roof, checking it with their lamps while they ate and drank and pee-ed.

Georgie's right hand was sore, blistered through the gloves. Both his hands were so stiff he wondered how he'd ever get them round the shovel shaft again, his back was so stiff he wondered how he'd ever bend again, his legs were shaking so much that Frank laughed and told him the only time he'd shaken like that was when he'd brought Tom back from the beating the fascists gave him at Olympia and delivered him to Annie at the hospital.

'Thought she'd damn near kill me I did,' he laughed, squatting on his hunkers.

'Did she?' Georgie asked, working his hands, rolling his shoulders.

'No, but I expect she damn near killed you when you said you were coming back down.' He tossed Georgie a piece of gum to chew.

'I guess you could say that but what about you, are you still in politics?' Georgie didn't want to think of Annie's attempt to nurse, her courage, her self-sacrifice, her nightmares, her rage and worry at his plans, he just wanted to be here, in spite of the pain and the tiredness.

Frank shook his head, his jaw moving in the same ceaseless rhythm that he had used when wielding his shovel. 'Kids' stuff, you get too old to stand there mouthing off at demonstrations somehow, and with Tom scratching away at the business idea he's had no time for anything but that and the union. You'll go into the business, will you?'

Georgie nodded. 'Aye, this'll keep us until it's off the ground.'

'Canny move too, the blokes'll get their wives to look out for your stuff, there's some who're good with sewing too. Get Tom on to that, then you'll not get any bad workers to be a bloody nuisance.'

Frank stirred, packed his tin away, looked at his watch but waved Georgie back down. 'Few minutes yet.' He leant back against the wall, and Georgie's lamp picked out the sweat which ran in rivulets down Frank's black chest and belly, just as it would be running down his. His back was too sore to lean against anything.

'So what d'you do with yourself now then, Frank?'

'Pigeons, that's what I do. Got a real good 'un.' Frank took his gum out of his mouth and stuck it on the sole of his shoe. 'Looks what he is, a belter. Got a good eye, make a good racer. You should get that old loft of Eric's fixed up, he raced a few good ones you know.' Frank checked his watch again and nodded. 'Best be getting at it.'

Frank came across and heaved Georgie up and for a moment he thought his legs wouldn't take his weight but they did and he could straighten his back, just.

After another two hours his blisters burst and Frank took gauze and cream out of his underpants and bound them. 'Full of surprises, my old lady says. Always happens first day back and you'll need to use them tomorrow lad, that's if you're going to make a real pitman.' He slapped Georgie's shoulder. 'You're doing well, Georgie, real well.'

He talked above the noise of the conveyor as they worked now and Georgie knew it was to ease the last hour for him. He learned about squeakers and then about ringing, training, and the race which had been spoiled by gale-force winds.

'You should get yourself a squeaker. Have one of mine if you like.'

Georgie laughed, heaving another shovel load on and then another, then breaking off to help Frank heave in another prop. 'Fat chance of that, any free hands around our house and you get a pair of pants stuffed into them, or a bra, or if you're really lucky, an apron.' They both laughed as the prop went in and picked up the shovels again, though Georgie had to use his to force himself upright and then lean against the prop as a wave of giddiness brought the nausea to his throat.

'Your Annie's got it right though you know, got to work hard at the beginning. She deserves success, she's a right bonny lass, Georgie.'

Georgie knew that she was, knew that she'd say nothing about his hands, his back but her eyes would flare until anxiety overtook the anger. He'd be all right though, and today had shown him that he could listen for the old sow's mumblings just as well as he'd always been able to, except for the noise of the conveyor.

Annie and Sarah stood at the yard gate waiting and watching for Georgie, Frank and the others and for a moment they couldn't pick him out because his walk now was that of a miner, measured, feeling the ground.

As he reached them he nodded to Frank, put his cap in his pocket, kissed Annie and stroked Sarah's hair with his bandaged hand.

'No need to scrub me back, little Annie, they've got pit showers now.' His smile was tired.

'Well, you can't win them all, then,' Annie said, her smile broad because that was how it must always be, though the anger had flared at his hand before anxiety had taken its place.

'Never mind, lad, nothing wrong with your fingers, you can still pick out the faulty stitching on the knicks.'

She heard Frank laugh further down the lane and then Georgie and Sarah too and now her smile reached her eyes, and her love was in her lips as she kissed his ear. 'I love you,' she whispered and left her relief at his return unspoken.

CHAPTER 4

Annie lay in bed and watched another rocket soar, then explode. Would that mean a stick in their yard in the morning? It was supposed to be good luck wasn't it? Maybe she'd get that big order they desperately needed.

'Four months gone and where is it?' she said softly to herself. 'Four months of slog and still I can't get my foot in the door, what on earth am I going to do?'

She ran her hands through her hair and could still smell the sulphur from their own fireworks, hear Sarah's shrieks as the Catherine Wheel had spun off its stand by the bonfire on the wasteground. Georgie had stepped forward, then stopped as Annie held him back. 'You're not defusing that, bonny lad,' she'd said and handed him a charred baked potato instead.

She turned away from the window, stretching her hands across the emptiness next to her. At least he and Frank had had time to come to the bonfire and at least on night shift they'd be turning over the conveyor rather than working behind the cutter but she still worried and she still missed him.

Annie turned again, then again and heard yet another rocket. Who was still up? Kids probably. She looked at the clock, two a.m. Oh God, she was tired. She must get some sleep or she'd be going to the market traders with bags under her eyes big enough to hold their week's takings.

She sat up now, resting her head on her knees. She'd try the traders to the west and north of Wassingham in early autumn. They'd taken the pants in the summer – now she would try them with the aprons with Christmas looming.

There were fifteen regular orders from stalls to the south and east but no money up front, that was the problem, and they were still asking for sale or return plus thirty days' credit and she had to go with that for now. At least though she'd hooked into two new shops in Newcastle. They were keen on the pants and bras which was good but they paid on thirty-day invoices too and even then they had to be chased. At least the markets paid up promptly.

She lay down again, watching the clouds scudding across the moon, pulling the bedclothes up around her neck, feeling the cold on her face. Would Georgie be cold? No, it was never cold deep down he said, and it might not be, but it was hard and she could see the tiredness more deeply etched on his face with each passing day and feel new cuts and ridges on his back. If they weren't getting enough garments into the retail outlets how could they sell? She must try harder, cut their profit margins if necessary, create a need and she just had to crack the big stores.

'I'll try offering the department stores a much bigger discount, even extended credit, but not too much, we can't carry it.' She could see her breath in the moonlight. Did everyone talk to themselves? But why worry, she wasn't growing hairs on the palms of her hands yet, Sarah had checked today and had said she might sound mad but so far wasn't.

She turned again and again but sleep would not come and so she went down to the dining room. There was no point in wasting time if they had to get more garments out. She walked over the thread-strewn floor. She must hoover in the morning – what was it Isaacs had said? 'A clean workroom is a happy room, Mrs Armstrong,' and then he'd handed her the Hoover. She touched the boxes of pants Gracie had brought in at the end of the day. She must put them into packs of twelve but that could wait until the morning. There were Bet's pants on the table, she'd re-do those now.

Her neck ached and her fingers were sore as she began

53

and she wondered how to tell Bet that her hands and eyes could not do the work, but even as she thought it she knew that she could never say the words and so she unpicked, re-sewed, stacked, unpicked, re-sewed, stacked as she always did for Bet, and then checked Gracie's and her own. The quality must be good right from the start. She stopped and wrote a reminder to ask Gracie to stack her garments into dozens, it would mean one less job for her.

Now she cut out the work for tomorrow and shrugged aside the ache in hands swollen from using the scissors too much. What did banana fingers matter just so long as the work was done – pain was nothing, it would pass but there were tears in her eyes after half an hour.

For a further hour she sewed samples of their bras, of the new pants because she had decided she must tour the Madam shops again. She wouldn't ring in advance this time, she'd just go. She sewed more aprons and gloves because she'd noticed two new kitchen and craft shops setting up on her way back from Gosforn market last week and she'd call in on them too. She'd do Durham, Newcastle, all the towns.

She needed to sound out Brenda Watson down Edmore Street again, make sure she'd really be available to help her train up the homeworkers if they got the big ones. No, not if, *once* they got the orders.

Tom and Georgie had talked to the men, they'd got four reliable wives picked out as homeworkers but how long would they wait, they might go and get other jobs.

'No, there *are* no other jobs, you idiot woman, that's why we're here.' Annie leant her head forward on her throbbing hands. Her back was stiff, her feet were cold, her lids were heavy.

She packed up the samples, checked through her list of calls, checked off the quantities against the orders – still needed twenty-four more vests and . . . she checked through the orders again, yes, there was an order for four dozen pants. It was for Fairway Market – how had she missed that? Gracie and she could have done them on Sunday. She gripped the chair. They were to be delivered tomorrow.

'For God's sake, we can't afford to be so careless,' she groaned and looked at the clock again, it was so late, she was too cold, too tired but then she shook herself. 'Get on with it.'

She went through to the kitchen, stoked the range, brewed tea, smoked a cigarette, stood in the open door looking out into the yard, there were no spent rockets and so she flicked her cigarette across the yard, watching it arc in the cold November air, watching it smoulder and die – 'Good as a rocket any day, Annie Armstrong, now sort it out.'

She drank her tea, curling her hands around the mug, ignoring the throbbing, wondering how many pants would be returned from the other stalls? Could she bank on twenty perhaps as part of the four dozen, but no, what if they'd sold the lot? She rinsed her mug, then cut and sewed the full forty-eight, checked and packed them, and the twenty-four vests.

If she had any returns she'd have to put them back into stock and sell those on at the next trader. She checked her route. Yes, she could do Fairway and still be back for Sarah because she stayed for piano until four.

Annie checked the clock again, her mind a blank, her eyelids heavy, she rubbed her eyes. Georgie would be in at half past six, she'd give him breakfast and finish packing before Sarah got up, but then she saw the invoices. She had to do those so that Georgie could look at them before she left. She insisted that all paperwork was checked because she was unable to trust herself. Maybe all orders should be too, but no, everyone had enough to do, she'd just make sure she checked through each evening.

Her hands were shaking as she wrote but then they were all exhausted. Tomorrow she must tell Gracie that they had to produce more than they were doing so that they could build up a reserve to call on, rather than going from hand to mouth like this. Could Gracie produce more? She'd have to, even though she had the two children. Could they work harder without telling Betsy otherwise she'd insist on doing more, which would only mean more unpicking? Annie slept for an hour.

The bacon was crisping and the sausages spitting as Georgie came through the door – safe, thank God, yet again. 'Sausages are almost ready, the bacon's crisp, the invoices are there.' She nodded to the table, then laughed as his arms came round her, as his hands stroked her breasts and he said, 'Since you don't have to scrub my back take me straight to bed, Mrs Armstrong. The sausages can wait, the bacon can burn, the invoices don't need checking.'

He pushed the frying pan off the hotplate and pulled her through the door, undoing her dressing-gown, leading her up the stairs, closing their door with his heel, stripping off his clothes, removing hers. He held her, stroked her, kissed her mouth, her breasts, her thighs and she could still smell the pits on him.

'I love you bonny lass, little, little Annie,' he said as he lay on her, moving with her, kissing her eyes now, her hair. 'I love you, I love you.'

Though she was tired she held him, kissed him and then felt her own passion rise as it always did for this man, for his strength, his kindness, his love. Later, they lay in one another's arms but only for a moment because Sarah must not be late for school, Annie must not be late for the rounds, so she eased herself from the bed, dressed and crept towards the door. She turned as he spoke.

'Forgot to tell you, love. An order was phoned through from Fairway on Saturday, I stuck it in at the bottom of the pile – it should have been on the top, shouldn't it?'

'Next time, Georgie, I shall murder you!' Annie blew him a kiss because this time the mistake had not been hers and so perhaps the days of carelessness were over.

Sarah ate Georgie's breakfast while Annie cooked another for him and packed up sandwiches and an apple for her daughter's lunch. She pricked the sausages, turned the bacon.

'D'you need another slice, Sarah?'

'No thanks, Mum, but I'll have his rind.'

'No you won't, your da likes it, you've got your own.'

'You're as bad as Miss Simpson. She's mean too.' Sarah was buttering her toast, putting on too much marmalade. Annie smiled.

'Surely not like Miss Simpson, she breathes fire, doesn't she?'

'Almost. She's been going on about the eleven plus but I don't want to go to the Grammar, it'll mean breaking up with Davy and . . .' Sarah waved her toast at her mother, 'and, it'll mean all girls, I'll get like Terry.'

Annie put Sarah's lunchbox into her satchel. 'I don't think we'd let that happen somehow.' She checked her watch, ten more minutes before they needed to leave. She turned the sausages, grilled more bread and looked across at Sarah. 'If you did pass, it would give you more opportunity you know, both of you. I mean Davy might want to go and if you're spouting about not splitting up he'd maybe hold back. You'd get the bus in together and meet up afterwards.'

Sarah was quiet as she finished her toast. Then she took Georgie's tray from Annie and ran upstairs with it while Annie hurried with the boxes out to the car, balancing too many, but Sarah rushed out and caught them as they fell.

'Well done – but go in and brush your hair, Sarah,' she laughed, 'and give Miss Simpson a chance and more importantly, don't influence Davy. Let him make up his own mind.'

She followed her daughter through to the kitchen and wiped the drainer. Then she shrugged herself into her coat, put on some lipstick and smoothed her hair. She straightened her daughter's collar.

'Are my seams straight?' She turned her back to Sarah.

'Yes, and Davy's made up his mind anyway. He wants to go to Art College so I'm going too.'

Annie picked up her handbag and looked carefully at Sarah, smiling gently. 'But you might not want to do art, darling.'

57

'I don't, not like he does, he wants to paint designs like Uncle Tom. I want to be like you, have ideas, make them work, learn how to move a strap and make something better but I want to stay here with you for the rest of my life. I don't ever want to leave Wassingham, or this house.' Sarah was moving towards the door as Annie reached out and pulled her close.

'I felt just like you when I lived here. I never wanted to leave but I did, and then I came back. You do that when you're grown up you know but the love never dies between families, it's always there. And I think it's a very good idea to go to Art College, if that's what you want to do but there's plenty of time to change your ideas. Listen to Miss Simpson though, she's maybe a wise old dragon. Now scoot, you'll be late.'

She watched Sarah walk through the yard and out into the alley, knowing she would pick up Davy outside Tom's, and was moved not only at the thought of the children's friendship but at the memory of Sarah's words. That night she wrote to the Australian newspapers in Sydney, Melbourne and Adelaide explaining that she was trying to trace Sophie and Eric Shaw and asking them to print her letter. Later she worked into the small hours because it might not just be the adults' future she was building up, but the children's too.

As November became December there seemed almost no time to eat, let alone sleep. She picked up orders for a further two Madam shops, and five market stalls, and still ran the Gosforn stall, though she never saw Maud or Teresa there. She spent her evenings with Sarah, her nights working.

She called on the kitchen and craft shops. The manager of one was rude and turned her away, the other took a dozen aprons and gloves, then rang for more. Tom suggested that they sewed holly on to the knickers with Christmas approaching and they did so, though Annie felt they would surely not sell, because there was no way she would wear a pair, or Gracie. But sell they did and once again she made a note not to allow her personal taste to influence her view of the market place.

She rang shops and stores offering larger discounts but only a few buyers from the smaller shops saw her and only one placed an order. In desperation she took Davy and Sarah to Newcastle for tea in the restaurant of the main department store.

They ate meringues with forks and watched the mannequins parade while she told them of the pantomime she had seen as a child and how she had clapped with all the other children when Tinkerbell was fading, and was convinced that it was only because of her longing that the fairy had lived.

She told how, long before that, she and Don had played jacks on the thick white cloth while they waited for Sophie and their father to finish talking in the front room, how she had wanted to turn herself into gossamer and float beneath the door so that she could listen to all that they were saying.

'I've not heard back from Australia,' she said. 'Sophie can't have seen my letter.'

'Mum, you're just putting it off. Go on, you wanted to talk to the buyer,' Sarah said, drinking her tea.

'Plenty of time for that,' said Annie, playing with her meringue. She still had a problem with rich food after the deprivations of the war. So did poor old Prue from the sound of her last letter from India in which she'd told Annie not to send out a Christmas pudding as usual. Just can't cope, darling. So unfair, she'd said.

'Oh damn,' Annie said, 'I haven't sent off Prue's biscuits.' She sat back in the chair, there had been no time, too much to do. 'I'd better nip off and get a tin and we'll send it on Monday.'

Sarah looked at her. 'Mum, just go and talk to the buyer, she won't eat you, she's not like Miss Simpson.'

'So, how is your work going both of you?' Annie asked, leaning forward.

'Auntie Annie, go and talk, we'll stay here and we won't

59

pinch the sugar lumps and we won't spill our tea.' Davy was picking up her handbag and scarf.

'Yes, go on, Mum, just put on some lipstick, that's right, you look great.'

Annie stood up, her legs were trembling. She hadn't rung to make an appointment, there was no point.

'Be good,' she muttered.

'You be good, sell it to them, that's what Da said.'

Annie nodded, well, he would, wouldn't he, tucked safely down a thousand feet under the bloody ground. She checked her samples, pulled her skirt, and had a word with the head waitress who nodded and smiled. 'Yes, I'll keep an eye on them, no bother.'

The lift to lingerie was crowded, carols were playing in the store as she weaved between the stands, checking the stock, the pants, the bras. There were none like hers.

'Can I help you, madam?' the salesgirl asked, her face fixed in a smile which disappeared when Annie said, 'May I speak to the buyer please? It's Mrs Armstrong from Wassingham Textiles.'

The girl ran her finger along her eyebrow, her nails were red.

'Have you an appointment?'

'No, I just happen to be in the area.' Annie pulled out the pants. 'We make pants and bras to any specification.'

The girl didn't even look but said in a flat, bored voice, 'Mrs Wilvercombe doesn't see anyone without an appointment.'

'Then how do I get an appointment?' Annie asked as first one woman came to the till and then another.

'You phone or write,' the girl replied. 'Now if you'll excuse me I have customers waiting.'

Annie stood for a moment, wanting to take the girl by the collar and march her to Mrs Wilvercombe – wherever that old battle-axe might be.

'I am in a hurry you know,' the woman behind her said and Annie moved to one side, her face flushed. She rammed the pants back into the box, then the box into the bag and walked towards the lift. She passed a phone by the stairwell and stopped, looking back at the girl. Damn it, cheeky little monkey. She fed in coins, rang the store, asked to speak to Mrs Wilvercombe.

'I'm actually in your store, at the stairwell, I have improved discounts to offer and an excellent range of underwear,' Annie began.

'I'm far too busy, it's pre-Christmas you know. Perhaps you could try again in February.' Mrs Wilvercombe's voice was brittle, hurried.

'But we're offering extended credit to big stores,' Annie said.

'Thank you no, try again in February.'

'Thank you so much,' Annie said, wanting to ask what she had to do to get a foot in the door – beg? Probably she told herself as she replaced the receiver. She walked up the stairs to the restaurant, paid the bill and shook her head at the children. They grimaced, took her bags, held her hands and came with her while she bought biscuits for Prue. All the time the carols played until she could have screamed.

In February she rang Mrs Wilvercombe again who said that she was too busy. She rang all the other stores and was told that there were no more appointments available, they had all been reserved for the wholesalers who would be touring with their samples in two weeks' time – didn't she know? No, she hadn't known, God damn it, and she sat that day and did nothing but think and use the telephone. That evening she called a meeting and discussed mail order with Georgie, Tom and Gracie.

'It's direct selling, the money comes in first then the orders are filled, none of this chasing for payment, none of this long slow build, this tortuous begging.' She had cleared the dining-table and lit the fire and she watched as the flames darted and curved around the coal. Her head was aching, she was tired. It was all so slow. Georgie was still in the pit,

61

the lines on his face more deeply etched with each week that passed. 'We're just not breaking in.'

Georgie tapped with his pencil. For God's sake don't do that, she wanted to shout. What was the matter with her?

'We knew it would take time, Annie, and we can't afford to gamble on mail order. What d'you think, Tom?'

Annie looked across at Tom who nodded. 'Too much outlay. We'd have to set up the advertisement, place it, order up the cloth, probably retain homeworkers to make sure we had them for the push and what if we guessed wrong and the design didn't appeal? We don't know enough yet.'

Annie tried not to hear the tapping of the pencil and looked at Gracie. 'What do you think?'

'Too much of a gamble and we are building, Annie, don't be too impatient.'

'But for heaven's sake, we're way behind the schedule we set ourselves.' She pushed the minutes in front of them. 'Look at Georgie, he's worn out.'

The pencil tapping stopped and Georgie looked at her, his eyes angry. 'Don't tell me how tired I am, bonny lass, you're panicking – we just need the big order, that's all. It'll come.'

'When though, Georgie, when? I'm your wife for Christ's sake, I know when you're tired, when Gracie's tired, we're all tired.' She was trembling. Was her face as tense as Georgie's? Tom's expression told her that it was and she sat down and hung her head, gripped her arms, took a deep breath. 'I think mail order is worth a shot, we can keep on the regulars as our cushion and we'll end up with direct and indirect sales. Please think about it, we're getting nowhere fast the way we're going.'

They did think and talk and argue and she told them how she'd rung and sounded out suppliers of second-hand rotary cutters and sewing machines during the afternoon, how she'd contacted the estate agents and yes, the warehouse was still vacant so they'd have premises to move into once the mail-shot got them off the ground.

She ignored Georgie's raised eyebrows and continued. 'I've

talked to the homeworkers, they've agreed to a retainer of two pounds a week once the advertisement has gone out but there'll be some capital outlay on training them up to the required standard. Brenda will help while Gracie keeps up with the regulars.'

'We'd need too much capital to fund it,' Georgie said.

'We've got it in the bank, we've built up that much of a reserve,' Annie countered.

'But if it fails, we're back to square one,' Tom said, drinking his beer.

'You've got a moustache,' Annie snapped. 'It won't fail.'

'I think we should respond to definite orders or we're working blind. Look how far on we are, after all, we only had two accounts in June,' Gracie said.

'But it's not fast enough, can't you see that? We had December blocked in for a big order, and it's February now. For heaven's sake, we're working flat out and the money's trickling in. We've got to make that leap so that we can employ others, push the goods out. At the moment we're working all hours of the day and night to virtually stand still – it's just not cost-effective.' She paused. 'Look, we need a shop window to show our wares, to tempt people in. Mail order would do that for us, and once the big stores see we've something good to offer they'll want us too.'

Georgie was writing, working out figures, he shoved the pad over to Tom who nodded, passed them to Gracie and then to Annie.

'Look at those, darling. It would run us right down. If we guessed wrong we'd jeopardise the house and we can't do that, not again. We'll just have to respond to orders, keep to the plan.'

Annie sat back, looked at her hands, at the carpet covered in threads, at the fire which had died down, at the ash which had spilt on to the hearth, the word 'again' ringing in her ears. Suddenly she wasn't as sure as she had been.

'I insist on a vote,' she said, but the crispness had gone from her voice.

It was three to one against and it was then that the frustration exploded and she banged her fist on the table and shouted, 'So what the bloody hell do we do now, I can't get through to the buyers, I can't get through to you, so what exactly do we do?'

There was silence and then Georgie said, 'For a start you can come out into the kitchen and help me make another cup of tea.' While they made the tea he told her that she was working too hard, that there was nothing to worry about, that she was over reacting, the business was fine and she said nothing but wanted to shout at him, at them all, Isn't it enough that you won't let me nurse, now you won't let me lead the business, don't you understand anything?

The next day she worked in the morning, and then sat and thought until Sarah came in. That evening she phoned Mr Isaacs and then called another meeting. Tom and Gracie came at nine p.m. and she barely gave them time to remove their coats before calling the meeting to order. 'OK, no mail order but we need to get professional. We need to get on the wholesalers' tour. I've rung Isaacs, he's told me the route, explained the wherewithal. One of us needs to take the samples to Edinburgh, Glasgow and all towns en route, then down to Liverpool and across to York. We need to phone ahead and make appointments with buyers at the time that other wholesalers are doing the same thing so we become part of the circus. I've got the timetable.' She pushed it towards Tom. 'We need to book into hotels, a cheap bedroom but a good room for the presentation and order up coffee by room service for each buyer and we mustn't try and sell the same stuff to competitors. I think I know those.' She passed round the list she'd written up earlier. 'We need to display the wares and discuss terms, they'll try and hem us in but as long as it's a reasonable margin we can deal with it, but we can't go any longer than thirty days' credit. We must have the cash flow. While Tom's doing that, we can do the same in Newcastle, Durham, and so on . . .'

'Hang on a minute,' Tom interrupted. 'I'm not going, this

is your patch. You have the expertise, the knowledge, you're the right sex for God's sake. Otherwise it's a damned good idea.'

'Not as good as mail order. I'm not going, I've got Sarah. You can use your holiday.' Annie insisted.

They argued long into the night again but Tom wouldn't go despite Annie's best efforts to persuade him. Georgie agreed with Tom, Annie was the one with the knowledge, and after all, for Tom is sell pants and bras personally to women alone in a hotel room wasn't right.

The next morning Annie was on the phone, ringing up buyers, talking her way into appointments, using Mr Isaacs' name as he had said she could – his only proviso that she should leave London, the South East and the West Country alone. That afternoon though, she left the phone and the samples and walked round to Betsy. She drank tea with her, talking of her plans, then took Betsy's stiff swollen hands in hers and asked her if she would mother Sarah and Georgie in her absence.

'They need someone they love, someone who will have a meal ready for them and ears to listen to them.'

'I'd love that, I'd really love it, pet, but what about the sewing? I'd not have time for much.'

Annie spoke carefully, gently. 'Listen, if all this goes well then we'll have made the jump, we can set on a homeworker so don't do anything while I'm away.' She still held Betsy's hands. 'The thing is, Bet, I'll need someone to mother me too, when I get back. I can't cope any more with the dinner, the ironing. I need to be out or in the dining-room for more hours in the day but how can I with Sarah?'

She looked at her stepmother and Betsy nodded, then said, 'Can I come and cook for you, lass? Can I be there for Sarah and for you? I don't like to think of you working when most folks are asleep and I'd like to have another go at looking after you.' She took her hands from Annie and reached for her cup. 'But I feel bad about letting you down with the sewing.'

'Anyone can sew, not many can keep the three of us in order,' Annie said, smiling gently.

A week later Annie took the train to the north to show the bras and pants 'in the hand', not on models. She and Gracie had worked into the night all week, cutting, sewing, checking the garments, listing them for insurance purposes, packing them in reams of tissue paper which Sarah and Davy pinched, wrapped round combs and blew until Annie shouted and their lips were numb. She arrived in Dundee, lugged her skips to the taxi, fell into bed and saw the first of the buyers at ten o'clock the next morning. She called for coffee but the buyer drank tea, then said that the the jute trade was in a bad way, had been since '53 and there wasn't a lot of money around. He couldn't take anything.

The last buyer said her budget was already committed but yes, she'd like coffee and perhaps a cake. At Stirling, Perth and the Lowlands they liked the samples and said they'd take a few 'to help her out', but they'd want extended credit. She refused but offered them another five per cent discount. One refused, the others accepted but when she took the train for Edinburgh she knew that so far their costs had not nearly been covered.

In Edinburgh a central buyer told her she should get her stationery and advice notes and invoices printed up properly. 'Can't expect anyone to take you seriously unless you put on a good front,' the woman said. 'Come round again in the autumn, let's see how you're doing then. May I have your card?' Annie did not have one, had never had one.

The buyer bought nothing, and Annie toured the Madam shops and sold six dozen bra and pant sets. A buyer in Glasgow liked the samples but had committed his budget almost before the tour began. 'Might be an idea to put out a catalogue,' he said as she left.

With what? Annie longed to ask.

She took the train to Liverpool, Manchester, Birmingham, Sheffield, Nottingham and York and sold a total of thirty dozen pants and bras, fifteen dozen aprons and gloves. It would perhaps pay for printed stationery but not for the train fares, the hotel charges or the taxi fares, she thought as she caught the train from Newcastle to Wassingham and wondered how she could tell the others.

Georgie was waiting for her at the station, running towards her, lifting her in his arms, kissing her, then hauling along the skips. She told him the total sales and then, when he seemed not to care, she set those against their expenses, but he just shrugged, heaved the skips into the boot and opened the door for her.

'We need proper stationery, proper advance planning, collapsible boxes for neat presentation, we must dip further into our resources, Georgie, it's not that much to ask.'

He smiled at her, touching he shoulder. 'Come on, we've got to get back, I'm nursing the phone.' He climbed into the driver's seat and started the car. 'I've had a call from a wholesaler, Nigel Manners, who supplies hundreds of small shops. Apparently his wife was in Newby's while I was trying to flog some to the buyer. She liked them, or so he says. I've sent him a sample and he's ringing back tonight at half past eight. Says if the terms are right he'll want thousands, so I've sorted it all out for you, darling, there's no more need for you to worry.'

Annie looked at her watch. It was eight o'clock. She looked ahead and made herself smile because all the months she'd worked, all the miles she'd travelled had been a waste of time – she'd been right in the first place, it was Georgie who should have run the business – and the knowledge churned deep inside her.

CHAPTER 5

There was no call at half past eight but at nine o'clock Nigel Manners rang and ordered eight thousand bra and pant sets as per the sample but with a few modifications.

Georgie mouthed to Annie, 'We're on, we're actually on,' his eyes alight. He turned back to the phone. 'My wife will drive across tomorrow.'

'Sorry, no, never deal with women. You've another director, surely?'

Georgie shook his head at Annie, raised his eyebrows. 'Fine, Tom Ryan will be with you at . . . shall we say eleven?'

Annie lit another cigarette as Georgie wrote down instructions and now she wanted to leap in the air, wave flags from the rooftops. What did it matter who had brought in the deal, the fact was it was here and her husband would soon be out of the pit and working in the firm alongside her and Tom and all regrets were gone. She stubbed out her cigarette, moved nearer to him, held him, kissed his cheek and mouth as he spoke to Mr Manners, feeling his arm coming around her, holding her close, squeezing her until she could hardly breathe, lifting her off the ground in a bear hug when he had finally put down the receiver.

'I love you, Annie, you little belter, and your ruddy knickers – we've done it, we're on our way.' His mouth and body were against hers and she could feel the heat of him through her dress. She had been too many nights away from him, and he from her.

The next day Annie ordered the rotary cutter and some new cloth. They needed more than end rolls for this though she would confirm in a few days, she told the supplier. Tom drove to Newcastle, arriving back at tea-time with a list of specification changes.

'Bloody nit-picker, wants the bra strap moved half an inch, the flowers in blue and the thigh line higher on the pants.' Tom handed her the sheets. 'I'll work on the new designs tonight, put them in the post tomorrow.'

She nodded. 'If you could, Gracie and I have to finish and deliver the regular orders. If he approves the new designs – which he must since they're his ideas – I'll run up samples for him. I've sorted out a printer for cards and stationery. We'll need a professional invoice, don't you think?'

Tom put the kettle on, nodding, turning, leaning on the guard, his face alive with excitement and pleasure. 'It's happening, isn't it, bonny lass? It's happening at last. We've just been talking and hoping for so long and now we're here. Give us one.' He nodded to the cigarettes.

Annie shook he head, tapping the packet. 'No, you've given up.'

'Oh come on,' he said, grabbing for the packet. 'It's a celebration and I need one after that Nigel Manners.'

Annie shook her head again, snatching the packet back, putting it down her cleavage. 'Just try and get them out of there and it'll be clipped ear time. We're celebrating tomorrow anyway, it's Saturday and we're off to the beach.'

Tom turned as the kettle boiled, pouring the water into the pot, bringing it back to the table, pushing aside the invoices Annie had been writing up. 'Brass monkey weather for the beach, isn't it?'

Annie smiled wryly. 'Bracing, the bomb man called it, the one who likes the edge.'

Tom grinned at her. 'He's coming out of the pit though, at last. We haven't heard much about his famous edge recently, have we? I think he's just about realising he's put on a few years since he was sixteen.' Tom held the pot over her cup and she nodded. 'Still, you were sensible to let him do it, Annie, he needed it.'

She reached for the milk, poured it, stirred it, heard the spoon click against the side, watched the spiral, thought of the three men who had been killed on Georgie's shift a month ago, and the countless others who were the walking wounded. 'I had no choice, Tom, you know that, no choice at all.'

The beach had been as cold as Tom had said it would be and now the children huddled in Annie's kitchen, pressing against the guard as their parents sipped hot soup.

'Come on, Rob, don't take all day,' Sarah said, rubbing her feet, brushing away sand. 'You're not the only one with chilblains, I've got some whoppers and Davy's are blinking away at me.'

She watched Rob take his time, stroking in the ointment until she wanted to slap him. 'You're such a little snot,' she said, hugging her knees, feeling her toes throbbing, smelling the salt on her skin, pinching it, making a bum out of her knee.

Rob grinned and threw her over the wintergreen. 'Your turn, and don't be vulgar.'

Sarah passed it to Davy. 'You have it first.'

Davy's chilblain's were belters and she winced as she saw him rub the wintergreen in harder, knowing how they were itching, because hers were too, but bye it had been worth it. She looked over her shoulder at her da. He'd run like the wind to catch her mum, waving seaweed until she screamed and then he'd come for her and she'd run and run as though she'd never stop, until there'd been no breath left, aching with joy and terror as she heard him coming closer and closer.

'That was a good tackle you did on me, Da,' she said to Davy, taking the wintergreen, stroking it on at last.

'Too good,' Georgie called over, 'I'll have a bruise for the next three weeks and just where did you put the seaweed you tried to shove down me neck?' He was laughing as he passed back Tom's new season designs.

'Outside the door, it'll tell the weather for us,' Sarah called back but he wasn't listening now, he was talking to Tom about the business and she was glad he was. She looked at her da's blue ridged hands, his coal-stained skin. Yes, she was glad he was because soon he would be out of the pit and then she'd sleep at night.

She looked at his shoulders, his arms, his legs. Norma's da had been a fast runner too, he'd won the fathers' race. He'd died a month ago in the pit, with his two brothers. Norma sat next to her in class and had forgotten how to laugh.

She rubbed the wintergreen in deeper, digging her nails into the chilblain, wanting pain, not itching. She screwed on the top, tossed it back to Rob.

'You're bigger,' she said, nodding to the shelf.

'Anything more, your worship?' he grunted, stretching, tucking it behind the clock.

'A few jelly babies would be nice,' said Sarah, her mouth rounded into posh, her little finger raised. 'But only the red and green ones, so sort them out first. I like to save the head till last, so cut those off too.'

She ducked as he flicked a paper pellet at her. 'Not nice,' she minced. 'Really, not very nice – common one might say.' They were all giggling now.

Annie smiled as she listened to Sarah.

'Did you hear me, Annie?' Georgie's voice was sharp.

'Sorry, I was miles away.'

'Well, get back here. We're trying to sort out the plans for the year. Now, are we all agreed that we need to send out a letter requesting an appointment and then a follow up phone call? Did you catch that, Annie, d'you agree?'

Annie looked at Georgie, sitting there with his pencil poised, and said gently, 'Of course I caught it, Georgie, I wrote it, remember?'

But he was already on the next point and didn't hear and

71

as she watched this man's confidence, his eagerness she knew it didn't matter that he'd take her place as chairman – the sharpness in his voice was only excitement, it would pass and soon he'd be safe.

'When's Manners coming back on the amended designs?' Georgie asked Tom.

'Monday,' he said. 'Strange man though, thought not dealing with a woman went out with the ark.'

Annie lit a cigarette, playing with her lighter, wondering where she'd heard that name before, pushing it around her mind as she'd done the first time Nigel Manners had been mentioned.

'Did you hear that, Annie?'

Annie looked at Georgie, 'Sorry, miles away again.'

'Who's going to train up Meg and Irene?' Georgie asked again, and Annie pointed to the notes she had written down for him. 'Brenda and I are, there you are, point six.'

Her voice was gentle and now Georgie looked at her, his face reddening and he touched her cheek. 'I'm sorry, I'm being an idiot, I just feel so impatient, I want it underway.'

She nodded at him, feeling the touch of his finger on her skin, seeing the softness of his eyes. 'I know, we all feel the same.'

They drank beer then and discussed the new designs properly and Gracie said, 'You've done dungarees here, Tom? I thought elastic wouldn't work?'

Annie nodded. 'By the autumn, we'll have premises and enough cash to buy a button holer, but we can hold buying it until we see if there's enough take-up on the design. Brenda said she'd do the button holes on the samples.'

They discussed the extra homeworkers they would need once the orders built up, and they would, once their stock came pouring out into Manners' outlets and their name became known nationally.

They discussed Briggs' warehouse. Bill the estate agent had told Annie they could relax, take their time because there was no interest at all, but soon they must think of planning permission so that they were ready to convert when they centralised the business.

It was then that Tom lifted his glass, looked over the top at them all. 'I reckon that day's not far away so I think there's a toast in order, to Georgie, who brought this whole thing off, and to Wassingham Textiles. We've finally made it.'

Annie drank, sitting back in the chair, looking at the children, the range where Sophie had baked, where she now baked. She ran her hand along the scrubbed wooden table and felt complete.

On Monday Manners required yet more changes but Isaacs had often had the same problem and so Annie and Tom worked late into the night adjusting the designs yet again, interrupted only by a phone call from Don, asking them all to the convent's Open Day in three weeks' time. 'Teresa's playing the piano at two. Perhaps you could be there in good time, Annie. Hats will be required, and gloves.'

'You will, of course, be wearing chiffon?' she asked, then wished she hadn't. 'I'm sorry Don, just a little tired.'

'Yes, I'd heard you'd landed a big one. Tell me more when I see you. Bye.'

Tom looked up as she put the receiver down. 'My what big ears he has,' Annie said. 'And my, how word gets around.'

'What did he want?'

'To tell us to be on parade in three weeks' time for the Convent Open Day.'

'Not bloody likely.'

'Oh come on, Tom, we should go. Terry's playing the piano and he's trying to make amends. They gave us nice presents at Christmas and now this. He wants his family there, in hats and gloves.' She was laughing now but Tom just groaned, then shook his head.

'God in heaven, he's such a pompous idiot. Come on, let's get on with these.'

Annie spent the next week training up Meg and Irene with

73

Brenda who had to be paid a full salary, she explained to Georgie, because she was already doing a job, not just sitting waiting for Manners' go ahead.

'But what's the hold-up?' Georgie said, shovelling down his breakfast, throwing on his coat and stepping out into the cold morning air.

'This is what's called business, my love.'

'Christ, it's worse than waiting for the coal to creak and the roof to come down.'

'Just call it the edge then, Georgie.' She pulled him back, kissed him. 'It will be all right, my darling. He's just fussy, he wants exactly the right thing, we'll have to go with it, it's no problem.'

She watched him leave, then hurried into the dining-room. She still had the regular orders to pack, the first of Tom's samples to make up, the invoices to draw up, Gracie's work to check, her own to complete and still a ruddy hat to buy.

In the middle of March Manners finally approved the samples and increased his order to sixteen thousand. It would take up all their capital, plus a loan to increase the order with the supplier, Annie told Georgie, who nodded. 'Just have to. I'll fix it.'

Annie alerted the suppliers, the homeworkers, Brenda.

'We'll be starting any moment,' she said. 'Just waiting delivery of the machines, the cloth and the trimmings.'

But Tom phoned from his pit office at eleven a.m. as she was sewing the last of the aprons for Gosforn Market.

'Annie, he wants exclusive use of the designs. He's just called. What the hell do we do?'

Annie said nothing, just held the phone. Exclusive use? Exclusive use, for God's sake. 'How dare he,' she finally said. 'How bloody dare he? He's messed us around and now this. Tom, we've used those designs for all the new market stock, the Madam shops, but put on different trim. He said that was fine. What's he playing at? Go back to him. Tell him they're out on the stalls but with different trim, just as he agreed. Just tell him.' She was shouting.

She hung up, leaning her head on the banister, then paced the hall, running her fingers along the wallpaper, twisting the door knob, dusting the mirror with her handkerchief, running her fingers through her hair. This was outrageous, dangerous, they mustn't agree. She pounced on the phone when it rang. 'Manners says the copies are to be off the stalls by tomorrow at the latest or the order's off,' Tom said.

Annie breathed deeply, who the hell did Manners think he was? The man was nothing more than a bully and she'd had enough of them to last a lifetime. Good God, it meant ruining their existing markets, it made the business too vulnerable, there'd be no fall-back if anything went wrong. And these traders were her friends, they were loyal, they'd been with her from the start.

Her knuckles were white on the phone, her arm was trembling, her head was aching. What the hell was going on? Did he really expect them to go along with this?

'No Tom, you'll have to tell him no. If I pull back the traders' stock it leaves them with nothing. We're their sole suppliers. We can't do that to them. Just tell him no. Call his bluff, we can't just be restricted to him, it's bad business, it's dangerous – we're out on a limb with debts to pay.' Her hands were shaking, her legs too. He'd gone too far.

There was a silence. 'I'll tell him we'll ring him back tonight, let's think about it – it's the big one, Annie. I know, see how many you can run up of the old stuff for the stalls.' Tom's voice was taut. 'I'll say I can't get a decision, catch Georgie as he comes off shift, discuss it with him. He'll know what to do, we don't want to blow it.'

There was a click as he put the phone down and Annie held the empty receiver. I know what to do, her mind shouted. I know what to do too – we wait until the new tour, do it sensibly. It was all she could think as she sewed up the oven gloves, one after another until her fingers were sore. Then she dragged out all the boxes she could find and counted through the stock. There was very little left. She checked through next season's designs, perhaps she could bring those

75

forward but she'd never get enough done in time for tomorrow's delivery and the traders hadn't approved them anyway.

She threw the sketches across the table. Why the hell should the stall holders suffer because of that man?

She stoked up the range, dragged on an apron, mixed flour and margarine, slammed the oven door, not caring that there was flour on the floor, waiting, because she knew that Georgie and Tom would come.

She watched them open the door, stand and look at her. 'We've rung Manners and agreed,' Georgie said.

She checked the scones, took them out, tipped them on to the rack. She had known they would, but they were wrong, they were being panicked, they hadn't thought it through, not properly, couldn't they see that? She washed the baking tray, trying to contain her anger as she spoke. 'If we agree to Manners we'll be putting all our eggs in one basket. We did it with Sarah's money, we'll be doing it again. We must just wait for the new tour.' Her voice was quite calm, quite quiet.

Georgie dragged out a chair, threw his lunch-box on the table, slumped into the chair. 'It's not the same thing at all, Annie, that was a stupid mistake, this is business. It's a good order, you can see that – you're the one who's been going on about it, pet. About needing it now and we might net nothing from the tour. At least we know we've got this.'

Annie rolled the words around in her mind. Stupid mistake, yes it had been, and hers too, but this would be as much of a mistake and she couldn't let it happen. Tom leant back against the draining board, looking at the clock.

'How did you get off work?' she asked, drying the tray, putting it way. She sat down again and tested the hot scones with the tip of her finger.

'They can dock me pay, this is important.' His face was drawn, his eyes anxious.

A headache was beginning to pound down one side of her head and neck. Georgie was pushing his bait tin round and round.

'Look both of you,' Annie said, still calm, still quiet. 'I've taken months to build up the traders. They've always been loyal, always paid, we're their sole suppliers. If we withdraw their stock they'll have nothing to sell, they could go broke, our name'll go down the Swanee. Manners will have us in the palm of his hand. If something goes wrong we're finished, we'll have nowhere to go, we'll have ditched everyone else. We must say no – we must wait. I don't want to any more than you but it's just too dangerous.' She turned the scones over, there was flour on her fingers and the smell of baking filled the kitchen.

Georgie rubbed his hand over his eyes, his movements quick, irritable. 'Don't be daft, Annie, what could go wrong? We'll have a contract for God's sake, we'll be covered.'

'Isaacs had a contract too. They rejected the order, said it was of insufficient quality.'

'Ours won't be,' Tom chipped in.

' "Said" being the operative word. There was nothing wrong with the stock, it's all just part of the game.'

'It's not like you not to gamble, not to go for the big one. It won't happen anyway, I've checked him out, he's bona fide,' Georgie said, his voice louder now. Annie swung round on him.

'It's more than a gamble, it's letting down the small men, it's exposing us and we can't do it. Manners can just go and bully some other idiots. Anyway, he's probably bluffing.'

Georgie pushed the tin round, faster and faster. 'Manners doesn't bully, and he doesn't bully idiots, or am I one, is that what you're trying to say?'

Annie flushed, shaking her head, wanting to pound the table. 'Of course I'm not, I'm just – '

'We need this,' Georgie broke in, his voice cold. 'We hooked in – I hooked in. So I'm saying we're going for it, we've got to.' His jaw was set, his eyes narrowed. 'I'm telling you, Annie, we're going for it, it's too important to bugger up. We'll just have to risk losing the traders, it won't matter when we're in the shops, we won't need them. It's not dangerous, it's foolproof, we'll have a contract. The stall holders are businessmen, they'll understand. Who did they dump to take you on? What d'you think, Tom?'

Tom was looking from one to the other. 'I don't know that I like the idea of the traders copping it. Annie's got a point, Georgie.'

He was looking at Annie now.

She felt the scones again. There were currants in six of them, which would Sarah prefer? But the anger was boiling up.

'As a matter of fact, Georgie, they didn't dump anyone to take us on, the old man died and we won the orders on merit, on my workmanship.'

'How's the old stock?' Tom broke in. 'Can we take that out to replace the exclusives so we don't let them down?'

Annie shook her head, waiting until she was calmer. 'I've thought of that but there's not nearly enough though there are the new season's designs. I was just wondering if we could pick one, make those up, take them out cold, no samples, do a straight exchange but I'd need to set the homeworkers on. We'd need to pay them over the odds to work round the clock so I could get them to the stalls before Manners' deadline.'

Georgie nodded, easing his back. 'Fine, get some of those out but we can't afford homeworkers, we're already down for enough of a loan, we can't afford to extend it. If you get a few out to them it'll be enough. If they're loyal like you say they'll wear it. We'll get some more to them by the end of the week. If they make a fuss, kiss them goodbye, they're not worth the hassle.'

Annie stood up, banging the table, shouting at her husband. 'But why the hell should they *wear* it? Manners is being totally unreasonable, the whole thing stinks, and it's we who will be damaged too, not just the traders. What's the matter with you, Georgie. Look, I'm telling you, watch my lips – without them we're just too vulnerable, we'll not just lose today's order but future ones. We need to supply them properly, we need to put money out or maybe you're going to sit up throughout the night sewing?' She gripped his arm.

Georgie shook free and now he was shouting too, his lips drawn tight. 'No, I'm not because I'll be down the bloody pit earning the money that's kept this afloat until someone like Manners came along and I'd like to remind you that I was the one who went out and got that, without a load of money being wasted on trains, taxis and bloody coffees. So no, I won't be sewing, I'll be down there with that bloody cutter screeching and the conveyor clattering until I can't speak, let alone think, that's where I'll be.'

He slammed back into his chair and there was silence until Annie said, 'I'll ring the traders at home tonight, explain, promise delivery of the new season's stock by the end of tomorrow, or at least enough to keep them going.' Because what else could she say? She knew from his face that the edge had finally gone, that it was the thought of more time in the pit that was pushing him and it should be pushing her – what the hell was she thinking of? This man had had enough.

She and Gracie worked throughout the night even though Annie thought her head would explode with pain and in the morning she set on Brenda, telling Georgie she would hock the walnut table to pay for her if necessary and so he said nothing.

In the afternoon she drove round, collecting back the Manners exclusives, restocking as far as she could, but there were not enough, not nearly enough and that evening she told Tom and Georgie that they were no longer the sole suppliers of most of the traders, in fact they had been dropped by half of them. She kept her voice neutral and didn't tell them of the comments that had been made to her, the disgust which had been voiced, because she agreed with every word. That night she didn't sleep and there was space in the bed between them because she couldn't bear the thought of him touching her. In the morning the rage was still there and she wanted to shake him for putting them in this position, for going down the pit in the first place.

Tom phoned to say that Manners wanted to change the delivery date from 1st July to 1st June and Annie clenched the receiver and said that she'd only begin work when she had a contract, until then nothing was going to happen. 'Nothing, do you hear?' she shouted.

On Wednesday the written order arrived and it was only now that Annie asked for delivery of the machines and the cloth and their terraced house shook as the lorries pulled up at Wassingham Textiles and off loaded. She called to the neighbours. 'Sorry about the noise.'

'That's all right, Annie, d'you need a hand, lass?' Mrs Warren called from across the street.

'If I do, you'll be the first I call on, Pat, bless you.'

The children took the machines round on their carts after school and Annie set up the rotary cutter in the dining-room. She cut out all evening and delivered to Brenda, Meg and Irene before breakfast. If they had to supply this man, then they'd do it perfectly.

She cut out and sewed the stock for the remaining market traders and the small shops throughout the day, and so did Gracie and they checked them as carefully as Manners' stock because they also deserved perfection.

She sewed for her own stall.

'But you won't be going in now,' Georgie said on Thursday evening. 'There's no need.'

'There's every need,' she replied.

'That's crazy,' he said, pulling off his boots, warming himself by the range.

'I need to be seen there, I need to recover the situation as much as I can.'

'It's not necessary any more, you'll get too tired. You won't be able to do the job you need to do.'

'We're all too tired and we're all doing the jobs we need to do, you more than anyone.' Annie left him in the kitchen, not wanting to discuss the markets, not wanting to think of the hours he was down there, for her. But for himself too, God damn it.

She sat at the sewing machine, working, her head bent low, nodding as Sarah and Davy brought in the completes from Brenda and Meg.

'Rob's gone for Irene's,' Sarah said and Annie nodded.

'There're some scones in the tin – and thank you, you've been wonderful.'

'Shall we sew some roses on, Mam? You look so tired.' Sarah's hand was on her shoulder and for a moment Annie leant her head against her daughter's and felt warm arms round her neck.

'You've done enough, my love, now go and have a scone.'

'Dad can sew them then, I'll send him in,' Sarah was following Davy from the room.

'No, your da's tired, I'll do it. He can pop you into bed through and I'll come up later.'

She watched as they shut the door. No, she didn't want Georgie in with her. She stretched her arms, rolled her shoulders, eased her neck then sorted through Brenda's, they were almost perfect, just seven rejects. She'd re-do them later. But Meg's smelt of cigarettes and there were ash marks on twenty-four of them. Dear God, as though things weren't difficult enough.

Annie threw her coat on, walked through the kitchen smiling at them, closing the door gently behind her.

Georgie took the scone that Sarah offered him, breathing in the scent that Annie had left behind, knowing that her anger would leave her when Manners paid up, knowing that they could hook back the traders when they had more time. He'd just go and talk to them as he'd talked to Manners – it'd be easy and then she'd see that all they'd been doing was prioritise. She just hadn't grasped how to kick-start a business. He tasted the scone and pulled a face – he didn't like currants.

Annie walked round to Sindon Terrace, walked past the

pigeons cooing in the loft. Frank had said that Geoff kept pigeons but they never won races, they were overfed.

Meg opened the door, her face surprised. 'It's nine o'clock, Annie, I'm just making Geoff's supper.'

Annie nodded. 'Yes, I'm sorry but, Meg, I've a bit of a problem. You see, I can't have you smoking when you're sewing. It's a fire hazard and when we move into the new premises it will be forbidden. But it's not just that, it makes the clothes smell and there are ash marks on two dozen of them.'

She was speaking quietly, not wanting the neighbours to hear, feeling her embarrassment making her blunt. 'I'm sorry, it's my fault, I should have told you, you weren't to know.'

Meg's face flushed. 'Keeps me weight down you see, smoking does. But I won't, not while I'm sewing.'

The next night there were no ash marks but there was still the smell of smoke and Annie had to walk to Sindon Terrace again. This time Meg told her that she hadn't smoked at all, though her husband had, and he wouldn't stop. Annie nodded, pressed the woman's arm, said, 'Not to worry, I'll just air them then.' There were tears in Meg's eyes.

She called in on Tom. 'Why did you suggest Meg?'

'Because her old man's a bugger. She needs the money, the sense of doing something for herself but if there's a problem we'll drop her, this is too important.'

Annie shook her head. 'There's been too much dropping and no, there's no problem, this is why we started this business, remember? I think she'll do very nicely, Tom.'

Each evening she aired Meg's garments and told Georgie that it was common practice to hang things up when they'd just come in.

The next morning she called in at the estate agents as Georgie had asked, checking that the rent was the same. Then she called in at the planning office on her way to the stalls, checking on their requirements, noting them down, referring them to Tom so that plans could be drawn up and presented as soon as possible. Once they were in premises there would be so much less rushing around and besides Meg could work in peace.

She worked eighteen hours a day, and so did Gracie. Tom redesigned the autumn collection and Annie ran up samples. The stationery was ordered, collapsible cardboard boxes for the presentations were costed. She checked and rechecked the homeworkers' garments and had to have one of the sewing machines repaired which held them up, but by the day of the Convent Open Day they were still on schedule with six weeks to go. At the eleventh hour she realised that she had forgotten to buy a hat and asked Pat Warren if she could borrow hers. It was pink, with flowers, and Sarah laughed.

'Well, I think you look lovely, Auntie Annie,' Davy said, 'Like a spring garden.'

'You're a smooth talker, Davy Ryan, just like your dad.'

Annie smiled as Davy flushed. 'You are, you know, just like your dad.' She made a note to speak to Tom about Davy, he must include him more, Rob took too much of his time.

They were driving up and out of Wassingham, Sarah and Davy in the back, Tom, Gracie, and Rob following. Betsy wouldn't come, she had too much cooking and washing and ironing to do, she had said, but give the lass my love, and Don and Maud of course.

'Bet just didn't want to come,' she said quietly to Georgie.

'Did any of us?' he replied and Annie didn't answer, just felt the tension coil around them. She watched the country-side as they travelled the road she felt she could now navigate blindfold.

They arrived in good time and as Georgie drove in through the school gates Annie looked at the sloping gardens she had not seen since she had left the school so long ago. The rhododendrons were still there.

'They grow wild in the foothills of the Himalayas,' she said over her shoulder to the children. 'Your dad's seen them, haven't you, Georgie?'

He nodded, smiling now. 'Saw them but missed your mam

too much to notice them.' Annie sat silently, watching his hands on the wheel.

'Will this do?' He swung the car into the car park and they all walked across the gravel to the front of the school where the yew hedges were still set in squares. 'I love you, I'm sorry I shouted, I can't bear it when you're angry.' He took her hand.

They stood close together seeing the spring flower beds within the hedges and Annie remembered her sense of loss when she had begun here, her sense of only being half a person because Georgie was not here. She looked at his face, the pit's deep lines, the love in his eyes, the weariness, and knew that nothing could really hurt their love, nothing. They were together, that's all that mattered. 'I love you too,' she said.

They strolled amongst the other parents, their hands tightly gripped, his thumb playing on her skin and she knew that he felt the same, that he always would, and now her smile came from deep within her.

They walked down the paths, and she showed them the runner beans the nuns had always grown, the cloakrooms where she had had her peg, the chapel which was still painted white with brown beams.

'There was a lot of spectacles, testicles, collar and cuffs, was there?' Sarah asked.

Georgie and Annie just stood and stared. 'What did you say?' Annie managed to say eventually.

'Norma told me they did a lot of that at convents, you know, made the sign of the cross. That's how they remember,' she said.' Sarah was looking at the lectern. Tom and Georgie were grinning, Gracie and Annie caught at Sarah's coat and hurried the children out, hoping that no one had been close enough to hear.

'Oh no, there they are,' Sarah groaned in front of her and Annie poked her with her finger.

'Smile,' she hissed, walking towards her brother, kissing

Don, clashing hats with Maud, asking Terry when she was playing.

'Time for a quick look round then,' she said, looking at Don and he smiled, his starched white shirt digging into his neck.

'Are you going to show us then, Terry?'

'Teresa,' said Maud.

'Or course,' Annie murmured not looking at Sarah, Davy, or any of the others.

They toured the hall where there had always been chrysanthemums in the late summer. That had been the smell she had remembered when the Japanese had come to the cathedral in Singapore to herd them to the camps. Annie shook her head free of the memory.

Terry led the way to the cloakroom again and Annie shook her head at Sarah. 'Be quiet,' she mouthed. 'Just look interested, again.' They passed the form rooms this time and Annie peered through the glass. Was 'Sandy loves Sister Nicole' still carved on the desk? Where was Sandy?

'Is the conservatory still cold?' she asked Teresa. 'Detentions were such a misery there.'

'Teresa has never had a detention,' Maud said, her heels clipping on the wooden floor.

'Of course,' Annie replied.

There was tea set up in the hall and Annie sat at one of the tables, gesturing to the other chairs. 'Time for a cuppa.'

Maud glanced around quickly.

'Sorry, time for a cup of tea I think,' Annie said, drawing out her cigarettes.

'It's no smoking in here, Annie,' Don said.

'Of course it is,' Annie replied, trying not to smile, looking across at the children, ignoring the grins of Tom and Georgie, suggesting to Teresa that she took her cousins to see the gym, and perhaps the music room.

'Miss Harding used to poke my hands with a pencil when I made a wrong note. She was a dreadful old witch.'

'I won the Miss Harding Prize, this year, that's why I'm playing.' Teresa's mouth was as prim as Maud's and Don's.

'Of course you did,' Annie said faintly. 'Well done, Teresa.'

'We're not going to learn the piano,' Sarah said, frowning at Annie who saw she had no intention of being shown anything by Teresa, who equally, had no intention of being the guide. 'We're going to play skiffle, aren't we, Davy, then we're getting guitars.'

Annie turned and looked at them, then at Georgie. 'Well, we learn something new every day, don't we? I thought the old washboard had disappeared.' She raised her eyebrows and accepted the tea that the senior girls brought round. Georgie caught her eye and grimaced, he'd have killed for a beer, and she was so glad they'd come to Gosforn and left the anger behind.

They sat in the hall for the performance, it still smelt of chalk and polish and while Teresa played Annie thought of the languid days, Georgie's first letters from the Army and she touched his hand, felt him hold hers, lift it to his lips and it didn't matter that Maud tutted, that Don frowned.

Teresa was very good and only stumbled once and Annie felt for the child as Don's lips tightened and he tapped his programme on his lap. She clapped all the harder because of this, and congratulated Don and Maud on Teresa's playing. 'It's so clever to be able to recover, says a great deal for her skill.' She was having to shout over the noise of scraping chairs as people rose and filtered out of the building. Georgie took her arm as they followed, calling to Don who led the way. 'Really must go, we've got a lot to do but it's been a great afternoon, Don.' She squeezed his arm because he was trying to be pleasant and she knew it was for her sake.

Don walked on, keeping up with the flow but stopping on the drive in front of the school, brushing at dust on his sleeve, smiling at them as he shook Georgie's hand. 'By the way, how's it going?' he asked. 'I heard about the Manners order on the grapevine, this is the breakthrough for you, isn't it, it'll give you the credibility you need – word gets round quickly, whether it's good or bad.'

Annie nodded, watching Sarah and Davy walking up to Teresa, pleased to see them smiling, knowing that Sarah had seen Don's irritation at his daughter's mistake.

She heard Georgie's voice harden as he said, 'Not likely to be bad at this stage so yes, it's what we've been needing. It'll set us up and we're already drawing up plans for Briggs' place.'

His shoulders were tense again but then Don said, 'I've heard that Manners is straight, shouldn't have any trouble. I should go for it.'

She felt Georgie relax, felt herself relax too at those words. Please God, let it be true. Don took out a cigar. 'Mm, taken out the lease have you?' He was rolling it under his nose.

'No smoking, dear,' Maud said and Annie was glad that she'd bitten back the very same words.

'Good luck to you both anyway. Thanks for coming. Hope it goes well – business is a tricky game.'

He was putting the cigar back into his pocket, shaking their hands, kissing Annie and she hugged him because it was the first time her brother had done that for more years than she cared to remember.

They worked day and night until the end of May but there were no more headaches because Georgie held her when she did finally fall into bed and touched her when she passed him. He sewed on the roses sitting next to her, and kissed her when the final set of underwear was completed, then handed them to Sarah and Davy to box.

'Brilliant, wonderful, you've been so good,' Annie told the children and Sarah said, 'Now he'll come out of the pit, won't he?'

'Yes, he'll come out, my love.'

'That's all that matters then.'

This time they didn't go to the beach, they bought

champagne and drank it in Bet's kitchen with the homework-ers and Brenda while the kids played their washboards in the yard and sang *Hound Dog* though Georgie called for *Mona Lisa*, or *Red Sails in the Sunset*.

'You're so square,' Sarah groaned. 'And we really need guitars for rock, not washboards.'

Annie looked at Tom. 'Maybe when the cheque comes in?'

He grinned. 'Maybe, after all, they could end up making us a fortune.'

They drank a toast to Manners and Annie downed hers in one because even Don had vouched for Manners and both he and Georgie could not be wrong.

During the next week they continued to provide stock for the stalls but there was no longer the need to work into the small hours and Annie put Brenda, Meg and Irene back on to the retainer but there were no complaints because they all knew it was temporary.

They submitted the plans to the planning office and Annie went over their figures and offered discounts to all traders to try to make amends and draw back those who had left them. But it was too late, they would not reconsider, and they were no more friendly than they had been last time.

Georgie shrugged. 'Who cares,' he said but Annie cared very much, and worried about it, but she wouldn't allow it to come between them again.

She looked at second-hand guitars but they seemed so large and she decided that there would be time enough for guitars when the children were older. But a gramophone at Christmas would soften the blow and maybe the adults' ears.

In the second week she hoovered the house free of threads, wielded the rotary cutter and sewed in the afternoon, helping Betsy with the supper, helping Sarah write up her project comparing the yearly pattern of an oak and a horse chestnut.

She slept eight hours again that night as she had done for the last ten days. 'I'd forgotten what it was like to be lazy,' she murmured to Georgie who was on late shift and could sleep in for much longer.

She packed Sarah's lunch, and checked her project, her collar and her nails. 'Good, sparkling clean, though I'm surprised you've any left after all that washboard work.'

'If I had a guitar I wouldn't have to suffer like this.' Sarah put her hand to her forehead.

'Out,' laughed Annie. 'Wait and see what Father Christmas pops into your little stocking, and no, it won't be Elvis Presley, so you can wipe that smile off your face.'

Sarah slung her satchel over her shoulder. 'Don't want Elvis, only his guitar.'

'Out.'

She washed the dishes, wiped the floor, heard the post. Picked up the letter. It had a Newcastle postmark and was addressed to Wassingham Textiles. She opened it. It was from Mr Manners telling them that their goods were of inadequate quality, that they had therefore defaulted on the contract and he would be returning the whole order later today. There would be no payment of course.

CHAPTER 6

Georgie passed the canteen walking in the midst of the other men, though not with them, Jesus, not with them. He took his lamp, handed in his tag. He stood still for frisking. No cigarettes, no matches – no bloody nothing – not any more. He'd lost them the lot. It was his order, he was the big I am who'd thought he'd cracked it for them all, thought he'd pushed them up when all he'd done was shove them down.

'Get on with it, man,' Frank said, pushing him forward into the cage. 'Left your brains back home, have you?'

Georgie nodded. 'Something like that,' but his throat hurt to speak, it felt swollen with rage, with anger, with hopelessness. The gates crashed into place, the surface disappeared, the cage dropped, dropped, thumped and they were out on to the paddy train.

'We're down the old workings today, setting the props.' Frank was squashed against him and Georgie wanted to break free, to smash his fist into the brickwork they were churning past. It was he who had pushed his way into the chair, taken over the meetings, insisted on the exclusives. God, if only he'd listened.

They walked inbye, crouching down, beneath the roof, the bloody creaking roof which could come down at any minute, which had come down on Wassingham Textiles. They stripped, ducked under the roadhead, their lights playing against the side, their faces in darkness, thank God, because he could feel the tears on his cheeks, dropping down on to his chest. She'd just held the letter out to him – 'it's part of the game' she'd said. 'Just part of the game. We'll get back on our feet,' and she'd smiled, held him. 'He's a bugger, we nearly made it, we very nearly made it, we couldn't have known, just think of that, nothing else.'

Georgie crouched lower, lifting his feet above the dust, feeling for uneven surfaces. There were broken props here, the roof had been working overnight.

'The old cow's splintered the buggers,' Frank said stopping, his lamp playing on the weakened props. 'There's another.'

Georgie turned away, wiped his face. No, she was wrong, she had feared it, had wanted to wait, had wanted to keep the markets but he'd pushed them – for Christ's sake he'd pushed them because he'd given her no choice, he'd shown her how he felt about this hot, dirty great hole which *he* had insisted he worked in. They'd never get back now, their name was gone – how long would he be down here now? A lifetime is what he bloody well deserved.

'Don't just stand there, man, let's get on with it.' Frank was heaving at the prop which had been left by the early shift. Georgie nodded. Yes, let's get on with it, there was nothing else to do.

He measured a prop, sawed it, erected it, tightening it into place, hammering it into position, feeling the judder up his arm, glad of it. He hit harder – harder – harder, feeling the coal dust falling on his face, in his mouth. Again and again . . .

'For Christ's sake, man.' Frank grabbed his arm. 'D'you want to bring the old sow down?' Frank's face was coal black, streaked with sweat, angry. Georgie dropped the hammer, heard it clang, coughing now, his mouth claggy with dust, his eyes sore, sweat and grime filled.

'You do the bloody thing then,' he snarled, snatching his arm away, wanting to smash his fist into the face of this pigeon man who held him, wanting to kick and pound the prop into nothingness.

Frank stood silently, watching him, then reached down for

91

the hammer, handing it back. 'For Christ's sake, Georgie, leave your rows with the missus at home and remember you're in a bloody pit. It's not just yourself you'll kill, it's your marrers.' Frank turned his back, tightened in his own prop, stopping, listening to the roof, watching for the fall of dust, and Georgie felt the hammer cold in his hand, felt the sweat running down his forehead, his chest, back, legs and arms.

He swung the hammer again, more carefully now, tightening the prop into place, hammering in a wedge of wood at the top, making sure it was straight, making sure that the pressure came down true and he felt the heat not just of the mine, but of his shame because he was part of a team, or at least while he was down here. Up there . . . but what was the point of thinking about up there any more?

They propped until all was secure, then drank in deep gulps of cold tea because the heat and the dust were thick. Frank went under the head with his pick, turning back what he'd loosened, cursing, swearing, toiling while Georgie shovelled the coal into tubs because there was no conveyor at this old, small face. And for once he longed for the noise of the conveyor's rumbling, or the harshness of the cutter because they filled his mind and his body, killing thought and feeling. 'Down the bloody drain,' he murmured, 'Down the bloody drain.' But he mustn't think of it, not now, not down here. Annie had said that. 'Don't think of it, we'll sort it out. Concentrate, Georgie, no need to worry, just concentrate.'

She hadn't wanted to show him the letter until the end of the shift, but he'd seen her face when he came down, and before that he'd heard Tom's voice, but by the time he reached the kitchen Annie was alone with the door open and a draught blowing at the ashes on the hearth. Her eyes had been guarded, her kiss intense, her hug too tight, her laugh too loud as she called him a lazy toad who probably wanted a three-course breakfast now.

Frank was easing out from beneath the head. 'Your turn now, let's see what you've remembered.' He was panting, his elbow had been rubbed raw, his side grazed. Georgie was glad to be handed the pick, glad to crawl beneath the coal, to lie on his side, dig the pick in, heave it out again, burrowing into the seam, panting in the heat, feeling his breath sore in his throat through thirst, not tears, straining his back, grazing his side because it kept him from thinking of her face smiling, her arms comforting him, her eyes shadowed and desperate, but not as desperate as his.

It kept him from thinking of her voice telling him it wasn't as bad as it looked, they could start again, work on the traders, repair the damage, go further afield where their name wasn't damaged – her voice telling him to concentrate, for God's sake concentrate. Calling him back as he crossed the yard, begging him not to go in, stay at home, get over the shock.

They stopped for snap but he couldn't eat. He sat back on his haunches and listened to Frank, hearing his words but thinking only of the future, which was this, nothing else. Christ, oh Christ. He thought of her eyes, her smile. What if she couldn't cope, what if she broke down again? Why hadn't he listened to her?

They moved on after snap.

'Roof's bad down at number six,' said Frank.

'No, it's fine now,' called a passing deputy.

It wasn't fine, the floor was dirty which meant the roof was a bugger. They crouched lower ducking under the jagged outcrops, by-passing the props bent out like crooked elbows.

'Jesus, that'd twist out soon as look,' Frank swore. 'Careful there, Georgie.'

Georgie didn't reply, just nodded; looking, feeling, listening, just as Frank was doing, then calling out. 'There's a bad one to your left, Frank.'

It was six feet to the face conveyor but the roof was so low they had to squeeze between the motors of the two conveyors.

'Timber up, the man said, so timber up it'll be but we've drawn the short straw today, Georgie.'

Georgie nodded. He knew that already. His lamp played

on the props in the new track, all pushed out of the vertical by fifteen degrees, even the new ones. They eased along the track under four yards of unsupported roof.

'Four broken.'

'I can see that,' Georgie snapped, then shook his head. 'Sorry man, bad day.'

Frank just nodded. 'I'd never have known it, but never mind, we all have 'em. Sometimes me birds don't win, sometimes the squeakers die – yes, we all have 'em.'

Georgie laughed. God, if only it was a question of a couple of bloody squeakers and he felt fury rise again at Manners, at Frank, at everyone, but most of all himself – then shook his head. Concentrate, the lass had said. Concentrate – and don't blame yourself. It's no one's fault, only Manners.

There were two middle sets broken too and they sawed, hammered, wedged, tightened. Georgie dug down to the solid floor to stand in the last prop, putting it side by side with the old broken one. He had to use his hands because there was no room between the props and the conveyor; he cut the prop with the tadge, set it, listening, always listening for the roof, watching for dust trickles, concentrating, always concentrating like the lady had said.

'Got to move on down to the undercut,' Frank grunted. 'Bloody long shift this is, with all this bitty work.'

Georgie nodded. He didn't want to go up now, he wanted to stay here, wedge, tighten, listen, look, hide because he didn't know what to do any more up in the open air, in the world of high finance he'd thought he'd conquered.

They cleared the gum beneath the undercut, shovelled it on to the conveyors and the noise was kind to him, filled his head, made it ache. His hands were kind to him because they were cut and sore. They worked in the heat and the dust and the noise, stopping, drinking warm water, wiping sweat from their eyes, easing their backs, stretching their arms. Frank looked across at him and grinned, his teeth white in his black face. Georgie realised that the anger was oozing out of him along with the sweat and he smiled now when Frank joked, nodded as he panted and talked of his squeaker.

It wouldn't be so bad Georgie thought, spending years down here. It wouldn't really be so bad, especially working with Frank, and he could go on the training schemes, work his way up. They could pay back the debts, they could supply distant traders, he could apologise to the local ones. Yes, perhaps after all, they could manage.

Just before the end of the shift was called they picked up their bait tins and started to walk to the paddy train, then stopped, they had no clothes. They were still in a pile down by the old face and they laughed as they trudged back down the jagged roofed roadway, crouching, wheezing, grinning in the light of their lamps, slapping one another's arms as they finally dressed, then eased their way back for the tadge which they had also forgotten.

'Let's take the tub road, catch up with the paddy train further on,' Georgie said, the laughter still in him, and hope too, because he still had his body hadn't he, he was still a pitman wasn't he – one who could read this old sow like a book.

They stepped over the tub rails, walking close into the walls, passing the manholes, easing back into one as a run of tubs trundled by, feeling the wind and Georgie remembered when he'd been a lad and they'd had a runner and he'd thrown himself hard back into the recess, almost cowering and had been ashamed until his father had told him that anyone who didn't do that was a bloody idiot. 'Bits of coal are a damn sight easier to pick up than bits of Georgie Armstrong.'

They were scrunching down an incline now, Frank ahead, his head down, his shoulders rounded. They were tired, and Georgie thought of the shower he would have and longed instead for a bath in front of the fire with Annie scrubbing his back. He would hold her when he clumped home, he would tell her how sorry he was, how he wished he'd listened. He didn't mind the pit any more, now that he knew it was for good, now that he'd stopped playing games with 'the edge', with the business.

He thought of the letter, felt the anger again, deep inside, churning, twisting, and he didn't hear the tubs behind him, way behind him, thundering and clanging, but suddenly he felt the ground, looked up, heard Frank yelling, 'Runner! runner!' There was nothing but darkness ahead though, he'd lagged too far behind Frank. Where was the bloody manhole? Georgie ran, stumbling, dropping the tadge, dropping his bait-bag, looking for the manhole.

The tubs were closer, louder, his lamp beam was jogging up and down, seeking safety, trying to hear Frank's voice above the noise, sucking all thought from his head except the need to hide because there was a bend in the track, he knew there was. How close was it? The tubs would come off – they'd come off over him.

He was running, running but they were close, so close and then there was the manhole, Frank was standing there, his light guiding him. He'd make it, thank God he'd make it.

But the leading tub leapt the track, the others smashed and spilled and there was only dust and debris and silence and Georgie thought that at last a bomb had got him, at last he'd been clumsy, that the CO would curse, Annie would cry and he wouldn't be able to tell her that there was no pain, just a growing lapping darkness.

Annie knelt on the floor, checking through the returned underwear box by box, the tissue paper piling high around her, but there were no faults and the workmanship was excellent as she had known it would be. She also knew that there was nothing that could be done. She sat back on her heels, then leaned forward, smoothing out the tissue paper, flattening it. It could be used again. She laid piece after piece on the pile, flattening, smoothing, not thinking, just for a moment.

She heard Tom enter the kitchen, heard him come through to the hall, heard the heaviness of his tread and called out quietly, 'Don't worry, lad, I'll think of something. We'll sort it out, but not today. Today, when Georgie and Sarah come in let's all go to the sea, blow the cobwebs off, paddle, let the kids drop seaweed down our backs. We'll leave the thinking until tomorrow – what d'you say?'

She turned. He stood so still, so white and there was no need for him to speak – she knew. The moment she saw him she knew.

There were no words either as he drove to the hospital, just agony at the slowness of the car, the length of the journey, the thought of the tubs, the coal, on top of Georgie, on top of the man she loved more than life itself.

She picked at the threads on her skirt, rolling them into balls, dropping them on the floor. Clenching her hands into fists, gritting her teeth, urging the car faster, faster. 'They don't know,' Tom had said. 'They don't know if he'll live.'

How could he live after tubs and coal had fallen on him? How could he live with that filth deep in his cuts? How could he live? But he must. He had to. How could he not? What did they know with all that dirt? They couldn't know.

'Gracie will bring Sarah, won't she?' Annie said, turning to Tom. 'He'll want to see her, he'll want to talk to her.'

Because of course he would live. He had to live. He'd have just caught a bit of the coal. Yes, that was it. He'd just have caught a bit.

'Course she'll bring her straight away. The coach was due back at three.'

Annie nodded. 'She'll have had a good day. She likes school trips. She can tell him about it. Take him when he's out.'

She felt Tom's hand on her knee and gripped it, the tears coming in great gulping sobs. 'We've come so far, Tom, through so much, he doesn't deserve this. He'll be all right, won't he? He's got to be all right, it's only fair that he's all right.'

Tom held her hand, nodding, but how could anyone be all right after they'd taken the full force of smashed runners for God's sake and who said there was anything fair about this bitch of a life?

Gulls were wheeling over the hospital, the light was brighter as it always was by the sea. Yes, they'd go to the sea, but not today, they'd go when he was better, when his cuts were stitched, his bruises gone. Yes, that's when they'd go. They passed the statue of Queen Victoria looking down her nose at the lobelia – they'd laugh about it, she and Georgie.

Tom stopped the car and they ran now, shoving at the doors, leaving them to slam closed, rushing through into Emergency. A nurse directed them down a corridor, towards a bench. 'Sit down, someone will be with you, I'll bring you a cup of tea.' Her apron rustled, her eyes were kind.

'I don't want tea. Where is he?' Annie said, putting her hand out to the woman. 'Please, where is he?'

'With the doctor, Mrs Armstrong. They've taken him upstairs. He needs surgery but he's in shock.'

Tom pulled her to the bench, went after the nurse, spoke to her, nodded towards Annie. The nurse smiled, spoke quietly and Tom came and sat down with her. 'They know you nursed here now. It'll help.'

Nothing will help, she thought. They've taken him straight up, he needs surgery but he's in shock. They can't operate until he's out of it and so he'll die. He's dead. But no, don't think those words. Don't you dare think those words.

They sat and waited, and she breathed in the smell of disinfectant, of cleanliness, of her past, and then Frank came through from the far end and on him was the dirt of the pit, the sweat-streaked dust and in his eyes was the same look that had been in them all those years ago when he had brought Tom to her here, after he had been beaten by the Blackshirts at Olympia.

He stood in front of her and she smiled, held his hand, drew herself to her feet, smelling the pit on him, 'You've seen him?' she asked.

'I travelled with him, Annie.' He looked at her, then at Tom. 'He thought a bomb had blown up. He didn't know

98

where he was. "Tell her it doesn't hurt,"he said in the ambulance.' He was still looking at Tom.

'How bad, Frank?' She was standing close to him, wanting to hold his face, make him turn to her so that she could see his eyes. It was always there that you saw the truth.

'Very bad, Annie,' He turned now and there it was, in his eyes, and she sat down on the bench again, her hands in her lap, watching the nurses in the distance, watching the clock leap and jump the minutes, seeing the glare of the white tiles, the shine of the floor – all so clean, so very clean.

Staff Nurse called her then, holding open the swing door. 'Sister Manon, come on through.'

'Annie Armstrong now, Staff,' Annie said gently as she left Tom and Frank. 'Annie Armstrong.' She walked with Staff past stretchers, screened examination-beds, then into the lift, up and up, then along another corridor. They stopped outside a door.

'The doctor is with him,' Staff said. 'He remembers you, that's why you're here but also it will help your husband. He needs to hang on, somehow he needs to hang on. Talk to him, Annie. Whatever the doctors say, just keep talking to him for as long as it takes.'

Staff's face was lined, her hair was grey at the temples. 'I don't know you but several do. They know what happened after Singapore too. Will you be all right?'

Annie nodded. The screen was cold in her hand, she breathed deeply, eased herself through, saw the doctor, walked to Georgie who was so clean, so very small somehow, and there was no colour in his face or in his skin.

She laid her hand on his cold fingers which were unhurt though nowhere else seemed to be except his face, his beautiful face. His legs were in splints, there were hot water bottles around his body, a cage to keep the weight of the blankets off. She could smell the shock on him.

'John Smythe, you won't remember me, I was a Junior when you were here.' The doctor's voice was warm, gentle, his eyes were almost the same colour as Tom's. He looked so young.

'Tell me,' she said. 'Just tell me what you've done and what needs doing.'

She listened as he explained how Frank had saved George's life by leaning on the femoral artery the moment he reached him. 'He'd have died then, without his mate,' the doctor said, standing the other side of Georgie, feeling the pulse in his neck. Annie did too. It was so faint.

'Look, how honest do you want me to be?' Dr Smythe said quietly. 'How much can you take?'

'As much as I have to.'

'OK then. I tied the artery, cleaned up the legs, the abdomen. The bones have torn through on both legs. The right is badly splintered, the left not so bad. Lots of dust and debris deep in. I've given him a heart stimulant. His chest is bruised but seems OK. His abdomen likewise. It's his legs. If he lives I'll try to save his legs. If being a very big word Annie. He's very poorly, lost too much blood, very damaged and is too shocked to operate yet.' He paused. 'Now, if we don't operate he's no chance. If I do, he has some chance so we just have to wait and hope that he comes out of shock soon enough to get him into theatre.'

Sarah was in the back seat, sitting with Betsy, not talking, no one was, not even Davy, not even Rob who sat in the front and read the map. Reading made her sick, made her throw up and she wanted to be sick now. Why, when she wasn't reading? She felt the cold sweat come again.

Sarah looked at the lunch-box in her hand. Why did she still have that? She shoved it from her lap and heard the clink of the stones they had collected from the river, heard the clatter of the spoon she had used to eat her strawberries. She'd probably been eating them and laughing while her da was . . . She felt the cold sweat again, the bile and now she was sick all over her lap, all over Bet, who mopped up and poured water from the flask Gracie handed over the seat saying, 'It's the shock.'

Davy gave her his handkerchief and she leaned back against Bet, feeling tired but she mustn't feel tired, not while her da was hurt because he was only hurt, nobody had said he was dead. No, not like Norma's dad. But on the hill Davy had said people died and Terry had said . . .

'Nearly there, we're nearly there.' Aunt Gracie said.

They were shown to the bench where Tom stood, where Frank sat and the grown ups talked of the river, of the wild flowers they had seen, drawn, of the diaries she and Davy would make for the teacher. They didn't talk of Da, why didn't they talk of Da? She sat and didn't listen to them any more. She sat and watched the nurses in their uniforms carrying charts, bringing them tea.

'No thank you,' she said. 'I want to see me da. Where's me mam?'

Gracie pulled her on to her lap but she was too old for that, stupid woman. Stupid, stupid, woman. 'Your mam's with your da.'

I want to be with me da, she wanted to shout and struggled to push herself from Gracie's lap but she was held firmly, soothed, when all she wanted was to be with her da.

A sister came and talked to Tom and he nodded, speaking quietly so that Sarah couldn't hear. Stupid man, stupid, stupid man. He turned. 'Come on, Sarah, let's go and find your mam.'

He took her hand and it felt good. They walked together, following the sister through the swing doors while he told her that her da was very ill. They wanted to operate but he was just too ill at the moment, she must be brave and help her mother.

They went up in the lift and she left her stomach behind. She'd done that when they went to the department store in Newcastle, trying to sell those knickers, those stupid, stupid knickers.

'You'll see your mother in a moment. She'll be able to talk

to you, to tell you more. Your mother is well known here, she was a wonderful nurse,' the sister said, putting her hand on her shoulder and now Sarah wanted to cry, wanted to stop the lift and run out anywhere, run and run and not hear what her mother had to say.

The lift stopped, the doors opened and there was another long corridor but it was lighter. They walked and the sister's shoes slurped on the lino. They waited outside the door. Tom sat down, his face looked so old. Gracie's had looked old too. Sarah walked up the corridor, her shoes were slurping too. Where was her mam? How was her da? She felt the cold sweat again, saw Norma again, heard Davy's voice telling her that people died, heard Terry telling her that her mam should have nursed.

She waited and waited and then her mother came out, her eyes red. She looked at Sarah and held out her arms. 'He's alive, my love, your da's alive, so far.'

Sarah ran at her then, reached her, hit her, slapped her, screamed at her as her mother reeled back. 'It's your fault. You should have been a nurse, shouldn't you? If you were so wonderful you should have been a nurse.'

Tom was up now, holding her arms down, lifting her off the ground as Annie was pushed against the wall. 'For God's sake, Sarah,' he said but Annie came to Sarah, held her, hugged her, and now Sarah wept, clung to her mother, sobbing and Annie looked up at Tom. 'It's all right, bonny lad. It's just too much for her, it's all too much and isn't she only doing what we all want to do – kick and scream and weep?'

Sarah and Annie drank tea that the sister brought. There was sugar in it. 'For shock,' the sister said.

Annie pulled a face when she had gone and Sarah laughed and leant against her mother, listening as Annie told her that they would stay because the doctor wanted to operate. 'If Da is well enough.'

'If he isn't?' Sarah asked.

'We'll have to see.'

Annie took Sarah back into the room with her and they sat one side, with a nurse the other, and talked to him, though he never moved and they could scarcely see, or hear him breathing. Sarah listened as Annie talked of the fright Tom and Frank had given her when they had staggered in from Olympia, how Tom had fought and become well, how the hospital had fought with him, how they would fight with Georgie too.

Sarah told him of her day at the river. The nets the teachers had bought out of the money from the jumble sale they had held last term, how they paddled, how he must get better soon, then they could all go paddling. She looked at Annie, who nodded at her to go on, and Sarah saw that her eyes were full of tears. She turned quickly, not wanting to see this because her mother mustn't cry – mothers didn't cry because if they did, there was nothing safe in the world.

Annie listened, dabbing her eyes as Sarah turned away. The anger had left the child, just as she had known it would.

Annie talked of the letters Georgie had written to her of the plains of Lahore, the corporal's stripe he'd got out of the fighting between the Muslims and the Sikhs – of the Himalayas; the clouds which gathered and dispersed, the geese and ducks that flew overhead, the bullock carts plodding by the stations, the musk-roses.

'Can you smell them, my love?' she murmured, nodding as Tom beckoned for Sarah to go and eat, shaking her head, feeling the pulse in his neck. Was it stronger now?

The nurse checked again too. She thought so too, the doctor also when he was called. Annie helped to refill and replace the hot water bottles, then talked on and on as the hours passed – of the whitebeams with their huge leaves and fruit which changed to colours of the English autumn and which he'd loved. Of the rhododendrons which were purple, not red as those at the convent were – and now she remembered that she had not told Don of his accident.

The doctor checked again, talked quietly to the nurse, left, brought back an older man who examined Georgie, then smiled at Annie.

'I'm Mr Adcock, the Consultant. I examined your husband when he first arrived. We're going to try and operate now. We'll take him into X-ray first but he's too shaky for thorough surgery.'

Annie nodded. 'Please let me fetch my daughter. She must see him – just in case.' Because otherwise she knew that anger could erupt again, and a resentment would be born that would never die.

Mr Adcock turned to the nurse. 'Bring Mrs Armstrong and her daughter down to X-ray, they can catch up with us there. Hurry though.'

They did catch up, they kissed him, touched his hand, though he never moved. Then they sat with Tom, though not the others because Gracie had taken them home, to sleep or to try. Georgie was brought out of theatre and he was still alive, Mr Adcock said in his white gown and cap.

'He has four broken ribs, lacerations of the abdomen, arms, back. I've patched, cleaned and set the right leg, cleaned and sealed the left, and injected a saline solution.' He nodded to the nurse who called Sarah over to hold the door for her as she carried things in and out.

Annie stood now, Tom with her, his arm around her shoulders as Mr Adcock lowered his voice.

'I couldn't do more. He was sinking. We've just got to hope that he keeps holding on. I've asked nurse to make up a bed for you and the child. You too, Mr Ryan?'

Tom shook his head and Annie too. 'No, we'll wait, but Sarah must sleep.'

They sat for the next two days as Georgie sank and rallied and sank. Don came, sat with them, said how sorry he was, brought fruit. They didn't talk. It was too much effort. Don left. They waited, waited, and Annie held Sarah who had slept the first night, but then not again. She stayed with them. Georgie rallied and Adcock said that if he lasted another night he would have a chance and he smiled, for the

104

first time, and the hours crept by until the dawn broke and
Georgie was still alive and now Annie dared to hope.

CHAPTER 7

Georgie opened his eyes to the sunlight streaming into the room and saw shapes to the right and left – what were they? He looked up – what was that? He lay and could feel nothing beneath him or above him. He could hear nothing, he just saw. He looked up again and slowly he knew it was a ceiling. He looked to the left and saw a jug, to the right, a person. It moved. It smiled. It was a woman, a nurse.

He could feel the sheet beneath his back. He moved his fingers and touched the sheet which lay on the frame. He spoke and his voice seemed too loud in the silence and the light.

'Where am I? Where's Annie?' and then darkness came again, floating him away to a warmth which nursed him.

Annie came in when the nurse beckoned and sat with him, pulling Sarah to her, holding her child against her because they must share each moment as it happened.

She spoke softly to Georgie, Sarah too and then paused, knowing that to listen, even sub-consciously, was tiring now that he was back with them.

That night she slept in the bed next to Sarah because Georgie's colour was better, his breathing, his pulse too and there was no pain. So far there was no pain.

Georgie woke before dawn and all he could hear was a clicking noise. The light was on above his bed, the nurse sat quietly, knitting. His mother used to knit, Annie too before she had to cut and sew and now he was remembering the past, Manners, the business. He stirred.

'I must be up tomorrow. I must be back at work. I need to work.' His voice was a croak, his throat was sore. Why was that? 'What's wrong with my voice?'

'You've had an operation,' the nurse said, putting her knitting to one side, feeling his pulse, putting her hand on his forehead. 'Any pain?'

Georgie shook his head. 'No, so I must be better, I need to work.'

The nurse said, 'Sh, no need to worry about work. There's plenty of time for that.'

'There's no time, no time.' But he was drifting again, sinking in the comfortable warmth and darkness.

Annie ate breakfast in the staff canteen, a breakfast which she had not been hungry for, but which she must eat for then Sarah would eat. The bacon was as she remembered, the tinned tomatoes too. She let Sarah pick up the rind and eat it with her fingers.

'I wish it was crisp,' Sarah said, chewing it, pulling a face.

'It never was,' Annie smiled, nodding to the Staff Nurse who had taken her up to Georgie on his first day.

'Mum, why didn't you nurse?' Sarah said quietly, laying the rind on the side of her plate, wiping her fingers on her napkin.

'Because it seemed better at the time for your father to go into the mine. It was just one of those things and perhaps it was a mistake but we must just try and put it behind us, try and live each day as it comes, help your father to recover. Perhaps you should try to finish that diary of the school trip, then you could show it to Da.' Annie drank her tea and longed for a cigarette to calm the ache in her chest because she knew it had been a mistake, of course it had been a mistake, but how do you tell a child her father wanted the edge above all else? You couldn't, especially now, because Sarah had said her father can't have really wanted to go back down if he loved her. Bet had said that it would all fade in time and so it would, it had to.

They sat with him while he slept and talked gently to him and Sarah promised him her finished diary. He opened his eyes and smiled at them, returning the pressure of their fingers and they talked gently, watching his eyes become heavy lidded, his mouth become slack as he drifted, then came back.

'I've got to get back to work.'

'Plenty of time for that,' Annie said, knowing that it would be months, if ever, though she had promised Sarah that he would never go into the pit again.

That evening Tom took Sarah back to Wassingham to sleep in Annie's old room next to Davy. 'It's school for you, young lady,' Annie insisted, 'and yes, don't worry, you'll be here tomorrow evening and I'll ring if I need you. I promise.'

She watched them go, feeling Tom's kiss on her cheek, Bet's too then sat with Georgie, sitting opposite the nurse, smiling when Dr Smythe came in, nodding as he said, 'So far, so good. Out of danger as I said this morning but we'll need to look at those legs again soon.' He checked the chart, smiled at Annie. 'Will you be all right here? I know you're competent. I must talk to nurse for a moment.'

Staff Williams blushed and Annie smiled.

'I think perhaps I can manage, I do hope you like the sweater she's knitting you.'

Dr Smythe laughed. 'The patients seem to like the click of the needles, that's all.'

Oh no it isn't, my fine lad, Annie thought, feeling old as she watched them brush hands on their way to the door. But yes, I expect the patients do like the timeless sound of knitting needles, I always did.

She looked at the chart now, straightened Georgie's sheets, checked the corners. Oh yes, very good, Staff Nurse, she thought, then sat again watching him, glad too be alone with him at last, glad to be able to lean over and kiss his eyes, his lips, his fingers one by one. The smell of his skin was coming back, the shock was almost gone and soon the pain would begin.

'I must get back to work, Annie,' he murmured and she bent over him, holding his face lightly in hers, brushing his lips with her kisses, feeling the response in his.

'No, there's no need.'

'There's no money, Annie. We've debts.'

'I said there was no need. I shall nurse, my love.'

He jerked his head. His fingers gripped hers, saliva ran from his mouth – she released his hand, wiped his lips with gauze. 'I shall nurse as I'm doing now – see, there's nothing wrong with me.'

His eyes were flickering, his mouth working. 'You mustn't, you mustn't.' His voice was rising, his breathing erratic, his head was turning from side to side. 'Get me up out of here. Get me back to work.'

The nurse came in, saw, called the doctor, asked Annie to leave. She sat on the bench, looking out across the city, out at the lightness of the sky above the sea and didn't think, didn't feel, just clenched her hands until they came and said he was asleep again, though he had been very disturbed and that was dangerous now. Very dangerous.

She cursed herself, knowing that she had nearly killed him.

The next morning he told her again that he must return to work and this time she said there was no need to rush, now that they had the mail order up and running. They had used Manners' pants – there was nothing to worry about, nothing, and his face cleared, his fingers touched hers and Staff Nurse smiled at her before she went off duty.

That evening Sarah sat with Georgie while Annie bought Tom tea in the canteen and told him about the lie she had told Georgie.

'But it needn't be a lie,' she continued. 'I'm going to put up the house as security, get a loan, set up a mail shot – it's all I can do.'

Her spoon was stirring, clinking, why did she do that when she was tense? Why did anyone do anything? Tom was

109

holding his cup between two hands, bending his head to it – he always did that when he was thinking.

'We should have done that in the first place, we should have listened to you, bonny lass.'

'No, you can't say that. Manners' order might have worked.'

'Then why didn't it, Annie? What went wrong?' Tom slurped his tea, his shoulders hunched.

'I don't know. It could have been that the outlets weren't as willing to take them as Manners thought or maybe he was over-extended, just couldn't pay us, or he found someone cheaper. We'll never know, but it's happened before and it'll happen again. Come on, let's go for a walk, I could do with some air.'

Tom grinned at her, putting his cup in the saucer, pushing back his chair. 'You could do with a fag, you mean.'

'How well you know me.'

The evening air was cool, the days were so long. Was it really still only the first week of June? It seemed as though it should be December. Annie smelt the roses, touched them. 'Has anyone watered my lavender?

'Bet's been in each day, don't worry.'

'So, what d'you feel about the mail shot, shall we go for it?' Annie asked, drawing deeply on her cigarette, blowing the smoke high into the air, looking back at the hospital. Which was his room?

Tom was breathing in her smoke. 'I'd kill for one of those.'

She shook her head. 'Shall we go for it?'

'It's all we can do, especially as we have Manners' sets.'

Annie stopped, dropped her cigarette on to the ground, stood on it, picked it up, tossed it into the waste bin. 'That's the problem, Tom, we can't use those.' She put her hand up as he turned to her. 'We can't. If Manners saw the advertisement he might just cause trouble, write in explaining that they had been rejected once. We can't risk it for the first one. We've got to make our name and we'll run those out for the next shot, just change the trim.'

Tom nodded. 'Yes, I can see your point.'

'So, I'll have to get a loan against the house, get supplies in not just for the first mail shot but for more of Manners' pants. We must get the same roll runs that we had for those while the suppliers still have them, put it 'under the counter' until we need it. But Georgie mustn't know about the loan or the new designs. Can you get some drawn up?'

They were walking out of the gates now, their heels clicking on the pavement. Were Staff Nurse's needles clicking in Georgie's room? Annie looked at her watch. 'I must get back, be within earshot, just in case.'

Tom linked his arm in hers, turning her, squeezing her. 'What about his legs?'

'I don't know, all I know is that he's alive and that's the first problem over.'

They walked in silence up the drive, into the hospital. 'We'll share the loan,' Tom said. 'I'll sort it out with the bank. I'll bring in the designs, I'll speak to Gracie and Brenda, get them alerted. You just relax, stay with him, get him better.'

'We'll need to set up the advertisement too, book the space, provide the copy and a sketch. Let's make it twenty-eight-day delivery; that will give us three weeks to clear the cheque, package, and a week for delivery.'

Tom smiled, 'Fine. Don't worry.'

The next day she sat with Georgie as he drifted in and out of consciousness and each time his eyes opened he said, 'Why are you here, why aren't you working?'

'Tom is doing it.'

'He can't be, he has work to do. I should be up. I shouldn't be here.'

His breathing was irregular again, his pulse weaker, and the doctor said that she should go, if only for the morning because it was hindering his recovery.

When he came to again he said once more, 'Why are you here, why aren't you working?' and she told him that she was waiting for Tom, that she would go home with him

111

this evening and return tomorrow in the afternoon and then Georgie rested, his breathing calmed, his pulse too.

Sarah wouldn't speak to her in the car, she sat stiff and straight until Tom stopped at the verge and turned. 'The doctors told your mam to come home, get the business going. They told her to do that because your da is worrying, it's making him worse. Now stop being such a claggy little beggar and smile – look, you've made the sun go down.' He pointed to the darkness ahead and around them and Sarah glared, then smiled, then laughed. 'It's gone down because it's ten at night, Uncle Tom, and if that's what the doctors said then that's all right.'

Annie and Tom raised their eyebrows at her.

'So all I have to do to get you to tidy your room next time is to give Dr Smythe a call, is it?' Annie asked, and laughed when Sarah sighed, and said, 'Bet and Aunt Gracie haven't made me do anything while you've been away.'

'Tough, I'm home now, so it'll be the hardship of Armstrong life again my girl, I just don't know how you'll survive.'

They rang the hospital when Tom dropped them off and all was well, then Annie cooked Sarah's favourite macaroni cheese, and they sat together for half an hour, just talking, thinking, stoking the fire. 'He'll be home soon will he, Mum?'

'Very soon I hope, but he needs another operation, just to check his legs.'

That night Annie sat up in bed drawing up plans for the mail shot, confirming twenty-eight-day delivery, deciding on just three sizes and a choice of two colours.

In the morning she rang the wholesalers, reserving more of the Manners cloth, white and cream cotton for the first mail shot. She spoke to the bank manager and they arranged that Tom would liaise for them both, then she drove back to the hospital for the afternoon, holding Georgie's hand and telling him of the advertisement Tom was drawing up. She pushed down the thought that it could all go wrong. It mustn't, it wouldn't.

She stayed at the hospital all night, driving back early the next day, calling in on Brenda and Meg, putting them on stand-by. She gave up her stall in Wassingham Market but arranged to supply the new trader. She ran up samples of Tom's designs. Yes, they were good, the trim was broderie anglaise, quite expensive but would look good on the advertisement. Could they get free publicity, a feature? She would write to the newspaper in which they set the advert. Tom had decided on *The Mail*.

She drove back to the hospital, taking Bet with her and now there were two pairs of needles clicking and Georgie smiled then and laughed and the doctor had a glint in his eye and the Staff Nurse a ring on her finger. Annie wished them well when the doctor called her out of the room, telling her that they were operating on Georgie the next day, they were concerned for his legs, especially the left.

She told Georgie quietly as Bet drank tea in the canteen with Sarah who had arrived with Tom and Gracie. He nodded, his eyes sunken now with pain, though he said nothing, and she wanted to hold him, take him far from here, but all he said was, 'But the business is all right? The mail shot is going through?'

When Tom took the others home, Georgie told her to go too. 'You must have work to do, or it'll not go well, you know.'

She drove home with Sarah and there was no stiffness between them now, there was just fear at the thought of tomorrow. They ate without appetite sitting either side of the range, their plates on their laps, and Bet stayed with them, taking Annie's plate from her as the phone rang and she ran to pick up the receiver. Was it the hospital?

No, it was a market trader from South Warnsted, one of those who had dropped her. 'We heard about your man at a meeting last night,' he said. 'Deliver what you can, we'll take the lot.'

Five more rang that night and two in the morning. She told Georgie as she sat with him and his smile brightened eyes that were clouded with pain and a face deeply lined.

He was wheeled to the theatre at two and Tom brought Sarah as Annie had asked. Together they sat in the corridor for the two hours it took, waiting for Mr Adcock to come out and tell them that he was fine, he had come through, his right leg and been tidied up nicely though his left was still giving cause for concern.

The Staff Nurse took Sarah for a cup of tea and Mr Adcock told Annie that he might have saved the left leg, he wouldn't know for a while and she nodded because what else could she do.

Tom held her though, when Adcock had gone, gripping her tightly, not speaking. How could he speak without his voice breaking because Annie was so tired, so thin, so brave, and so was Georgie and none of this was fair.

That night Georgie was in post-operative shock but rallied in the morning, then sank, then rallied, and sank again. His cheeks were hollow, his eyes too and Annie signed the forms that Tom brought in from the bank, reading them line by line because there were to be no mistakes this time. Georgie would need a firm to run. Yes he would, he bloody well would she said inside her head, pushing aside the look of him, pushing aside the smell of him, the weakness of his pulse, the quietness of his breathing. She wouldn't let him die.

She took Sarah in to see him when she arrived, telling her it was much worse than it looked, much much worse. He stabilised in the afternoon and the pain tore at him, and his eyes sank deeper into their sockets until they gave him pain killers and he drifted again.

Annie used Staff Nurse's phone to ring Brenda and Meg, setting them on to work on the traders' stock, telling them to give the completes to Tom and he would bring them in for checking. She couldn't get home tonight.

'How is he?' Brenda asked.

'Holding his own.' And he was, just.

She sent Sarah to bed in the hospital room at eight p.m. and checked through the stock. All but ten were perfect. Meg's smelt of smoke again and she told Tom to hang them on her airer overnight. Brenda could re-do the rejects. Could Gracie deliver to the traders tomorrow?

Tom nodded, showing her the figures for the week. Thanks to the traders there would be enough to pay the household bills. He also brought her a letter for Georgie from Don, asking when he could come and visit.

'Not yet,' Annie said, looking towards Georgie's room. 'Best not yet.'

The next day Adcock told her that the antibiotics had lost the battle, the leg was gangrenous and must be removed if he was to be saved, and Annie nodded. Somehow she had always known it, and her heart broke for Georgie and for Sarah when she told her because the child looked old and crushed and in pain – just as she felt.

In the theatre Adcock worked fast, severing the left leg well above the knee, sewing the flap of skin over the bone but Georgie was weakening, his pulse was becoming faint. He tidied, finished. 'The heart's stopped,' the anaesthetist called.

There was a stillness, a silence, then Adcock jabbed with a needle, took Georgie's wrist, and felt nothing. He waited and then there was a thread, a flutter. 'He's there.'

Adcock finished, and George was wheeled to intensive care.

Adcock spoke to Annie. 'He's in shock again but he should recover, he's very strong, though there's always a risk, my dear.'

Annie nodded. She knew that, oh yes, she knew that. She and Sarah waited. It seemed to be all that they'd ever done.

Georgie woke fourteen hours later and Staff Nurse was there, but no knitting – how strange – then the darkness came.

He woke again to streaming sunlight, to searing pain, to parched thirst, to a nurse who was holding his wrist.

115

'Please, it hurts.'

'It'll ease,' she soothed, wetting his lips which were cracked and dry.

It didn't ease, even when Annie came it didn't ease and he couldn't bear the touch of anyone's hand, even hers. He couldn't bear the pain.

They gave him more pain killers and for a moment he slept. When he woke the pain was there, digging deeper, deeper, and Annie was gone. He called but she didn't come. He was alone with it and he couldn't bear that, it was coming again and he needed her.

Then she was there, thank God she was there, but don't touch me. Don't touch me he screamed, but his lips didn't move. She hadn't touched him. She knew, she could see inside his head because she was part of him but why wasn't she stopping the pain?

Annie made Tom take Sarah away. She mustn't see this, she mustn't see her father's glistening, grey, waxy face, the eyes which knew no one, which sank deeper with each hour into the darkening hollows.

Georgie called again, Why? The pain was fading, then it was here again and there was sunlight. It hurt his eyes. The pain was sweeping through him, clawing at him and he groaned and groaned again and then darkness came, and there was nothing.

Annie let Sarah into the room now. 'He's in shock, he's unconscious, now you must go back to the children's ward, help there until I call you.' Her voice was quite calm, she was too tired for it to be anything else.

She helped the nurses to roll him, to avoid lung congestion. She checked the garments that Tom brought over, checked the advertisement. It would go in in two weeks' time.

'Three,' Tom said, coming again the next evening. 'One of your Glasgow buyers rang. He wants me to take up some samples. He's decided he underspent his budget after all and wants a presentation but is it OK if I leave you?' He nodded towards Georgie's room. 'I'll be away two nights.'

'Yes, go. You can't do anything and by then it'll be decided one way or another.'

Georgie came to in the afternoon of the next day and Annie gave him a drink, putting the spout to his lips, letting the water trickle into his mouth. There was a stubble on his chin and his face was less waxy. The pain killers were given again and took the edge off the pain more efficiently now.

They changed the dressings as they had done each day and Staff Nurse peeled off the last of the lint from the raw wound as Annie leaned across, hiding the stump from Georgie, talking to him gently. She saw the naked agony in his face even though they had soaked the dressing in warm water and was glad that when he was unconscious at least he was spared this.

She sat and talked with him in the afternoon, telling him of the Glasgow buyer, of the diary Sarah had at last finished.

'Why aren't you working?' he murmured, too filled with pain to speak properly.

'I am, I have it here.' She held up the traders' pants.

'Those aren't Manners' pants.'

'No, these are for the traders. The mail shot goes out in three weeks.'

The pain came through the pain killer, it roared and raged and took him away from Annie, took him down dark tunnels, twisting and turning with him until day became night and now he woke again and there was a rim of light, a nurse but no knitting, thank God, for the click, click would have jarred on the pain.

He looked for Annie. She was there, watching him, smiling.

'I wish they'd cut the bloody thing off,' he groaned, wanting to touch her, but not being able to bear the pressure.

'They have, my darling,' she said.

'No they haven't, I can feel my toes. Why don't they cut it off?'

The morning came and he woke again and there was Tom with Annie and he was holding her hand. Georgie was glad someone was.

117

'It hurts,' he said to Tom. 'If they took it off the pain would go.'

Tom looked at Annie. 'They have bonny lad, they've taken it off.'

'That's what Annie said, but they haven't because it still hurts.'

The nurse told Annie she must get some sleep that night and Tom insisted too, and she fell on to the bed and slept though she dreamt of the camps, of Prue, of Lorna, of the parade ground.

Again Georgie woke and there was the nurse, and the light, but no sun. It was night then. His mind was clearer, the pain was less, wasn't it? Yes, a bit less, he felt different, stronger. He turned his head. Annie wasn't there.

'Is she sleeping?' he asked the nurse. She nodded.

He lay still, thinking of Annie's face, her eyes, her laugh, her voice. What had she said? Tom had been here too, holding her hand, talking. He'd been talking. What had he said? Georgie looked up at the ceiling, floating, drifting in and out of pain. Oh God, why didn't they take it off?

Then he remembered what Annie had said and Tom too, so it must be true, but what did it matter – there was still the pain, which was swelling, growing, taking him back into the darkness.

CHAPTER 8

Georgie improved a little that night, more the next day, the greyness went from his face and the pain eased though they still injected pain killers to calm his tortured nerve endings. He didn't ask again about his leg, so Annie just waited.

At the end of the week he told her that she shouldn't be sitting here while Tom and Gracie did all the work and he smiled at her. 'Get on, or there'll be nothing for me to do when I get back on my feet.'

Annie felt despair. He still didn't know. She looked at the nurse, who shook her head. So she grinned. 'OK slave driver, I'll be back at four.'

'Make it six,' Georgie said, 'Then I can have me tea in peace.'

He watched her go, seeing the looseness of her clothes, the tiredness in her shoulders. It would give her time to eat hers in peace too. He lay back on the pillows and now, with just the nurse there, he lifted the sheets. Yes, they had taken his leg off. He really was a cripple. They had been telling him the truth and he wept the tears he had not wanted any of his family to see, knowing that they must be hidden again by this evening.

Annie sewed most of the day, then checked the Glasgow garments which Brenda and the homeworkers had been sewing. Oh God, there was still the smell of smoke on Meg's and they needed to be packed tonight. Annie walked round to Meg, standing on the step, asking her if she'd work in Annie's house because if there was no time to air the clothes

119

now, what would it be like when the mail shot began next week – if it worked that is, and it had to.

That afternoon she talked to Tom, checking that last month he had put in for planning permission for Briggs' warehouse. He had. 'We should know if it's been granted this week, then we'll be set up for when we need to take on the premises.'

'Thank heavens for that. Well done, Tom, we'll have to take it the moment we can. It's going to be chaos next week, absolute chaos.'

'We hope,' Tom said.

'It's just got to be. It's going to sink in soon about his leg and he'll need something to get hold of, to work at.'

Georgie listened to Mr Adcock telling him that losing a leg was a great inconvenience but not fatal. 'Mobility can be obtained with a false leg and of course, wheelchairs. We'll be getting you along to physio soon, and then to the special unit where we'll fit your leg.'

Georgie nodded. He smiled until Adcock left, then sank back on to the pillows, slept again and dreamt that he was running across the sand with Sarah, chasing Annie, catching her, pushing seaweed down her neck.

He smiled again when Annie came, kissing her, smelling the summer on her hair, her skin. He'd forgotten about seasons, it was just dark or light in here. He listened as she talked of the last minute preparations for the mail shot and Meg's sewing machine which they had installed on the kitchen table.

'Geoff smokes, that's why I used to hang them on the airer, I just didn't want to tell you but of course you'd have understood.'

'Of course,' he said as she bathed him, washing his arms, his chest, his leg.

'I know about my leg,' he said then, quite quietly, casually, and he was proud of himself. 'I know and it doesn't matter, I can learn to walk again, it's just an inconvenience.' He looked at the ceiling, at the wall, and then at her. 'It's all right, Annie, tell everyone it's all right.'

She touched his face, kissed his lips gently. 'Inside you must be destroyed but I shall tell them because it will be. I promise you it will be.'

He wouldn't talk about it any more and so Annie told him of the greenfly which were annoying Bet, of the kids' gang and the carts they were making out of old prams, of the world which seemed a million miles away to him and he was glad he was here, hidden behind the nurses and these walls, out of sight of that world which hadn't yet seen him as he was now and into which he must one day stumble.

Annie came in over the weekend with Sarah, dressing his stump and she didn't speak then, just concentrated, as he should have done, he thought.

'Where did you get the capital for the advertisement?' he asked when she had finished, when he could trust his voice not to shake from the pain.

'Don't worry about that,' Annie said, taking the bowl from the room. But couldn't she see that he did worry? But then he felt tired again, so tired and the agony that was his stump took all his energy.

'Where did you get it?' he asked Annie again when she returned.

'The profit from the Glasgow deal,' she replied because she had had time to think in the sluice.

But he didn't hear, he was asleep.

'He's just not thriving at the moment,' Staff Nurse told Annie. 'It often happens when they discover the facts. Just keep on as you're doing, it's fine.'

The advertisement appeared on Tuesday and the first orders came through that morning.

'They must be from the newspaper staff,' Gracie said, opening the envelopes, stamping the coupons, passing them to Annie who entered them into the book, packing up their orders, stacking them under the window, going out to bank the cheques, to wait for them to clear before sending the orders off.

On Wednesday there was a deluge of mail, and they opened the envelopes, stamped coupons, filled the orders from stock, and told the homeworkers to keep on with the traders until their orders were filled and only then moving on to the mail shot, since they had enough in stock.

That evening Annie delivered the traders' stock on her way to Georgie, grateful that they didn't ask for sale or return any more – smiling when they asked how Georgie was.

'Coming on, he'll be riding a bicycle soon,' she laughed. That night she told Georgie of the two hundred orders already received, that she needed him alongside them, longing to be able to lift the darkness which hung behind his eyes.

He was even quieter tonight, feverish and he wouldn't eat. 'Ring me,' she told the staff. 'I must know if he's any worse.'

'It's because he knows, he's trying to adjust, he's depressed, but you're doing fine.'

She sewed all night, without rest, she had to re-order from Glasgow, she had to write up the schedule for the homeworkers. She rang the hospital at dawn. His fever was down and his spirits too. Is it any wonder, she thought. 'Shall I come?'

'No, he'll only start fretting because your nose isn't actually on the grindstone. He needs some time to himself to accept things.'

At eight-thirty the postman knocked, emptied his sack on to the floor. 'Mrs Norris is right glad you warned her of this,' he said, pushing back his cap. 'Me wife sews you know.'

'No, I didn't, get her to bring round a sample, Joe, today if possible.' One of the homeworkers that Tom had picked out had moved with her husband to Nottingham last week.

Annie packed, stacked, then cut and sewed until lunch, then checked through the girls' work, approving Joe's wife's sample, keeping her in reserve. She drove with Sarah to see Georgie in the evening, her head aching, her eyes and fingers sore, but her smile was warm though he looked no better – and so quiet.

They sat and she knitted because he liked it, but her hands were sore as the wool rasped and rubbed. She dressed his stump again, soaking the old dressing, easing it, feeling his pain as though it were her own. Her hands were trembling, the air was heavy, the smell of healing flesh strong. She tried not to breathe, then to take shallow gasps. Don't rush, you'll hurt him. Don't rush, whatever you do don't rush. There, it was done.

She took the soiled dressings to the sluice, putting them in the waste, the dishes in the sluice, leaning against the wall, then putting water on her face, more and more. She was tired, that was all.

She sat with him, knitting, always knitting, until eight-thirty.

'Sarah must get to bed, she has school, my love,' she told him, though he was sleeping again.

'He'll be all right, you're doing fine,' Dr Smythe told her and she wanted to scream because if she was doing fine, why wasn't he improving?

She worked when Sarah was in bed, and the same again the next day, but only after her visit, and the next, and still the orders were pouring in and she should have felt excited, pleased, but she didn't because still he was not thriving and exhaustion was clawing at her. Now she couldn't get the smell of the dressings out of her head, and when she grabbed at an hour's sleep she dreamt and woke herself up chanting ichi, ni, san, yong.

On Saturday there were more orders, many more orders, and they opened, stamped, entered, banked, then Tom sent her to the hospital because they could sew, package and check between them, he said.

'Now scoot.'

As she drove she talked to Sarah about the fields of ripening wheat they passed, of the villages they drove through, of Bill Haley's new song which Sarah loved, of the need for a

123

catalogue that they could send out with the orders to save on advertising costs.

'I must get Tom to design some more sets. We could extend our range.'

'I wonder how Dad is?'

'Better, much better I think. Do you think we should have a catalogue?' Annie asked because she didn't want to think of Georgie's despair which she couldn't touch, or the dressings she must do yet again.

'Oh I don't know, Mum, I just want to see Dad.'

There was silence in the car. Yes, I want to see him too. I'm just tired, she thought and her hands felt slippery on the wheel. She wiped her left one on her skirt.

It was as though the car drove itself now, down the drive, parking near Adcock's reserved space. It was as though her feet knew their own way to his room, it was as though her smile flicked on independently as her eyes took in the darkness in his, the flatness of his voice. Her hands became busy and they were nothing to do with her, soaking the dressings, peeling them, redressing. They washed themselves in the sluice, again and again, then dried themselves, again and again.

She walked back to the room, but they were still not dry. She rubbed them down her skirt, putting on her smile, walking into the room where Sarah was sitting, where the nurse was taking his temperature.

'Fever again today, Annie,' Staff Nurse said, 'and he won't eat you know. Can you try him with some ice cream?' She handed the bowl to Annie who sat down by the bed.

'I'm not a child,' Georgie said faintly. 'Just not hungry.'

Annie held the spoon in her hand, then dug it into the ice cream, lifting it, carrying it to his mouth. 'Into the hole then,' she said, 'the rabbit wants to go into the hole,' and the room was so hot, her hands so slippery and it was Prue that she saw there, the light of madness in her eyes. It was the sound of the guards, shouting and screaming that she heard and she couldn't breathe, couldn't move and then she turned, looked at Sarah.

'Feed him,' she said thrusting the bowl at her, walking from the room, down the corridor, down the stairs, not the lift, out into the air, breathing in deep gulps, clearing her head of images, of sounds, gripping her own arms, holding herself tight.

She sat on the bench, feeling its cool hardness and then she heard the gulls, saw the dark brick of the hospital, felt the cotton of her dress, looked at her hands. They were quite dry. She looked at them again, they were scored with needle marks, they were sore from opening envelopes, from entering, from stamping. They were sore from knitting, God damn it.

She rose then, walking back to the entrance, taking the lift, going back into the room, taking the bowl from Sarah.

'He won't have it, Mum.'

'Oh yes he damn well will.' Annie said because there was no time for either of them to sink, they had a future to get on with. 'Oh yes you will, my bonny lad. Open up.'

Georgie looked at her. 'I don't want any.'

'Well I want you to have some, because until you start really getting better, my love, we can't have you home. We need you there, for us, and for the business. We can't manage without you, so come on, eat up.'

Staff Nurse came back into the room but Annie didn't care.

'Come on, Georgie, you're not doing justice to yourself. Get this down you, get yourself sorted out and come home.'

Annie held the spoon, looking into his face, into eyes which were still dark and dead.

'Mum,' Sarah shouted. 'Stop it, how can you, he's ill!'

Staff Nurse said, 'He's not ill, he's better now, or he could be, your mother's quite right – just you remember that my girl. It doesn't do anybody any good to spoil them. We've been waiting for this to happen.'

She stood behind Annie and neither of them looked up as Sarah ran from the room.

'Come on, Georgie,' Annie said again. 'I can't do it all on my own. I need you to get better, to come home.'

He opened his mouth then and his eyes were brighter, she fed him once, then gave him the spoon. 'Come on then, you know you like strawberry.'

'I like you better, Annie Armstrong,' his voice was still faint but now there was a smile and it lit up both their eyes.

They managed to keep their supply level-pegging with demand and Annie pinned up a series of coloured stock control boards giving an instant picture of availability. These she updated as the garments came in and went out. They needed to set on another homeworker, to set up another design, plan for the next mail shot, sort out that catalogue.

'We need some coverage too, I'll chat to the newspaper, tell them of our success, try and swing it this time, they weren't interested for the first one. Talk to the nationals as well can you, Tom? See if the fashion page will mention it in *The Mail* since we're placing the advertisement with them. We'll set Joe's wife on, isn't her name Jean?'

They received requests for outsize and filled them – it was surprising how little sleep a person really needed, Annie thought, brushing aside her headaches, her trembling hands.

She asked Mr Adcock to move Georgie into the general ward and Staff Nurse concurred. 'He needs company, he needs to be eased into other people,' Annie said.

Adcock agreed and asked her if she'd like a job. She thought he was joking but he wasn't, or only half.

'Sorry, I've got to get this lot on the road,' she answered because she didn't need to prove anything any more did she, she had pushed back the shadows, hadn't she?

'We'll send out a catalogue with the next one or two, shall we?' Annie asked Georgie the next day as he sat up in bed, squeezing his hand round rubber balls, trying to build up his strength.

'Yes, let's sort that out, it's a good idea. By the way Don's been in, talked quite a lot. I told him about you, and the business. He was surprised, I was proud.'

'Did Maud come?'

'Towards the end. Still flashing her nails. Thought I'd be in a room on me own, she was quite put out – all these beds, all these people and no one quite knowing where they'd been.'

'Nice of them to come. Did they eat your fruit?' Annie looked at the spidery grapeless stalks. Georgie nodded and they laughed.

'Left me some chocs though, take them home, pig yourself, you've got too thin, bonny lass.'

Annie left them in the cupboard, 'Share them with this lot,' she said, looking round the ward, grinning at the other patients, and visitors.

Georgie nodded. 'I'll lick all the nut ones first though. What about the tour, are you going?'

He didn't look at her as he said it. Annie looked out across the ward.

'Couldn't, I'll need to be home when you get back. I shall expect to be snatched up and tangoed down the street, just to shock the neighbours.'

He laughed. 'Maybe a waltz.'

'I'll settle for that and we shall picture Tom presenting his knicks and bras to all the female buyers. They'll love it.'

Two days later they received another large order from Glasgow and they were tripping over one another in the dining-room, trying to check, trying to pack, snapping at each other, making errors, and in the kitchen there was nowhere for Annie and Sarah to eat because Meg's sewing machine was on the table and her garments had to be moved from there each evening or they smelt of the food they cooked.

The mail-shot coupons were still arriving in sacks. Annie ordered a further roll from the supplier. He was pleased, surprised.

'Really taking off then?'

127

'It's wonderful, and we've a buyer's re-order from Glasgow too, so stand by your phone in the autumn after the tour, we'll need more, if your prices are still competitive, Jack.' Annie laughed, knowing that word would travel fast via Jack, or Big mouth as he was known in the trade.

'So eat your heart out Manners,' she said to herself as she poured the tea.

Tom came in that afternoon, leaving the door, open, propping himself up on the drainer.

'Planning Permission's come through for the conversion of Briggs' place, so come and go over these with me, Gracie's just coming.' He waved the balance sheets at her, hauled her into the yard, pushing an upturned tub towards her with his foot, shutting the door.

Annie sat there, relishing the peace of a sewing machineless world. 'This is where I need to set up my office, on an upturned tub next to a downbeat pigeon loft. What more could I want, and if it rains, I shall just roost *in* the loft – perfect. I can even smoke.' She pulled out her cigarettes, tapped one out, lit it, inhaled. God, she was tired. God, it was noisy in there. God, it was a mess and this evening she must take time to clear up, then just sit and talk to Sarah, and most of all listen to her day – there had been no time last night, or the night before.

'Well, while you're sitting there, puffing, have a read of these.' Tom handed her the balanced sheets, smiling at Gracie as she came through into the yard. 'Look at the profit so far.'

Annie looked. She couldn't believe it. She'd been working so hard she hadn't even thought of profit and loss, of money. She had just paid the bills that had to be paid, worked, visited the hospital, and slept when she could.

'Tom this is wonderful, we're in profit. It's that Glasgow one that's done it. It's tipped us over, well over.'

'Right, and we've already paid up for the next mail shot because we're using Manners' stock aren't we?'

Annie smiled. 'Yes, we'll get away with that now. We'll

128

change the trim, it wouldn't be worth his while to start rumours, the success of this will stifle anything like that. We can just get on and set up the next range, and the wholesale range. The traders are really picking up now and I've had three more Madam shops this afternoon. Big-mouth has done us proud.'

She passed the sheets to Gracie, drawing in on her cigarette, arcing it out over the garden.

'You are so disgusting. That'll have to stop.' Tom groaned.

'It's for luck, bonny lad. It brings us luck, don't you know anything?' Annie said softly, leaning back, looking at him. 'Because you're thinking what I'm thinking, aren't you?'

Gracie looked up at Annie, then at Tom who was nodding, grinning. 'What are you two up to?'

Tom raised an eyebrow. 'Briggs' place.'

'We can afford it.' Annie leaned forward, her arms on her knees. 'We could move in over a weekend. We'd need lights, shelving, tables immediately, heating by the end of the month and we've just about enough money for it. We'll get everyone under one roof, Gracie and I wouldn't have to deliver cutouts, or pick up completes, or liaise between the two houses. We wouldn't have to eat on our knees, our kids would have their homes to themselves – and we've got to get set up and out of here before Georgie comes home anyway.' She stood up. 'Let's do it now – move in when the lease is finalised. Shouldn't take long. Bill's been in the picture about it and he'll know about the planning permission being granted – or he will when we get round there.'

Tom stood up, walked to the cigarette butt, picked it up, dropped it in the dustbin. 'The only thing is . . .'

'I know. There'll have to be a no smoking rule. It's going to bleeding well kill me, lad.'

Annie and Tom called in on Bill the next morning and she had been right, he had heard that the planning permission had come through. He had also been informed late last night by his area manager that Briggs' Warehouse was part of a

129

parcel of properties taken over by a London-based consortium. The lease was still available but the price had tripled.

Annie looked at Bill, his face reddening, his eyes flicking from her to Tom. 'I'm so sorry. There's been no interest for months. I can't understand it but it's all part of a bigger deal that's been handled in Newcastle. It's been on offer there as well and they didn't let me know this was going on. I'm sorry Annie, Tom.'

She looked at Tom who had gone pale and clenched her hands to keep them steady, hardly able to believe what she had heard, knowing that all their profits would be wiped out. They needed heaters by the end of the month, phones installed, electricians paid, carpenters for the work benches, the shelving, and there was the material Jack was keeping under the counter for the next mail shot. She looked at Tom.

'It's the only place here and we've got to stay in Wassingham, we promised ourselves that. Talk to them, Bill, talk to them.' Annie was standing now, turning to leave. 'Ring me at home when you have. Come on Tom.'

She cut out, checked, packed, talked to Sarah as they drove to Georgie, asking how long she could bear to eat on her knee, laughing when she said, 'I like it, Mam, you don't nag about me keeping me elbows in, or putting me elbows on the table, or clattering the plate.'

They walked down the ward, nodding, waving, chatting to the men. She told Georgie of the packing, Big-mouth, the three Madam shops. She showed him the preliminary sketches Tom had done for the autumn tour and asked for his go-ahead.

'There'll be more for the next mail shot.'

She didn't tell him that they would be using Manners' stock because he had thought they were using that first. She would merely bring in the designs they had used on the first shot, the samples too. Neither did she tell him of the premises because he would ask to see the figures and would veto it because Annie knew that another loan would be needed and she knew that Georgie would not go into debt, not after

Manners. And she knew that they must move, because Sister had told her that on Monday they would be trying him in a wheelchair, that soon he would be transferred to the special unit where he would learn to walk again, and soon he would be home.

Bill had spoken to his area manager who had asked for a revised price for the lease. It was refused. The bank agreed a loan, shared by Annie and Tom again because they had no choice but to accept the consortium's terms – Georgie was coming home, there were no other suitable premises, there never would be in Wassingham. Their solicitor forced through the paperwork. The consortium co-operated because otherwise Annie threatened to withdraw and open up in the next village. 'Eager to have their bloody money,' Tom cursed.

'Afraid that they'll be left with a pup,' said Annie.

It was agreed that they would move in over the weekend.

'It's as though some bugger is second guessing us, Tom,' Annie said. 'It's as though every time we have enough to make it just that little bit easier the rug is pulled from under us.'

They moved in at nine a.m. Saturday morning, brushing, washing paintwork, until their hair was thick with dust and the air too. The children painted the woodwork when Annie had finished the whitewash.

She cleaned the lavatories, remembering Uncle Albert's and how she had hoped that he had chilblains from the cold and an inky bum from the newspaper he used because he was too stingy to replace it with proper stuff. 'Horrid old man,' she murmured, then raised her voice and asked Tom to start the tables out in the yard. 'We'll cover them with tarpaulin if it looks like rain and no sawing and hammering when I've just painted or you'll know what its like to be glossed from head to toe.'

They ate bread and cheese at lunchtime. The men drank beer but not too much for there was still the wiring to be done, the shelves to be erected, the tables to be finished.

Annie and Gracie pretended not to hear the curses as drills

were broken or hammers dropped though Davy and Sarah kept a notebook and wrote all the new words down.

They ate fish and chips on the floor by the light of hurricane lamps and laughed at the sight of Tom's back which was white from the gloss paint he had leaned against.

They laughed the next day too, as the tables were put together and Rob asked where the union man was to have his office.

'Union woman you mean,' Sarah said. 'Or hasn't Uncle Tom told you all about the birds and the bees.'

'No unions necessary here yet, lad,' Tom said wagging his finger at Sarah.

'No unions necessary at all,' Annie said. 'We've only got six workers and that includes Gracie and me.'

'We're all in it together – like a big family. There'll be a bonus scheme with the profits. Some will be ploughed back, the rest shared,' Tom added.

Sarah looked at Annie. 'Well, we kids deserve a share too, look how hard we've worked.'

Annie looked at Tom and Gracie, then at Betsy. 'We'll see, when the weekend's over.'

The electrics were finished at three, the tables too. Brenda's husband had helped Tom without charge.

They moved in the machines, stacked the cloth, the trimmings, everything. Annie put up her stock-control charts and asked Tom about printing up some two shilling discount vouchers 'off the next purchase' to be put into each packaged order.

'Good idea. They'll come back to us. We can build it into the price to some extent.'

They moved in her rotary cutter, Tom's design board. The carpenter erected a partition for Annie's office. The phone would be installed on Monday. 'I'll ring round and tell everyone our new number then send a circular to all potential customers.'

They erected a partition for Tom's design department. He

placed his board beneath the skylight, and asked for just one more shelf.

Betsy brought them flasks of tea at nine o'clock. 'Bloody ambrosia,' Tom said, drinking his in great gulps.

'I've brought in a kettle, and put in a box of provisions,' Bet said. 'We'll not be able to run a business without a good cuppa.'

Annie sat back on a table, took out her cigarettes, put one in her mouth, then looked up as a silence grew. Bet, Gracie, Tom, Rob, the carpenter, Sarah and Davy, even Brenda's husband were all shaking their heads and she took it from her mouth, put it back into the packet and joined in the laughter and the conversation which swelled and continued until late into the night.

In the morning Annie told the staff that they were forbidden to eat or drink and especially to smoke at their tables. They could make tea in the restroom and smoke there in their breaks.

She told them of the revised Glasgow order which she had taken this morning when she rang the store. She pointed to the coupons which Joe had brought to the premises.

'We're still inundated but it's getting better so there'll be a new mail shot soon. Don't worry, we can cope with the existing Manners' stock, we'll just be altering the trim to fill the first orders, and only then making up new ones. We are paying a basic wage – I don't believe in piecework, as you know. And there will be a bonus as and when we are operating at a profit. Sadly the leasehold has tripled. It has swallowed our profit and we now have debts to repay but the direct and indirect orders are pouring in and growing all the time. Things will improve,'

She worked throughout the day, walking to the restroom frequently to light up, sucking the smoke in deeply, wishing the trembling in her hands would stop, and the headaches too. Brenda said, 'It's not fair you know, Annie, Jean smokes and she can't keep leaving her machine.'

Annie nodded, 'You're right,' she said and walked back to

her office, then to the cutting machine. She must keep her hands busy and her mouth shut. How had Tom stopped and not screamed at them all every minute of the day? Didn't Brenda know what it was like to starve yourself?

Gracie took over in the afternoon and Annie visited Georgie with Sarah. As they walked up the stairs to the ward Sarah said, 'When we were laughing yesterday I forgot Da, forgot he was in here.'

Annie nodded. 'I did too, but that's what he'd want. It means things are getting better. We're not so worried. Soon he'll be home.'

They walked down the ward, waving to the men, saying hello, waving to Georgie who was sitting up in his bed at the end of the row.

'Cor, been riding up and down the ward in his throne today he has,' Old Jed said.

Annie smiled, not understanding, then Andy called from the left. 'Proper little Hitler. Telling staff to turn left, right and then fast forward. Come and have an apple, Annie, lovely they are, the Missus brought them.'

Annie moved across as Sarah ran down to Georgie. 'Hello Mrs Ganby, how do you put up with this husband of yours?' Annie took the apple, feeling Andy grip her fingers, pull her closer.

'He's been in the wheelchair today. He was faint, frightened. He's not himself,' Andy said quietly.

'Thanks, Andy.' Annie touched his hand, smiled at Mrs Ganby, took the apple across to Georgie, watched his empty smile as they talked, his shoulders which were straight and tense. She told him of the move, of the help that Sarah had been.

'You can see from her hair,' she laughed.

His laugh was strained.

'The girls are busy. Everything's set up, there's a new order from Glasgow and there's talk of another from Edinburgh.'

Georgie nodded, she waited, listening as Sarah told him of her new cart, the latest Elvis Presley, Bill Haley's *Rock around the Clock*, of Annie's quick temper now that she wasn't smoking, then there was silence.

'So, how are you, darling?' Annie said.

'Fine, just fine.'

Staff Nurse took his temperature, his pulse, straightened his sheets, caught Annie's eye and gestured towards her office. Annie nodded, she would stop and talk when visiting ended.

'You look better, you've some colour.'

'So I should, I've been having my exercise. I've been having my constitutional. I've been pushing myself up the ward in a wheelchair, practising to be a cripple.'

Sarah's face went blank with shock, she turned to Annie as the bell rang and the wives bent to kiss their husbands, squeeze their hands, tuck in their blankets. Annie did all these, then took Sarah's hand and his, saying to both of them. 'There will be days like these but it will improve. You'll be frightened now, it'll seem strange to be upright, to have to be helped. You'll feel faint but just remember, you'll come home and pick up your life again and that's what we want more than anything else because we love you, we admire you.'

She held Sarah's hand as they walked down the ward, turning to wave at Georgie, feeling her own tears but knowing he must never see them fall at the thought of him in a wheelchair.

Georgie watched them go. God, she looked so tired and Sarah so small – he must be crazy. 'Annie, Annie,' he called but she was gone and he hadn't told her that he'd wanted to cling to the bed, stay where it was safe, that he hadn't wanted to look down once he was in the chair and see the gap where his leg should have been. He hadn't wanted to be pushed down the ward so that everyone could see it too. He couldn't tell her that he loved her, wanted her to hold him, make him better, bring back his leg, take him to a time before any of this had happened.

He couldn't tell her that they would be moving him to the special unit now that his stump had healed sufficiently for a leg to be fitted. He would practise walking again and then he could come home and pick up his life. He couldn't tell her that that thought frightened him more than death, because what sort of a life would it be? They had all moved on without him.

CHAPTER 9

Georgie wheeled himself down the ramps on to the grass of the special unit. It was his first morning and the scent of roses hung in the August air. All around were other patients in chairs, wheelchairs and on crutches. It made him feel at home.

He sat and watched the breeze ripple the lake.

'You'll be able to walk down there soon,' a passing nurse called. 'I'm telling you, just you wait and see.'

He looked after her, watching her stride across the lawn towards the building. Could she also tell him how to join a firm which had not existed before this had happened, a firm which he had had no hand in, which had only thrived once he had gone?

Could she tell him how to show his body to his wife, make love to her? Could she tell him how to break free of this great black bird of depression which hovered over him, day and night?

The next morning he wheeled himself down corridors which did not shine as they had in the hospital. 'Don't want you all slipping and sliding about do we?' the nurse said, walking behind him.

He eased himself up on to the bed, hitched up his dressing gown and watched as a man in a white coat smiled at him and then slipped a thin sock over his stump.

'Taking a cast for the pylon,' he said. 'I'm Bill by the way.' Bill whistled through yellowed teeth as he slapped plaster on.

137

He needed his white coat Georgie thought, as the plaster splashed him, we all need a bloody white coat, as some landed on his own lapel.

In five minutes it had set.

'OK. I've got a pair of your shoes, haven't I? Come back in a week, same time, same place, I'll be waiting.' Bill grinned. 'I'm not as tempting as Marilyn Monroe but who cares.'

It took a week to build up his strength – a week of physiotherapy and exercise, a week without Annie and he was glad because then there was nothing to remind him of the world outside.

On Sunday she came with Sarah and they walked across the lawn towards him, Annie so thin, so tired, Sarah so eager and it was at Sarah he looked, at Sarah he smiled because she wouldn't see that behind the smile there was only uncertainty and fear.

They drank tea and watched the ripples on the lake and the glitter of the pale afternoon sun and talked of the following week, when he would begin to walk.

'At last, darling,' she said, 'you'll be up on your feet, and soon we'll have you back terrorising the neighbourhood. Remember that waltz you promised me?'

They could only stay for one hour because the drive back was long and besides, Sister Barnes had said that he was tired, depressed, and needed his peace.

She watched Sarah and Davy crouching on the grass making daisy chains and Annie remembered how Georgie had made one for her at the beck when they were children, his strong brown fingers sewing the stems through the eyes, his fingers lifting her hair as he settled it round her neck, and the smell of his skin had hung between them.

'She's growing so much,' Georgie said.

'I know, the time just seems to rush by somehow, one minute they're babies, the next they're singing rock 'n' roll.'

'I don't want to talk about time,' he said quietly, his voice flat and empty.

Annie put her hand on his, wanting his firm grasp but

there was nothing and so she talked of Brenda because that at least was safe.

'You see, Georgie, she feels one girl should just sew seams, another the gusset and so on. Apparently it's how it was done in her old workshop. I don't agree, I think there's a pride to a finished garment. What do you think? You've such a steady head on you. I wish you were back – we need you.'

Georgie looked at the trees. The leaves had already begun to change and soon there would be a chill in the air. Sarah and Davy were down by the lake now, running round it, counting how many times they could do it before they had to give up, out of breath.

He looked at Annie. What did he know about gussets and seams? It was a world away. He shrugged. 'You'll sort it out.'

Annie drove away from the white building with its columns, its sloping lawns, its roses. The gravel crunched beneath the wheels, the children chatted in the back. She looked in her rear-view mirror hoping to see him waving but he had turned and was pushing his way back to the lake. He hadn't been interested in her, or in the business, but it was only uncertainty, she knew that, she was a nurse, goddammit, and she knew that his battle was not nearly over, that he was in danger of drowning and that she could do nothing to help.

Georgie wore trousers down to Bill's. The sister had pinned his empty leg up. 'Tidier,' she'd said.

We must be tidy, he thought, remembering how he'd told his men this. For God's sake be tidy or the bomb could blow. Isaacs had told Annie that. What was it – be tidy or Georgie Armstrong will mess it up?

Sister held the swing doors open and he wheeled himself through and there was his leg standing against the wall, shiny, new, tidy, covered in rivets, nuts and screws, wearing his sock, his shoe.

'Shapely, don't you think?' Bill said, lifting the leg, pointing towards another set of swing doors. 'Come into the Palais then, just don't jive the first day.'

Georgie's hands were damp as he pushed himself through into a whitewashed room with a large rubber mat on the floor and a huge mirror hanging at the end of low parallel bars.

Bill steadied him as he heaved himself from the chair on to a stool. He wriggled his trousers down as Bill asked, feeling unsafe, glad of Bill's help as he lifted first one buttock then the next, easing his trousers from beneath him, removing his shirt. 'Good, Sister said she'd told you to wear a vest. Leave it on, you'll need it. The harness is a bit like a new pair of shoes which rub your heels – have to wear them in a bit.'

'I knew there was a good reason to lose a leg,' Georgie smiled, nodding at his false leg. 'No blisters to worry your heel any more.'

Bill laughed. 'That's the spirit. Gets some people down, this does.' Bill pulled on a short woolly sock over the stump then eased the deep socket of the pylon over the leg, buckling the leather belt which was attached to it round Georgie's lower abdomen, then buckling his leather braces to the body-belt. Georgie felt helpless, uncomfortable, ugly. 'It's like harnessing up a bloody horse,' he said.

'Not a bad comparison – you're going to be working like one in a minute and if you're good you can have a carrot,' Bill said rechecking the harness. 'Now listen to me, there's a hinge in the knee and the instep to "give" when you walk. It'll all feel very strange and you'll have no strength in that stump. Upsadaisy now, time to take your partners for a glide across the floor – you've drawn the short straw – two blokes.'

A younger man had come through the door and they each helped him up, steadied him and let him sink his weight on to the pylon. Christ, he had no strength at all. He was going to fall, he felt faint, so high up. Christ. Georgie took deep breaths, his body trembling, the pylon was pinching, his stump squeezing it, hurting. For God's sake he couldn't bear

140

any more pain. The harness was digging into him and cutting. Don't let go. For God's sake don't let go!

'I can't, sit me down. Sit me down,' he was shouting.

Bill said, 'That's what they all say so don't worry, we're here. I might look small but I'm tough, or that's what I tell the girls. So's John. Put your arm round me – I promise not to kiss you.'

Georgie leant on them both.

'Look up, Georgie, pretend that chap in the mirror isn't you but our Marilyn walking over a vent. Go on get your head up.'

Georgie couldn't move. He'd fall if he moved even his bloody head just a fraction, couldn't they see that?

'Go on, look in the mirror, see that man standing looking at you?'

Georgie lifted his head now, slowly, very slowly and saw a man, thin-faced, pale with hair which hung over his forehead and a metal leg. It was the man who had once run on to the beach with his family, the man who had fought in the jungles, who had struggled over passes and down through valleys. It was the man who had once been Georgie Armstrong.

'Try a step,' Bill suggested.

Georgie looked at him then, turning his head slowly, slapping the smile back on to his face. 'Just one, I thought we were going to have a jive Bill?'

Bill's face was gentle now. 'Just one and we'll trip the light fantastic tomorrow, eh, make your wife jealous.'

Georgie looked back but not at the mirror, as he tried to swing his leg forward but nothing moved. 'Hold me, hold me,' he panicked, feeling his right leg trembling, feeling nothing but pain from his stump. Bill's arm tightened around his waist.

'Try flicking the stump forward, the knee will bend automatically. Then when it's forward, kick the stump down and it'll straighten out on the heel. Imagine you're at home and the wife's cracking the whip.'

He did, the knee straightening as the heel hit the rubber mat. He jerked, lost balance, felt Bill tighten his grasp, felt his own arms bearing down on their shoulders. 'Don't drop me.'

'OK, you've got that far, now finish it,' Bill said.

Georgie couldn't move, the leg was stopping him, it was just stuck there in front, obstructing him. It was lifeless, dead. 'I can't move.'

'I know, no one can because that leg isn't part of you, it's not listening to your brain. It's got no spring because there are no muscles. It's an obstruction you have to push yourself over, using the momentum of your body.'

'I haven't got any bloody momentum,' Georgie ground out, the sweat of the effort running into his eyes, down his chest, staining his vest and the leather of the harness.

'Imagine it's Marilyn over there and the draught from the vent's becoming a bloody hurricane.' Bill was laughing and Georgie joined in, though there was no mirth in him.

'Pull me,' he ground out, ashamed of his failure.

'They all say that too,' Bill said. 'You're doing fine.'

They pulled him forward until he was balancing on his stump, frightened that he would fall. Oh God, if he was like this with two men holding him what would he be like alone? It was all too difficult, too damn difficult.

'Move your good leg then,' Bill urged, gripping his arm. 'We've got you.'

He didn't dare. He'd never thought about lifting a leg to walk but you did. You lifted it off the ground, and that would leave him balancing on a bit of metal. He couldn't – he'd fall, he'd never be able to do it.

'Hold me,' he begged.

'It's all right we've got you. You're doing fine.'

They held him, he balanced, lifted his leg, moved it forward so slowly, very slowly, don't jog, don't fall. There, it was in front.

'Now the other one.'

He flicked his left stump forward and they pulled him up

142

and over it. He moved his good leg but not quite so slowly this time. He was closer to the mirror but he couldn't see himself because of the sweat in his eyes. Now the left again. He flicked it, it stuck. God, it was going to push him backwards. It didn't but there was sweat all over his body now.

'Keep going, we've to reach the stool by the mirror and then we can all go and have a nice cup of tea.'

He kept going, jerking, flicking, balancing. So much to remember, so difficult. Too difficult. Try, just try. Keep on trying. He looked up, almost there. Once more, flick, stop. 'Pull me, please.' Over and down. Thank God. He felt Bill and John take his weight as he sank on to the stool, glad that the sweat was rolling down his face, his chest and his body because he feared that there might be tears there too.

'It's always the same the first time. We'll try you on shorter steps this afternoon.'

They did and it was slightly easier, but that was all.

He dreamt that night of the beach, of Annie when she was fifteen, of their bodies lying together, of his hands on her, his lips on hers and she was calling him a beautiful bonny lad, and stroking his legs, both his legs. When he woke he was bathed in sweat and he longed for her to be here, to be with him but that was before he remembered.

The next day and the next he worked and still it was hard, frightening, and so bloody difficult and by Thursday his stump was chafed and raw and Sister Martins said he must rest it but only for two days. He wished Sister Barnes had been on duty because she would have said a week.

He pushed his wheelchair into the garden and watched the lake, it didn't matter because at least for this moment he wasn't in that room streaming sweat, struggling, despairing. He breathed in the freshness of the morning savouring his solitude, glad that he was here, alone, where the hours blended and life moved on without him and there was only dark nothingness for company.

The weeks passed and by the third he was flicking, balancing, pulling himself over without help. By September he was

143

turning himself round, lurching in a tight semi-circle. In September too, Sarah told him of her first week in her new class, showed him her satchel and he nodded and smiled but it seemed too far away.

Annie told him that Mrs Norris was talking of retiring but that she wouldn't until he was home for the farewell party.

'I've dried the lavender, made pot pourri for the bathroom. You'll think you're back at Gosforn. Oh Georgie, I can't wait until you're home. You look better, my darling. I love you so much, miss you so much. The house is all ready for you. I hope you like the wallpaper in the bedroom.'

She talked of the town, of the independence of Malaya, Frank's pigeons and he nodded, but what had any of this to do with him?

'I had to insist that Brenda go back to the girls sewing complete garments because production's fallen off, they need the satisfaction of seeing the finished article, is that all right?' Annie said, wishing he would say he loved her.

He nodded.

She told him that the children helped them with packaging the garments each evening because they were saving towards a gramophone, that the new mail shot was up and running, that they all missed him, loved him.

'We need to replace two of the machines though. They have no interlockers and just one wrench will pull apart the seams so Meg and Jean have to hand-finish, it's ridiculous. I've some on order – do you agree?' She wanted him to feel part of it, to feel necessary.

He listened, though what was it to do with him? Here it was the lake that was important and the roses which were past their best, and his leg. Her world was too far away. It was too dark, too difficult.

As Annie walked back through the building towards her car Sister Barnes called her into her office, telling her that Georgie would be ready to leave before the end of September. 'He's very much better physically and should be independent by then and confident in his mobility,' she said. 'But there's always a psychological adjustment to be made, Mrs Armstrong, and it can take some time.'

Annie nodded, looking out at the lake, at Georgie sitting there, his hands resting on his stick.

Sister Barnes continued. 'Georgie's depressed, uncertain. Can you manage?'

Annie didn't like Sister Barnes, she was blonde and silly, she giggled. She wished that it was Sister Martins sitting there. 'He'll need great care, these men have suffered a great deal, they turn inward and need kindness, forbearance, patience.'

Annie nodded. She wanted a cigarette and she did not want to listen to his silly woman telling her how much her husband had suffered. Did she think she was blind, or deaf, or just plain stupid and had noticed nothing over the days and weeks? All she wanted was to have him home and then she would make him come alive.

'Now, do you have a downstairs room? I suggest you set up a bedroom for him there. He says the stairs are narrow. It would be a problem for him, especially at first. He's asked us especially to mention this to you.'

Annie looked at the clock on the wall, then back at the lake. Yes, the stairs were narrow, yes she would set up a bed but it would be their bed and she tried not to feel pain at the thought that he could not make that request himself and wanted to go and drag him to the car, back to Wassingham because it was more than time that he came home.

The hospital rang Annie at the end of the third week in September to ask her to collect Georgie at ten o'clock the next morning, Sunday. Tom came round and helped her to dismantle her double bed and lug it down the stairs into the front room. Sarah and Davy brought down the bedside cupboards and the dressing table when they came home from school.

145

Annie bought food from the market. Plaice because it was his favourite and strawberry ice cream.

Sarah said, 'Oh, Mum, it's going to be so good to have him home, have him here eating with us, talking to us.'

'He'll be rather changed, he'll need time to adjust. He'll be depressed, my darling.'

'No he won't, he'll be glad to be home.'

He was quiet on the journey, sitting with the seat pushed as far back as possible, his false knee bent, and Annie let him just absorb the countryside, which must seem strange and threatening after the restrictions of the world he had lived in for nearly four months.

They approached Wassingham from the north, coming in below the slag heaps. 'Nothing changes,' she said, knowing that everything had.

He gripped his stick.

She turned into Wassingham Terrace and there were Tom and Sarah, Davy and Rob, Gracie and Bet and the neighbours, so many of them, waving, smiling.

'Oh God,' said Georgie.

'They're so pleased to see you, so thrilled you're home.' She touched his knee and he jerked away from her, staring through the windscreen.

Annie pulled up, and came round as Tom opened Georgie's door. She saw him lever himself erect, smile at the neighbours, at Tom, Sarah and the others, saw him walk towards the door, flicking his leg out, kicking, moving over, his jaw set in concentration, his smile rigid. She hardly breathed until he reached the doorway and then she relaxed until she remembered the step.

She moved forward to steady him, but it was too late. His foot caught, he toppled, grabbed at the door, at her, fell out and into the street and there was silence.

She bent down, put her hands beneath his shoulder, saw Tom doing the same. 'I'm so sorry, Annie,' Georgie said and the smile was still fixed on his face, and there was nothing

146

in his eyes and her heart broke for this man she loved so much.

'Bloody step,' Annie said, heaving him up, looking across at Tom. 'Daft bloody step, it's tripped me up more times than I can count. We'll go in and have lunch.'

Sarah moved ahead of them, the others behind, but Georgie stopped at the door to the front room.

'I'm tired. I'd like to sleep.' Annie saw Sarah's face and Davy's too but said, 'Fine, we'll eat later.'

He wouldn't let her help him change and whilst he slept they talked in the kitchen about anything but how dark Georgie's eyes were, how lonely, how cold he looked. He wouldn't eat all that day, he just lay in the front room until everyone had gone, until Sarah was in bed and when Annie came to him at last, he said, 'I toss and turn. I don't want to keep you awake.'

She lay upstairs in the camp bed in what had been their room thinking of the shape of just one leg beneath the blankets and she didn't sleep, and so she worked because the tour was coming up in two weeks and the catalogue needed to be proof-read, the samples finished off, their forward planning rechecked because it stopped her thinking of the bleakness in his eyes and her helplessness.

Georgie didn't get up the next morning. He ate breakfast in bed. Annie worked all morning and though she knew that Bet was in the house she still rushed home at lunchtime to give him salad and tea. Bet and Sarah gave him scones at four, tucked him in tightly, talked to him, soothed him and when Annie came in she helped him to the bathroom, pinning up his pyjama leg before she did so.

'Can you pass me my crutches?' he asked.

'Why not put your leg on?'

'I'm too tired.'

She handed him the crutches Sister Barnes had put in the boot saying that they might be useful and she liked her boys

147

to have them. If she had been here now Annie would have slapped her.

He wouldn't allow her to stay. He locked the door and she wanted to shout, I'm your wife, let me in and throw those crutches away but she didn't know what harm that would do.

She didn't sleep that night either. How could you sleep when your husband was in the depths of despair and you didn't know what you should be doing? But anyway, she had only slept for a few hours at night for so long, what did lack of sleep matter? It didn't make the headache any worse, or the trembling in her hands.

All week she soothed him, talked to him, told him she loved him, kissed his lips but there was no warmth in his. Did he blame her? She asked him and he said no.

'Does it hurt?'

He said, 'No.'

'Are you very tired?' He said yes and there were dark circles beneath his eyes and that night she wanted to come down to his room, hold him, comfort him but he had said he wanted to be alone.

She sat and talked to him over the weekend, Sarah brought him tea, books, biscuits, love, and by Sunday Annie knew that in spite of what that stupid blonde Sister Barnes said there was too much love around him, too much care. Her husband was drowning and none of this was helping and so that evening she sat on his bed.

'Darling, it's time you got up. It's time you helped me, became a father, a husband again. Please come into work with me in the morning. Eat with us this evening.'

'I'm tired, Annie, can't you see that? I'm bloody tired.'

He lay down, closed his eyes and she left him, closing the door quietly and he wanted to call to her. Annie, I need you, stay with me, hold me, love me, stroke me, but how could he ask that of anyone when he was as he was?

How could he go into work when all he had ever done was

misjudge Manners? How could he go out into the street and fall again and see the pity in everyone's eyes?

On Monday morning Annie looked into his room before she left for work.

'I won't be back for lunch, Georgie. You'll have to make you own because Bet won't be in today.' She didn't tell him she had instructed Bet not to come in and neither did she wait for a reply but sat in the office all morning, working, but not properly, wanting to smoke, but not doing so, wanting to run home but sitting, just sitting.

She returned at half past five. Sarah was not yet in, Georgie had gone without lunch. She stood in his bedroom looking at this man she loved and knew that she had fifteen minutes before Sarah arrived and that she must use those minutes to try and break through to Georgie and to do that she must speak words that must only ever be heard by the two of them.

'Help me with the tea, please, Georgie.'

'I can't, I'm too tired.'

'Yes, you bloody can, George Armstrong, you just won't. There's nothing wrong with you, you're not ill, you've just lost a leg – now just get your bum out of that bed, perch it up on that leg and get going. I need help. I'm the one who's tired, I'm the one who's busting a gut trying to keep this business going. You're the one who wanted an edge, you insisted on it. Well, you've got one for the rest of your life, so face it and get on with it.'

He looked at her now. 'Yes, that's right, you're the one who's keeping the business going and I'm the one who nearly ran us on to the rocks so I'm best out of the bloody way. Get off my back, woman.' He was leaning forward, his lips thin, his eyes hopeless. There was no anger in his voice, no resentment, nothing and Annie turned away, not knowing what to say or do now only knowing that a great despair was pouring over her.

'Mum!' Sarah was standing in the doorway, her face white

149

and there was enough anger there to make up for any lack in Georgie.

Annie stood still, Oh God, Sarah had heard. She grabbed her daughter's arm, shut the door, and pulled her to the kitchen as the words spilled out of Sarah's mouth, white hot, wounding as she had known they would be. 'You bitch, you cruel bitch. You're just mean. He's me da, you can't say anything like that to him. You don't love him, you just want him working. He's not well, he's hurt, he needs . . .'

'A bloody good kick up the pants,' Annie shouted back, then said more quietly, 'Listen to me, do you remember the nurse in hospital who said I was right not to spoil him, not to make it easy? She was right, Sister Barnes is wrong. I should have had more sense because if we don't get him up off that bed I don't know what'll happen. You've just got to try and understand and if you can't, then be quiet, because I can't cope with any more.'

Annie sat down as Sarah spun away from her, rushing out of the room, running up stairs, screaming down, 'I hate you, I hate you. You went off and left him today, all alone and then you shout at him. You don't care about anything but that bloody business. I hate you and if you'd nursed none of this would have happened.'

Annie sat at the table, running her trembling fingers up and down the grain, feeling the headache worsen. How could that be when it was already such agony all the time? She held up her hands, trying to hold them steady. They were clammy. She ran them over her face. God, she was hot and she didn't know what to do any more.

She went into the yard. It was dark, her hands were wet and she leant back on the wall, looked up at the sky, closed her eyes and heard the sound of screaming, of shouting, of counting getting louder and louder. It was even louder than the pounding in her head and it was taking her away from this. Thank God it was all coming back and taking her with it, into the darkness again.

There were the smells, Dr Jones, her face smeared, kind,

her hands coming out towards her, waving her on. Where was Prue? There at the end of the rope. 'I'm coming,' Annie called. 'I'm coming back.'

But then she heard the small sound of crying. A tiny sound and it was coming between her and Prue, between Dr Jones, between the smells and the noises and the counting, between the pounding in her head and they were fading, growing weaker and she couldn't hear the counting, she could only hear the crying.

Annie felt the wall behind her. It was cold, rough, she opened her eyes, the sky was dark, cool. There was a wind, the crispness of autumn all around her and from Sarah's room there was the sound of crying.

She walked over to the pigeon loft, feeling the rotten wood at the ends, remembering the fluttering of Eric's birds, the soft cooing and now her head was not even pounding any more, there was nothing but cool, clear thought and she knew that she would never again be visited by the past – it was over, her family had pushed it away, consigned it to its proper place.

She went to Sarah's bedroom, kissed her damp hair, and held her while her daughter cried and then Annie told her that tomorrow her da would be up, but that she must help. She also told her that from now on she would be home from work earlier, that life was too short to be working when there were children to enjoy.

That night she slept and there were no dreams and no headache in the morning, there was only the same clear freshness. The next morning she phoned Gracie asking her to open the factory.

'Sarah and I have a few things to do.'

She rang Tom at work and found that Frank was on the afternoon shift.

'God, you're not getting him sewing knickers too, are you?' Tom asked. Then his voice became serious. 'How's Georgie, have you got anywhere?'

151

'Let's just say, we're about to.'

Frank came round just after she called him. Sarah played the radio in the kitchen. It was *Worker's Playtime* and she sang along loudly to it while Annie and Frank hammered in the yard, then piled their tools and the wood near the back door.

'You can stop now, Sarah,' Annie called.

They cycled round to Frank's and came back with one of his wicker boxes which they carried into Georgie's room.

'Since you won't feed yourself, perhaps you'll make sure you feed this,' Annie said nodding to Sarah.

Sarah lifted the squeaker out, then looked up at Annie.

'Yes, please darling, put it on the bed.'

Sarah hesitated and Annie smiled gently. 'Shall I do it?'

Sarah shook her head and put the squeaker on Georgie's bed.

'Now, we're going. We shall be back at the end of the day. Frank says they're like kids – only two things on their mind – food and a place to roost. He's left food but you need to mix it. There are small pots out in the yard. It's a late bred bird, too late for this year's races but it'll need exercise and training. There's a note explaining everything.'

Georgie said nothing, just looked at the bird and then at Annie.

'It'll do plops if you leave it there, Da,' Sarah said.

They left. Annie dropped Sarah into school with a note which said she had needed to be at home on a medical matter and then sat in the office, looking through the mail-order catalogue proof. They would enclose one with each order and get spin-off sales. She looked at the clock. It was midday.

She checked the invoices, then walked to the restroom, needing a cigarette, asking Brenda for one of hers. She refused.

'Oh go on, I need one. It's a special day.'

'Georgie?'

'Yes, I can't go home for lunch. I have to stay until five

and then I hope he'll be in tomorrow. Go on, let me have one.'

Brenda shook her head. 'No, you've done so well, I'd get fired if I let you.'

'But I'm the boss.'

'I know and you'd fire me tomorrow.'

Annie laughed, walked from the room, as Brenda said, 'I'll keep my fingers crossed for him. You look so much better today, different somehow.'

Annie knew she did.

She checked the design table and approved the smock Tom had sketched. He had one more week to do at the mine and then he was coming in full-time. Their turnover was high enough now to support the two families, and there would be a bonus at Christmas for the girls.

She looked at the clock. One o'clock. Was he up? Would he ring?

By two there had been no call. She walked round the machine room, checking the garments. She had two girls on mail order and two on wholesalers and traders. It worked well but was too much work for her – she desperately needed Georgie to carry the mail order. More could be done if they could spread the workload.

She rang the hotels, confirming the bookings for Tom's tour next week, they were going later than they should be, but the buyers had said they would see him anyway.

It was three o'clock.

What would she do if Georgie didn't make it – if her husband, and Sarah's father, gave up?

She rang the reporter that she'd met at Terry's sports day and talked him into doing a feature on Wassingham Textiles using the angle of a local employer employing only local people and growing fast. Maud would be annoyed that she had dared approach a fellow parent but then Maud was always annoyed.

It was four o'clock.

The phone rang at five past four and it wasn't Georgie,

but the Central Buyer of T. Jones and Son, the Midlands department store chain and he was interested in the look of the mail order shot and wanted to discuss a pants, bra and slip set.

'It must be exclusive and our own label.'

So what's new, she thought. 'I think we can help, Mr Harborne. Can we arrange a meeting between you and our Chief Designer. He's tied up for the next two weeks but will be in your area on . . . let me see,' Annie reached for her diary, flipping through until she found Tom's tour dates. 'How about lunch in the week of tenth October? I'll get him to call you tomorrow to finalise.'

She put down the phone. Twenty past four. She beckoned to Brenda and told her the news. It was what they'd longed for and an exclusive to a Central Buyer was safe as long as the quality was good. This wouldn't be another Manners.

It was twenty-five past four, and he still hadn't rung so even this good news meant nothing.

She couldn't stand it any longer. She picked up her coat. 'I'm going . . .'

'Yes, I think you're right, I can't stand the waiting either. I'll lock up.'

Annie kissed Brenda, then ran out to the car, throwing her briefcase into the back, starting the engine, roaring into the street, rattling over the cobbles, pulling up at the kerb, turning the key in the lock, passing his door. It was open, the bed was gone, the cupboards too and the table was back.

The kettle was on the range, steaming quietly. The back door was open and there was the sound of hammering and then a curse. 'Bloody woman, bloody finger.'

She walked to the door and stood there watching him. He had wedged himself for balance between three tubs. His leg was on, his stick was leaning against the loft, the squeaker was fluttering in the basket.

'That's a grand loft, bonny lad. Eric would be proud of you. I'm proud of you.' Annie was surprised that she could speak through the tightness of her throat.

154

He turned and put his arms out to her and she went to him, holding him gently, feeling him find his balance, kissing her.

'No point in having any plops on the bed. Our Sarah couldn't sell them for rhubarb, could she?' he said.

Annie felt his lips on hers, so soft, so gentle, so full of love. 'Frank and Bernie moved everything back upstairs – it's where I belong.' He kissed her again. 'I lost my way for a moment, Annie.'

Annie stroked his hair, his cheek. 'Tonight I'll race you up the stairs,' she said and now she cried because at last there was time.

CHAPTER 10

After a week it was as though Georgie had never been away but it was so much better – the worst had happened and they had survived, he told her when he first made love to her again, tentatively, differently, but completely.

He said it again at the end of the week, as they lay in the moonlight.

'Now all I have to worry about is you getting jammed in an interlocker,' Annie said.

Georgie laughed. 'Never mind the interlocker, it's the pigeon loft we need to worry about.'

Annie shook her head. 'Tell you what, let's not worry about either now.' She turned, kissed his eyes, cheeks, lips. 'More physio I think, my darling?' She was laughing and so was he and then the laughter faded as passion came, and Annie relaxed into his arms knowing that there would still be adjustments, tears, and for him there would always be bouts of pain, but that they were now going forward.

By the end of October they had taken on another worker because Tom had brought back two large orders from the tour, and several smaller ones. 'We were as professional as the next man,' he told them as they sat on the beach in the mildness of the Indian summer. 'I was flashing me cards about all over the place.'

'As long at that's all you were flashing,' Gracie snapped, then shrugged and laughed. 'Daft really, but I don't like the idea of you sitting there having lunch with all these smart women, then holding up knickers and bras for them.'

Annie nodded, hearing the shrieks of the children as they ran in and out of the foam, seeing Gracie's face and the hurt in her eyes.

'You go with him in February,' she said firmly, squeezing Gracie's shoulder. 'We should have thought of that, I'd have been upset if it had been Georgie. It needs two anyway. We can manage.'

'Does it matter that Jones wants exclusives?' Georgie asked and Annie felt Tom's eyes on her, because they had wondered when Georgie would say this.

Annie chose her words carefully. 'Jones is dealing with an established company. If he messes us up, it will do him more harm that it will us. From the business point of view, you know, it was a blessing that Manners happened when it did. It shook us up, it made us very careful with our quality, taught us a few lessons.'

She looked at Georgie, then at Tom.

Georgie said, 'Set you up with the mail order anyway, didn't it?'

The children were running up the beach now, trailing wet seaweed behind them.

'Not exactly,' Tom said and Annie looked at Georgie, at Gracie who was sitting quite still, as she was now, because she knew Tom was going to tell Georgie the truth about the loan. 'We've been trying to find the right time to tell you about this but you see, we had to put the houses against a loan to get mail order underway and we saved the exclusives for the second shot. We couldn't risk Manners putting the word about that we were selling rejects. It all worked out, Georgie, and we paid off the loan, but had to put up the houses again for the premises.'

They told him then about the consortium, about the need to keep their salaries right down in order to repay their debts and build up their capital reserves again in order to update the machines, increase bonuses, and then go on into textiles.

Georgie's face was set. The children were close now, Sarah was panting, laughing and then suddenly Georgie was too.

157

'I thought, way back in hospital, that you'd both lost your touch when you said you'd used the rejects for the first shot. Seemed crazy to me but I was too busy trying to live at the time and then I forgot. Sounds about right, all of it. Sounds pretty bloody wonderful. Now let's have this picnic.'

They ate chicken with sand in it, bread and butter with sand in it and laughed as it grated between their teeth because there were no lies between them any more, the last hurdle had gone. 'Ambrosia,' said Tom. 'Bloody ambrosia. Now all we need is Jones' order.'

'Come into the sea now, Uncle Georgie,' Davy said, throwing his crusts to the gulls.

Sarah looked at her father, at the trousers he wore, at the other children on the beach, some from Wassingham.

Georgie watched the gulls calling, swooping, soaring, then the fathers wading into the surf with their children, jumping the waves. He felt Annie's hand on his, the softness of her grasp, her love. 'No, not this year, lad. Me leg would go rusty.' He smiled but cutting through the laughter of the afternoon came the pain as they had both known it would, on some days.

Sarah looked away, at the men who were lifting their children and dipping them into the sea and felt anger so sharp that it took her breath away and when her mother brought strawberry ice cream out from the bag, unwrapped sheet after sheet of newspaper, and passed one to her, she pushed it back.

'I hate strawberries. I hate them,' she shouted and ran down to the sea, away from them all, away from the memory of her mother feeding her father strawberry ice cream and shouting at him in the hospital. Glad that he hadn't paddled, glad that her friends hadn't seen him hopping with his stick because you couldn't go into the sea with a false leg, didn't Davy know anything? And she wondered where all the anger had come from.

The Central Buyer of T. Jones and Son confirmed his order

in early November and Brenda insisted that the machines needed updating immediately.

'You're absolutely right,' Annie said and rang the supplier, ordering them for immediate delivery, explaining to Tom and Georgie, vetoing another worker at this stage in favour of better machinery, showing them the outgoings against the incomings. 'It'll be cheaper and the girls are coping. They're interested, busy, and the new machines will be a better investment right now. Brenda is doing a training session when they arrive to get maximum efficiency, though it might be an idea to do that on a regular basis anyway, just to keep them up to the mark. I'll talk to her, but not tonight, it's five-thirty, time we were home.'

She drove them, taking the accounts and designs with her. She and Georgie would discuss these later, but only when Sarah was in bed. The beach had shown them that Sarah needed to make her own adjustments and that they must be there for her.

'Sarah's been very good and done half Miss Simpson's work,' Bet said as she put supper on the table. 'But only half mind.'

Sarah pulled a face. 'I don't have to get it in until Friday and it's only for this eleven plus and I might not want to pass, even if I do.'

'I think perhaps you need to finish that work, judging from the muddle you got yourself into there,' Annie said, easing herself on to the chair next to Bet.

'Frank brought round those three youngsters for you Georgie,' Bet said, shaking pepper on to her stew.

'Sit down,' Annie laughed as he started to get up again, nodding as Sarah pleaded to be able to see them before the next round of homework.

They ate, talked, laughed and then later they held the birds in their hands, pulling out their wings, fanning their tails, listening to Georgie's plans for his Red Chequers, feeling the silkiness of their feathers as he told them that they would fly dry even in the wettest weather. 'They'll win, I know that, but they'll not beat Tiger. He's just a beaut.'

'When are you going to teach them to trap, Da?' Sarah said, holding the bird against her chest, stroking it gently.

'Pretty soon.'

'Can I help?'

'Course, and Davy too, and your mam.' Georgie put the youngsters back in the loft. 'But finish Miss Simpson's work first. It's good of her to give it to you, she doesn't have to, you know.'

'Oh, can't I stay? Go on, Mum.'

Annie smiled at her, 'Homework, or you can clean the loft if you'd really rather.'

It was no contest and Sarah was in the kitchen faster than she'd ever been whilst Annie laughed softly, cleaning the loft with the scraper, hearing the fluttering, the cooing, the soft sound of Georgie's voice. 'Ambrosia,' Annie said quietly, blessing Frank for all the months he had talked pigeons to Georgie in the darkness of the pit, because it had bred the same love in him for them and in Sarah too. It was holding them all together, it was pulling them forward because Georgie's disability made no difference in this sport.

All through the early winter they gained new orders, working themselves hard, their staff hard, and in the early evening and weekends they trained the pigeons lightly. 'But never when my washing's out,' Annie insisted.

They trained them to trap – taking them from the loft, keeping them in their basket overnight across the other side of the yard. Annie barely slept that night, glad that their neighbours had moved and taken their damn great cat with them and hoping that whoever bought the house kept goldfish instead.

Before work they released them, watching them flap and flutter. Would they go to the landing board or soar away, into the freedom of the skies? Sarah clung to her hand and they watched as they lifted.

'Oh no,' Sarah wailed.

'Sh,' Georgie said.

The pigeons were straining up, up, then they came back down, on to the landing board, then through the trap, heads deep into the food hoppers.

'Greedy little pigs,' Annie murmured.

The next week, before feeding time, they allowed them out of the loft on their own, having cut their morning feed in half. Again they stood and watched and Annie whispered between clenched teeth.

'Your bloody pigeons are going to give me a nervous breakdown one day. It's worse than Manners' orders, all this. What if they fly away and cats get them? What about the hawks?'

Georgie laughed softly. 'That's why I've got Red Chequers. Hawks like white ones, they're always picked off first.'

'I'm glad I'm a brunette,' Sarah said, holding her da's hand, feeling his warmth, her eyes on her own bird, Buttons, as he flew higher and higher.

'OK,' Georgie said. 'Call them, Sarah. Use the feeding tin, rattle it and call as well.'

Sarah looked at him. She didn't want to, what if they didn't come? What if she wasn't loud enough?

'You do it, Da.'

Georgie didn't want to. What if they ignored him, what if they kept on flying?

'Go on, Sarah, pretend it's Terry running off with your drum sticks.' Annie's voice was gentle. 'They'll come back, kids always do when they're hungry, just think of yourself.'

Sarah called them, again and again, until they circled lower and lower and trapped.

'Greedy little pigs,' Annie murmured again, feeling her muscles relax.

On the weekend before Christmas they put them in their basket, hearing their scratching, their fluttering, driving out past the slag heaps towards the north. Only one mile, Frank had said, then turn left, down the track. They bumped and rocked and Sarah and Davy said the birds must wish they were flying already.

They stood in the whipping wind and Annie's hands were numb as she fumbled with the leather straps because Georgie still found it difficult to reach to the ground.

'God, worse than your harness, Georgie,' she grimaced, smiling as he laughed, noticing that Sarah laughed too and she felt relief wash over her.

'I hope they're ready for this, Uncle Georgie,' Davy said, squatting next to Annie.

'So do I lad, but they had no supper last night and they've been flying round in a flock for a week or so now, so they should be fine. They'll race against one another, just like you kids. If they're on their own, they'll mess about.'

'Just like you kids,' Annie laughed, looking up at Georgie. 'Shall I let them go?'

He nodded, checked his watch and she lifted the lid, letting it drop back, standing up as the birds left, watching them soar, dip, rise again, keeping together. Just like Sarah's gang. She looked at her daughter, at Davy. Yes, they'd all keep together but would they if some got through to the grammar? She still wished that Don had not pulled apart as he had.

The birds were at home, waiting for them and Frank's grin was all they needed when they told him the exact time that they had been tossed.

'They're good, aren't they?' Georgie said.

'They'll do,' Frank replied.

By Christmas, Jones had re-ordered because their exclusives had sold so well.

'The wholesale division,' Tom called out over the remains of the Christmas lunch at Bet's, waving his cigarless hand, blowing imaginary smoke rings. 'The wholesale division is thriving.'

'Mail order could still do better,' Georgie said patting his stomach.

'Your stomach's really fat, Da,' Sarah said. 'You're gross.'

162

Georgie grinned and patted it. 'There, sounds better than your drums.'

'Urgh. It's because you've only got one leg for all the food to go down. You'll have to eat less, Da.' Sarah was laughing, they were all laughing because there had only been humour in Sarah's voice, and acceptance again.

Annie caught Georgie's eye and they both knew what the other was feeling and, if they could, they'd have tangoed round the kitchen. She grinned, watched Tom lean forward, hand Georgie the wishbone, saw their little fingers pull, leaving Tom with the wish. It didn't matter, they had all they wanted.

She looked round the kitchen at the red and green decorations, there was tinsel on the tree that they'd helped to hang last night and the smell of turkey all around. No cigars this year.

'Don looked well, and Maud.'

'They should have come today instead of last night, then they'd have seen the gramophone,' Sarah said.

'We could have taken Terry down to the club, let her have a go on the drums.'

'Does she go to a Youth Club?' Bet asked.

Sarah shook her head. 'No, she says her mother wouldn't like it, she might meet the wrong people. People like us, she meant.' She and Davy were laughing, Rob too, but Annie, Tom and the others looked at one another, seeing the same anger until the children pulled them to their feet, dragging them out through the yard, down to the football field where Georgie refereed as they kicked a ball around on the frost stiffened grass until the breath jogged in their bodies.

Tom looked at his watch. 'Time you kids were at the club,' he called and Annie sank on to the cold ground, grateful that there was a halt, moving her toes inside her shoes, walking back slowly with Georgie, taking his arm in case he slipped on the frost.

'It's OK for you,' she murmured against his sleeve. 'You only get chilblains on one foot, we get them on both.'

163

Georgie laughed, 'But I've got a fat stomach, your daughter said.'

'She's always my daughter when she's in trouble.'

Georgie squeezed her arm, then called to Tom. 'You know mail order needs perking up – what about an outsize department? I know we wouldn't get enough response to make it worth a special mail shot but what about a special catalogue mailed out to all those who've ordered outsize before, plus including it in all the orders sent out.' He turned to Annie. 'What d'you think?'

'Good idea and we could extend the ordinary offers to include outsizes, not just respond to specific queries.' They were nearing Bet's, walking through the yard, into the house, stripping off their coats, drinking the tea Bet brought over, working out figures on the paper she brought to them when she heard their conversation. They decided on a thirty per cent ratio to hold ready. Tom would run up catalogues. Not glossy, they decided. Keep that expense for the tour. Just run off some copies.

'And what about a special kitchen mail shot next year, using red and green fabric and special Christmas motif. I haven't seen any but maybe we could find some?'

'Or maybe we'll be able to set up the printing sooner than we thought, make our own?' Georgie said, grinning at Tom.

They drank more tea, smiling, talking, feeling the same excitement, loving it.

Outsize went well. By the end of January 1958 the turnover was higher but Brenda said that the girls were bored with underwear and aprons. What about fashions – would that be a good idea?

Annie put it to them all at one of the monthly meetings which had been held since the firm began but explaining that there was no falling off in underwear demand, no reason to take a risk just at the moment. They needed to consolidate, because their profit margins were still tight. 'Remember how small the bonuses have been?'

The workers nodded.

'Have a look at the balance sheets, but we won't forget fashions. Tom has a smock he's playing around with.'

'He hasn't got the legs for it,' Jean called out.

'Couldn't agree more,' Annie said, passing round the balance sheets. 'We'll go into fashions one day, girls, don't worry, but we must be patient, think how far we've come and very quickly. We must just be careful.'

Georgie felt his birds were not just bored with their loft, but cold because the wood was so rotten it was crumbling, letting in draughts. Annie told him that he must be patient because there was no way she was going out and building a loft when they were in the middle of a mail shot.

At the end of February, once another mail shot was up and running and the tour over, he said he'd have to start rubbing wintergreen on Tiger's legs if this went on. So Annie spent her evenings with him, mapping out a new loft tight against the left-hand fence, its front facing the house, leaving space at the side for later extensions.

Annie groaned. 'Why don't we just move in there and let Tiger and his mates have the run of the house?'

They sawed, screwed, hammered, banged their thumbs and cursed but not seriously because there was the same excitement inside them for the pigeons too. It was all part of their lives, which were going forward.

It was fifteen feet long and seven feet deep, divided into three compartments. They made it seven feet high, covered the roof with corrugated asbestos and Annie said they needed to make their underwear out of it to keep out the wind.

'Must keep the air moving,' Georgie said, covering the window frame with fine-mesh wire netting.

'Rather them than me,' Annie said, pulling her woollen hat down over her ears.

They could only work a few hours each night and then only by the light from the kitchen and it wasn't until the middle of March that it was finished, just as they were starting to send out summer samples to the traders who had promised that their orders would be up on last year.

'We'll be increasing too,' Georgie said as they transferred the birds into the new loft. 'Should be some eggs in a couple of weeks but Frank says we've got to breed lightly as they're late-breds. Says not to start their yearling training until July. They're OK on the youngsters' schedule.'

They made nesting bowls in the evening and Annie laughed as she wrote to Prue, saying that she wondered quite what she'd done with her life until pigeons came into it.

'Sat back and eaten peeled grapes,' Prue wrote back a few weeks later. 'I'm glad Sarah liked the sari and the ring. Did she know that all saris should be able to go through a ring, or did she think I'd gone bonkers and sent her a large napkin?'

By the end of March the pigeons were settled and had laid eggs and an overseas buyer had written, saying that he would be arriving in Britain in the near future and would like to see them with a view to placing an order.

They drank a bottle of beer on the yard step to celebrate. Sarah and Davy had lemonade and told Annie that the Youth Club Committee were trying to win the table tennis league, but that they all really wanted a tennis court.

'Raise funds and build it yourself,' she said watching Georgie checking the birds, knowing that he wanted to lift them off their nests. 'Leave them alone, poor little things. You've already taken one egg away and now you're poking about.'

The yard gate opened and Don came in. 'What's he poking?'

Annie stopped with the glass midway to her lips. 'Good heavens, where did you drop from?'

'Just passing and thought I'd see how you were, didn't know you'd built a new one. Bit grand, isn't it?'

'Only the best for his pigeons,' Sarah said, getting up, sidling out, grabbing Davy, taking him with her. 'See you later, Mum.'

Annie poured Don beer, sat with him in the weak sun and listened to tales of Teresa's success at school, of Maud's ambitions for her, her piano, her ballet, and it felt strange to be here, standing in a Wassingham yard, just talking with her brother. It felt good.

'What does Teresa want to do?' Annie asked gently, watching as Georgie weighed out the food for the birds.

'I don't know. What her mother wants of course.' Don sipped his beer, took out a cigar. 'May I?'

Annie was surprised, he didn't usually ask. 'Of course.' She wanted one herself. She would have smoked old socks, anything because she still missed her cigarettes, still dreamt about them.

They sat and she breathed in his smoke, laughing at Georgie's face as he saw her do it. They talked about his business, about cigarettes and how difficult it was to stop.

'Try cigars,' Don joked and Annie smiled, wanting to hug him, to keep him as he was at this moment because she hadn't seen this Don for a very long time.

They talked about Wassingham Textiles and the Central Buyer's order, the success of the tour, the overseas buyer.

'He'll be coming here, will he?' Don asked, blowing smoke rings as she had known he would.

Annie shook her head. 'No, we'll have to go to him. I'll get Tom to meet him wherever he is. Take our samples. It'll be so good if we break into that market without having to plod round the European Trade Fairs – it just saves so much money. We hadn't even thought of expanding abroad just yet, though we can handle it.'

She offered tea as the beer was finished but he had to go, he had people to see, cocktails to drink. Of course, Annie thought, as they waved him away, glad that he'd been, warmed by his interest, eased by his chatter – perhaps Georgie's accident had done what nothing else could.

'Come again,' she called as his Jaguar purred away. 'He was nicer than he's been for ages,' she called to Georgie.

'Makes you wonder what he's up to.'

'For goodness sake, can't he be nice without that sort of remark?' Annie stood with her hands on her hips. 'It's her, she gets him on edge. He was perfectly pleasant then, so maybe he's trying to reach out again.'

'Are you going to give us a hand?' Georgie asked, cleaning the loft. 'And I hope you're right, pet.'

'I'm sure I am. He's not a bad lad, not really. He was nice once and no way am I helping with that loft, I'm making the picnic for tomorrow.'

'Will it work do you think, taking her?'

'It's got to, but I'm wearing three vests.'

The sun is as warm as it ever is in March, Annie thought, and for that they must be grateful. They'd certainly be the only fools out on the beach at this time of year but that was the idea wasn't it, to beard the beach alone, just the three of them, so that Sarah would not say any more that she wouldn't go to the sea because it was too childish. Annie saw Sarah's face in the mirror, so tense, so angry and knew that it had nothing to do with childishness, but with embarrassment and the fear of seeing her father without his leg, and of others seeing it too.

'One step at a time,' she thought, hoping that Bernie and his family would not be late.

Annie drove along the coast road, down the track, seeing the white-capped waves rolling, fragmenting, sucking the sand back into their depths.

They struggled against the wind as they walked down to the beach, sheltering in the dunes, seeing the sand whipping, dusting, along the beach.

'Are you sure, Annie? This early season bathing seems a bit stoic for me. We can come again.' Georgie's voice was low and Annie heard uncertainty as well as cold, but it was no surprise, she had known that he too needed today.

She nodded. 'I'm coming in too, darling. Just think of that – that no woman, in the field of human . . .'

He groaned. 'I thought you might just say that,' then

raised his voice, looking across at Sarah. 'This dune is as good as any, gives us a bit more shelter than the last. Come on, let's get 'em off.'

He eased his trousers down over his bathing costume. Sarah watched as he unhitched his leg. She'd never seen his stump before. She'd never seen him stand like this, balancing on crutches not his stick, with that great gap there, where his leg should have been. She turned and Annie watched her do so, as did Georgie.

He nodded to her. 'Come on then, Annie, get your clothes off, I'm getting cold hanging about for the pair of you. I'll meet you down there.'

Tom had put a base to each of his crutches to stop them sinking into the sand and he swung himself along, feeling the cold, feeling Sarah's eyes on his body and knew she would be feeling the same revulsion that he had felt, but knowing that she must face it, come to terms with it in all its forms. He looked either way. No others thank God, or perhaps he couldn't have gone through with it.

Sarah watched him, swinging across the great expanse of beach, all alone. So alone. She looked either way, remembering how he'd chased them last year, how he'd played cricket, how he'd swung her up in the air on Bell's Farm Hill.

Swing, swing, swing his leg was going now and he was so alone down there.

She turned. 'Come on, Mum.'

'You go on, darling.' Annie was doing up a strap, watching Georgie nearing the sea. He couldn't go into the water on crutches, he might fall.

'Quickly, someone needs to be with him,' she gasped, wrenching at her strap, the cold drawing her skin up into goose bumps, knowing she must stand and fiddle for a while longer.

Sarah looked either way again and saw another family coming down from the dunes, the children running on, then seeing Georgie, stopping. Annie saw them too. Well done, Bernie, hope the grandchildren are wrapped up well. 'He's too near the sea and he's alone,' she called to Sarah. 'Don't worry about the other people. There are these accidents so often in the pit. Remember Gracie's da?'

Sarah watched the children stare, then turn, call to the adults and point at Georgie. 'But you never saw him without his leg, like this, did you?' she shouted at her mother. 'Those kids haven't either.'

'It's another world now. Men like your father have a right to paddle without fear, without embarrassment.'

Sarah was still standing. Georgie was nearing the sea. He'd fall if the waves caught him. Annie ran as fast as she could, down the beach, but then Sarah passed her, her breath heaving in her chest, the sand squeezing up between her toes, slowing her, but then she reached him, held his arm, looked up into his face.

'Don't let the sea knock you over,' she shouted above the noise of the surf and the wind, though what she wanted to tell him was how much she loved him, how proud she was of him, because he was about to paddle in the sea and that other man, with two legs, had a damn great coat on and two silly kids with wellingtons.

They came back to Wassingham, their skin stinging from the wind, the sand and the sea spray, their hair thick with it and Sarah was laughing and saying that they should bring the gang in the summer, then Georgie could get out really deep with them all around him, that people would scream and think he'd been bitten by a shark when he came out.

They lugged the empty picnic box through into the yard and there was a man there, in a dark suit and briefcase, measuring the pigeon loft. He turned.

Georgie said, 'Just what's going on? What're you doing?'

Annie put down the picnic and stood with her hand on Sarah's shoulder, listening as the man told them he was John Evans, from the planning office. They'd received a complaint about the height of the pigeon loft from a prospective purchaser of the property next door.

'They claim it takes their light,' he said. 'It is higher than usual.'

Annie looked from Evans to the house, to the pigeon loft, then started to laugh. 'You've got to be joking. This is ridiculous.'

'I'm most certainly not joking but I do agree, it does seem ridiculous, though we've had stranger things happen. The thing is, you're going to have to take it down, or lower the roof.'

Georgie touched the loft. 'The pigeons are about to hatch out. There's no way I'm taking this roof off. Who's buying the bloody house? I'll go and speak to them.'

Annie left the yard now, tried the door into next door's yard. 'Come here, Georgie, give me a bunk up.'

She stood by the gate, waiting, hearing him limp up to her.

'What're you doing, Annie?'

'I'm going over to open the gate so that Mr Evans can see that we're not taking anyone's light. I'm just not having it. Now give me a bump up.' Her voice was angry now because no one would tell her husband to lower a roof after he'd had a leg off.

Sarah came out, and Mr Evans too. 'Oh, Mum, you'll show your knickers.'

'Good advertisement – they're ours,' Annie grunted, putting her foot in Georgie's hands after he'd wedged himself against the wall. 'Get over here, Mr Evans, in case he falls.' It was not a request, but an order. Georgie was lifting her up.

'Well, I don't know . . .'

'Get over here. There's a man with only one leg under me.' She looked down at Georgie and winked, he grinned.

She was up then, straddling the wall, swinging herself over, unbolting the gate, pulling Mr Evans in. She pointed to the loft. 'Look, you can see for yourself, it takes no light from them at all.'

Mr Evans looked around, up at the sun, measured, then

171

smiled. 'You're right. Quite right. You're quite safe – keep the loft as it is. I'll report back.'

As he left Annie asked who it was who'd lodged the complaint. 'A Mr Jones,' he said.

She rang Bill at the estate agent's. He'd shown quite a few people round, but hadn't a Mr Jones on the list, but if he was lodging a complaint perhaps he'd used a false name – or perhaps he was a disgruntled neighbour.

'Never a dull moment,' she murmured to Georgie. 'For heaven's sake, who'd do something so petty?' They stood outside the loft with its especially wide doors, its extra height. 'Everyone knows you need it as it is, for God's sake.'

Georgie was standing quietly, looking from the loft to the back alley. All their neighbours had had plenty of time to complain. The only person who'd been recently was Don – but no, not even he would do that.

The phone was ringing and Annie answered it. It was Tom. 'Jurgen Schmidt's been in touch. He'll be over soon he says, and would prefer to visit our showroom since he can come via Newcastle to Edinburgh.'

'Our what?'

'Exactly. We'll need to set one up. Jones wants to come up too so it would be worth it. Did you have a good day at the sea, did it work?' His voice was anxious.

Annie shook her head to clear it. There was so much to think about. 'Yes, it worked,' she said. 'And yes, we'll get a showroom, somehow. When's he coming exactly?'

'Within the next three weeks. He's going to confirm.'

Annie nodded. 'Fine, we'll sort it out.' She didn't know how but they would. It was their entry into the export market, but who had tried to mess up Georgie's life?

CHAPTER 11

On the Monday of the following week, Jurgen Schmidt rang to say that he would be in Wassingham in two weeks' time, on 14 April. Annie had located an old haberdashery off Armore Terrace, just round the corner from Briggs' Warehouse.

'We don't want him coming to the machine shop,' she told Bill, the estate agent. 'There are too many designs, too many samples, too much hassle.' She sat back in the chair. 'OK, break it to me gently. Has the lease tripled on this, just because we're after it?' She was grinning but tension was pulling at her neck.

Bill shook his head. 'Don't go paranoid on me, Annie, that was just business. No, this is fine. Really cheap. It's been hanging around for ages and I've more news for you. There *was* a Mr Jones, my wife took the call. He was from Whitley Bay apparently and he hasn't been back. A rather nice elderly couple are buying it so you can relax.'

Annie told Tom and Georgie in the afternoon as they sat round her desk at the office. They looked at one another and Tom said, 'Maybe I'll buy him a cigar.'

'What d'you mean?' Annie asked, checking the small print of the lease, signing where their solicitor had marked with a cross, passing it across to Tom.

'Nothing, nothing at all,' Georgie replied, reading over Tom's shoulder, adding his signature when they had finished, passing it on to Brenda to sign as witness.

That evening, Georgie lifted the hen and the eggs were hatched, there was a squeaker covered with down. 'A right little beauty,' he breathed, leaning to one side so that Annie could see, and then Sarah.

There were bits of white shell in the nesting bowl.

'It must prick them,' Sarah said, trying to pick them out.

'Leave it, lass, they'll sort it out.'

'How'll it feed – should we put out some food?' Sarah whispered.

'No, it'll put its beak in her mouth and her mam will throw up into it.'

Sarah snatched away her hand, stepping back, looking up at Annie and Georgie. 'That's disgusting.'

'Mm, the things we mothers do for you,' Annie said, 'Now, get back to homework please and only then can you come with us to give Tiger a toss.'

While Sarah worked in the front room Annie and Georgie went through the designs for Schmidt at the kitchen table, hearing the kettle simmering on the range and the shouts of children in the back alley. 'I'll make up the samples myself,' Annie said. 'The girls have too much work on and Brenda's on holiday next week. Can you help Gracie and me check through the work, and we'll need to pack too, though Sarah and Davy can do some at the weekend. It boosts their pocket money.'

'Shall we put the other stock forward as well?' Georgie was looking at one. 'I don't like this.' He passed it to Annie.

She looked. 'Yes, you're right. It's a young style and the fabric's wrong. We need a really fresh design on it – cotton can be so versatile but this is dreary. We'd better talk to Tom about it.'

Georgie leaned forward, resting his chin on his hands. 'We need to design our own fabric as soon as we can – it would give us so much more flexibility and our own voice. It would boost the mail order division an' all.'

Annie laughed. 'Wouldn't hurt mine either, or are we in competition?'

Georgie reached across, took her hand, kissed it. 'Never in competition, my darling, but now that you mention it, there is a race planned for the eighth of April. Just to get the "new boys" used to the procedures.'

Annie shook her head. 'Tiger knows all about the procedures – he just has to flap his wings and tuck his legs up.'

Georgie grinned. 'No, the human "new boys". The committee's arranged a practice run. I'm taking the time clock round tonight for it to be checked. The trouble is the eighth is the Saturday before Jurgen's visit.' He looked down. 'It was set up before we knew about Schmidt and I didn't quite know how to tell you then and I don't now.'

Annie leaned back in her chair. 'I'm not surprised you didn't – that's when all the hard work needs to be done. We've got to decorate and fit out the shop.'

'I won't go of course. I'll just do the best I can in the youngster races.' Georgie was leafing through the designs again.

Annie was laughing now. 'Don't be so daft. Of course you can go. Take Sarah and Davy too, have a day out. Is Frank going to be convoyer?'

Georgie looked up, his face in a grin. 'Yes, it's his first time. He's nervous.'

'Then how could you not go and hold his hand, my love, but tell the committee from me that if they ever coincide with Schmidt again I shall personally murder the lot of them. You'd better be the one to tell Tom and duck while you do it.'

Georgie nodded at her. 'I've told him and he's OK. He wants time off in the winter to see Sunderland play.'

Annie crunched up a sheet of spare paper and threw it at him. 'Fine, just fine. So Gracie and I need a few days off too eh, and incidentally, what did you mean about a cigar today?'

Georgie told her that he had suspected Don had been 'Mr Jones', just for a moment that was all, and now she really was angry and wouldn't go with them to toss Tiger but stayed in the house, not turning the light on as darkness fell, because she knew her brother would never hurt anyone like that. But her anger was directed at herself because she too had thought it for a brief moment and she was shocked at herself.

Another bird hatched the next night and by the next weekend their Union Rings were fitted and each evening they checked to see how the nestlings were 'making up'.

Annie showed Sarah how to pinch the youngster's crop. 'This is Button's nestling, so you must look after the bairn, grandmother,' Annie said gently, watching as Sarah pinched the crop lightly, hoping that it would appear to be full. It was.

She showed her how to lift it, belly upwards, to check that the breastbone was straight and the skin wasn't blue, it was red. It was fine.

'Put it back in the nestbowl now,' Annie instructed, noticing how carefully Sarah did this – she was a gentle child as well as a handful.

She looked at Sarah's nestling again. It wasn't standing up in the bowl, it was crouching. Good. 'Now put your finger near it. Don't touch it, just near.'

Sarah looked at her. 'Why?'

'I want to make sure it rocks back, and doesn't stand up. If it's feeding properly its crop will be full of soaked grain, and it'll be too heavy to scramble to its feet.'

'Did Da say that?'

'Yes, don't worry, he showed me last night.'

'I was still up, he could have shown me too.'

Annie nodded, surprised at the anger in her daughter's voice. 'I know, we were so busy talking we forgot. I'm sorry, darling.'

'You always forget me when you're together.'

Sarah turned away, put her finger forward and the nestling rocked backwards. She grinned at Annie, who felt her tension ease, not only because the bird was 'making up' and would not have to be destroyed but because the anger was gone from Sarah. Though the child was quite right, they did forget and it was unforgivable.

The next week was busy. Sarah had to be reminded to do Miss Simpson's work and the exams were getting nearer but Gracie put her foot down with Davy too, and sent Paul home to do his work, so that made it easier.

They had a new order in from Edinburgh too, and were organising the next mail shot. Late into the night she and Georgie planned the showroom with Tom and Gracie and wished they'd their own fabrics to hang at the windows, and wallpaper to match.

'One step at a time,' Tom said. 'We haven't the capital yet. Let's see how the export order goes, if it goes at all.'

Georgie checked with Annie that he'd ordered enough fabric for the apron and gloves mail shot, and she said he had. He checked with her that there was a car available to collect Herr Schmidt. There was, Tom's.

They talked then about a converted car for him. 'You need one,' Annie said. 'For business and for pleasure.' For your dignity too, she thought and your daughter, because she had decided that he must take Sarah, not her, out with him on training tosses and races – she must never feel forgotten as Annie had done as a child.

She discussed it with Tom when Georgie was talking to the newspaper about the mail shot, coaxing them into a feature. Ringing another, telling them about the possibility of an export order, arranging to ring them the following week if it was confirmed.

'Yes, he should have one,' Tom said, sitting on the corner of her desk, smiling as she flicked a piece of gum into her mouth. 'What's it worth not to tell the kids that Auntie Annie is chewing like a Yank?' he asked.

'Anything you care to name, my lad. But if I don't chew I shall smoke right now. It's the Schmidt thing. I want it Tom. I want it because then we'll be that much nearer the textiles. It's what you and Georgie want. It means we've done what we said we'd do. But I want that car more and I can't have it without the order.'

She ran Georgie and the children to the station on Saturday morning. They had been to the club the night before and a member of the committee had set the clock by Greenwich Mean Time, it had then been sealed and handed back to Georgie. Annie had smiled at the tension of those who stood around her, but she had felt it too and was glad she'd held Tiger this morning, stroked him, wished him well, told him to beat those wings hard for Georgie and Sarah, duck the hawks, for God's sake, duck the hawks.

'Did you remove his hopper after supper last night?' she asked now.

Georgie nodded. 'Just as Frank said.'

'Is the forecast good? You won't let him out if it's too windy?'

Georgie shook his head, he was laughing. Why was he laughing?

'Fifty miles seems such a long way. He's still so young.'

'Oh, Mum, no he's not. He'll be past it in a few years, stop fussing. You always fuss, doesn't she, Da? Fuss, fuss, fuss, no one can get a word in edgeways.'

Was she fussing? It was only a bird for heaven's sake. Of course she wasn't fussing but Sarah was right, no one else had squeezed a word in.

Annie said nothing more, pulling up at the station, seeing Frank unloading the panniers from his truck, seeing the committee taking the panniers into the station, on to the train.

'It'll be so strange for him. He hasn't been on a train before,' she said.

'Oh Mum,' Sarah said, pulling at Georgie's hand. 'Come on Da, Davy, let's go. We'll miss the train.'

Georgie was looking at her. 'Will you be all right? I feel bad about leaving you.'

Annie looked down at Sarah's face, at the way she held Georgie's arm, pulling him, the eagerness with which she was talking to Davy. 'Well don't. You and Sarah should

178

share a day out more often – this must be the first of many, Georgie, she needs you, really she does.'

She waved to them, watching Sarah talk to Georgie and hold his hand. Yes, they must get a converted car for Georgie, even if the export order came to nothing, because then he wouldn't need her to drive him everywhere and he and Sarah could spend days together as father and daughter should.

They decorated the showroom a light green with white woodwork, leaving the windows open all day and all night.

'No one will break in, there's nothing to steal,' Tom said, locking the door. 'And there's enough of a wind to clear the smell of the paint out.' He looked at the clouds scudding across the sky. 'They won't have let them fly today, will they? Your lad won't be home until tomorrow you know.'

Annie did know, she'd been monitoring the weather all day. 'Will Gracie mind about Davy? Do you?'

'No, I'm off to a debate with Rob tonight anyway – bit late now but we'll catch the end of it. See you bright and early tomorrow then?'

Annie caught his sleeve. 'Do you take Davy to these debates?'

'No, he's always with Sarah.'

'Not always, Tom, and he needs you, it isn't just Rob who does.'

They worked all Sunday and the weather was better, so Tiger would be flying. Annie hung the curtains, ironed and hung the slips, the aprons, the smocks that they thought they'd try out on Schmidt. They hung the bras and pants and pictures on the wall. They had arranged for the phone to be reconnected.

'It'll be worth it,' Annie told Bet. 'We can keep this up and running for the other buyers who might want to come. Jones is visiting in May.'

'It's getting big isn't it, Annie. What would your da have thought?'

Annie paused, then continued to put the iron in the box. 'I doubt that he'd be pleased. He wanted us both to leave Wassingham, didn't he, Bet, to make it big elsewhere and certainly not in trade.'

'But he'd have been glad you're happy and you are, aren't you?' Bet took the iron.

'I've never been happier in my life and I think he'd have been pleased about that.'

Annie closed up the ironing board and walked to the car boot with it.

'He loved you, he just couldn't show it and a father should, you know.'

Annie did know and on Monday after Schmidt had been she rang a car dealer in Newcastle about car conversions. 'I'll send you the details,' he promised.

It had been a good day, Schmidt had left leaving a large order for two sets of underwear and he would have ordered the aprons too if the fabric designs had been more appealing. As importantly, Tiger had survived the hawks and won his race. Sarah sat and told her all about it while Georgie and she listened, directing their questions at her, not one another.

'And so we learn,' she groaned that night. 'But who said it would be so difficult being a parent – running a business is so much easier.'

Throughout April and May they taught the young birds how to trap and toss and in June Georgie had his car, paid for by a loan which Annie had arranged, because it was unfair that they should draw more from the profits than Tom or the workers.

He drove out each weekend on training flights, taking Sarah and Davy with him, and sometimes Annie, but only sometimes.

In early August some late birds hatched and a further order arrived from Schmidt who was eager for aprons but still didn't care for the designs.

In mid, August Tom and Gracie took the boys to Scarborough on holiday and Annie and Georgie worked late into the night, covering for them. On their return they did the same for Annie and Georgie, who took Bet to the sea for days out, though they didn't go away, for who would look after their birds, Georgie asked.

Annie just smiled and lay on the dunes feeling the tiredness draining from her body, hearing the gulls, the shriek of laughter, the thump as Georgie swung his crutches, and then his leg, thinking of how relieved Sarah had been when Davy also passed his eleven plus, and Paul too. The gang could stay together.

'I'll make your uniform this week, shall I?' Annie said as Sarah dug into the sand and began to bury her. It was so cold. 'Not so deep, you horrible child.'

'Mum,' Sarah's voice was hesitant. 'They'll laugh if I wear home-made clothes. Teresa said you'd make them, she said everyone would make fun.'

Annie lay quite still. 'We can't have that, can we? I remember how I felt. Of course I shall buy it, darling.'

'You don't think I'll get like Terry, do you? It's just girls you know.'

Now Annie laughed and the sand fell from her shoulders. 'Mum?'

'Well, let me tell you, my dear girl, that there's no danger of you becoming like that particular child, she's a one off, and so are you.'

In September they received a postcard from Don, Maud and Teresa in Spain and nobody was rude because they all felt guilty about thinking Don was Mr Jones. The night before Sarah started school she didn't sleep and neither did Annie, but she need not have worried. She, Davy and Paul caught the same bus in and the same bus out and as long as she could do that, Sarah said that it didn't matter where she went to school.

They ran another mail shot and this time there were features in two of the dailies and mention of the export order

181

and the response was bigger than ever, and the wholesale orders were greater too.

They worked long hours building up the new season's designs and samples, though Tom would not have to include the Jones department stores in the February tour because they had visited the showroom and placed their own order.

The people of Wassingham were also visiting it, so it was decided that Bet should open it each morning and sell direct to the public at prices slightly cheaper than the shops. It gave them a greater profit but when Bet suggested opening more retail outlets they decided against it.

'Too much capital, too much hassle with staff, and supervision. We're not big enough yet,' Tom said and the others agreed.

'Let's see how the printing works out when Tom and Gracie get back off tour.' Because they'd decided to print off some tea towels and table mats and try them on the Christmas market and only if they worked would they invest in premises, continuous printers and curing ovens.

'Retail outlets are part of the future I think, but a good idea, Bet,' Annie said.

At the end of October Tom built a silk-screen printer in Bet's kitchen because she said they could use her oven if Gracie would put her dinner in the upstairs oven.

'Better than that, you'll come and eat with us until we see if this idea works,' Gracie said, kissing her cheek.

Tom bought wood and built a frame but it wasn't sturdy enough and it flexed.

'Damn it, it'll print badly, and the colours won't register,' he said.

He tried again, laying it on the kitchen table when he'd finished. This time it rested evenly with all four corners on the surface.

Annie called Georgie in from the stable where he'd been cutting wires which they would string up in the kitchen for drying, and others which he would make into racks for the oven.

'I glued and nailed the corners together and reinforced with angle irons screwed to the top,' Tom said, showing it to them, bringing Davy forward so that he could see and Annie was pleased.

'Get me the silk, Davy,' Tom said and then unrolled it on the table, putting the frame on it. 'Check the weave's parallel, Annie.'

It was.

Tom fastened the silk to the frame with drawing pins. 'Thank God Prue sent us a load of silk. Perhaps we should cut her in if we get it off the ground,' he said.

'Not if, when,' Georgie said.

Tom looked at the silk. 'It's no good, it's uneven. I know, let's take it off. I remember what we did at college now.'

They all helped to lever out the drawing pins and he turned up one edge of the silk and pinned it to the centre of one side of the frame, putting two further pins on either side of the first, pulling towards the corners for tension.

Annie watched Davy and he looked as pleased as Sarah did when Georgie and she went off together.

'Come on Annie, fasten the centre of that side, pull the silk as you do it.' Tom was frowning with concentration. It was his face as a child, it was Davy's face.

She fastened and pulled, then Davy did the other side and Sarah the last. Tom turned it over.

'Tight as your drums,' he grinned at the kids.

They watched as he masked the inside edges to prevent the ink from seeping underneath. 'Don't want a load of duff ones. Give old Manners a real Christmas treat wouldn't it?' Tom said.

The next day, Sunday, they covered Bet's table with a blanket and waterproof sheeting, stretching out the creases while the children mixed the dyes.

Tom had converted Annie's idea of a red star on a green background edged with red berries into a simple two-colour design and Bet had prepared the fabric the previous night, boiling the heavy cotton oblongs to remove the dressing and hanging them on Georgie's wires to dry.

Tom printed the green background, passing the fabric carefully to the others. They hung them over chair backs, airers or hoisted them up on to the wires suspended across the ceiling and did the same the next night, and the next, all of them coming to Bet's kitchen, mixing, printing, drying, baking in the oven to fix the dyes. Then drinking cocoa in Gracie's kitchen upstairs – which used to be my da's dining room, Annie told Sarah, wondering what he'd think of the cottage industry downstairs.

Each day they responded to orders which were coming in from the July tour, and at the end of the week Tom repeat-printed the red star and the border. They sent samples of the tea towels to Germany, and to Jones Department Store. At the end of the week there were more and Annie took the afternoon off and drove round the market stalls, showing them the tea towels, telling them there would also be matching table mats in time for Christmas – if they were interested.

They were and phoned in their orders all the next week.

Tom phoned Bill at the estate agents and he called them in during their lunch break. He checked for them that Steadman's was still available. It had been last year, and still in the summer.

'Yes, seems OK, but there's a stirring of interest, my boss says. Just a few questions being asked.'

'Not the consortium.'

'Yes, I'm afraid so.'

They didn't work that afternoon, instead they visited the planning office and discussed with them their requirements for the printing business, asking if there were any other sites within Wassingham that would be suitable. There weren't. There was only one sewage works.

That night they decided to have plans drawn up and submitted, even though they were not in a position to move on it and each of them tried to keep the panic at bay.

'If the bloody consortium's getting interested we'll have to be sharp or it'll cost us a fortune,' Tom said.

There was no word back from Germany, that week, or the next. Neither did they hear from Jones but they continued to print in the kitchen, refusing to believe that Schmidt would not like the towels, but prepared to believe that perhaps they were too primitive for Jones.

The pigeons were in moult and each morning and evening Georgie checked them, fed them, cleaned them out and by the middle of October they had shed their primaries and some of their secondaries and so there were no long training flights, just local flights and a mess about from the loft.

'Couldn't have timed it better, pet,' Georgie said as they mixed more paint, because the children were scavenging for Wassingham's bonfire that weekend. 'But I wish to God we'd heard back.'

At the end of October Schmidt placed an order, and Jones too but they wouldn't commit themselves to further goods until they saw how the Christmas take-up went on the existing stock.

It was a long two months and as Christmas came they were tired because the stalls had re-ordered three times and Jones had sold out and come back for more for their post January sale period. 'But not Christmas designs of course.'

On Christmas Eve Jurgen Schmidt rang, ordering two thousand aprons, to be delivered by Easter in a two-colour design, the rough sketch of which he would send.

They drank champagne with Don and Maud on Christmas Eve, and all the children drank too, though Maud said it was foolish and could lead to trouble in later life. No one took any notice, they were too excited, too happy, too tense.

Immediately after Christmas they heard that they had received planning permission. They also heard that the consortium had finally bought Steadman's, though the lease was still available, Bill said, his voice tired and defensive.

'Don't tell me,' Annie said, gripping the receiver. 'At triple the cost.'

185

'I'm afraid so, Annie, and a landlord inspection clause too.'

'Tell me,' she said this time, listening as Bill said that there would be an inspection each year and any repairs deemed necessary must be undertaken.

'Well, this is a wonderful start to 1959 isn't it?' she said.

They talked that evening as they worked in Bet's, wondering if they had ever smelt roast beef where now there were only chemicals. They talked and raged and could have wept.

'But there's nowhere else,' Georgie said finally. 'That's it in a nutshell, we'll have to take Steadman's or move out of Wassingham.'

'Which we promised ourselves we'd never do,' Annie said as Tom nodded.

'It's as though . . .' Georgie said, and then trailed off.

'Could it be personal?' Bet asked.

'Don't say that, we'll be thinking it's Don next and that's not fair. They're a London-based consortium, nothing to do with us,' Gracie snapped.

Annie listened, making herself think back to the yard, his jokes at Christmas, the kiss he had given her. No, it couldn't be Don. Yes, he'd run that loan business with Uncle Albert, yes, he'd been tight and mean but no, he wouldn't hurt his own family. He couldn't, and losing their money had been a mistake which she had instigated. For God's sake, Gracie was right, look at Mr Jones – how wrong they'd been then. Her head began to ache.

'It can't be Don,' she said, her voice firm because she could see that Georgie was filled with doubt. 'Look at the loft – that was a real Mr Jones. Look at the showroom – if we hadn't rented that we'd probably not have landed the export order.'

Georgie said, 'There were other shops we could have gone to for the showroom, but look, we needed Briggs, and we need Steadman's and it's wiping out our profits again, we're always back at square one.'

'There weren't other shops, not then.'

Bet spoke up then. 'Don was difficult, but never wicked, not as you are saying. You've asked Bill and he says it's a consortium, he's said it's being done all the time. I think you've got to stop wondering who it is and sort out what you're going to do. It wouldn't be the lad. No one would be that devious.'

Annie clasped Bet's hand. 'I know it's not him and so do you all. He's a right little bugger, we all know that but Bet's right. This is just business.'

Tom looked at Georgie, then at Annie, 'I didn't want to tell anyone but I've got to now. I've checked the names of the consortium. I'm sorry, I shouldn't have done because he's our brother but he isn't named. There's Samual Davis, James Merriott, Albert Sims, oh, and others. It isn't Don. I'm sorry, but it just gets on top of me when we make all this effort and then we're clobbered.'

That night Georgie held Annie and said, 'It gets on top of us all, my love, but you're right – it's just business and a collection of people out there that're bloody shrewd. Just wish we had them on our side.'

They paid the price and Georgie sold his car to help towards the cost of the ovens and the continuous printer. Annie hocked her walnut table to try and get it back, but it had been sold and by the time there was another there was no money left, it had all been sucked up by the printer, the shelving, repairing the heating, the ovens, and they were unable to sub-let the Briggs Warehouse at the price that they were paying for it.

Annie said to Tom, 'If I hear those politicians saying once more that we've never had it so good, I'll scream.'

CHAPTER 12

Sarah sat at her desk, leaning back against the radiator, feeling the heat in strips, waiting for Miss Bates to call her name, watching as first one girl and then another walked down the row of desks. It was the first day of the new school year and she had just been appointed window monitor, together with Hannah.

'Do we open or close them for fire practice?' Hannah whispered, her long hair hanging down her face as she drew pictures of Elvis Presley on her rough book.

'They'll tell us,' Sarah said. 'They always *tell* us everything but perhaps we'll change that this morning.'

Deborah was walking past them now, on her way to Bates's desk. Deborah always won the posture prize. Sarah sat up, put her shoulders back, then saw her breasts and hunched them again. They were a nuisance, they made her feel different, made her feel more of a girl beside Paul and Davy but they hadn't noticed, nothing had changed.

She drew guitars on the cover of her rough book. They were rehearsing tonight for the show at the Youth Club – Geoff was bringing his guitar, Paul was playing the bass they had made from a tea chest, a broom handle and a piece of string. Her fingers were sore from the washboard and Davy's looked the same but they'd have to practise or they'd never get it right and the families had said they were coming. What if they waved? No, they wouldn't, she'd tell her mum and she'd tell everyone else.

Hannah was called up to Miss Bates now and Sarah

188

watched her friend walk to the desk and sit down, her face
hidden by her hair. She had spots. Why did people get them?
Sarah felt her own skin – so far so good. Paul had spots but
then he didn't want to kiss anyone, he'd said, so it didn't
matter.

Hannah was walking back now. 'Piano,' she mouthed, then
louder, 'Your turn, Sarah. Good luck.'

Sarah nodded, picking up her slip of paper with guitar
written down. She handed this to Miss Bates who looked at
it, then at her. 'Another one. As I said to the others, it is out
of the question. You have a choice of violin, recorder or
piano.'

'But I want to play the guitar.'

'The guitar is not a proper instrument, it's just something
that's used to make a noise, these days anyway.'

Sarah nodded. That's just what her da had said. 'But I
want to learn to play it properly. I'm fed up with the washboard and anyway, skiffle's gone out really. Did you know,
Miss Bates, that rock 'n' roll is our present-day folk music.'

'Nonsense.'

Sarah smiled, she'd hoped Miss Bates would say this. 'It's
not nonsense, skiffle was a strain of American country blues,
played by blacks and rock 'n' roll's the same really. It's like
our folk music and we listen to that in musical appreciation,
don't we? I mean, if we could all learn the three basic chords
around which the music is geared all of us could play it and
write pieces, instead of plonking along learning piano chords
and taking exams.'

Sarah knew the whole class would be listening. They had
talked about it this morning, decided that each of them would
ask for guitar and one of them would have to try to talk Miss
Bates round – no one else had volunteered.

Miss Bates sighed, fingering her hair which was grey at
the temples, but only sometimes. Davy said she dyed it, but
Bet said only fast women dyed their hair. Sarah looked at
Miss Bates. No, she wasn't fast, never had been, never would
be. Had Bet been a fast woman – she'd had Tom when she

wasn't married. But Sarah didn't want to think of that, didn't want to think of old people being fast – it was revolting.

'I'm putting you down for piano,' Miss Bates said. 'It will give you a musical sense and in due course you can pursue your guitar playing on your own, if you must.'

So that was that, Sarah thought, walking back to her desk, hearing the whispered 'Bad luck' 'Never mind' 'Good try'. At break they huddled around by the milk crates and wondered why adults were so stupid, so set in their ways. Why did they have to be so narrow minded? Why did they always know best? Why did they never listen? Their parents were the same – nag, nag, nag.

On the way back to Wassingham she told Davy that it hadn't worked – that they'd just have to keep on with the book. She dragged the beginner's guide out of her satchel and as the bus jerked and rattled from village to village they played imaginary chords and talked of Elvis and Haley and Buddy Holly, who had died in February, and they still couldn't believe that.

They practised that evening at the Youth Club hall, working on *Rock Island Line* until their fingers were too sore and their throats too dry to sing another note.

Roger, the Youth Leader, was sitting on a chair at the front of the stage, calling instructions to the ballet girls who were going to dance to *Swan Lake* on the gramophone.

He shouted to Davy over his shoulder. 'Much better, but still needs work. Remember that when you take the world by storm, no good without practice.'

Sarah told Annie and Georgie that when she arrived home half an hour late but it didn't help and she was packed off to bed without cocoa, but who cared, she thought, lying in her bed, hearing the cat yowling next door and the pigeons fluttering. She pulled her radio into the bed and listened to Radio Luxemburg beneath the covers, trying to cut out the interference, wishing it was her group playing, promising herself that one day it would be.

At the end of September 1959 Annie set on another worker, this time a mother with a child. They partitioned a room, brought in sand and camp beds and Gracie and Bet shared the running of the creche whilst Annie, Georgie and Tom shared the printing between them as well as their normal work. Brenda took on the supervision of the staff completely but there were still not enough hours in the day and while Sarah practised, or did her homework, Annie and Georgie worked in the kitchen and they knew that Tom and Gracie were doing the same.

Mrs Anders from next door came in each morning to clean the house and peel the vegetables and each afternoon she popped in to put a casserole in the oven.

'Better than Mr Jones,' Georgie would say to Annie each week.

As October turned to November the weather grew colder, snow fell and Annie was glad that the birds were in moult because they didn't have time for long journeys any more and besides, there was still no car for Georgie.

He fell twice the day of the snow, and twice the next day, and so Annie lugged down the wheelchair from the attic, heaving it down the stairs, dragging it into the kitchen, dusting it down as he ate bacon and eggs and Sarah played drums on her lunch-box.

'There you are m'lord, your carriage awaits. We'll bung it into the car and keep it at Steadman's, then you don't have to skid yourself across the car park.' She felt tense, he hadn't used this at all.

Georgie looked at it, and then at her, his eyes shadowed, then cleared. 'You ought to wear a cap, I insist on it. I like my chauffeurs properly dressed.'

'You'll get them as you find them, or I'll haul you to the top of a high hill and let you go.' Annie was laughing, pushing the chair through the yard, out and into the boot of the car. It wouldn't close but who cared, Steadman's was only round the corner.

She turned and Sarah was there, her face angry. 'He

shouldn't be in the chair, he should be in his car. Why can't we get that one converted, Mum, it's not fair.'

Annie felt the wind tear into her and pulled her cardigan round her, taking Sarah's arm, pushing her before her into the yard, seeking the shelter of the walls. 'Do you think I haven't thought of that? Really, Sarah. Brenda uses the car for deliveries, so does Gracie, and whoever happens to be on the run that day. It's just not possible. I'm saving as hard as I can, now don't worry.'

Sarah shrugged out of Annie's grasp, her face sullen. 'Well, someone's got to.'

She turned but Annie grabbed her arm again. 'Just what do you mean by that? And look at me when I'm talking to you.'

'I mean just what I said,' hissed Sarah, looking at her mother now, her cheeks red. 'You're all right, you can get about. You're like everyone else, rushing around looking after yourself, never listening, never seeing what people need or want.'

Annie felt anger flare. She shook her daughter. 'How dare you talk to me like that? You know I've done all I can for your father and I'm still doing all I can. I just don't know what's the matter with you these days, Sarah, you're so difficult. I think you're spending too much time up there in your bedroom listening to that damn music, you need to sit with us in the evening, or something.'

'I like that damn music, and I like my damn bedroom.'

'Don't swear.'

'Why not, you do. But then adults can do anything they like, it's just us who can't, even though we're not kids any more. We just have to do as we're told – play the piano, not the guitar.'

Annie threw up her hands, and wanted to put this child over her knee. 'So, that's what all this is about, is it? I really cannot believe I'm hearing this from you. Go in, put your sandwiches into your lunch-box, fill your flask because I'm

192

not doing it any more if you're so very grown up, and hurry up, you'll miss your bus.'

She watched as Sarah stalked into the kitchen. She listened to the bangs and crashes. She waited until her daughter came out again, walking past her, and Annie itched to slap her. Sarah stopped by the gate. 'Anyway, it wasn't about me, not really. It's about you and poor Da.'

Annie said. 'Just go to school.' Her voice was quiet with rage.

She went into the warmth of the kitchen and stood in front of the range, gripping the guard. Kids, bloody kids, she thought to herself – and I thought the nappy stage was difficult.

That day Annie called a meeting and discussed the possibility of using their own textiles on a mail order shot. It wasn't scheduled until spring 1960 but demand from wholesalers was increasing. 'I know it'll go,' she said because they had to improve their profits. Sarah was right, it wasn't fair that he should not have a car and somehow that had been forgotten.

The workers agreed and so did the family. Georgie rescheduled and Tom suggested that they took on Bernie to help with the printing. 'He's retired from the pit, but he's bored out of his mind. We can't do everything you know, bonny lass,' he said.

'I know,' Annie snapped.

'You had a row with someone?'

'No.'

She rang the bank that afternoon and explained about the mail shot, that Georgie would need to be mobile – it was just too much for the rest of them. 'Too inefficient,' she said. 'I just need to extend the overdraft.'

The bank manager agreed. That was the easy part. The difficult one was to convince Georgie.

She sat on his desk after lunch, playing with the papers she'd brought in, knowing that she looked tired, knowing that they all looked tired. 'Now, with this mail shot, we're going to be under even more pressure so you'll need to do your own running about. I've arranged a bank loan. Tom's agreed, so will you do the same please?'

Georgie put down his pen, laid his hands flat on the table. 'We can't afford it.'

'We need to spend money to make money sometimes. We can afford it. We will afford it.'

Brenda interrupted her. 'Sorry Annie, call from Jones. They want a further supply of aprons. Interested in some children's dungarees too.'

Annie nodded. 'I'm coming. Now, just give me a break will you Georgie, take some of the load.'

He picked up his pen again, bent his head, began to write. 'Georgie, are you listening?'

He looked up. 'Sometimes I feel I want to punch my fist through a brick wall. It's so bloody difficult being like this.' He tapped his leg. 'It's so bloody difficult for everyone connected with me, and today it aches, the cold's got into it.'

Annie smiled at him. 'You have no idea how easy it is to be connected with you.'

Sarah walked from the bus to the back yard, pushing the door open, calling to Mrs Anders that she was home, hearing her reply from the kitchen.

She opened the door. The range was burning, the kettle was on and the kitchen smelt of macaroni cheese. She slumped into the chair, dropped her satchel on the floor, then stood up and walked down the road, through Steadman's car park, into the machine shop, then into her mother's office. She was on the phone.

Sarah sat down and listened to the strain in her mother's voice, saw the lines running deeply to her mouth. She looked so tired and Sarah hadn't noticed. She felt the raffia beneath her legs. It was warm and she could hear the sewing machines all around, music from the radio – Alma Cogan, Frank Sinatra, no rock 'n' roll. Sarah looked at her hands, sore from the washboard and covered in ink from her leaking pen. Her stomach tightened again as it had been doing all day. She felt the tears close again, though they hadn't fallen yet, and they mustn't. Girls of twelve didn't cry.

'Sarah, how nice. Shall I get you a cup of tea?' Annie put down the phone, started to rise.

'I'm sorry, Mum. I'm sorry. I shouldn't have said it, I know I shouldn't. I don't know why I say these things.'

She was crying now but her mother's arms were round her, holding her, smoothing her hair. 'I deserved it,' Annie said. 'I had sort of forgotten, other things to think about, other priorities but he'll have it within the next two weeks. It's all been sorted out.'

Sarah let herself lean into her mother, let her stroke back the hair from her face but the tears were still coming. 'In PE today Miss Smithers said I needed a bra and the other girls laughed.'

Annie held her more tightly. 'Growing up is very difficult, my darling. I'll bring some home tonight.' She looked over her daughter's head at the machine shop, the design office, the printing shop and wondered where all the years had gone, and knew that the coming ones were going to see more of this and the best she could do was to keep the lines of communication open. It would need a light hand.

That night she sewed yards of petticoats for Sarah's skiffle costume, then the skirt, the wide belt, the top, and then sat on her daughter's bed and talked about growing up, all the uncertainties, the conflicts, boyfriends, kissing, petting and Sarah was glad that the lights were out and wished that her mother would stop, because they'd talked all about sex at school, and then on the bus going home with Davy and Paul and it hadn't been embarrassing like this.

Her mother bent forward and kissed her, 'Don't listen to Radio Luxemburg for too long,' she said. She smelt of lavender and now Sarah hugged her, holding her tight, not wanting to grow up, but impatient for it too. 'I love you, Mum.'

Annie remembered this as she and Georgie sat in the

audience with Gracie, Don, Maud and Teresa on Saturday evening and winced at the ballet, tapping to the African drums, swaying to the English madrigals played by the organist and his friends.

'It's music through the ages and from many lands,' she told Don, pleased that he had come.

'How quaint,' said Maud, looking round. 'But no Tom, no Rob?'

No, there was no Tom, he was at a debating competition, supporting Rob. 'We had to split up,' Gracie said, 'So each of the boys had someone there.'

Annie drank her tea and wished that just for once it had been Tom who had listened to Davy.

They talked of the new mail shot, the clauses in the lease, Don's business and Teresa looked at the programme and asked if there was any piano playing. There was not, Annie said, taking Bet's cup, moving away as Teresa told them all in a loud voice about her success at her own school concert.

After the interval there was jazz dancing and then Davy and Sarah, with Paul and Geoff, rasped out *Rock Island Line* and now Annie's feet were tapping, and her hands clapped out the rhythm with the rest of the audience, though Don, Maud, and Teresa kept silent. They were good, really good and Sarah's voice was confident, powerful, brilliant, and Annie felt such pride that suddenly she couldn't clap, she could only grip her hands together because her throat was tightening and her eyes blurring and at the end she wanted to stand on her chair and whistle and shout like the kids in the audience were doing.

That Christmas Gracie and Annie took Davy and Sarah into Newcastle, gave them tea at the department store, wafted into Lingerie and said 'Good afternoon,' to Mrs Wilvercombe, who preened and asked them to stay for more tea and told them how well their garments were selling. 'Such a pleasure to do business with you.'

Annie wanted to say that she wished she could say the same, but didn't.

They refused tea. 'So sorry, no time. We have guitars to buy.'

She and Gracie smiled as they heard the children gasp and then took them out to the music shop that Roger, the Youth Leader, had suggested and stood while the kids looked, then fingered, then tried, watched them blush because no sound came from one. It was electric.

Annie shook her head, pointing down to the far end. 'Oh no, a cheap one first, just to see if you really like it.'

They each left with an American six-string National with a metal body and groaned when their mothers took it from them, saying that they must wait until Father Christmas dropped it down the chimney.

All Christmas Day, while the parents and Bet drank champagne and wine to celebrate the success of their first textile mail shot they fingered the strings, moving up and down the frets, until they were banished to the upstairs sitting room, taking their *Learn the Guitar the Easy Way*. Georgie said, 'Why aren't there any good tunes any more, that's what I'd like to know.'

In spring 1960 the consortium's inspector insisted that they update the lavatories and it did them no good to insist that it came within the landlord's province because the small print stated clearly that it didn't.

In the summer Tiger won the Club cup and Buttons took second place and Frank's grin was almost as wide as Georgie's. Sarah told Miss Bates at school, and also told her that she had learnt to play the guitar, and would teach the others if she liked.

Miss Bates said no, but she could write her project on pigeon keeping if she liked. Sarah did like and worked hard, charting the daily routine, the trapping of the youngsters, the tossing, the destruction of those who didn't 'make up', calm and analytical now, leaving out of the project her tears, her pleadings with Georgie to let them remain. But he was right, they'd never have thrived, she could see that now.

In the autumn the children were banished out to Black

197

Beauty's stable to practise because they had been joined by Geoff on guitar and Paul on drums. 'It's too much for an old man's eardrums,' Tom said, though he drifted out from time to time because Annie had said that he should pay more attention to Davy. Sarah still sat in her room for half an hour before sleeping, picking out the tunes that were played on Radio Luxembourg, wanting an hour, but being refused.

In the early spring of 1961 Tom and Gracie toured the European Trade Fairs and brought back so many orders that they took on three more workers and there were now four children in the creche. Annie loved to walk in and hear the sound of their laughter, their singing, because these were the simple sounds of childhood and a relief from the minefield of the teenage world.

In June the inspector called again and this time insisted on redecoration and replacing of the external doors, which had been damaged by the comings and goings of the textile workers, or so he said. They had to overhaul the heating system because the flue was dangerous. It took too much from their profits and Tom said that the creche was a drain on the business. He showed them the books when Georgie and Sarah returned from a training race but as they sat back drinking tea they knew that they couldn't close it.

'This business is not just for us, it's for Wassingham,' Annie said and the others agreed.

'It's just that our overheads are so high we're never in profit as we should be. Christ, I wish we had an alternative to Steadman's.'

'Perhaps we should build our own premises?' Georgie said, as Sarah made herself cheese on toast.

Annie felt hungry just smelling it. 'Would you put some on for me, darling. Anyone else?' Everyone else. Sarah sighed and Annie grinned.

'Tough being the cook, isn't it?' she said.

'Oh, Mum, I've got practice for the fête.'

'Be quiet, Sarah, this is important.' Georgie was leaning forward.

'So's my fête.'

'I said be quiet.'

Annie intervened. 'Leave the cheese, take yours and Davy's, half an hour's practice only and then homework, then clean the pigeons.'

'Oh Mum.'

Annie stood up. 'Go on, there's been a compromise, don't push it.'

Sarah paused, then smiled. 'Thanks Mum.' Annie grinned wryly, then grated the cheese, whipped the egg, mixed it, listening as Georgie and Tom thrashed out the possibility of building, but there was no possibility, they all knew that. They were trapped.

'Don't worry,' she said. 'In spite of everything we're still in profit, we're growing – we have domestic and export markets, and pretty soon we'll have rebuilt that damn building so they can't cream any more off us. Now eat this up.'

In August the children played at the fête and Annie heard them before she saw them, driving up to the grassed wasteland beneath the slag, laughing at Georgie's face as he heard his daughter's voice, his daughter's guitar playing, heard her growling out from the tannoy, beating across the air.

'Why aren't there any proper tunes any more? Why do I feel so old?' he said, heaving himself from the car, walking with Annie to the tombola, buying tickets.

'They're good you know.'

Georgie nodded, moving on to the coconut stall, throwing and missing, thank God, Annie thought. She hated coconut. 'Yes,' he said, tossing the last ball up. 'But where's it all going to end?' He threw and hit one and Annie's heart sank.

She carried the coconut towards the roped off area where the kids were playing. Teenagers were jiving all around them, their skirts whirling up, their arms flailing, their hair back combed and bouncing.

'I mean, Annie, they ruin their hair. She was scrunching it all up this morning.'

'Back combing.'

199

Georgie walked on. 'They throw themselves around. Look at that.'

Annie looked at a girl being thrown over her partner's shoulder, then back down again between his legs. She wanted to join in.

'I mean, we didn't have time for this,' Georgie said. 'I mean, what are they going to get up to? There's this music, all these strange fashions. I liked those pretty skirts with lots of petticoats.'

'Mm, but the children are deciding what *they* like, not following what we like and perhaps it's not before time. It's a different world, my love – careful.' The grass was tufted, uneven and the smell of it was in the air. 'They've more money, people are catering for them. We've got to forget what it was like for us, and try and understand what it's like for them, much as it goes against the grain, and go on being patient.'

Annie said that again to Georgie in December when Miss Bates told them at the parents' evening that Sarah was not working to her full potential, that she had too many interests in her life, that her guitar playing should stop, and that she should put the group to one side until her 'O' levels were over, and perhaps her 'A's.

Annie spoke to Sarah in her bedroom that night. She sat on the edge of her bed, feeling the ridges of the patchwork that Bet's mother had sewn so many years ago, looking at the ivory paper knife that had been her father's and wishing she felt old enough to be this child's mother.

'Now look, Miss Bates feels you have too much to do now that you are starting to work for your 'O' levels. Something has got to give. She would like it to be your music.'

Sarah hugged her knees and nodded. 'Yes, piano's a waste of time.'

Annie knew she would say this. She spoke quietly but firmly. 'No, not the piano, the group.'

Sarah straightened, flicking her hair back from her face. 'That's not fair. I won't give it up. I just won't.'

'There's no need to shout.'

'Mum, I won't.'

Annie took her hand and Sarah snatched it back. Annie said, 'Listen, let's leave that for now, let's talk about what you want to do in life, we never seem to discuss this sort of thing, everyone's too busy. It's our fault as well, don't worry, I'm not blaming you. Now, what do you want to do?'

Annie walked to the window, leaning against the frame, looking out across the town that she loved, hearing Mrs Anders' cat, and the pigeons in the loft outside, wishing she'd done a degree in diplomacy.

'I want to go to Newcastle to learn fashion design.' Sarah's voice was muffled.

Annie turned. Her daughter was leaning on her knees, her mouth against the quilt. 'Are you sure? I remember you saying that years ago but I don't want you to feel you have to do it just because of the business.'

Sarah shook her head. 'No, it's not because of the business. Anyway, you can't call it fashion can you – a few dungarees, aprons, smocks and underwear – but I do want to work with you.'

Annie raised her eyebrows, well pardon me for living, she thought, but merely said, 'So, if you want to do fashion design you will need your 'O' and 'A' levels. You will need to do more work.'

Sarah looked up at her. 'Mum, it's not the music I want to give up.'

Annie looked out again at the pigeon loft and nodded. She had thought as much.

'I don't know how to tell Da.'

Annie smiled gently at Sarah, walked back to the bed, straightened the quilt. 'Don't worry, I'll do a deal with you, I'll tell him – you may keep your music going, but only if your homework is done. I'm not sure what Tom will say to

Davy, because he's in trouble too. You might find yourself going solo.'

She bent and kissed her daughter.

'I'll never go solo, it'd be no fun without Davy, no fun at all.'

Annie was quiet for a moment then left the room, thinking as she walked down the stairs that her daughter's love for Davy was very deep, but was it the love of a sister for a brother as her love for Tom was, or was it something quite different? Only time would tell. That night Annie barely slept because all she could think of was how Sarah would cope with the loneliness of college without her friend, whichever love it was. But thank God it was only as far as Newcastle.

CHAPTER 13

On the Saturday after she had spoken to Sarah Annie and Georgie drove ten miles north of Wassingham, through wind-flattened moors and huddled villages. She could hear the wind screaming in from the north and soon she'd feel it. She drew her scarf round her neck, turned up her collar. Would it be a white Christmas?

'You shouldn't have come, pet, it's too cold for you. Sarah'll be here next week. I could have come by myself.'

Annie looked at his strong hands on the steering wheel. Oh no, he couldn't come by himself because what if he fell, damaged his false leg, damaged his stump? He could die in this cold, but to tell him that was to admit his limitations and that she must never do.

'The thing is, my darling, she can't bear to give up music and she has to give up something.'

They were turning into Rowen's Track and she felt Georgie turn to her, then to the front again, wrestling with the wheel as the car lurched on the rutted ice-cracked tracks.

'Oh I see.'

She could tell from his voice that he did.

'These few years have given her so much Georgie, not just success with Buttons but time with you. She'll have shared memories.'

They were approaching the farm gate, Georgie stopped the car whilst she leapt out, the force of the wind stopping her, taking her breath. She bent her head into it, her nose already numb, her lips too. She slipped the wire, pushed back the gate, stumbling over the frozen hummocks, but the sun was already coming out as Georgie drove in past her. She shoved the gate shut and ran for the shelter of the car, pushing her hands between her thighs as they lurched and bounced across the field.

'I'll miss her, she's sliding through our fingers isn't she?' Georgie said quietly.

Annie nodded. 'Just as we did. Everyone does.'

Georgie steered the car towards the north-east corner, to the lee of the hawthorn hedge and already the air was warmer.

'The wind should drop,' Georgie said, making no effort to leave the car, just sitting back. 'Let's wait and see, don't want them battling too much, it makes me stump ache and God knows what it does to their wings.' He paused. 'I love her, I worry about her, I'm glad I had all those days with her. You're a generous woman, Annie.'

He kissed her now, held her close and she remembered Bet saying to her as they stood and watched Georgie and Sarah leave one day. 'Aren't you jealous?'

Yes, she had been jealous – of Georgie's time with Sarah, of Sarah's time with Georgie but it had been necessary for them both. His lips were on hers now, kissing softly, gently and then with passion. 'I shall just have to do put up with you now,' he said at last, drawing back from her, pushing her hair off her face. 'Cold nose and all.'

They carried the basket across to the usual place and now the sun was warm as she dropped the lid back and watched Button's and Tiger's youngsters wheel, dip, then fly for home.

They drank coffee out of the thermos, cupping their hands around the mugs, moving their feet. 'I can still feel my toes, after all this time,' Georgie said. 'Come over here and let me feel your nose.'

She laughed and leant against him as he pressed his cheek to her face. She kissed him, heard him tip his coffee away, felt him take hers and toss the mug to the ground, felt his arms around her, his lips on her eyes, her nose, her lips, his hands undoing the buttons of her coat, stroking her breasts, her body, then holding her tightly to him, so tight she could hardly breathe.

'There's a time for them to grow up, isn't there, if only to give us time together,' Georgie said, his mouth on hers. 'I'm glad you're back, I've missed you.'

Both domestic and export sales rose steadily in the spring of 1962 and Annie redeemed her walnut table. Throughout the Easter holidays they agreed to take on Sarah, Davy, Geoff and Paul as temporary packers and cleaners. The tennis courts were finished – they had managed to build two – and now they wanted decent tennis rackets, shoes, and the group needed amplifiers.

'We're screwing on pick-ups beneath the strings, Mum,' Sarah said, 'and wiring them into amplifiers. All groups need them.'

Annie shuddered. 'Not in our house they don't – your father would flip and I'd die.'

'Oh Mum, it's not for the house, it's for our gigs.'

'Your what?'

Sarah flicked her hair back from her face. 'Our gigs, we're going to try and earn some money, get around, let people hear us, it's the only way to improve you know, to work for something, otherwise we just mess about – just like Da said the birds did if they didn't have competition.'

Annie looked at Davy, shaking her head, that child would take the ground right from under Georgie's feet with that particular argument as she well knew. 'So, whose idea was this?'

Davy grinned. 'Guess.'

Annie shook her head. 'You should stand up to her Davy, don't let her push you around – and there's the small matter of your work.'

Davy laughed. 'She's all right, she just knows what she wants and it's a good idea isn't it, Aunt Annie? It'll get us

205

out of earshot of you and me parents and that way we can buy ourselves better guitars.'

That evening Annie talked Georgie into employing the kids, telling him that he was always going on about being in the pit at their ages, so they could do a bit of slave labour 'at mill' instead.

'But homework must be done. You're fifteen and working towards those exams,' she warned.

As summer came the sales were still increasing and the inspector found only that the outside needed redecorating and they felt like sticking out their tongues and blowing raspberries as he left.

In May the graph in Annie's office showed just a steady rise since December, no dips as there had been the year before. They were selling to France now and had stabilised the size ratios at last, accommodating slimmer French figures, whilst judging Holland and Germany on the British shape. Georgie's mail order division was expanding, bringing in further orders for the wholesalers.

'You were right, it's a good shop window, my love,' Georgie said as they worked out the bonus for the workers, the increase in salary for them which this year would be larger, though their overheads were rising along with their sales.

'It's not enough just to divide the profits, we need to do something together this year, to celebrate, all of us – everyone in the firm. We're so busy we never have time to talk, even at the meetings we just discuss business,' Annie said one evening as she dished out new potatoes from Bet's allotment since they had been too late with their own this year, again.

Sarah watched the butter melt on the potatoes, darkening the mint. She remembered how her mother used to scrape parsley off her food at Sarah Beeston's, not knowing that it was to be eaten. Parents were embarrassing.

Georgie reached for the salad cream. 'Good idea – how about a trip to the sea.'

'No, not the sea – if it rains we'll have Bernie grizzling

and everyone sitting on the coach steaming up the windows wishing they hadn't come.' Annie cut into her tomato. 'Bet's had a really good year with these. I like the small ones.'

Sarah looked up. 'How about Spanish City at Whitley Bay? There's lots to do.'

Georgie nodded. 'Not a bad idea. I haven't been for years and they're bringing their families aren't they Annie? The kids would love a fair.'

Annie nodded. 'Oh yes, I've been through the books, we can afford it and never mind the kids, *we'd* love it.'

Sarah smiled. 'Can the Easter packers come too?'

'If you want to but I'd have thought it was a bit square for you. We'll probably be wearing Kiss Me Quick hats and eating candy floss – can The Founders' image take it?'

Sarah just nodded and smiled. Some of the best American rock 'n' roll music was played there, or so Geoff had said but there was no need to tell them about that.

In June Gracie, Bet and Annie took Friday off and cooked chickens, sausages and sausage rolls, wrapping them in greaseproof paper and stacking them in the fridge until the morning. When Sarah came in from school she sliced and buttered seven loaves of bread, then helped Annie boil eggs for fifteen minutes. They filled containers with squash but when they arrived at the coach the next day they saw Georgie and Tom loading bottles of beer into the luggage hold.

'Too hot for squash, or tea,' Georgie grinned, nodding as Bet handed him the thermos flasks which the women had brought.

'Well, you just keep your eye on Bernie,' Annie warned, laughing as Tom rolled his eyes. 'And yourselves.'

They sang all the old favourites as they travelled – *Knees up Mother Brown*, *The White Cliffs of Dover*. Davy and Sarah sat staring out of the window, mortified by their parents who were standing up at the front conducting.

The coach driver took them via the scenic route as he had promised and they stopped for half an hour on moorland where the heather was lush and the gorse spiked dark green and yellow. There were peewits, and hawks, and the sound of insects as Annie lay down and looked up at the sky, hearing the laughter, the voices of people she employed, children the creche looked after. She heard Sarah giggling as Geoff pounced on Davy, then her, rolling her over and over down the slope, her flared jeans picking up dirt but what did it matter, they were going to the fair, weren't they?

She smiled up at Bet. 'It's a good day isn't it, Bet?'

'Aye, bonny lass, and you've done a good thing, all of you, for Wassingham. Your Sarah Beeston would be proud of you, and your da.'

When the coach finally pulled up at the fairground they could hear the music. Annie caught Sarah's eye, grinning at her, then at Davy. 'Well, well,' she said. 'Just as well your da's had a few beers and the sun's shone on me. This could lead to a severe sense of humour failure.'

The rock 'n' roll was pounding as they all arranged to meet in an hour's time for the picnic. Annie shrugged off thanks as she handed out spending money to each family.

'It's yours, it's part of the profits and you deserve it,' she said. 'We've all worked hard, just don't fall off, we want you coming back in one piece.'

She felt Georgie stiffen at her side and wondered why there were so many sayings that involved the body and why she was so stupid. She turned, touching his arm as he smiled at Meg and her husband Geoff, waiting until they had gone, then said, 'I'm sorry.'

He looked at her. 'Don't be – it's just that every so often it still gets to me. I still wish it had never happened. I wish I could grab you and run off as they're doing.' He nodded at Sarah, Davy and the other two boys, racing one another to the dodgems.

Annie held his hand, slotting her fingers between his, holding him tightly. 'There aren't many people of our age running anywhere right now,' she said, but she understood, and from his kiss she knew he realised that she did.

'She's a little devil though, isn't she? Just listen to all this,' Georgie said, but he was laughing. 'Davy's just told me he wants to do textile design so that'll please her majesty – I'll bet any money you like they'll be going to the same college, so they'll keep one another company and we can easily get to Newcastle to see them, make sure she's not getting out of hand.'

'*Getting* out of hand, I just hope she's not already there,' Annie said walking towards the music, seeing the candy floss stall and feeling the relief spreading through her at the thought that Davy and Sarah would stay together, and close to home.

'We must do this more often,' she murmured, 'it brings us luck.' Because she had feared they would disappear to London and it seemed so far away, especially in today's world.

Sarah and Davy ran with Geoff and Paul through the crowds, feeling the heat on their faces, hearing the music blasting out from the huge speakers, almost drowning the chugging of the generators, smelling the diesel, candy floss, hot dogs. They stood on the steps, watching the cars crash and thump, the drivers grimace and jerk, waiting until the music slowed, then running for a car. Sarah and Davy in the yellow one, Geoff and Paul in the green, chasing one another as the power came on, screaming, screeching, groaning, jolting.

They ran off to the Big Wheel and flew through the air, and Sarah felt the wind rush through her, like it did when she tumbled over the bar at the allotment and she gripped Davy's arm. 'Isn't life wonderful, just so wonderful and you're right, we should go to your da's college. It'll get us away from here, give us a change. This is what London will be like – the two of us and music like this, and people who understand op art, and like it too. Oh Davy, I can't wait.' She turned and looked out across the flashing lights to the sea.

On the coach back Sarah and Davy conducted the singers in *Hound Dog* and *Living Doll*, then organised them into groups using their voices to create rhythms, singing Platters songs, and Coasters numbers while Rob sat next to Annie and talked about Ban the Bomb marches and the escalation in the United States military aid to Vietnam until his father reached over and said, 'Shut up and sing.'

Annie saw Davy turn towards them, he had heard and the love in his face was for Tom. She smiled gently. Everything was going to be all right. It wasn't until the next morning that Sarah told her about London, about Davy's need to go to his father's college, about their need for a change.

Annie merely straightened her daughter's collar, gave her a kiss and said that of course she understood, they would all understand. She walked to the allotment and wouldn't allow the ache to take hold, she just hoed and dug and watered, and thought of the places she had been, and how Sarah Beeston had let her go with never a murmur – how Georgie had travelled far further and his mother had allowed him – how Tom and Gracie had spent three years in London.

By the time the evening came her back ached and her hands were blistered but she was comforted, because London wasn't so far away, Sarah would be practically an adult and she must learn to let go, it was as simple as that and this is what she told Georgie as they made love. 'I know,' he said. 'It's what I've been thinking. I'm quite looking forward to life on our own while we watch her grow. It'll be a new stage for them and us.'

His lips were as soft as his voice and she held him close to her because she knew that he was right.

Throughout the summer the kids worked as packers again, standing alongside the machinists who had voted to take turns in the packing room to ring the changes during the day.

In the autumn the kids bought second-hand amplifiers and fixed them to plywood, taking them to the Youth Club for the Christmas gig which was the only one they had secured.

They had new guitars for Christmas, ones with good solid wide bodies and black inlaid trim. They had cutaway necks for easier manoeuvrability on the lower frets of the finger board, or so the man in the shop had told Gracie and Annie.

They sat round the table, fingering them, playing desultory chords, talking of the geometric patterns of op art, the visual effect they created, and Annie asked Tom if they could be incorporated into the soft furnishings they were considering for the summer if they found they could afford new printers.

He shook his head. 'Too adventurous.'

'Oh Da,' groaned Davy.

'Oh Da nothing, just think what it would be like to live with. Interesting to create, a problem to sell, just you remember that, both of you, when you're down there in that big city.'

'And just remember too,' said Annie, pouring the last of the beer, 'that nobody's going anywhere unless these exams are passed, so rehearsals are restricted until July.'

The kids didn't groan, just nodded because they had their guitars, they had their amplifiers and after their 'O' levels they would have two years to penetrate the clubs of Newcastle before they left for London, then they'd have everything.

In the spring of 1963 Annie took on a cutter because there was too much work for just one. They took on two machinists, a bookkeeper and a clerk and at last her office was tidy, Georgie's and Tom's too.

'I feel like a real boss now,' Georgie said that night. 'I really must get myself a cigar.'

'Over my dead body,' Annie replied.

In the summer there was no maintenance for the inspector to throw at them, just profits, and so the bonus was higher, but not too high because they'd decided at the monthly meeting to invest in new printers, pad mangles, and a boiler so that they could respond to the upholstery requests which were pouring in.

'Next year,' Annie said, 'our turnover should be so much higher that the bonus, and the salary increases, should be much bigger. Hang in with us, everyone, we've nearly cracked it.'

At the end of June, Don rang and she told him of their expansion, of their increased bonus for the workers, the escalating graph, the lack of repairs on the inspector's list.

'So the consortium can go and take a jump,' she said and he was pleased for them, really pleased, she could tell from his voice.

'Come over,' she said. 'We haven't seen you for ages.'

'Can't, we're going to the Canary Isles tomorrow.'

Sarah said, 'Tweet, tweet,' when Annie told her and Annie asked Georgie that night whether London knew quite what was going to hit it.

In July, they reorganised the factory, reshuffling, making room for the two flat-bed printers, one Buser printer, two pad mangles, a step and repeat machine and the boiler. They could now print eight colours, not just two. It took a month to set up and start producing and they took on three extra print workers and a machinist called Pat who was a new-comer to Wassingham but who needed a break, Brenda said. They also took on a van and driver for distribution.

'Should we try our own retail outlets?' Bet asked.

No, they said, they couldn't cope. Not yet.

'Should we try wallpaper?'

No, they said, not yet, next year perhaps because they must recoup their outlay first and then they would reconsider. Now they should start building up their reserves because the new machinery had taken their capital, though there was no loan involved and that in itself was a victory. 'It's going to be good, just up and up from now on,' Annie told everyone.

On 1 August Sarah showed Annie details of a talent competition in Newcastle in three weeks' time. 'We want to enter. We want to get as far as we can while we're here. It'll improve us so much, hold us in good stead for London.

They're more sophisticated there, sharper. We'll need much more experience.'

That night in bed, Annie and Georgie lay and worried and the next day as she cooked breakfast Annie said, 'Where is this music taking you – will it push aside your art? Do think carefully, you need qualifications to fall back on, and we hear such stories of the music world.'

She turned the bacon, hearing it spit, watching the fat cook, the rind warp, waiting for her daughter to reply.

Sarah was reading the paper, turning the pages, speaking with toast in her mouth. 'Oh, we're only going to use it to earn a bit of extra money. It's just a hobby, Mum, like Da's birds, then we'd like to come back here and help in the business, if that's all right, because the north's our home and besides you'll need us when you start the retail outlets and the wallpaper.'

The bacon was burning. Annie flicked it on to the plates. 'That's all right then,' she said quite calmly, though she wanted to leap in the air and cheer.

The kids practised in Annie's front room because Tom's neighbours had complained about the noise coming from the stable. Mrs Anders complained about the noise coming from the front room, but no more loudly than Georgie did, stamping into the kitchen on Friday night, storming out into the yard, talking to his pigeons, complaining to Annie that the whole thing was ridiculous.

Annie laughed gently. 'It would be ridiculous if it was serious, just remember that, but they're being sensible, so count your blessings.'

Georgie slumped down on the step. 'I'm tired, you're tired. We can do without this bloody racket. There's so much to do at work, there's the pigeons to race . . .'

'There are the children to nurture,' Annie interrupted. 'And that's the most important thing of all, Georgie Armstrong.'

She joined him on the step, putting her hand on his false leg as he leant back against the door frame. 'And what about

213

that dress she's made for the show, Annie? It's above the knee, for goodness' sake. It's a disgrace. She'll get herself into all sorts of trouble, and imagine that in London. I suppose you made it for her.' He was leaning forward now, holding her arm.

'No, I didn't make it for her, I just showed *her* how to do it, so stop being so stuffy. All the girls are dressing like that now.'

'But she's only – '

'Sixteen,' Annie interrupted again. 'Not a child, so stop panicking and treating her like one. Give her some freedom and she'll . . . oh, come back and perch, just like your youngsters do. Lock her up and she'll break out. They might not want to come back to Wassingham if you start all this, just think on that.'

Georgie rubbed his forehead, then rested his back against the frame again, looking up at the sky. It was so clear, the stars so close.

'What can we do then? I can't stand this noise, and neither can the Anders.'

Annie stood up, brushing the back of her jeans. 'I know and I've been thinking about it for a while. We've got space in the packaging area. Let them use that. There's no one there.'

Georgie moved his head slightly, looking at her, and she bent down and kissed his mouth. 'Give them a hand, we've only got them for two more years,' she said.

He nodded, putting his hand behind her neck, holding her mouth against his. 'You look very lovely in those jeans, very, very lovely, and I adore you.'

'Then get up, go in there, give them the good news and then we can have some peace.'

She handed him his stick and went to the pigeons, put her fingers in the wire. 'Poor little birds, I'm surprised you came back to this mad-house each day,' she crooned, laughing as she heard the whoop of joy from Davy and then, 'Oh, Dad, you're brilliant,' from Sarah and wished that she had been able to say that just once to her father.

After work that day Annie waited in the office, looking out across the car park, seeing them struggling along with their guitars, their amplifiers. She showed them the packaging room, reminded them of the no smoking rule, gave them the keys and drove Georgie mad at home, until Sarah came in and said everything was as Annie had left it. In the morning, she found that it was.

They practised there each evening for the next two weeks and sometimes Annie would stay late at work to listen to them. They were good. Sarah explained that they were practising the descending introduction to *Move It*, a Cliff Richard song.

'We're trying to get the question and answer lead breaks right at the end of each line.'

Annie nodded, though she didn't understand a word.

'We're trying to broaden our appeal, Aunt Annie,' Davy said. 'We're covering *Living Doll* as well as rock 'n' roll. We don't know what we really want you see, which way we want to go.'

'One doesn't,' Annie murmured, 'but you seem to be doing better than most.'

As she walked away she recognised *Blue Suede Shoes* and felt very proud of these children – only they weren't children were they, not any more, but neither were they quite grown up. Was anyone every really grown up? Annie wondered, as she sat at her desk, drawing doodles, filling them in. Did anyone ever feel fully wise and in control, because she didn't, not when she looked at her daughter and knew that one day she would leave.

Three days before the talent show Georgie came into her office with Brenda. He held slips, pants and bras. 'We've got a problem,' he said, passing them to her. 'And I've got a meeting in Newcastle in two hours. We can't have this, darling. I think you should sack her, whoever she is.'

215

Annie looked at the burn marks on the garments, touched them with her fingers, looked up at Brenda. 'For God's sake, what's been happening?'

Brenda shook her head. 'I can't understand it. There's your check mark on those . . .'

There was a knock at the door and Tom came in, with tea towels in his hands, showing her the holes, sticking his finger through them, shouting at her, 'What the hell are we going to do? I've had Jones on the phone. These are his returns. He's furious – says can't we run a proper business.'

Annie stood up, taking the tea cloths. 'Keep your voice down, Tom, for goodness' sake. I'll sort it out, go and soft talk Jones, tell him it won't happen again.'

She hurried out into the machine shop with Brenda, walking round slowly now, calmly, both of them looking for cigarette ends, trying to smell smoke. It couldn't have happened here, they were sure, the workroom was under constant supervision. Annie reached the end of the room. No, nothing. It had to have happened where people worked alone, which only left the packing room.

Annie felt sweat start on her hands. That was where the children practised but they wouldn't, they didn't smoke. Surely they didn't. She'd told them, again and again. She'd told them. She walked ahead of Brenda, down the machine shop, down the corridor into the room. What would she say to Georgie? What would he do? What would she do?

They were at the door now, opening it. Pat was in there, packing clothes, her forefinger nicotine-stained against the white of the cotton. Her clothes smelt of smoke. Brenda touched Annie's arm and Annie nodded, feeling relief swamp her, walking round, checking the boxes, moving to the corners of the room, seeing Brenda doing the same and Pat packing all the time with those fingers.

Brenda stooped, picked up a cigarette butt and brought it to Annie. It was still warm.

'When did you come on packing duty, Pat?' Annie asked,

standing with the cigarette butt in her hand, hating the smell of it, glad that she'd given up.

'Few minutes ago,' Pat replied, not looking up, just packing.

Brenda checked the duty roster on the wall. 'Half an hour ago, according to this.'

'So, it might have been.'

'Pat, what do you know about these?' Annie said, standing quietly in front of the woman, whose roots were dark against her bleached hair.

Annie held out the damaged goods, showing the holes, the burn marks. 'You do know don't you that there is a no smoking rule? We explained – I can remember both Brenda and I telling you.'

'Course I know. That's not me, and I don't know whose that is either. All I know is that it isn't me.'

'Feel it, Pat.'

She watched the fingers touch it. 'It's cold.'

Brenda touched it and nodded. 'Yes, it's cold now, but it wasn't.'

'I can't have smoking. It's not just the damage to the goods, it's the fire hazard. There's so much cloth in here and chemicals that it would be a disaster if anything happened.'

Pat turned from her.

Annie put the butt in her pocket, watching as Brenda brought over other butt ends from beneath the shelves. They were a different brand, Kensitas.

'See, it's not just me. I smoke Players, not those. Those are someone else's, probably your kids. I didn't burn anything, anything at all. OK, so I had one but that's all. You know yourself they're all stacked up when you've checked them. It's them who've done the damage.'

Annie looked at Brenda. There was doubt in her eyes, and in Annie's too, she knew. She took the butts, looked at them, then at Pat. 'OK then, Pat. You'll have a warning. If I ever find you smoking, you'll go. I shall speak to the children tonight.'

Annie said nothing when Sarah arrived home, and would not allow Georgie to either. She said nothing as they washed the dishes and Sarah did her homework, just smiled and said she'd be spending the evening at home tonight, they'd have to practise on their own, without the benefit of her wisdom and experience.

Sarah laughed and left them.

One hour later with Tom and Georgie, she entered the machine shop quietly, stood outside the door of the packing room, listening to the chords, to the singing, the coughing, and Annie felt her shoulders tighten with tension as Georgie opened the door.

The kids were moving, right foot forward, backwards, sideways, trying to keep their steps in time with the music and with one another. Davy's hair was too long, she thought. But then Geoff's and Paul's was also and she was smiling because there was no smoke, no thickening of the atmosphere, their throats were just dry from too much singing.

'Just thought we'd drop in, see how you're getting on.'

Tom took a packet of cigarettes out of his pocket. 'I found these, anyone want one?'

No one did.

'We don't smoke thanks, Mr Ryan,' Geoff said, straining to get his fingers on the right strings, frowning with concentration.

They left, closing the door, checking the machine room again, then the cloakroom where the overalls were hung. And it was there that they found the Kensitas in Pat's overall pocket.

Annie showed the packet to Brenda in the morning and then called Pat into her office and dismissed her on the spot. At the end of the next day she saw her again, stopping the machinists at the entrance to the car park, stopping the printers, even Bernie and Brenda, showing them the papers she had in her hands.

Tom said it was probably a petition which no one would sign and besides she was gone when they left, hurrying to

218

get home, packing both cars with speakers, guitars and people driving to Newcastle, telling the kids to do their homework while they were waiting to go on – it was school in the morning as usual.

They sat round the tables which were wedged into the club with Geoff's and Paul's parents and thought that no one was as good as The Founders, who kept in step and in tune and who played their question and answer breaks perfectly at the end of each line.

Annie applauded along with everyone else, while Rob and Tom whistled with approval. She looked round and people were smiling and laughing but some youngsters were just sitting, smoking sweet-smelling cigarettes and from their glazed eyes she knew that it was pot and hoped that Georgie hadn't seen.

He had and was quiet all the way home whilst the others talked of the thrill of coming second and how next time they would be first. He said nothing to Sarah but held Annie when they finally fell into bed. 'If it's like this here, what's it like in London?' he said quietly.

'They'll be together and just think, the vast majority of the kids there were just smoking cigarettes and ours don't even do that.'

But even so, she wished that Sarah had chosen the pigeons over music and she knew that Georgie felt the same. She knew though that they must trust their children, it was all they could do, but it didn't stop them worrying.

It was a relief to arrive at the office in the morning at eight, to sit behind her desk, sorting through her schedule, drinking coffee, calling across the partition to Georgie, calling along the shop to Tom. She would talk to Brenda about Pat's severance pay when she arrived, she'd laugh with Bernie about his racing tips, check on the children in the creche when they came.

But by eight forty-five no one had arrived, there was just a note from Brenda, telling Annie that they were out on strike and perhaps would never return to work, because employers who were so basically unfair and dishonest didn't deserve loyalty. Annie held the paper, saw the words, but understood none of it.

CHAPTER 14

Annie heard the phones ringing, Tom and Georgie answering them. She would never have heard their voices usually, there would have been too much noise – why hadn't she noticed the silence earlier?

She walked into Georgie's office, showed him the letter while he was still on the phone.

'I'll ring you back,' he said, putting the phone down, looking up at her, his jaw slackening with shock.

She took it from him, called Tom, heard him come, his heels ringing on the floor. Hadn't he realised that there was no one here either? What was the matter with them all for God's sake?

She handed it to him as he walked in, saying, 'Christ, is that the time? Where is everyone?'

She told them then, word for word, what had happened with Pat and they agreed that there had been nothing else she could have done.

'But they must all think it's the kids, that we're protecting them, making Pat take the blame,' Georgie said. There were phones ringing in all the offices now, insistent, noisy. She'd never noticed before.

She grabbed her jacket. 'I'm going to see Brenda, this is absurd. You two man the phones until I've sorted it out, try and keep the lid on it, say nothing. I'll get Gracie in from the creche, she won't realise because Moira and Pam come in later with the kids. Georgie, you ring Bet, tell her to shut up the showroom and get on down. If you each take an office we can try to keep things as normal as possible.'

The morning air was fresh as she walked from the car park, down street after street – the slag was churning up the heaps, as it had done for years, there was smoke coming from the chimneys as it had done for years, there were women sweeping their steps and she dug her hands deep into her pockets. This was Wassingham, this was her home – all this could be sorted out but why did things have to keep being sorted out, for God's sake? Why did everything keep going wrong? She bunched her fists in her pockets, thinking of the idle machines, the printers, the ovens, the orders, their name for reliability. Good God, all over a stupid woman who smoked cigarettes – what was wrong with everyone?

She turned into Stanley Street, her heels clicking. She nodded to Mrs Arthern who was polishing her letterbox. The woman turned away, hostility in her eyes, and Annie slowed, faltered, put out her hand, then walked on. She would speak to Brenda, she would clear this up – she had to. These people were her friends.

The postman passed and she called, 'Good morning.'

He said nothing but at the sound of her voice his face set just as she remembered other faces when the bosses passed by after a strike had been called and she felt lonely and wished that Georgie was with her, because she had never thought of herself as being on the other side.

She went down the back alley, hearing a dog barking, pigeons fluttering in the yards. What would they say at the club when they heard about this? But it would all be over this morning. She'd talk to Brenda, explain, though she thought she already had, and then the machine shop would hum again, and the radio would drive her mad as it always did.

She pushed open the gate, ducked in under the washing and knocked at the back door. She did not go in as she would have done yesterday, or the day before. She waited, hearing Brenda's footsteps, her voice hushing the dog, saw the door

222

opening and there was no smile on Brenda's face, just the same look that had been on Mrs Arthern's and the postman's.

'So, Annie,' she said.

Annie stood in the yard knowing she would not be invited in, knowing that others were listening in the yards on either side.

'Brenda why? Is it the smoking? It wasn't the kids. You know and I know the cigarettes were found in her pocket. Tom and Georgie were there.'

Brenda folded her arms. 'But no one else was and how can we believe anything any of you say?' Her hair was pulled back into a bun, her eyes heavy-lidded, tired, as though she'd not slept and Annie put out her hand to touch her arm, but Brenda moved away.

'I don't understand what you mean. How can you say you can't believe us, what are you talking about, Brenda?' Annie stepped back. 'Look, what's changed since yesterday?'

Everything, her mind replied but I don't know why.

'Listen to me, Brenda, you were the one who picked up the cigarette end, it was warm, Pat *had* been smoking. I know you weren't there when we found the Kensitas but we did find them in her pocket. Our kids don't smoke, their friends don't smoke. We actually went along to check up on them in the evening.' Annie dug her hands into her pockets again, seeing the hostility still there in Brenda's eyes and not understanding why. 'Even though we trusted them, we still checked.'

'That's what we should have done years ago, checked on you, but we trusted you. Next year, you kept saying. Next year the bonus will be bigger. Stick with us, grow with us, work harder and it will be all right. It's not the money, it's the lies you see, Annie. You can't get away with that in Wassingham, you're just like your brother, Annie Manon. Just like that thieving brother of yours.'

Annie jerked back at the anger in Brenda's eyes, at the thin mouth, the words which leapt out at her.

'Yes, just like Don. He was taught very well by that uncle

223

of yours, only he didn't pretend to be doing good. He acted a bastard, we knew he was and just had to accept it and pay his bloody interest rates on the loans. But at least he was honest about being a bastard. I just don't understand why you promised bonuses you never had any intention of paying. Why did you bloody well bother? You've made fools of us by cheating us and we don't forgive that.'

Annie couldn't grasp the words, only the tone, which was one of contempt.

'I don't understand, Brenda. I just don't understand what you're talking about.'

Brenda stepped back into the kitchen, holding the door. 'Well, let me spell it out to you. I know you've cheated us, lied to us about your profits. We all know now because we've seen the proof and so we'd rather do without your grand Wassingham Textiles. We've had enough of your sort of boss to last a lifetime Annie.'

'What proof?' Annie said, stepping forward as Brenda began to shut the door, leaning on it, trying to stop her, shouting, 'What proof?'

'Go away Annie, I don't want to talk to you ever again,' Brenda shouted back and the door closed. Annie tried the handle and heard the key turning in the lock. She beat on the door, shouting, calling, but Brenda wouldn't answer and so she walked back through the streets which seemed cold, empty, full of people who set their faces against her and turned their heads – and still she couldn't understand.

Neither could Georgie and Tom, who rang Brenda but the phone was off the hook. They made coffee and Bet walked through the streets to see Brenda and Meg, but neither would open the doors, though people weren't rude to her, just embarrassed, just sorry for her, she said when she returned, her voice distressed, her hands trembling.

All morning they answered phones, checked and packed what clothes were completed, though Tom refused to help.

'I can't break the strike, Annie. I can't be a scab, not after all these years.'

'Then go home,' she snapped. 'We've got to give them a business to come back to because they will come back.'

'When and how?' Tom asked, putting on his coat.

'You try and think of a way,' she shouted, sitting at a machine and beginning to sew. 'While we get on with all this.'

Gracie made sandwiches at lunchtime but no one could eat, all they could do was talk but still they couldn't understand and didn't know what to do. In the afternoon Tom came back.

'No one will talk to me. They don't trust us any more and I don't know why.' He took off his coat, threw it over a chair and started the rotary cutter, looking at them as they sat in silence watching him. 'You're right, we need to make sure there's something for them to come back to. I'm a boss now.' And there was such sadness in his eyes that Annie could have wept.

All afternoon Annie and Gracie sewed to complete the orders which should leave today, but there was no way they could do it all and by four o'clock only half of Jones's order was complete. At least the traders would receive theirs because nobody could forget their earlier loyalty.

They filled the van and Tom and Gracie drove it out through the gates, through the pickets who jeered and cat-called, and Annie's breath steamed the window as she watched. She wanted to run out, grab them, shake them, make them tell her what the hell was going on, because this dream of theirs, not just hers, was going down the drain and nobody would tell them why.

She drank tea with Bet and Georgie, then sewed more slips, her fingers sore, her neck aching, her mind leaping and jumping. She stretched and looked at the clock. Four-thirty. The kids would be coming home soon. She stood, looked out. They were still there, milling, talking, leaning up against the gate post. Bernie, Meg, Geoff her husband. Did they remember the fair, the dodgems, the candy floss? Did they? Did they?

She looked at the clock again and now panic surged within her and she ran to the door, calling to Bet, 'The kids, they don't know. I must go, there might be trouble. Tell Georgie.'

She ran through the car park, past Meg and Bernie, shouting at them, 'Get out of my way, I'm sick of the lot of you.' On down the street, to the right down Sylvester Alley, left, then left again, feeling the wind cold through her cardigan but not caring, feeling her shoes rubbing. Left again. She looked at her watch. The bus would have dropped them, for Christ's sake. She ran faster still.

Sarah stood at the bus stop, gripping her satchel, seeing the angry faces of the boys who usually lounged outside the pub, whistling and cat-calling at the girls. She heard the voices which clamoured, jostling, closing in, felt Davy's arm around her.

'What the hell's going on?' he said, his voice tight. 'What the hell's going on?' he shouted now, putting his arm up, pushing John from Ardmore Street back, struggling to keep his feet.

What were they doing here, these roughs from the back streets, what the hell were they doing here, they should be at school? No, don't be daft, school was over, that's why she was here. Sarah felt herself being grabbed from behind, her hair was pulled, it brought tears to her eyes. She hit out, grabbing Simon, pushing back.

'What're you doing? What're you all doing?' Not understanding what was happening, for God's sake. They'd been sitting in the bus, they'd jumped off, they'd walked to the corner and then this. Her satchel was grabbed and now she heard the chants of 'Scabs, bloody scabs.'

'Bloody crooks.'

'Rooking me mam, that's what you've been doing, all you bloody Manons.'

Sarah snatched at her satchel, held it, but it was torn from her grip again.

'That's ours, it's our money that's paid for that.' Pat's boy

226

threw the satchel over her head towards the arms raised at the back. 'Go on, let's share it about, like her mam said they'd do. Only they didn't.'

Davy lunged at him, battling to reach the satchel. He was pushed back, she couldn't move, she couldn't hear, all she could feel was fear, deep wild fear, and then the stone was thrown and there was blood on Davy's forehead and he was falling, crumpling and now she heard again, quite clearly, 'Milk the profits will you.'

'Go back to Gosforn, you grammar school pigs.'

And Sarah saw, quite clearly, the blood, so red against Davy's shirt, and she hurled herself at Simon, beating at him with her fists, hearing the growls and shouts, feeling them pulling at her clothes, her hair, and then there were no more voices, no hands pulling at her, no voices raging, just the sound of her mother's voice.

Sarah fell back, turned and there was her mother gripping one boy by the collar, shaking him, dragging another by the hair, shouting at the boys, 'Go home, you silly little children. Go home and stay out of things you don't understand. Don't you ever lay one finger on my family again or I'll tear the hair out of the lot of you, like I'll do to this one.' She jerked and the boy yowled.

She shook the other one, then let them go, no longer shouting but her face was white with rage. 'You yobs, how dare you come here and start all this? But of course you dare, there are – what – twelve of you and two of them? Of course you dare – they're just about the right odds for you, aren't they, John?' Annie pointed to one boy. 'Oh yes, I know you and I know your father, and you too, Simon. I grew up with your mum, Nellie.'

The boys were muttering, dodging back behind their mates, leaving. 'Yes, that's right, disappear but I'll remember you, and you too, Steve, Jack.' Annie was pointing to others. 'Your da used to give me jelly babies, Bob. Go on home and ask him what I do to little boys who push me around, or my family. Get him to tell you about Old Mooney's rag and

227

bone mare. Your mother will know too, Simon.' But Annie was only talking to their backs as they stuck their hands in their pockets and melted away into the shadows and alleys.

Sarah held Davy in her arms, there was grit digging into her knees. 'Get up. Please get up.' She felt her mother's arms around her, holding her, wiping tears that she didn't even know were falling and she felt safe and didn't know why she was shaking, because it was all right, Mum was here. It would all be all right.

They supported Davy back to the house, passing women on their doorsteps who looked away, though not in hostility any longer but in shame, and now the rain was falling, and the blood on Davy's forehead ran more quickly. Mrs Arthern brought the satchels back to the house, leaving them on the doorstep, saying that the boys were stupid, angry. 'I'm sorry for what happened, though not for the strike,' she said.

Annie shut the door because she didn't want to speak to any of them.

Georgie wheeled his chair towards Brenda's yard. He had no coat deliberately, just as he had the wheelchair, quite deliberately. He was not averse to evoking pity on this occasion. In fact he was banking on it and welcomed the rain which soaked him, and the shivering that had begun.

He knocked with his stick on the door. 'Brenda. It's Georgie. I'm wet, I can't walk because it's too slippery and me stump's too chafed so I'm in me chair and I'm staying here until you open this door.'

He waited for five minutes then banged again. He waited another five and the cold was seeping through and his stump was aching, as it always did in the wet, and Brenda knew that. He waited for another five minutes, then banged again as he saw her face at the window. The door opened.

'You fool,' she said. 'You'll be ill.'

'Then let me in,' Georgie said, putting the brake on more firmly, putting out his hand to her. 'Pull me up and let me in.'

Brenda stared at him and he felt the drips from his hair running down his face and knew that his trousers were soaking and dripping on to her yard. He took the hand that she offered.

They talked in the kitchen and Brenda handed him the accounts which Pat had shown to all the workers. They showed a vast profit and were false.

Georgie nodded, said nothing and left, wheeling himself to Pat's house, knocking on her door, not wanting pity now, but trying to control his rage, heaving himself up from the chair, ignoring the shivering which had begun again.

He stuck his stick in the door when she tried to slam it, pushed it open and heaved himself into the kitchen which smelt of unboiled tea towels, standing with his back to the range, watching her as she sucked deeply on her cigarette, her shoulders hunched. She was too thin and her face was nervous.

'Who gave you the accounts, Pat?'

'Someone who knew what he was talking about.'

'Who Pat? Describe him to me.'

'Why should I?'

'Because if you don't I'll report you to the police too.'

Pat ground out her cigarette. 'What for? I've done nothing.'

'The paper's a fraud. You'll be in it too so just tell me who gave it to you.'

'I can't, he made me promise and he let me have this house cheap. He's helped me a lot and I promised.'

Georgie felt the heat on his back, on his leg and the shivering slowed.

'So where did you meet him, Pat, in Newcastle was it, where you worked before?'

'What's that got to do with anything?'

'Just answer me.' Georgie's voice was quiet, firm, cold. 'Did you meet him where you worked before? Where did you work, Pat?'

229

Georgie knew before she told him, somehow he knew. 'I worked at Manners. He sacked me.'

Georgie touched her Kensitas packet with his stick. 'Same old problem, eh? You need a job where you can smoke Pat, didn't you ever think of that?'

Pat took another cigarette, her fingers were almost brown with nicotine. 'Yes, I did. I went for one in an office but the boss said he could fix me up with a house and a job, if I moved. I wanted to move. Me old man knocked me about see. That boss was good to me. He gave me the accounts. He knew what you were up to, see.'

Georgie nodded. 'Just tell me who he is, Pat.'

She wouldn't, she drew deeply on her cigarette, once, twice, and still she wouldn't, so Georgie described him to her, in minute detail because, in a way, he had known all along.

'Give me your rent book, Pat,' he demanded when she nodded at his description, his voice still cold, firm, quiet. She did and he put it in his pocket, heaved himself back out into the rain and wheeled himself home, because Annie must be told and it was she who must deal with it, not any of them, because he knew that that was what she would want.

Annie drove to Newcastle the next day, through cold and rain and there was only the swish of the wipers to keep her company, but she was glad she was alone because this must be between the two of them.

She parked, climbed the stairs, walked straight past the receptionist, past his secretary and into his office.

'Good morning, Mr Jones,' she said, standing in front of the desk looking at Don's hands, tanned against the pristine white of the blotter.

She held out the accounts and a copy of the rent book, saying nothing, just watching as he glanced at them, then threw them on the desk, rotating his chair, taking out a cigar.

'If you smoke that, I'll ram it down your throat,' Annie said, her voice quite calm.

230

He put the cigar down on the mahogany desk, steepled his hands and looked at her, and now she could see the hate that had been there all along.

'Why, Don?' she asked, still standing.

He didn't answer and so she handed him another sheet of paper. This time it was the copy of a statement written by Pat in the presence of their solicitor. It contained everything she had told Georgie.

'If you don't tell me why, and how, this will be sent either to the newspapers or to the police, who will, of course, be aided by us in all their investigations.'

He sat looking first at her then out of the window.

'You shouldn't have come back and taken the house,' he said finally. 'Sarah Beeston gave you everything and me virtually nothing.'

Annie just looked, then said, 'You had so much from Uncle Albert and all I had were clips round the ear and his lavatory to clean day in and day out. He loved you, he gave you everything.'

Don shrugged. 'He had no class. Sarah had and she gave it to you and how dare you move ahead of me, and how dare you come back and move into my territory and take the house from me?'

'Was that enough reason to try to destroy my life?'

Don steepled his hands again. 'Yes, I rather feel it was. I wanted you back down where I had been, I wanted you all down there, with your college degrees, your nursing experience, your officer's pips – your neat little gang, all closed up together again, leaving me outside. You never gave me a hand up, you never asked me to share your life in Gosforn. She was my relative too, you know.'

Annie watched the man and remembered the boy who had jeered at Gracie's plumpness, who had jeered at their father, at Bet, at her, at Sarah Beeston. The young man who had sided with Albert, run his business, inherited it, sneered at Gosforn. She hadn't known what he really wanted and he'd never said. If he had done so, Sarah would have helped him to achieve that, not just given him money for his partnership with Uncle Albert which was what he had said he wanted. Was it just a warped justification? She didn't care, finally she didn't care, because now she knew that this was the man who had arranged for Pat's brother to view the house next door, and then to complain about the pigeon loft using the name of Mr Jones.

'So, you fixed for Tommy Mallet to do a runner. Did you share Sarah's money with him? Val's too?'

He shrugged. 'He was going to leave anyway, got a nice little place abroad.'

'And I never did sign a form, did I, there was no letter?'

Don laughed. 'You're so bloody thick I knew you wouldn't remember whether you had or not.'

Annie felt no anger, there was nothing.

'And Manners, that was you too?'

'He was a good friend in the old days and put a number of loans my way. That little bit of business suited us both, but you're so bloody difficult, Annie. You won't give up but you'll have to now.'

Annie said, 'The consortium, that was you too, but under a different name?'

Don pursed his lips, his voice interested, objective as he replied. 'More or less but I didn't get the showroom in time though – you didn't tell me about that before you did it. As I said, you're so thick, Annie, you never twigged did you, none of you?'

Almost, thought Annie, but we just couldn't believe it. Could anyone, of their own brother?

'So what did you promise Pat to burn the clothes; she wouldn't say.'

There was silence.

She looked out of the window, through the venetian blinds, to the tall buildings and the heavy rain-sodden skies, then back at him, his thin face, his hands so carefully manicured and without any blue-stained scars.

'Come on, Don, might as well or I shall just have to show

232

this little paper to people who matter.' Annie reached for Pat's statement, waving it backwards and forwards.

'Well, I offered her an office job, but only if it was successful. She can go to hell now.'

Annie shook her head, looking at him as he pushed his chair back, watched him cross his legs, picking imaginary fluff off his dark suit.

'No, I rather think she will come to you.' She waved the paper again, even more slowly now, still watching his legs – his two legs.

'Is that quite clear? She works for you from now on.'

She was still waving the paper, and now she felt its draught on her face. 'Is that quite clear, Don Manon?'

He looked up at her, his lips thin with rage, his eyes narrow, but she just waited, waited. Finally he nodded.

'Good.' She looked out of the window again, the clouds were still heavy, grey. There would be more rain today.

'Is that all then?' His voice was tight.

Annie didn't look at him. 'More or less but I shall never forgive you as long as I live for hurting our family, for soiling Sarah's house with your presence and her money with your dishonesty. Most of all I shall never forgive you for trying to deprive Georgie of his pigeon loft, when you had already taken his leg.'

Don frowned at this, putting up his hand. 'No, you can't blame me for that. I wasn't to know.'

'You played the game Don, you were responsible for the consequences but that doesn't matter now. It's happened, it's over. You and I are over, all finished, Tom and Bet too, but I'm going to stay in this office until you write a letter to our workforce, telling them exactly how you falsified the accounts. You will write another to us explaining in detail your other activities. This will not be used against you unless anything further happens to disturb the smooth running of our business. As a family we will maintain a civilised demeanour because of the children, who need know nothing of this, but that is all.'

She held out her pen, took paper from the pile on his desk, walked to the door, called in his secretary and made her wait while Don wrote, his face red with rage.

'Please witness this, Miss Archer,' Annie said.

Miss Archer did, her hair falling across her face as Sarah's had done when she had held Davy – was it only yesterday?

'Thank you, that will be all.' Annie watched as Miss Archer left, then picked up the pen Don had thrown on the desk. She threw it in the waste-paper basket.

'Now, Sarah's money you "invested". Keep it. We don't want it now it's been through your hands.' Annie saw the glint of satisfaction in his eyes but wait for it, Don, just wait, she thought. I'm not going to take money because that won't hurt you, you have so much. You see, you need to feel pain, you need to be taught never to do this again.

Annie waited, and then said, 'But the house is a different matter. You're to get out – now. I shall sell it and set up a trust fund for the children. None of us wants to live there now, it's spoiled for us. You'll have to think up something to tell Maud, won't you?'

Annie saw shock take the place of satisfaction, then the shock became hatred and anger and she was glad, because now her own rage and hate were stirring for this man who had dared to harm those she loved. 'One more thing, Don. I will ruin you if you ever try anything again – and then where will you be? Not with Maud, I can assure you, she'll move her little painted fingernails somewhere else.'

She picked up the papers, all of them, including the copy of the rent book and the accounts, and walked to the door across the deep pile carpet, wanting to be away from this man who had once been her brother.

He called out to her then. 'What makes you think your workers will believe any of this? When people think someone's been lying they'll never trust them again.'

Annie didn't turn, didn't stop, she just opened the door and left but she knew that Don was right. There was no guarantee that their workers would believe them, or the evidence, but at least she and her family knew the truth, at last.

CHAPTER 15

Annie sat in the kitchen on Saturday morning, hearing the kettle simmering on the range, tasting the hot strong tea which she sipped from the mug Sarah had given her before she left for London – was it only a week ago? It seemed so much longer. So, she thought – 1965 and my daughter's first letter home. She reread Sarah's account of their first days at college, the enrolling, the queueing for stationery, for the meals in the refectory.

She smiled at Sarah's description of the lecturer who had explained how to use the sewing machines step by step and Sarah felt unable to tell her that she'd been using one for as long as she could remember.

She's not a bit like Brenda, Mum, tell her she'd cope with all of us with her arm tied behind her back. How's she getting on with the new machinist?

A man showed us how to cut patterns, so when we come back, if you haven't got a second cutter, I can help out. Next week we learn how to design. Davy is loving his foundation course, keeps telling me about dyes and fabrics. He's keen on African dyeing or something. It's great, Mum, really great but we're missing you all, so much.

Annie put down the letter, smoothing it, glancing again, touching the writing, imagining Sarah in the bedsit they had chosen in July. God, she'd forgotten how huge London was, how small her daughter and her nephew were in comparison.

'London nowadays is very different to pre-war London,' Tom had said as they waved them off last week. 'I hope to God they can cope.'

Annie had echoed that again and again as they drove back from Newcastle to the factory. She smiled now, clasping the mug between both her hands. Were Sarah's as sore as hers had been after her first experience of cutting, poor girl?

She rose, restless, lost, wishing it were a working day. She washed her mug, dried it, watched Georgie cleaning out the loft. He was restless too, missing his daughter, but at least they'd managed to find a second cutter. She leant against the sink watching Georgie turn and smile. He looked younger somehow and she knew that she did too.

She smiled at him, then checked through the minutes of the monthly meeting again. Yes, no wonder they were both looking better, they'd gone from strength to strength since she had shown the workers Don's letter and the bonus this summer had been as good as she had promised it would be. Georgie opened the door and called through, 'How many times have you read it now?'

'Almost as many as you, bonny lad, but I can't sit here any more. Let's go and pick Bet up and take her for a run.' Annie pushed the minutes away but tucked the letter into her pocket, grabbing her coat, throwing Georgie his and the car keys. 'Come on or I shall get maudlin but do you really think it's great for them, Georgie? God I hope it is.'

Sarah sat in the bedsit, looking at the books she had bought in the student shop, opening them, then shutting them again, sketching out a design, screwing it up, throwing it in the bin. She buttoned up her coat, rubbed her hands and then moved to the window, leaning her head on the pane, seeing her breath misting up the glass. It was so cold, so different, so big, so busy and she wanted to go home.

She looked across the roofs, at the lit sky. It was always

237

bright in London and she longed for the dark of home. It was noisy, too many cars, too many people, too many strange faces and she wanted Wassingham, its neighbours, its shops, its slag heaps. She turned to pick up a book but the tears were falling now, and she sank on to the bed. 'Only two months, then I can go home – we can go home,' because Davy was as lost as she.

He knocked on her door now, 'Sarah, can I come in?'

'In a minute, wait a minute, I'm changing.' She rushed to the sink, splashing water on her face, drying it, looking in the mirror. Yes, it was all right. 'Come in then.'

She sat on the cane chair and it wobbled as Davy opened the door and she said, 'Toss us that piece of paper then, Davy, I'll bung it under the leg, there's one shorter than the other and it's driving me mad.' She strove to keep her voice strong, because he mustn't know that she had been crying.

Davy brought it to her. She dug her fingers into the palms of her hand, smiling as he squatted before her, handing her the paper. She folded it, then leaned back in the chair, handing it back to him. 'It's better if you do it and I sit here getting at it at the right angle. OK, now stuff it under the one that's up in the air.'

She watched as he shoved it beneath the leg, then stood, looking down at her. 'Strange how you always get the sitting down jobs,' he said smiling but it didn't reach his eyes. 'It'll get better, bonny lass.'

He moved to the bed and sat down. Tell me that and mean it, Davy Ryan, she thought because she knew it wouldn't get any better, how could it? They'd been here a week and no one had spoken to them properly, no one had smiled in the refectory, or called them over to sit with them. Everyone seemed to have someone else to talk to, so many friends. She looked around the room and wanted to be back in her mother's kitchen, in own bedroom, she wanted to hear her parents' voices, their radio, the pigeons. She wanted to go home and now she felt her throat thicken, and knew that she

238

would cry again and so she said, 'Oh come on, let's get out of here.'

She hurried to the door, pressed the timed light switch and rushed down the stairs, hearing Davy following her, not wanting him to see her face, not wanting to speak because then the tears would come. She squeezed past the bikes in the hall. The light went off, she knocked her shins on a pedal, and heard Davy doing the same. She banged the light switch by the door. 'Damn bloody thing, can't even have enough light to get out in one piece.'

She wrenched open the door, hearing Davy begin to laugh. She waited for him on the steps, leaning back against the railings, hearing the laughter growing louder as he came down the hall, out of the door, slamming it behind him, and now she was laughing too, holding on to the railings and on to his arm. 'Damn bloody light,' she gasped, knowing it wasn't funny, wondering where the laughter was coming from, unable to stop it.

They clung to one another and he said, 'We could always jump out of the window you know and save our shins.'

Sarah could barely speak, just nodded, clutching her sides then pointed at the railings. 'That's right, we'd break our necks but we'd have lovely shins.'

They sat on the steps, laughing, winding their scarves round their necks, then moved to one side as Tim from the end room came down the street and bounded up through the middle of them. He'd never spoken, just nodded as he did now, opening the door, going into the still lit hall, which plunged into darkness as he squeezed past the bikes. They heard 'Christ all-bloody-mighty,' and the laughter burst from them again.

Sarah ran up the steps and banged the light switch, her sides heaving, and Tim called from the end of the hall, 'I owe you a drink for that, I'll be down in a minute, we can curse Ma Tucker's bloody light together.'

Sarah looked back at Davy, and now they grinned. 'Maybe it's getting better,' he called.

It was getting better. Tim took them to Soho, strap-hanging on the tube which lurched and swung, then they walked along Wardour Street, Frith Street and Dean Street, and Tim told them that he had to repeat his last year because he'd spent too much time hanging out here. 'Got into a group,' he said, 'all play and no work got Tim the big stick. Lesson one, kids, you've got to do a bit or you get slung out.'

Sarah felt the pain in her thumb and fingers from the cutter. 'Trouble is,' she said, 'all work and no play makes you wretched, makes you want to go home.'

Tim stopped in the street, swung her round, arched his eyebrows, grabbed Davy's arm. 'Oh, we thought that's what you wanted. Always together, always serious. Didn't know you wanted to play too, that's why we left you alone. Can't have you going home, come along, see what London can tempt you with.'

He dragged them past French, Italian and Greek bars, restaurants, snack bars and delicatessens, and the smells mixed, the languages too. They heard the sounds of laughter, of conversation, of singing, of living and Sarah turned to Davy. 'I've never seen anything like it.'

'I bet your mam would laugh at that.' Davy nodded to a strip club. 'Probably try to sell them her knickers.'

They laughed, told Tim why, and he grinned, pointing out the prostitutes in dingy doorways, the teachers of French in the second-storey bedsits and Sarah felt that her world was being cracked wide open.

'Don't bother to write to your mam about them,' Tim warned, 'The last thing they need is knickers.'

He led them into a coffee bar which oozed steamy warmth. The hiss and spurt of an espresso coffee machine was drowned again and again by laughter and talk. They sank into chairs which nudged others, slipping off their coats, their scarves, while Tim bought the coffees.

'Not bad, bonny lad,' Sarah murmured, looking round at the garlic and onion strings which hung around the room, at the students who crammed round the tables. One of them looked up and smiled. She was on Sarah's foundation course and had never acknowledged her before. Sarah smiled back, blushing, pleased, and she held Davy's arm. 'I didn't know any of this was here.'

He nodded. 'Makes you feel better, doesn't it?'

They spooned sugar on to the top of the froth, watching it sink through to the coffee, drinking it, wiping away moustaches, talking of their courses, their homes and Tim nodded when they spoke of Wassingham.

'Knew you were from the north east. My uncle worked there for a while. Long way to come, long way to run away home too.'

Sarah looked down, scraping the froth from the inside of the cup with her spoon. 'Where's your home then?' she said, because she didn't want to talk of running away. It wouldn't be running away, it would just be not returning after Christmas, that was all.

Tim came from Guildford and told them of the cobbled North Street, the second-hand bookshop run by the Thorpes, one younger, one older, the younger being as old as Methuselah.

Davy said, 'What group do you play with?'

'I don't, not any more. They eh, got sent down, shall we say. Got too heavily into drugs so it's just me and my guitar now, looking for a home.'

Davy bought more coffees and more people came in, squeezed past, slapping Tim on the shoulder, telling Davy and Sarah that this man had to do some work this year or he'd never cast himself upon the world.

'We play,' Sarah said. 'We had a group at home.'

Tim looked at them both, his face serious now. 'What d'you play?'

'Most things, we've been trying to broaden our scope, covering the Beatles, the Stones, Cliff Richard, the ballads but now we're trying to write our own too.' Sarah stopped because they hadn't tried, not for the last week, everything had stopped, sucked into the long dark tunnel of loneliness.

241

'Fine, let's get together. We'll need a fourth but Arnie's free,' Tim shouted across the room, waving Sarah's scarf in the air. 'Arnie, over here a minute.'

Arnie shambled across, dressed in a long sweater with holes in the elbows, his hair long and unkempt and Sarah knew that her da would love to get his hands on it, cut it, slick it down with Brylcreem.

He sat with them, playing the drums on the table, listening. 'Great idea, we can audition for the Christmas gig, where'll we practise?' He spoke with a drawl.

'Mid-Atlantic,' Tim said, grinning. 'The furthest this man's been is Watford.'

But where would they practise? It could only be back at the digs and then only when Ma Tucker was out and she was always out on a Monday, Wednesday and Friday but returned at varying times. They drank more coffee and devised a system whereby they would take it in turns to keep watch at the window while still playing.

'But what about the room next to Sarah's? Doesn't anyone rent that – will they complain?'

Tim shook his head. 'Someone called Carl has taken that. Arnie knows him, he was in his house last year. Didn't say he was going to move, but here he is. He drifted in and out of Arnie's place – didn't turn up until halfway through last term. He's at the LSE but isn't there much, he's got his fingers in the pop pie and God knows what else. He was in Morocco this summer so he's probably still there – bet he brings back some good pot. Anyway, don't worry about him, we can square it if he turns up. *If* being the operative word.'

'Mm, sounds great,' Arnie said, rising. 'We can fix up some gigs for next term, still a few clubs who'll give groups a chance and we can try and talk Carl into helping.' He shambled away again and Sarah finished her coffee.

Next term was another matter, she thought as she lay in bed that night, because now that the lights and the warmth of the coffee bar were gone, the room seemed darker, colder, and Wassingham even further away.

In November she read her mother's letter and laughed gently when Annie told her that her father had nearly had apoplexy at the Beatles' MBE.

He wanted to take my scissors to their hair, and plaster it with Brylcreem. He still aches for Vera Lynn and the *White Cliffs of Dover* you know but he'll make do with Alma Cogan or Donald Peers! I'm glad to hear that you are practising again and just hope your system of signals works. I'm sure the packing room misses its nightly vibrations, I know we do.

Business is good, and getting better. It's all a great relief and Bet spends more and more time in the creche – I'm sure it's because all you birds have fled the nest. We're so looking forward to Christmas, my darling. Incidentally, Prue sent you over this sandalwood box, thought it might bring some sun into your bedsit. Are you happy? I do so hope so.

Sarah held the box, smelt it, ran her fingers in the carved grooves and wanted to write back that the lavatory was horrid, a bath possible only once a week, the gas fire gobbled shillings, that she was sick of baked beans and wanted to come home.

She put the box on the table near to the designs she had been drawing and passed the letter to Davy. She washed the dishes. Tomorrow Davy would cook – and it would be beans – and she wanted to be a child again, leaning into Bet's arms, into her mother's, her da's.

'It's better now, isn't it?' Davy said, pulling the table to one side, stacking up her designs. 'It's better now we've got the music, now we know Tim.'

Sarah nodded. Yes, it was better but only while Tim and Arnie were here, the rest of the time they were still too far away from home, from friends and family.

That evening they played the music that they would perform at the audition, playing the riffs again and again,

243

drinking instant coffee and then beer which Arnie had brought, taking turns to stand at the window peering left and right. Taking a break, talking themselves through the score, picking out the chords.

'We're getting better. Sarah's got a good voice,' Arnie said, drawing on his cigarette.

Tim tossed him his cigarettes back. 'Yes, and we're getting better as a group, what d'you two think?'

Sarah and Davy nodded. They were getting better but they weren't as good as they had been with Paul and Geoff, there wasn't the understanding, the years behind them. They played again, practising the vocals, the breaks, the repeats, the riffs until her throat and fingers were sore.

She sipped water and they played again practising the descending introduction over and over. 'Louder,' Davy said. 'Louder.'

The air was thick with smoke, their fingers strained on the strings, Sarah's voice cracked, she cleared her throat, caught up with them, sang again, and then there was a knocking on the door and they fell silent – utterly silent.

Then Tim whispered, 'Oh God, Ma Tucker.'

They'd forgotten to watch for her. They looked at one another, then the knocking started again.

'Somebody died in there?' It was a man's voice, cultured, creamy.

Tim laughed, dumping his guitar, opening the door.

'Nearly, Carl, thank you very much.'

He was tall with blond, sun-streaked hair and his skin was tanned against his cuff as he shook Sarah's hand. 'We're neighbours I believe. I hope I won't disturb you when I turn over in the night.'

Sarah could think of nothing to say. He moved along to Arnie, slapping his arm. 'Got a new group then, you old reprobate.'

Arnie just nodded, fingering his guitar and smiling, the smoke from his cigarette drifting up, mingling with the hazy

cloud which hung above them. Davy grinned. 'Good to meet
you. We thought it was Ma Tucker.'

'So, a little northern laddie – and how d'you like the big
city?'

Carl was bringing out two bottles of wine from the bag he
carried. 'Thought we'd have a welcome home party for Carl.'

Sarah said, 'We were practising.' And her voice was hard
and more Geordie than usual because this man had made
Davy flush.

Carl looked at her, smiling slowly. 'A little northern lassie.
Good. The Animals are quite something and so are you. I was
talking to them just the other day. Have you a corkscrew?'

'Of course,' Sarah took it from the drawer, blessing her
mother for giving her one, 'just in case'. Her voice was cold.

Davy was smiling now, because what had seemed to be an
insult now seemed to have been a compliment and Sarah felt
confused. Tim brought glasses from his room, Davy one from
his and they drank to the new group, to Carl's return, and
his eyes met Sarah's, deep brown, almost black and his
eyelashes cast shadows on his cheeks. 'Cheers,' he said, raising his glass to them all, and again to her. 'Cheers.'

They drank and he put another shilling in the gas fire, it
spluttered, hissed and then burnt steadily as he told them of
the heat of Morocco, the yacht his mother had bought for
the holiday and then sold at a profit, the flight he had taken
to India with friends, the boat they had taken down the
Ganges.

'You'd have been interested in the designs, Tim,' Carl
said, blowing smoke into the air.

'These two as well,' Tim said, pouring more wine for them
all.

Carl smiled at Sarah. 'Textile designer too?'

She shook her head. 'No, dress design, and I agree with
you about the designs of India.'

Carl looked at her more closely. 'Oh you've been?'

'No, I'm just a wee Geordie lassie, aren't I? My parents
have lived there and have told me all they know about

the place.' Sarah heard the anger in her voice and didn't care. How dare this man come into their room and flash his tan, his accent, his wine at them like this?

Davy was grinning at her, Tim too and now Carl nodded. 'Touché, I feel.' He sipped his wine, looked away at Arnie. 'So how's it going? You licking them into shape?'

Arnie sucked on his cigarette. 'More like these two licking us into shape. They're good.'

Carl looked at Sarah again, surprise in his face. She looked not at him, but Davy. 'We'd better practise harder on Friday, we've lost an hour tonight.' Her voice was cold.

Carl smiled at her. 'Please, do go on. I shall be the audience.'

'We're not ready for an audience,' Sarah snapped, covering her glass as he moved the bottle towards her.

Tim asked Carl, 'So, who've you been mixing with then, apart from The Animals?' He was lounging back on the bed, whilst Davy and Arnie sat on the floor, their glasses between their legs. Sarah sat on the chair and thanked God that the legs were balanced or she'd be wobbling about and my God, wouldn't this prat enjoy that? She looked at him as he answered Tim, sitting across from her, facing sideways, his face thin, his lips so perfectly formed, his shirt so clean, his neck as tanned as his hands.

'Talking to a guy at a party the other night. The Stones were there of course.'

Of course, Sarah thought.

'A couple of new female singers too, but I don't know, their managers just seem set on pushing them towards Blandsville, they're just copying and magnifying the fifties ballad singers. I mean, just look at Kathy Kirby and Pet Clark, Sandy Shaw – we've seen them all before. They're just jumping on a bandwagon that's gone before.'

Arnie murmured now, lighting up another cigarette. 'Bob Dylan's just done that too. Gone electric, for God's sake, what's the matter with the guy?'

Carl laughed, scratching his neck. His nails were short,

clean, his fingers long and thin, an artist's fingers, Sarah thought, hiding her own which were swollen and scored from cutting and sewing.

'Got a good head on him, that's what's the matter. He's going for the money and what's wrong with that? He could get a new sound, who knows.'

Davy said quietly, his words slurred, glass at his mouth, 'It's a betrayal.'

'No way – I'm telling you, these guys are in it for the money, nothing else. That's the bottom line, for you lot too.'

Sarah spoke now, her voice cool. 'These "guys" are where they are courtesy of the kids and they couldn't produce the music they do if it was only for the money. It's got to come out of the core of the group. They're got to have a commitment.'

Tim and Davy nodded and she looked only at them, not at this man whose blond hair was too long and rested well below his collar.

'So, Sarah. Perhaps you're right, who knows. Perhaps you are.' Carl's voice was soft now, serious and he nodded at her as she turned to look at him, at those brown eyes which caught and held hers.

Arnie drawled. 'So, what's the demo about this week at the LSE, still the Vietnam war?' He held out his glass for more wine but Carl turned from Sarah and shook the empty bottle, putting it down, taking out a silver cigarette case.

Davy said loudly, 'For God's sake, not politics. I thought I'd got away from that.'

Sarah looked at him then said quickly, 'What music do you prefer then, Carl?'

He passed the cigarette case to her. She looked at the three large joints. 'No thanks.'

He smiled. 'What's up, hasn't pot reached Newcastle? Is it still just beer and pigeons?'

She stiffened, turned from him again. 'Of course it's reached us but I don't want one, not tonight.'

She watched as he offered them to Arnie, Tim and Davy,

247

all of whom took one, Davy avoiding her eyes because he had never smoked before.

Arnie lit the joints and Sarah watched Davy draw in too deeply, cough, choke, his eyes watering, the others laughing, but not unkindly. Carl was bringing out a pouch and papers, laying them on the table, saying over his shoulder to Arnie, 'Open the window or Ma Tucker will have hysterics.'

As he pulled out the pot and laid it on the paper she smelt the heavy sweet scent of the marijuana – Davy was coughing no longer, but taking more shallow draughts, his lids heavy, his smile relaxed. He looked happy, he looked as he had done in Wassingham. Sarah looked around the room at the people they played music with but didn't know. Strangers. So many strangers.

Carl held out the reefer to her. She shook her head again. He shrugged, lit it, sucked deeply, leaning back in his chair, watching her with kind, brown eyes and there was silence in the room. Sarah looked at her hands, so tense in her lap. She looked at Davy, sprawled and happy, at Tim and Arnie, who were strumming imaginary guitars, beating imaginary drums, and felt alone.

Carl leant forward, tapped her arm. She looked at the reefer he held out to her, damp from his mouth. 'Sure?' he said. 'Alcohol does your throat far more harm and you should look after your voice, it's good, I heard it through the door. Trust me, I wouldn't hurt you.'

She hesitated, then put out her hand but he placed the reefer in her mouth, his fingers brushing her lips.

'Just draw lightly,' he said gently.

She did, and felt the heat, the taste enter her. He took the reefer from her mouth and she breathed smoke on to his hands. The tension left her body, her shoulders dropped, she leaned back in her chair.

'I came in because I wanted to see if the body was as lovely as the voice. It is.' She watched him reach forward and pull the velvet band out of her hair, she felt him touch her cheek, her neck, pull her hair forward over her shoulder so that it fell on her breast. He brushed it away, touching her. She felt a flare of heat shafting down, taking her breath from her, the strength from her fingers, and now her hands lay limp on her lap.

'Play for me,' he said but how could she, her lips felt too full, her fingers too weak. All she wanted to do was to lay her head in the hand which still held her hair.

'Come on then,' Tim said, heaving himself to his feet. 'Check for Ma Tucker then, Sarah.'

Sarah turned. Everything seemed so slow, so easy. She checked the window. 'All clear,' she said and her voice seemed distant.

She held her guitar, easing the strap over her head, tapping her foot. 'One, two, three.'

Then they played their own songs for him and she sang, and all she could think of were his fingers brushing her lips, her breasts, and all she could see were his eyes watching her, then Davy, then the others, but always back to her. Her shoulders felt loose, warm, and for the first time since leaving Wassingham she felt secure.

They stopped and there was silence. 'Very good. Very, very good, but you need more muscle, the songs are anaemic. Let me know if I can ever help you. Good luck with the audition – see you at your Christmas gig.'

He was standing, moving to the door, leaving them. The door closed but the others were talking, laughing, joking, they hadn't really heard, they were too drunk on wine, on pot and he was gone, he hadn't even looked back. She looked at the ashtrays, full of ash. She sat down, so tired, so empty and then so full of anger. How dare he say their songs were anaemic, how dare he say they needed more muscle? And now she felt cold again and slammed the window shut.

Carl was gone again the following morning and his room remained empty. She was glad she wouldn't have to see his blond hair, his thin face, his bloody tan. She was glad.

They practised three evenings a week, remembering to look for Ma Tucker each time and she also looked for Carl, but it was only so that she could stop singing at his approach, wasn't it?

She worked hard during the day, cutting, sewing, pressing seams, remembering Brenda's instructions, remembering her throaty laugh, her mother's grin and though she still wrote home saying that everything was great she crossed off the days on her calendar. Davy, though, was relaxing, enjoying the music, the fabrics he was working with, enjoying the pot which Arnie bought from 'a friend' and sometimes Sarah smoked as well, but not often, and then only with a sense of guilt.

They failed the audition. 'Your songs are too weak,' the Student Union Entertainment Committee told them and that night Sarah lay in bed, watching the lights from the passing cars on her ceiling, remembering Carl's words, his touch, his tan and she reached for one of the joints she kept in Prue's sandalwood box, drawing deep, leaning back on her pillows, two cardigans around her shoulders until at last her lids felt heavy, her body limp. She stubbed it out, replaced it in the box and slept, dreaming of pigeons, of her mother's kitchen, Bet's voice, and she knew when she awoke that she would not return to London after Christmas.

They went to the gig, packing before they did so, stuffing things into cases, cleaning the rooms. 'We'll catch the early train,' she said and Davy nodded.

'I like your skirt,' he said. 'But your da'll have a fit.'

Sarah smiled. 'I'll wear them good and long up there.'

Tim and Arnie were there, Deb and Sally too, and the girls from her year. They bought drinks at the bar, chatted, talked as they'd never done before and Davy brought his year over and there was laughter, dancing, fun. Sarah twisted with Tim, with Davy, laughing as they dragged in Sally too, listening to the group which was playing and knew that they were good, better than she and Davy had been, but it didn't matter now. None of it mattered because she was going home.

Arnie draped her in tinsel, and Sally too and Sarah picked

250

pieces off and hung them over Davy's ears. 'Now, just what do you think *your* da would think of that, bonny lad,' she giggled, passing him her beer to drink from, sipping it herself, then smelling pot close by. She turned, Carl was dancing close, so close to a blonde girl, who clung to him, and he to her, his joint wafting sweet smoke.

Sarah turned away, back to Davy who still had tinsel behind his ears, and tried to laugh again, but all the fun had fled and she couldn't understand herself. The music was too loud now, far too loud and her head ached and her throat as she strained to speak, strained to listen to Arnie's drawl, Tim's Jokes. She looked at her watch – nearly midnight, thank God – this time tomorrow she'd be far away from London.

She eased her way through entwined couples who moved with the music, through balloons which floated and were tapped back up into the air, feeling the streamers which caught at her, but never held. She sat at their table, drawing dress designs in the spilt beer, thinking of the train which would carry her home.

'So, Geordie lass, come and dance with me.' It was Carl, his breath heavy with wine and pot, his eyes soft, but his hands firm as they pulled her to her feet. She danced with him, felt his knee pushing again and again between her legs, his hands on her arms, gently holding, stroking.

'Forgive me for saying your songs were anaemic,' he said bending his head to speak into her hair. 'I shouldn't have done, but let me help you. There's a need for a good strong girl singer. I could make you big.'

Sarah smiled because she was going home. 'No thanks. Davy and I stay together. He's family and besides, we're going into my mother's business.'

He was still so close. 'Trust me, I'll help you both while you're down here, and then you can go back to your mother.'

Sarah just smiled again, remembering the suddenness of his departure, the rudeness of his words, knowing she would never see him again after tonight, knowing that she was going into the business now, not in three years' time. His arms

251

tightened around her and she pushed away, looking into his face, his deep brown eyes, seeing only kindness when she had expected derision, feeling his kiss light on her forehead, when she had expected coldness. 'Have a good Christmas, Sarah. I'll see you when I return from skiing.'

Then he was ducking and weaving between the dancers, waving, smiling as people stopped him, took him aside, until he was gone from her sight.

'No, you won't see me,' she said quietly. 'I'm going home.' But she could still feel his kiss on her forehead, and his hands on her arms.

CHAPTER 16

The journey had been long. They had changed trains at Newcastle and now they were approaching Wassingham, they were coming home. Sarah stood at the window looking out at the slag heap being lowered because of Aberfan, at the houses, the pitheads and it seemed so small, so very small.

The train stopped, and there was Annie, and behind her Georgie, Tom, and Gracie. Sarah ran now, throwing her arms round her parents, dropping her duffle bag with her presents, promising herself that she wouldn't cry, proud that she didn't.

They drove her back and Davy called, 'See you tomorrow,' his face as settled and happy as she knew hers was.

The kitchen was warm, the kettle simmering. Bet had cooked a casserole and hugged her, kissed her, her plump cheeks warm and her arms strong, pushing her into a chair while Annie stroked her hair, then they made a cup of tea and Georgie brought Button's grandson in to see her. She laughed and stroked the bird, wanting to sink into the warmth of her home, of her family, not able to understand how small the room seemed, how old Bet looked, how grey Annie's hair was, how different it all seemed, how different they all seemed.

That night she stood by her window, looking out over the town, hearing the birds fluttering and cooing in the loft, seeing next door's cat prowling in the yard, remembering the new dinner plates, the plants that had not been there when she left, the new fireguard, and none of it was as she had remembered, even the loft. It all seemed so small.

The next day, she and Davy went into the factory where new machinists had been taken on, where schoolkids were doing the jobs that they had done in the packaging department and there was no room for Sarah and Davy this Christmas.

The next night they went to the pub for a drink and people said hello and told them the news – the Post Office's new counter, Meg's daughter's baby, the new Mine Manager, and they smiled when Davy talked about African dyeing, or Sarah of the new line in design, but they didn't listen, because what had this to do with them?

On Christmas Eve Sarah and Davy walked to the beck and talked together of Arnie, Tim, Ma Tucker, the lights, the bikes, Soho, and they laughed, smoking their last joint, chewing gum to take the smell from their breath, shaking their hair, running back through the frost-filled mist and that night Sarah couldn't sleep because she didn't know where she belonged any more.

On Christmas Day she and Davy were given guitars with pearl inlaid trim and a wonderful resonance, and a sewing machine. 'For you to make yourself more clothes in London. You'll need it – their fashions move so quickly.'

Sarah smiled and knew that she must tell her parents that she would not be going back but not now, it wasn't fair, it would upset their day. But when would Davy tell Tom and Gracie, because he had said he would not return if she did not?

He hadn't told them, he said as they walked to the football pitch and kicked the ball around. 'But just tell me when you do,' he said.

The pitch was frosted white and the hummocks ricked their ankles, tripped them, the ball slid from her hands, hurt her leg when it slapped into her and there was no laughter as there was with Rob, her parents and Uncle Tom, just irritation, and she could see it in Davy too.

254

She kicked the ball towards Tom, then stood with her arms folded, not running when Gracie kicked it towards her, just watching as it sped past. Her mother moved closer to her. 'At least pretend you're enjoying yourself, Sarah, for heaven's sake.' Her voice was low, angry.

Sarah shrugged. 'I'm cold.'

'Then go back, don't spoil this for everyone, and for God's sake, grow up.'

'But this is so childish, Mum. It's not me that needs to grow up.'

That night Sarah sat by the range, rubbing wintergreen on her feet, smelling her knees, wondering what was wrong with her and why she was such a bitch, and now she was crying, holding her knees, feeling the tears running down her face until her mother came into the room, holding her, rocking her. 'Sh, it's all right. It's all right.'

Sarah said against her shoulder, 'It's not all right. I didn't want to go back because I don't belong there but I don't belong here any more and I hate myself for it.'

Annie held her tightly. 'I know, and it is all right. I should have guessed, I'm sorry. We should know how you feel, after all, we've been through it too. Be kind to yourself, give it all a bit more time. But Sarah, you really must remember that you do not spoil things for other people, no matter how fed up you feel. Is that clear?'

In the New Year they met up with Geoff and Paul, and Annie let them use the packaging department and they played but they were out of synch. Geoff was too slow, or perhaps Sarah and Davy were too fast? They tried again and again, but it had gone and they were all embarrassed as they drank beer afterwards, struggling to find things to talk about, grasping at old school stories, old gigs but it wasn't enough and as they walked home together, Sarah said to Davy, 'How can things change so quickly?'

'It's not things, it's us,' Davy replied.

Lying in bed that night Sarah knew that it was true, that

255

they had changed, moved on, and that she would return to London.

'Will it work if we come back when we're qualified?' she asked her mother as she saw her off at the station. 'Will it all be too difficult – will we have changed too much?'

Annie shook her head. 'That's up to you. We'd love to have you and you will remake your old friends and make new ones if you do come back, but just live each day, Sarah, my love. Don't try to answer all the questions now, just go with it for a bit – stretch your frontiers, enjoy yourself.'

The train was coming in, screeching, doors were slamming and Sarah hugged her, held her tight, wondering at how small she seemed, kissed her father, her aunt, her uncle, then told her mother again. 'I'll be back in the spring.' The words gave them both comfort.

Snow was falling as the train drew out, thickening, cocooning them, and she just wanted to stay here, in amongst the white silence, not arriving anywhere, just sitting with Davy, feeling safe.

The windows of their bedsits were crusted with ice. There was a deep chill in the blankets, the mattress and the gas fire ate her shillings all night. In the morning they bought paraffin heaters and lugged them up the stairs, and then paraffin from the corner shop, trimming the wicks, lighting them, watching the blue flame waver, leaving it as they went into college on the first day, cycling with Tim, careering round corners, their scarves flying, their breath visible.

Sarah walked into the sewing room and Deborah turned and smiled. 'Come on over here, Sarah.'

Sally joined them and they talked of how strange Christmas had been, how different, how sad they were to leave, then they walked to the refectory together, ate lunch, cut, designed, laughed together. Sarah cycled back to the bedsit, ringing her bell for no reason, wanting to sing, wanting to shout because it was all right, the darkness had gone, she had friends, they felt as she did. She wasn't alone, her confusion was gone.

She propped up her bike, smiled at Ma Tucker, ran up the stairs, listened at Carl's door. Nothing – but she couldn't remember what he looked like, sounded like, felt like and tonight they were practising because Arnie said they could get some gigs this term, and so they bloody well would.

They played in her room, putting more muscle into the songs but keeping the fragility of Davy's melodies, running the riffs again and again, looking for Ma Tucker, drinking the beer that Tim had bought with money from the joint kitty, then drinking cocoa which she made on the Belling, sipping it, talking gently, singing through the numbers quietly until midnight struck. Nodding to one another as they left because they all had work to do.

Sarah sat at her desk, writing up her notes, writing to her mother, looking up at the condensation running down the windows and at two o'clock she fell into bed and slept as she had not done since she had come down in October.

On Sunday she cooked a stew with dumplings for Davy and Tim because they were beginning to look and feel like a can of baked beans. Davy had cooked rice in his oven and carried it into the room when the stew was finished, dumping it on the table and they drew straws over who should have the skin, which was dark and crisp.

Tim had brought beer. 'Because I'm not safe around food,' he said.

'You seem to be doing quite well,' Sarah murmured, looking at his empty plate. 'And don't you worry, my lad – I shall teach you and then you can do your share.'

'You lot must be gluttons for punishment.'

Davy leaned back, reaching for the sugar from the draining board. 'No, just gluttons.'

They walked in the park in the afternoon, calling in on Arnie for tea, then wishing they hadn't because he and some friends had bought take-away curry the night before and it was still in cartons on tables, on the floor. 'Have some,' Arnie nodded at the food.

They laughed, shook their heads. 'Another time.'

'What would Bet say?' Davy said, flinging his arms round Sarah's and Tim's shoulders as they left.

'A great deal I expect,' Sarah replied, looking up at the crisp blue sky, 'A very great deal.' She was happy, for the first time since October she was happy. She looked at Davy and nodded as he smiled. He was too. 'Race you,' he said, starting to run, jumping up to reach the lower branches of the trees that lined the street. 'Race you back,' he shouted.

She and Tim ran, leaping, whooping, their scarves flying – down street after street, then up the steps, through the hall and into her room. They sat on the floor and drank tea, still laughing, groaning when curry was mentioned, writing a song when they should have been working. They called it *Curry Afternoons*, and spent the rest of the day picking out rhythms on their guitars, singing the words, testing how they hung together.

By the end of the second week Sarah had taught Tim how to cook liver and bacon. He cooked it again for Sunday lunch and they groaned. 'Not again.'

'Then teach me something else,' he said, grinning at them, his hair lank from the rain which had poured down on the way back from the off-licence.

The following week she taught him how to cook smoked haddock. 'But I'm doing Sunday lunch and we'll have Arnie round – we don't want to see smoked haddock or liver and bacon until February!'

Arnie forgot lunch next Sunday, but they were not surprised, the only thing he was ever on time for was rehearsals and so they ate his lamb, drank his beer and looked out at the rain, shaking their heads at the thought of the park, and ran through their numbers again, very quietly because Ma Tucker was downstairs. There was an audition on the first of February at a new club which was giving spots to newcomers. 'I want to get it,' Davy said. 'I want to be able to stuff that under Carl's nose when he finally does come back.'

Sarah looked at him and at Tim. She'd almost forgotten about Carl. They played at the audition and were taken on for a spot every two weeks and that night they drank too much in the pub, and stumbled back along the road, arm in arm, then up the steps, banging the light switch, giggling, squeezing past the bikes, yelping as the pedals caught their shins, creeping up the stairs, along the landing, into Sarah's room. She fumbled for the light and basked in the damp heat of the paraffin stove. They boiled the kettle for coffee and sniggered as Tim tiptoed across to her bed, with Davy following, his finger to his mouth, giggling as they collapsed and made more noise than a herd of elephants.

There was a knock at the door. Carl stood there, more tanned than before, his face relaxed, smiling. 'So, what time d'you call this then?'

Sarah felt her hands shake as she put coffee into the mugs, her face had flushed at the sound of his voice. How could she have forgotten what he looked like, sounded like? How could she when he was so beautiful? She turned away, back to the kettle.

'We're celebrating,' she said, her voice tight. 'We've been taken on by Max's – he liked Davy's new song – *Curry Afternoons*.'

She looked across at Davy and winked. He grinned and Tim slapped his back.

'I heard,' Carl said. 'Well done. Is there a coffee for me, Sarah?'

He was moving towards her and when she turned back to reach for another mug he was there, next to her. 'I've missed you,' he said quietly, taking the spoon from her shaking hand, heaping it with coffee, pouring the water into the two remaining mugs.

She didn't turn, couldn't because he was so close. She just stood there looking at the cracked tiles, the grouting which was covered in mould.

'I skied down the moguls and all I thought of was you. Am I forgiven yet?'

Sarah wiped down the drainer, rinsing out the cloth, wringing it again and again. 'There's nothing to forgive – you were right.' Because, damn it, he was.

'Oh yes, I think there is. I was unkind, tactless, I didn't say how good you all were too, not really.' He moved away and now when she turned she could still smell him. She leant back against the drainer, clutching it, feeling the heat in her face, in her body and wondered if this was love.

He stood there, talking to the boys, his stance easy, his voice level, calm, his fingers sure as he flipped them cigarettes, offering her one, looking at her with those eyes, smiling as she shook her head, turning from her to speak to Davy.

'Come to a party with me tomorrow to celebrate. Seven o'clock, here.'

'Arnie too?' Tim asked.

'As if we could go without him – you lot are like the four musketeers. But make sure he's on time and clean. It's in Chelsea.' Carl looked at the ash on his cigarette, then at Sarah, his eyebrows raised. She brought him a saucer and his fingers stroked her hand as he took it from her. She felt his touch in her belly and wanted to feel his hands on her face, wanted just to be near him for every minute, every second of each day, and she couldn't understand how she had not thought of him, not longed for him every minute since she had last seen him.

That night she lay in bed and heard him turn. She reached out and touched the wall, then kissed her hand where he had touched her, running her tongue over her skin, wanting the scent of him inside her. She turned, brought the blankets up round her neck, then turned again, hearing the cars in the street outside, seeing the lights across the ceiling, because she never drew her curtains.

She turned again, counted the hours, thought of him dancing with her, his shirt so fine and soft, his legs so long and then she stiffened, leapt from the bed to the wardrobe, searching through her clothes. Chelsea, he had said. Chelsea, for God's sake.

In the morning she dragged Davy from his room and they cycled to Carnaby Street, where they rushed in and out of shops, looking at shirts, trousers, ties.

'I can make the shirt but I can't do the trousers,' she panted as they hurried to the next boutique, hearing the music thumping out, sorting through the racks, smelling the cotton, the joss sticks. They found a shirt Davy liked with a large collar and pockets.

'It'd look nice in pale green, bring out the auburn in your hair,' she said.

Davy nodded. 'I'll get that tie.'

They bought the trousers from a boutique which was painted dark green and had lights that flashed on and off. 'God, like a bloody party already,' Davy said, shouting above the music. 'It's going to be great – I was wrong about him. I thought he was a bastard but he's nice, Sarah, he likes you too.'

Sarah said, 'He likes us all.'

Davy just grinned.

They bought an offcut of green cotton from the market stall. It was darker than they had intended but better, Davy thought, holding it up against the tie. Smoother.

Sarah smiled. 'Oh, creating an image, are we?'

Davy nodded, blushing. 'That's what Carl said last night – image is all important. There'll be music people there tonight and he wants us to be seen. I told you he was nice – he's trying to help us, bonny lass.'

They cycled on to the Kings Road and locked their bikes up again, dashing from one boutique to another, looking for ideas. It was hot in the shops and Sarah flung off her coat, handing it to Davy, trying dresses up against her, pressing them to her, swinging left and right in front of the mirrors.

'I think the one you've got on is better than any of this,' Davy said in the third shop. 'You got some real good ideas, Sarah, a real eye for fashion.'

Sarah hung the dresses back on the rack, and flicked through the rest. 'But I can't wear the one I've got on, he's seen it, it's not posh. It's Chelsea we're going to, Davy.'

They rushed on to the next one, then Davy made them stop for coffee and a Chelsea bun.

'To give us inspiration,' he said, 'and me a bit of stamina.'

They tried the next, and then the next and now they saw something that caught her eye – a simple shift with cut-away shoulders and another with a huge leather belt.

'You could do that easily enough,' Davy said. 'I'd like to have a go at creating a waxed batik design for something like that, it would be stunning.'

Sarah held it up against her, turning, twisting, liking it. She turned it inside out to look at the darts, the seams, and stretched it while Davy held it.

'Can I help you at all?' a woman's voice said and Sarah snatched her sketch to her side, then fingered the material. 'Not quite what I was looking for,' she replied, smiling at the woman whose lipstick had run into the lines dug deep along her upper lip.

The woman looked at her, then at the dress. 'Do you make clothes?'

Sarah paused, then shrugged, bringing up her sketchbook. 'Yes, I'm sorry, I was just looking for ideas.'

'Did you make that?' The woman pointed to the shift Sarah was wearing with its scalloped neckline, its thick deep purple belt which she had made of Indian cotton that Prue had sent at Christmas.

Sarah nodded, looking back at the dress that Davy still held, trying to hold it in her mind.

'Can you make me some?'

The music was flashing in time with the lights and Sarah could feel the vibrations through her feet.

'How many?' Davy asked.

'One dozen in a dark colour, one in a light, one muted, one vivid. Four dozen altogether and I want this sort of textile design.' She whipped a dress off the rack. It was a simple two-colour design.

'How much?' Sarah asked.

The woman told them.

'By when?' Davy asked.

'One week.'

They looked at one another, then nodded.

'Yes, we'll be here, in one week's time.'

They left then, running to their bikes, talking as they did so, stopping at the market for an offcut for a remake of her own dress, buying an Indian scarf to pick up the colour.

'I'll make your shirt and run up another shift for tonight, then a sample for Mum because it's too big a job for us. We'll have to talk them into it somehow – we'll ring them tonight. It's cheaper.' The traffic lights were red but they kept going, sliding round to the left, ignoring the hoots, pedalling into the wind, turning right, then left. 'Oh God, Davy,' Sarah called over her shoulder, 'Deborah's friend was asked to do this by a boutique and she made a mint. These shops are just following along after the kids now, the designers aren't dictating the fashion any more. It's just . . . oh I don't know.'

'Grand's the word you're looking for.' Davy was leaning forward, pedalling hard. 'What lectures are you missing?'

'Only pattern design. Debs will cover for me, I'll get the notes off her. What about you?'

'The history of dyeing.'

'Who needs it?'

Davy laughed. 'Not many, but I hope they bloody well need our dresses.'

They worked all afternoon and as she cut and sewed Sarah thought of Carl, then of the clothes, then of Carl again. They brewed one another coffee and worked until five. Then Sarah sneaked into the bathroom to run a cold bath because Ma Tucker would only heat the water once a week, leapt in and out quickly, then opened the door a crack, her hair wet and dripping. Was Carl home? He mustn't see her. She listened, waited, then ran for her room.

She dried her hair, wondering whether to have it cut short like Mary Quant and the women in boutiques. She brought out the iron, folded a towel on the floor, knelt to lay her head on the towel and ironed her hair, wanting it straight, wanting the kinks out of the side just for once. 'Come out, come out, just this once,' she begged, rushing to the mirror. No, they were still there.

She pressed the samples, Davy's shirt, her dress and checked her watch. Oh God, it was twenty to seven. 'Davy,' she yelled, banging on the wall. 'Come on, get your shirt. We've got to phone.'

She threw it to him as he came in, his hair still wet, sticking up. 'Get your hair dry. I'll go down and ring.'

Sarah hauled on her tights, rammed her feet into shoes that she had bought from the market. They were too tight, but never mind, they looked good. Bet had always said you could tell a person's class from their shoes, she thought as she rushed down the stairs to the pay phone behind the bikes, shoving them along, squeezing in behind them, putting the money in, dialling. 'I should be a bloody princess from the looks of these, but the bikes spoil it,' she murmured, listening to the ringing tone. 'Be in, be in.'

Annie answered, Sarah pushed the button. 'Mum, it's Sarah.'

'Oh darling.' There was pleasure in Annie's voice, then anxiety. 'What's wrong?'

Sarah laughed. 'Nothing, Mum, or there won't be if you think we've done the right thing.'

She told her then about the dresses, the money, the quantity, the delivery date.

Annie laughed. 'You don't give us a lot of time, but why not? Perhaps it's time we kicked off into fashion. All right, darling, put the sample on the train tomorrow. I'll get someone to pick it up. Make sure you've put all the details down. The sizes and so on.'

264

'Oh God, I didn't get them.'

'Never mind. Give them a ring in the morning, and me a ring in the evening with those. Well done, darling. Tell Davy well done too. Hang on, your da's here.'

Sarah leant against the wall, then heard Carl calling down to her. 'What are you doing, it's nearly seven. Come on, Sarah, get off the phone, we've got to go and you haven't put your make-up on.'

Georgie was speaking then, telling her how Geoff had called in to see them today, with copies of the photographs he had taken when they were up at Christmas. 'I'll send them down to you.'

'Good, Dad, that's great but I've – '

'Come on, Sarah, we'll be late. Get yourself ready.' Carl was hanging over the banister, nodding to Arnie as he squeezed past the bikes and ambled up the stairs.

'Buttons' great-granddaughter is thriving, her squeaker's coming on nicely.'

'Come on, Sarah.'

Sarah nodded at Carl. 'Da I've got to go, I'm just off out. Mum will tell you all about the clothes. It could be good. Bye, love you.'

She hung up, her hands wet with tension.

'For God's sake, Sarah, get your make-up on.' Carl was running down the stairs.

'I don't wear make-up,' she said, catching the coat Davy dropped down from the landing.

'Will you lot be quiet?' Ma Tucker shouted from her room.

She followed Carl out of the house and stood behind him as he hailed taxi after taxi but none had their lights up. She ran her hands down her hair, felt her skin. They were going to Chelsea, she should have worn make-up. She'd show him up. Oh God.

'We could take our bikes,' Davy said.

Carl spun round. 'Give us a break – that'd show a lot of class wouldn't it, arriving on our bikes?'

Davy and Sarah looked at one another, then at Tim and

the laughter came, stupid silly wonderful laughter. 'Me grandma always said your class shows in your shoes,' Davy said.

'And try not to sound so bloody Geordie, will you?' Carl said, flagging another which swung towards them and stopped, just as their laughter had stopped.

They sat in the taxi silently. 'Can you hurry please?' Carl said, sliding the glass partition open. The cab lurched round the next corner and the next and Arnie slid from the dicky seat and now laughter came again, from Carl too, but Sarah could still not forget.

Carl put his arm around her. 'So why did you have to ring then, what was it all about?'

Davy told him.

'But why ring when we're going out?'

'Because it's cheaper after six,' Sarah said, her voice crisp. 'We're not all like you with money to burn and besides, they're not home from work until then, and we don't want to disturb them at the factory.'

She felt the pressure of Carl's arm, his hand as he stroked her shoulder. 'I didn't realise they actually worked in the factory, I thought they just owned it. It's tough on you though, little Sarah, having a mother who works, they say it harms the kids.' His voice was soft, whispering into her ear. 'Poor little girl, I shall look after you.'

They turned another corner and Arnie slid off again and again they laughed, then Sarah turned to Carl. 'It didn't harm me, I'm fine.'

'Hardly, darling.'

They were drawing up at a house which had steps as Ma Tucker's had, but they were white, and the pillars were white too. The number was in brass and Davy raised his eyebrows at Sarah, as Carl rang the bell, then opened the door.

'Shouldn't we wait?' Sarah said, clutching at his sleeve.

'Oh no, I'm almost one of the family.' A blast of light and music hit them, the scent of perfume and pot as they walked into a hall filled with people holding wine glasses, smoking cigarettes or joints. Carl turned and grabbed her hand, pulling her after him, up the stairs past family portraits on her left and a hung chandelier on her right which hung over the people below.

On the landing he stopped to take wine from a waiter, handing one to her. She looked behind. Tim and Davy had stopped and were leaning over, pointing to Arnie who was accepting a joint from an older man.

'What did you mean, it has done me harm? What's wrong with me, apart from my voice and my make-up?' Her voice shook with anger, with hurt.

'Oh darling, don't be cross. It's just that you're so clingy, look at you, looking round for poor Davy. You should let him live his own life – and you ring your mother or write every week. I mean, isn't it time we cut those apron strings? This is London sweetie, the sixties, not the forties.' He kissed her cheek with his soft lips and waved to a blonde girl who lounged pouting against a mahogany table, her pan-stick make-up pale, her eye-liner dark. 'See you in a minute, darling,' he said to Sarah, kissing her lips this time, and even though the hurt and anger were harsh in her, so was the surge of passion at the touch of his lips.

She stood in the doorway, watching him leave her and thread his way through groups of people, seeing them brightening at the sight of him, slapping his back, and then he was gone. She watched the crowds, daring herself not to look for Davy, trying to smile, sipping her wine, gripping her glass with both hands until an old man with hair below his collar came up, smiled, shook her hand. 'We were just discussing how the Vietnam war has fostered a solidarity among the youth, bound you together against authority, against parental power as you watch your brothers being felled. Do you agree?'

His breath was sweet with pot and wine, his eyes unfocused. He didn't wait for an answer but ambled away.

She looked for Carl and saw him kissing the cheeks of the women, his briefcase with him as always. He was patting it

267

now, mouthing 'Later,' to the young man in the flowered shirt. So, he could do business night and day, but not her mother during working hours?

She drank her wine, plonked it on a passing tray and took another, drinking faster this time, joining the drifting crowds, smiling when a girl came and gripped her arm. 'Dr Timothy Leary is right, this nirvana is the surest means to tune in to the higher consciousness, to break with the traditions of one's parents – we need to break free, to explore everything, after this decade, nothing will ever be the same again.'

Sarah wanted the girl to stay so that she was no longer alone, so that when Carl saw her he would see that she was mixing, holding her own, damn him. 'Who's Timothy Leary?' she asked, speaking as she had done so many years ago, before they came to Wassingham, her mouth rounded, her words clear.

'He's God,' the girl said, leaving her.

Sarah took another drink, moved closer to a group to the left of her, smiling as though she was one of them, then becoming one of them as they widened their circle to let her in, asking if she had seen Thomas Henson's surrealist art exhibition, telling her she simply must when she said no, shaking her head at the joint which was offered, looking round casually for Carl, feeling the pain when he saw him dancing with another girl. What am I doing here? She saw a man come, put his arm round Carl and speak quietly, then lead him to a table where a champagne bottle stood in ice.

'So that's her is it, Carl?' Sam Davis nodded towards Sarah.

'My backer's right, she's got the looks if she uses them properly, it's all image, Carl – come on, get going on her – and it is just the girl they want, not the group, those are the backer's instructions, and I agree, having seen her. It's a solo artist I'm after.'

Carl brought out his cigarette case and offered Sam a joint. 'I know it, but I've got it all in hand.'

Sam sucked on the joint. 'Nice stuff,' he nodded approvingly. 'So you'll ditch the group, and make sure she ditches the degree? We're not fiddling around so someone can have a fling for a couple of years and then walk away from it, it's got to be a long-term thing. Mark you, you'll have to get her trained, take her on the circuit, we'll try a recording in sixty-seven probably.' Sam leant forward. 'I had a scout there at the college audition, just to check that my backer was right and my boy said she was good. There's nothing wrong with the boys, they just don't fit with the plan, so get rid of them, especially the Ryan boy and the family. Apparently she's close to them, and that always leads to trouble. We want kids we can nurture, mould, you know what I mean? We don't want any clever sods in on it and I gather they're business people. It won't do, so sort it or you'll have no one to help you with your big break, and no more contacts, ever – got it.'

Carl nodded. 'You worry too much, far too much.'

Sam poured more champagne. 'I got where I am by worrying, my boy. You're only twenty-two, still wet behind the ears where this business is concerned. Got your gear have you? I'll give you your due, you've got that side of your life sorted out.'

Carl smiled. 'It's in the safe – I'll be in the library in half an hour. See you then.' He downed his champagne and stood looking for Sarah, waving at her, languidly passing through the crowded room. She watched him come, his walk, his hands, his face and turned to listen to the man next to her, then felt his hand on her arm, pulling her towards him, his arms sliding round her, his body moving in time to the music and she moved with him, sinking closer as his fingers slid beneath her shoulder straps, warm against her back.

'Little Sarah, come and sing for my friends.'

Carl's breath puffed her hair and she pulled away, looking for the others. Davy was drunk and so was Tim, leaning up against the wall, talking to two girls who were also drunk.

'No, we can't, not tonight. They're past it.'

Carl looked at her, kissed her mouth gently, softly, his

tongue stroking her lip, and her limbs felt weak. 'Then sing to us yourself,' he murmured, his mouth still on hers.

She drew back. 'I told you I can't. We're a team.'

'For God's sake, Sarah, I'm not asking you to divorce him, just sing without him, and don't shout, people will hear.'

Sarah looked around her now and saw a girl blowing a kiss at Carl, saw his answering smile. She said, 'I should have come with a brown paper bag stuck over me head and a cork stuffed in me mouth, having dropped Davy off down a bloody drain, shouldn't I, and I don't care if people stare, bonny bloody lad.'

She wrenched herself from him. 'And I don't cling.'

She stormed to the door, looking for Davy, Tim or Arnie but they were all drinking, laughing, enjoying the night, and so she hailed a taxi, and used the money that she was saving for another gallon of paraffin to pay for it.

'Damn you, damn you all,' she cursed as she lay in bed, not knowing what to think or feel, not knowing what to do with the anger inside her, but then she leapt from bed and tore up the music she'd been writing. That was all over, she'd stick to what she knew, she'd just work, and work and work.

She left the house early, took the samples to the station, rang the shop about sizes, and went back to lectures, her head aching, her hand aching from the notes she wrote because she must not think, she must not remember the feel of his hands, the unkindness of his words. She couldn't eat her sandwiches at lunch and there were no lectures that afternoon so she cycled home, lugging her bike up the steps, seeing the headless chrysanthemums in the garden, shaking her head at the kids who had done this.

The stairs seemed steep, her legs tired and then she stopped at the sight of Carl sitting on the top step, holding a bunch of chrysanthemums, Ma Tucker's chrysanthemums, his face contrite.

'I'm doing everything wrong, Sarah, but it's just because you're special to me. I get tense, the words come out back to front and I don't mean them. I love your group, and I love Davy and I love your mother. Please forgive me.'

He held out the flowers and their scent was heavy as she held them to her face, feeling the coldness of their petals, the dampness of their stems.

'Will you come and walk in the park with me, please?' he asked, holding out his hand.

They walked all afternoon and he told her of his mother's yacht, his mother's life and how he had brought himself up, how she had been away, or busy, or both and how he longed for someone to love him, just him.

'That's why I feel so strongly that mothers should be with their children. That's what I would want for my child.' He squeezed her hand. 'I've been waiting for someone special, Sarah, for the whole of my life.'

She told him then about her parents, their life in the Army, the building of the business which was her mother's dream, her father's accident, the problems which seemed to have stopped two years ago, though she didn't know why. She told him about Bet and Davy who was like a brother to her, as Uncle Tom had been to her mother.

'So he's no threat to any love I have,' she said gently, feeling so sorry for this young man who had so much, but also had nothing.

He kissed her then, holding her close, his mouth opening, his tongue seeking hers, his arms holding her up as her legs became weak and she wanted to stay like this for ever – in a park, with his mouth on hers and no space between them.

Annie received the samples and called Tom and Georgie in, showing them Davy's designs and Sarah's pattern design and sample.

Tom nodded. 'Good for them. Yes, the design department can do that in two days, what about your side, Annie?'

Annie ran her fingers through her hair. 'Even if I have to sew them myself we'll get it done. They're keen and I think it's important that we encourage them because things seem

271

to be improving down there, they're sounding so much more lively, so much keener about everything. I think we should try their designs in the showroom too, see how they do. Then cut them in on all profits.'

Georgie laughed. 'They'll be buying electric guitars and hiring the Albert Hall for a gig next.'

'Yes, you're right, Annie, cut them in.'

'You write and tell them, Georgie,' Annie said, knowing that he had been hurt when Sarah had put the phone down on him and this would be an opportunity for her daughter to write back to him.

Sarah opened the letter, read it, called out to Davy to come in. Carl came too, standing in the doorway.

'Da says we're to have a cut of the profits, that Mum's really pleased and so's your da.' She handed him the letter, feeling Carl's kiss on her forehead, his hand on her back.

Later he murmured that his mother had never had time to write either.

Sarah said, 'It's not like that.'

That evening he brought them pizza and strawberry ice cream to celebrate. She ate it, even though she hated it and as she did so she remembered how her mother had shouted at her father in the hospital, forcing him to eat the ice cream. Sarah put her hand to her forehead, rubbing her skin, forcing herself to eat. She remembered that the nurse had said that her mother was absolutely right, but why hadn't she nursed in the first place, she remembered asking, then her da wouldn't have been hurt?

She finished the ice cream and accepted a joint, sucking deeply, welcoming the haze, the relaxation, the numbing of the senses, the deadening of an anger which had come. She drew more deeply, to blot out the memory.

CHAPTER 17

Annie and George decided that the take-up on the clothes had been enthusiastic enough for them to extend into the retail trade.

'Just in Newcastle to see how it goes, and later in the local towns,' Annie suggested and Tom agreed.

Bill, the estate agent, scouted for premises and at the end of February, in good time for the spring season, they took on Jessica, a middle-aged woman who had been a shop manager in Surrey. Annie wrote to Sarah.

> So keep on sending up samples, darling and let's see how it goes. Your dad has organised a few local advertisements but we're hoping that word of mouth will do the trick. Tom's decorated it in green and white and all of them will be the same. I say 'all' but it depends on how it goes. Brenda and the girls are right behind us. I hope you and Davy are pleased too.

She handed the letter to Georgie to finish and took a cup of tea from Bet, stirring it because the milk was yesterday's and cream floated on the top. She hated that, it was like the skin of custard – it stuck in her throat.

'Have you heard from them this week?' Bet asked, undoing the top button of her blouse and wiping her neck with her handkerchief. 'Oh dear, I don't know, I get so hot these days, must get some more pills from the doctor.'

Annie smiled. 'Well, it can't be a hot flush, Bet, I'm getting all of those. Yes, you must go back, your blood pressure might be up again.'

Bet nodded. 'So have you heard?'

'Yes, they're back into the music again and want to go up to Scotland on what they call a chewing-gum tour. I gather this friend Carl has fixed up a lot of gigs, so they're going there in early December, by coach, stopping off along the way.'

Georgie was still writing, his head bent over the table. Bet poured more tea. 'Are you letting her?'

'How can I stop her? It's always been so important to them – it just shows that they're enjoying life, getting the most out of it. It's better than them wanting to run away home.'

Bet pursed her lips. 'I don't like it, you know, it's not healthy the way kids today live, eating vegetables, all this s – e – x.' Bet spelt out the letters. 'There's this pill now and all these other drugs, it's in all the papers.'

Georgie looked up. 'I know, but you don't want to believe all you read, that's just a few of them. Ours are good kids, sensible and they're together – and they eat meat, so perhaps the other is all right too.' He smiled. 'Oh, they'll be all right, it's like I said to Annie – look at my birds, give them a safe warm home and they'll come back after they've felt the wind beneath their wings.'

Annie walked to the sink and looked out of the window, wanting to shout at him to be quiet about his bloody birds, this was her daughter and she was growing up, growing away. Was it as wild as the papers said? And who the hell was this Carl that Davy had mentioned, but Sarah hadn't?

She added a postscript to the letter, asking Sarah to let them know their itinerary and they would come to support her if there was a show nearby.

Sarah read the letter, passed to to Davy, not wanting Carl to see it but he did, and smiled at her. 'So, the apron strings are being drawn a little tighter, are they?'

She didn't send her mother the itinerary and boarded the coach with the boys and Carl, sitting with the other acts as they drove through pouring rain to Northampton, unpacking their luggage, sleeping in a boarding house that Carl had arranged, playing that night to a half-empty drill hall, moving on the next morning to Newcastle.

It was still raining but much colder and Carl helped her drag her case from the luggage hold, saying that they'd have to go straight to the club, they were late.

They played and Davy caught her eye. 'We should have told them,' he said, as they eased back for Arnie's break, listening, moving in time.

'I know, but it just seemed easier for them, they'll be so busy with the spring season coming up and the shop's doing well. They've got more than enough to do without traipsing through the rain to sit in amongst all this smoke and these drop-outs.' She nodded at the audience who were drinking and talking, doing anything but listening.

'Yes, you're right, bonny lass.' His smile was gentle, but became a grin as Arnie wiggled his hips and the waitresses screamed, but momentarily Sarah lost her rhythm because she had felt such a wave of guilt. She listened, skipped a few bars, came in again concentrating on the music because Carl was right, they must grow up. Tim's mother hadn't asked for an itinerary, or Arnie's, just hers and Davy's and it was no excuse that they were touring the north, not the south where the others came from. It was ridiculous.

They drove on up to Scotland and now they knew the others well, and had jam sessions on the coach, leaping off at garages to use their lavatories since there were none on the coach. Sarah was the only girl but she was with Carl and so no one pinched her bum, or spoke sweet nothings and she was proud of him as he extolled the Beatles and their experimentation, their anticipation of future tastes, their originality, their foresight in putting in the sixth chords into their numbers.

'So simple,' he said, 'and it's the simple things that work.'

Her mother said that too, but she didn't tell him that, just watched his lips, his hands as they touched her knee, his mouth as he laughed.

He left them in Glasgow, flying down to London to meet some business friends who were taking a skiing lodge, waving to her, grinning. 'See you after Easter, my sweet little Sarah. Look after her, Davy. I'll talk to them about you all.'

The gigs in Chester and Wales were dull, the hours dragged, the music seemed flat and slow, like the train which took them from London to Newcastle at the end of term.

They worked hard during the day, catching up on the notes which Deborah's and Davy's friend had copied for them, and played together in the evening in the packaging room, and Annie stood and listened.

'The tour was a good idea,' she said on Good Friday as she took Sarah hot chocolate in bed. 'You're sounding more solid, more substantial, you're looking well too, my darling. Was it better this term?'

Sarah held the cocoa between her hands, feeling the steam on her face. 'Yes, much better. The sun seems to be out, if you know what I mean. There's so much to do, it's all so interesting.'

She didn't mention Carl, somehow she couldn't and she didn't know why. She looked at her mother's hands on the quilt, her nails were dirty. Carl never had dirty nails. Annie saw her looking and shrugged her shoulders. 'Bet and I have been putting the potatoes in.'

Sarah nodded. Yes, that's what they always did on Good Friday, it was all so predictable.

Annie lay awake that night, knowing that her daughter was growing away from her as she had done from Sarah. She eased herself against Georgie, wanting the warmth of his body, the comfort of his familiar shape, wishing she had asked Sarah why she had not told them that the group were appearing in Newcastle, why she had to read it in the newspaper. But she knew she mustn't ask, that she must let

276

go. In the morning she checked that the cutting was safely hidden from Georgie, because he must not know.

In the summer term life was wonderful, Sarah felt the sun warming her, the wine in the evenings loosening her. She bought pan-stick, eye liner and mascara and talked at parties about the extension of consciousness and the limitlessness of life as it now was, and heard Davy do likewise though they failed to understand their own words.

They went to a Rolling Stones concert and found themselves twenty feet from Mick Jagger and Keith Richards, blown away by the music, blinded by the lights, surrounded by hot jostling bodies.

They played at a Young Farmers gig and here there were no jostling bodies but restrained dancing until too much beer had been drunk and then raucous choruses and jiving shook up the whole room.

She and Davy bought their own pot now, because Carl could not keep supplying them out of his own pocket, he said, his face red with embarrassment, neither could he pay for all their taxis to and from the parties, so they worked harder to design and sell clothes to their friends at college and to local market stalls.

They auditioned for a college gig and were accepted. They also had more commissions from the students for shirts, dresses, skirts specifically for the gig and by June were working each morning, evening and lunchtime, copying notes when they could, eating when they could, remembering also to send up new samples to Annie from the shops they had gathered into the circle, until Sarah's head was splitting and Davy looked drawn and pale.

Carl took them to another party that week and they were too tired to smile and talk of Dr Timothy Leary, or the duty of the young to explore and push back the frontiers of the mind, or the brilliance of Bob Dylan. 'I can't understand his songs,' Sarah said to the man who had spattered canapés in her wine and now had some on his beard. 'I think he's a pseudo-intellectual.'

277

She felt Carl's hand on her arm, saw Davy mouthing 'ouch', and didn't care, she was too tired. She didn't care that Carl pushed her out before him, that his voice was sharp in the taxi. 'For God's sake, you can't afford to be tired, nobody can. If you do that once you've made it, it'll be splashed all over the bloody newspapers and that'll be that. And when did you last rehearse?'

She laid her head back on the seat, her hands sore from cutting and sewing, knowing that Davy's were too.

'We haven't time, for God's sake. We're running a business here and trying to get through college, then we did your tour, all the tour, not skiving off for a bit of skiing like some of us here.'

'There's no need to run a business.'

'There's every need if we're to afford our lives, especially all this.' She waved at the taxi, banged his cigarette case, shouting now. She leapt from the cab when it arrived at Ma Tucker's, storming from him, slamming her bedroom door, locking it, just needing to sleep but she couldn't and then she heard a scratching at the door.

She opened it a crack. He pushed in a joint and whispered, 'I'm sorry, I know you're tired, have this to help you sleep.' She rested her head on the door and wept for his kindness.

The next day she was up early sewing, cutting, pressing, then cycling to college, returning early and sewing again while Davy sat with her, checking, cutting, designing. Arnie and Tim came round to practise but there was no time tonight, Sarah said, jerking her head at the coffee. 'But you can make us all a drink.'

She lifted the mug with hands swollen from the scissors, refusing a joint because she couldn't relax yet, shaking her head at Davy as he took one. He grimaced and put it back.

'I'll just breathe in deeply,' he said, chasing Tim's smoke across the room, making them all laugh. They worked again when the boys left, necks aching, heads pounding, not looking up when Carl knocked, just calling, 'Come in.'

Carl stood there. 'Where're the others, it's rehearsal night, for God's sake, not your mother's bloody factory. This is no good, you've got to dump this and get on with the music.'

Sarah pushed harder on the pedal, heard the machine whirr, listened to that as Davy said, 'For God's sake, Carl, it's OK for you to work, I see you've got your briefcase as always, but it's not OK for us – and that's ridiculous because we need to do it. Anyway, we've nearly finished for tonight, we've just got the samples for Auntie Annie now.'

Sarah looked up now, seeing Carl stare at the floor, then at her as he spoke slowly. 'Oh yes, of course, the gig can go to hell, all my efforts too – but we must make sure Auntie Annie gets her pound of bloody flesh.'

Sarah lifted her foot from the pedal. 'Leave my mother out of this, we learn from it as well, don't we? Davy's right, you're bloody well working, you always work, wherever we go. I'm sick to death of that case, of your friends, and of you.'

Her head was pounding, nausea rose in her throat and she didn't care as he stormed out, slamming the door. She just worked and then smoked with Davy, too tired to talk, too tired to ache at the thought of Carl's anger, almost too tired to sleep when Davy stumbled from her room.

Carl's room was empty in the morning, his door locked and in lectures Sarah couldn't concentrate, all she could think of was his beautiful face, his hands, his tan, his lips. Had he kissed another girl, had he slept with her? Had he? Had he?

Would he come back? Would he?

That evening she smoked the joints that Davy had brought, one, two, three, and the room faded until there was nothing but warmth, looseness, peace and she smiled as Davy left, smiled as Carl came in, held her in his arms, cradled her on the bed.

'I'm sorry, my darling girl. I just felt worried about you, so worried. Please stop sewing this weekend, stop working, stop rehearsing and come with me. Sam Davis is having a party at Bracklesham Bay in a house he owns.' He was stroking her arms, undoing her blouse, running his fingers beneath her bra, touching her nipple, easing the strap from her shoulders, taking her in his mouth and she arched her back, wanting more, knowing that he had wanted it for weeks, but she was too frightened.

'Come away with me, my darling,' he said, against her skin.

'All of us,' she said.

'Just you.' His tongue stroked her breast, her shoulder, her lips.

'No, Davy should come too, it's not fair, he's been working too.'

His hand was on her thigh now, gently stroking. He undid her jeans, stroked her belly, her groin and then his fingers were between her legs, probing, gentle and his lips were on hers, his tongue deep.

'Davy too,' she gasped, because she was frightened of being with this man alone for a weekend – it would be so hard not to sleep with him.

Carl lifted his head. 'He needs to practise, he's not as good as the rest of you.'

Sarah felt his fingers leave her as her own anger rose. She pushed him aside, scrambling to her feet, feeling faint, falling back on to the bed, tasting the marijauna.

'He's just as good, he's better. Arnie says so.' She was wrenching at her zip.

Carl still lay on the bed, resting on his elbow. 'So, Arnie's the expert now is he – our fine electronics whiz-kid knows all about it, does he?'

Sarah was buttoning her blouse, her fingers trembling, her head swimming. 'I know he's good, and that's what's important and I'm not going without him, if I go at all. We do nothing but row, it's all so pointless, the whole damn thing.' She sat with her hands between her legs, her shoulders slumped. 'So damned pointless.'

His arms came round her then, holding her, pulling her back beside him, not kissing her, just rubbing his cheek on her hair, cupping her face in his hand. 'Fine, we'll take him then.'

It was Friday the next day and they were leaving in the evening so Sarah cycled to Marks & Spencer and bought new bras and pants, not wanting to wear her mother's any more because it wasn't only Sarah's hands that knew them now.

They took the train, then a taxi which entered a sweeping drive, gravel crunching beneath the wheels, light pouring from the latticed windows of the old redbrick house with its moss-spattered roof.

Sam Davis met them at the door, kissing Sarah with his moist lips, drawing her into the dark panelled hall, his arm about her waist, moving from one pool of soft yellow light to another, introducing her and Davy to quietly spoken men and women, handing them plates for the buffet, guiding them to the table, tempting them with lobster, crayfish, crab.

'It's a lovely evening, lovies, take it into the garden, there are tables and chairs.' He wafted away from them, his cravat matching his gold watch perfectly. They walked on to the terrace, smelling the sea in the soft wind, and ate the crab with their fingers as they found a table, sitting down to listen to muted Beatles music and it was as though everything had slowed, as though she'd stepped off the roundabout for a moment.

She felt Carl's hand on her knee, saw him wave to an auburn-haired girl who was dancing alone on the terrace to *Love's Just a Broken Heart* by Cilla Black. The girl came over and Carl pointed to Davy. 'You two match, sit down and share his lobster.' His voice was gentle, his eyes kind and Davy flushed, looked at Sarah and she nodded. 'You do make a pigeon pair, you know.'

She leant back in her chair, feeling the cushion behind her, watching couples who ate, drank or danced.

'I hope love isn't just a broken heart,' Carl said, his arm around her, pulling her towards him.

Sarah drank her crisp cool wine which she recognised as Chardonnay. He had never spoken of love before.

Carl spoke again, very quietly low. 'Let's dance, I'm not hungry, not while I can hold you.'

He laced his fingers through hers, pushing back his chair, slipping his arm round her as she joined him, pressing his body against hers as they danced and the music was *We Can Work it Out* by the Beatles.

'We can, can't we?' he murmured into her hair, running his hands down her back, holding her buttocks, pressing her to him.

She leant into him, breathing his scent through his shirt, watching Davy laughing with the girl, his arm round her, their two heads close together and she relaxed. 'We have worked it out, we're here and it's as though we're in another world. Carl, you've given me so much.' She looked at the pop singer on the next table, the photographer smoking pot and nodded to the woman he was with, smiling as she came across and talked to them of *The Secret Of The Golden Bough* which Sarah had bought from the Indica Bookshop, and of John Coltrane.

'Brilliant, of course,' Sarah said, wondering if anyone in Newcastle had ever heard of him, knowing that no one in Wassingham had.

'I'm not too keen on jazz though,' Carl said, rubbing his hand up and down her back, then whispering into her ear, 'Just on you.'

He eased her away from Marlene and walked her away from the patio across level sweet-smelling grass, kissing her, stopping, holding her close, running his hands down her sides, her bare thighs, the outside of them, the inside, easing his fingers into her pants, stroking her gently. Oh God. Then he withdrew and held her buttocks, breathing, 'Thank God you came into my life just when mini skirts arrived.' He pulled her after him, towards the trees which edged the lawn, stopping again, undoing her dress now that they were far from the noise of the music, the chatter, undoing all the buttons, letting it hang loose.

'Jesus, you're lovely,' he murmured, standing back, pushing the dress aside, running his fingers from her shoulders to her thighs and she felt as though she was swollen, exposed, raw-nerved, on fire but frightened. She pulled her dress to her again, doing up the buttons, because it didn't matter if she recognised Chardonnay and John Coltrane, she was just a girl from Wassingham who was too frightened to give herself.

Carl pulled her to him. 'Trust me, darling, here let me do them up properly.' He bent his head to see by the moonlight, then took her hand, leading her further into the wood, down a beaten path and there were lights at the end.

They approached a stone pavilion hung with lanterns and with cushions strewn about. Sarah hesitated at the foot of the steps.

'Come on, my darling,' Carl said, pulling her with him, taking her inside the one-roomed building, holding her to him, kissing her gently, so gently, licking her lips, her cheeks, his eyes looking into hers, his hands holding her face. Kissing her again and again but there was nothing else, just kisses and she relaxed again.

He moved to the table which was laid with bowls and a burning spirit stove. He took a silver spoon from a cut glass bowl, removed the lid of a porcelain jar and dug deep and she saw the hash gleaming darkly as he tipped it into the glass bowl, kissing her again as he put the spoon down, touching her mouth with his fingers.

'I love you, darling,' he murmured, looking deep into her again and she saw that he did, and knew that she loved him too.

He lifted the glass bowl, heated it and she saw the glass turn cloudy, then thick grey, watched him as he trapped the smoke, turned and held it to her, his lips glistening with moisture from her mouth.

'Breathe it,' he commanded gently, bending her head down to the glass. She looked into his eyes and again saw the love and nodded. He removed his hand and she breathed deeply, so deeply and now he did too and she gripped his shoulders, kissing his head, holding his arms, kissing his hands as he breathed in the smoke, taking the glass from him, breathing again, feeling a stroking begin inside her head, the kisses on her face.

He laid her on the cushions and took the clothes from his own body and he merged into the soft light of the lanterns, the soft sound of the music which drifted around them, in them, through them, then he came to her, kneeling over her, and she stroked him, pulled him on to her, kissed him and then he was gone but there was no sense of loss, just the floating of her body.

Then she felt his hands again and they were pulling apart her dress, ripping the buttons and she watched as they rolled across the paved floor, spun then fell, one, two, three.

She felt his hands on her breasts, tearing at her bra, ripping it from her, kissing her body, licking it and now she was floating so high, and her limbs were loose and lost.

'Please,' she begged, 'please.' But the words were so far away, the stroking in her mind so strong. 'Please,' she whispered, kissing his smile, running her hands down his body, finding him, stroking him then pressing his body on to hers. 'Please.'

He raised himself to kneel over her again and now his hands found her, easing off her pants, stroking her gently, bending, kissing her, licking her and she moaned from the pleasure that rippled from his tongue, again and again until she could hardly breathe, and the ripples grew and the pleasure surged, again and again, inside and out.

She shut her eyes, and all she could see was a golden light. There was no fear. She looked at him, so golden too in the light, his lips parted and swollen, his eyes half shut.

'Please,' she said, lifting her arms to him and he looked at her and took a condom from the pillow behind her, easing it on.

'No,' she said. 'You, just you.'

He shook his head. 'No, we don't want babies yet, my darling.'

284

She wanted to weep for the babies she wanted to have with him, and for his love which protected her, but the stroking was still there, the floating, the pleasure and now he was on her, pushing himself gently into her, so gently and after a moment's pain there was nothing but a surge of light, of being, and another, and another, again and again until she thought she would die.

That night they lay together on the cushions and loved again, and then he held a joint to her lips and they breathed in deeply, before walking across the dewed lawn when dawn was breaking, sinking into the bath which led from their room, his legs round her, his hand soaping her body, hers soaping his.

As the sun warmed the day they lay on the lawn with the others, smoking pot and she smiled at Davy, who lay with the auburn girl, and they tapped to the music of the Beatles together and Sarah could still feel Carl inside her and knew that she would only ever love him.

They drank coffee and she smiled at Sam as he dropped sugar lumps into all their cups.

'I don't take sugar,' she murmured, lying back in Carl's arms.

'You'll like this, my darling,' Carl said, rubbing his finger down the curve of her neck.

She drank, sipping slowly, and the music began to pound and then to slow, to thump, to pulse faster and she turned to Carl in fear. He held her.

'LSD, darling. We're getting all the treats this weekend; don't worry, I'll look after you, just remember that your mind will fly open, this will open doors to unbridled creativity, to another world. I know, believe me, I know.'

She lay back in his arms, feeling the waves of euphoria sweeping over her, gasping in wonder at the swirling colours of the sun through the trees, the flowers in the bed, the dresses of the girls, but then it was too bright, it was swirling too fast, she was breathing too fast, the music was pounding, rushing and then a flower opened up inside her and she basked in the sun which was warmer than it had ever been and the flowers brighter, the scent of Carl sharper. She didn't have to talk, to think. All she had to do was to be.

The following week, she went on the pill and to more parties with Carl. They took LSD tabs and as they cycled to college in the morning Davy told her that it was as though he had never tasted, smelled or heard anything before, that he wanted to keep that depth and clarity of perception all the time and she understood every word he said.

They played at the gig and Sarah explained to Carl that Davy fumbled because of the LSD. That was why his timing was wrong, his voice too quiet. Carl took her to bed, loved her and then heated hash for her.

She replied to Annie's letter, telling her that the gig had gone well, that she was sorry she hadn't written for three weeks but life was hectic, busy, and such fun.

She wanted to write and tell her of her love but she didn't, neither did she tell her of the drugs because how could she understand that it was not as harmful as they had always told her it was. It was just light, love, the unlocking of doors, an explosion of talent, because Davy's art had broken new boundaries and leapt into psychedelia and their rooms were festooned with his work.

'But don't send any up to them,' Sarah warned. 'They'd freak. They wouldn't understand.'

They played at a party of Sam Davis's the following week and Sam praised them, but said that Tim and Davy needed just a bit more polish, a bit more experience. In bed that night Carl said, 'Don't worry, I know how you feel about him, I'll think of a way to brush up his style.' Then they sucked hash and she sank into its arms, and Carl's, not thinking, just being, just accepting.

In July Davy went to Hamburg with Carl and another group, who took him along as lead guitar.

'To give him that edge, darling,' Carl said as he kissed her goodbye at the station.

'Write,' she called as the train pulled away. 'Please write and don't be sick on the ferry, Davy.'

Her bags were heavy as she lugged them on to the train, heaving them into the luggage rack, smoking cigarette after cigarette and stubbing them out in the ashtray, watching the countryside unfold, the blackened verges, the wheat ripening to the colour of Carl's hair and she ached for him and the glow which surrounded their lives together.

She slept, woke, tried to read her course notes. She'd passed her exams, but only just, there were no flying colours for her but who cared, life was too short. That's what Davy had said too, when he got his results.

Wassingham was as small as she remembered it, and just the same, always the same, and so were her family, the pigeons, the neighbours, the smell of coal, the grime. She lay in bed that night and ached for Carl again then walked to the beck in the morning, smoking pot as she sat by the willow, wondering if they were there yet, wondering why she couldn't have gone too.

'It's business, not a holiday,' Carl had said. 'I only just managed to swing it for Davy, couldn't get them to take Tim.'

She smoked another joint, holding her face to the sun, exhaling slowly, feeling her thoughts become submerged beneath the haze, and she preferred it that way.

That evening her mother asked why she hadn't gone with them and treated it as a holiday.

'Because it's not a holiday, it's business. You of all people ought to be able to understand that.' Sarah flung down the tea towel and slammed up to bed.

That night Annie held Georgie in bed. 'She's in love, in pain. She's not sleeping, you can tell that. She looks so drawn and pale – I'd like to meet him, just to see what he's like.'

Georgie sighed. 'She needs to keep busy – let her have this

week to settle down, she seems so jumpy – then give her some work to do in the design department, Tom's all for it.'

The next day Georgie took Sarah with him to the tossing point three miles to the north and she sat in the car, wanting to scream at the creaking of the basket, the fluttering of the birds, the boredom of it all, the rawness of her nerves. God, she must be tired.

She stood in the north-east wind, turning up her collar, thinking of the warmth of Bracklesham Bay, the touch of those hands, the feel of his lips, the feel of him inside her, the glow of the hash, the softness of a joint, the vividness of a tab.

'Let 'em go then, Sarah,' Georgie said, leaning on his stick, gauging the wind. 'Easily calm enough for them.'

She stopped, undid the straps, let the lid fall back and watched as the birds fluttered and took flight, wheeled, dipped, then soared.

'It's so good to have you home, to do this with you again, bonny lass,' Georgie said.

Sarah smiled. 'I'm so glad I'm here, Da,' but she wasn't. She wanted to be with Carl, wanted his hands to undress her at night, heat her hash, roll her joints. She wanted all that and none of this, and she hated herself for it.

A letter arrived from Davy at the end of the week and she tore it open, scanning the page, skimming over the flea-ridden digs, the smoky club, the heckling British sailors calling for the Beatles, then slowed and read again and again of Carl taking photographs of them all outside the Kaiserkeller, then walking them all down the Reeperbahn dodging the prostitutes.

Finding it tiring, the sessions are so damn long, but Carl's helped me out, he's a great guy, Sarah, he really looks after us both, doesn't he?

Sarah waited for the second post, but there was no letter from Carl. There was none the next week either, and she shook her head when her mother asked her if she would help out in the local shop while they moved the manager across to supervise the opening of the new one in Gosforn.

'I've too much college work to catch up on, Mum,' she said, bending her head over her file.

Another letter came from Davy the following week and his writing was scrawling, untidy and there were psychedelic motifs beneath his signature.

Annie leant over her shoulder and picked up the envelope. 'Good lord, is he writing it on a bus or something?'

Sarah smiled. 'Yes, he's off on a trip.' Not your sort of trip though, Mum, and she went up to her room, looked out across the levelled slag heap and could have screamed with boredom and frustration and the pain of getting no letter from Carl.

At the end of August Annie cooked supper while Georgie was at the pigeon club and said, 'Would you like us all to go on holiday, it might make the time pass more quickly for you, Sarah? You still look tired.'

Sarah lit a cigarette, avoiding her mother's eye, waiting for the comment again but Annie said nothing, after all, she had smoked, how could she complain about her daughter?

'No thanks, Mum, I'm too old to go with you and Dad, if you know what I mean.'

'Then go and give Betsy a hand tomorrow in the creche. I'm not asking you this time, I'm telling you. We're all working very hard and you are not.'

Annie put down the pork chop, passed the apple sauce. Sarah looked at it, stubbed out her cigarette.

'We have lobster quite often you know, I find it suits me more than meat.'

Annie put down her knife and fork. 'Well hard bloody luck, you'll just have to put up with this.'

The next day Sarah helped Betsy in the creche and she wiped noses and read stories to the children, sitting them on her knees, but hating it. She wanted to be in the world she knew, not here, with all these people and kids who never looked beyond the bloody slag heaps.

That evening she arrived home and there was a postcard from Carl.

Should be having a lovely time, but am not. Miss you, miss you, miss you. Carl.

She made tea for her mother and cooked steak because Betsy was coming then sat with them all, talking and laughing, feeling the card in her pocket, touching it, smiling to herself. That night her mother made cocoa and brought it into her, sitting on her bed, sipping.

'So, you've heard from him.' Annie's face was kind.

Sarah nodded.

'A long one I hope.'

'Yes, sort of.'

'Oh?' Annie said quietly.

'A postcard if you must know.' Sarah's voice was hard, defensive because what right had her mother to ask? She had no right, for God's sake.

'He cares for me, he's there for me, always there.'

Annie said dryly, 'Not this minute though, business comes first eh, even before letters?'

Sarah flushed and put her cocoa on the bedside table, it was revolting, thick, horrible. She wanted a joint, speed, anything but this woman sitting on her bed criticising Carl.

'You should know about business coming first,' she hissed. 'And why are you still in this stupid little house – you own a factory, we could be in Gosforn, somewhere smart.'

Annie just sat there, gripping her cup, then she said slowly, 'We're here because it's our home, and besides we can't afford anything else because we plough the profits back into the business and then split what's left over. You know that.'

'But it's so boring, so small. There's a world out there, Mum, a world that left this place behind ages ago.'

Annie stood up, looking into her cocoa. 'I know there's a

world out there and that it's exciting, stimulating. I felt I had to leave once too, Sarah, and I did, and then I came back because I wanted what it had to offer. I do understand how you feel.'

She stopped and kissed her daughter but there was no warm arm flung around her neck as before, just the heat of her daughter's damp skin and the confusion in her eyes.

Annie walked from the room. Dear God, why weren't there any lessons in being a parent?

Sarah left for London early, she couldn't stand being suffocated by her family any longer, she would rather be alone.

CHAPTER 18

Carl and Davy arrived back in October, just before the start of term when the leaves were falling from the trees and there was mist morning and evening and a crispness in the air. They burned their paraffin heaters and Sarah put Davy's pale drawn looks down to sleeping in dank rooms and too many hours playing in smoky bars.

Carl agreed. 'Oh yes, it was tough, but it's done him good.'

They rehearsed on Wednesday and there was a hard edge to Davy's playing, and his fragile melodies were gone. In bed Carl said they were the best he had heard in a long while and flipped her a tab, and they made love as she had remembered, though better, deeper, surer, sharper.

Carl planned more gigs for them, including a week's tour in November in the Midlands so they all played sick at college and laughed and sang in the van as Carl drove up to Leicester where it was cold, and the audience uninterested. They slept in the van too, eating in a fish and chip bar, using public conveniences which were cold and smelly. Carl made a phone call the next day, before they should have left for Northampton.

'I have to go back, bit of business has come up. Tim's got the itinerary, I'll see you in London on Sunday. Just be good, all of you.'

They drove to Northampton and Sarah cursed his business, his college work, his contacts, because she wanted to be the whole of his life and if they had to sleep in a van she wanted to be next to him. They played Davy's music that night and the audience roared and clapped to it, dancing round the tables, calling for more.

That night Sarah couldn't sleep because the adrenalin was pumping in her body and the van was cold, the floor hard, the whole bloody thing was impossible, she thought, turning over and over. The next day she felt sick with tiredness, and her voice was flat when she sang. Davy handed her water during the break and she saw that his hands were trembling.

'For God's sake, you're tired too. why are we doing this?'

He grinned, his thin face creasing. 'I'm not tired, Carl sees to that. Here, take one of these tonight.' He handed her an orange and blue pill. 'It's Tuinal, it'll help.'

She looked at it. 'Mm, I always did like the orange smarties.'

She sang and played but Davy started to make errors and she was glad Carl wasn't there. In spite of what Davy said, she knew it was only tiredness. She used the public lavatories that night then crawled into her sleeping bag, taking the pill, feeling her mouth becoming sticky, then dry and she slept as though she'd never wake, and couldn't wake when Davy shook her, beating him off, feeling her head pounding, her mouth dry.

'Go away, let me sleep.'

He laughed. 'Come on, let's have the Prellies, they help, I promise you, it makes it all possible.'

She took his flask from him and swallowed the upper, hanging her head on her knees, watching as Arnie took one too, Tim refused. 'I'd sleep through an earthquake.'

They drove hard the next day, making for North Wales, sweeping along the rugged coast where the waves broke on to the shore, and she wanted to run along the beach and dance and shout and so they sang all day instead because their hearts were pounding so fast, their energy bubbling as it had never done before.

They played and it didn't matter that they made mistakes, because they were leaping on the stage, repeating riffs, bending towards one another, eyes glistening, voices shouting, lapping up the applause, the whistles, the screams.

They took downers in the van, uppers the next morning and there was no ache for Carl, no guilt about Wassingham, just success, exhilaration, excitement and again the next day, and the next and it was all so easy. They bought more pills from a guy at the last club, refusing cocaine and heroin. 'We're not into that,' Sarah said. 'We're not druggies.'

They worked hard the next week to catch up on college work and used the Tuinal and Prellies to keep them going for that too. On Saturday Sam Davis asked them into a studio to do a practice demo tape. Sarah's hands were trembling too now but all she had to do was sing, not play, and she rasped out the hard edged music.

It was a one-track studio and when they made a mistake they had to repeat the whole number again, and again and again.

'For Christ's sake,' Carl shouted at Davy, 'get it right.'

Sarah looked at Davy's trembling fingers, at her own. 'Leave him alone, for God's sake. He can't help it, can't you see he's tired?'

They tried once more but even after three hours the engineer was not satisfied with their performance and Carl threw his coat over his shoulders and talked to Sam, shaking his head, looking across at them, while Sarah stood with Davy. 'It's OK, we're just tired.'

Sam walked them to the taxi. 'You should think of going solo, you know. Davy's a better composer. He could write your stuff for you, he knows you so well.'

Sarah nodded, kissing the old man's cheek, smelling the gin on his breath and she smiled. 'We're a group,' she said, then slid across the seat. They drove back in silence with Carl sitting stiffly beside her. He left them at the bottom of the steps. 'Bit of business,' he said, not turning, leaving them there.

Tim and Arnie left. 'Get some rest, Davy, it's not the end

of the world,' Tim said, walking with Arnie back to his pad for a curry.

Sarah put her arm through Davy's. 'Come on, let's get on. We've those designs to finish for Mum and you've your course work, remember.'

That night Carl returned and dropped some hash on to Davy's lap. 'Try this, it's new. Arnie told me where I could get some.'

Sarah paid him from the tin, watching as Davy heated it, wanting it, wanting Carl, glad that his anger was over, that he said nothing more about Davy. She did not need Tuinal tonight, and neither did Davy. They didn't have any uppers left for the morning but they woke in time, cycling to college, feeling the cold sweat beneath their macs, the pounding of their heads.

'We'd better be careful of those smarties, bonny lad, hash is safer and the tabs. Let's stick to those.'

Carl held her in bed that night, having spent the evening with her and Davy, listening to the Beach Boys, to Dusty Springfield, to the Rolling Stones and it was better than any party, it was heaven, just the three of them, Sarah thought.

'You do understand now why I won't leave the group?' she breathed in his ear that night as she floated into sleep.

'Yes, I understand, my darling, never doubt that.'

There was a letter from Annie in the morning, asking if they had managed to sort out any more samples as they hadn't received any for three weeks.

But not to worry at all, if you haven't time. We are getting the hang of it here now, so can just carry on.

Sarah swore and knocked on Davy's door, entering, looking at the design he was drawing, the swirling, swooping shapes, the vortex of colour. 'Brilliant, but not for Wassingham, lad. And our masters call. We're very late with the samples. I'd forgotten.'

They sewed all week, their hands steadier now, their seams

straighter, but Davy couldn't get the textile design right, and so they left it for a few days then went back and rechecked the students' dresses which were far from perfect. They unpicked seams, working far into the night, drinking too much coffee, and Carl slept in his own room because he was trying to catch up on lectures and seminars – when he wasn't out, doing business.

'What business?' Davy asked, as he unpicked the last of the mini skirts.

'He never says,' Sarah replied, her voice muffled with pins, and they laughed together. 'I'll swallow one in a minute and probably end up top of the hit parade.'

Davy looked up at her. 'D'you want to go solo, Sarah? I don't mind. I love me art you know.'

Sarah put down the shirt she was working on. 'I know you love your art but it's fun isn't, this music business? I mean, it's opened so many doors, we've met so many people, so why should I want to go solo? Anyway, Carl's forgotten about that particular bee in his bonnet.'

Davy grinned. 'Rob's still in the debating society at Leicester, you know. Wonder if he ever lifts his head out of his books, or opens his mouth to sing.'

'Don't ask for miracles, Davy. Anyone who stays on to do an MA is seriously deranged. I mean, he even works when he gets home.'

'Or goes debating with me da,' Davy said, picking up the shirt again, finishing off the seam, throwing it on to the pile. 'That's about it.' He smiled but there was an edge to his voice.

Sarah switched on the iron. 'Don't forget you're named after your da's cousin and me mum says he loves you very much.'

Davy just nodded.

They completed the designs on Saturday afternoon, but Sarah still had her own clothes to make for the party they were going to that night with Carl. As she lined up the seam beneath the needle, she suddenly remembered that she should have met him for lunch at the Bistro. It was the second time she had forgotten that week and she closed her eyes, enraged at herself, running to his door, knocking to apologise but he wasn't back.

She packed up the samples, boxed and addressed them, then pressed her own dress and heard him come up the stairs, heard him stop outside her door and she turned, holding the last sample as he came in.

'I'm so sorry, darling,' she said. 'I was so busy, I just forgot.'

He walked over to her, snatching the dress from her, ripping it, throwing it in her face, punching the boxes to the floor, kicking them, then turned on her, his face furious, red, thin-lipped and she flinched as he raised his hand, then dropped it.

'For God's sake, now I know how your father felt,' he raged. 'You're just like her, working working. You "forgot" on Wednesday, you "forgot" today. And what about the parties you missed on Thursday, and on Tuesday. It's important to me that you're there, you help me, you help *my* business but it's only you that matters, isn't it? You're just like your mother. If I lost my ruddy leg you'd leave me in the hospital too wouldn't you, and rush back here and get *your* business on the road and bugger anyone else. You use everyone, like she does, look at her making you and Davy work like this. Just like you make me work for you, fixing up gigs, tours, God knows what . . .'

He slumped on to the cushions. 'And what about your rehearsals? Those go to the wall too, damn the group.'

Sarah picked the ripped dress from the floor. There were threads all over the table, all over her tights, her skirt. She went to him but he brushed her off, striding from the room.

'The address of the party is in my room, come and find me if you've got bloody time.'

She bathed in cold water, smoked a joint, collected Davy and took a taxi to Fulham, hearing the sitar music as she climbed the stairs, and thinking, always thinking.

She looked for him. He wasn't there. Would he come or would he think she was like his mother, leaving him alone? Would he still think she was like her own mother, using h:m? There was a deadness inside her, a vacuum of darkness and she smiled at Davy and took the wine he brought.

'It's my fault you rowed, isn't it?' he asked, his pale face thin and worried.

She kissed his cheek. 'No, bonny lad, it's not your fault, nothing to do with you, just with me.'

They sat with the others on cushions covered in Indian cotton, listening to the eerie twang of the sitar music, drowning in its resonance, sinking into its dreams and all the time she thought but felt nothing, gripping the cushion, wanting to jump off the roundabout again, stand and sort her mind out, in peace.

The musicians stopped and drank wine, and she leaned back on cushions watching as the men rose, stretching their limbs, easing their fingers and she was surprised that they did anything so mundane in this darkened room, full of incense and India.

There were drawings of Hindu gods on the walls between the hanging carpets, and she looked around, sipping the wine which was not Chardonnay but just plonk. There was one drawing beside the window which looked familiar and she moved closer, peering at it.

'Do you like it?' a sing-song voice asked behind her.

Sarah nodded. 'I have a paper knife at home with that design on it.'

'So, that is Tara, one of the Hindu goddesses, or you would say Star but whether you use Hindi or English, it is still a beautiful name. Shall we call you that. Aren't you to be Carl's star?'

She turned now, slopping her wine, dusting off her dress as she looked at the Indian who had been playing the sitar.

He smiled. 'Forgive me, I have the advantage of you. Your Carl rang earlier to say he had been held up and asking me to take care of you, if you arrived. He described you rather well. I am Ravi.'

Sarah smiled, the vacuum filling now because Carl had thought of her, had forgiven her.

'I think Tara is a little previous, don't you? I'm a student and my name is Sarah Armstrong. My father was in India, you know.'

Ravi led her back to the cushions. 'No, I didn't know. Where?'

Sarah told him, asking him if the plains were really as hot as her parents had said.

'They certainly are much hotter than your English summers.'

She asked him then where he lived. 'North of Delhi. My father runs a clinic which is open to all castes, all faiths, but run by Christians, many of them converted. I am finished here now, a truly fledged doctor and soon to return to add my help.'

Annie nodded. 'And you also play music rather well. We like music too but there isn't time for everything, is there?'

Ravi leant back, waving to the saffron-robed shaven-headed monk who was now leaving, having tapped out mantras on his prayer beads since Sarah arrived.

'It's kind of you to say I play well. I'm not sure how well but I was taught by an old man who was one of the Maharajah's musicians. The poor old thing is living in splendid solitude near my father's compound but that is what he wishes and it is to our benefit because he has told us many stories of those glittering times.'

Sarah listened to tales of splendour, of indulgence within the fort and longed for a joint, feeling restless, feeling the trembling in her hands, longing for Carl. She looked for Davy, he was taking a tab and she tried to catch his eye, but he wouldn't look.

She looked down at her hands, gripping them tightly, seeing the red weals that the scissors had made. Carl was right, she was doing what her mother had done, forgetting everything for her own ends. She no longer heard Ravi, just thought of her mother who had rushed from hospital to start her dream business, who had shouted at her da, forced strawberry ice cream down him. He wouldn't have lost his leg, but for her bloody business. She should have nursed, even Terry and Aunt Maud said that.

Ravi was taking the glass from her hand. 'Let me get you some more.' He rose easily and she looked towards the door. Carl still hadn't come, but he had rung, he had cared.

Did her mother care about anyone, or did she just use them?

She watched Davy staggering over by the far wall, hanging on to the picture frames. Just like she was, hanging on to the past, hanging on to her mother. She took out a joint then, lit it, inhaled deeply, holding it, longer, longer, and then exhaling, sucking in again, feeling the world slowing, her head floating. She arched her neck. But no, her mother loved her, she'd come to them when the strike had flared. Of course she loved her, she didn't use her.

Ravi said, 'Do you use a great deal?' He was nodding towards Davy who had sunk on to the floor.

Sarah smiled. 'No more than anyone else, we need it to break into another dimension, to experience and explore just as everyone else is doing.'

Ravi handed her the glass. 'By no means everyone, Sarah, and there are other, slower ways.'

Sarah shrugged. 'There's no point in taking life slowly if you don't have to is there?'

The door opened and Carl came in, looking around, but she was already on her feet, moving away from Ravi, as he said, 'But it leads to other things. Be careful, I beg you.'

She didn't look round, but went to Carl and held him. 'I'm so sorry, my darling, there will always be room in my life for you, just as there is room in my mother's life for me, there is no need to feel insecure. But I promise there will be less sewing, and that way I can help Davy practise too. We must make room for everything.'

300

The next week she and Davy bought posters of benevolent gods, from Buddha to Brahma, from a shop near the British Museum and asked Annie and Tom for money from their account to buy sitars. For some weeks the music gave them no time to suck hash or trip. Ravi came on Fridays to teach them, sitting, smiling as he showed them, plucking the strings, telling them they needed to go into their own temple once a day for the benefit of the soul, that there was no haste, no need for short cuts.

He took his hands from the sitar and tapped his head. 'It is better than the chemicals you take. You should try to chant the mantra like our friend the monk did. Perhaps I should send you some *japa mala*, to finger while you chant. Perhaps you should come to visit me, return to the land your father once knew, my Sarah.'

He guided Davy's hands on the strings. 'Perhaps,' she said, looking from Davy to Carl. 'Perhaps we could all go.'

Ravi nodded. 'You land at Delhi and you travel the whole country, staying at Gurdwaras, Sikh temples open to those of all faiths, that way you will sleep and eat with the people of my country, and we are very diverse – and then you come to us.'

Sarah grinned at Carl's face. 'Bit different to Sam Davis's pad?'

Carl grimaced. 'Too right.' He paused. 'Maybe one day Ravi, but not yet.'

Sarah listened as Ravi played, then Davy repeated the sound and it was as gentle as his melodies. It was right for him. She said. 'I think we should go, one day, when we've finished. We can get all sorts of design ideas, Davy, and there's all that Indian cotton.' She turned. 'You've really got to get more work done, Carl, or you'll end up without a degree. You just spend your time wheeling and dealing like Uncle Don.'

Davy laughed. 'Oh, Carl's nothing like Uncle Don, don't insult him.'

They practised with Tim and Arnie and at the next college gig they played a number of Davy's using a sitar, an Indian drum and two guitars and a hush fell on the dancers as they stopped and listened to the fragile melody easing out across the smoke-filled hall. There was silence when they finished and then applause and Sarah kissed her cousin, seeing the joy in his eyes, feeling the fullness in her own throat.

She told Carl that night but he laughed and said, 'That gig's just amateur night. Trust me, and keep that stuff for yourselves, might save you having to go into your own temples too often.'

Ravi left for India at the start of December and Carl brewed them all hash that night and the next he took Davy out for a drink and Sarah was grateful to him because Davy was fond of Ravi. 'I'll miss him, he understood what I was trying to say,' he told her as they climbed the stairs after seeing him off.

'I understand,' Sarah said, 'really I do,' but Davy had just squeezed her arm.

Each night now, Carl took Davy out, sometimes with her, sometimes not and they came home too late for love. She missed Carl in her bed but at least she had written up Davy's notes for him, and sorted out his project into some sort of order and sucked hash to help her sleep.

She and Davy travelled to Wassingham for Christmas, and as the train rumbled and rocked towards the north she closed her eyes and thought of the passion of Carl's lovemaking last night and wondered how she would last for a month without him.

There was the same smell of coal in the air, the same bitter wind, the same small kitchen in which she and Davy worked, bringing their projects up to date, sketching new ideas for next term, hoping to run them up on Annie's machine.

'It'll give us more time for music if we do it now, Davy. She needn't know, I'll put them in my case and send them up every two weeks or so.'

302

On Christmas Eve she cleaned out the pigeons for Georgie and cursed at the smell, the echoes of a childhood which seemed miles away now and so dull.

She watched as they had their afternoon flight, trying to pick out Buttons' great-grandson, unable to, though she pretended to Georgie that she could.

On Christmas Day they opened presents in Betsy's kitchen, drinking sherry and wanting a joint, Christ, she wanted a joint. She picked up Teresa's present to her, and peeled off the paper, to find slippers, the same as Bet's.

She looked at Annie and grimaced, then laughed as she did. It was the first time she had laughed since she had come home. She put them on, then stood by Betsy. 'I reckon you and I should start a chorus line then, Grandma, how about it?'

She felt Bet's arm come round her, hold her tightly. 'If I were a few years younger I'd take you up on that, my love.'

They shuffled their feet, lifted their left leg, their right leg, and shuffled it all about.

'Steady, Mam,' Tom called. 'Remember what the doc said, not too much excitement until we've got that blood pressure down.' He grinned as he picked up Teresa's psychedelic wrapping paper. 'So I'd better put this away or you'll end up blowing the top of your head off. Blimey, if you two ever send me up anything like this I'll be down like a shot to see what's going on in that den of vice.'

Sarah laughed and helped Bet back to her chair. 'If only it were a den of vice. It's just like here, but bigger.'

They had turkey, plum pudding, and mince pies, but Davy left most of his.

'I'm just tired,' he said to his mother, picking at his napkin, his fingers restless, his eyes active and Sarah felt the same. She wanted a joint.

They sat on over brandies. 'Bad for the voice,' Sarah told her father, leaning forward, listening as Annie talked of the wallpaper they were thinking of introducing into their shops, and the wholesalers.

'We thought we'd reproduce the design of the curtains so that there is a matching effect,' she told Sarah.

Davy put down his brandy goblet, turning it round and round, saying slowly, 'Wouldn't it be better to invert the design, have the curtains the reverse of the paper. I think the same would all be a bit too much.'

Annie thought for a moment, then nodded, calling out to Tom. 'Tom, will you and Rob stop talking about the Americans in Vietnam or whatever it is, and listen to your son for a moment. He's come up with a brilliant idea.' She was smiling but her voice was sharp. 'Say that again, Davy.'

He did so and Tom turned in his chair, putting his arm on the back of Davy's chair. 'That is so simple, but so good. Yes, we'll do that. Now tell us more about your term.'

Davy told them how much he liked silk painting because the light could shine through the silk and create brilliant transparent effects.

'You see, you can achieve subtle nuances of colour with colour blending, it gives a feeling of other-worldliness, or of something quite unique. I feel it could be incorporated into the business, though I'm not too sure in what way.'

Tom was looking at his son, at his tired face, his hollow cheeks. He'd been working too hard, he'd immersed himself in the world of design, just as Tom had done as a student, and he felt immeasurably relieved because they had all been so worried at the look of him, and Sarah too.

After lunch they didn't go to the football field, but into the stables where Tom kept the old silk-screen he had made and they stood around Davy as he blended paints while Tom cut a length of silk. He placed it on the table, running inside to bring water for dampening the silk, as Davy laid two intermediate colours next to each other, standing back while his father rubbed the silk under more water, looking at Davy.

'Go on, a bit more, the shading's not quite right.'

Sarah saw him blend more blues, saw the look of concentration on his face, the expertise with which he added more colour. She had never seen him at work like this before.

He brushed on more colours, one above the other, working with Tom, their faces both with the same expression, the same intensity, the same love of the medium.

By five it was finished, a landscape in tones of blue, in which the lines and contours had been created simply by colour displacement. It reminded Sarah of his sitar compositions and she knew that her cousin had the soul of an artist.

They talked all evening about its application. 'It'll just have to wait until you have time to set up a branch line to handle it,' Tom said finally. 'It's your interest, it should be you that develops it. We'll talk about it more tomorrow.'

Annie sat up in bed with Georgie, her glasses slipping down her nose as she read her letter from Prue.

> Thanks for the biscuits – wonderful to have good old
> England tucked away in a tin. Are you any less worried
> about Sarah? Do remember ourselves at her age and
> today life's so much more exciting, demanding. They'll
> make mistakes, but we've all had to do that. Just help
> them pick up the pieces afterwards. This Carl may not
> be such a bad lot, you know, just because he didn't write
> to your daughter. And remember, she and Davy have
> one another.

Annie took off her glasses, passing the letter to Georgie, reassured not so much from the letter as from this evening.

The next day Tom didn't talk to Davy about painting or design, because he and Rob were off before the others rose to plan a demonstration about the American build-up in Vietnam.

'On Boxing Day, for God's sake,' Davy said to Sarah as they walked by themselves to the beck.

'I'll do some silk-screen painting with you,' she panted as they walked quickly beneath the frosted branches of the lane. 'Slow down a bit.'

Davy shook his head. 'No, I don't want to, it's boring, it's all boring.' His head was down, his hands in his pockets, his breath cloudy in the sharp air. There were traces of snow on the ground, frost hardened in the ruts. There was snow in the meadow and ice at the edge of the beck and the willow hung lifeless and still.

'So damned boring,' he repeated as they stood there watching the water pass beneath the ice. 'You know, I'd be all right if I drew silk paintings of Trotsky.'

Sarah took his arm. 'Remember he loves you.'

'I know,' Davy said, his face as white as the snow on the rocks near the willow. 'So everyone says. I'd have gone with them, but they never asked. They never do. They never even said they were going. If they had, I could have butted in and invited myself.'

He looked at her and his eyes were dark, then he smiled. 'Life's too short, Sarah, it's too damned short to be feeling sad. Come here, this is my Christmas present to you, something a very good friend introduced me to.' He took her arm, led her across to the rock, took out a polythene packet and laid a line of cocaine near snow which lay in rivulets.

He handed her a straw and together they snorted the coke and she felt the euphoric delights immediately, sitting with him on the ground, not feeling the cold, only hearing Davy as he said, 'The road to excess leads to the palace of wisdom. Do you think they know that Balke said that, bonny lass?'

She didn't know and she didn't care because it was the first time she'd tried coke and it was wonderful.

They played and sang for Annie that night, sitting in front of the fire, smelling wintergreen, still floating, still dreaming, playing *Afternoon Curry* with the new hard edge.

'I don't like it as much, it seems so hard, almost like the Rolling Stones. Davy's songs were always so fragile, so delicate, like his silk painting.'

Sarah looked at her mother as Davy fingered the strings, his eyes heavy-lidded. 'Don't be absurd, Mother. This is what the punters want. You're always saying that we shouldn't allow our personal preferences to come between us and the market.'

'This is different, isn't it? This is Davy's soul. Who's altered you so much?'

Sarah sat back. 'You don't know anything about it. Music isn't a roll of bloody wallpaper or a pair of pants.' Sarah took out a cigarette, tapped it on the pack, lit it, inhaled.

'But that's my point, you're treating it as though it is, or is it someone else who's treating it like that?'

'Why don't you just come out and say it's Carl? You don't like him, do you?'

Annie reached forward, held her hand. 'Darling, I'm not saying that, I don't even know the boy.'

'He's not a boy, he's a man, I'm a woman, Davy's a bloody man and music's our world. We know it, we understand it, you don't.'

Annie said nothing for a moment, just looked at her daughter who looked almost as pale and thin as Davy. It was nearly 1967 and Sarah was nineteen – did that make her a woman? Dear God, she was fifty-two and she still felt like a child in the face of this changing world.

'You're right of course, I don't understand it, but I do love you and I'm proud of you, you've achieved so much but don't get too tired, you both look so exhausted.'

Sarah and Davy left on 29 December when Carl phoned with news of a New Year's gig. Tom and Annie took them to Newcastle and asked if they would like to send up some up-to-the-minute wallpaper designs. 'As you say, darling,' Annie said as she held Sarah on the station, 'I don't understand your world so you must lead us, but only if you have time. We don't want you getting tired.'

They fell into their bedsits, laughing and calling out to Carl, heating the hash, lying on cushions on the floor, hearing of his skiing, groaning at his falls, laughing as they told him of the beck, of the white of the coke alongside the snow. That night she and Carl made love for hours, drifting in and out of the night, heating more hash, snorting coke in the morning, playing at the gig in the evening, just the two of them, without Tim and Arnie and it didn't matter that Davy's errors left them little applause, nothing mattered in the world they were swimming in.

They drifted from party to party and it was so much better than Wassingham, than pigeons, than slippers and chorus lines. In the second week of January Annie rang, asking if they would like to send up any designs. Sarah left a note for Davy as she left with Carl for a party at Sam Davis's London pad.

In the morning she crawled from bed, shrugged into her dressing gown, pulling it round her as she slapped to the bathroom, seeing the ice on the windows, feeling the cold water on her body, rushing back to her room, a room without Carl who had stayed on with Sam to work out more business.

She lit the paraffin stove, made tea, sat at the table drinking it, feeling the pounding in her head from the LSD of the night before, lighting a cigarette with trembling hands, watching a match fall, still alight on to the papers on the table.

She doused it with the palm of her hand and brushed it to the floor, seeing Davy's designs for the first time, holding them, not believing that he could have done this off-the-page psychedelic design for their parents, the fool.

She dropped it, ran to his room, banging on the door, opening it knowing it wouldn't be locked. He was sitting on the bed, tripping. She shook him. 'For God's sake, what have you done? They'll be down, you fool. Oh Davy. What the hell are we going to do? They'll take us back.'

Davy watched her leave the room, still feeling her hands on him, her lovely warm hands and then he wept, because at last his father would come and take them back.

CHAPTER 19

Annie took Tom's phone call two days later and rushed straight round, in through the yard and into the kitchen, snatching the designs from Tom.

She looked at him and Gracie. 'It could mean nothing.'

Tom nodded. 'I know but then on the other hand . . .'

Annie let the designs fall on to the table. 'I've left a message at the club for Georgie, he'll be round any minute. Oh God, I just don't know. They seemed so different, so thin, so difficult when they came up, or Sarah was.'

Gracie took the tea that Bet put on the table before easing herself into her carver chair. 'Davy wasn't difficult, he was just too quiet, so different.'

Bet took out her handkerchief and patted her top lip. 'I don't know what to think about the bairns. I don't understand this world any more.' Her lips were trembling and Annie patted her hand. 'It'll be all right. I mean, these designs are all the rage, it doesn't mean they're into drugs and things, we'd know, surely we'd know. Look at all the work they brought back, all the parties they go to, I mean the kids of today never rest, it's no wonder they get frayed. I mean, I've never seen them with anything, well, any drugs, have you?'

No one had and now Bet said, 'You and Tom looked tired and pale after your time in London, you know, Gracie.'

Annie nodded. 'I certainly felt it when I was nursing. I remember being so tired I couldn't write, my hands shook so much.'

Georgie came in through the door. 'What's happened?'

Tom slung across the designs, telling Georgie what they'd been saying, looking at Annie. 'We must go down. We have to see what's going on – but they wouldn't be so stupid, surely?'

Georgie shrugged, his face anxious. 'We mustn't let them think we're checking up though. We must think of a good reason for going down.'

Tom was looking at the designs again, then he pushed them from him. 'I'm disappointed in him either way. These are a load of rubbish.'

Annie sat forward. 'Tom, that's completely unfair, nothing your son does is a load of rubbish. He's so talented, why can't you see that? Whatever else we do, you will not tell him you think of them in that way. You must not reject him. Anyway, I don't know about anyone else but I'm worried sick about them and I want them back here where I can look after them and make sure they eat properly, sleep properly. I hate that bloody city and I want them back for good.'

She walked to the sink, washing out her mug, wanting to rush down, bring them back, look after them, wipe the differences from them.

Gracie said, 'I want them back too.'

'Oh, for God's sake,' Tom snapped. 'It's 1967, we can't just go and bring them back here because some silly little sod's drawn a mindless doodle.'

'Tom,' Gracie and Annie shouted together.

Georgie spoke now, his voice measured, his hand beckoning to Annie, pulling her close to him, leaning his head against her body. 'Now look, we can't bring them back, it's just not on. We were allowed to fly, weren't we, make our own mistakes? This design is just a mistake. What is there here for them until they're qualified, until they've got the excitement out of their systems? Let them finish their courses then let them decide what to do. Remember, it's a different world down there, we're so out of step, I can see it when they come up.'

'But I just feel there's something wrong,' Annie said.

Georgie squeezed her. 'Women always feel there's something wrong. It's only a young man and woman putting their heads together and coming up with a modern design – exactly as we asked.'

Tom shook his head. 'I still feel we need to go down, we just need a good excuse.'

Annie suggested that they went down to discuss the design. 'Because Tom, it really would be quite good if it was changed to black and white.'

Gracie objected. 'But there's no need to go down to tell them that, we could do it over the phone and they'd know.'

Bet spoke now, still patting her lips. 'Well, why not take some stuff down there for their friends to try out? Tell them it's a bit of market research – weren't you thinking of running up some of those PVC blown-up armchairs, Annie, and some Indian cushions? They'd believe that.'

There was silence and then Annie grinned, left Georgie's side and hugged Bet. 'You are a bloody marvel, woman. You're wasted here, you should be Prime Minister.'

Sarah brushed the carpet, wiped the paintwork, put the magazines into a neat pile, straightened the bed and checked that there was nothing of Carl's still here. She checked Davy's room too, piling up his records, standing the sitar and guitar in the corner, taking down the psychedelic swirls as she had done in her room.

'You've got to shave, boil the kettle. Come on, they'll be here soon.'

She looked at him sitting on his bed smiling at her, his eyes sunken, his stubble as auburn as his hair, his shoulders sharp beneath his shirt and something caught in her chest. She went and sat with him. 'Look, we've got to cut down on the stuff we're taking. I know we hardly ever take coke but maybe we shouldn't take any at all and cut down on the hash. I just don't want to eat any more and we've got so thin. It's so expensive as well, especially the tabs. We don't need to trip so much, look where it's got us. Anyway, I've been pulled up at college for non-attendance and poor effort. What about you?'

'You could say that. OK, we'll cut down.' His voice was tired from too much hash. 'What time are Auntie Annie and Da due?'

Sarah looked at her watch. 'In half an hour. Oh God, I hope I haven't missed anything.'

'You've missed nothing, it's as clean as a whistle. They'll think nothing's wrong.' His voice was flat and she looked at him again and now she took his hand. 'Davy, you're not on anything else are you? You're so thin.'

Sarah gently pushed up his sleeve but there were no needle marks as there had been on Sam's friend Lou before he overdosed at a party over Christmas, and she felt a flood of relief.

'Yes, we'll cut down,' she said. 'You can do more of your silk painting, think about the future.'

Davy watched her as she walked to the door, seeing his dream of returning fading because she wanted to stay so much, and he would die for her.

Sarah boiled the rice, then put it into an enamel dish, adding sardines and tomatoes, grating cheese on top. Carl liked her rice hash. She checked the table, tidied the napkins she had sewn to match the tablecloth, stood back and adjusted the mats. She looked at her watch again, glad that they were coming, that they cared enough to be worried and take the train to London to check on them, because that was why they were coming, there could be no other reason. They would meet Carl and see him as he truly was, not as they feared.

Davy came in, washed, shaved, a sweater on that hid his thinness. 'I'm just going to get some beer, can I borrow your scarf?' He unhooked it from the back of the door.

'But Carl's bringing back wine from Sam's.'

Davy smiled gently. 'Me da's a pitman, he likes beer.'

She heard him walking down the stairs, past the bikes. Oh God, the bikes.

She rushed down, pushing them against the wall, standing back, seeing one wobble, adjusting it until they were all stable and there was more room to pass. She ran back up the stairs and opened a tin of peaches and another of pears. She tipped the cream into a jug, the milk too. She put on the kettle, then heard them ringing the bell, pushing open the door and she leaned over the banister, calling, 'Come on up.'

She saw them inching past the bike, lifting large cartons high above the handlebars, knocking the phone and laughing as Annie propped hers on Tom's back whilst she put back the receiver.

They struggled up the stairs and into her room, dumping the cardboard boxes, hugging her, looking round. 'It's so lovely, so fresh,' Annie said, taking off her gloves and coat, looking at her daughter keenly. 'You look well but still tired.'

Sarah laughed. 'I am tired, there's a lot to do, but what're those?' She pointed to the boxes.

Tom laughed. 'We'll tell you later.'

Sarah nodded, puzzled, but now she could hear Carl coming up the stairs, along the landing and she was nervous as he knocked before opening the door. Thank God, he'd remembered not just to barge in.

He stood there so beautiful, so golden and she took his arm, leading him to her mother. 'This is my mother, Annie Armstrong, and my uncle, Tom Ryan.'

She watched as they shook hands, as Annie smiled and Tom too, though there was reserve in their voices, in the shortness of the handshake.

'I brought wine,' Carl said. 'Where's your opener Sarah?'

Thank God he'd remembered that he shouldn't know where it was.

Tom started to shake his head at the glass Carl offered him, then smiled as Annie pressed his foot. He took the wine.

Sarah felt tension tighten her shoulders because Davy had

313

gone for beer for his pitman father. 'I thought you liked beer, Uncle Tom?'

Tom stood awkwardly sipping. 'No, no, I like wine, just don't have it much somehow. When in Rome, you know.' He laughed and Annie talked then of the crowds, how it seemed to have become so busy since her day. 'But these bedsits are lovely. Is Davy all right? I thought he'd be here?'

'He's just slipped out,' Sarah said, as she checked the rice, stepping back as the heat billowed up into her face, wishing she had stopped him, wishing Tom had refused. Oh God, it was all going wrong.

Davy ran up the stairs as they sat talking of Carl's skiing holiday and burst in, his scarf flying, his arms full of beer. His smile faded as he saw the wine in his father's hand. Annie stood up, glancing at Sarah, concern in both their faces.

'How lovely to see you Davy. The designs were very interesting. We were fascinated.' Annie was taking the beer from him, kissing his cheek as Tom came across.

'Yes, lad, we couldn't wait to see you so that we could discuss them but we were wondering if they could be in black and white? Didn't like to do it before we had spoken to you but it would give a greater feeling of perspective – what d'you think?'

Sarah smiled at Carl, whispering, 'You see, they do care, they don't use us, they've come all this way to check, using the design discussion as an excuse. I knew you were wrong, my darling.'

She watched as she saw Davy's slow smile, his brief nod as he unscrewed the beer bottle, pouring it for himself, lifting it towards his father, who looked at Annie, then grinned and said, 'Well, I'm not a Roman, am I?'

Sarah laughed with her mother, though Carl stood there silent. She squeezed his arm, knowing that the warmth of her family had taken him by surprise, that there was regret in him at all he had said, at all he had not experienced with his own mother.

They sat down at the table, listened as Davy talked to his father about the salt method he was using to obtain different effects with his silk painting.

'You see, Da, the salt absorbs water which has paint dissolved in it, and this leaves traces behind on the fabric. They can form all sorts of different outlines, some clumsy, some delicate. I've some in my room.'

Tom laughed, his hand restraining Davy, his elbow nudging Annie who sensed his delight in the enthusiasm, the lack of any signs of drug abuse. She toyed with her rice, putting small amounts in her mouth, forcing herself to swallow because Sarah wasn't to know that after the camps she had never been able to face it again.

Davy went to his room when he had finished eating. Annie forced down more rice, but with it half eaten she put her fork down. 'It's the excitement of London getting to me. I can't eat but it was lovely, my darling.'

Sarah cleared away, bringing the tinned fruit and the cream as Davy showed Tom and Annie the salt effects on twill, satin taffeta and chiffon, and Sarah was pleased that his hands trembled only a little.

Annie held them up, comparing them. 'I wonder if this could be used for evening dresses – it's so beautiful, each one's different.'

'That's it exactly, Auntie Annie – it is unique and the punters like that.'

Tom finished his beer. 'Mm, but it would still need to be run as a department on its own. Let's think about it some more when you next come home.'

Annie washed the dishes, understanding now how they had become so thin in London – there was so much to do, so much self-exploration. Just look at Davy's salt effects, his enthusiasm. Of course the nights were a waste of time when there was all this to discover.

Sarah called her for coffee and they laughed at Davy's story of the art lecturer who was so vague he not only forgot which lecture he should be taking, but at which college. Carl passed Annie the sugar. 'What are those boxes?' he asked quietly, nodding to the cartons.

Tom looked at Annie. 'Well, it's the reason we're here really. You see we thought we'd try out this new fad for PVC and we've run up some inflatable chairs that we thought we'd bring down for you to try for us, and ask your friends. It's a bit of market research. There are some cushions too, which we gather people like to sit on – like that one over there.' Tom nodded towards the one Sarah had bought from the market.

Sarah felt something die in her. 'Fine, I'll ask.' Somehow she didn't cry. Somehow she laughed and talked until they'd gone, somehow she kissed her mother and nodded when Annie said, 'If you ever need me, ring me.'

Now, as the door closed she looked at Davy and knew that they were both feeling the same. She put her arm through her cousin's and leant her head on his shoulder but then Carl called her back into the room. He stood by the boxes, pushing at one with his foot. 'So, they came because they were concerned, did they?' he said, his voice tight with anger. 'Did they hell. They came so that they could use you again, and me this time. When's it going to bloody stop?'

They heard Davy slam the front door and she ran to the window, shouting 'Davy, come back, let's talk about it, all of us.' But he didn't turn, just waved his hand and kept on walking.

Carl pulled her back. 'Leave him, he's the one who nearly blew it, he's the one who always nearly blows it while you pick up the pieces.'

'That's not – ' but his mouth was on hers, hard, savage, his arms about her, holding her. 'They're all a dead loss,' he said at last, heating up hash for them both which she drew in deeply, wanting to ease the pain because at last she saw he had been speaking truth for all these months.

That evening she and Carl blew up one of the armchairs, taking turns, feeling their sides aching, their heads bursting as they did so, and then they shared a joint, and kissed, hard, deep but all the time she listened for Davy.

Carl undid her buttons, and she his. Their naked bodies were against one another. She clutched at him, holding him close and still there was no Davy and anger rose in her from the dead coldness there had been since her mother left. She gripped Carl's head between her hands, kissing him. He pulled back and kissed her breasts her belly, her thighs, her mouth again, then pulled her down on top of him, on top of the chair.

She pressed her body against him, then she was easing him inside her, moving with him, cursing the bloody chair. Then she eased herself away from him, pulling him to the bed, and lighting a joint. They smoked, and as her head began to float she crawled to the chair and pressed the butt into it, watching it shrivel and deflate beside her and now she laughed again until the laughter turned to tears.

That night she didn't sleep but lay with Carl and thought of her mother who hadn't eaten the meal she had cooked, who hadn't come because she cared but because she'd wanted to use them. She thought of her shouting at her da, forcing him into the mine, who lived for her life for the factory and had been too busy to come pigeon-racing with her daughter and husband. Carl had been right all along and it was time she grew up and let them go.

Tom and Annie sat on the train, their feet throbbing, their heads aching.

'What did you think, bonny lass?' Tom asked.

Annie rubbed her eyes, pressing her fingers into her forehead. 'If I lived in London I'd look pale and interesting too – I think they're all right. They say you can smell pot. I didn't smell anything.'

'You didn't eat much either, but you did well to get through as much as you did. Yes, I think they're fine too. It was great, Annie, seeing that enthusiasm in their eyes. I mean, that salt technique is very interesting and I'd forgotten. I'd also forgotten how hard I worked when Gracie and I were down. I painted murals to make extra money, d'you remember?'

She did. She remembered the Mickey Mouse gasmasks too, when Tom told her of his journey back up. 'One little horror kept blowing raspberries with his, blimey I pity the family that got him.'

'Did you like Carl?' Annie asked Tom, looking at her hands, at the broken Ruby Red.

'No, he reminded me of Don.'

Annie nodded, rubbing her finger. 'I thought so too – so why does she love him, because she does you know?'

Tom shook his head. 'Because he's handsome, blond and she hasn't been through everything we have. We might be wrong. We were wrong to panic over those designs – Georgie was right. Anyway, didn't you ever make mistakes with your men?'

Annie blushed and looked at him. Oh no, Tom Ryan, you're not going to hear about my mistakes. She laughed and shook her finger at him. 'Just you make sure that you keep in touch with young Davy, not just Rob. You didn't tell him you were going away to the conference with Rob, did you?'

Tom blushed. 'I had to, he asked me to come down for an exhibition he was interested in seeing. I had to tell the truth.'

Sarah and Davy didn't go home for Easter, but pleaded pressure of work, telling Tom and Annie that the cushions had a market but there were too many down here doing it already and the armchairs hadn't taken off at all. She and Davy still sent samples because they were smoking as much pot and hash, taking LSD, and needed the money. But no coke, they promised one another.

Sarah had started driving lessons in February, and never smoked before them, though she often smoked afterwards as she made the others laugh about her kangaroo jumps, her back to front hand signals, her terror, but she did well and loved the freedom of it all. Davy wouldn't learn. 'It's too much hassle,' he groaned. 'And one lunatic on the road is enough.'

Sarah's letters home were short, but she did write or they would be down again, taking them back, hauling them from this life they loved. There was no anger in her, just nothing and she didn't bother to answer her mother's query about the turmoil at the LSE. What did they understand about students up in Wassingham?

In May she took her test and passed and they celebrated with champagne and LSD. In June they played at even more gigs and she and Davy bought a Mini to share which they painted purple and decorated with sunflowers. Increasingly Davy could barely stand, let alone play at the gigs.

'I'm fine, bonny lass,' he said when they played at the club behind their digs as heat beat down on the city at the end of June. His arms hung limp on stage, his eyes were glazed, the smell of beer was on his breath, the smell of pot on his clothes.

Tim hissed. 'Get him off, Sarah.'

She called into the microphone, 'Time for a break, kids,' and guided Davy down the stairs, feeling the thinness of his arms, the brittleness of his ribs as she put her arm round him to steady him.

'You mustn't drink so much with the pot, Davy. Come and sit down,' she said, shrugging at Carl.

She sat with them, watching Tim and Arnie threading their way through the tables, sweat dripping off them, staining their shirts. The air was thick with smoke and dark beneath the shaded lights.

She took Carl's hand in hers, asked whether he'd caught up with his work yet and seen Sam's phone message. 'Have you rung him back?'

Carl nodded. 'Just business, I'm seeing to it tomorrow. Could you write up the economic notes I've borrowed from Charles? I've a seminar on Monday.'

She smiled and nodded. Oh yes, she'd type up his notes,

wash his back, give him the time that her mother didn't give, that she herself had been in danger of not giving. 'Buy me another tonic and I'll walk barefoot to India for you.'

Carl laughed. 'That's not likely to be necessary, thanks madam.' He beckoned to the waiter and ordered.

'We should go to India in the summer, Davy, and see Ravi. We could all go.'

Carl laughed, passing the tonic to her, beers to Tim and Arnie, and a lemonade to Davy. 'I think he's had more than enough booze tonight,' he murmured, then raising his voice he said, 'Summer's a bit too hot for India, even if you head for Kathmandu like the rest of the weirdos.'

Sarah punched his arm lightly. 'Well, thanks for that, it's nice to think my boyfriend thinks I'm weird.'

Carl leant across and kissed her. 'You'll be an unemployed weirdo if you don't get back on that stage, but leave Davy with me.'

They played well into the early hours of the morning and she waved as Carl took Davy back to their digs at midnight. He was so wonderful, so kind.

She worked on his notes the next day, then sorted out the designs for the wallpaper, sifting through Davy's ideas while he slept, then their joint ones which were better, infinitely better. Sarah sat back, chewing her pencil, looking at the lines of Davy's sketches. They were uncertain, and there was no core to the design, no theme, no skill or talent, no soul.

She brewed herself coffee, drinking it as morning turned to afternoon and still Davy didn't get up, but then he seldom did now she realised and she wondered why she had not noticed before. She completed her notes, putting together the last of her end of term collection. She pressed the seams, wanting to show someone, wanting to send them to her mother, but there was no point, because they were not for the business. Annie wouldn't be interested, and besides, there was no love in her for her mother any more, and no need either.

She looked again at Davy's designs, walked to the window,

leaning her head on the pane, looking out at the plane trees in full leaf, the dusty road, and thought of the beck, so clean and clear, the black-eyed daisies, the meadow grass. She thought of the coke lines on the boulder. They had promised there would be no more coke.

She looked at her watch. It was six o'clock and still Davy slept and she walked quietly from her room into his, stepping over the sitar which lay on the floor, picking up his mug which he had dropped, seeing the coffee stains on the floor. It was so hot in here with no windows open, no curtains drawn. She pulled them back and opened the window. Davy lay sprawled on the bed and Sarah remembered how Tim had said he would be in trouble if he didn't appear at lectures more often. She hadn't registered.

The bed sank as she sat on the edge. He smelt of stale sweat and dirt. She hadn't registered that either. Now he opened his eyes, so blue, so gentle, and he smiled and put up his hand to touch her long hair.

'We promised to use no more coke. Have you, Davy? Have you used anything else?' Sarah said softly.

'I'm fine, bonny lass,' he said, smiling at her, his eyes no longer seeing her, closing.

'Roll up your sleeves, Davy,' she said but he no longer heard her.

She took his arm, unbuttoned his sleeve, rolled it up and saw the needle marks she'd known would be there. She rolled down the sleeve again, buttoned it, stroked his hair and couldn't see him any more for the tears were falling down her cheeks, staining his shirt. She bent and held him, and wondered how she could not have known before that this boy was now a heroin addict.

She rang her mother that night and told her that she and Davy would not be coming home that holiday, they were going camping in Cornwall.

'Just the two of you?' her mother asked.

321

'Yes, Mother, just the two of us, you're quite safe, Carl is not coming with us.'

'I didn't mean that, Sarah, really I didn't.'

But she did, Annie told Georgie that night. 'I'm just so glad they're going away together, getting some fresh air in their lungs, spending time with one another as they used to. Perhaps the relationship with Carl is weakening.'

Georgie looked at her as he put Buttons' great-grandson in his basket. 'If that's the truth, perhaps it is.'

'Oh, Georgie, that's so unlike you. Of course it's the truth, she's never lied to us, ever.'

Sarah sat in the dark that evening and when Carl came in she told him that she was taking Davy away because he was main-lining.

She watched the shock on his face.

'I don't know where he got it from or how he can afford it, and I don't know why, that's the worst thing. Why? Why? But I'll make him stop. Deborah's old schoolfriend was taken to a Scottish island by her parents and they cured her. She was new to it and he must be. He was clean at Christmas. Will you come?'

Carl squatted in front of her, taking her hands. 'How can I, I'm going to Morocco with my mother but anyway he needs proper treatment – you don't know enough. He needs to go home.'

Sarah shook her head. 'No, he won't want to go home. He'll want to stay with me. I do know enough, I talked to Deborah about it tonight, I know what those other people did. I wish you were coming.'

Carl kissed her hands. 'Poor little bugger, what was he thinking of? Where did he get it? Has there been any talk?'

'No, there's nothing. Tim doesn't know and I can't find Arnie but none of that matters, it's just Davy that's important.'

Carl kissed her and held her gently and she needed the

322

strength of his love at that moment more than she had ever needed it from anyone.

CHAPTER 20

Sarah drove through Somerset and Devon, then over the Tamar Bridge into Cornwall, heading always onwards, wanting to put as much space behind them as possible.

'We need to be as far from London as we can. Deborah said we need a different environment,' she told Davy, who sat with beads of sweat on his forehead, his nose running, his eyes too, his mouth opening and shutting in prolonged yawns. They stopped on the moor and she looked away as he rolled up his sleeve, tightened the fixing belt round his upper arm to pop his veins, and inserted the needle. He pushed the plunger, withdrew the needle and passed it to her.

She bleached it and put it in the box he kept at his feet, seeing the blood trickling down his arm, the haze coming into his eyes. She looked at her watch, five o'clock, they'd be at Polperro in an hour. Deborah had rung her farmer friend and he expected them by six. The sun was still hot and the shadows were long. Please God make it stay fine, if only to put the tent up.

'Don't tell him why you're there, for God's sake,' Deborah had said. 'Just remember, weaker and weaker doses, and then cold turkey. God help you. It'll take weeks before he's ready to come back.'

They drove on but she stopped at a pub for lemonade and pasties, bringing it outside to one of the tables, wanting Davy to eat. 'Not hungry,' he murmured, leaning back on the bench, his head loose, his limbs too.

'You must eat,' she insisted, breaking his pasty in half, holding out a piece on her napkin. 'Please, for me.'

'For you?' he queried and then opened his mouth.

She pushed it in and saw the family at the next table looking at them. 'Come on, Davy, do it yourself.'

She broke off another piece and put it in his hand which lay limp on his lap. The pasty fell to the floor and she wanted to shout at him. She didn't. She broke off another piece and fed him herself – what did it matter what people thought? She stared back until they looked away.

They drank their lemonade and she walked with him to the lavatory. 'You must go in there, Davy. We're camping, let's have our last taste of luxury.'

He looked at her. 'A pub lavatory – we've come a long way, bonny lass.' His grin was the old grin, his eyes sparkled. She laughed and left him.

He was waiting by the car, leaning against it, his hands in his pockets, his shoulders so thin under his shirt. The sun was being overtaken by clouds, there was a chill in the air and he was shivering.

She unlocked the car, leant in and brought out his pullover, put her own on. 'Rain is all we need,' she groaned.

She looked at him but the sparkle had gone, there was just the haze. 'Come on, in you get. We've still half an hour to go.'

She checked the map, then drove on, missing the turning, reversing, driving down the track, bumping over the ruts, seeing honeysuckle in the high banks, smelling it through the open window.

'It's so beautiful, Davy. I'll get you better, I promise.'

She stopped at the farmhouse. The farmer pointed out the field they could use.

'You can stay in the house if you like, we've spare rooms.'

Sarah shook her head. 'No, that's fine, we love camping, we're all-weather idiots but I'd like to buy some milk, please, and eggs and butter perhaps some tomatoes.'

The farmer's wife bustled out smelling of newly baked bread. 'You sure you don't want a room?'

How could a drug addict take a room, how could he slump and sleep, and moan when the drug wore off, when there was no more and the cramps began? Sarah shook her head but bought the provisions, waving to them, glad that the far corner of the field was out of sight. That's where they would pitch the tent, overlooking the sea but sheltered by hedges.

Davy sat in the car while she took the tent from the roof rack, put the aluminium frame together, banging in the pegs, tightening the guy ropes, cursing as the rain began, feeling it soaking into her back, dripping down her hair.

'Blimey,' she said to Davy as she urged him from the car to the tent. 'Tim didn't tell me it was the Ritz. Look, you can stand up. Here's the cooker, and there's the bedroom. Sorry you'll have to share it with the staff.'

Davy said nothing, just sat cross-legged on the floor of the tent. She ran to the car, carrying back sleeping bags, loose sheets, boxes of plates, cups and food because soon, when the doses had decreased to nothing, they would not be leaving the tent for days on end.

The rain was pattering on the roof. She blew up the lilos and laid out the sleeping bags side by side. 'Sorry, you'll have to put up with me next to you,' she said, setting up the camping stools, taking his arm, pulling him up, sitting him on the chair. 'I don't snore.'

She lit the petrol stove and heated milk in an old aluminium pan of Tim's. She looked around. Everything was Tim's and she had kissed him when he brought them round but he had said, 'He should go home. You need more help.'

'No we don't,' she'd replied. 'He doesn't want to go home because they won't let him back but I'll get him well, then keep an eye on him.'

She poured the milk on to the cocoa, stirring it, watching the blobs of cocoa rise to break on the surface.

'One or two?' she called above the rain.

Davy didn't answer so she put in one and carried it to

326

him, watching as he took it in two hands. 'Hold it tight.' There was no ground sheet and she could smell the grass.

She cupped her own and sat next to him. 'D'you remember putting the sheet over two sticks at the beck, there was the same smell.'

Davy said nothing, the mug was tipping over in his hand. She took it from him, emptied both drinks on to the grass. She poured water into the bowl.

'Wash,' she said.

He did.

She peeled his clothes from him and couldn't bear the thinness of his body, the scarred veins of his arms, the scabs.

'Into the sleeping bag,' she murmured, standing at the opening to the inner tent until he was comfortable.

She washed, undressed and lay beside him, sleeping lightly, hearing the rain, Davy gasping beside her, turning, and with dawn there came the moans, the sweat on his forehead. She handed him a syringe with a decreased dose.

She cooked breakfast, bacon, eggs, tomatoes. He ate little. The rain was still strumming lightly on the tent.

'More like a sitar than a guitar, sort of fragile, like your music. Would you like to play, shall I bring it in from the car?'

Davy shook his head, sitting in his sleeping bag, his plate on his lap, the bacon congealed.

'Get dressed, Davy.'

He did.

The rain stopped and she tied back the tent opening, stepped barefoot into the wet grass. 'Come out here, Davy.'

He came.

The sea was grey, the sky too and there were white tops, rolling and rolling to the shore. She looked towards the small bay to the left. 'We'll swim when you're better.' Polperro was to the right but too deep in the valley to be seen. She felt the wind lift her hair, tasted the salt on her lips, took Davy's hand and held it tight. 'Yes, we'll swim.'

They wrote cards which she had bought at the pub – to Gracie and Tom, Georgie and Annie.

'Write three, Davy.' Deborah had said that while withdrawing all life stopped except survival. She'd post them when she could.

She lit a joint, counting the number she had in the sandalwood box. They would need them for withdrawal.

There were seagulls circling, screeching, blackberry flowers in the hedge. 'Draw this, Davy.'

He couldn't. He just sat in the sun until the stomach ache came again and sweat beaded his forehead and this time she wouldn't let him have another fix immediately.

'Not yet.'

'I want it,' he moaned.

'Not yet, we've got to do it like this.'

He stood up and grabbed her arms. 'I want it.'

'No.'

He turned from her, his hands to his eyes. 'I need it, my eyes hurt, my belly hurts. Give me some.'

He was stumbling from her into the tent, lying down on the sleeping bag.

'Soon,' she said, sitting in the entrance, knowing that he watched her every breath, her every move. She looked at her watch. Another hour – just another hour. This is how the girl's parents had done it, but there'd been two of them. She put her face in her hands. Carl, couldn't you have told your mother to go alone?

Davy was quiet, lying with his face to the tent wall, his hair deep copper against the lilo, his sweat staining dark beneath his head. He turned. 'Please, give it to me.'

His eyes were dark, desperate, in pain, his skin sunk blue. 'For Christ's sake, you bitch, give it to me.'

She rose and said, 'Another half an hour.' He stood, then fell as the lilo shifted beneath him. He crawled towards her, on the ground, grabbing for her leg. 'Give it to me.'

She shook her head, prising his fingers from her. He

328

grabbed her hair then, pulling it, his lips thin, twisting his fingers in it, pulling again and again. 'Give it to me.'

She pushed him back and he fell and didn't rise, just lay there with his legs pulled up. Deborah had said this would happen too but the tears were falling because of the pain in her scalp and the sight of her cousin in ruins at her feet.

Annie read their card the next week, sitting in the kitchen with the door open on to the yard.

'It looks so lovely,' she called to Georgie, turning it over, looking at the fishing village, the crowded cottages, the small harbour. 'They say they're having a lovely time – mixed weather, lots of swimming when the sun comes out, lots of pasties.'

'Just what they need,' Georgie called back. 'Any chance of a beer, it's hot out here with me head stuck up a pigeon loft.'

Annie laughed, made herself a coffee and poured Georgie a beer, carrying them out, handing him the card as well.

He said, 'You're right, it's a canny place. Makes me wish we were there.'

Annie sat on the back step as Georgie perched on the old stool. 'Could we, do you think? I mean we could take a week off, drive down, surprise them.'

Georgie was looking at the froth on his beer, holding it up to the sun. 'Bye, you've got a head on this, Annie, what'd you do, give the bottle a good shake before you poured it?'

'That's the problem isn't it, my love, you can't get the staff these days, can you? You'll just have to sack me.'

He was laughing, scooping the froth off with his fingers and shaking it on to the ground, then drinking, lifting his face to the sun. 'It's an idea though. We could drive down in two days, find Polperro and then try and locate them.'

Annie reached for the card. 'They don't say where they're staying. How big is Cornwall?'

'Big, when you're trying to find two kids.'

Annie stretched out her legs, kicked off her shoes. 'I wonder whether they'd want us, they sound so happy, so well – perhaps we'd be interfering – perhaps we'd better leave them to it.' She wanted to go, to spend time with her daughter to laze in the sun, swim, eat pasties in pubs and talk of nothing very much, just be there, but it was crazy. Two cousins had just taken off, dusting the city from their heels, they didn't want parents popping up at every available opportunity. 'Yes, we'd better leave them but if they can be by the sea so can we. Come on, I'm packing a picnic. Finish the birds and we'll take Bet to the coast.'

Tom and Gracie came too and they parked behind the dunes, walked across sand which was hot beneath their bare feet, spreading rugs, propping up thermos flasks, beer.

Gracie and Annie walked with Bet to the sea, standing in it, cold against their hot skin, their words fighting against the breeze which swept their hair from their faces, laughing as children ran past, splashing them, taking the breath from them as it hit their bellies.

'Little devils,' Annie said, thinking of Sarah at that age, always with Davy, back with Davy now.

'They seem happier,' Gracie said. 'Their letters have been so short, they've been busy but if they're having a breeze like this it'll blow a thousand cobwebs away, do them so much good. I remember feeling as though I could never get a good lungful of air in London.'

Annie held Bet's arm and they walked a little deeper, feeling the waves slowly breaking against their legs, the sand running away beneath their toes.

Bet growled. 'They needed to get away, relax, paint, talk. Perhaps it'll see that Carl off.'

Gracie laughed. 'You've never even met him.'

'I heard what Tom and Annie said and that's enough for me. I think he's on the way out, or they would all have gone together.'

Annie was silent, looking out to the horizon. God, she hoped so.

They joined the men for lunch, cracking and peeling hard

330

boiled eggs and talked of the holiday they would have next year.

'Wonder who's doing the cooking in Polperro?' Gracie said.

Annie laughed. 'No one, they'll be having sandwiches and eating at the pub, makes me wish I was young and carefree.'

It was the end of the second week and today there had been no more heroin, just a boy who cried out to her, swore at her, hit her or who lay still while she bathed his body free of cold sweat and wiped his chin of the saliva he dribbled, and the mucus which ran from his nose and eyes.

That night the stomach cramps clawed at his guts, his limbs jerked and kicked and she was bruised, but never felt the pain, just sat and watched and waited, and longed to do more, but there was nothing more she could do.

She bathed him in the morning but he pushed her from him. 'It hurts. It hurts,' he gasped. 'Please give me some. Please.'

'No, I'm going to get you well.'

He lay back and she lit him a joint, which he sucked, again and again, and another, and then he slept but it was so hot, for God's sake, Sarah thought, as she fanned his naked body, kissed his forehead, touched his hand.

She threw back the tent flaps, and undid the windows. At last there was a breeze. She took the basin out into the sun, pouring water over the flannels, washing, wringing, but they still smelt. She dragged the cooker from the tent and pumped up the petrol stove, putting them on to boil.

She tore off her shirt, feeling the sun on her back, pouring water over her body, dragging on a T-shirt, shorts, hurrying to the farmhouse for more water, asking if they would post the cards for them as they were shopping, feeling her shoulders straining as she lugged the water back, rushing to check on Davy. He was still there, lying motionless but the flannels had burned, for God's sake. She'd forgotten and they'd burned. She dragged her fingers through her hair, knocked

331

the pan off the stove, kicked it across the grass. She wanted her mother, wanted Bet, anyone.

'Sarah,' Davy called. 'Sarah, help me, please.'

She looked across the field, to the sea, to the birds which wheeled above her. Oh God.

By night time the tent was fetid from his vomit and she sat outside under the awning, watching him in the moonlight because he could bear no light, not even the glimmer from the hurricane lamp. She rested her head on her knees, her sleeping bag unzipped and wrapped around her for comfort, there was no need of warmth on a night such as this.

All night she sat, or bathed him with towels she had ripped apart, took his slaps, his despair, his rage, his calm and knew that she must have slept because time had passed for which she could not account.

The next day was the same but this time she didn't burn the cloths, but boiled them properly, wrung them out, hung them on the guy ropes, drank coffee, but she didn't smoke a joint, because she mustn't sleep, she must only doze. She must eat. She cut bread, opened a tin of corned beef. He called her. She went.

'No,' she said. 'Hang on Davy, just a while longer. Hang on.' She lit a joint for him, stayed while he smoked it, left when he was asleep. There were flies in the corned beef. She just ate the bread and was surprised at the tears which ran into her mouth.

The next day she gave him a book on silk-screen painting to read.

'They're jumping,' he said. 'The words are ants scrambling, jumping.' He threw it at her. 'You bitch.'

She took the book and sat outside in the sun, reading it, listening to him rage, watching him crawl to the entrance, then curl into a ball as the cramps came again.

She sketched the honeysuckle the next day and the birds which called and wheeled, and wondered how she could survive for another seven days.

On the sixth day she talked to him of the beck, of the

332

cool water, the soft willow fronds, of the honeysuckle which surrounded them here, in this field, of her sketches which were not as fine as his.

'We'll sketch soon, both of us. Not long now Davy.'

He rolled over and looked at her then. 'I want to die. I need it or I shall die.'

She shook her head and looked into those violet eyes which were not the eyes of Davy, but of someone she didn't know. 'You'll die if you do take it.'

His abuse followed her but she just turned her face to the sun as she left the tent, picked up her pencil and drew the headland with its wind-whipped gorse, and then picked a sprig of honeysuckle and sketched each leaf, petal, stamen, listening all the time to his foul mouth, and then his pleadings, and then his sobs.

She took him water as the sun went down and he told her that when his eyes were closed they stayed open and looked into the back of his head and all he needed to be better was a fix, just one.

By the eighth day his skin was yellowing, his hands shaking, his body shivering and Sarah wondered how all this had happened. 'Why?' she asked. 'Why?'

'Because it takes me to a better world.'

She looked at him and thought of the boy he'd been and walked into the sun. She drew the blackberry flowers meticulously, carefully, again and again, because she didn't want to think any more.

By the ninth day the vomiting had ceased.

'I hurt with a deep, deep ache,' he said, reaching for her hand.

'So do I, Davy,' Sarah whispered.

The next day he sat up and took the flannel from her and wiped down his own body, hiding his nakedness beneath the sheet, accepting the tea she gave her, drinking it without vomiting, then he slept for hours, coming to her as she sat at the entrance, the moon soft in the sky.

'Will I ever stop needing a fix, Sarah?' he said, standing there, looking out across the sea.

'Deborah's friend has, but you have to really want to stop, bonny lad.'

She looked up at him.

'Have I been very . . . difficult?' he asked, still looking at the sea.

'No, you've been grand.' Sarah laid her head on her knees, feeling her shoulders relax for the first time since they'd been here.

The next day she posted another card, washed her hair, plaited it, feeling its weight between her shoulders, cooked bacon and eggs. Davy ate a little, sitting under the awning, out of the sun because it still hurt his eyes, his skin.

'Would you like to swim?' she asked. 'There's a track down the cliff?'

He shook his head. His muscles felt as though they'd been hammered, his bones as though they had been cracked, his skin as though it had been peeled.

She handed him his sketch pad and pencil, brought him honeysuckle but instead he drew the tent, the stove, the Mini, her. The next week the weather was cloudy and he drew the sky, the sea and Sarah in her flares lugging water back from the farmhouse.

'Soon, my lad, you'll be fit enough to carry these, not just that little bitty pencil,' she said, smiling gently as she dumped them by the stove. She poured water into a bowl, rinsed out a flannel and wiped his forehead. But not fit enough for a long while she thought.

At night he was restless, still needing heroin but no longer cursing her, no longer needing to be watched every minute of every day, and so she slept and in the day they talked of the beck and he drew it. They talked of India and he drew Ravi at his clinic, or as he imagined it.

'We'll go one day, when we've finished our degrees. It would be interesting. Think of all the designs, the colours,

334

the cotton,' she said. 'It'll give us time to think about what we really want to do.'

They walked around the field slowly and sketched the valerian, the lichen on the boulders.

'Ravi said the landscape as you fly into Delhi is like lichen on a stone. He said the colours of the land are muted, a perfect backdrop to the richness of the cottons.' Davy picked at the lichen. 'You're right, perhaps one day we should go.'

The days passed and there was time to talk of the art of Andy Warhol, of the new wave architecture.

'One day I shall go and see the Sydney Opera House, it will be wonderful when it's finished,' Davy said.

There was time to do nothing, say nothing, just be together as they had been long ago. At the end of July they walked down the cliff path to the beach, easing themselves into the water alongside children who splashed and screamed. She stayed with him as they swam because he was still so weak, but stronger, definitely stronger.

He turned on to his back, kicking his feet, moving his hands and she did the same, feeling the water lapping at her face, over her breasts. Where was Carl now? She turned and trod water. It was the first time she had thought of him for so long.

They ate hard-boiled eggs on the beach and then climbed slowly back up the cliff path, their skins tight from the salt, their shoulders sore from the sun. She rubbed lotion on him and he on her and they sat cross-legged on the grass as day became night and talked of the beach above Wassingham, the seaweed they had chased one another with, the dreams they had had.

She looked at him. 'They've come true. We're at college, in London and it will be all right now. We'll play in the group, you'll do your silk painting. But not in Wassingham. We can't go back can we, not after the "market research", not after everything.'

She pulled at the grass. 'That's what made you take drugs, wasn't it?'

Davy looked at her, saying nothing for minutes and then he shrugged. 'Who knows what makes people do anything – perhaps it's the thought of being suffocated.'

She nodded. She knew what he meant, Wassingham and their families took the breath from around them.

He continued. 'And perhaps it's always failing. I wish I was like Rob, political, brave, standing in the front line, just like Da. I don't know how they do it, all those police, standing there. Those fascists with Da, I couldn't have done it. I froze at the bus stop that day in Wassingham, so I know. I'm so proud of him. I'd love him to be proud of me.'

'He is, he really is. He loves your art.'

The next week his skin was tanned and there was flesh on his bones and laughter burst from him as he chased her around the cove with seaweed, draping it around her neck when he caught her, dragging her back into the sea, ducking her, being ducked by her. It was as though he'd never been ill, Sarah thought, or almost, because he still shivered, still craved the drug in idle minutes.

By mid-August they were swimming each day and there was laughter in both of them as they basked on the sand and ate pasties from the wooden café at the rear of the beach, or played their guitars outside the tent deep into the night, feeling the wind on their backs, hearing their voices in harmony.

In the last week of August they packed the car, paid the farmer and drove to the 'Festival of the Flower Children' at Woburn Abbey.

'We need to go somewhere like this, Davy,' she said. 'Just to see how you cope. I don't want us going straight back to London, in amongst the old scene, without you feeling confident. I'll be with you here, I can help if you need it.'

She touched his hand and he held it. 'It's been like old times,' he murmured.

Sarah nodded, changing gear. Yes, it had and she remembered the sound of his laugh on the beach, the feel of the seaweed and felt a deep ache and didn't know why.

They slept on the ground with the rest of the hippies, smelling the joints all around, smoking a little, but not much because Davy now relished the taste of food, the smell of the grass – all of which had been lost to him since heroin.

They listened to the music, joined in the dancing, wove flowers in their hair, painted their faces, but didn't trip. They didn't need to, not today, not in the sun as they danced and talked of peace and all the love that there was in the world.

She walked to the lavatory tent with him. 'If you're long, I'm coming in, so it's your fault if all the men have to run out screaming,' she said, laughing, but she meant it.

'I'm fine now. I want to be better. I want to stay like this for ever,' he said as they walked through the dancing bodies, or stepped over bodies loving on the grass.

She asked him again that night where he had bought the heroin. 'Just a mate,' he said.

'What will you do when you see him again?'

'Nothing, I've told you, I don't need it any more. I'm me now. I'm happy. I don't need it.'

They looked at the fashions, the bells, the beads, the multi-coloured clothing.

'If we go to India we can bring back some of their cottons. Look at these colours, it's really catching on in a big way,' Sarah said, drawing an overskirt of muted blue over an underskirt of vibrant purple.

'You've just got a thing about purple,' Davy said, quickly sketching the detail of a silk-painted design. 'That'd look better.'

'Cost a bit too.'

'There's money around, and I still think we could adjust the technique to work well on cottons. Think of that sari Prue sent you, it's wonderful.'

They played fragile melodies on their guitars and the other kids danced around them, singing with them long after the light had died as they picked out the tunes of *San Francisco*, (*Flowers in your hair*), *Strawberry Fields Forever*, *Mellow Yellow*.

They left on the third day, along with everyone else,

winding in a long trail from the Abbey, with flowers still in their hair and beads which a girl had given them.

They approached London and she looked at him, gripped his hand. 'Ready?' she asked.

'Ready.'

They sent off for visas for India on their return and she sewed long shirts for him, and skirts for her, cutting up Prue's sari, using it as an overskirt, preferring the floating drifting length to the minis she'd been wearing.

They worked all day on their projects and notes. They ate in pubs, drawing out money from their joint account.

'There's plenty left,' she said, as they finished their lagers, and twisted spaghetti round their forks, splashing the bolognese on their chins.

They sent up Indian designs to Annie who loved them.

. . . and yes, I think it would be a wonderful idea to travel to see your friend Ravi, you and Davy will get so many ideas from that country. It's so very different. I know we've talked about it but you need to see for yourself.

Carl returned at the beginning of October, knocking on her door, coming in, scooping her from the chair, his lips and tongue hungry on her mouth. She pushed away from him. 'He's fine. It worked, Davy's better.'

His arms came round her again and his mouth was on hers and she pulled back because there was so much she wanted to tell him but he was pulling at her clothes, and so she held him to her although she would have preferred to talk, not love, but there was such eagerness in his eyes. His hands found her breasts and his fingers her crotch, and finally, his body found hers.

She talked then, telling him of the tent, the flannels that had boiled dry, Davy's courage, his thinness, his swimming.

Carl put a joint in her hand.

'No, I'm all right thanks.'

338

He took it from her and lit it, sucking it, putting it in her mouth. 'A welcome home present,' he insisted. 'And this.' He held up a bracelet. 'And this.' It was hash.

She smiled. 'I love the bracelet but we're trying not to take drugs. I don't want Davy getting back to anything.'

Carl laughed. 'This is safe, darling. This will just relax us all, nothing to worry about.'

She was relaxing and her voice was quiet as she told him of Woburn Abbey, the increase in Davy's confidence. 'It shows in everything, his art, his music, his bearing. Deborah said we had to get his confidence back and then he'd be all right.' She inhaled again. 'They loved his music at Woburn, so you see there is a place for his sort of touch.'

He passed her another joint, going next door to fetch Davy, handing him one. 'But only one,' Sarah insisted.

'I'll look after him now, you've done so much,' Carl said. 'I'm here to help.'

They played at the club behind their digs when Tim and Arnie returned to college and the audience fell silent at the skill of Davy's playing and the close harmony of their voices.

'You see,' she said to Carl as they walked home. 'There's no need for me to go solo any more, we can stay together.'

In November Arnie shambled into her room on a Wednesday evening telling them that he couldn't practise on Saturday morning as they'd intended because there was to be an anti-Vietnam demonstration at his college.

'We'll all go,' Carl said.

'No, we won't,' Sarah said, looking at Davy. 'There's no need for us to go – it's not our college, it's Arnie's.'

'For God's sake, don't be so wet. What were you talking about at that festival? Peace and love – only talk then is it?'

Sarah felt the anger rise because she had told Carl about Davy and his father.

He apologised that night. 'I'd forgotten. We won't go, I'll say we're too busy.'

On Saturday they put on scarves and coats and went with

339

Arnie, because Davy insisted that they should. 'Never let it be said that we're wet, eh, bonny lass.'

She put her arm through his, following the others to the meeting place, slowing their pace so they could be at the back though there had never been any trouble, Arnie had told them. But Davy was still too fresh from drugs for any of this, God damn it.

'Come on,' Arnie called, beckoning them forward.

'There's no need to be at the front,' she said, holding him back.

'Yes, there is,' Davy replied, his eyes dark.

The march began and they were in the fifth row, pressed between too many people. They walked slowly, chanting, holding up fingers in the peace sign, looking out for hecklers, seeing only support from the passers-by.

They sat on the ground in the road while a sociology lecturer talked of the obscenity of war, the hopelessness of the US involvement, this bullying by a superpower. The ground grew colder and harder and the police just stood in front of them, waiting until the cold soaked into their veins, smiling at them, joking with them.

'Load of bloody rubbish,' Tim said. 'I'm getting nothing from this but piles.'

He stood up as others were doing and Davy grinned at Sarah. 'So this is what Rob spends his weekends doing, is it? We could do a few more of these. I'll write to Da tonight.'

They ambled away with the crowd, seeing the banners held high, hearing the chanting, feeling hungry. They peeled off with others down a side street of small shops, following a banner, which suddenly dipped and disappeared. There was a scream and now they were piling up one on top of the other, and those in front were turning, pushing through them, rushing, knocking into them. Sarah looked at Carl.

'For Christ's sake, what's happening?'

He was standing on tiptoe, trying to see. 'Wait here, we'll go and find out.' He grabbed Davy's arm, pulling him through those who were trying to escape.

'No, leave him here,' Sarah yelled, rushing after them, forcing her way through, seeing a crush of black leather jackets, the bicycle chains that were being swung round the air, the punches. A gang had attacked the marchers.

'Bloody flower people,' she heard.

'Don't like war? Take a bit of this.'

A stone was hurled and there was Davy, still being held by Carl, still being dragged forward. 'Let him go, come back.'

Carl turned and saw her, let Davy go. She saw him turn to look at her, and there was blood on his forehead so red against his white face.

She moved towards him, looking for Carl. 'Get out, get away,' she screamed then looked for Davy again, but he was pushing through the scrum, running away, running. 'Wait for me,' she called, turning to follow him, seeing his face as he swung round. She tried to shake off the hands which held her.

'Leave him, let him go.' It was Carl holding her arm, but she still struggled to be free because she had seen the look in Davy's eyes.

Arnie came running from the front, his clothes dishevelled, one eye swollen. 'Come on, let's get out of here too.' They ran, with Tim catching them up, his shirt torn, Arnie shouting out, 'I can't understand it, there's never been any trouble before. Why pick us?'

Davy came back late that night and went straight to his room. She went to him. He was sitting in the dark, plucking the sitar.

'Don't turn on the light,' he said, his voice flat, slurred.

She knelt next to him, smelling the beer on his breath. 'I ran too, we were so frightened.'

'You ran towards me, I ran away,' he said, his voice calm. 'Now I want to be alone.'

She kissed his cheek, unable to forget the look of self-disgust in his eyes as he had run that afternoon.

'Your da would have been proud you were on the march at all,' she said, but he didn't reply.

341

CHAPTER 21

Annie looked up at the sky on 5 November, seeing the rockets explode in the air, hearing Betsy's soft laugh as she stood by Black Beauty's stable. 'I wonder if the kids have fireworks in London.'

Betsy shook her head, her breath coming quickly. 'Too busy playing their Indian guitars, what did you call them, sitals?'

Annie smiled. 'Nearly there – sitars. Gracie and I have been back to the shop in Newcastle where we bought their first guitars. They're getting us new sitars for them in time for Christmas. Tom's going to tell them about his decision to start a one-off silk printing division the year after next. Then it's there if they want to get involved. They might not of course but they're so talented and Tom can't wait to work alongside his son.'

'Took some time for him to wake up, didn't it?'

Annie smiled. 'I know but we all make mistakes. I know I have, but I never thought being a parent would be so difficult. How did you cope, Bet?'

Bet shook her head, moving slowly over to Annie. 'I didn't, lass.'

Annie put her arm round her. 'Oh yes you did. I remember you covering for us with Da when we hammered out those lead coins in the allotment for the fair. I remember you coming and holding me after I heard Mrs Maby and Francy talking about Mam taking poison. Oh yes, you did cope, Betsy, and don't let anyone tell you different. Now, inside and get your feet up – do as the doctor said or he'll be round with a big whip. We've got to get this blood pressure down so no more chocolates.'

She squeezed Bet's arm, helping her into the warmth of the kitchen, loving her.

Sarah did enjoy fireworks on Guy Fawkes Night, laughing with Carl as the catherine wheel whizzed off its nail in Sam's London garden.

'Bit of a damp squib,' Carl shouted and everyone groaned.

'Davy would have enjoyed that,' Sarah said, taking a glass of wine from Sam.

'How is he, still off the hard stuff?' Sam ducked as a rocket exploded well above him. 'Damn things, don't know why I have them.'

'Oh yes, either Carl or I or one of the boys stays with him when he's out. He's with Tim tonight, but you'd have been proud of him at Woburn, Sam. He played so beautifully, the hippies loved him.'

Sam sucked his cigar and the smell reminded her of Uncle Don. 'Hippies don't buy records,' he said. 'We need what the market wants.'

Sarah shrugged. It didn't matter, she wasn't fussed about music any more. All that mattered was that Davy was well.

'You just wait until you hear him,' she repeated.

They ate caviar and smoked salmon and she refused LSD because she had work to do when she returned home, and she must check on Davy.

She smoked pot, enjoying the taste, the drifting, and nodded as Carl kissed her and patted his briefcase. She murmured against his cheek, 'Fine, go and do your business, I'll just stand here and wish I had a sparkler,' she smiled at him, caught his hand and kissed it.

Sam walked into the study, shutting the door behind him. 'My backer wants her in a proper recording studio by the New Year, what the hell's going on, Carl? The bum recording didn't work, heroin didn't. He's still there for God's sake, larger than life.'

Carl lit a cigarette, picking a piece of tobacco off with his finger. 'Not for much longer – trust me, we're almost there. I organised a nice little diversion at a demo the other day, should just flip him over. The rest of the family's out of the picture so she'll be ripe for the picking soon, then we'll all get our money.'

Sarah found Davy in his room, drunk, lying in a stupor on the bed. 'Must have been one hell of a party, bonny lad,' she said quietly as she eased his shoes from his feet. He struggled up, kicking her from him. 'Leave me alone.'

She laughed. 'OK, but you're going to have a head like a punch bag and a mouth like the bottom of a budgie's cage in the morning.'

She kissed his forehead and he gripped her arm and whispered, 'Better than a pigeon loft though.'

She was still laughing as she eased into bed beside Carl, feeling his arm around her. 'He's going to be all right,' she said. 'I thought the demo might push him over but he's going to be fine.'

Carl took Davy out the next night while she wrote up her notes, and then finished the long skirts that the girls from Arnie's college had ordered. Davy didn't get up the next day.

'Delayed hangover,' Carl told her as she cycled away in the morning.

In the evening he told her that there was a gig the next week. 'So Sam can hear the *new* sound, he'll tell us how he thinks it will go.'

Davy was too tired to practise much in the week, and when he played at the gig he was clumsy and the hard edge was back in the music. That night she checked his arms for needle marks but there were none.

Carl shook his head. 'He's just lost his touch, that's all.'

'He'll never lose his touch, he's too good. He's just tired, too much booze. He's not on heroin again, I know, I've just

344

checked. I'm getting paranoid about this, it's ridiculous. I'll be ripping everyone's sleeve up the moment they have a runny nose, or feel knocked out.'

She couldn't settle, thinking of the change in Davy, in his music, what could she do? She smoked the joint that Carl gave her and sucked the hash, it made her sleep.

Carl took him out the next night, and the next and she was grateful, kissing him with passion, moving with him into the small hours of the morning, smoking the present he had brought her back, drifting because it was easier than thinking, than being paranoid.

On Saturday morning Carl talked to her of going solo but she shook her head. 'No, I told you, we do everything together and we *do* make a good sound – if only you could have heard us. But I'd rather not bother at all if it makes him this tired.'

Carl's voice was angry as he replied, 'It's not music making him tired. He's just weak, you know, physically, emotionally, look at the way he broke and ran at the demo. God, the booze he's put away since then – it's all too much for him, you'd be doing him a kindness you know. Tell you what, I'll bring it up when we go out tonight.'

Sarah laughed. 'Again, that's every night, no wonder he's so tired in the day. He's got work to catch up on at college, he was late in this morning, Tim told me. Don't be too late tonight, darling, we mustn't get him run down again.'

Carl put his hand on her arm. 'You're right. I just thought I'd take him for a light meal, take him out of himself. Come with us if you want to, but I was hoping you'd run up a shirt for Sam. I'm getting him interested in your gear – could be another opening for you and Davy.'

Sarah stayed in and worked, wishing that her parents could see Carl and the way he cared for them both. She smoked the joints that Carl left her.

On the Wednesday of the first week in December the phone rang.

Sarah ran down the stairs when Ma Tucker called up.

'It's a Teresa Manon for you, Sarah.'

'Terry, what are you doing in London – are you in London?'

'It's Teresa actually, and yes I am in London. Doing a Cordon Bleu course, you know. Mummy's idea.'

'Of course,' Sarah said.

'Thought I'd pop round Friday, catch up with the cousins.' Sarah smiled with relief.

'Sorry, no can do. We're playing at Smokey Joe's, what a shame.'

'Lovely, I'll meet you there.'

'Wonderful,' Sarah said.

She told Carl that night, and he laughed. 'God, not another one of you.'

'Oh she's different. Our Terry's a one-off, but Teresa please. Must make sure Davy knows, he's none too keen on that particular little item.' She started to move towards the door and he grabbed her. 'Give the lad a break, he's having a rest – Tim's taking him out later.'

Sarah gripped his hand. 'Tim said he thought he must be taking too much hash, he thinks he's too . . . oh I don't know.'

'For God's sake, you're like a dog with a bone. You've got to learn to trust the lad, though he's so well chaperoned he must doubt that anyone does. Or don't you trust us either?' His voice was cold and Sarah hugged him. 'I just get worried.'

'He'll be all right. We'll put on a good show for the cousin and have a look at how he's coming along at the same time. I mean, Sarah, if he's not interested and is slacking off we ought to let him take a back seat. It's not fair to drag him to rehearsals if he's bored.' Sarah felt his arms tighten around her.

'He's not bored, I'll never forget his face at Woburn, he looked so happy. It'll come back, you wait and see.'

Davy went with Tim and Arnie to Smokey Joe's and was

sitting with Teresa at a table when Sarah and Carl arrived, listening to her talk nineteen to the dozen, smiling gently and, dear God, he looked as he had done when he was on heroin, but how could he be? He played as though he was. Sarah felt the coldness in her as they sat at the table in the interval, drinking tonics and she looked again at Davy's arm, but he wore his sleeves rolled up, and there were just old scars. Nothing.

She turned to Carl whispering, 'I don't understand, I know there's something wrong. Has he been doing coke?'

Carl shook his head, taking her hand, whispering back, 'I told you, I've been looking after him. He's just tired, bored. He doesn't want to play any more and he's had a bit of hash.'

Perhaps then, they should stop these gigs, all of them, though she didn't say that, not yet. She would tell him tomorrow because she didn't want to play without Davy, but neither did she want to drag him down as it was doing.

Teresa was telling Tim about the profiteroles they had made today, and how Daddy loved them.

'How did you get my phone number, Teresa? I keep meaning to ask you.'

'Daddy gave it to me. I suppose he got it from your mother – how is your mother? Still nicking people's houses from under them?'

Teresa was smoking a joint which Carl had given her, her lips were glistening and her breath smelt of gin. Sarah said, 'My mother doesn't nick houses. She owned it in the first place, you always seem to forget that.'

Her voice was tight with rage and she wanted to slap this stupid drunken girl.

Carl pressed her shoulder. 'Joe wants you back on.'

She shrugged him off, then felt sorry. She looked at Davy lolling next to Teresa.

'Take him home,' she begged Carl. 'We'll talk about it in the morning. I'm due to finish at two.'

She, Tim and Arnie played, and Sarah's voice was rough

347

with anger at her cousin but why? She didn't like her mother, did she? She looked for Davy, not knowing what the hell was going on, but they were going, Teresa too, and now there was more rage and fear because Carl was smiling, his hand was on Teresa's back.

They played until midnight only and by then her throat was raw and her feet swollen but the applause was loud.

'I'll pay you until two. You were good but we've got this Blues group who want to do a couple of hours. You'd do even better on your own,' Joe said, paying her.

'I don't like being on my own,' she snapped, walking out of the club, her eyes stinging from the smoke, looking for a taxi. Where the hell were they all?

'Coming on to a club?' Tim called to her. She shook her head.

She started walking, looking over her shoulder, hailing one. It stopped. 'Hurry please,' she said, telling him her address.

Davy's door was ajar, she pushed it open, turned on the light and saw him lying on the bed, a syringe dangling from his ankle vein. She moved so slowly towards him, her arms like lead as she touched him. 'Who gave this to you Davy? Who?'

He turned to her, his eyes opening slowly, his mouth in a gentle smile. 'He's so kind to us, always so kind.'

'Who, Davy?'

'Why, Carl, of course, he helped me. He's got it in his case. It's always in his case.'

She touched his cheek and let him lie quietly now, but took out the syringe, bleached it, put it away in his box, cleaned up his ankle and only then went to Carl's room.

She tried the door quietly. It was locked. She inserted the key that he'd given her so long ago, turned it, then the handle and entered.

Teresa was in his arms, both were naked, groaning, heaving, their skins sheened with sweat in the lamplight. She threw the key on the bed. It glinted.

348

Carl saw it, saw her, started up. 'I thought you were staying until two?'

He pushed Teresa away, throwing her clothes at her. She stared at Sarah, then laughed. 'I rather like your golden boy.'

'Get your bloody clothes, Terry, and get your stupid little backside out of here, or do you want to end up a junkie too?'

She stopped and threw the girl's shoes at her, not looking at her now, only at Carl who was scrabbling for his pants, and trousers. 'Get out, I said.' Sarah shrieked now. 'Or I'll tell your bloody father.'

Teresa stopped dead at this, then scrambled into the rest of her clothes. 'Don't tell him, Sarah. Please don't. I'm sorry,' the girl was edging past her.

'Get out you little fool and stay away from filth like this, you'll save yourself a lot of grief.'

Carl stopped, his trousers almost on. Sarah heard the door slam behind her. She moved towards him. 'Why have you tried to destroy him? Why?'

Carl brushed back his hair with his hand. 'Come on, darling. I'd had too much to drink, Terry was coming on strong, I'm sorry, I only love you, you know that.' He moved towards her. She pushed him away.

'Why did you give him drugs?'

Carl looked amazed. 'Me, drugs. He's not on drugs, is he? We took such good care of him.'

She looked around the room, looking for the briefcase. There, by the window. She dived for it, clicked it open. There were the packets, the syringes, the fixing belts, the pills, the uppers and downers. He was moving in on her. 'Put the case down, Sarah. Don't do anything stupid.'

She stood with it poised at the lower pane. 'One shove and it goes through, Carl. Why?'

He shrugged. 'Because I wanted you, loved you and you wouldn't leave him alone so we could get on with our lives.'

She said again, bringing the case back, ready to smash the pane. 'Why?'

His face was ugly with anger now. 'OK, you silly bitch.

349

Because I had a contract to get you as a solo artist and would you listen? Oh no, "we must stay together," ' he mimicked. 'So I gave him back the habit which you thought you'd cured, the big I am, eh? He was grateful the first time, more grateful the second. You only cured him so that you could still cling to him – never able to stand on your own two feet, were you?'

She lowered the case now, walking past him, feeling him grab her. She slapped him hard across the face and his hand came up and hit her, jerking her head back. She was glad of the pain, it unleashed her thoughts. She moved quickly now, along the landing, down the stairs.

'Going to phone, Mummy, are we? She won't come. When did she ever come? Only when she can use you. Just as you used that poor little sod in there.'

She dialled her mother's number, resting her head on the wall. She heard Annie's voice.

'Mum,' Sarah whispered.

Annie said, 'Thank God you've rung, when are you coming, we need you, it's – '

'Mum,' Sarah cut across her. 'I need you here. You said you'd come if I ever needed you.'

'But darling, we can't come, we left a – '

Sarah put down the phone, feeling the anger surge again. Carl called over the banister. 'Didn't think she'd come, did you? Has she ever come? She rang earlier you see, some crisis with a strike. Can't leave dear old Tom on his own. Wanted you to ring her.'

Sarah ran up the stairs now, pushing past him, dragging out her rucksack, shoving in her clothes, pass book, passport, papers, money, address book. She rushed into Davy's room, and packed his things, shaking him awake, slapping him, feeling the blood from her own swollen lip.

She pushed him before her down the stairs, dragging the rucksacks, stopping, saying to Carl, 'What'll you do now you've got no solo singer, now you've messed up the life of a lovely boy?' She was no longer quiet, she was shouting with rage, spittle spraying on to his shirt.

Carl shrugged. 'Doesn't matter – I've made enough contacts through all this, and had a nice bit of sex.'

She looked at him, her golden boy, and followed Davy who stood on the steps, arms hanging at his sides. She unlocked the car and pushed him into the front seat, the rucksacks into the back, and drove to the nearest phone box. She rang the police, giving them Carl's name and address, but not giving her own.

She started the car and left their area, her hands shaking. She stopped again, looked in her address book for the Dutch clinic that Deborah had told her about because she couldn't do it alone again.

'Davy, we're going away. We've got to get far away. No one here can help us, no one cares enough. Mum wouldn't come. Do you understand me? Mum wouldn't come.' She was shouting now, shaking his arm.

'I'm fine, just fine,' Davy said smiling at her. She put her head in her hands. I must think. The ferry. A map. Money. Customs. He'd need some heroin to last the journey but not enough to carry.

'Davy, how much stuff have you got left?'

He was lolling against the car door. 'Davy,' she shouted. 'Where's your fix?'

He shook his head. 'Carl's got it, he's very kind.'

She gripped the steering wheel, letting the engine idle. 'Look, we've got to get some more stuff, we're going on a journey. Have you any money?'

He had and so had she. 'Where can I get some heroin?' She kept her voice very calm.

He smiled again, his eyes unfocused. 'Davy,' she shouted. 'By the bridges, just by the bridges.'

'Which bridges?' she shouted again.

'The workshop bridges. Carl showed me.'

She knew now and put the car into gear, driving carefully, not wanting to be stopped, down to the bridges where the road was unmade with deep holes. She steered in between them to the end where the squatters had taken over the empty terraces.

'Where, Davy?'

He pointed to the one with shutters and she took him with her, knocking quietly on the door, smelling urine in the hall when it opened, buying one fix of heroin, a syringe, and one snort of cocaine. It was all they could afford.

She drove through the night to Harwich, stopping once for petrol, once so that Davy could snort cocaine, and she saw traces on his jumper, as though he'd been baking bread, and she remembered the farmer's wife, the sunshine, the hope. It was on his lip too but he didn't care, did he, because it was taking him away and she brushed him gently, kissed his cheek. 'We're on our own Davy, but I'll look after you. I always have, always will.'

She made the bank in Harwich phone their London bank and she withdrew all their money. She got a berth on the ferry, but before they drove on she pulled into a side street, looked both ways and handed him the syringe. 'It's got to do until we get there.'

He nodded, his nose running, his eyes too. She squeezed his arm to fix his vein, unable to look as he inserted the needle, depressing the plunger, withdrawing. She wrapped the syringe in newspaper then put it in the box, wrapped the box in old newspaper and put it into a wastebin.

Then they drove on to the ferry, and up the steps to the deck, leaning on the rail as they left harbour, and she wanted to see her mother running towards the quay, wanted her to see the boat leaving with her daughter on it, because she had left her alone in London for a strike.

Annie sat in Sarah's bedroom, watching Betsy's shallow breathing, knowing that she would die before the night was out. She held her old friend's hand. Ring again, Sarah, she begged inside. Ring again.

She called softly to Georgie. 'I should have told her it was

352

Betsy straight away. I just didn't want her to drive up here distraught. I should have told her. I tried but she put the phone down. Oh God what's wrong with her?'

Georgie stood in the doorway. 'Nothing much. I've just rung Carl, they've had a tiff, he says, and she and Davy have gone off to a club, would you believe. Selfish little buggers.'

Betsy died at dawn.

CHAPTER 22

The ferry rode the winter waves, rising and dipping, and they stood at the rail, their hair whipping their faces and Sarah was too cold for anger, for pain, too tired for thought.

They drove off the ferry at The Hague and now there was no time for speech because she had to drive to the clinic, looking at the map on her knee, keeping to the left. She went the wrong way round a roundabout. Oh Christ. Took the right road, driving fast as the daylight faded.

'The countryside's so flat,' she said, her voice tired.

Davy said nothing as the sweat beaded his forehead. She gave him three joints. 'Smoke these. Just two more miles.'

'Are we nearly home?' he murmured.

The clinic was white-tiled, clean, with ochre chrysanthemums in a bowl at reception.

Davy sat shivering on a grey leather chair.

Sarah said she must see a doctor. She would not leave until she had. She knew Vanessa Morgan who had been treated here.

A doctor came, his broad face tired, his smile calm. He took them into his office where a stove burned and delf tiles were set in the fireplace.

'You know Vanessa?' He spoke good English.

Sarah shook her head. 'I know of her. It's Davy. He's on heroin. I've tried to get him off, it seemed to work but it hasn't. You've got to take him. He's so important and I can't bear it.'

She looked at her hands on her lap, wet from the tears that were streaming down her face. 'Please, help us.'

He told her how much it would be and she nodded. She would sell the car.

He called in Davy, and sat him in the chair next to Sarah whilst he propped himself on the edge of the desk.

'So, Davy, you want to be rid of this addiction?' The doctor's hands were clasped, his voice was casual, his eyes serious and fixed on Davy.

Davy looked at him, at Sarah and then at the doctor. 'Yes.' That was all, but it was enough.

'Please wait out in reception. You may wish for a coffee?'

Sarah sat on the grey chair and drank the coffee and another, stirring in sugar this time, round and round, hearing the click of the spoon against cup, watching the spiralling bubbles, not thinking of anything, not feeling anything, not yet. There was no time.

The doctor called her in again after an hour. Davy wasn't there and now the doctor waved her to a settee in the bay window. He sat opposite.

'He's been taken to his room. You may go later. Now I have to tell you some of the things that I have told him. The first is that his addiction is recent, months not years. He is the same as many others. That I have also told him and it comes as a shock to the ego to learn that one is not unique.'

He crossed his legs, his white coat falling open. 'There is a way to get off drugs, and stay off. That I have also told him but there must be a great need within that person to rid themselves. You see, heroin is stronger than anything. It takes so much of your life, so much time. You come off and then what do you do with that time? You need help to come off. You need help to stay off.'

Sarah pulled out her cigarettes. He shook his head.

'That is also an addiction. It is very hard to come off those for some people.'

She put them away again. Her mother had come off, but then she had wanted to, because of the business. Always the

355

business and now there was some feeling, but she shoved it away, deep inside. Not yet.

The doctor smiled at her. 'As long as an addict believes he has any control at all over drugs he will never come off. Davy has come to that knowledge, but you knew that, of course?'

No, she didn't know that and now she looked down at her lap. Somehow they hadn't talked since Cornwall, somehow the days and weeks had passed and there had only been Carl, standing between them. But she couldn't think of him. Not yet.

The doctor spoke again. 'Working together, Davy and I will get rid of this drug. We will take it from him, but what will we put in its place?'

'I'll help. I've always helped. I always will.'

The doctor didn't look at her. 'You should speak to him, I think. He has been given methadone. He is coherent, able to make decisions. Do you understand me, Miss Armstrong?' He was looking at her carefully.

'Yes, your English is very good,' she replied.

He smiled gently.

He led the way to a room which was carpeted, clean, bright, but the lights were low now and Davy smiled at her as she stood by the bed and held his hand. 'We'll kick it, together,' she said.

The doctor looked at Davy. 'Shall I inform your parents?'

Sarah shook her head. 'No, there's no need, we'll handle this together.'

The doctor just stood there and looked at Davy.

He took his hand from Sarah and the smile was gone. 'Yes, please. I want them here, and then I want to go home.'

He looked at Sarah as she shook her head and clutched his hand. 'But we can't go home, I told you what she did. How can we go home? I'm here. I'll look after you, I always have. You need me. We can do this together.'

He withdrew his hand and leant back on the pillows. 'I want to go home. I, Sarah, me. This is my mouth, not yours.

You keep talking for me and I've let you, but I need to breathe, to think. It's you that suffocates me, no one else until I don't know anything any more and I've got to know my own mind, if I'm going to live. I've got to be free of you. Please, just go away.'

She looked at the doctor whose face was grave but kind. 'Now do you understand me?' he asked again.

Sarah nodded and turned to Davy. 'I'll go.'

She left the room and didn't look back. She slept that night in the Mini, then sold it the next day, taking the money back to the clinic, keeping half for herself.

'Will you go home?' the doctor asked as he walked with her to the door.

'I have no home.'

Tom had received the phone call at seven that morning. He couldn't speak as he listened to the calm kind voice of the Dutch doctor. Then Gracie came and took the phone and it was she who spoke, taking down the details, thanking the doctor, telling him they would be there as soon as possible.

It was Gracie who walked to Annie's because Tom was hunched over Betsy's table, wanting his mother's arms around him as they had been when his cousin Davy had died.

Gracie told Annie that the kids were at a drug rehabilitation unit in Holland, that Davy had been a heroin addict for some months, that Sarah was with him and now she couldn't speak either but crumpled against Annie, who held her, holding her tightly against the horror of it all.

Georgie stayed to arrange Bet's funeral whilst they flew to Holland, then hired a car to take them to the clinic. The doctor ushered them into his room and told them that the treatment had begun, the methadone would be decreased, the withdrawal would begin but not before they had spoken to their child.

Annie waited with the doctor as Tom and Gracie went into Davy's room.

357

'Where is Sarah?' she asked, understanding now why her daughter had needed her, hating herself for denying her.

'She's gone, I'm afraid.'

Annie looked at him, not understanding. 'Gone where?'

The doctor shook his head. 'I don't know. You must talk to Davy.'

Tom called her in some time later and she sat with her nephew, her brother and his wife and listened to Davy tell them of Carl and the drugs, of the psychedelic pictures he had painted and the cover-up they had carried out, of Cornwall, of the phone call, how Carl had said that Annie wouldn't come because there was another strike. How she and Tom had only come down after the pictures because they wanted them to carry out market research. How Teresa had slept with Carl and Sarah had found them.

Tom raged at Carl, standing at the window, banging his fist on the sill while Gracie held her son's hand and Annie sat silent, thinking of their trip down, the inflatable chairs.

'Where is she now?'

Davy ran his fingers through his hair. 'I sent her away. I wanted to go home, I wanted me family here. I wanted time to think. I just wanted her away from me. I didn't mean her to go for ever.'

Annie said, 'Do you believe we didn't care?'

'I did for a while, but then I didn't know what to think, or feel. And there was Carl, you see, always talking. We didn't know anything by the end. She doesn't even now. She's on her own out there and she's frightened of being on her own. I sent her away because I had to be alone. I'm sorry, Auntie Annie. I'm just so sorry.'

Annie walked in the garden of the clinic, looking up at the windows which were yellow in the low light of winter. The trees were leafless. Sarah, how could you use this boy as you did? she raged, anger tearing at her, you selfish little brat. How could you keep him down in London, in Cornwall when we could have helped? Davy's right, he needs to be on his own without you. She turned from the sun and looked out across the miles of marsh, her arms folded tight, until the anger died and then she wept, the sound harsh and loud because her daughter was out there, all alone and neither of those kids from Wassingham had stood a chance against Carl. And finally she wept because over all the years she must have failed her daughter.

Sarah walked along the busy road, her rucksack rubbing on her shoulders. She didn't know where she was going, she was just putting one foot in front of the other, walking away from them all, hating them all for the love she had given them, when they had given her none.

She walked until dusk and then a red van with huge marigolds painted on its sides stopped.

'D'you want a lift?' the young man drawled. He wore a band on his forehead, his hair was long, his smile lazy.

Why not?

The rear doors opened and hands pulled her in.

Tom stayed on at the clinic when Gracie and Annie returned for the funeral. He wouldn't leave his son, and it was right that he shouldn't, Annie thought. Betsy would have approved.

The days were dark and Christmas came and went. Sarah's sitar stood in her bedroom, waiting for her return. Annie and Georgie alerted all their export contacts, sending photographs of their daughter, telling police who said there was very little they could do, but what could be done, would be.

It didn't help, nothing helped their anguish, the sense of loss, the sense of self-blame, and so they worked. What else was there, Georgie said. 'Do we drive all over Europe, looking?'

'Yes,' Annie said, hunched by the fire.

'No, she could come here and find us gone.'

'Gracie would tell us.'

They took the ferry and spent a month driving round

359

looking, thinking they had found her, stopping girls who were not her, ringing home to see if she had phoned.

In February Gracie said, 'There's a card here from her. She read it out to them. "I'm alive. Don't look for me, I'm with friends." '

They drove home, read the card, Italy. They alerted their contacts but Gracie was needed in Holland and so they stayed, installing an answering machine in the house, and one at the office for when they were not there. They hired detectives in Italy and then they waited but there was no lifting of the darkness.

Tom brought Davy home in the second week of February. Annie held him in her arms, smiling, hating him for being home, for being safe, but only for a moment, knowing that she loved this boy as if he were her own son.

They set up a silk printing division in the factory and it was this that filled Davy's hours, the hours that were empty now that heroin had left him. And Davy knew, as he lay at night in his room, or talked to others at Narcotics Anonymous in Newcastle that he loved Sarah, always had, always would, but that he had needed the time without her to understand that. But could he ever forgive himself for sending her away? Would she ever come back?

Sarah sat in the front seat with Fred, the US draft dodger, as they drove into Venice, smoking the joint the others had made up in the back.

'So, where're we staying then – is it somewhere your mother fixed up?'

Fred nodded, edging the van in through an archway, his headlights reflecting back in the mist. 'The things mothers do for their kids.'

Sarah shrugged. 'Don't knock it, she's taken good care of you, at least you're not being blown to pieces in that little bit of "trouble".' She blew her smoke up into the air, running her hands through her short hair, cut by Sally last night.

'Short, really short,' Sarah had commanded.

She felt it now, two inches left. They left the van, took a water bus, then walked down alleyways until they entered a courtyard. Ahead of them were double doors standing ajar. They heaved their stuff into the building. There was a smell of damp, and the plaster was crumbling on the walls.

'Not a palace but who cares? Good old Mom.' Fred led the way into a room on the right. 'Marco,' he called. 'Marco.'

Sarah followed him. 'Who's Marco?'

'He's the guy who looks after it for Mom.'

Sarah looked round at the heavy furniture, the carpets on the walls. Ravi's flat had carpets on the walls. Did his clinic? She shrugged, not caring. She was happy with her friends – why want anything else?

'You own it?'

'Sure, lots of Italians in America. We're some.' He bent and kissed her mouth, she kissed him back, liking the taste of him, that was all.

They slept on an unaired bed that night and he kept her warm.

They painted the next day, sitting in coats in San Marco Square and the glowing gold and white, the gold and grey of the façade took her breath away and her fingers moved, her mind worked.

'Kinda good,' Fred said, 'But like I said, you've got to have some soul there too.'

Sarah shrugged. She had no soul any more.

They drank wine that night which they bought in Venice, and spaghetti cooked by Marco. They sucked at the strands and the bolognese stained their shirts, their chins, and she wouldn't think of how it had once stained Davy's. He had sent her away.

They all took LSD and spun in the colours and the extension of consciousness and then lay in bed in the morning, all of them, and later played their guitars in the afternoon sunlight which was thin and cold, but what did it matter?

Tom left Wassingham for Newcastle a month after he had

returned with Davy. There was a chill wind and snow lay on the ground. Would the winter ever be over, would the waiting ever end? He parked his car and walked up the steps into reception.

'I have an appointment with my brother,' he said, shrugging out of his coat.

She spoke into the intercom. Don came to the door of his office, his hair sleeker, greyer, his smile cold. 'Come in, this is an unusual pleasure.'

Tom shook the hand that was offered, holding it for a moment. It was soft and flabby. Davy's was still so thin.

Don returned to his desk, gesturing towards the chair Tom stood by.

'Such a sad day when we said goodbye to Betsy. We were all most affected.'

Tom nodded, sitting quite still. He wanted to smash his fist into that face again and again.

'Yes, it was a great loss, especially at that time, with Davy as he was, and Sarah gone.'

Don nodded gravely, his hands steepled, his fingers against his lips. 'Yes, it's been a very bad time for you all.'

Tom nodded. 'It has been the worst time of our lives and it's far from over. You see, we don't know where Sarah is, we don't know what condition she's in. It's not fair, Don. Annie's had more than enough in her life.' His voice was level.

Don nodded. 'Ah yes, indeed, but life isn't fair – these things happen, especially with children who . . . well you know, headstrong children.'

Again Tom looked at that face, so empty, so cold. 'Sometimes things are helped though, aren't they, Don?' His voice was still level, his eyes steady as he held his brother's gaze. 'I know who Sam Davis's backer was.'

Don's eyes weren't empty now, they were scared and his arms had slipped from the chair. He said nothing.

'You see, Don,' Tom's voice was still quiet, level. 'You see, I talked to my son as he groaned and wept and pleaded in

362

the clinic for the drug Carl gave him. I listened to him in the weeks leading up to his discharge. I came home and looked up the names of the consortium because I knew that I'd heard the name of Sam Davis before.'

Tom sat quite still, watching as Don wiped his mouth with his handkerchief. His hands were trembling. 'I went to see Sam.' Tom's voice was conversational as he rose and walked round the desk and stood close to Don. 'He told me that you had found out from Annie where the kids were staying. Sam moved Carl in. You gave your orders – that on the pretext of creating Sarah as a solo artist he was to break up the family by any means possible. Sam knew Carl was a drug dealer. You knew too.'

Tom put his hand on Don's shoulder. 'I want to kill you, Don.' His voice was still level. 'I want to tear you limb from limb so that you suffer all the pain that can be suffered. I can't though, can I, Don?'

Don looked up at him, leaning back into the chair. 'You see,' Tom continued, 'we live in a civilised society where people don't ruin other peoples lives, or do they? What would you say, bonny lad?'

Tom shook Don's shoulder. 'What would you say, I said?' His voice was no longer level but full of hatred.

'I didn't know he'd get them on drugs. I was never told what was happening.' Don was rearing back, his head arched away, waiting for the force of Tom's blow.

Tom removed his hand, wiped it with his handkerchief, which he dropped in the bin.

'I remember others saying that – was it in 1946?' he said, standing with his back to the window. 'The thing is, Don, I don't know what to do with you because I can hardly believe it, even of you. You did know he'd get them on drugs, didn't you – now it's important that you answer me properly.'

The phone on the desk rang. Tom moved quickly, put his hand on it. 'Tell your secretary on that thing,' he waved to the intercom, 'to hold all calls until further notice.'

He waited while Don did so, his voice cracked and dry.

'So tell me now, Don, you did know, didn't you?'

Don patted his mouth again, looking round the room, then back at Tom. 'All right, I knew it was a possibility I suppose.'

'Just for the hell of it, was it, Don? Or to get back at us finally, since you hadn't killed the business. Kill the kids, kill the hearts of the parents? Hatred is a terrible thing. I should know. I feel it now.'

Tom sat down again, leaning forward. 'Did you know Teresa was with Sarah and Davy on their last night in England? She rang them, went to the club with them, went back with Davy and Carl. Did you know that Sarah found them having sex together?'

He stared at his brother as the handkerchief fell from Don's hand. 'She was high on pot. Where is she now Don? Still in London?'

Don gripped the table. 'It's not true, she's a good girl.'

'Oh it is true. I can get you the written statement if you like. Carl's in prison now. He wrote it for me. I thought I'd show it to Maud.'

Tom stood and walked to the door. 'Don't you come near us again. Don't you come near any of us again and see to your own family, Don, not ours.'

'The statement,' Don gasped. 'Maud.'

'I don't know what I'll do yet, Don. I really don't know.'

He drove to Wassingham and walked into Annie's kitchen where she sat by the range, her eyes sunken. She smiled when she saw him. 'You look like Rudolph,' she said. 'You could lead an army to safety in the dark with that nose.'

He stooped and kissed her. You could lead an army anywhere with your courage, he thought.

He handed her Carl's statement, watching as she pushed her hair back from her face, put on her glasses and read, waiting until she had finished before saying, 'I've been to see him.'

He told her all that had been said. 'I don't know what to do,' he ended.

364

'Nothing. Too much damage has already been done. But I hate him with all my heart because our children didn't stand a chance and we couldn't protect them, Tom, or we didn't, I don't know which it is.'

Sarah and Fred took the public boat to Torcello at the end of March, feeling the sun on their backs, their sketch pads and lunch in the bags they carried. They skirted the long brick wall of the island of San Michele, the white chapel and the blue-grey cypresses and she took out her crayons and matched up the colours, merging them, overlapping them.

They passed Murano, saw the Grand Canal, then shingle, then glass factories and she sketched the shape of those, matching the colours again, falling and rising with the boat, taking no notice of the passengers, of Fred.

The boat increased speed along the open avenue and Sarah sketched the *pali*, three, four, five to a bunch. She noted the electric lantern on one, the seagulls on another. They skirted the islet of San Giacomo in Palude and she sketched the trees choked with ivy.

They slackened speed and chugged down the wide canal of Mazzorbo, past ugly little modern houses with their varnished and glazed front doors, their varnished and glazed little families. She turned away.

They accelerated into Torcello.

Fred led the way, walking ahead of her along a towpath beside the stagnant green canal which smelt of drains and fish. She stopped and sketched the marshland either side, and some vineyards. It was flat like Holland. How was he?

She walked on, looking only to left and right, not thinking.

'There's honeysuckle and hawthorn in the summer,' Fred called.

There had been honeysuckle in Cornwall.

They arrived at the cathedral. She sketched its plain brick façade, its six blind arches. They moved inside and Sarah sketched the simple, rich interior and the light which came through small circular panes on the south wall.

365

'The wind's too icy from the north,' Fred said, looking over her shoulder. 'There are some peacocks over there, on the inner *plutei*. They symbolise the Resurrection and the new life given by baptism.'

She moved along, drawing their long, stretched necks as they pecked at the grapes in a bowl. Did she have a new life? She ate, drank, breathed, talked, slept, loved. She looked at Fred. No, she didn't make love, she just kept warm. No, this wasn't life – but what was life? She didn't know any more.

They ate lunch outside back to back, not talking, just eating, drinking. Afterwards Fred pointed to the campanile which stood a few yards from the east end of the cathedral. 'We should climb that at twilight but now will do.'

They climbed it and she sketched the island spread out all around, and the sea, and she noted the colours with her crayons.

'At twilight the Adriatic seems pale, to the south the lagoon can be purple or green, depending on the sky. It's kinda nice.'

She looked at Fred, his beard, his loose shirt, his hands which drew competently, but not like Davy. She shut her mind, sketching Fred as he stood there. Was he nice? She supposed so.

They walked back along the towpath, caught the boat and now the wind was fresh and cool and the light was fading. Another day had passed, thank God.

They disembarked and walked silently from the boat, through a Venice sunk in shadow, the light behind the buildings turning them azure, lilac, violet, their shutters hard-edged and black. They turned into the courtyard, past the marble well-head, the empty flower urns standing on the moss-covered paving slabs, into the house where the sound of guitars and singing drifted from above.

Marco came, his apron greasy, his face worried. 'There are men at the trattoria asking about a girl called Sarah Armstrong.'

That evening Fred took her to the station and put her on a train for Rome. 'Let me stay,' she said.

'Look, Sarah, it's been fun but I can't have cops checking up on me. They'll kick me out and I'll be in Nam before I know what's hit me. You'll have to go. Use the money for a plane ticket. Just get the hell away from here.'

'Please let me stay.' She grabbed his arm.

'Look, don't cling, you're a big girl, time you made it on your own. Don't always need someone else, for Christ's sake.'

Sarah stood at the window as the train drew out, waving, but Fred had turned and was walking away. He didn't look back. She was alone, quite alone, and his words echoed round her mind.

Rome was like London, crowded, chaotic, noisy. She stayed in a small hotel that had bed bugs. She walked the streets, looking up at the Spanish Steps, at the stalls in the markets, at the artists, the students. She looked into the cafés but hadn't the courage to go in alone and always Fred's words echoed and that night she dreamt at last, of Carl, of Davy, and woke in the morning bathed in sweat.

She ate breakfast alone. She bought a map and toured the Colosseum, looking up as a pimp sidled up to her.

'All alone? Come with me.'

She turned and walked away quickly, frightened, checking the map, going back to the hotel, lying on the bed. Don't cling. Don't cling. She didn't eat that evening. She just lay on her bed, thinking. She lay awake all night, all the next day, hearing Fred's voice, hearing Carl's. 'You only cured him so that you could cling to him.' She heard her mother say years ago, 'Let him decide. He might not want to go into art.' Again and again she heard their voices until her head ached with the echoes of them all and in the morning she had travelled many miles and many years. She went out again to the Colosseum waiting as a pimp came up. 'All alone? Come with me.'

'Piss off,' she said, staring at him. 'It's time I was alone.'

367

He moved away and Sarah finished looking at the Colosseum, before eating at a café. She rang the Dutch clinic from the café. The doctor said Davy had gone home. So far, there had been no relapse.

She walked to the river and stood there, knowing she would never be the same again because she acknowledged now the fact that *she* had decided that they must cover up after Davy's psychedelic pictures. She hadn't asked him. It was *she* who had taken him to Cornwall. It was *she* who had changed from Newcastle to London to be with him. It was *she* who had not listened to Ravi as he warned her of the drugs. She hadn't wanted to listen.

She had never asked Davy what he wanted. It was what she wanted that had mattered to her. He had wanted to go home and she hadn't seen it, or if she had she had ignored it because she wanted to stay, and now she knew that he had once loved her, and that she had seen it, and used it. She was as much a user as her mother and the knowledge broke her heart because all along it was Davy that she had loved, she knew that now. It had never been Carl.

She stood until the sun went down and it was dark and there was just the sound of the city around her. She walked back to the hotel and packed her rucksack, heaving it on her back, and took a taxi to the airport, knowing at last where she was going.

Annie listened to the Italian, straining to understand his broken English, her heart sinking as she did. Sarah had left before the private detectives reached her. Her friends had no idea of her destination.

CHAPTER 23

Sarah lay in the dormitory wondering how she could bear such heat for another moment. She rolled over and checked her watch. Midnight.

'Lie still,' the old woman in the next bed called out. 'If you lie still the heat is not so bad.'

Sarah eased on to her back, feeling the sweat running off her, smelling India all around her, hearing its music, seeing the shadows the street lamps cast through the curtainless windows. Ravi had been right, the landscape as she had flown into Delhi looked like lichen on a stone but nothing had prepared her for the smell, the noise of the streets, the number of people, the bikes, rickshaws, tongas.

In the morning the old woman brushed her hair, twisted it up into a bun, her arms scrawny, her fleshless skin hanging, shaking.

'I should have mine cut like yours. Have you had a broken love affair – my mother always said that those with broken hearts need to despoil themselves.'

Sarah looked out of the window at the people who were buying from hawkers, eating chapattis in the street, others were scrabbling for scraps in the gutters. Some were still sleeping in corners.

'I need to get to this clinic,' she said, digging Ravi's address out of her bag, handing it to the woman.

'Take a bus, number nine. It'll get you there. I'm going the other way. Every year I come – it beats Worthing.'

Sarah stuffed her clothes into her rucksack.

'So, you're working at a clinic – atonement, is it?' the woman asked.

Sarah heaved the rucksack on to her back.

'Something like that.' She left the room.

'Boil your water, don't eat food from the street stalls for the first week, then you'll be immune,' the old woman called. 'Remember, broken hearts can mend.'

She walked out into the heat and the dust and the noise, joining the stream which ebbed and flowed, bright-coloured. Men hawked, spat betel juice. Street vendors called, children begged, pulling at her long cotton skirt, she kept walking. Past silk wallahs squatting cross-legged on the ground, past the derzie sitting on an old durrie sewing on a hand machine. She stopped to look but she had a bus to catch and sewing was of no interest to her now.

'Carry your bag, missy?'

She shook her head.

An old Sikh in a white tunic and turban was weighing rice, lentils, flour, from baskets that stood on wooden planks. Their colours were good together. She should draw them but that was of no interest to her now either.

On past the betel leaf shop, the toddy shop, stalls where ghee and cooking oil were sold, on and on through the hot bodies, with the heat on her head, the heat beneath her feet, in her lungs – and everywhere there was the ordure of India.

Bikes were piled high on the roof of the bus, the seats were crowded, people stared but she turned from them as the driver lurched forward and eased into the sea of bikes, rickshaws, lorries. She looked out at the suburbs, peeling, shabby, dirty, the blacksmiths by their wagons, the VD clinic, the rickshaws which had died together like a farmer's yard full of rusted equipment.

She sat still because the heat was too much and it was only nine in the morning. They were out now amongst short scrub grass and there were flat-roofed houses squatting beneath the sun. She closed her eyes, feeling the sweat bead her forehead, then run into her eyes, her mouth. She felt the flies on her lips, everywhere, hearing them all around.

They drove and drove, stopping at midday for fuel at a broken-down shack. She shook her head at the food hawkers and just drank warm water from her bottle, standing beneath the shade of the awning, looking out across the plain which shimmered and danced and she could hardly breathe. It was only April.

They drove all afternoon and the woman who sat next to her, her body pressed too close, smelt of curry. They passed scrub, and the horizon danced as villagers squatted beside cow-pats kneading them.

'To cook,' the woman beside her said.

Sarah turned, surprised. 'You speak English.'

'Many do. I am having a little.' She smiled, slight against Sarah's European build. Ravi had made her feel coarse, huge. Would he remember her? Would he let her stay?

They drove past a fair. The bus stopped and everyone clambered off, buying food from the fly-specked stalls, and music blared from a loudspeaker tied to a tree. She ate nothing but thought of the fair in Whitley Bay, the cool east wind – Davy. Did broken hearts mend? She thought not and wanted to die, but that would be too easy.

They drove on until well after dark, when the driver stopped at the crossroads of a town.

'Missy,' he shouted above the chatter, standing up, pointing at Sarah.

She struggled through the people, murmuring, 'So sorry, I'm sorry.'

They smiled or shrugged – all stared.

She took her rucksack from the driver and walked towards the bazaar where old natives were smoking pipes, fruit and vegetables were being sold and derzies were sewing. Did nothing alter? She hired a tonga and now it was cooler but the mosquitoes were biting. The horse was thin, his hooves kicked up dust, it was in her mouth, her nose. The moon was bright and she could see to the horizon. They turned off

371

the road, on to a track between fields until they came to the gates of a compound, the shapes of the buildings flat black against the moon.

She paid the tonga wallah, heaved her rucksack on to her back and walked through the gates, towards light which came from behind a building. She reached the entrance to the courtyard and stood looking at the women who sat on charpoys around a fire of cow-pats.

'Ravi,' she said into the silence that fell. 'Is Ravi here?' Did her voice sound as desperate as she felt? Did it sound raw with pain and despair?

He came to her, hurrying across the compound from a long low building. She stood, letting her rucksack fall to the ground, wanting to run to this man from her past but she didn't need to because he was here, holding her, leading her away out of the circle of light, away from the silence and the stars, holding her hands in the soft light from the moon. 'You came,' he said. 'I hoped you would. But you have come alone?'

'Yes.' That was all.

He looked at her and nodded. 'You are tired, but you are also different. We will talk tomorrow.'

She held his arm. 'No, I don't want to talk, I want to work. I want you to use me, please.' There was the sound of cattle moving, lowing, the soft voices of the women, and Ravi's eyes were gentle.

'You need sleep, come with me. I will use you, but – forgive me – perhaps not yet in the clinic.'

'I will do anything.'

Ravi nodded. 'Come with me, you need sleep, my dear Sarah.'

She followed him to a room beyond the courtyard. She sat on the charpoy.

'Wait here, I will be back.' Ravi left her and Sarah lay back in the coolness of the windowless room. Tomorrow she would work in the heat, the dust, the dirt, with the flies, until she dropped and at last there was a sort of peace within her and she closed her eyes and slept.

Ravi returned carrying chapattis and water. He stood over Sarah, seeing the exhaustion in her face, the shortness of her hair, hearing again the pain in her voice. Where was Davy, whom she had loved?

Davy stood in Annie's office, waiting until she had finished the phone call. She was so drawn, so grey and though she smiled at him, at everyone, there was always agony in her eyes.

Annie put down the receiver. 'Hi, how's it going? Did the design work as well in practice as in theory?'

'I think it did, Da's looking at it now. May I sit down?'

Annie nodded, leaning back in her chair. There were daffodils on her desk.

'I want to go and find her, Auntie Annie.' Davy said. 'I love her so much and it's my fault. I'm better, fitter, I feel like I did before I went to London.'

Annie smiled at him. He was fit, he was the boy they'd known, gentle and strong. She shook her head. 'No, don't go. Where would you look?'

'I've been getting all the names and addresses of friends abroad. I wrote to them all last night, telling them I was coming. I'll just comb the streets until I find her.'

'The trouble is, my dear, she just doesn't want to be found.' Annie's voice was quiet. 'We've had private detectives trying to trace her. They've found nothing. They've checked the airports in and out of Venice, Rome, everywhere. They've checked the airports into and out of India, America, everywhere, the seaports too.'

Annie touched the daffodils, the yellow was so brilliant. 'Wait until you hear from your friends. If they've heard anything, then do go. Please don't rush off, Davy, just stay until you hear, or we might lose you too.'

Sarah woke at first light, and heard the animals moving in

373

the byre. She lifted the mosquito net, eased her feet on to the dirt floor, searching for and finding the Indian sandals she had bought at the fair. There was a broken cane chair at the end of the bed. Her rucksack had been unpacked, her money, passports and address book were on the small table by the bed. Had Ravi noticed the second, false, passport and visa that the pimp in the Colosseum had provided?

She stood in the doorway looking out across the land which seemed huge, the sky which seemed even bigger. In the distance was a derelict fort, at her feet was dust and in her face was heat.

Ravi waved to her from the entrance of the courtyard.

'Come, Sarah, you must be hungry, but first you will need the more basic things of life. Maji will help you.' He smiled and beckoned to her.

Maji took her to the thunder box which her da had told her about. She shut her mind to her past and washed in bowls of water, standing behind the wall by the pump, stripping, throwing it over her body, letting the heat dry her.

She ate chapattis, drank water with the women around the fire, squatting as they did, her skirt in the dust.

'Ravi?' she said, feeling the panic in her. She must work, couldn't he see that? There was not time to eat or talk or feel.

They smiled and pointed towards the clinic.

'He will be here,' Maji said.

He came, his feet kicking up the dust, telling her that he had to go to the outlying villages for three days. His father was away and so a male nurse was in charge of the clinic.

'Do you wish to rest or to work?' he said.

'To work.'

That morning she took the four beasts out into the fields to graze, eating their dust, tapping them with her stick, looking across at the yellowed wheat, sparse and limp, the same colour as the huts. Within minutes the sky grew pale with heat and she walked on widening cracks. Did the cracks go

374

down to Australia? Was that how Annie's Aunt Sophie had gone? How absurd and who cared anyway?

She moved slowly in the heat and Maji gave her lime juice and salt to drink and said she must stop in the heat of midday, everyone did. She didn't want to but her head was bursting, her tongue swollen and Maji was calling her, so she came in from the fields and lay on the charpoy, her hands and arms and feet burned and blistered by the sun. Sleep wouldn't come, there was only Davy's voice, her mother's. There were only memories.

She brought in the beasts when the sun went down, carrying fodder on their backs, she carrying it on her head, as Maji did. The dust was no longer wheat yellow but deep ochre from the low tired sun – it cloaked her and Maji. She watered the beasts and cared nothing about her blisters as she sat around the fire with Maji, with Ritu, feeling her head aching, her feet burning, wanting total exhaustion, wanting more discomfort. Sleep didn't come that night, only echoes, and for God's sake she didn't want those, she ground out into the darkness of her mind.

The next day she took the beasts to the fields again and then squatted and kneaded the cow dung for fuel, carrying it in, dropping it in the courtyard.

'This is not for you to do,' Maji protested, shaking her head.

'Yes, it is for me to do,' Sarah said.

Maji gave her a basket then, but said, 'It is too hot, it is too dirty for you.'

Sarah said, 'I like the heat.'

She drank lime juice and salt and when the sun went down she ate chapattis with dal and sat with the women again, still smelling the stench of cow dung, and that night she slept a little but not enough. She did the same the next day and this time worked through the midday heat, ignoring Maji's pleas to rest. That night the ache in her head was too bad for echoes, for feelings, for anything and so the next day she worked in this way again.

Ravi came back as night fell, easing himself down from the old Morris, walking towards the courtyard. She was too tired to feel pleasure at the sight of him and that was good. She watched as Maji walked towards him and spoke quietly in the darkness of the compound. She watched as he nodded and then approached Sarah, taking her hand, pulling her to her feet, easing her away from the light of the fire.

'I need you in the kitchens tomorrow,' Ravi said, his brow furrowed, his smile anxious and Sarah knew that Maji had spoken of her fieldwork.

'No, I like the fields,' she said, her voice quiet.

'Please,' Ravi said, squeezing her hands. Sarah welcomed the pain on her blisters. 'Please, no one else likes to do it.'

'Yes,' she said at that.

'And then we should talk, my little Sarah.'

'No,' she replied, looking away from him, not wanting to see or hear the gentleness that came from him, because it opened up her heart.

The next morning she helped Maji light the fire and brew the tea, then scoured last night's pots with yesterday's ash and straw. She set new milk on a slow fire to make yoghurt and churned butter in an earthenware jar. She watched the sweeper brushing the verandah of the clinic, and the sun as it crept over the roof.

They mixed chapattis before the sun rose hot and baking, rolling the dough on a circular board, chopping fresh vegetables.

'For the patients?' Sarah asked.

'No, that is cooked over in the hospital, though many of the families bring food, if they have any. This is for the staff.'

When they had eaten she washed her clothes under the hand pump, using a block of hard yellow soap, which stung her blisters. She washed other clothes, boiled up lightly soiled bandages, rolling them in the shade of the awning, watching the queues forming for the clinic, seeing the heat shimmering, knowing that she needed to be back in the fields.

That evening she flavoured the eggs and dal with ground coriander, pepper and black cardamom and they ate by the light of a paraffin lamp, slapping at the mosquitoes, and so it went on, day after day. Now there was a pattern to the days that was comforting, predictable, safe – but she didn't deserve that.

'This is like any village, like yours in England,' Ravi said one evening as they all sat together round the fire.

'I have no village,' she said and the pain was so sharp for a moment that she could hardly breathe.

She washed and cooked the next day and the next and the harvest was brought in and the heat became even more intense and now she wasn't sleeping again because the work was too easy. Instead she walked up and down the courtyard throughout the night, counting her steps, anything to stop herself thinking.

'You will work in the clinic tomorrow,' Ravi said, as he ate his dal that night. 'You are ready, I think, and Maji tells me you walk in the night, instead of sleeping. Perhaps the ward work will help. Perhaps talk would too?'

His eyes held hers and she shook her head. 'No, I just want to work, not talk.'

She walked across the square the next morning, before the heat burnt the very air she breathed.

'We have pregnant women, we have children, men. All sorts. We can operate or we can just nurse,' Ravi told her on the verandah. 'You will work with Pitaji today. He will tell you all that you need to know, all that you need to do.'

He left her then and Pitaji smiled and walked before her into the wards which were wood-lined, white-painted. Fans whirred and moved the hot air.

'Here,' Pitaji said, walking down the ward, 'we have pregnant women whose bones, especially their pelvis, are disintegrating because they do not eat enough and so their babies eat their calcium. They cannot give birth normally. We try and feed them properly, we help them give birth but still seventy per cent of their babies are diseased. They will become semi-invalids.'

Sarah followed him, looking at the large-eyed women. 'Can nothing be done?'

'How can we feed the world?' Pitaji pushed open the door at the end of the ward and stepped through into an annexe where a man was putting food into a huge pan.

'Can you dole this out to them? We give them rice, vegetables and lentils. Then yoghurt.'

Sarah moved down the ward with Pitaji, ladling stew into the bowls the women held up.

They washed the bowls later, as the heat beat down on the corrugated iron annexe before moving into a ward of elderly women. They distributed stew here too.

'You come to the clinic now,' Pitaji said.

Sarah stood behind Pitaji who wrote down the details of those who had queued since before the sun rose. One by one, they filed in, filed past, into the day clinic.

'Ravi's father is away, he is very busy,' Pitaji said.

'Can't I do more? I'm doing nothing. I want to be used.'

Pitaji smiled at her. 'Go with this man, take this form and see Ravi.'

Sarah walked beside the native, holding the form which she could not understand. 'Can I help?' Sarah asked.

Ravi read the notes, then looked at her. 'Yes, I think you can. Help Bhim to remove the foreign body from this man's nose.' He handed her the card. Bhim beckoned to her, leading her to the cubicle, washing his hands, telling her to do the same, then handed her a light.

'Please hold this quite still,' he said, taking an implement from the steriliser, patting the man on the shoulder, making him lie down.

Sarah held the light as Bhim dug gently, while blood and mucus ran. He said, 'This man is a stone breaker. It is a familiar problem.'

The old man's eyes sought hers.

Bhim said, 'Wipe him clean please.' He withdrew the pebble.

Sarah picked up a swab and wiped the old man's face, nose, lips. She smelt disinfectant and there was blood and mucus on her fingers. She dropped the swab, looked at her fingers and felt the bile rise in her throat. She swallowed, wiped with a new swab and collected up the soiled pieces as the old man stood, salaamed and left.

Ravi called through. 'Pitaji is returning to the wards now. Perhaps you could go too, Sarah.'

She walked into the heat, feeling it beat into her face, across to Pitaji. They bathed the old women, and the stench of their illnesses brought the bile to her throat again. They moved from bed to bed drawing back the sheets, sponging them, smiling, drying, moving on, but the woman in the last bed was dying. 'Just her face,' Pitaji said, handing her the last of the clean water, leaving her.

Sarah wiped the lined brow, smiled at the woman who did not smile back but lay with her eyes wide open, and there was no breath from her nostrils, no movement of her body, and Sarah dropped the cloth and ran from the ward, vomit spewing from her, on to the parched cracked earth.

She ran then, back to her room, lying on the charpoy, vomiting again, crying because she had never seen death before, never touched it, because that is what she had done.

Ravi came to her that night as she lay unmoving on the bed. He sat on the cane chair and took her hand.

'Now we talk,' he said.

'No,' she replied, her voice dull.

He gripped her arms. 'Sarah, you are in pain, you will harm yourself. You came here to talk, not to die, for heaven's sake.'

'I came here to work, not to talk, or to die. One is too difficult, the other too easy.'

Ravi looked at her and his shoulders slumped. He touched her cheek. 'Oh Sarah,' he said. Then left.

She sat up, not looking after him but at her hands which

379

had swabbed an old man, and hated it, bathed an old woman who had died. She had hated that too. She was just like her mother. Even where nursing was concerned she was like her bloody mother.

'So, where is Davy?' Ravi said and now she looked up. He hadn't gone as she had thought. 'Tell me, Sarah, because I shall not leave until you do.'

She looked at him, then back at her hands. She didn't want to talk, she didn't want anyone to know what she had done, but the words were coming, tearing themselves from her throat. 'He's alive but I nearly killed him. I used him you see, even at the very beginning. I clung to him because I couldn't bear to be alone.'

Ravi said nothing, just stood silently.

'I even changed colleges from Newcastle to London right at the start.' Her words were stilted, abrupt. Ravi waited but she said nothing more. Her mind couldn't produce any more words. There was just a darkness.

Ravi moved towards her now. 'Of course you did,' he said. 'You loved him, it is what anyone would have done, you just did not know that you felt this for him.'

The darkness was pushed aside at the sound of his voice and the words came back, harsh and dry. 'You don't understand. I cling. Fred said I did, Carl said I did. I used him, Ravi, I nearly destroyed him.'

She told him about the drugs, about covering it up with Tom and Annie that day, about Cornwall. 'I used him.'

Ravi was silent and now he reached for her hand. She felt his warmth on her skin, but it didn't reach inside her.

'Yes, you did use him, but it wasn't you, it was the drugs, it was the madness of the times – for you both. It was Carl. You couldn't think when your mind was blurred, when someone was pulling in another direction, dripping poison as he was doing.'

Sarah dragged her hand from his. 'No, it wasn't the drugs. I'm like my mother, you see. People aren't important, it's only our own needs that are, our own ambitions.' She lay

380

back and turned her face to the wall and wouldn't speak any more.

That night she ran a fever and for the next three days the hate raged in her, for herself, and for her mother who had always put her business before her da, before her. She hadn't come. She hadn't come.

Annie took Don's phone call at the end of April. He asked her to meet him that evening. She walked to the allotment, past the bar, to the shed. He stood there, his face pale, his eyes uncertain.

She felt nothing as she looked at him. 'Well Don, what do you want?' He reached for her and she moved back. 'Please don't touch me, Don.'

His hand dropped.

'I want to say I'm sorry. Teresa is home in Gosforn. She's going to the local secretarial college. She didn't get into heroin, or cocaine, or LSD.' His voice broke. 'I don't deserve that luck. I don't deserve your forgiveness but I'm asking for it. You see, I know now a little of what you must be feeling. I thought for a moment Teresa was in danger, and my world crashed. It just stopped. I didn't even know I loved her until then. All I knew before was rage and envy for you. I was mad. You took back the Gosforn house you see. I went crazy inside. I just wanted to say I'm so sorry and that I've told Maud and she can hardly believe what I did, and now neither can I.'

Annie looked across the allotment. She had come on Good Friday and planted potatoes as she and Bet had always done. Sarah liked them fresh from the ground – translucent, tasting of the earth.

'Thank you, Don,' she said, turning from him, walking back towards the bar because what did it matter how sorry anyone was when her child wasn't here and what did forgiveness have to do with anything?

Sarah was weak when the fever ebbed and Ravi brought her

381

a boiled egg, because he had remembered that she liked them. He brought her tea too and talked quietly as she ate and drank.

'You must rest for a few days, you know. You have worked too hard. You need time to think, my Sarah. To come to terms with all that has happened.'

'No, I don't want to think. I want to work.'

He shook his head. 'You are too weak and I repeat, you need to come to terms with your life. However, I am going to another village today and I cannot leave you here because you will not promise me to stay on your charpoy will you?'

Sarah didn't answer.

'Then you must come with me.'

Her legs were weak as she moved towards the Morris and the heat drenched her. They drove silently as the plain unfolded before them and there were no thoughts in her head, there was nothing. How could he think she wanted to come to terms with anything? She knew all there was to know about the past, about hate.

They entered the village, driving past buffaloes which grazed on parched grass and wallowed in the pool. She stepped out of the Morris, following Ravi to the mud house, where people were already queueing. She stood with him, handing him forms, whilst Bhim, who had travelled with them, swabbed, bathed, comforted. They sat with the villagers as the midday heat rose and worked again in the afternoon.

At the end of the day, Ravi walked her round the village as the heat eased. They passed black-trunked acacia trees.

'The villagers make furniture and doors, tools and charcoal from these,' Ravi said. He broke two twigs, handing one to her. 'They make good toothsticks too. Chew it until it makes a brush, Sarah.'

She did, tasting the bitterness of the twig, stopping as Ravi did, turning round to look at the village.

'Everything on this land is used by the villagers. The mud is for building and plastering, the wood for rafters, hemp fibre for charpoys, and so on and so on. But the young men are leaving, going to the towns, to England. The villages are changing. Their parents are so brave to allow them to leave. It takes courage to let your children go. Come with me, over here, Sarah.'

Ravi took her hand and they walked over to one of the houses. He spoke to the woman who smiled and showed him into the grainstore. 'Look at this, Sarah.'

She peered past him into the darkness and saw a loom. Ravi was close to her. She could feel his heat and that of the mud walls.

'The village women still weave daris for the family from the cotton they grow. People need clothes, and families need to be clothed, to be fed, to be provided for, my Sarah. Had you never thought of that?'

She pushed herself away from the building, walking back to the Morris. 'I'm tired,' she said. 'I'll wait for you in the car.' She stumbled and his arm was there.

'Yes, you are tired and we will go home. Perhaps when you have thought more, we shall talk again?' Ravi said, nodding to Bhim who was loading the boot.

But there were no thoughts in her head as she travelled back, just an anger that was growing.

The next day she rolled bandages, and then followed Pitaji into the children's ward, smiling at the children, telling them stories they could not understand, giving lunch to those whose parents brought them nothing, because they had nothing. She gave Polo mints to one child, though Pitaji said she must not.

'One won't harm her,' she replied.

Pitaji fetched Ravi who took her outside, his lips thin with anger. 'That child was to have an operation this afternoon. Now she cannot, not until tomorrow. There is no goodness in spoiling, there is only stupidity, Sarah.' His voice was firm, hard. 'Now go and roll bandages and do not again enter the wards.'

She rolled bandages, feeling the panic inside her, hearing

his anger again and again. She cooked chapattis when the sun went down and sat alone, because she had been stupid, foolish, and Ravi stayed in his office.

There was no sleep that night, and as she lay on her charpoy her head wasn't empty, it was full of shame, and Ravi's voice, firm and angry as it had been this afternoon. It swamped the night sounds, and then it was joined by another voice and it was her mother, shouting at her father because he wouldn't eat.

She sat up, shaking her head, feeling the sweat running down her face and neck, but the image and the sound would not go away and now she heard the nurse who had taken her to one side and told her that there was no goodness in spoiling a patient, it was too easy. Her mother was quite right.

She thought of the loom in the grainstore, the women who wove to clothe their families, and now she pushed back the mosquito net and stood in the doorway, hearing the chatter from the courtyard, seeing the lights from the clinic. She gripped the doorway, making herself think, making herself face up to her past, opening her mind to things she had forgotten because the anger was dying, the hate was gone, replaced by doubt as she remembered her mother sewing outfits for her auditions well into the night, when her hands were already shaking with tiredness.

Sarah looked at her hands which were trembling at the memories which were seeping back. She walked across, stood at Ravi's door, knocked, opened it. He was working, his head bent over the desk.

'Please, can I talk? I have been so very wrong.'

Davy's letter reached Ravi after Sarah had left but Ravi had already written to say that Sarah was safe, and loved them, and would one day be home.

Davy took the next flight to India. Annie and Georgie let the birds out for their evening toss, watched them dip and rise and return, and as the spring night closed in they held one another as though they would never let go.

CHAPTER 24

The plains were hot and dry, the train rattled and clicked, Indians hung from the sides and lay on the roof. The smell of curry and India was with her day and night but the heat was made bearable by a fan which stirred the air. She shared her compartment with a middle-aged woman who smoked cigarettes in a holder and put her lipstick-covered stubs into a brown paper bag. She seldom spoke except to curse this godforsaken land.

'I love it. My parents were here after the war,' Sarah said, looking out of the window at the landscape which was no different to Georgie's and Annie's descriptions. She wanted to talk of them, to draw them nearer, to somehow make them know she loved them, because she did, so very much – she knew that now.

'To love a land like this is very strange,' the woman said, turning from Sarah. 'You must have had very little of beauty in your life.'

Sarah looked at the sweat which streaked down the woman's neck. A week ago she would have agreed but now she knew she had grown up amongst great beauty. It was there in the beck, the sea and even in the mines and the narrow streets. It was there in her home, in her parents, her aunt and uncle, in Davy, but she mustn't think of him, because that love was closed to her. She didn't speak to the woman again.

The next day it was the dust which bothered her, cloaking her skin, hair and throat, especially when a sand storm blew up and turned day into night. But none of this really mattered because she was impatient now, all doubt had gone. She had been wrong about her mother, she was sure of that and now there was so much to do, so much to discover, so many bridges to mend.

She left the train as dawn of the third day broke, pale through the cloudy sky. Would it rain? Of course not, the cloud cleared and the heat baked the ground again. She shouldered her rucksack and pushed through the throng of hawkers, beggars, stallholders, weaving through the tongas to the bus station, waiting as bicycles were heaved on to the roof, and the driver shouted and waved his arms.

She listened, watched and longed for the bus to start because she had much to do, and more to discover about her mother. She looked into the distance where the Himalayas soared. Would her mother's friend Prue Sanders still be there? Would she talk to her? She must, Sarah wouldn't go until she had.

The bus left at last and they journeyed towards the foothills. The air was clear, cooler and sweet smelling and at seven-thirty in the morning they stopped near a dhak bungalow and drank tea. Soon the driver was shouting again and they boarded the bus, driving on in increasing heat until they reached the level of the pines. They stopped and Sarah ate cold vindaloo from the rest house and then lay on pine needles as the others did, resting until four, before continuing. The Hindu girl sitting next to Sarah left the bus as they entered the next village. 'This is my home. You may stay with me,' she told Sarah. Sarah smiled but shook her head. 'No, I shall stay at the rest house, but thank you.' She didn't want to stay with anyone, she didn't want to have to talk, to smile. She just wanted to train her thoughts on Prue, on the truth.

The next day they left early again and Sarah watched the Himalayas unfolding before her, their white peaks, their shadowed foothills, the terraced and irrigated slopes. Where was Prue's village? Was she looking at it?

The road was winding endlessly through rolling heights of grassland. They crossed a long precarious bridge of logs. Sarah looked down and it was as though she was looking at her life over the past few months, a bottomless drop. Then they were climbing to the pass. Above them Sarah could see five tiers of road winding away into the distance, at times it seemed to end in space and was so narrow she wondered how the party of Indians approaching with ponies could pass but they did. Were they much bigger than her mother's pony had been? One day perhaps she could ask, if she felt she could ever go home after the grief she had caused them.

The bus stopped at the top of the pass. Sarah climbed out with everyone else, and looked at the river which formed a semicircle at the base of the mountain thousands of feet below her. Had her father seen this? Had her mother?

She sat on a boulder and breathed in the clear cool air and looked at the wild flowers and the rose bushes which were not yet in bud. Yes, Ravi was right. There must have been reasons why her mother hadn't nursed. There must have been reasons why her mother hadn't come with them to race the pigeons. There must have been reasons why she hadn't come that last night.

She lifted her face to the sun. How could she have been so stupid, how could she have remembered Carl's words above all others, when Carl had always lied?

'Have I been mad,' she had asked Ravi, 'to have been so cruel?'

He had shaken his head. 'Just young, just confused, just muddled by life, and by drugs. Go home.'

But she couldn't go home yet. How could they still love her?

'Love in a family doesn't die,' Ravi had said. 'But grief tortures. Let me tell them you are safe, but that your journey isn't finished.'

No, it wasn't finished, not nearly because, after Prue, there was still something more she had to do.

The driver hooted his horn and everyone clambered back

on board. Sarah smiled at them, talked to those who had English, marvelling at the river valley as they wound slowly downwards, then up again through silent pine forests, gazing at the massive snow-covered peaks which came into view and then were hidden by the trees again.

The bus set her down in the late afternoon near old shacks on the outskirts of Prue's hill station. She took a tonga which plodded past brambles and heather, seeing butterflies the size of sparrows, remembering the nettles by the allotment shed, the tortoise-shells. There was a church on their left and now they were coming into the town.

The tonga lurched as the wheel mounted a rock, then straightened. Sarah hung on, settled again, then looked down to the valley and over at the bazaar. Further away to the left were old buildings set amongst trees.

That must have been where Dick Sanders had worked after the war. She craned her neck round, knowing that behind the trees she would just see the clinic and there it was, as Prue's letters had described. She sat back. It was almost like coming home.

The hotel was old with a sagging verandah; so they hadn't replaced it as Prue said they had hoped. Sarah was glad. She paid the tonga wallah and heard him hawk and spit betel as she walked towards the steps. Crows were rising from the trees, there was a slight breeze. The verandah creaked and then she was into the darkness, ringing the bell at reception, booking a room for just two nights.

The dining room was on one side, the lounge on the other. She sat on a red cretonne sofa which was worn and old. Palms stood in brass pots that were smeared with finger prints. New brass spittoons gleamed. The tables were draped with dark red cotton. She drank the tea that was brought and heard sitar music as the office door opened, then silence as it was shut. Fans hung motionless above her.

'Your room is ready, Miss Armstrong,' the manager said, bowing over the key.

She smiled as a boy carried her rucksack up the stairs. She

bathed in the old mahogany bath. The water was cold, fresh. She changed her skirt for another, and her blouse also. She walked to Prue's, following the directions with which she had grown up. Past bungalows with compounds, keeping the valley to her right, the sounds of the bazaar to her left. Not yet, not yet because she hadn't reached the clump of pine trees which stood between the Sanders plot and all the others. Here they were.

She walked towards the verandah where crimson canna lilies grew. Oh Mum.

She climbed the steps and stood there, not knowing what to do now and frightened. What would she do if Prue wouldn't speak to her of the past? The door opened and a plump, pale-skinned, blue-eyed woman with long lashes and blonde hair stood there, dressed in pastel shades.

'Prue? It's Sarah Armstrong.' Sarah could think of nothing more to say. She just waited, wanting to grasp this woman and shout, Help me to know my mother.

The woman said nothing, her eyes widening and Sarah's hopes plummeted because this must not be Prue. Where could she now look? She must search until she found her. Sarah half turned, then turned again as the woman put up her hand.

'I'm Annie's daughter,' Sarah said, feeling the hand on her arm.

Now the woman smiled. 'Did you really think I wouldn't recognise you? You are her image. I was just too moved to speak.'

Prue's arms were round her now, holding her gently and Prue's kisses were on her cheek, her hand stroked her hair as her mother used to do. Sarah put her head on the older woman's shoulder and felt tiredness sweep over her as she cried for the first time for a long while.

Prue held the thin body and knew if she spoke she would cry too because she had shared each day of Annie's pain.

She led Sarah to a chair set back against the verandah wall and called, 'Ibrahim, tea please.'

390

She sat opposite and Sarah heard the creak of the cane chair under Prue's weight. Sarah took the handkerchief that was offered and smiled. 'I'm sorry. I didn't know if you'd be here and I had to talk to you.'

Prue thanked Ibrahim and poured the tea. 'Yes, I'm usually here, but Dick's in Delhi I'm afraid, on business. Never mind, you'll see him on his return.' Prue put the cup in front of Sarah, her bracelets jangling as Annie had said they always used to. 'Now look, my dear. Your mother is sick with worry. Please, may I telegraph or telephone her to say you are here?'

Prue looked across and now Sarah saw the deep lines to the corners of her mouth – they were the same as her mother's.

'She knows I'm safe, she knows I'm sorry and that I love her.' Sarah broke off because it was as though the tears would come again. She drank her tea, it was strong, good – now she could speak. 'Please don't tell her yet – tomorrow will do.'

Prue looked closely at her, then agreed. 'Now, where's your baggage?'

'At the hotel.'

Prue laughed, throwing her head back. 'No child of Annie's will stay anywhere but under my roof. Ibrahim,' Prue raised her voice. 'Please send the mali to bring Miss Armstrong's bags.'

Sarah put down her cup and leaned forward. 'Prue, I need to talk to you.'

Prue poured more tea, her finger on the silver lid. 'And I to you, my dear, but not tonight, tomorrow. Tonight we have guests for dinner – you will like them. It is a girls' night.' Prue waved at the Chinese lanterns hanging on the trees. 'You see, it will be fun. Now, in a moment I shall show you your room and then I have to go and supervise affairs in the kitchen. I have this total fascination with my stomach, as you will know already – it and I spend many happy hours together planning its next extravaganza.'

Prue led her now to the bedroom. 'Good, Ibrahim has organised towels and so on. Do please make yourself at home. You will find your clothes in the wardrobe. Please leave anything you would like washed in the bathroom. We now have flush lavatories my dear. Such a treat, one almost wants to go in there, just to admire.'

Prue smiled at her and Sarah grinned. 'There,' Prue said. 'That's the Sarah I remember from the photographs. Tomorrow we will talk.'

At half past seven Sarah was introduced to Mrs Carter, Mrs Smythe and Mrs Taylor. She sipped her gin and tonic and looked at the lanterns, the town, its lights, its noise. It was so cool, so fresh – how Ravi's patients would improve if they were here.

Mrs Carter sat next to her. 'I just love your skirt, the colours are so vibrant. Did you make it yourself? I expect you've been on an ashram somewhere, have you, exploring Hindu philosophy and religion, or some such thing? One hears that so many are doing that sort of thing these days. So many lost souls.'

Prue cut across the conversation, leaning back in her chair which was beside Sarah's. 'Oh Veronica, for heaven's sake, let the poor girl get a word in edgeways.' She patted Sarah's knee. 'This old girl has chronic verbal diarrhoea, always has had. We were at school together in Devon, you know, and she looked as though butter wouldn't melt in her mouth, but she was a devil.'

Veronica held up her glass. 'Enough, Prue, good grief, this child doesn't want to hear stories from the past.'

Sarah smiled at her. Oh yes she did, but she'd hear those tomorrow. Tonight it was enough that she was here.

Ibrahim poured more gin and they ate canapés while Prue told them how they had been 'talked to' by the biology teacher, about men's and women's 'things', which had puzzled them all greatly until they read *Lady Chatterley's Lover*. Whereupon Veronica had been sent from morning service for changing the words when singing *All Things Bright and Beautiful* from 'he made their glorious plumage, he made their tiny wings', to 'things'.

Sarah laughed with the others and moved to the table where coq au vin was served. Prue winked at Sarah. 'I do so like a treat from time to time.'

Mrs Taylor asked. 'Where have you come from?'

Sarah drank her wine, it was cool, dry – a Chardonnay. Where was Sam Davis, still giving parties? Where was Carl?

'I flew into Delhi, then on to a clinic north of there.'

The chicken was good. She ate carefully, listening to the women talk of Delhi as they had known it, long ago. The parties at Government House, the silver plates, the toast to King-Emperor, the desserts.

'Oh yes, the desserts, darling,' Prue gushed. 'I mean those sugar baskets, girls.' Prue's eyes were bright. 'Sarah, they were magnificent, stuffed with fruit salad. The cooks would compete, positively compete, to create the most splendid and fragile concoction, spinning crisp brown sugar until it looked like a translucent amber dish. The trick was to serve the fruit salad and then crack the bowl and serve that. It must have broken their hearts to have seen all that work go down the gullet. But so delicious. I just can't tell you.'

Prue looked down at her chicken. 'Sorry, girls, tonight we just have fruit salad, couldn't rise to the sugar basket. Chocs after, I promise.'

'I remember sleeping under an apricot tree when I was very young,' Mrs Smythe said quietly as she finished her chicken. 'I can remember the crickets singing me to sleep and being woken by Daddy's regimental band – it all seems so long ago.'

Sarah sat back and looked at these women, lined, content, at home. 'Did you never want to go back to England?' she asked.

There was silence for a while and now there was the scent of jasmine on the breeze. Mrs Taylor spoke at last, smiling at Ibrahim as he took away their plates. 'It's not the same as it was before Independence, but something about the country gets under your skin.'

Prue poured more wine. 'There's a spiritual quality to ⁺his land. It haunts you somehow, and the richness of its history soaks into your bones. I missed it when Dick and I came to England after the war. We couldn't stay, it wasn't home. You see, Sarah, we were born out here, we know its patterns, its rituals, its timelessness. Daddy couldn't go home either.'

Mrs Smythe said, 'I remember our parade ground on Independence Eve. We dined at the House, then sat in stands around the parade ground. The whole place was floodlit, I remember, and we watched the small British contingent march on behind all the Indian troops. The band played as all the floodlights were doused, leaving just the flagpole lit. I remember the Union Jack fluttering, there was a slight breeze, you know, quite chilly really.'

They were all silent now, not drinking, just listening.

'I remember the Union Jack being lowered as everyone stood to attention. It was so quiet. It must have been the same all over the country. I dropped my programme. As midnight struck the Indian flag was raised. We all sang the Indian national anthem. It was so strange, so dark, so different.'

No one spoke or moved until Mrs Taylor said, 'We all thought it was the end but it was a new beginning. We stayed on, lived differently, better because we weren't contained within a cantonment, having to abide by rules, by tradition. We could be ourselves.'

Prue looked at Sarah and lifted her glass. 'To new beginnings,' she said softly.

Next morning Sarah woke to see pale light spreading over the mountains and slowly filling the town, the valley. They ate *chota hazari*, little breakfast, and Prue sat in her dressing gown, buttering toast, drinking fruit juice. 'Squeezed by Ibrahim,' she said, pouring some for Sarah. 'We'll bath, then

394

go to the bazaar for food. Then we can have bacon and eggs if you wish?'

Sarah smiled. 'No, I've had sufficient.'

'Oh how disappointing, then I may not indulge either.'

'I would like to talk to you, please Prue.'

Prue smiled. 'Then we will return for coffee and to talk.'

They walked down the road the tonga had taken and always there was the freshness of the air, the glory of the mountains, the valleys, the trees.

'Are there walnut trees here?' Sarah asked.

'Many. Your father wrote to your mother about them, didn't he? It made her feel closer to him because Sarah Beeston had a walnut table in the hall.' Prue pointed out the trees. 'And over there is an apricot.'

'Is there anything you don't know about my mother?'

Prue spoke softly. 'Very little. We had many years to talk to one another, many long years.' She wasn't smiling now and the lines were deeper around her mouth.

They were in the bazaar. Sarah stopped at a khadi stall.

Prue stood with her. 'It's the locally woven cloth, a relic of Mahatma Gandhi.'

Sarah loved the colours, felt the loosely woven cloth, talked of the designs that would suit them best, the muted colours of the landscape transferred to them, the vibrant colours also.

Prue laughed. 'You're your mother's daughter all right.'

They bought vegetables from the stall. 'It's produce our mali sells from our kitchen garden.'

'Why d'you let him?'

'Why not, it's a sensible cycle, leaves everyone with some dignity.'

They walked back past the cinema, into the garden, passed the delphiniums, stocks. There was a garden shed amongst the vegetables. Did this smell the same as the one at home? She stopped, opened the door. No.

This time they took coffee in the sitting room, leaning back on cane furniture whose cushions were covered with

Wassingham Textiles upholstery sent by Annie, and now Sarah could wait no longer.

'Please tell me why my mother couldn't nurse.'

'It wasn't a question of your mother being unable to nurse.'

'Well, why wouldn't she nurse?'

'Neither is it a question of your mother being unwilling to nurse,' Prue said quietly. 'I need to explain some things to you, so that you can understand others. It is a time of my life that I discuss with no one, just as Annie does not because its shadows could reach out and scar us all over again. But you have your own shadows, my dear Sarah, and they must be seen off.'

She told Sarah then of the camps – of the endless years of brutality, of heat, hunger, misery. 'We nursed in the hospital that we built ourselves. We had no medicine, no tools but a wonderful doctor, Dr Jones from Australia. All day, every day we nursed, scooping ulcers, calming the dying, boiling bandages, rags, burying our friends. We were beaten for many things. Have you seen your mother's finger? Yes, that was because she was late on parade. They beheaded our friend Lorna Briggs. It was raining, her blood was so very red.'

Prue wasn't looking at Sarah, she wasn't looking at anything but the past.

'They made us write postcards. Your mother was frightened to write to your father in case it tempted fate and put the mark of death on him. They found the cards at the end of the war in a box. They'd never been sent. They found medicine too, and Marmite, boxes and boxes of Marmite – we could have saved so many of our friends. Dr Jones wept, they all wept. I say they, because I was not there, not in mind, only body.'

Prue touched her lips, swallowed and then continued. 'Near the end of the war diphtheria raged. I became ill, your mother nursed me but I lost my mind. I wandered the camp and was almost shot, so she tethered me to her wrist, day and night with a piece of rope and fed me, because I wouldn't eat. She would take a spoon and make the rabbit go into the hole.'

Sarah sat quite still remembering her mother running from her father's side after she had tried to make the rabbit run into the hole. It was when she returned to the room that she had spoken to him firmly and Sarah had hated her until the nurse had told her that her mother was right.

'I ate,' Prue continued, 'though it was rice, which by then made us want to vomit because we had eaten nothing else for more than three years. I still can't eat it today, neither can your mother.'

Oh yes she can, Sarah thought. She ate it when she came down with the inflatable chairs, she forced it down through love.

'I wondered why she wouldn't nurse. I've always blamed her for it,' Sarah whispered. 'I couldn't have done what you both did. I know, I've tried in a very small way and I couldn't bear it either.'

'Let me finish,' Prue said, her hands clasped together, her bracelets still on her motionless wrists. 'Please. Your father found her camp after the war and took her back to India, where he was stationed. One night the rains came, hammering on her roof whilst he was away defusing a bomb. 'Does he want to die, is that why he does it?' she asked me before I left her that evening. Later she took too many sleeping pills – it had all been too much – her life had been too much. You see, her father killed himself and left her alone. The war had nearly killed her, now perhaps her husband wanted to die too. So she tried to leave this life, Sarah, and the only way your father and I could make her walk, make her drink in order to save her life, was to shout at her in Japanese. She obeyed out of fear.'

Prue's voice was quite calm though there were tears running down her face, like an endless stream. 'It nearly killed your father and it was he who refused to allow your mother to nurse, though she had conquered her past. He refused through fear for her and through the need for an edge to his

397

life, the same edge that defusing bombs had given him. The same edge that your mother now had to live with again. She agreed out of love, though it nearly broke her again.'

Prue rose now and still the tears were falling but it was as though she didn't know. 'Now, come with me, Sarah, and read the answers to all the questions you would like to ask me. It is better that way for both of us.' Sarah followed Prue into the study stacked with the Peak Frean tins that they had sent her every year.

Prue touched the tins. 'I sorted these out last night, while you were asleep. There is nothing in this box that is personal to me, but it might hold the answers you need. If not, come and find me. I shall be in the garden. It is where I go when I need to hold on to the present.'

Sarah sat at the desk and touched nothing for a long moment because her tears were also falling and she could not see to read. She began after Ibrahim entered and brought her lime juice with ice. All morning she read and by noon she knew the truth of her mother's love for both her and her father, her respect for their dignity and the death of her beloved Betsy.

She left at two p.m. taking the bus back down the winding road. She had borrowed money from Prue and had asked for the address of Dr Jones in Sydney.

At two-ten, Prue telephoned Annie, telling her that Sarah had been and gone, but she didn't know where or why.

'Be patient, my darling Annie,' Prue said over the crackling line. 'Be patient for just a bit longer.'

Sarah barely noticed the long journey back through the Himalayas. She stopped at the same rest house and slept on the verandah, she ate vindaloo at lunch time and mangoes at breakfast but tasted neither. All she could think of were the letters she had read in her mother's writing, the love, the pain, the hope, the steadfastness of the woman whom she loved and now respected above all others.

As the train rattled across the plain she didn't feel the heat, or the stirring of the air as the fan whirred, she just felt the love her mother had always borne her and grieved for what she had done. She grieved, too, for the life her mother had led, not just the war and after, but her lack of a mother's love. So many had come and gone. First her real mother, then Aunt Sophie, then Betsy until Sarah Beeston had taken her away. They were all dead now, except perhaps for Sophie. Sarah looked out of the window, willing the train to hurry. Except perhaps for Sophie, she echoed.

Sarah flew from Delhi to Sydney and it was strange to travel without the cacophony of hens clucking, or the sing-song of Urdu, or the smell of curry, or the beating heat. She missed India already.

Sydney was bright, smart and still warm, though the summer was nearly over. The buildings were clean and European. There were cars, but no rickshaws or tongas, no dust. There was a harbour that glistened, the clipped accent that was almost, but not quite, like home.

She stayed in a hostel with other girls. She nodded and smiled when they asked if she too was travelling round the world, filling in before or after college, breaking free from the family, seeking experience.

'Something like that,' she said, lying on the bed in the dormitory which in some ways was the same as in Delhi, but also so very different. She looked at the address that Prue had given her. Dr Jones lived in Vaucluse. She would take the bus out there tomorrow and hope that the woman her mother had worked with in the camps still had access to hospital records. After all, Aunt Sophie had borne a child, perhaps it had been delivered in a hospital. Perhaps there was an address.

The bus left at ten and this time there was no driver gesticulating, no dust, no sea of humanity into which the driver eased. In Vaucluse the houses were large, gracious, moneyed. There was so much space, so much sky, established gardens, an air of ease.

Sarah stood at Dr Jones's front door. This time the woman who answered the door would not know her, would probably think she was mad.

Dr Jones did not think she was mad. She drew her out to the back garden, sat her down with coffee and listened as Sarah spoke of her mother's wartime life and some of the years that had gone before, and all the years that had come after.

Dr Jones cupped her mug in her hands. 'I remember your mother. I remember everyone and everything about those years. How could any of us forget? Prue writes occasionally and so I knew Annie Manon had married her Georgie Armstrong. I knew, too, that you were missing. I did what I could here.'

Dr Jones frowned at Sarah, and now the lines that Sarah had thought could be no deeper on that thin, old face, were. She continued. 'But that is past. Your mother knows you are safe so why are you here and not at home with her?'

Sarah put down her mug, looking out across the clipped camellia bushes with their glossy leaves, their blooms had been and gone. 'I can't go home yet. I've hurt her too much. All along, people have hurt her too much. She's gone to them with her arms open, only to see them slip away. I want to try to bring one of them back to her.'

Sarah explained that Aunt Sophie had left for Australia when Annie's father had returned to Wassingham after the First World War.

'He took her away from Sophie and Eric, Don too, to live at the shop with him and Betsy. Don had already been staying on and off with his Uncle Albert, he didn't care about Sophie and Eric – I wonder if he cares about anyone – but Annie loved them, and they her. They sent her letters and cards and in one they told her that their own daughter had been born. She was called Annie too. Mum never replied, she thought she had been replaced. The correspondence died out after she moved to Sarah Beeston's. A few years ago she placed advertisements in the Australian newspapers trying to find them again, but there was no response.'

Sarah handed Dr Jones the details she had written down last night – the year of Sophie's daughter's birth, the date of their arrival in Australia, all that she knew of them. 'Please, can you use your contacts – perhaps the new Annie was born in hospital. Or perhaps I should trace the registration of her birth, but then I won't have an up-to-date address, though there would be something to go on.' Sarah was leaning forward, pushing the paper towards Dr Jones.

The doctor took it, read it. 'I would like to do this for Annie. I respected her, held her in great affection. But what about you, what will you be doing while all this is going on?' Dr Jones's eyes were sharp, piercing. 'I don't approve of posteriors on chairs while others are busy.' She poured more coffee.

Sarah smiled as she lifted her cup. 'I could do anything you like to help. I was going to go round the markets and retail outlets, to see what gaps there are in the markets, see what possibilities there are for Wassingham Textiles. Mum and Dad haven't an outlet and Australia's growing, isn't it? But I can do that later. I'll do anything, Dr Jones.'

The old woman stirred her coffee and smiled. 'I think you are doing quite enough my dear. Let me use my contacts, it is more efficient. You do what you know most about.'

As Sarah left Dr Jones said, 'Give me a week – I won't tell your mother you are in Sydney. But Sarah,' Dr Jones added, 'don't get your hopes too high, Sophie will be elderly, she might be dead.'

For the rest of the day Sarah walked around the shops, stopping at the small outlets, the kitchen shops, talking to the managers, making lists. She stayed on at the hostel and that evening a boy brought his guitar on to the steps where they were all sitting and they sang. He handed it to her and she played *Curry Afternoons* and then more gentle ones, for

Betsy. Now there was a calmness in her that she had never known before.

All week she toured the city making notes, thinking of the fabrics she had seen in India, telling the traders of these, writing down their comments.

In the late afternoon, she would stand and look at the incomplete Opera House. Yes, it would one day be as wonderful as Davy had said. She watched the yachts in the harbour, the bridge, the blue of the sky and wished that he were here with her, but knew that part of her life was over, there were some things that love could not survive and her behaviour had been one.

At the end of the week she talked to the market traders, then rang Dr Jones, scarcely able to breathe with tension.

'I have the address you want, my dear,' Dr Jones said and read it over the phone. 'But remember, Sophie is old, she might not have her faculties, she might be ill, oh, any number of things. Good luck.'

That afternoon Sarah wrote to Yerong Creek and took the train two days later to Wagga Wagga where she hired a taxi and drove along a straight road with red parched earth either side, and now there was dust again. In places there were gum trees that hung limp, their bark stripped and loose. The taxi turned left over railway lines into the small township with a garage on the left, a Post Office on the right. They drove on until they reached a small bungalow with rose trees in circular beds.

Prue had grown roses. Did the English abroad always do so? Her hands were trembling. Why was she thinking of roses? Sophie had to be the same, she had to remember Annie. Sarah tried not to rush. She closed the taxi door and paid the driver. She walked up the path hearing the cicadas, feeling the warmth, seeing the corrugated iron roof.

There was a fly door on the verandah. Her pace quickened but before she could reach the wooden steps the door opened. An elderly woman came down on to the path, her face tanned to leather. An older man came after her, his leg stiff.

Sarah said, 'Sophie? I wrote to you. I'm Annie's daughter, she's been trying to find you for years.'

Eric was beside Sophie now and it was he who pulled Sarah to him, holding her so tightly that she could hardly breathe. 'You're the image of your mam,' he said and his voice had all the flavour of Wassingham in every syllable and so too did Sophie's when she touched Sarah's cheek. 'I never thought this would happen,' she said, holding the girl's arm, then kissing her forehead as she had kissed Annie's when they had left for Australia so many years ago, unable to bear living without that lovely child.

She held Annie's daughter in her arms now and Sarah smelt lavender as her mother had done.

'You must come and meet our own Annie,' Sophie said. 'She's a bonny lass, with grown bairns of her own.'

Sarah returned to Sydney that night, but sent a telegram to her mother before she left Yerong Creek, telling her Sophie's and Eric's address, knowing they would come, knowing it would complete her mother's life and that was the least Sarah could do for her.

The next day, and the next, and the next, she went to see the Opera House, to stand and stare at the ferries ploughing through the water, the boats, their sails so white. Would they come? She had left a message with Sophie, telling her mother she would be here each day, if they wanted to see her. Would they?

On Saturday, six days after she had left Yerong Creek she watched the sun cast long shadows across the water. The ferries were crowded, carrying people who would one day buy clothes and furnishings made by Wassingham Textiles, and Indian cotton and silk printed as Davy would wish. Yes, one day, whether she was there or not.

She turned and walked away from the water. 'I'm sorry,' she said, moving out past the people who stood behind her, brushing the hair from her eyes.

'You have no need to be, my love,' her mother said. 'No

need at all,' and all the flavour of Wassingham was in her voice.

Sarah looked now, and there was Annie, her face older, thinner, her hair grey, but the smile was so wide, the eyes so full of love. How could she not have seen her? Then Annie's arms were round her daughter, holding the thin body as close to her as she could, never wanting to let her go, feeling Georgie put his arms round them both. 'Oh Mum,' Sarah said and that was all. There was no need for words, not any more.

Annie kissed her daughter's forehead, stroking her hair, her poor shorn hair and now they walked, their arms around one another until Annie stopped, laughing. 'Oh God, I've left my bag where we were standing.'

Sarah squeezed their arms. 'I'll go.'

They watched her run, their arms around one another, and saw her stop when she saw Davy standing where they had been, saw him walk towards her and Annie felt her breath tighten as he put out his hands, and then she breathed again as her daughter took them.

Davy said, 'I love you, Sarah, I always have. I love you, I'm in love with you. I can't stand life without you. Will you come home now and swing from the bar?'

Sarah looked at his tanned skin, his strong face, felt the pressure of his hands. She turned and looked at her parents, at the smile on her mother's face, her father's too. 'I've never wanted anything so much.'